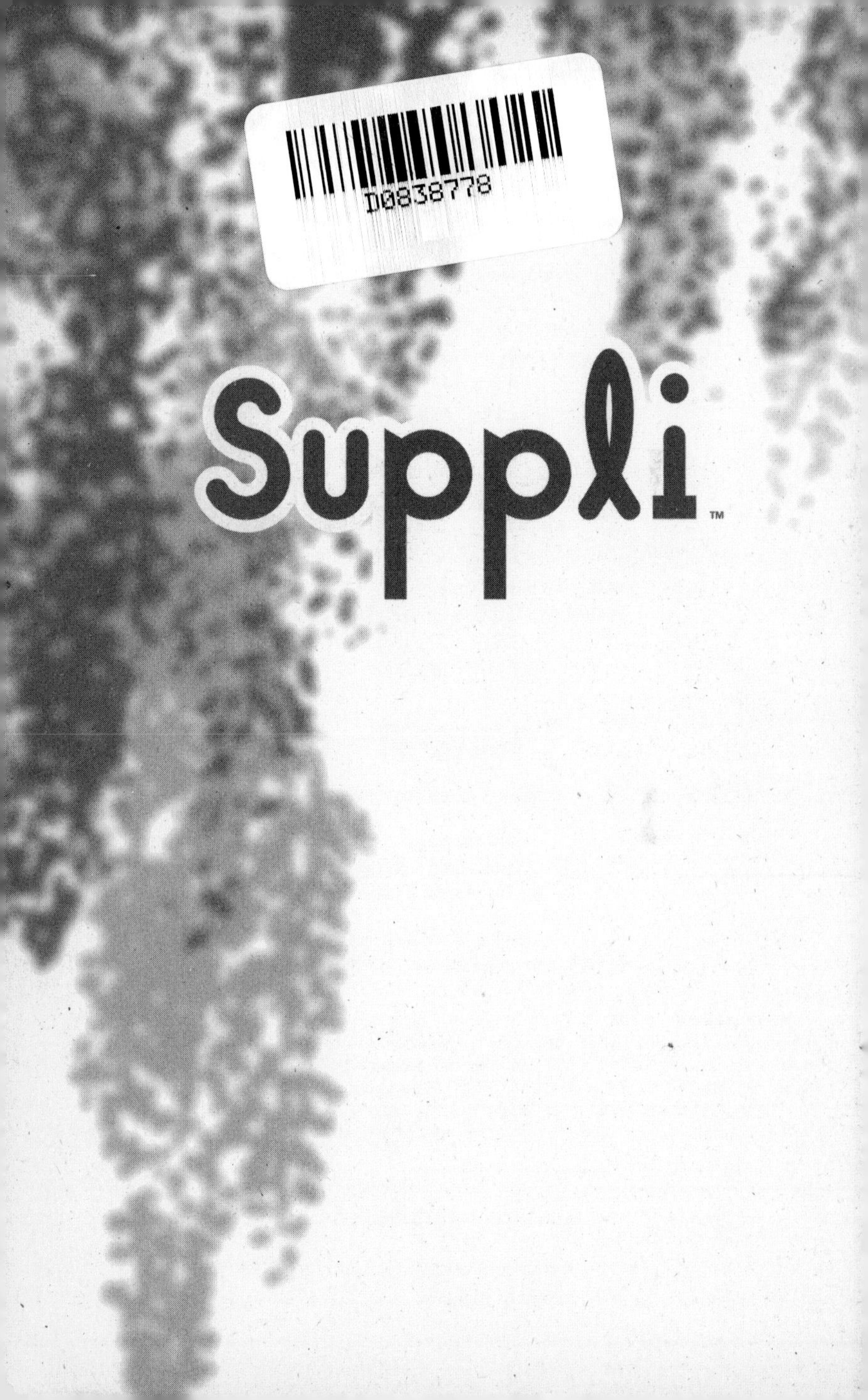

Suppli™

Suppli Volume 4 + 5
Created by Mari Okazaki

Translation - Angela Liu
English Adaptation - Liz Forbes & Hope Donovan
Retouch and Lettering - Star Print Brokers
Production Artist - Rui Kyo
Graphic Designer - James Lee & Al-Insan Lashley

Editor - Hope Donovan
Print Production Manager - Lucas Rivera
Managing Editor - Vy Nguyen
Senior Designer - Louis Csontos
Art Director - Al-Insan Lashley
Director of Sales and Manufacturing - Allyson De Simone
Associate Publisher - Marco F. Pavia
President and C.O.O. - John Parker
C.E.O. and Chief Creative Officer - Stu Levy

A **TOKYOPOP** Manga

TOKYOPOP and are trademarks or registered trademarks of TOKYOPOP Inc.

TOKYOPOP Inc.
5900 Wilshire Blvd. Suite 2000
Los Angeles, CA 90036

E-mail: info@TOKYOPOP.com
Come visit us online at www.TOKYOPOP.com

ISBN: 978-1-4278-0468-6

First TOKYOPOP printing: July 2010
10 9 8 7 6 5 4 3 2 1
Printed in the USA

Suppli™

BY MARI OKAZAKI

4

⚙️ TOKYOPOP®

HAMBURG // LONDON // LOS ANGELES // TOKYO

Mizuho Tanaka

Fujii's rival and Ogiwara's ex. She balances being a married woman and being a working woman with enviable feminine grace and beauty.

Satoshi Ogiwara

The company golden boy, who can't choose between his old flame Tanaka and his new fling with Fujii.

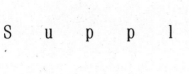

S u p p l i

Minami Fujii

Would you believe that outside of work this highly-organized 27-year-old can barely boil water? After a seven-year relationship ended, she was flung into the raging sea of broken hearts and is navigating the rough waters of the late twenties dating scene, with varying degrees of success.

Etsurou Kouda

aka KouEtsu, a prodigal
producer with several
hits under his belt.

Yugi

A freelance copywriter
who sometimes works at
Fujii's company. Currently
in a romance with Kouda.

Touru Sahara

A cameraman who works with
Kouda. Potential partner for
Fujii or professional playboy?

Watanabe

Perhaps her frustration at
being middle management at
the advertising company has
led her to lay claim to Ishida.

Ishida

Two years Fujii's junior.
Dating Watanabe hasn't cooled
his attraction to Fujii.

S T O R Y

Fujii has lost the battle against sensible work hours, and continues to commit
herself to long hours and all-nighters at her advertising company. On the bright
side, she won the battle against Miss Perfect Tanaka for Ogiwara, and much to the
other woman's dismay, Fujii and Ogiwara are starting to get serious. Still, Tanaka's
feminine charms unleash Fujii's worst insecurities about her femininity...

CONTENTS

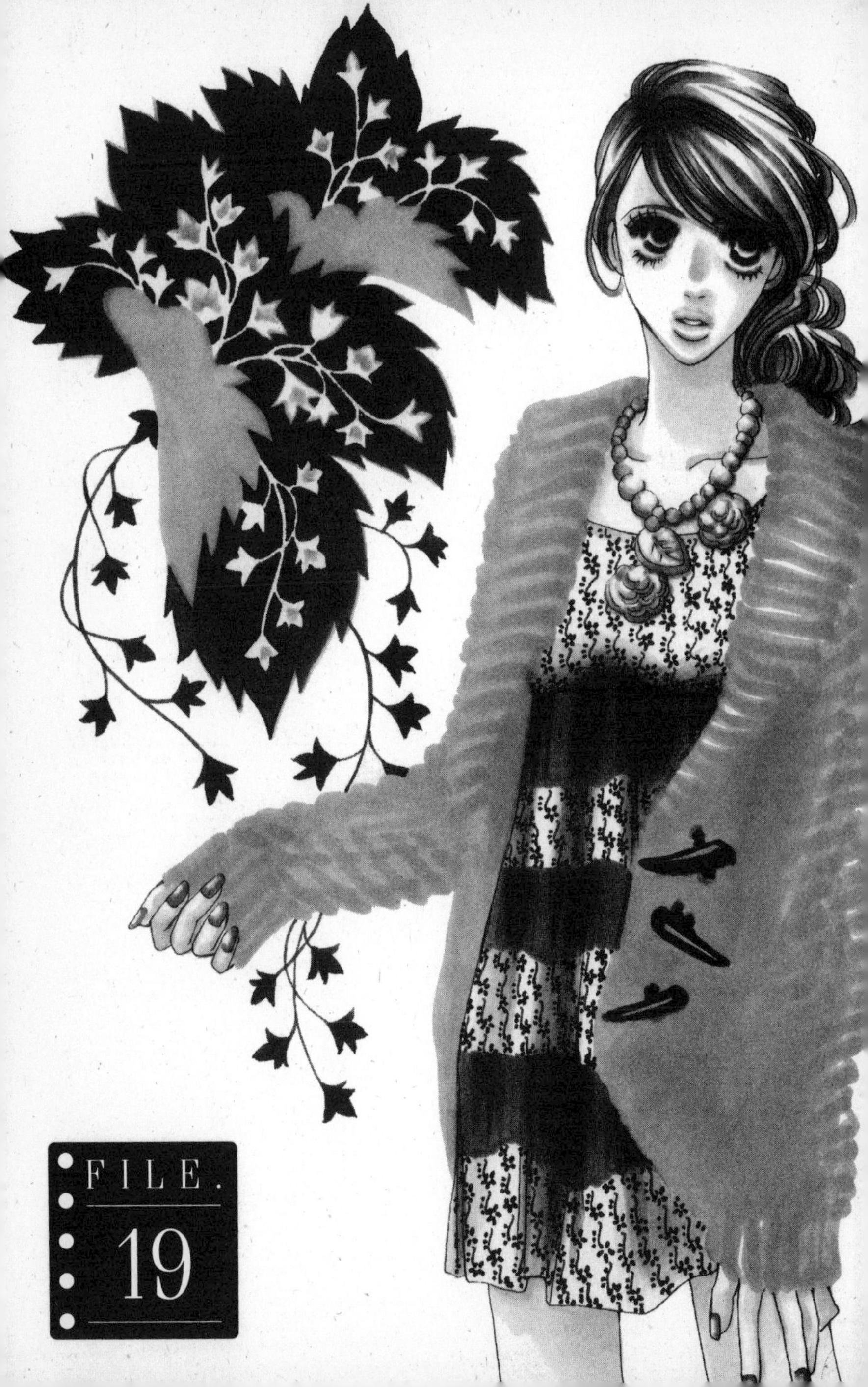
FILE.
19

Suppli 4

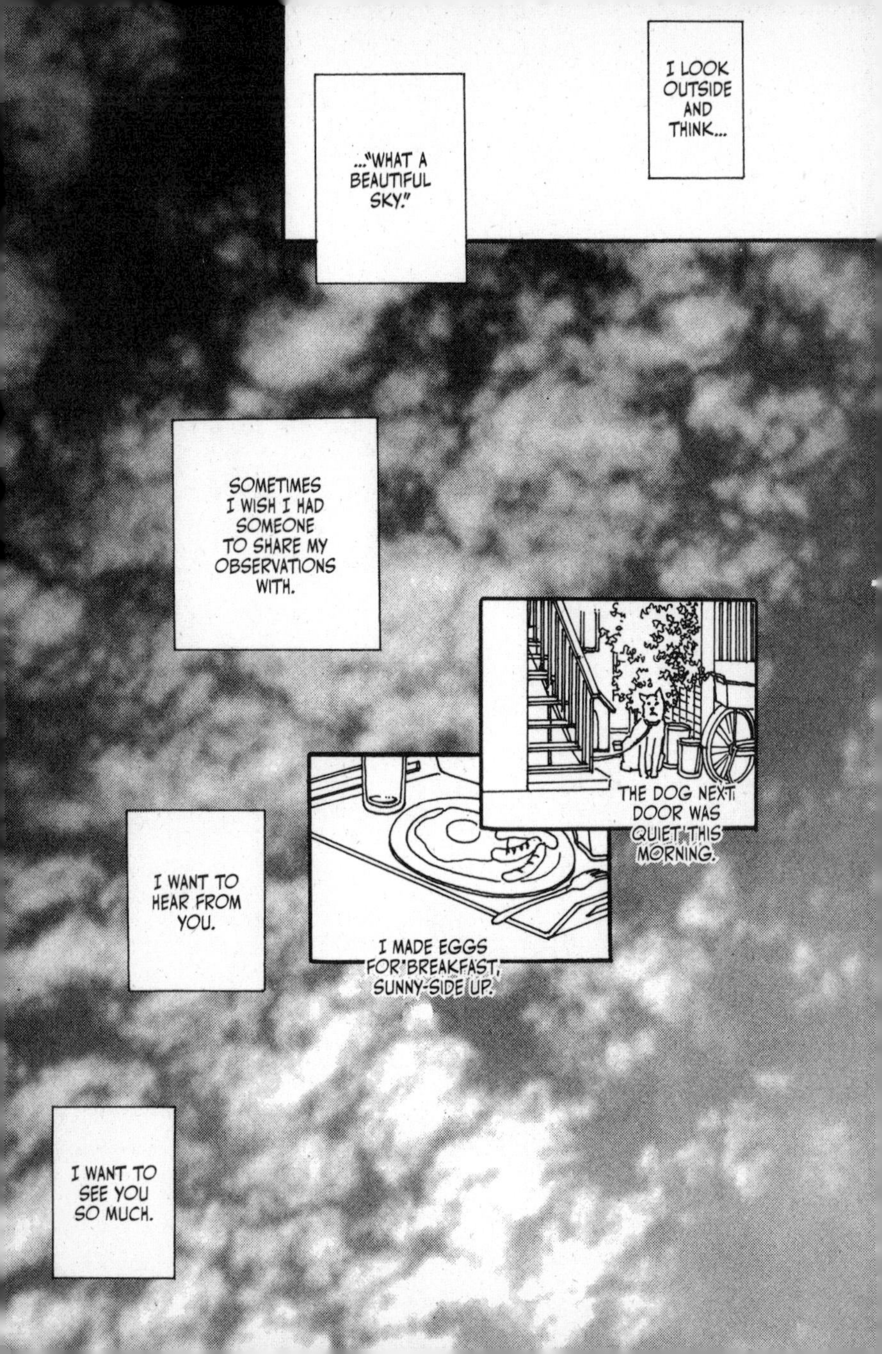
I LOOK OUTSIDE AND THINK...
..."WHAT A BEAUTIFUL SKY."
SOMETIMES I WISH I HAD SOMEONE TO SHARE MY OBSERVATIONS WITH.
THE DOG NEXT DOOR WAS QUIET THIS MORNING.
I MADE EGGS FOR BREAKFAST, SUNNY-SIDE UP.
I WANT TO HEAR FROM YOU.
I WANT TO SEE YOU SO MUCH.

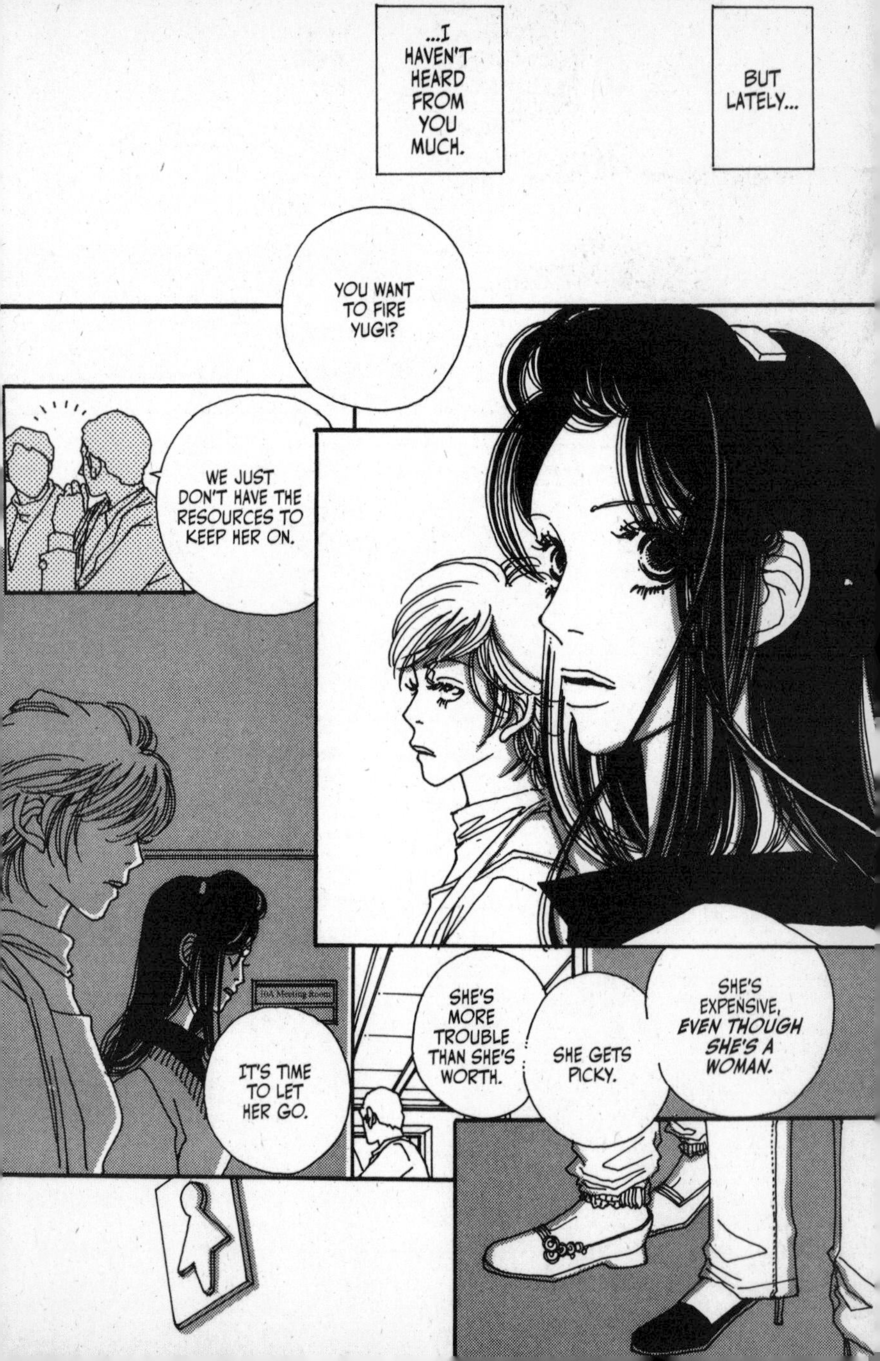
BUT LATELY...
...I HAVEN'T HEARD FROM YOU MUCH.
YOU WANT TO FIRE YUGI?
WE JUST DON'T HAVE THE RESOURCES TO KEEP HER ON.
SHE'S EXPENSIVE, *EVEN THOUGH SHE'S A WOMAN.*
SHE GETS PICKY.
SHE'S MORE TROUBLE THAN SHE'S WORTH.
IT'S TIME TO LET HER GO.

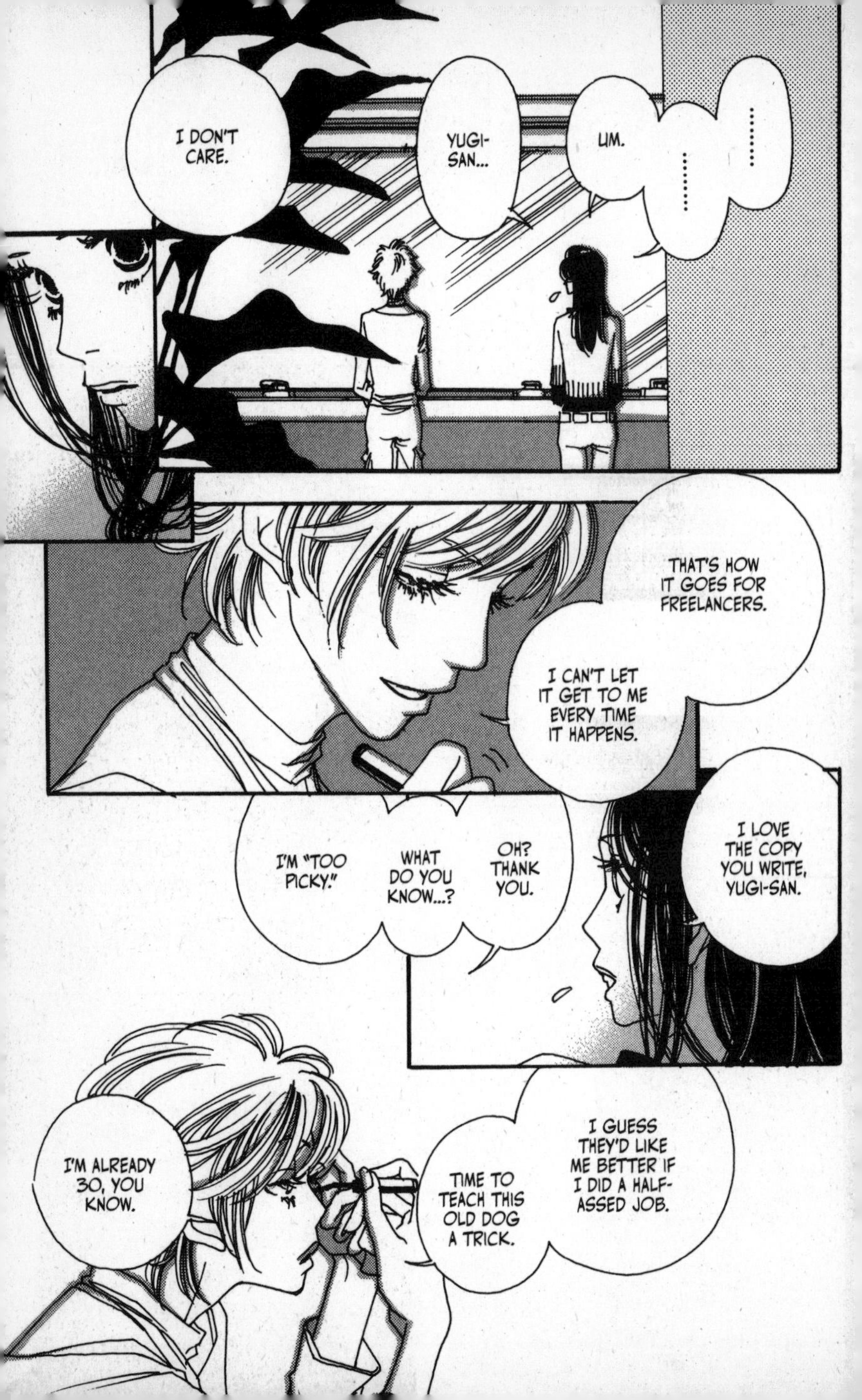
……
UM.
YUGI-SAN...
I DON'T CARE.
THAT'S HOW IT GOES FOR FREELANCERS.
I CAN'T LET IT GET TO ME EVERY TIME IT HAPPENS.
I LOVE THE COPY YOU WRITE, YUGI-SAN.
OH? THANK YOU.
WHAT DO YOU KNOW...?
I'M "TOO PICKY."
I GUESS THEY'D LIKE ME BETTER IF I DID A HALF-ASSED JOB.
TIME TO TEACH THIS OLD DOG A TRICK.
I'M ALREADY 30, YOU KNOW.

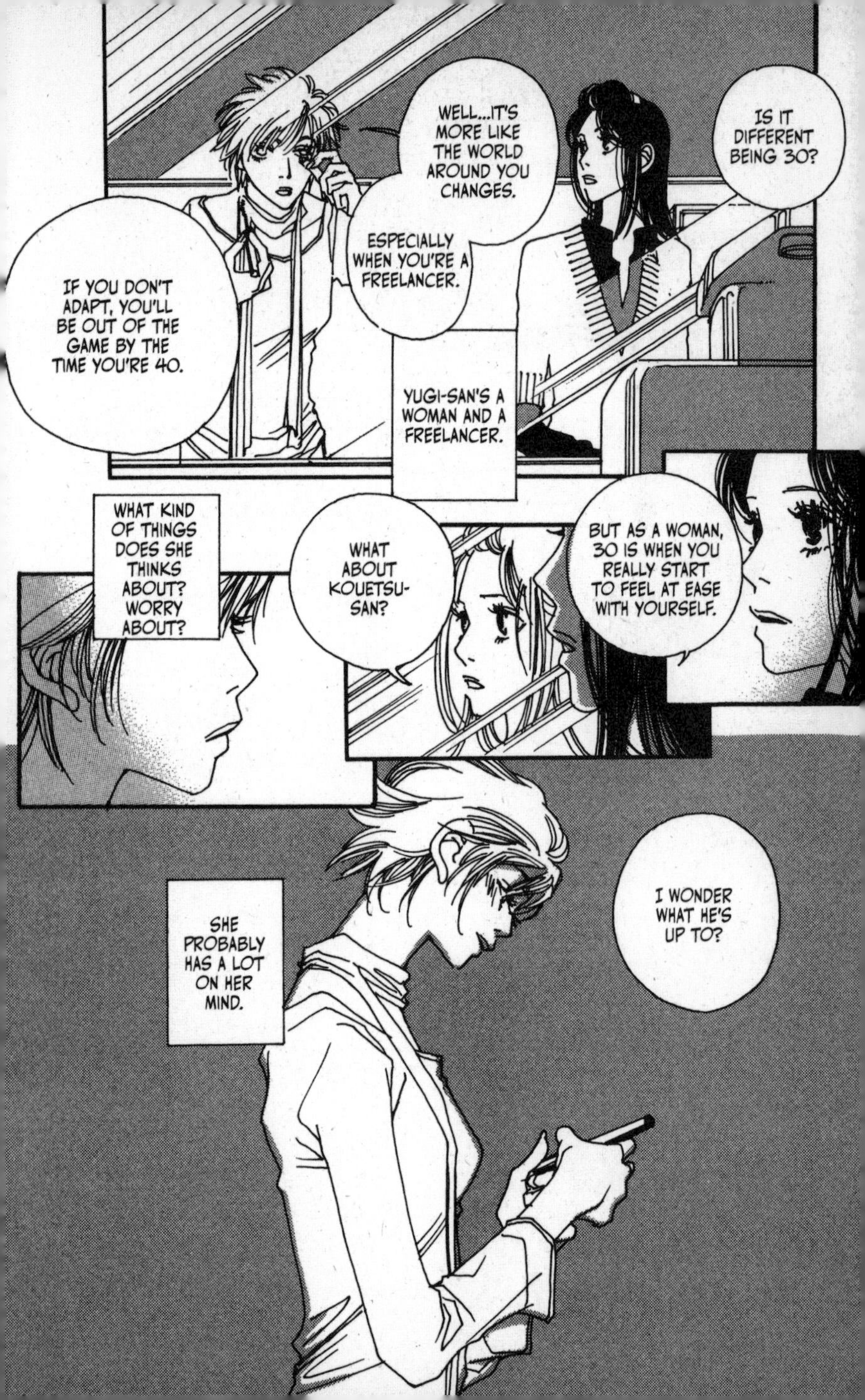
IS IT DIFFERENT BEING 30?
WELL...IT'S MORE LIKE THE WORLD AROUND YOU CHANGES.
ESPECIALLY WHEN YOU'RE A FREELANCER.
IF YOU DON'T ADAPT, YOU'LL BE OUT OF THE GAME BY THE TIME YOU'RE 40.
YUGI-SAN'S A WOMAN AND A FREELANCER.
BUT AS A WOMAN, 30 IS WHEN YOU REALLY START TO FEEL AT EASE WITH YOURSELF.
WHAT ABOUT KOUETSU-SAN?
WHAT KIND OF THINGS DOES SHE THINKS ABOUT? WORRY ABOUT?
I WONDER WHAT HE'S UP TO?
SHE PROBABLY HAS A LOT ON HER MIND.

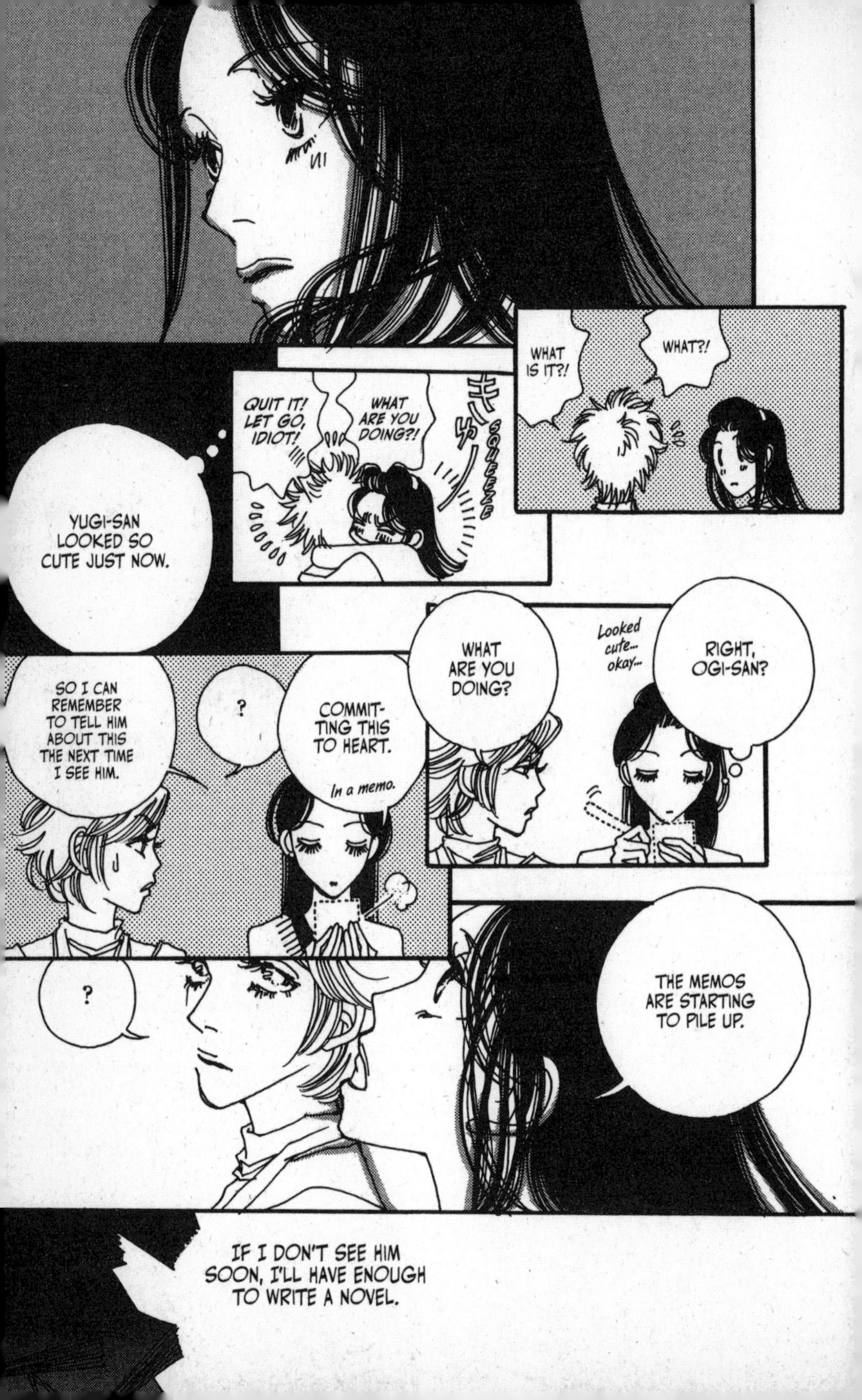
WHAT?!
WHAT IS IT?!
SQUEEZE
WHAT ARE YOU DOING?!
QUIT IT! LET GO, IDIOT!
YUGI-SAN LOOKED SO CUTE JUST NOW.
RIGHT, OGI-SAN?
Looked cute... okay...
WHAT ARE YOU DOING?
COMMITTING THIS TO HEART.
In a memo.
?
SO I CAN REMEMBER TO TELL HIM ABOUT THIS THE NEXT TIME I SEE HIM.
THE MEMOS ARE STARTING TO PILE UP.
?
IF I DON'T SEE HIM SOON, I'LL HAVE ENOUGH TO WRITE A NOVEL.

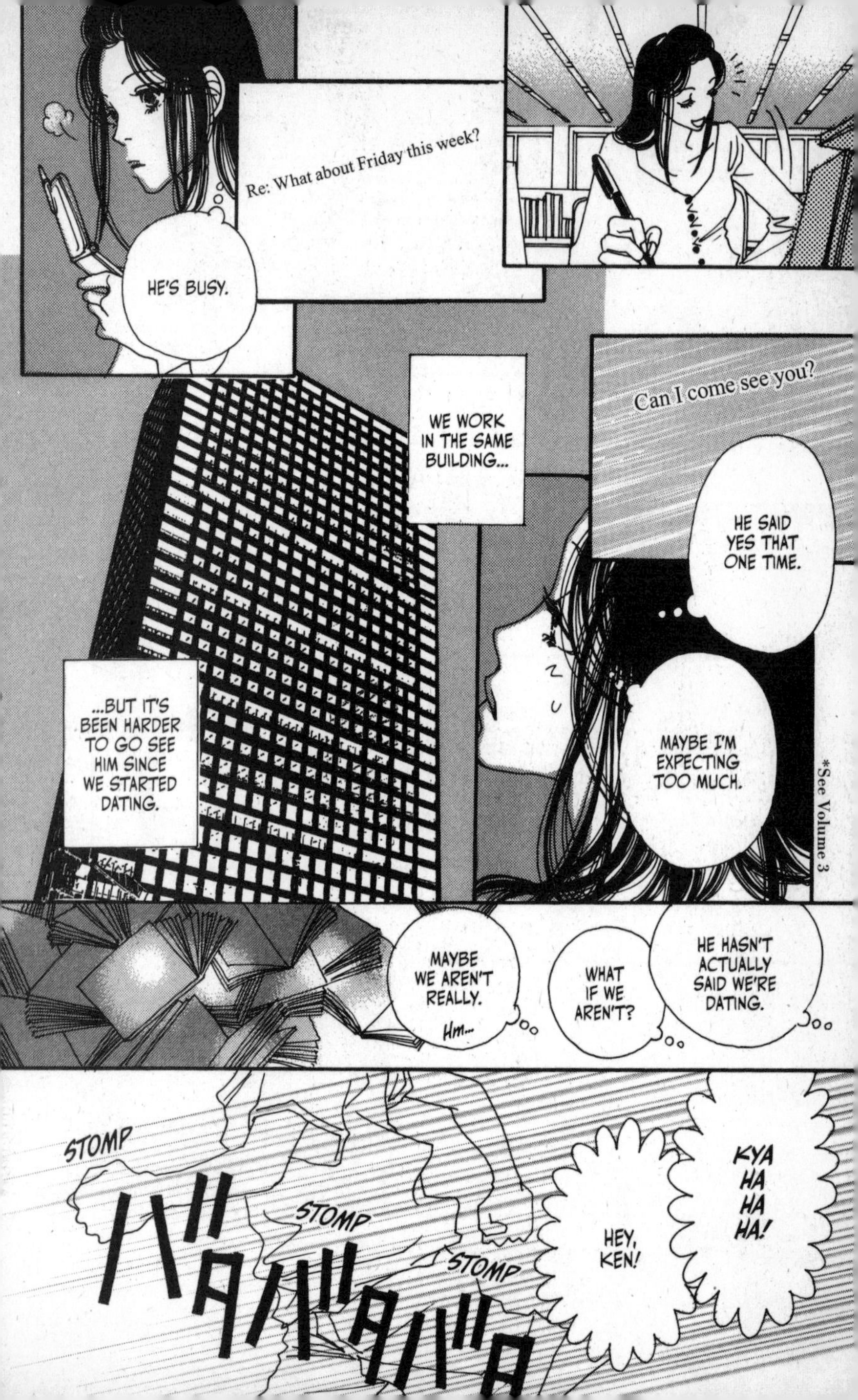
Re: What about Friday this week?
HE'S BUSY.
Can I come see you?
HE SAID YES THAT ONE TIME.
*See Volume 3
MAYBE I'M EXPECTING TOO MUCH.
WE WORK IN THE SAME BUILDING...
...BUT IT'S BEEN HARDER TO GO SEE HIM SINCE WE STARTED DATING.
HE HASN'T ACTUALLY SAID WE'RE DATING.
WHAT IF WE AREN'T?
MAYBE WE AREN'T REALLY.
Hm...
KYA HA HA HA!
HEY, KEN!
STOMP
STOMP
STOMP

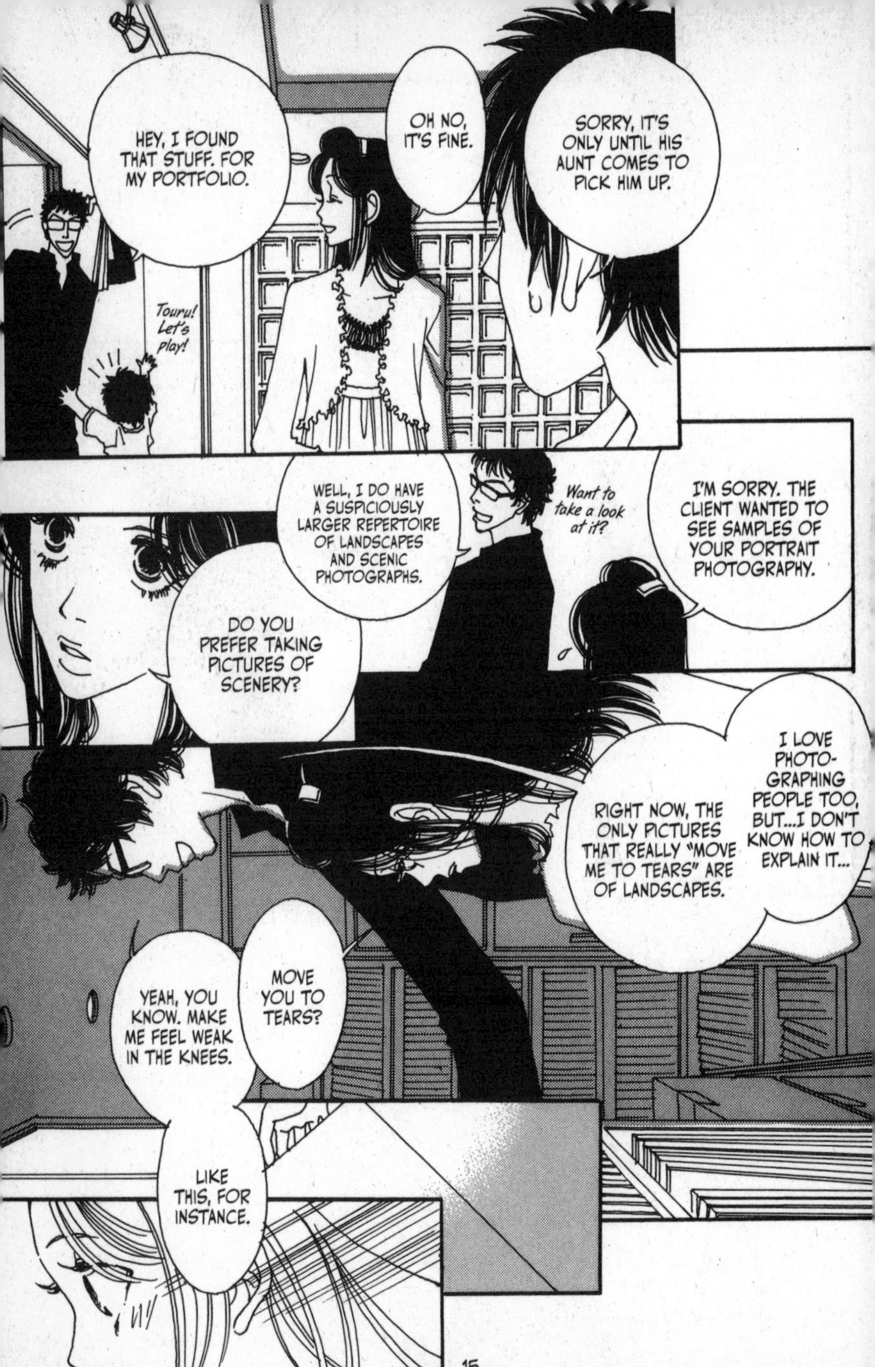
SORRY, IT'S ONLY UNTIL HIS AUNT COMES TO PICK HIM UP.
OH NO, IT'S FINE.
HEY, I FOUND THAT STUFF. FOR MY PORTFOLIO.
Touru! Let's play!
I'M SORRY. THE CLIENT WANTED TO SEE SAMPLES OF YOUR PORTRAIT PHOTOGRAPHY.
Want to take a look at it?
WELL, I DO HAVE A SUSPICIOUSLY LARGER REPERTOIRE OF LANDSCAPES AND SCENIC PHOTOGRAPHS.
DO YOU PREFER TAKING PICTURES OF SCENERY?
I LOVE PHOTO-GRAPHING PEOPLE TOO, BUT...I DON'T KNOW HOW TO EXPLAIN IT...
RIGHT NOW, THE ONLY PICTURES THAT REALLY "MOVE ME TO TEARS" ARE OF LANDSCAPES.
MOVE YOU TO TEARS?
YEAH, YOU KNOW. MAKE ME FEEL WEAK IN THE KNEES.
LIKE THIS, FOR INSTANCE.

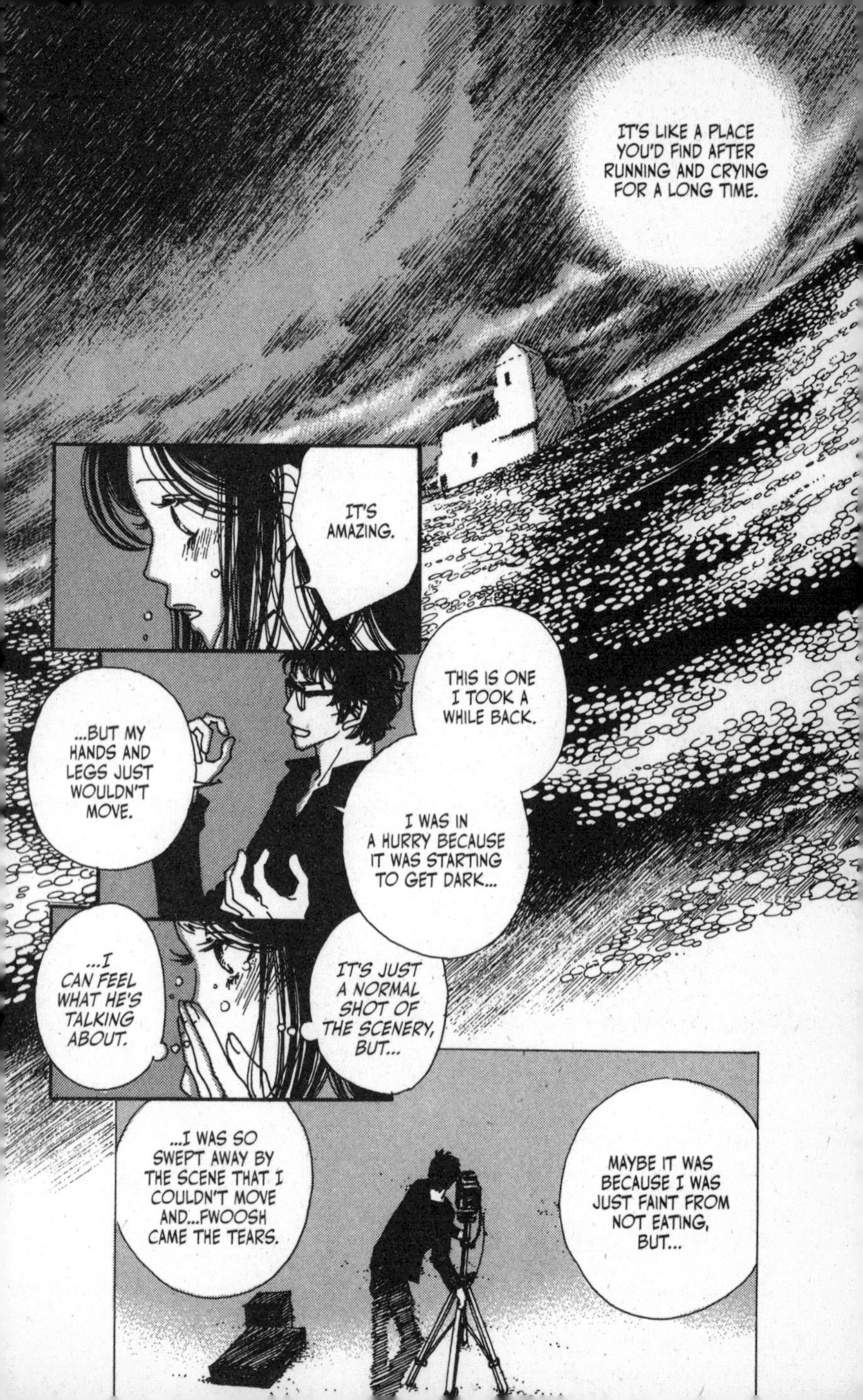
IT'S LIKE A PLACE YOU'D FIND AFTER RUNNING AND CRYING FOR A LONG TIME.
IT'S AMAZING.
THIS IS ONE I TOOK A WHILE BACK.
I WAS IN A HURRY BECAUSE IT WAS STARTING TO GET DARK...
...BUT MY HANDS AND LEGS JUST WOULDN'T MOVE.
IT'S JUST A NORMAL SHOT OF THE SCENERY, BUT...
...I CAN FEEL WHAT HE'S TALKING ABOUT.
MAYBE IT WAS BECAUSE I WAS JUST FAINT FROM NOT EATING, BUT...
...I WAS SO SWEPT AWAY BY THE SCENE THAT I COULDN'T MOVE AND...FWOOSH CAME THE TEARS.

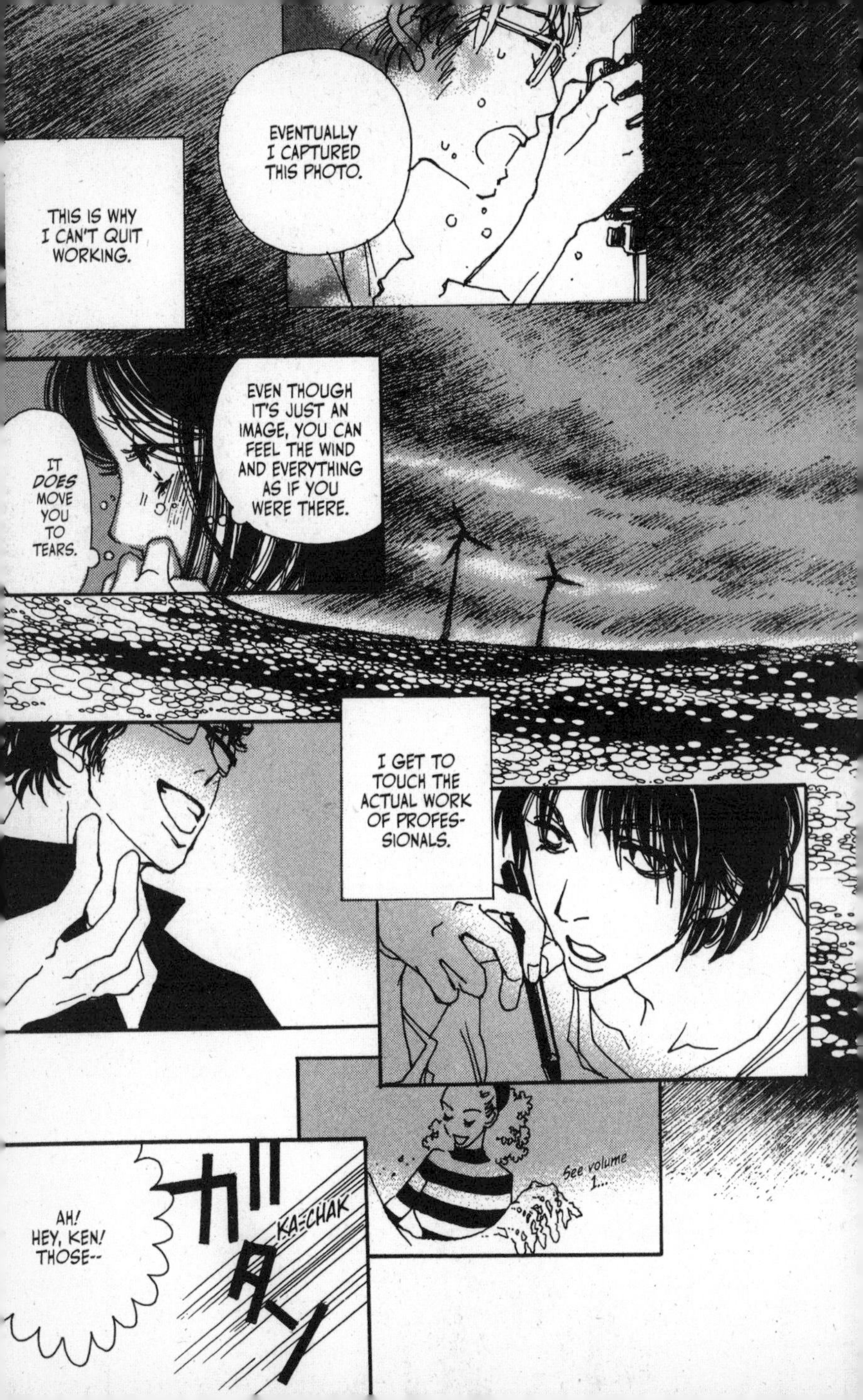
EVENTUALLY I CAPTURED THIS PHOTO.
THIS IS WHY I CAN'T QUIT WORKING.
EVEN THOUGH IT'S JUST AN IMAGE, YOU CAN FEEL THE WIND AND EVERYTHING AS IF YOU WERE THERE.
IT *DOES* MOVE YOU TO TEARS.
I GET TO TOUCH THE ACTUAL WORK OF PROFESSIONALS.
See volume 1...
KA-CHAK
AH! HEY, KEN! THOSE--

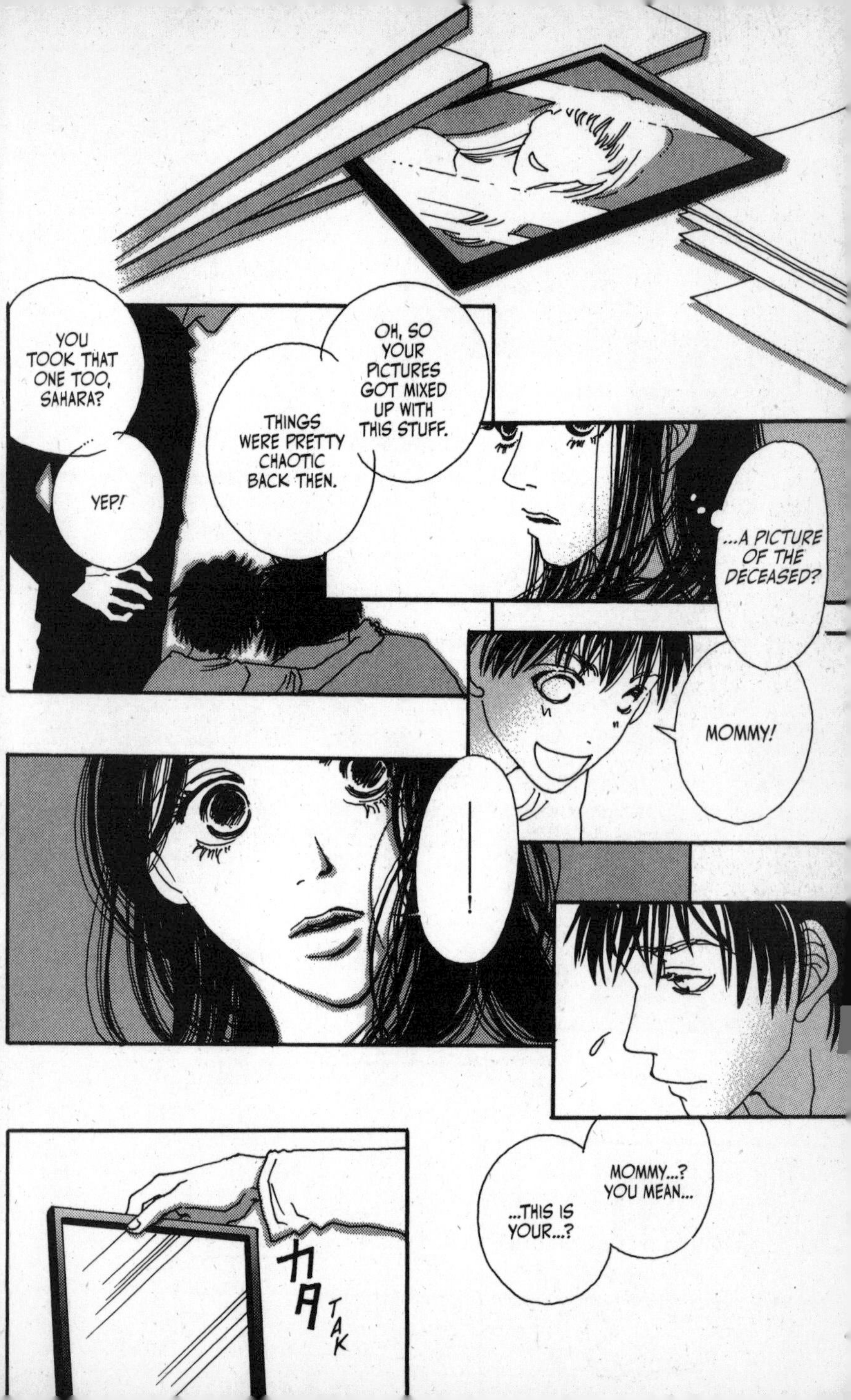

OH, SO YOUR PICTURES GOT MIXED UP WITH THIS STUFF.
THINGS WERE PRETTY CHAOTIC BACK THEN.
YOU TOOK THAT ONE TOO, SAHARA?
...
YEP!
...A PICTURE OF THE DECEASED?
MOMMY!
!
MOMMY...? YOU MEAN...
...THIS IS YOUR...?
TAK

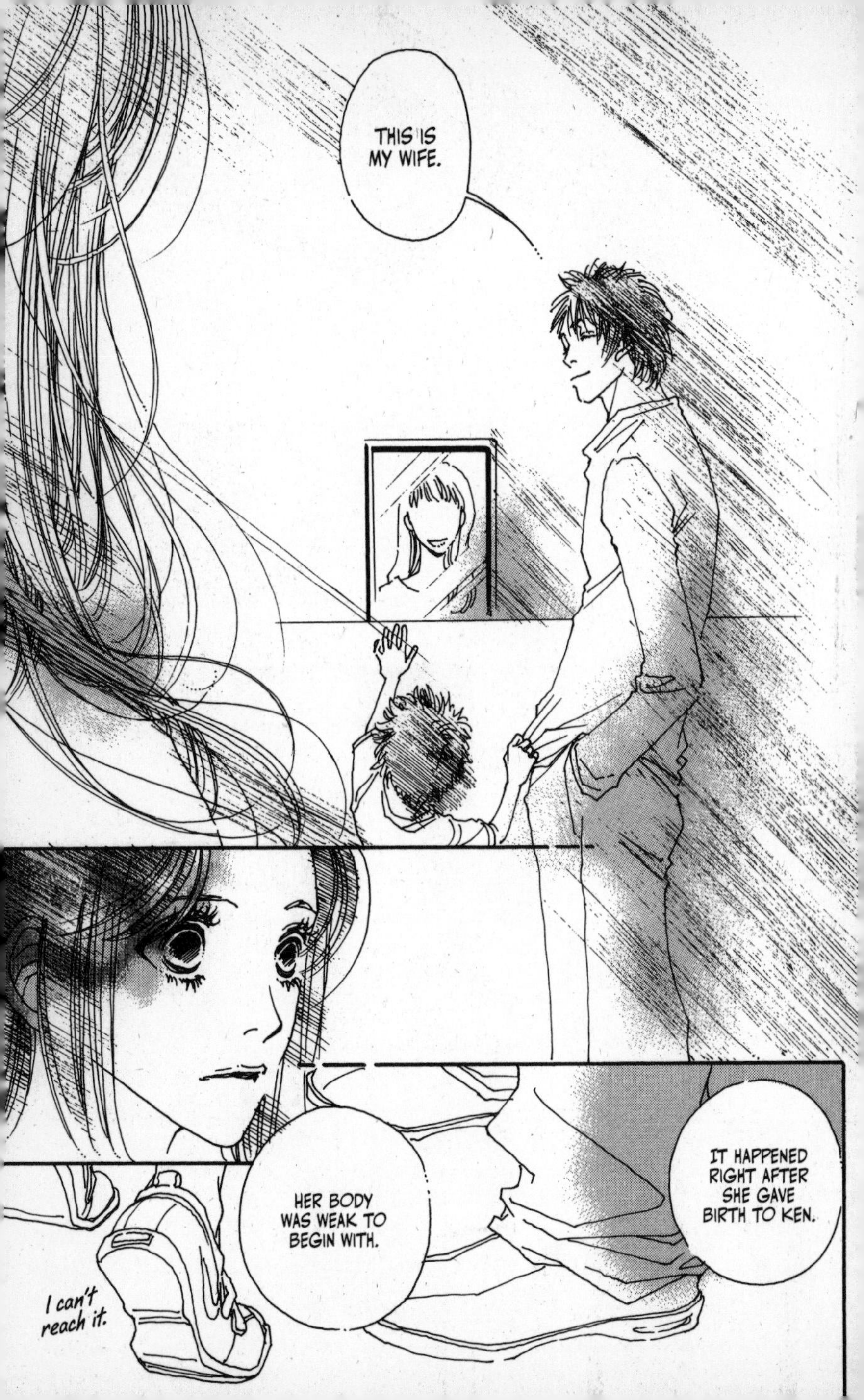
THIS IS MY WIFE.
IT HAPPENED RIGHT AFTER SHE GAVE BIRTH TO KEN.
HER BODY WAS WEAK TO BEGIN WITH.
I can't reach it.

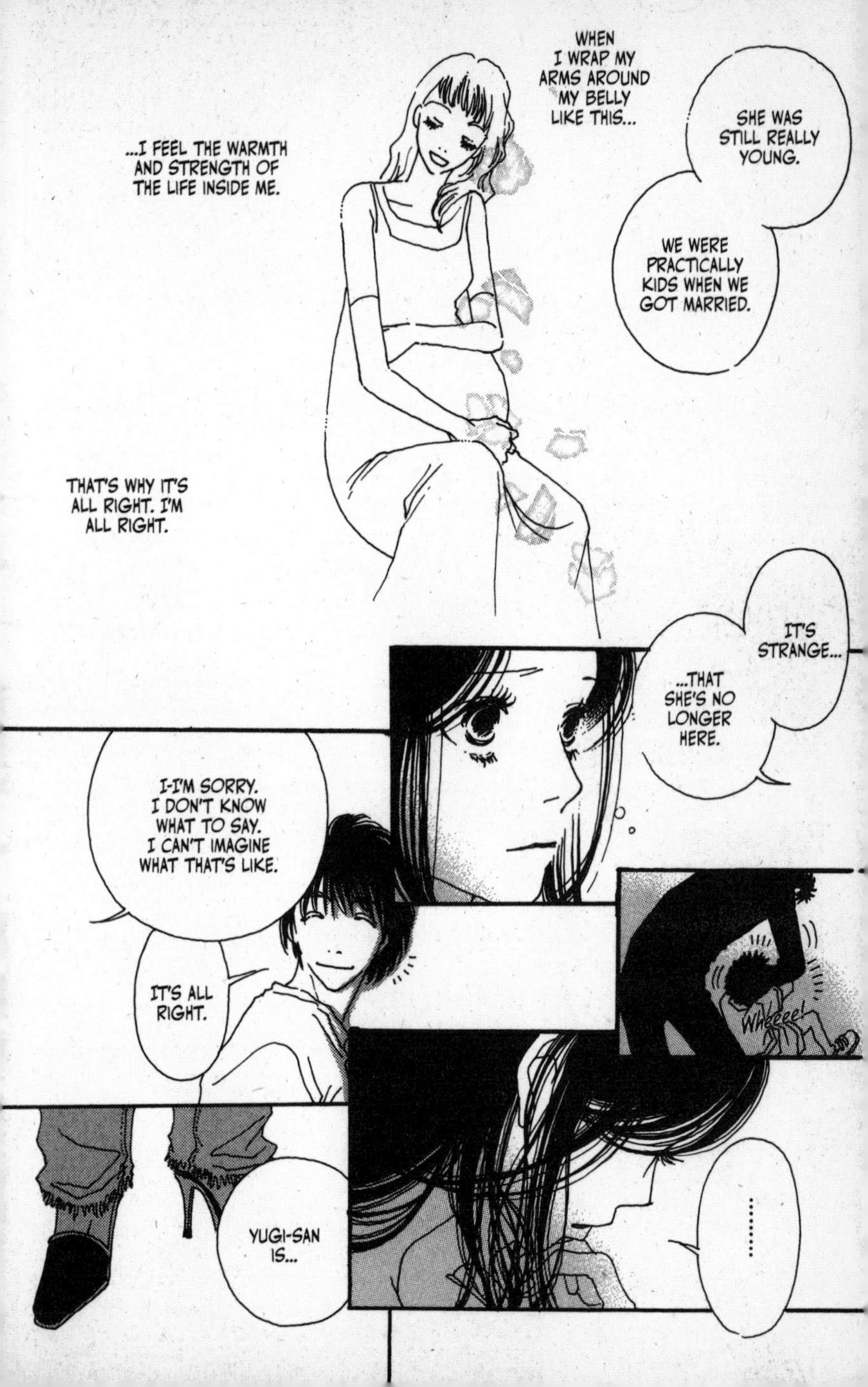
SHE WAS STILL REALLY YOUNG.
WE WERE PRACTICALLY KIDS WHEN WE GOT MARRIED.
WHEN I WRAP MY ARMS AROUND MY BELLY LIKE THIS...
...I FEEL THE WARMTH AND STRENGTH OF THE LIFE INSIDE ME.
THAT'S WHY IT'S ALL RIGHT. I'M ALL RIGHT.
IT'S STRANGE...
...THAT SHE'S NO LONGER HERE.
I-I'M SORRY. I DON'T KNOW WHAT TO SAY. I CAN'T IMAGINE WHAT THAT'S LIKE.
IT'S ALL RIGHT.
Wheeee!
......
YUGI-SAN IS...

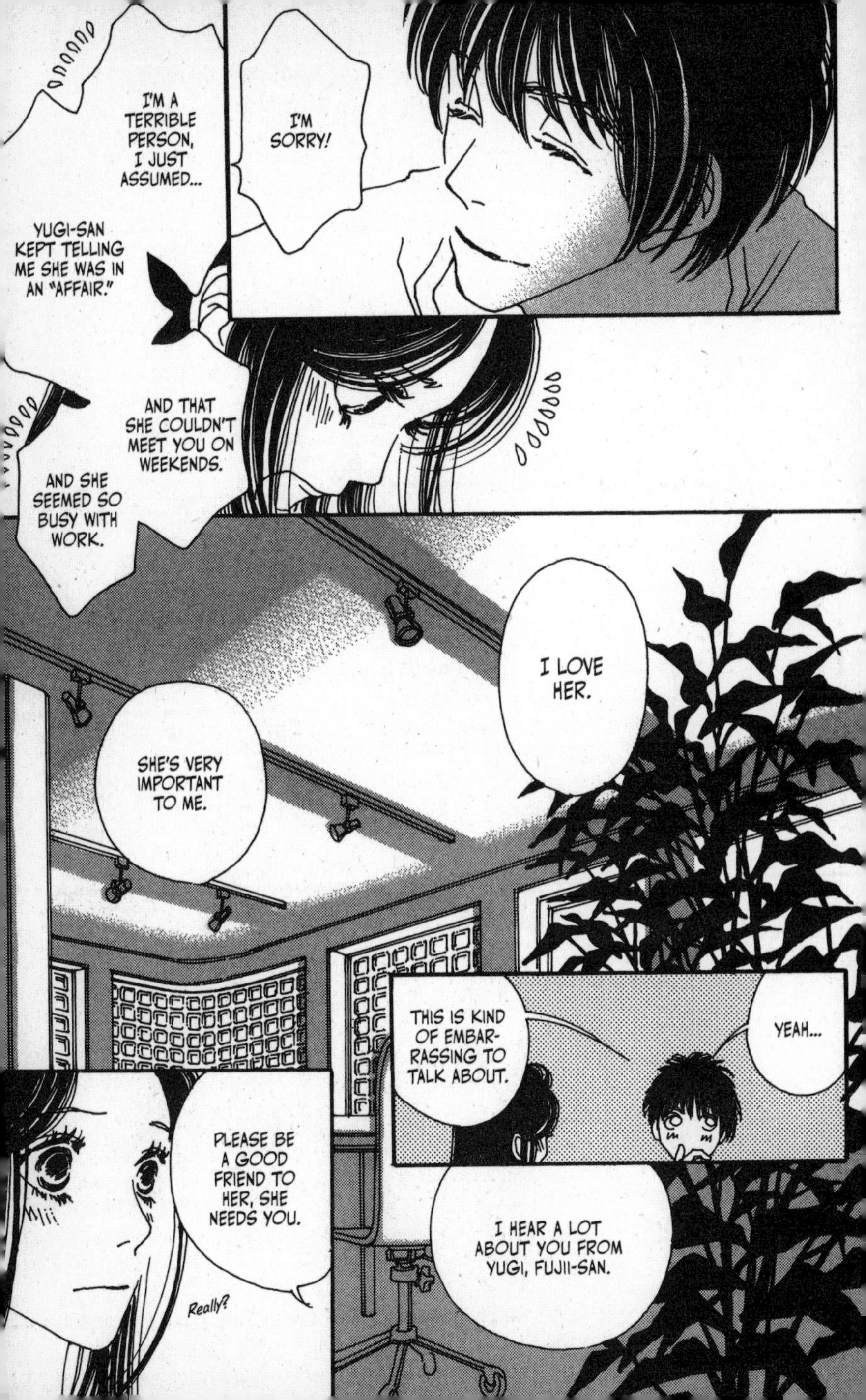

I'M SORRY!
I'M A TERRIBLE PERSON, I JUST ASSUMED...
YUGI-SAN KEPT TELLING ME SHE WAS IN AN "AFFAIR."
AND THAT SHE COULDN'T MEET YOU ON WEEKENDS.
AND SHE SEEMED SO BUSY WITH WORK.
I LOVE HER.
SHE'S VERY IMPORTANT TO ME.
YEAH...
THIS IS KIND OF EMBAR-RASSING TO TALK ABOUT.
I HEAR A LOT ABOUT YOU FROM YUGI, FUJII-SAN.
PLEASE BE A GOOD FRIEND TO HER, SHE NEEDS YOU.
Really?

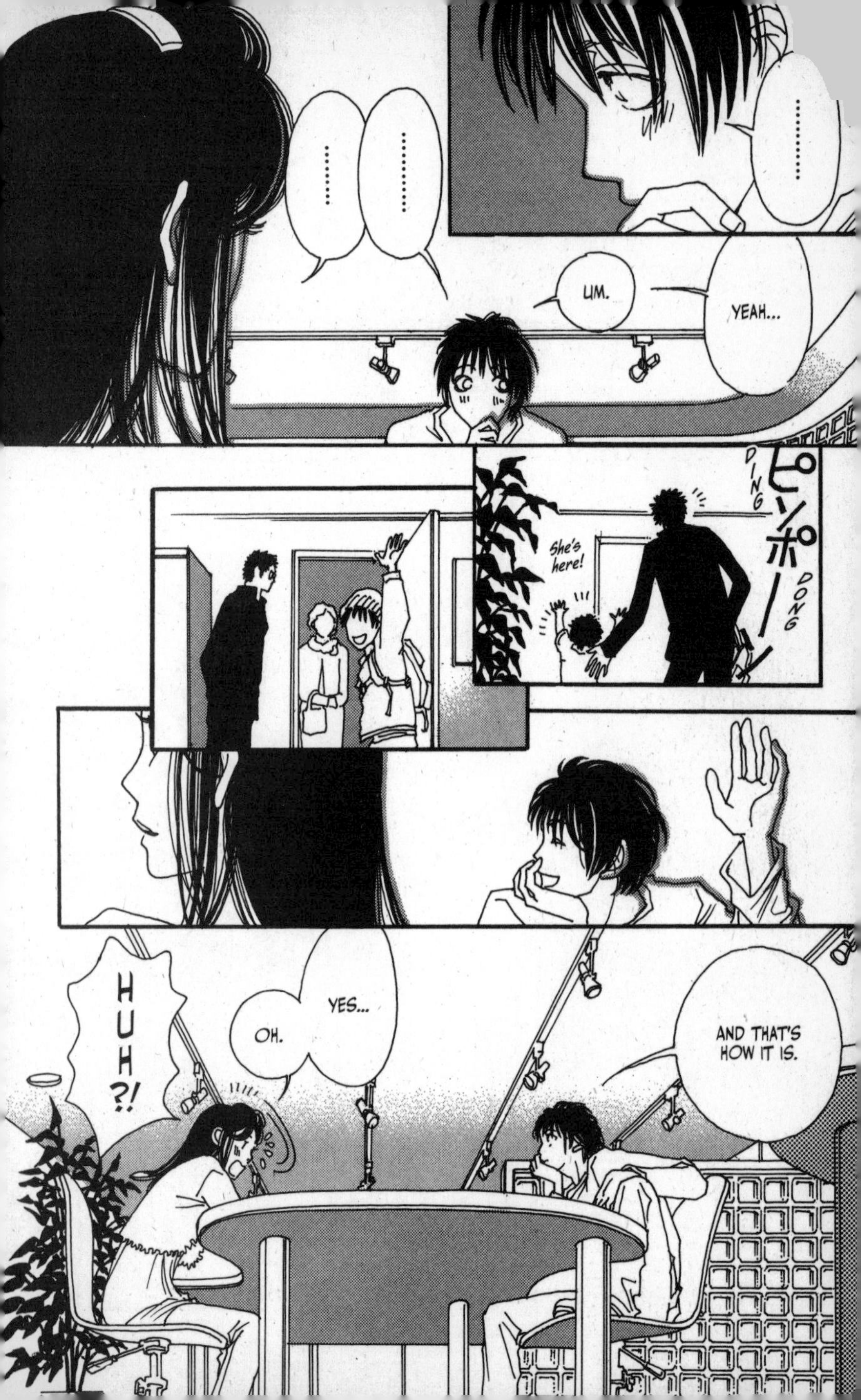

......
......
......
YEAH...
UM.
ピンポーン
DING
DONG
She's here!
AND THAT'S HOW IT IS.
YES...
OH.
HUH?!

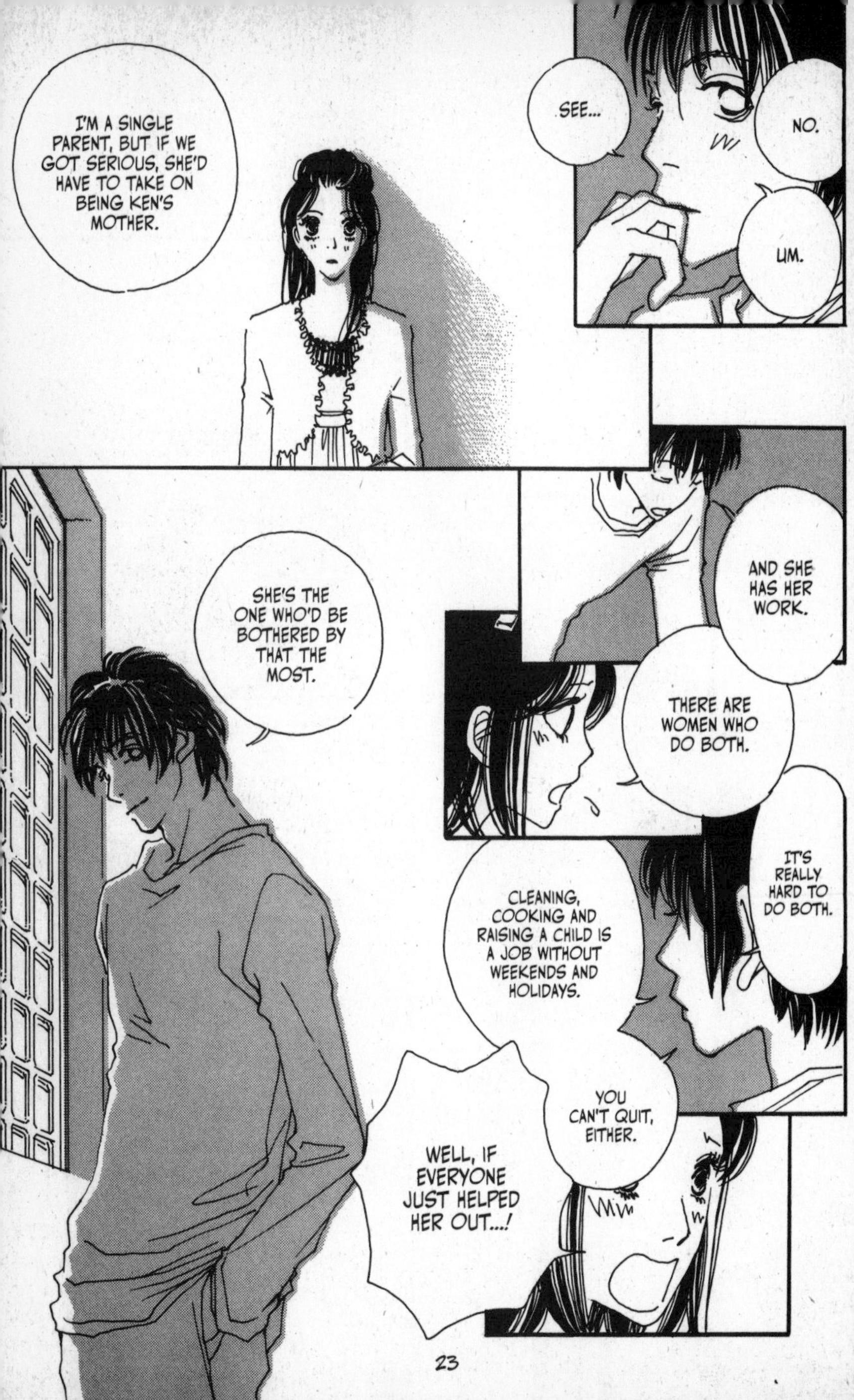
NO.
SEE...
UM.
I'M A SINGLE PARENT, BUT IF WE GOT SERIOUS, SHE'D HAVE TO TAKE ON BEING KEN'S MOTHER.
SHE'S THE ONE WHO'D BE BOTHERED BY THAT THE MOST.
AND SHE HAS HER WORK.
THERE ARE WOMEN WHO DO BOTH.
IT'S REALLY HARD TO DO BOTH.
CLEANING, COOKING AND RAISING A CHILD IS A JOB WITHOUT WEEKENDS AND HOLIDAYS.
YOU CAN'T QUIT, EITHER.
WELL, IF EVERYONE JUST HELPED HER OUT...!

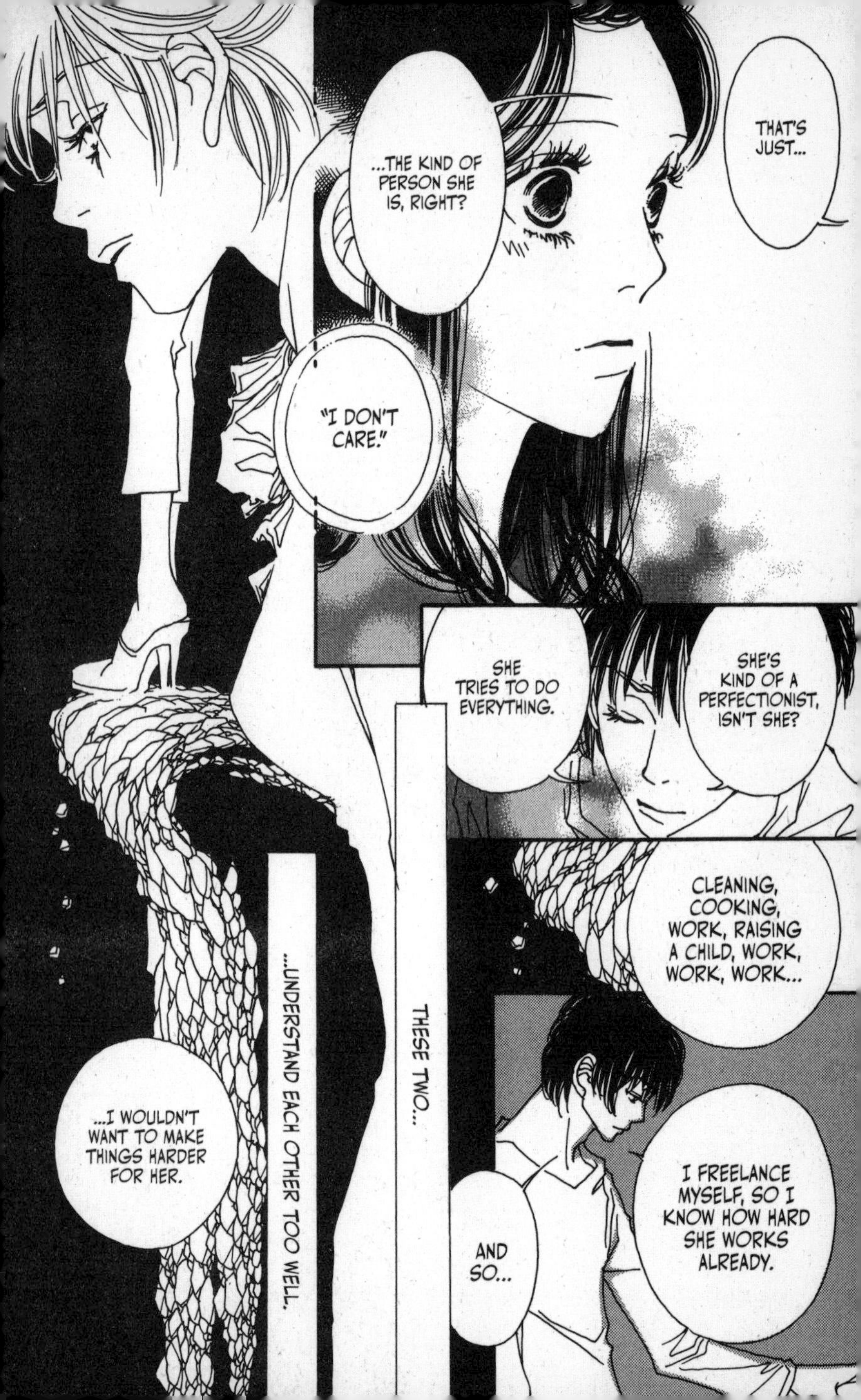

THAT'S JUST...
...THE KIND OF PERSON SHE IS, RIGHT?
"I DON'T CARE."
SHE'S KIND OF A PERFECTIONIST, ISN'T SHE?
SHE TRIES TO DO EVERYTHING.
CLEANING, COOKING, WORK, RAISING A CHILD, WORK, WORK, WORK...
I FREELANCE MYSELF, SO I KNOW HOW HARD SHE WORKS ALREADY.
AND SO...
...I WOULDN'T WANT TO MAKE THINGS HARDER FOR HER.
THESE TWO...
...UNDERSTAND EACH OTHER TOO WELL.

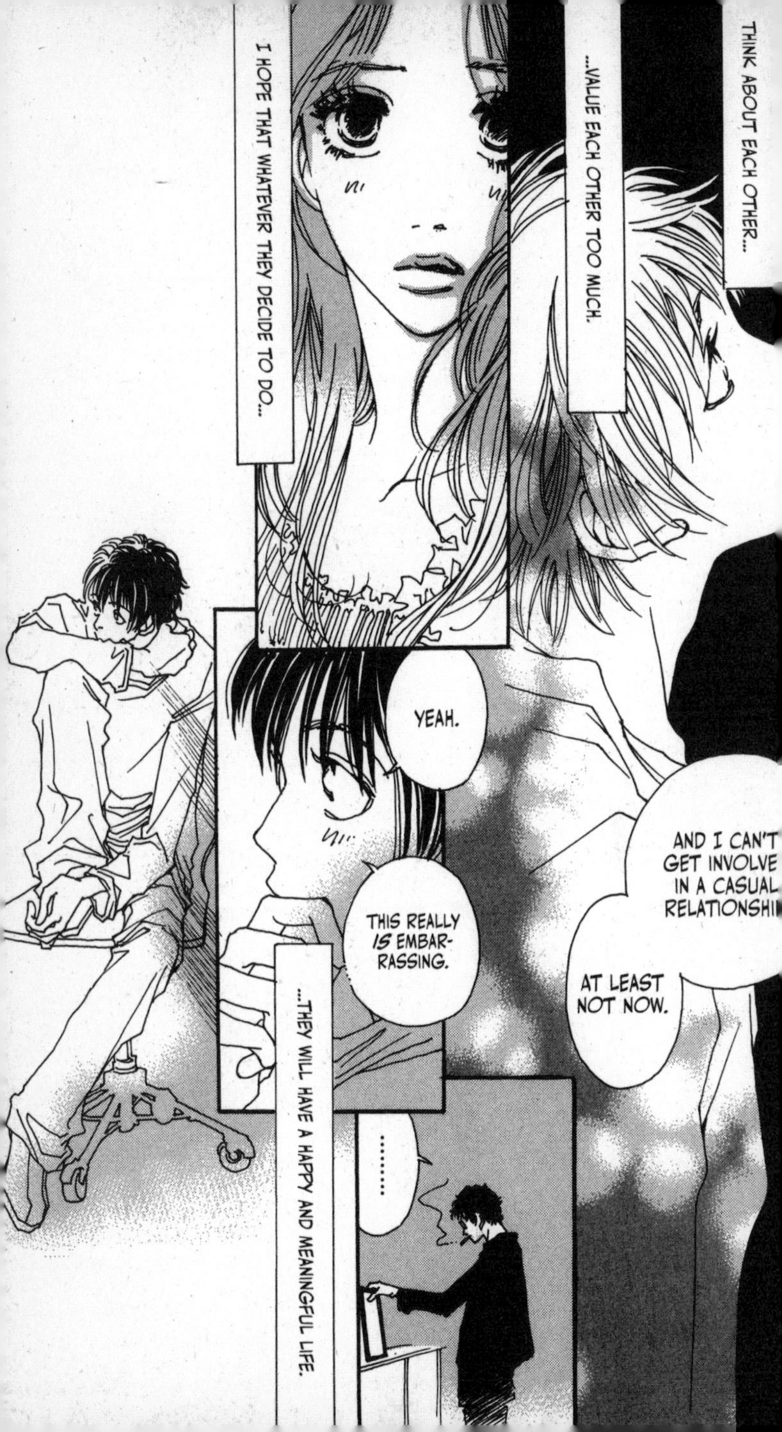
THINK ABOUT EACH OTHER...
...VALUE EACH OTHER TOO MUCH.
I HOPE THAT WHATEVER THEY DECIDE TO DO...
AND I CAN'T GET INVOLVE IN A CASUAL RELATIONSHI
AT LEAST NOT NOW.
YEAH.
THIS REALLY *IS* EMBAR-RASSING.
....
...THEY WILL HAVE A HAPPY AND MEANINGFUL LIFE.

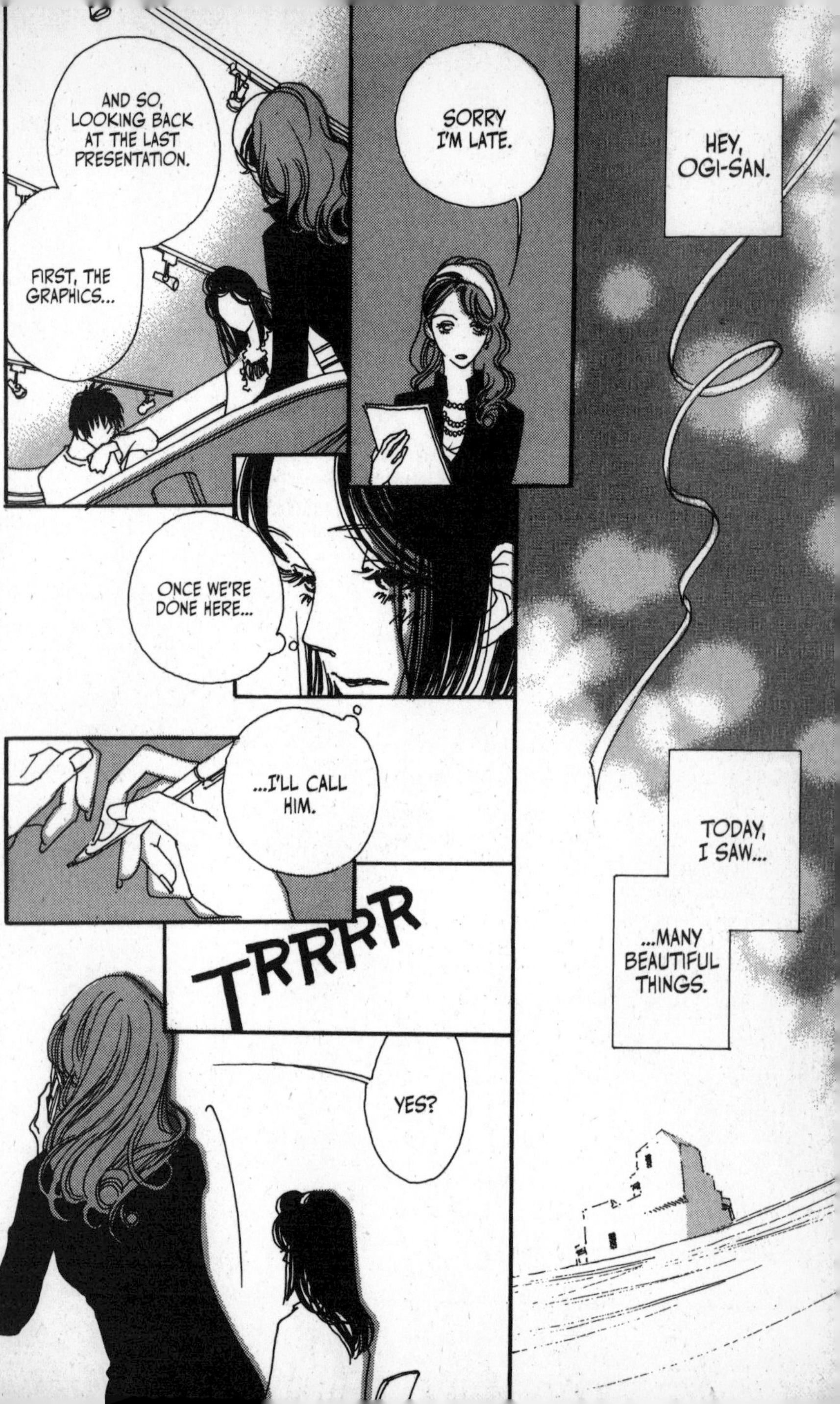
HEY, OGI-SAN.
TODAY, I SAW...
...MANY BEAUTIFUL THINGS.
SORRY I'M LATE.
AND SO, LOOKING BACK AT THE LAST PRESENTATION.
FIRST, THE GRAPHICS...
ONCE WE'RE DONE HERE...
...I'LL CALL HIM.
TRRRR
YES?

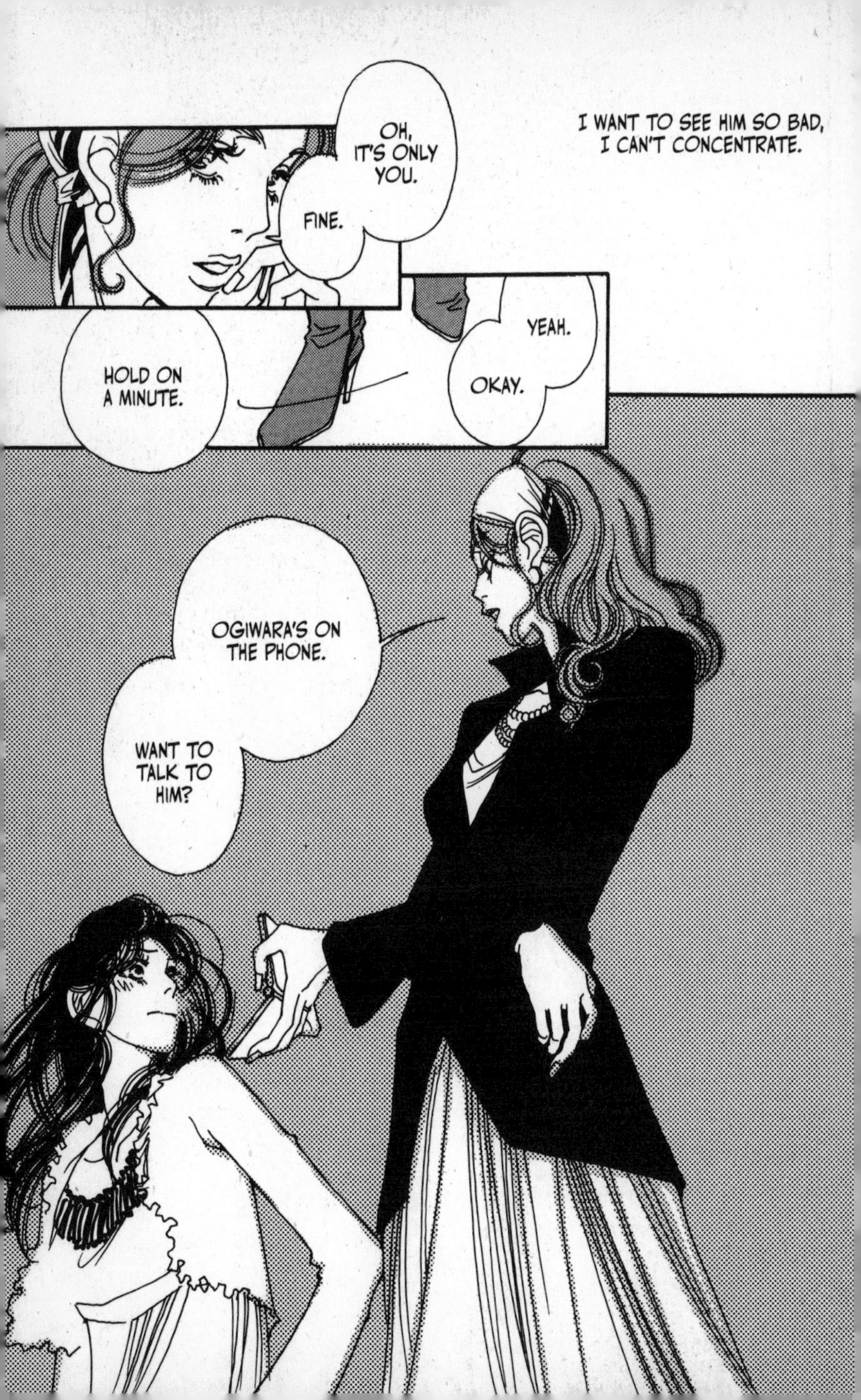
I WANT TO SEE HIM SO BAD, I CAN'T CONCENTRATE.
OH, IT'S ONLY YOU.
FINE.
YEAH.
OKAY.
HOLD ON A MINUTE.
OGIWARA'S ON THE PHONE.
WANT TO TALK TO HIM?

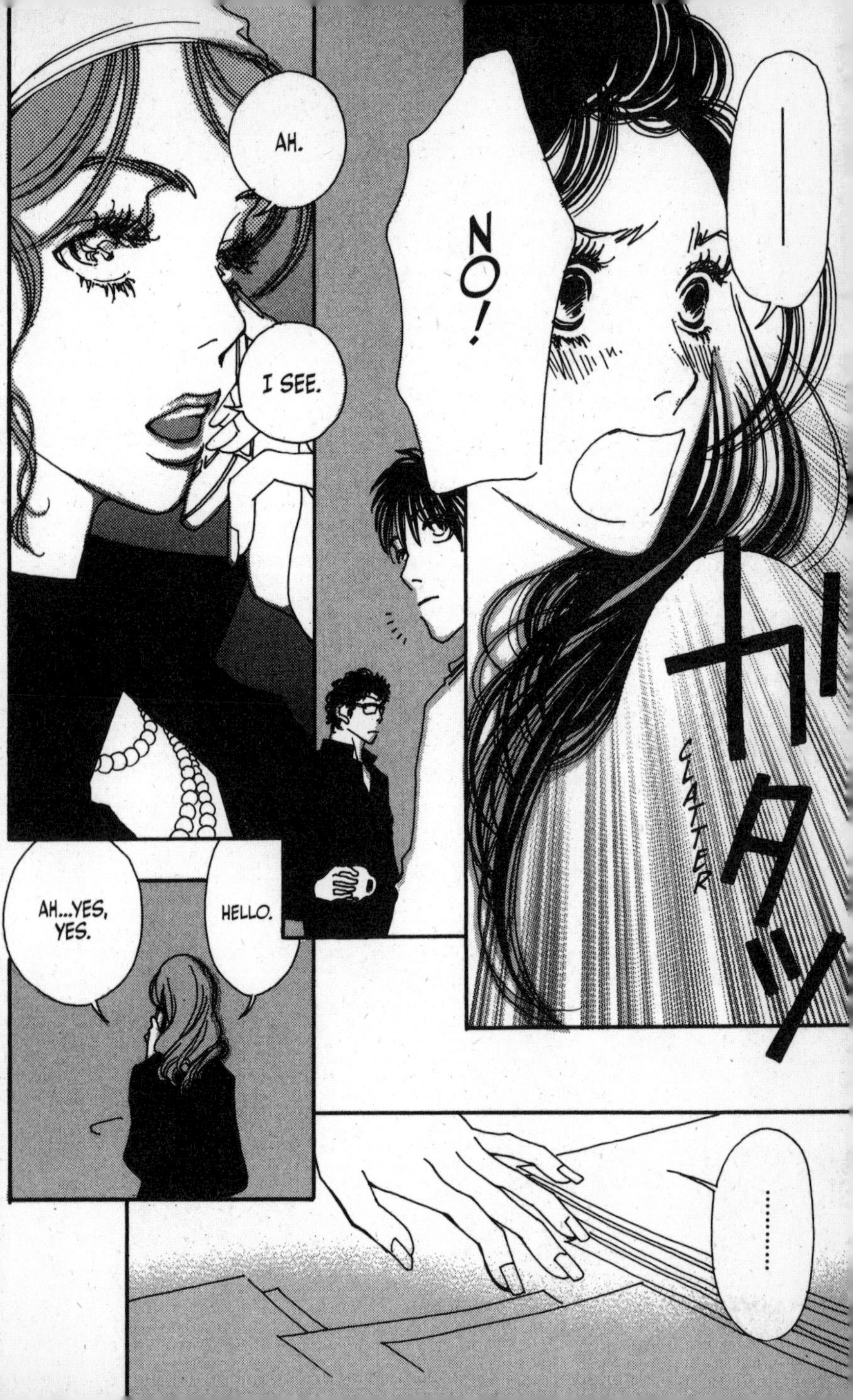

—
NO!
ガタッ
CLATTER
AH.
I SEE.
HELLO.
AH...YES, YES.
......

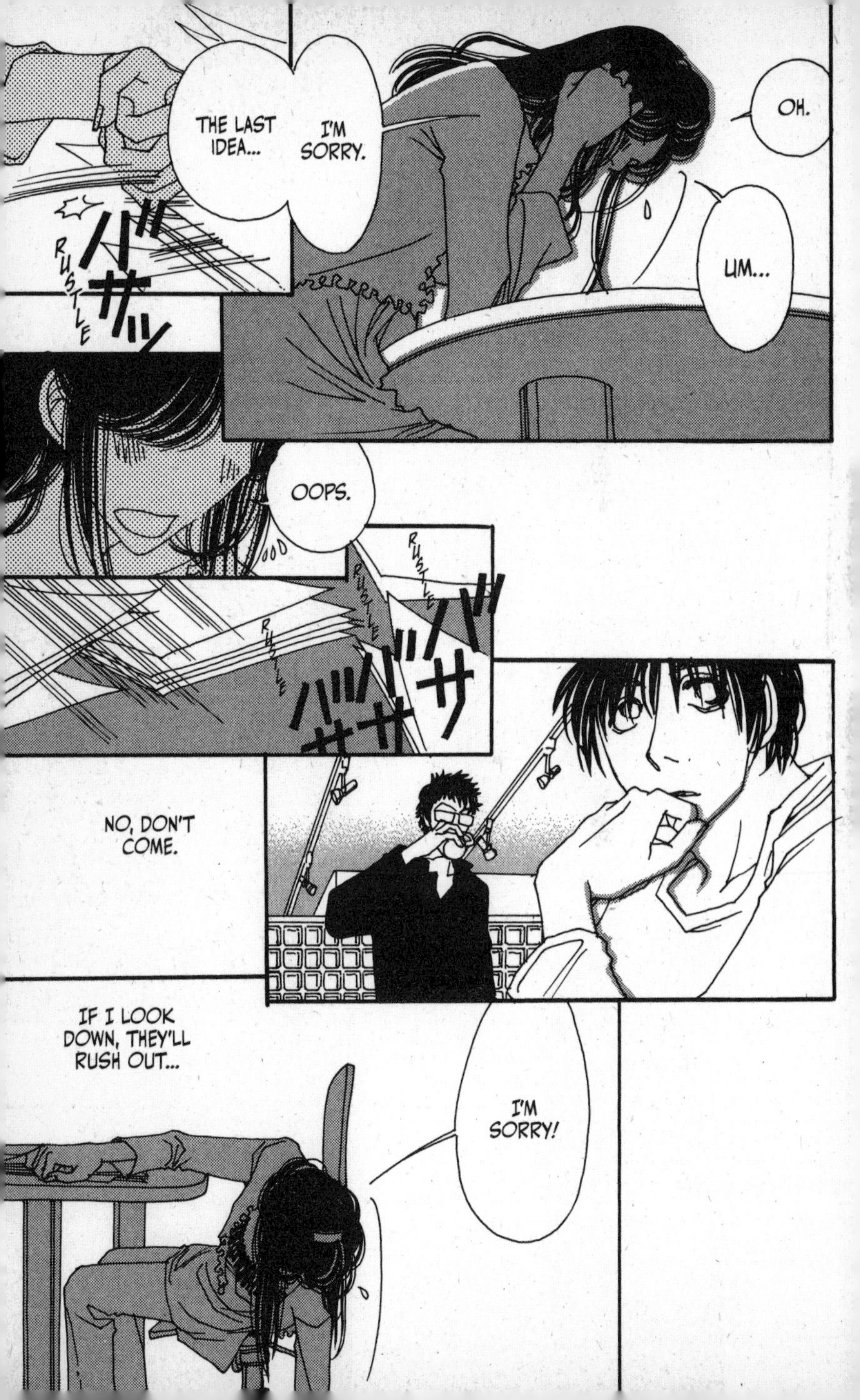
OH.
UM...
I'M SORRY.
THE LAST IDEA...
RUSTLE
OOPS.
RUSTLE
RUSTLE
RUSTLE
NO, DON'T COME.
IF I LOOK DOWN, THEY'LL RUSH OUT...
I'M SORRY!

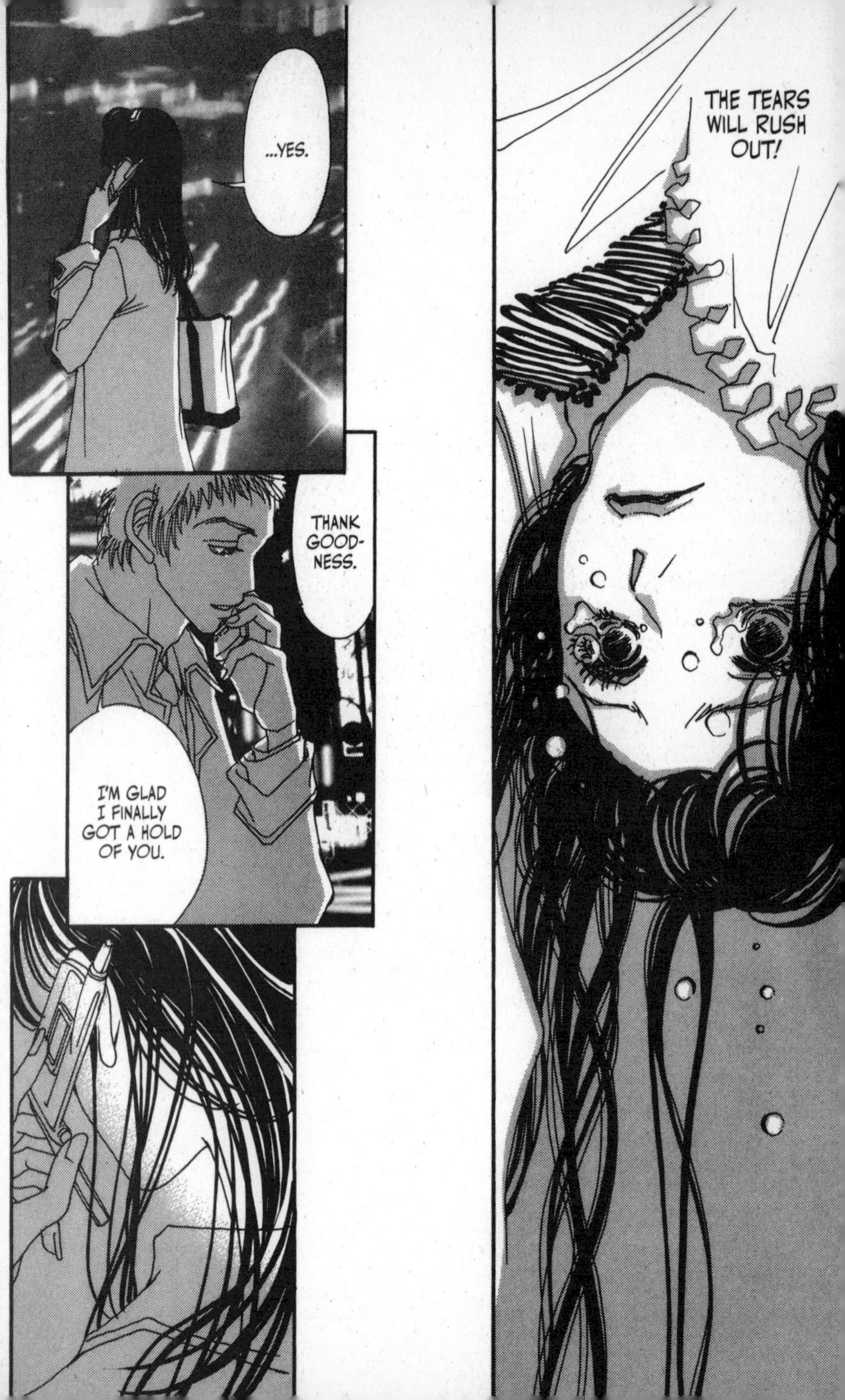
THE TEARS WILL RUSH OUT!
...YES.
THANK GOODNESS.
I'M GLAD I FINALLY GOT A HOLD OF YOU.

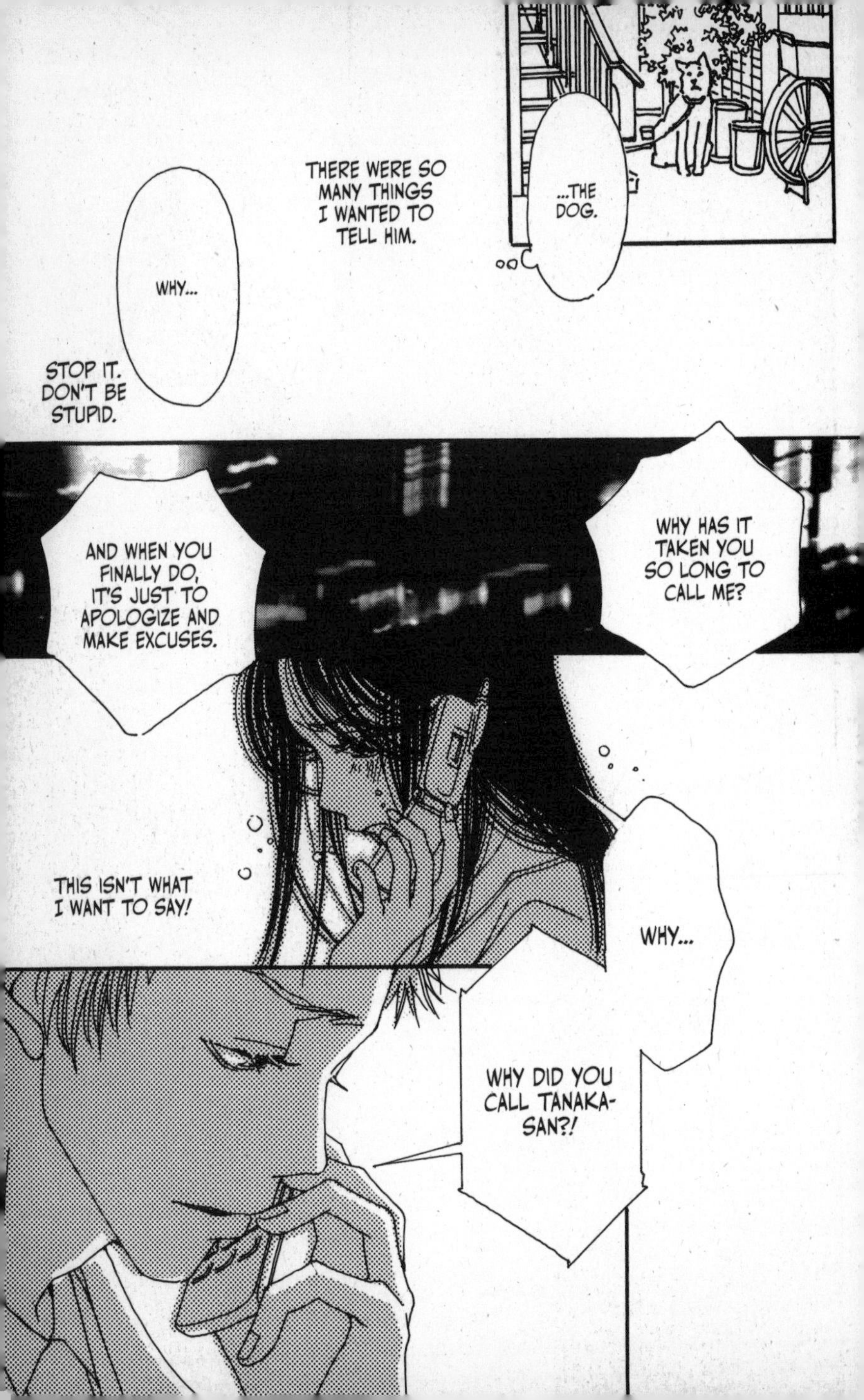
...THE DOG.
THERE WERE SO MANY THINGS I WANTED TO TELL HIM.
WHY...
STOP IT. DON'T BE STUPID.
WHY HAS IT TAKEN YOU SO LONG TO CALL ME?
AND WHEN YOU FINALLY DO, IT'S JUST TO APOLOGIZE AND MAKE EXCUSES.
WHY...
THIS ISN'T WHAT I WANT TO SAY!
WHY DID YOU CALL TANAKA-SAN?!

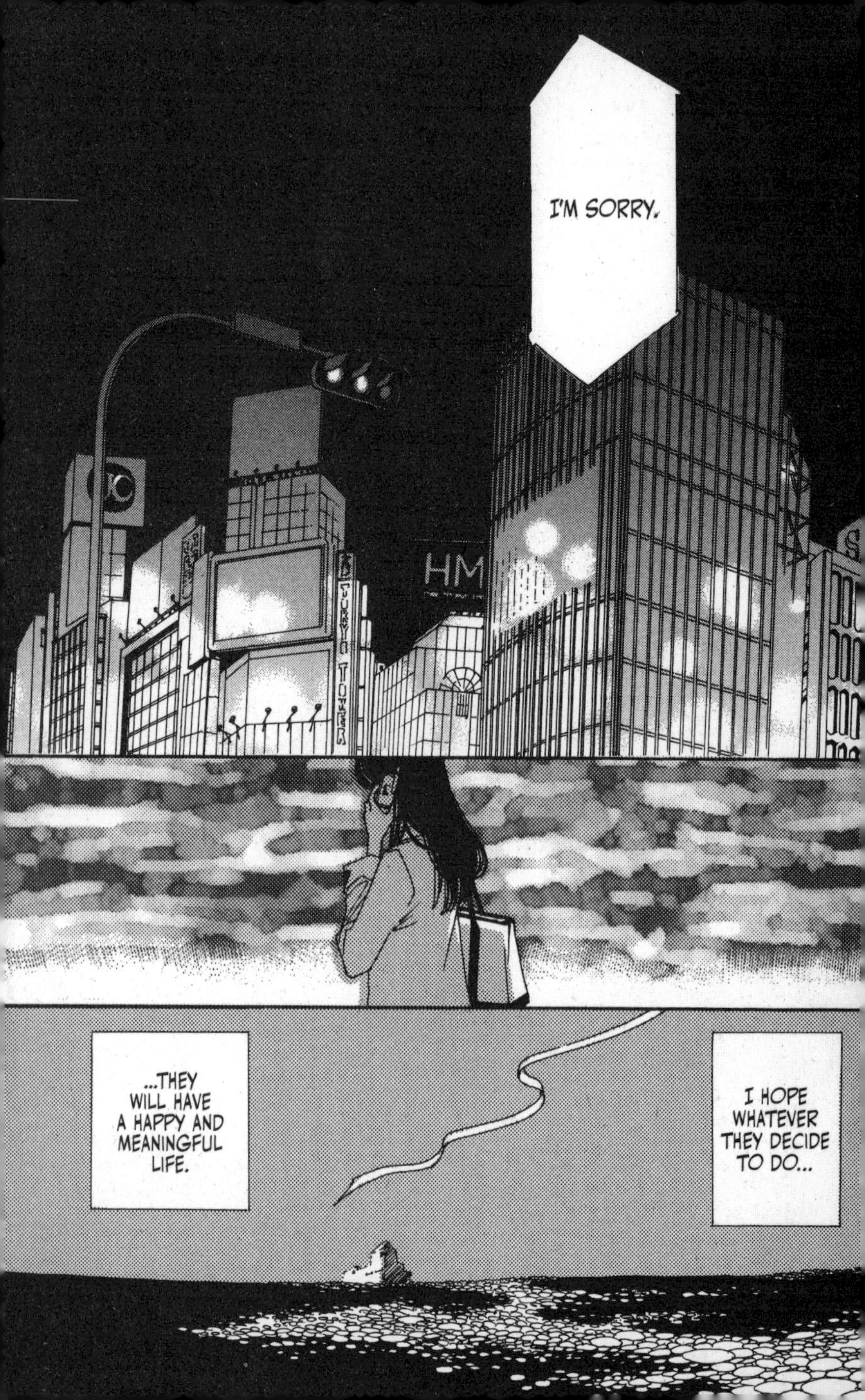
I'M SORRY.
I HOPE WHATEVER THEY DECIDE TO DO...
...THEY WILL HAVE A HAPPY AND MEANINGFUL LIFE.

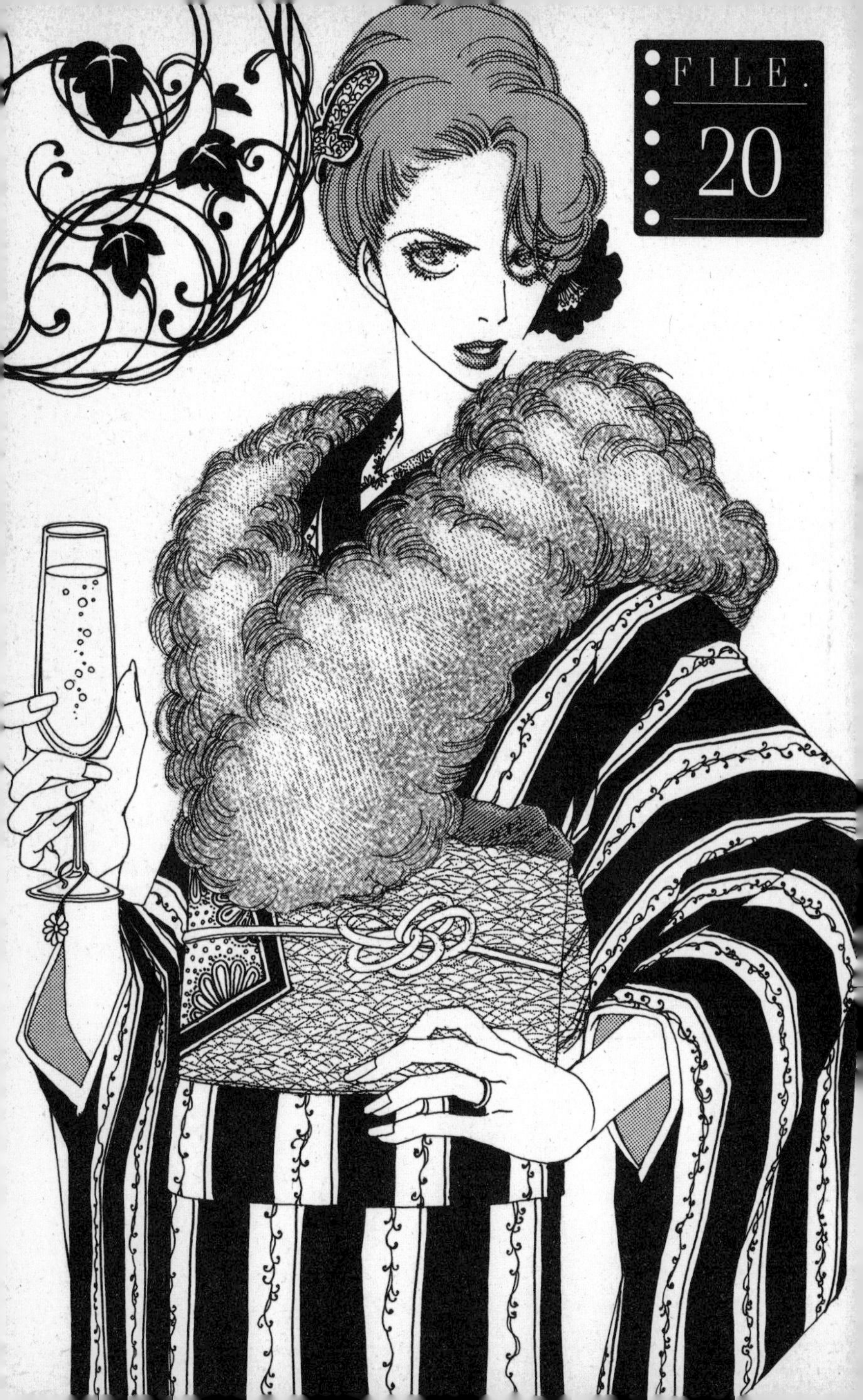
FILE.
20

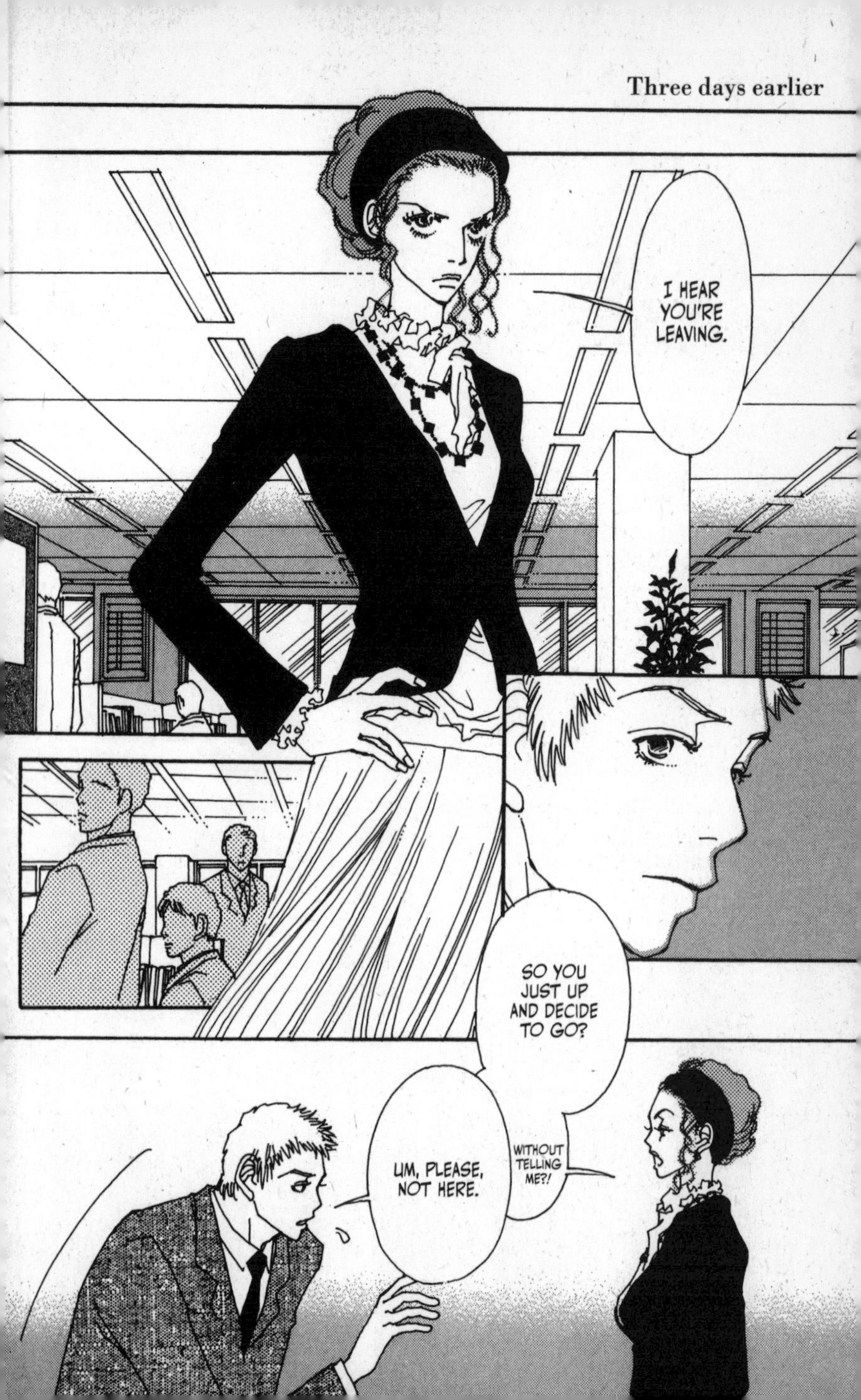
Three days earlier
I HEAR YOU'RE LEAVING.
SO YOU JUST UP AND DECIDE TO GO?
WITHOUT TELLING ME?!
UM, PLEASE, NOT HERE.

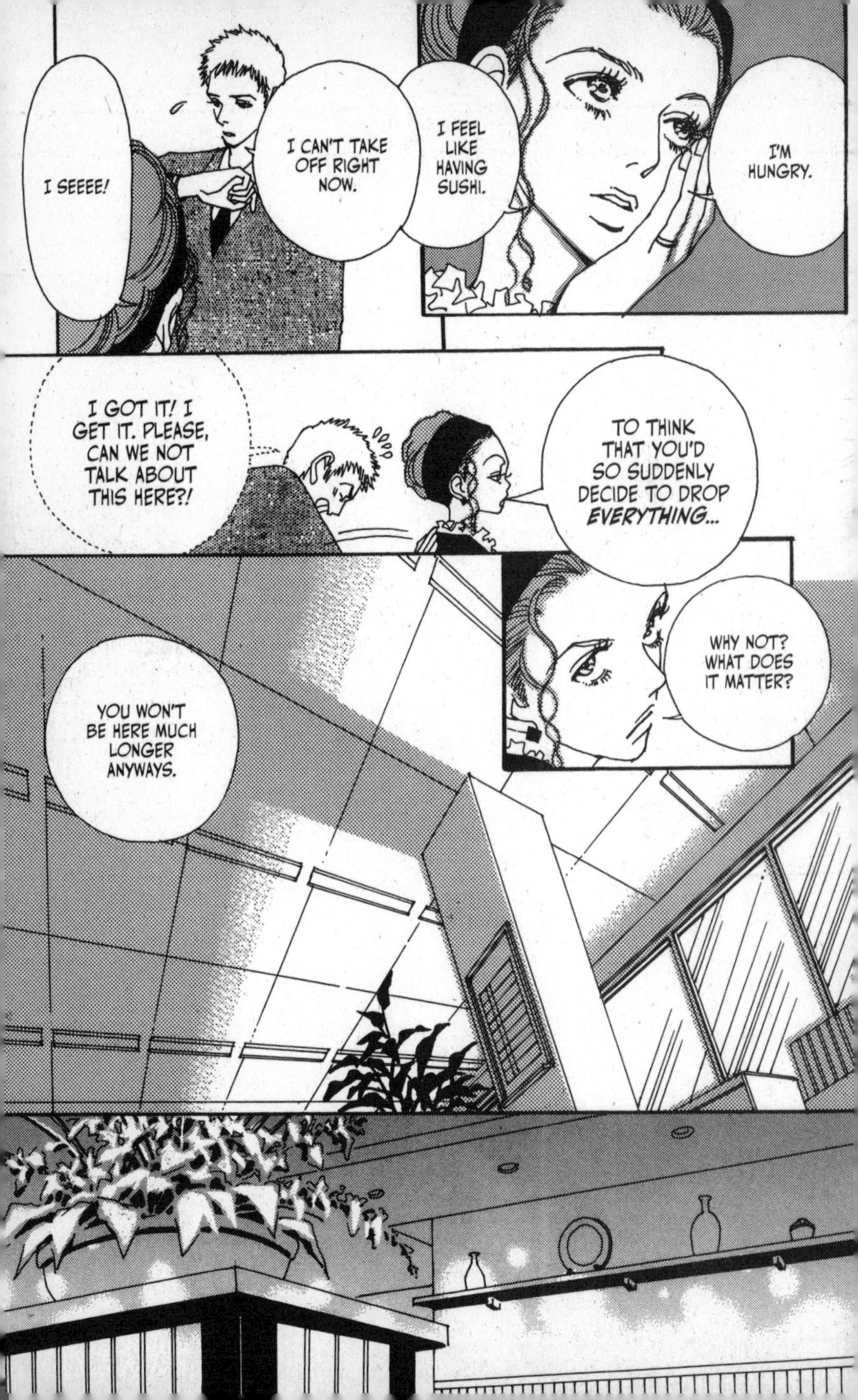
I'M HUNGRY.
I FEEL LIKE HAVING SUSHI.
I CAN'T TAKE OFF RIGHT NOW.
I SEEEE!
TO THINK THAT YOU'D SO SUDDENLY DECIDE TO DROP *EVERYTHING*...
I GOT IT! I GET IT. PLEASE, CAN WE NOT TALK ABOUT THIS HERE?!
WHY NOT? WHAT DOES IT MATTER?
YOU WON'T BE HERE MUCH LONGER ANYWAYS.

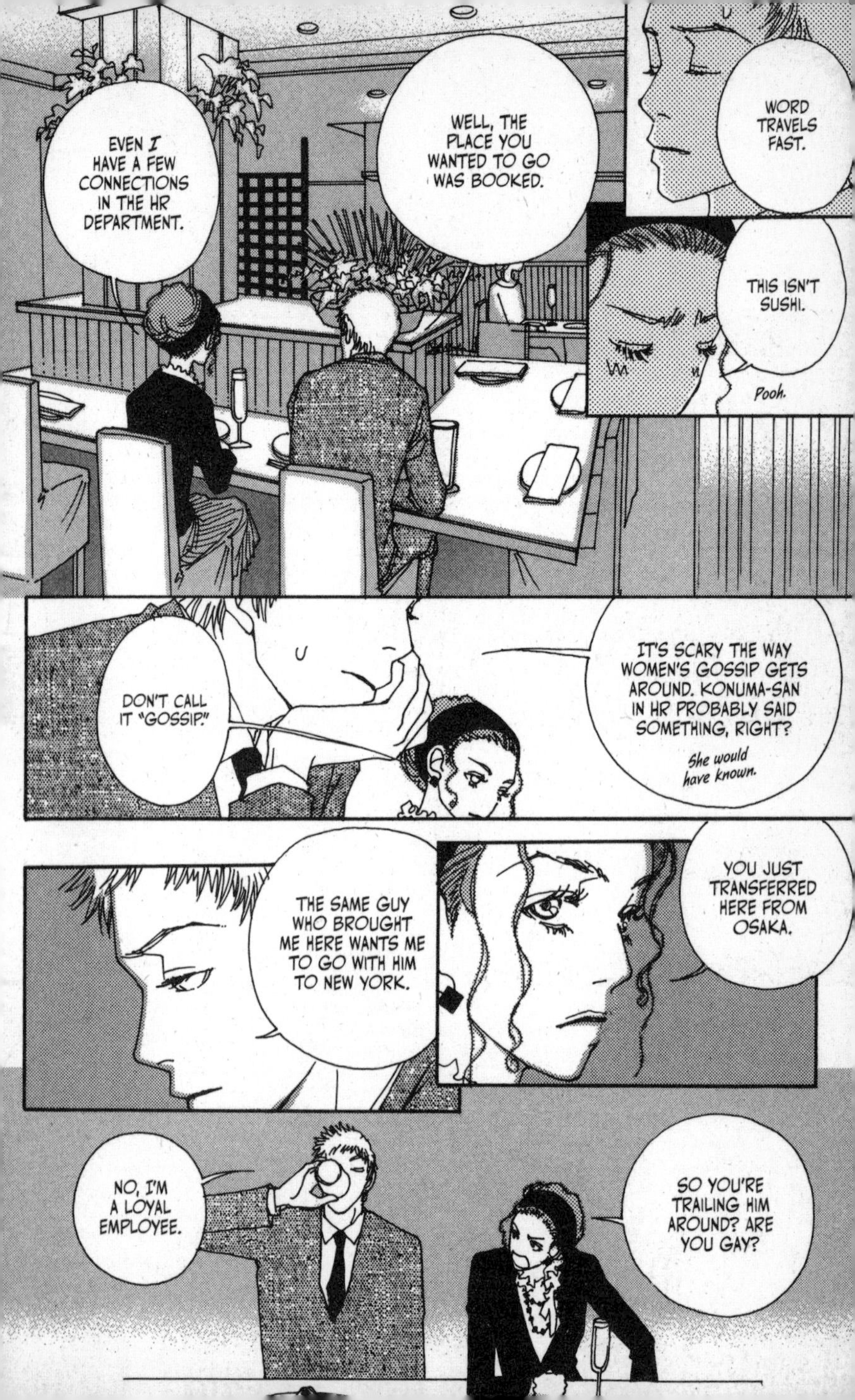

WORD TRAVELS FAST.
THIS ISN'T SUSHI.
Pooh.
WELL, THE PLACE YOU WANTED TO GO WAS BOOKED.
EVEN I HAVE A FEW CONNECTIONS IN THE HR DEPARTMENT.
IT'S SCARY THE WAY WOMEN'S GOSSIP GETS AROUND. KONUMA-SAN IN HR PROBABLY SAID SOMETHING, RIGHT?
She would have known.
DON'T CALL IT "GOSSIP."
YOU JUST TRANSFERRED HERE FROM OSAKA.
THE SAME GUY WHO BROUGHT ME HERE WANTS ME TO GO WITH HIM TO NEW YORK.
SO YOU'RE TRAILING HIM AROUND? ARE YOU GAY?
NO, I'M A LOYAL EMPLOYEE.

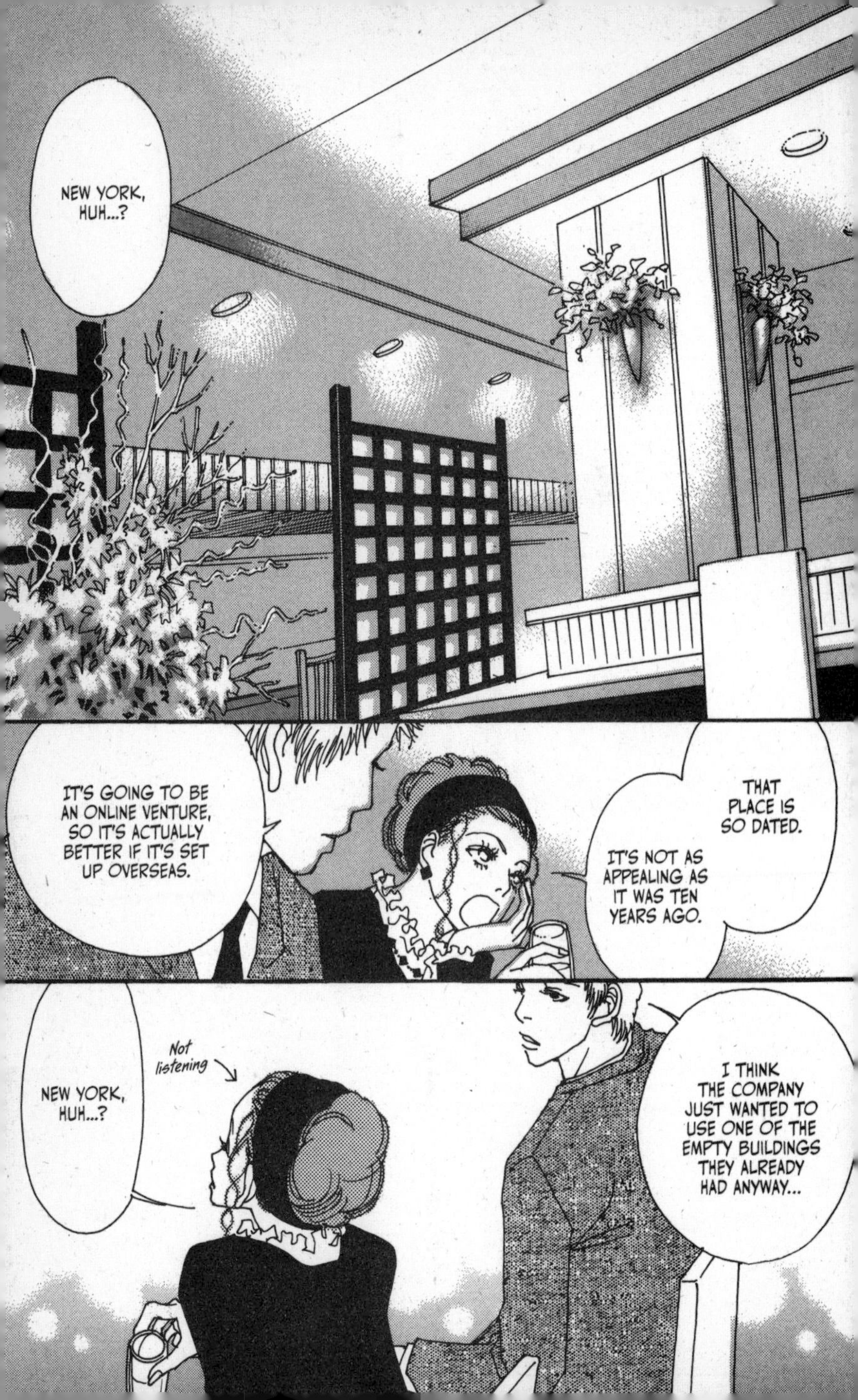
NEW YORK, HUH...?
THAT PLACE IS SO DATED.
IT'S NOT AS APPEALING AS IT WAS TEN YEARS AGO.
IT'S GOING TO BE AN ONLINE VENTURE, SO IT'S ACTUALLY BETTER IF IT'S SET UP OVERSEAS.
I THINK THE COMPANY JUST WANTED TO USE ONE OF THE EMPTY BUILDINGS THEY ALREADY HAD ANYWAY...
Not listening
NEW YORK, HUH...?

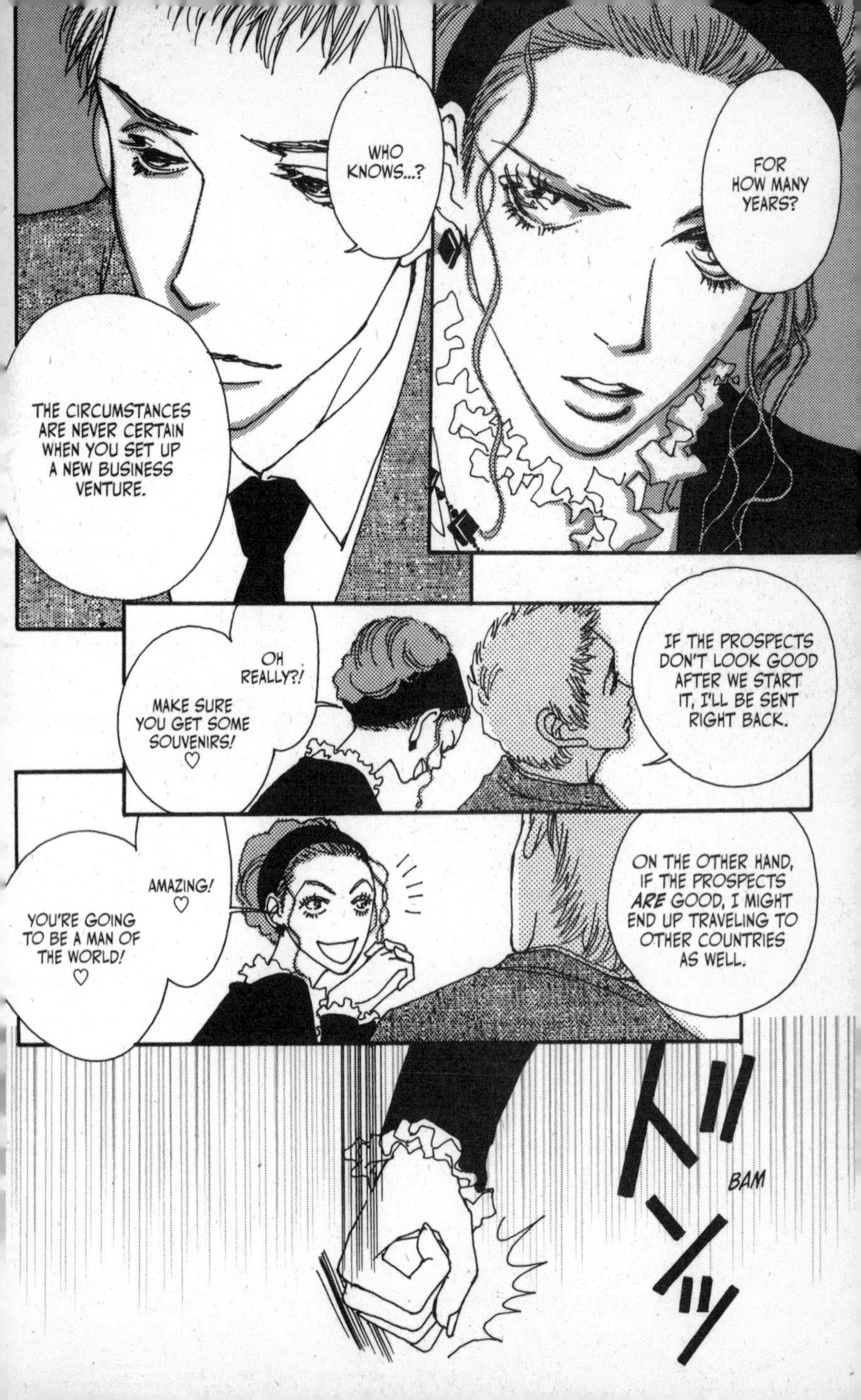

FOR HOW MANY YEARS?
WHO KNOWS...?
THE CIRCUMSTANCES ARE NEVER CERTAIN WHEN YOU SET UP A NEW BUSINESS VENTURE.
IF THE PROSPECTS DON'T LOOK GOOD AFTER WE START IT, I'LL BE SENT RIGHT BACK.
OH REALLY?! MAKE SURE YOU GET SOME SOUVENIRS! ♡
ON THE OTHER HAND, IF THE PROSPECTS *ARE* GOOD, I MIGHT END UP TRAVELING TO OTHER COUNTRIES AS WELL.
AMAZING! ♡ YOU'RE GOING TO BE A MAN OF THE WORLD! ♡
BAM

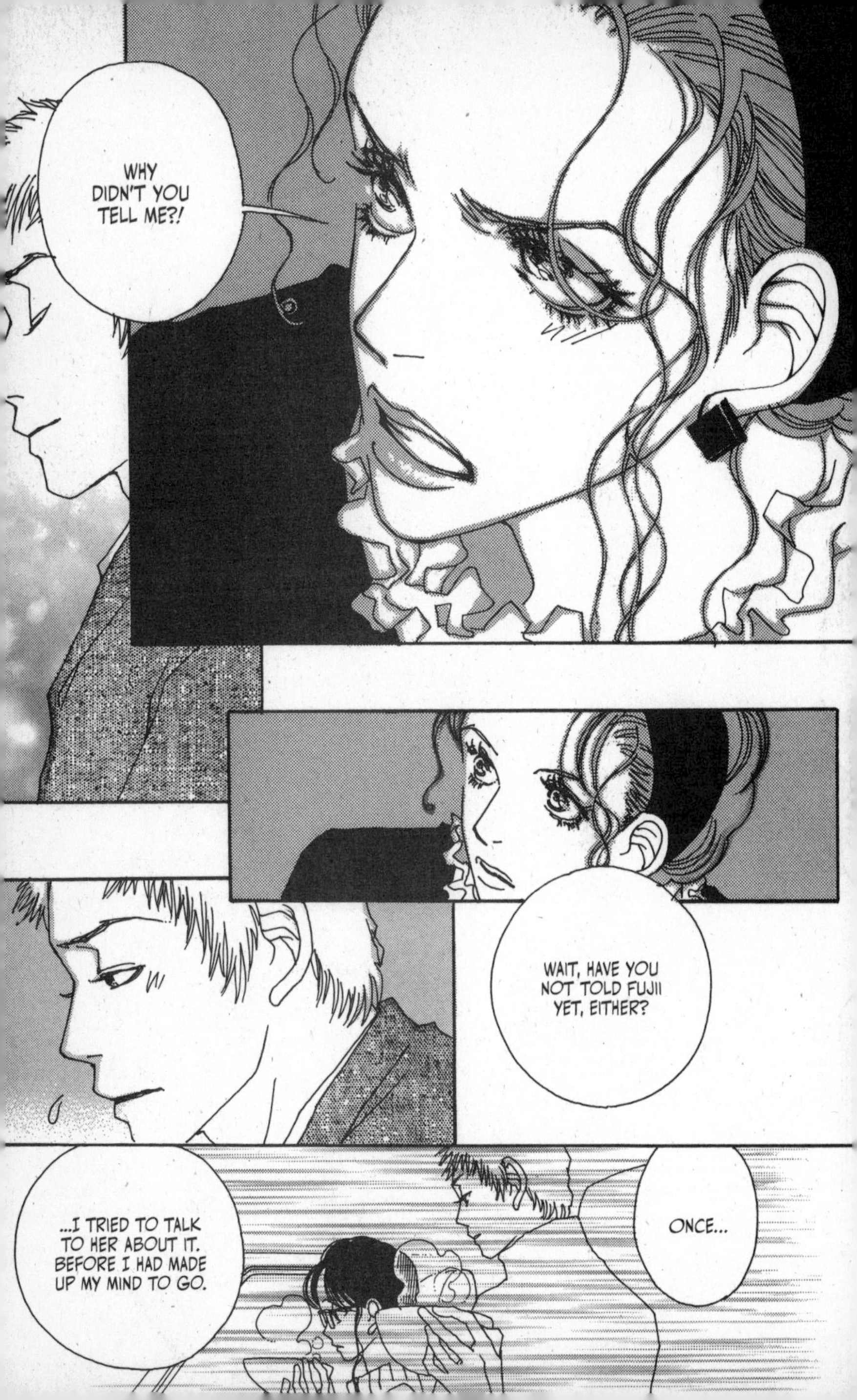
WHY DIDN'T YOU TELL ME?!
WAIT, HAVE YOU NOT TOLD FUJII YET, EITHER?
ONCE...
...I TRIED TO TALK TO HER ABOUT IT.
BEFORE I HAD MADE UP MY MIND TO GO.

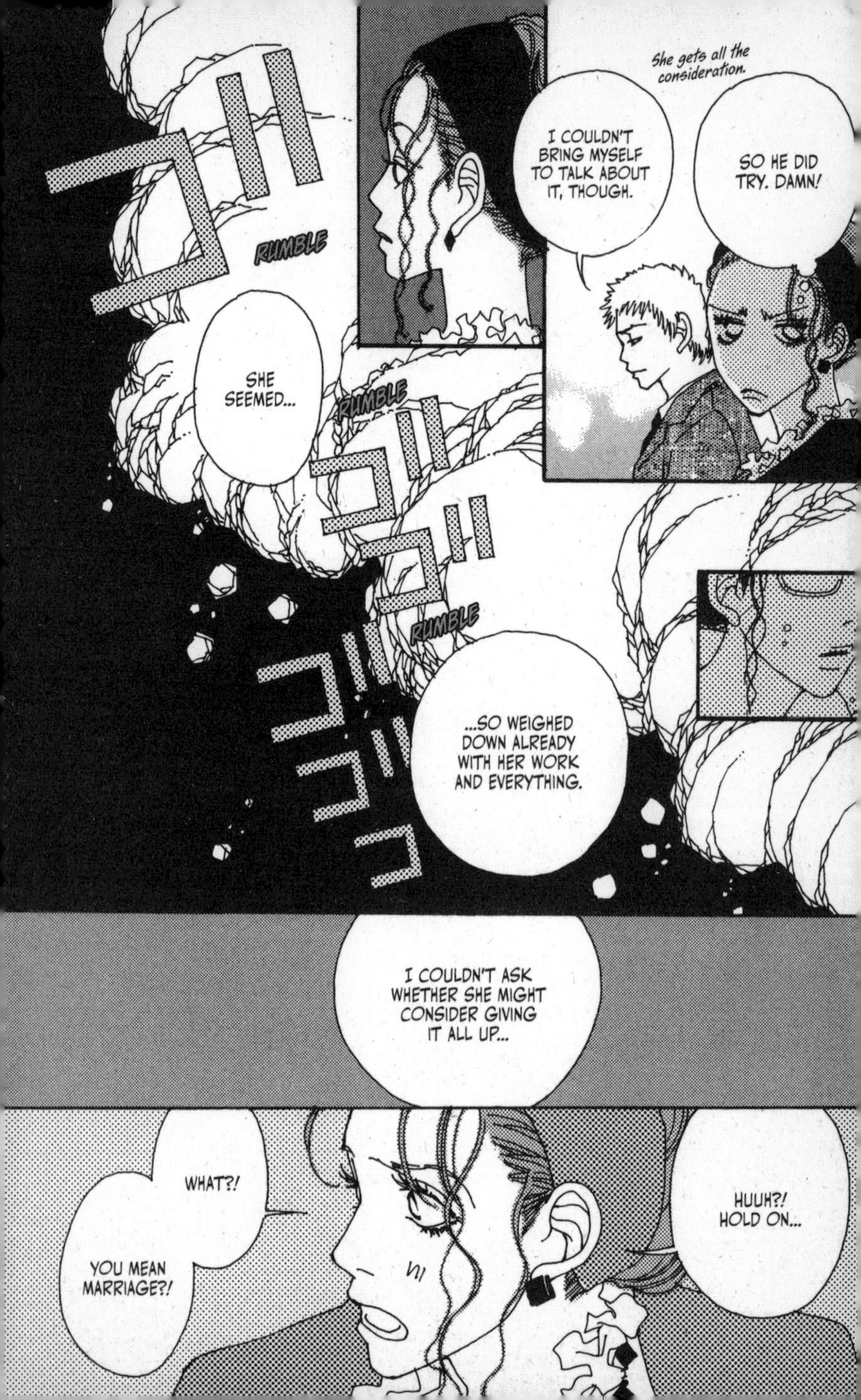
SO HE DID TRY. DAMN!
She gets all the consideration.
I COULDN'T BRING MYSELF TO TALK ABOUT IT, THOUGH.
RUMBLE
SHE SEEMED...
RUMBLE
RUMBLE
...SO WEIGHED DOWN ALREADY WITH HER WORK AND EVERYTHING.
I COULDN'T ASK WHETHER SHE MIGHT CONSIDER GIVING IT ALL UP...
HUUH?! HOLD ON...
WHAT?!
YOU MEAN MARRIAGE?!

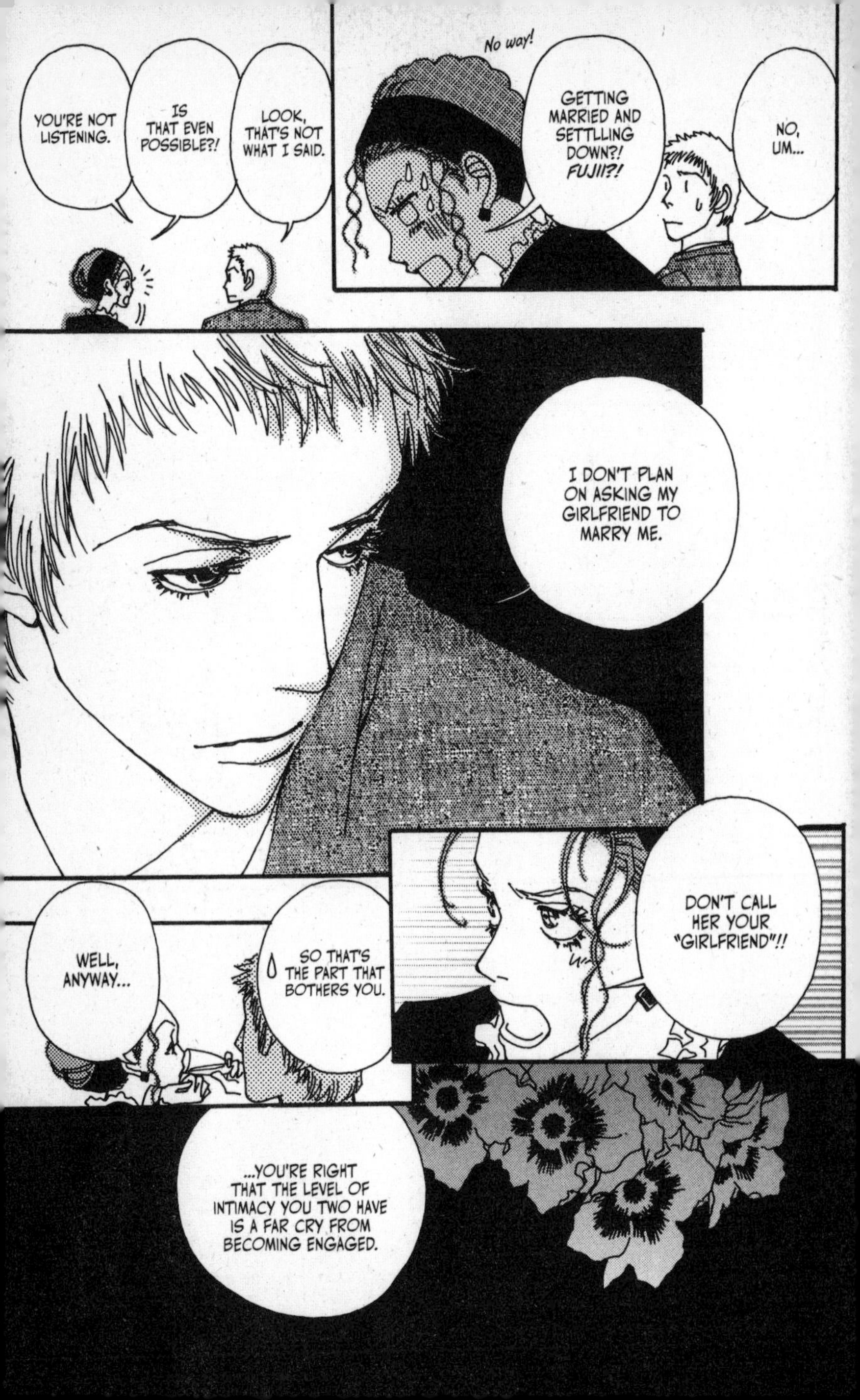
NO, UM...
GETTING MARRIED AND SETTLLING DOWN?! FUJII?!
No way!
LOOK, THAT'S NOT WHAT I SAID.
IS THAT EVEN POSSIBLE?!
YOU'RE NOT LISTENING.
I DON'T PLAN ON ASKING MY GIRLFRIEND TO MARRY ME.
DON'T CALL HER YOUR "GIRLFRIEND"!!
SO THAT'S THE PART THAT BOTHERS YOU.
WELL, ANYWAY...
...YOU'RE RIGHT THAT THE LEVEL OF INTIMACY YOU TWO HAVE IS A FAR CRY FROM BECOMING ENGAGED.

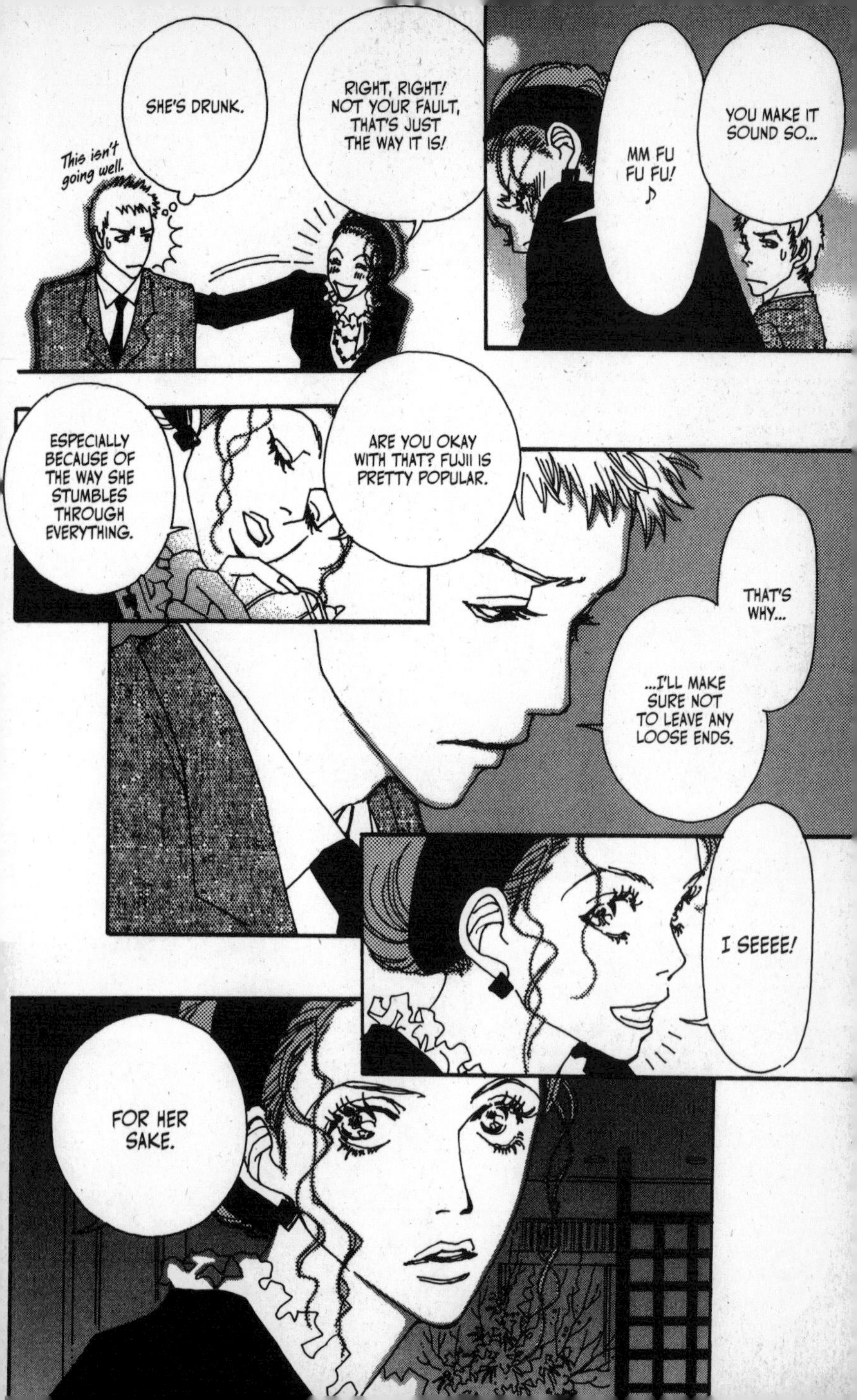
YOU MAKE IT SOUND SO...
MM FU FU FU! ♪
RIGHT, RIGHT! NOT YOUR FAULT, THAT'S JUST THE WAY IT IS!
SHE'S DRUNK.
This isn't going well.
ARE YOU OKAY WITH THAT? FUJII IS PRETTY POPULAR.
ESPECIALLY BECAUSE OF THE WAY SHE STUMBLES THROUGH EVERYTHING.
THAT'S WHY...
...I'LL MAKE SURE NOT TO LEAVE ANY LOOSE ENDS.
I SEEEE!
FOR HER SAKE.

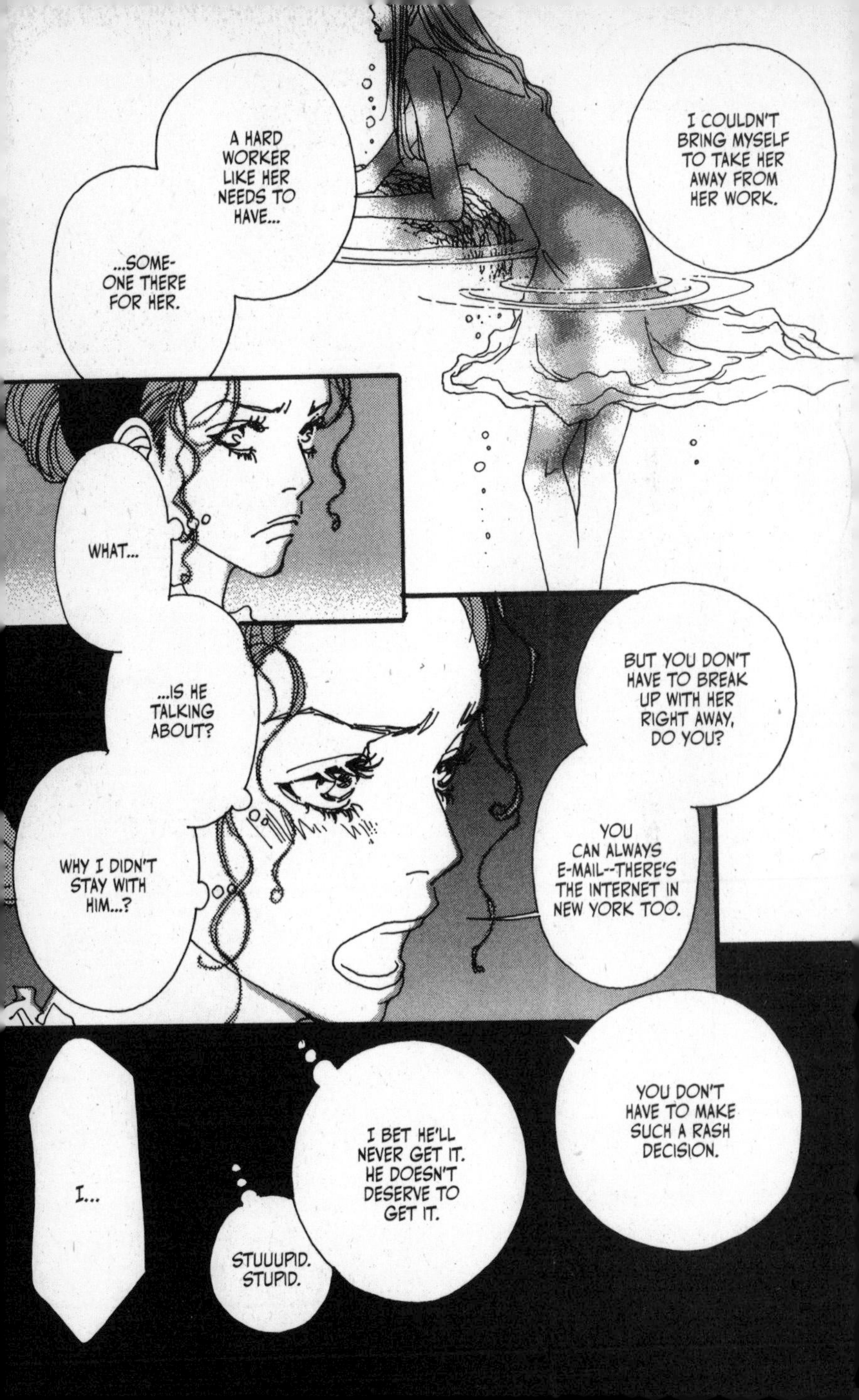

I COULDN'T BRING MYSELF TO TAKE HER AWAY FROM HER WORK.
A HARD WORKER LIKE HER NEEDS TO HAVE...
...SOME-ONE THERE FOR HER.
WHAT...
BUT YOU DON'T HAVE TO BREAK UP WITH HER RIGHT AWAY, DO YOU?
YOU CAN ALWAYS E-MAIL--THERE'S THE INTERNET IN NEW YORK TOO.
...IS HE TALKING ABOUT?
WHY I DIDN'T STAY WITH HIM...?
YOU DON'T HAVE TO MAKE SUCH A RASH DECISION.
I BET HE'LL NEVER GET IT. HE DOESN'T DESERVE TO GET IT.
STUUUPID. STUPID.
I...

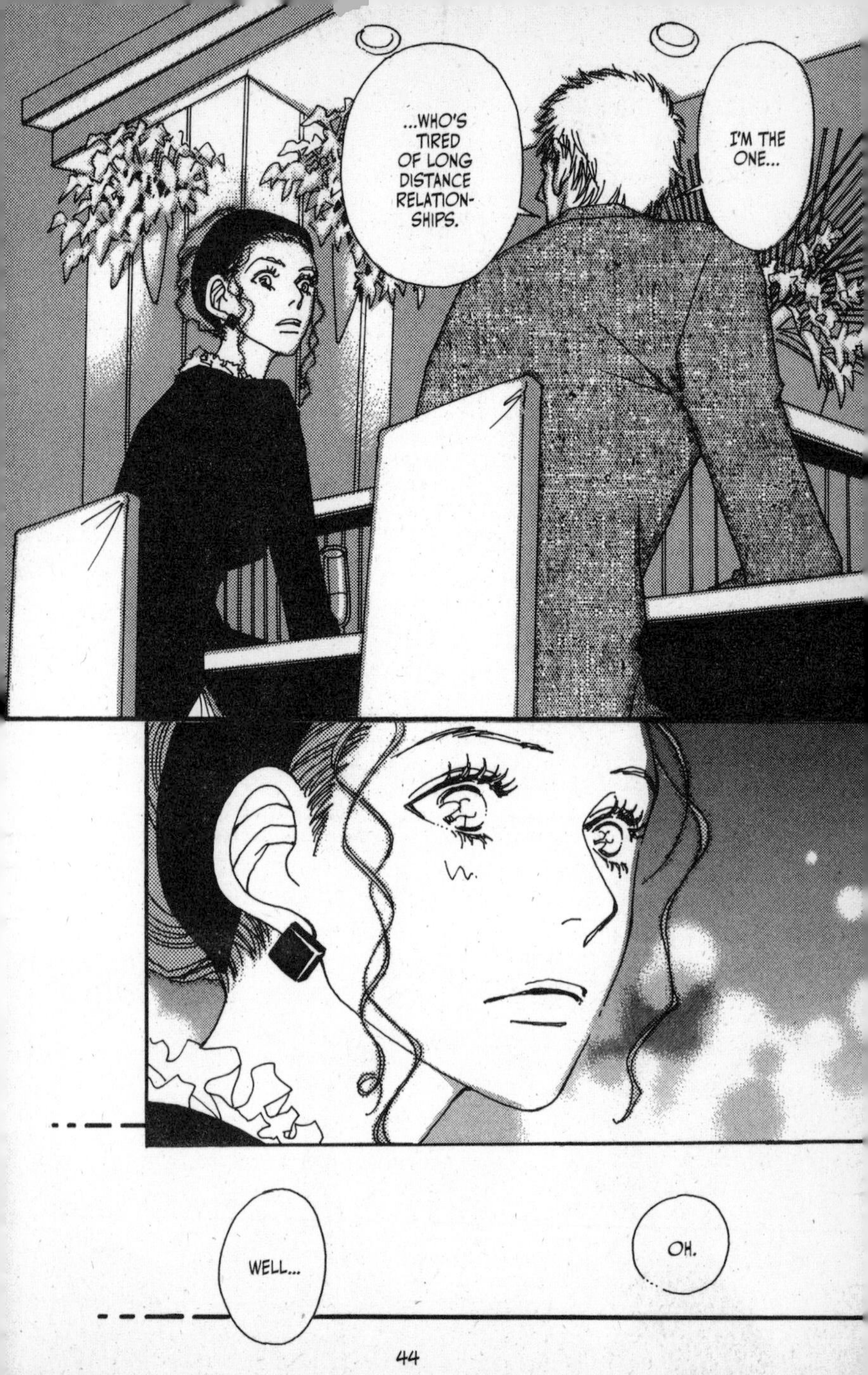
I'M THE ONE...
...WHO'S TIRED OF LONG DISTANCE RELATION-SHIPS.
OH.
WELL...

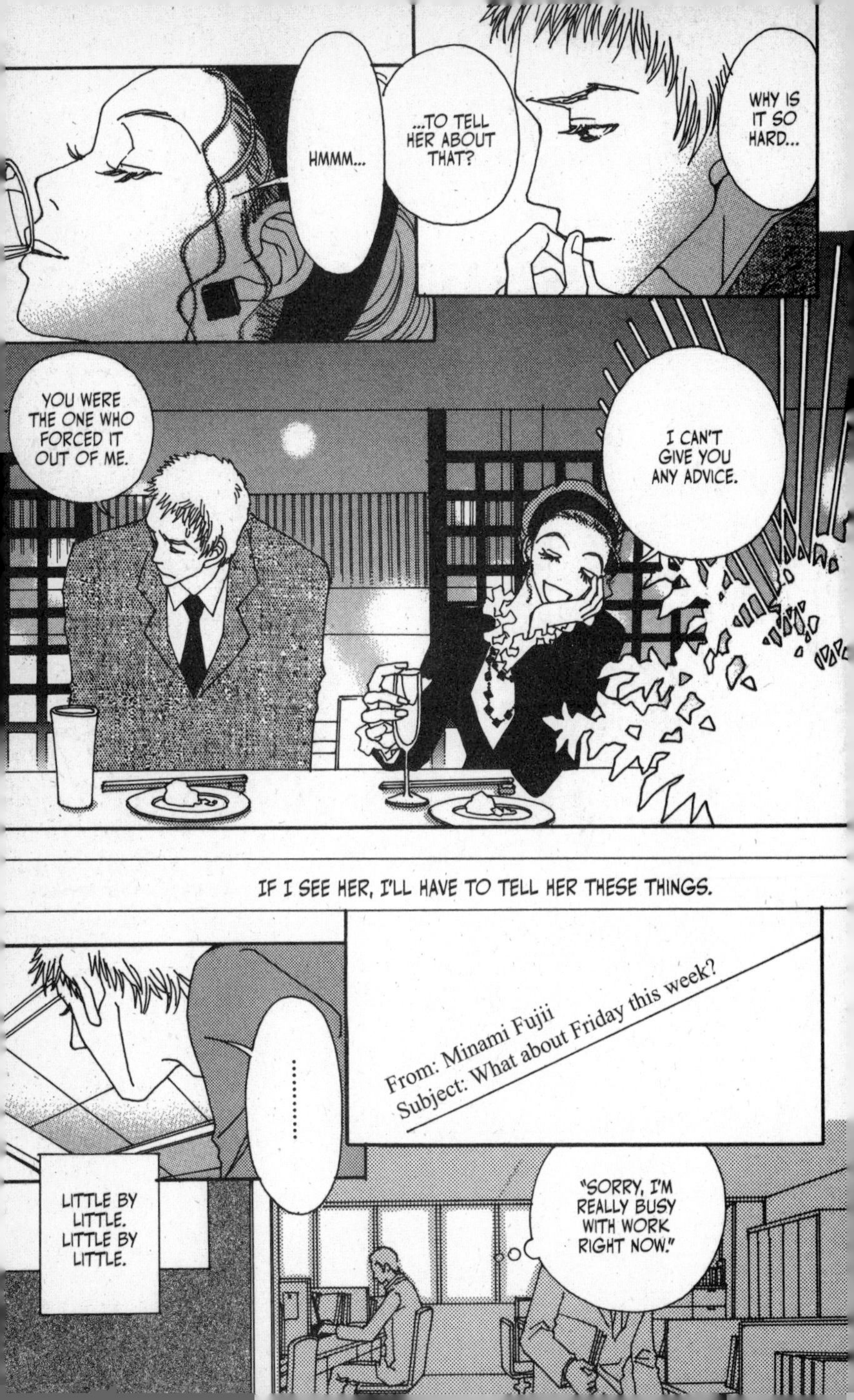
WHY IS IT SO HARD...
...TO TELL HER ABOUT THAT?
HMMM...
I CAN'T GIVE YOU ANY ADVICE.
YOU WERE THE ONE WHO FORCED IT OUT OF ME.
IF I SEE HER, I'LL HAVE TO TELL HER THESE THINGS.
From: Minami Fujii
Subject: What about Friday this week?
"SORRY, I'M REALLY BUSY WITH WORK RIGHT NOW."
......
LITTLE BY LITTLE. LITTLE BY LITTLE.

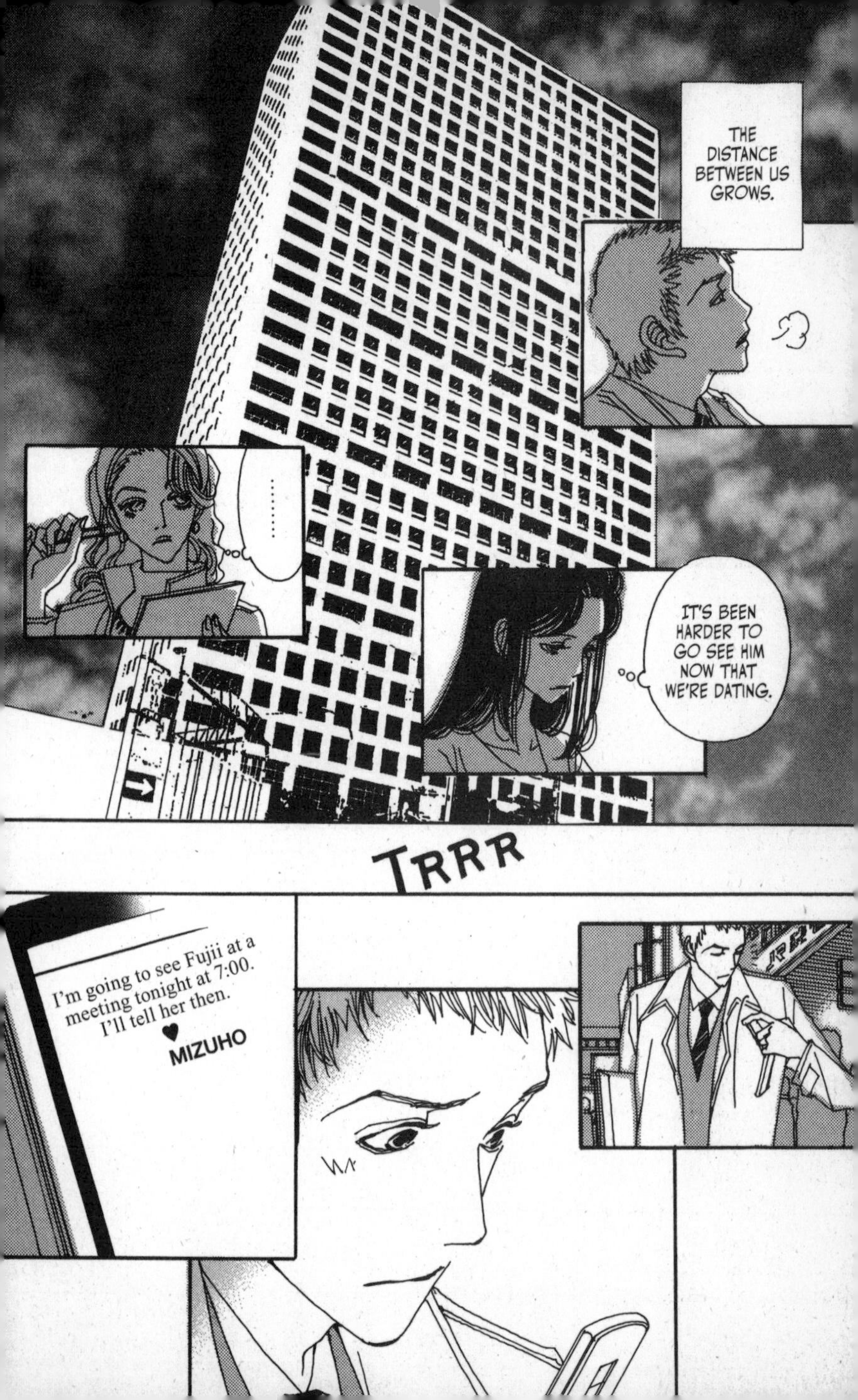
THE DISTANCE BETWEEN US GROWS.
IT'S BEEN HARDER TO GO SEE HIM NOW THAT WE'RE DATING.
......
TRRR
I'm going to see Fujii at a meeting tonight at 7:00. I'll tell her then.
♥
MIZUHO

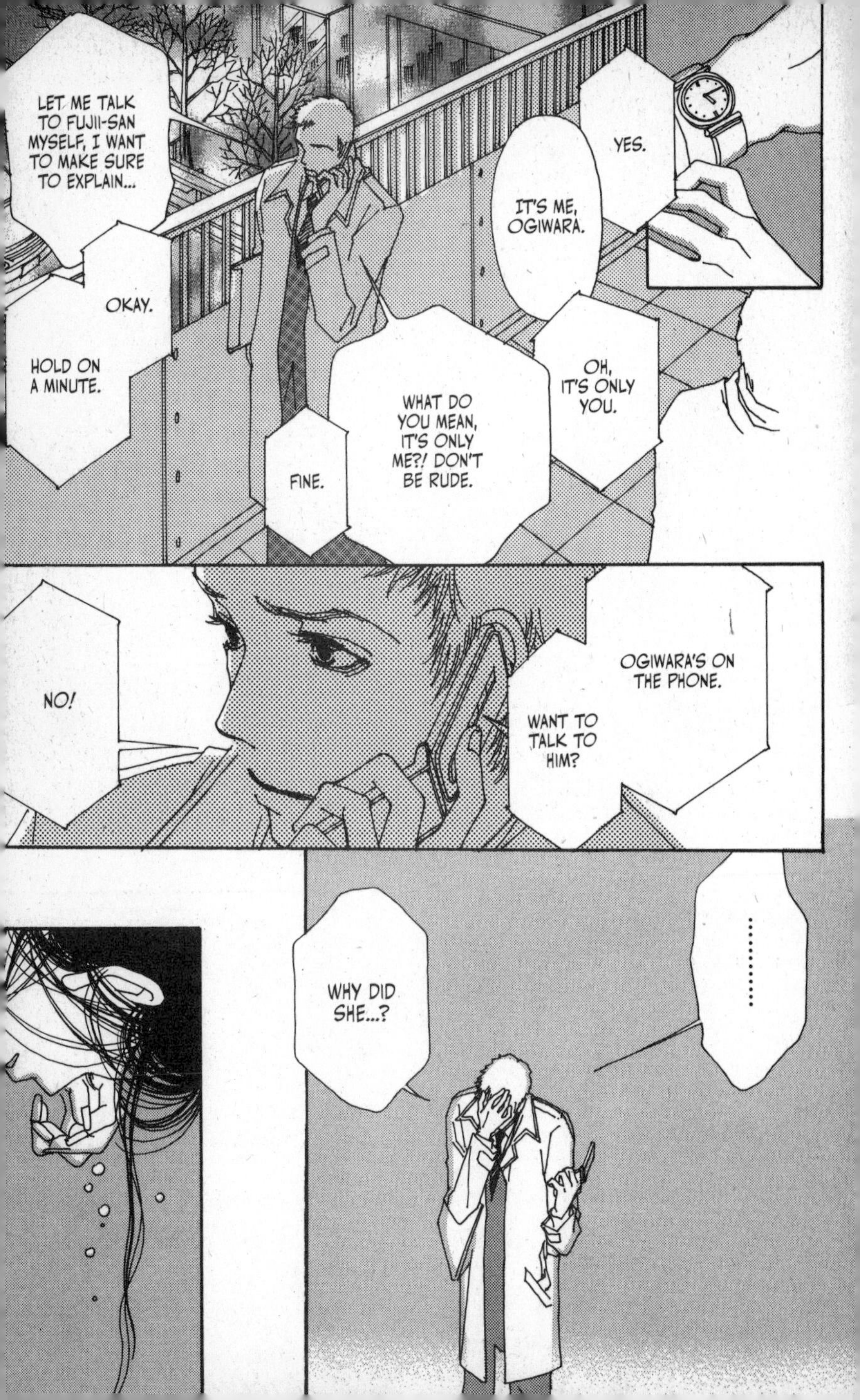
YES.
IT'S ME, OGIWARA.
OH, IT'S ONLY YOU.
WHAT DO YOU MEAN, IT'S ONLY ME?! DON'T BE RUDE.
FINE.
LET ME TALK TO FUJII-SAN MYSELF, I WANT TO MAKE SURE TO EXPLAIN...
OKAY.
HOLD ON A MINUTE.
OGIWARA'S ON THE PHONE.
WANT TO TALK TO HIM?
NO!
....
WHY DID SHE...?

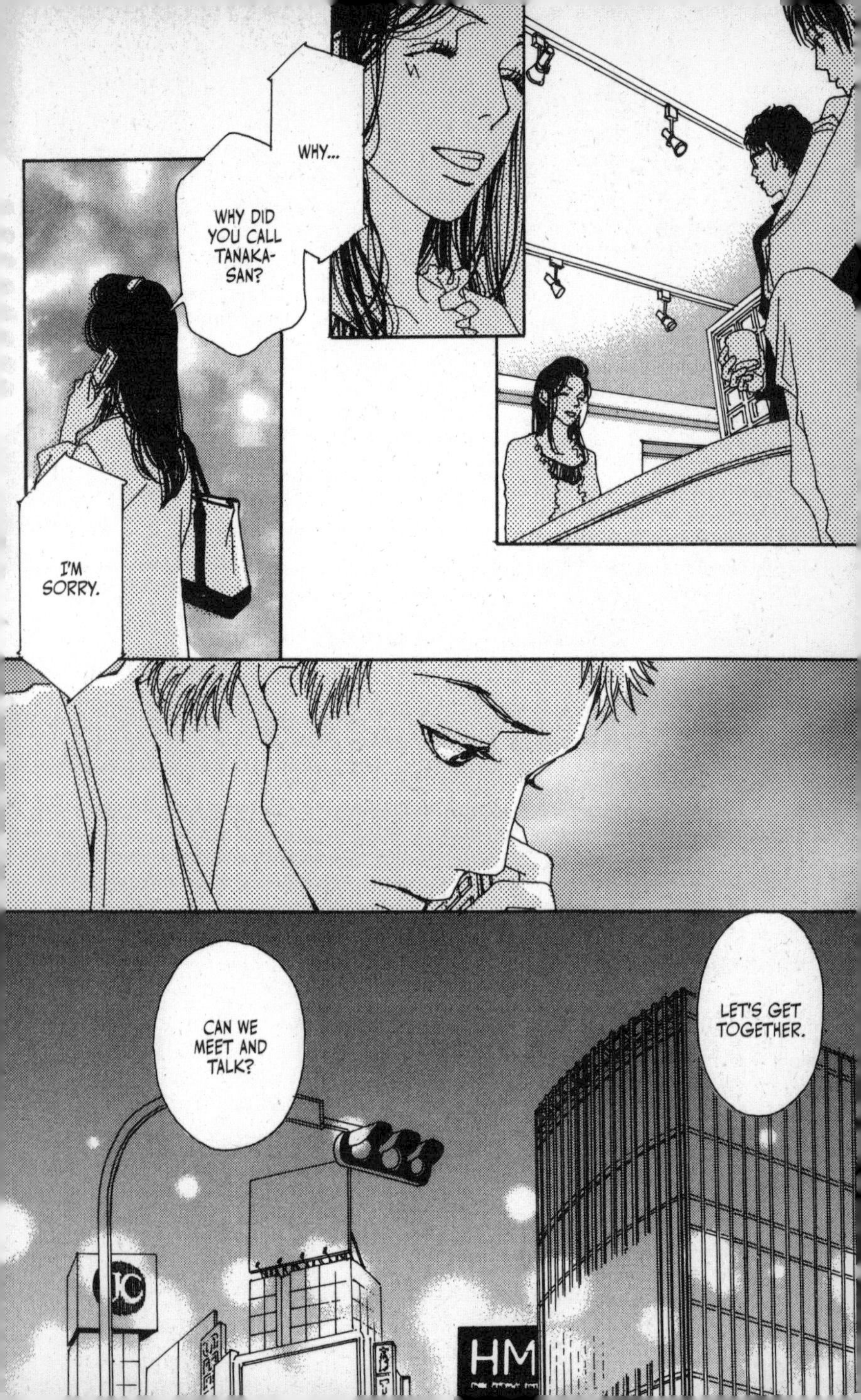
WHY...
WHY DID YOU CALL TANAKA-SAN?
I'M SORRY.
LET'S GET TOGETHER.
CAN WE MEET AND TALK?
HM

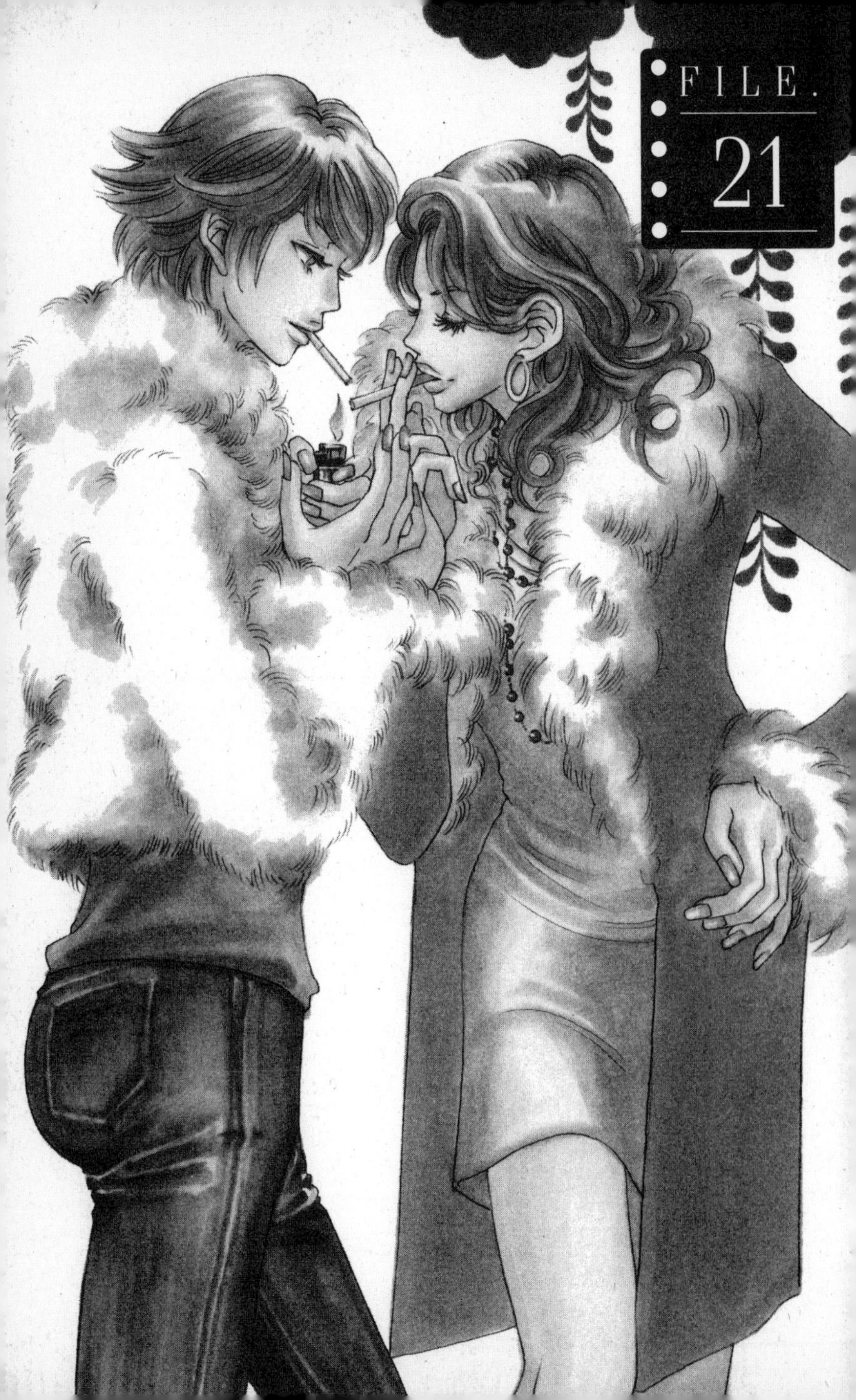
FILE.
21

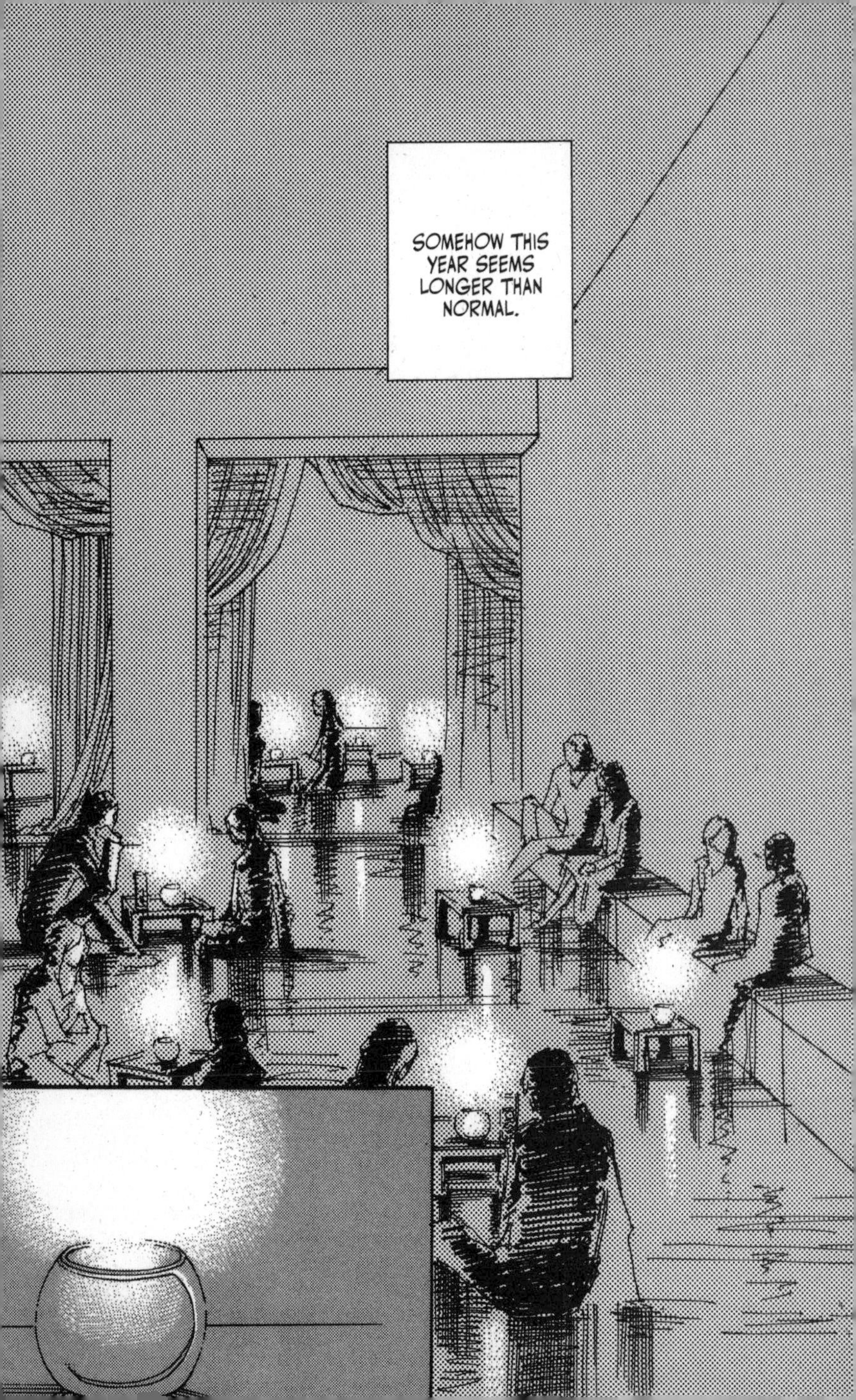
SOMEHOW THIS YEAR SEEMS LONGER THAN NORMAL.

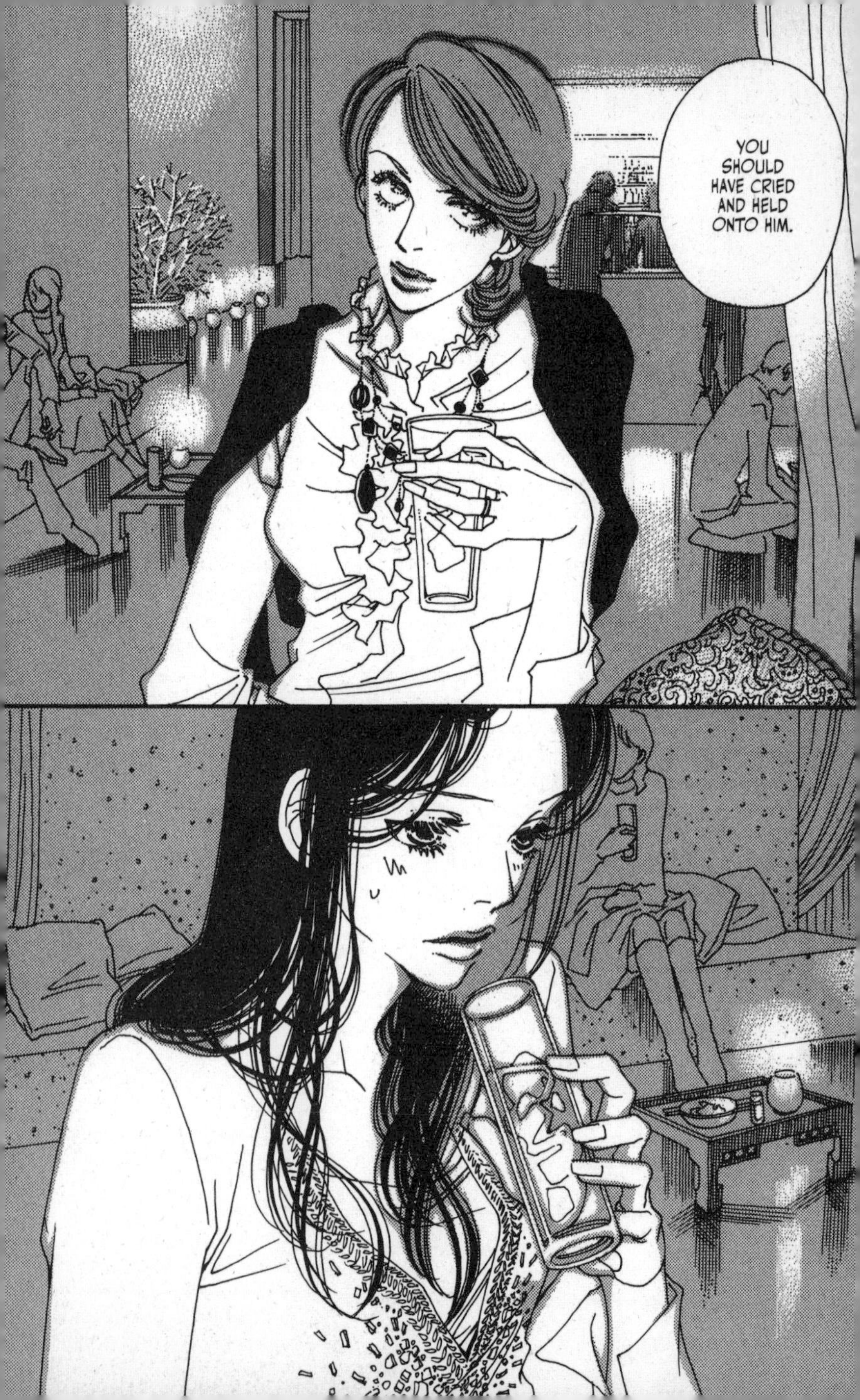
YOU SHOULD HAVE CRIED AND HELD ONTO HIM.

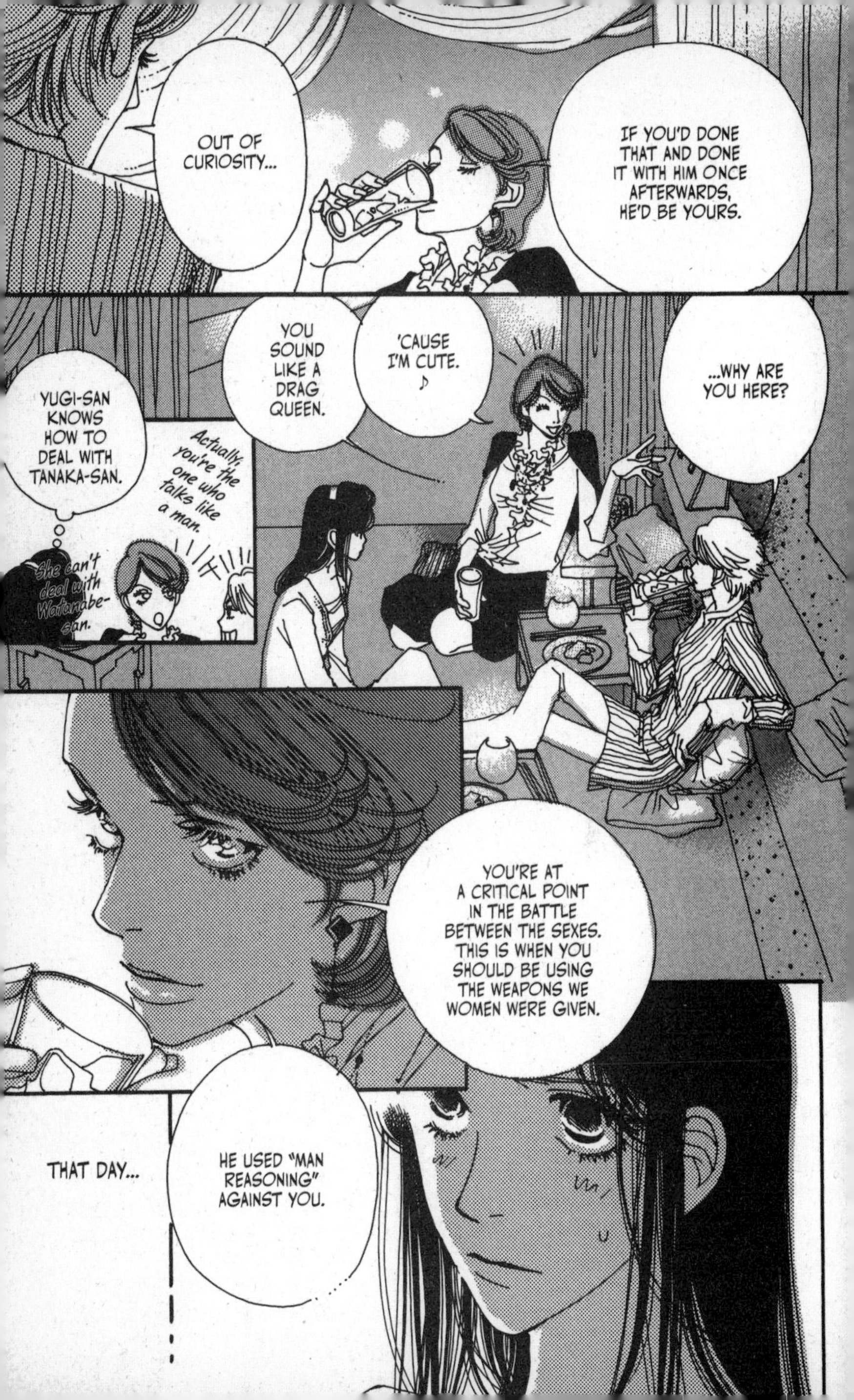

IF YOU'D DONE THAT AND DONE IT WITH HIM ONCE AFTERWARDS, HE'D BE YOURS.
OUT OF CURIOSITY...
...WHY ARE YOU HERE?
'CAUSE I'M CUTE. ♪
YOU SOUND LIKE A DRAG QUEEN.
Actually, you're the one who talks like a man.
YUGI-SAN KNOWS HOW TO DEAL WITH TANAKA-SAN.
She can't deal with Watanabe-san.
YOU'RE AT A CRITICAL POINT IN THE BATTLE BETWEEN THE SEXES. THIS IS WHEN YOU SHOULD BE USING THE WEAPONS WE WOMEN WERE GIVEN.
HE USED "MAN REASONING" AGAINST YOU.
THAT DAY...

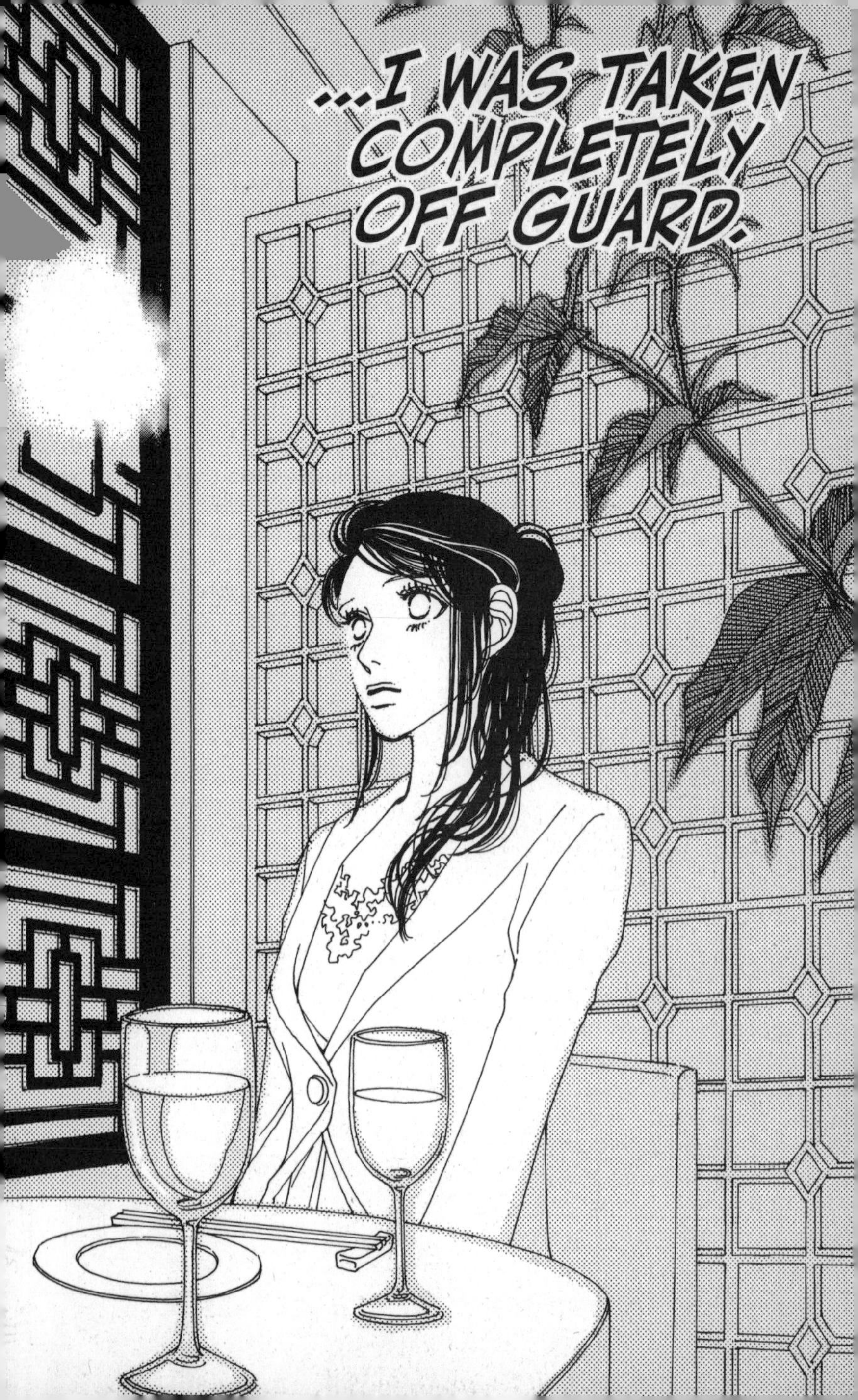
...I WAS TAKEN COMPLETELY OFF GUARD.

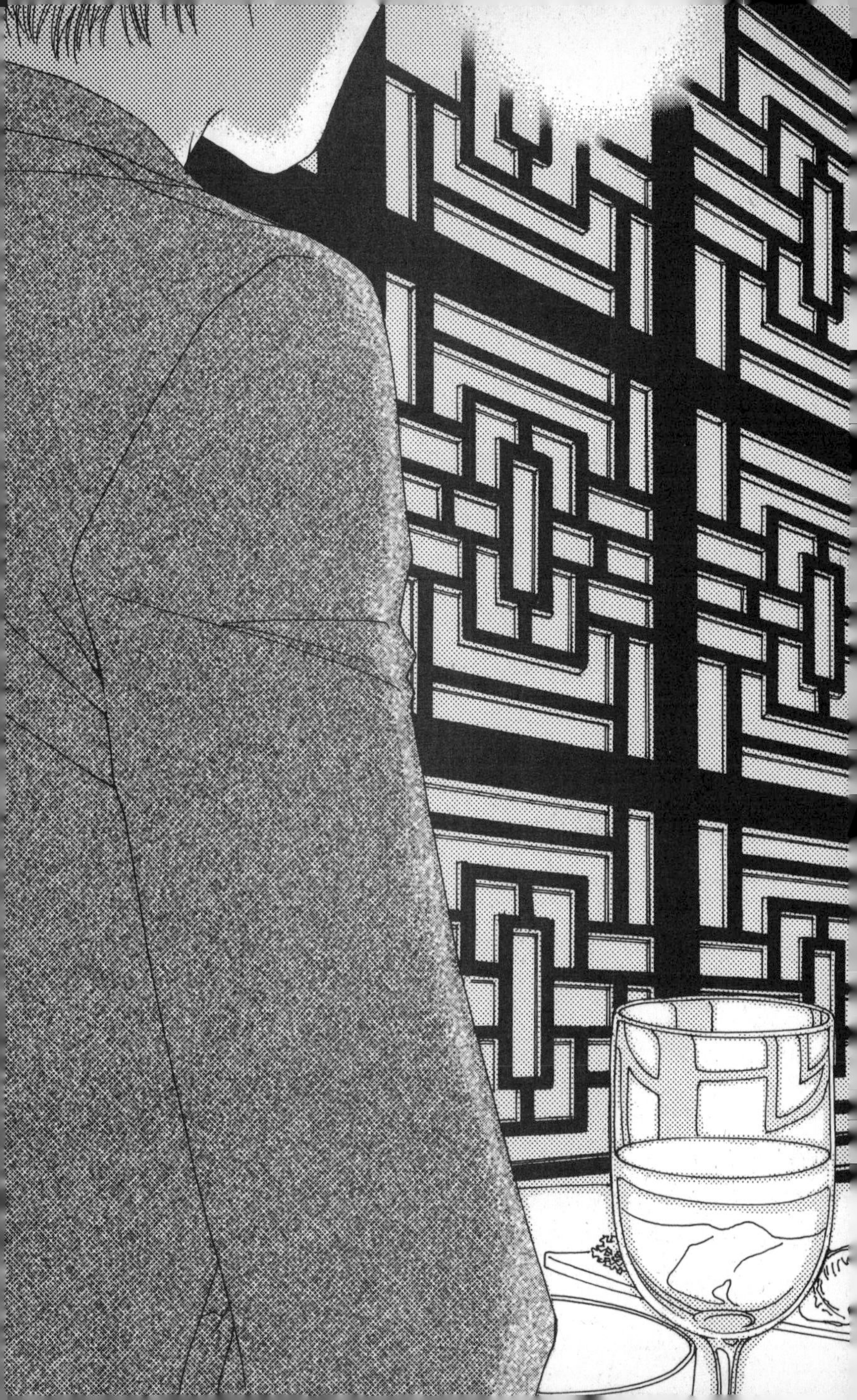

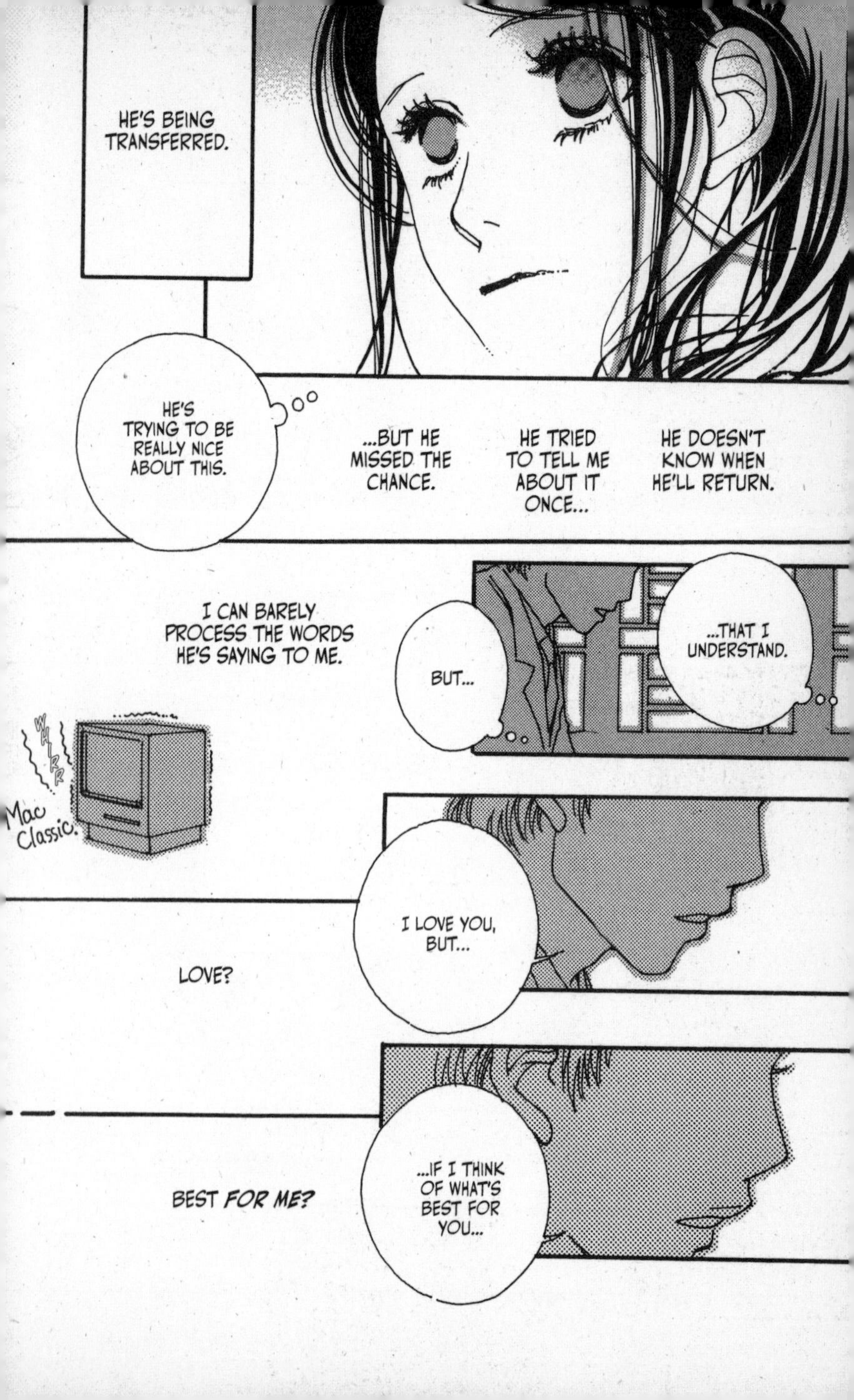
HE'S BEING TRANSFERRED.
HE DOESN'T KNOW WHEN HE'LL RETURN.
HE TRIED TO TELL ME ABOUT IT ONCE...
...BUT HE MISSED THE CHANCE.
HE'S TRYING TO BE REALLY NICE ABOUT THIS.
...THAT I UNDERSTAND.
BUT...
I CAN BARELY PROCESS THE WORDS HE'S SAYING TO ME.
WHIRR
Mac Classic.
I LOVE YOU, BUT...
LOVE?
...IF I THINK OF WHAT'S BEST FOR YOU...
BEST FOR ME?

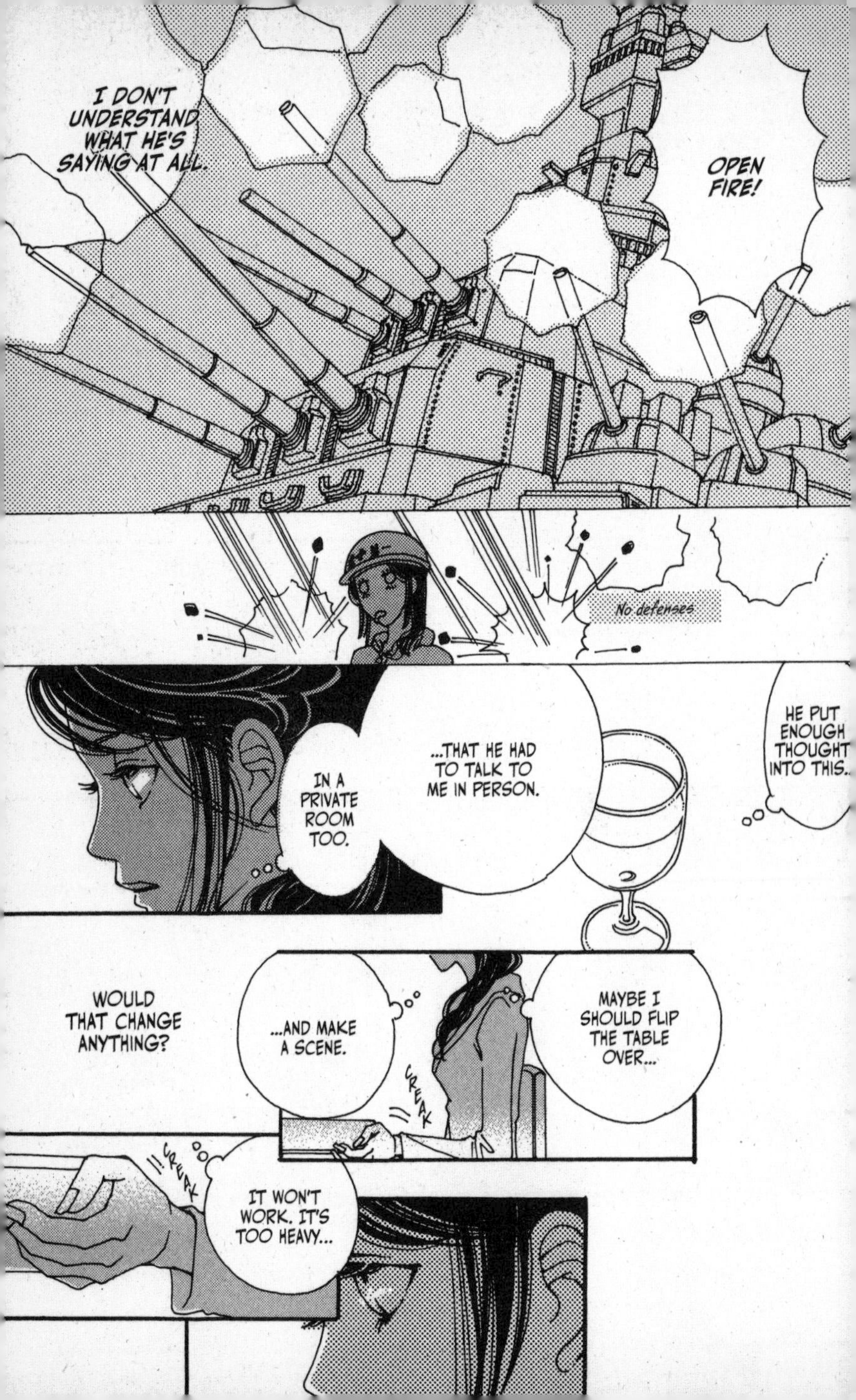
OPEN FIRE!
I DON'T UNDERSTAND WHAT HE'S SAYING AT ALL.
No defenses
HE PUT ENOUGH THOUGHT INTO THIS...
...THAT HE HAD TO TALK TO ME IN PERSON.
IN A PRIVATE ROOM TOO.
MAYBE I SHOULD FLIP THE TABLE OVER...
...AND MAKE A SCENE.
CREAK
WOULD THAT CHANGE ANYTHING?
CREAK
IT WON'T WORK. IT'S TOO HEAVY...

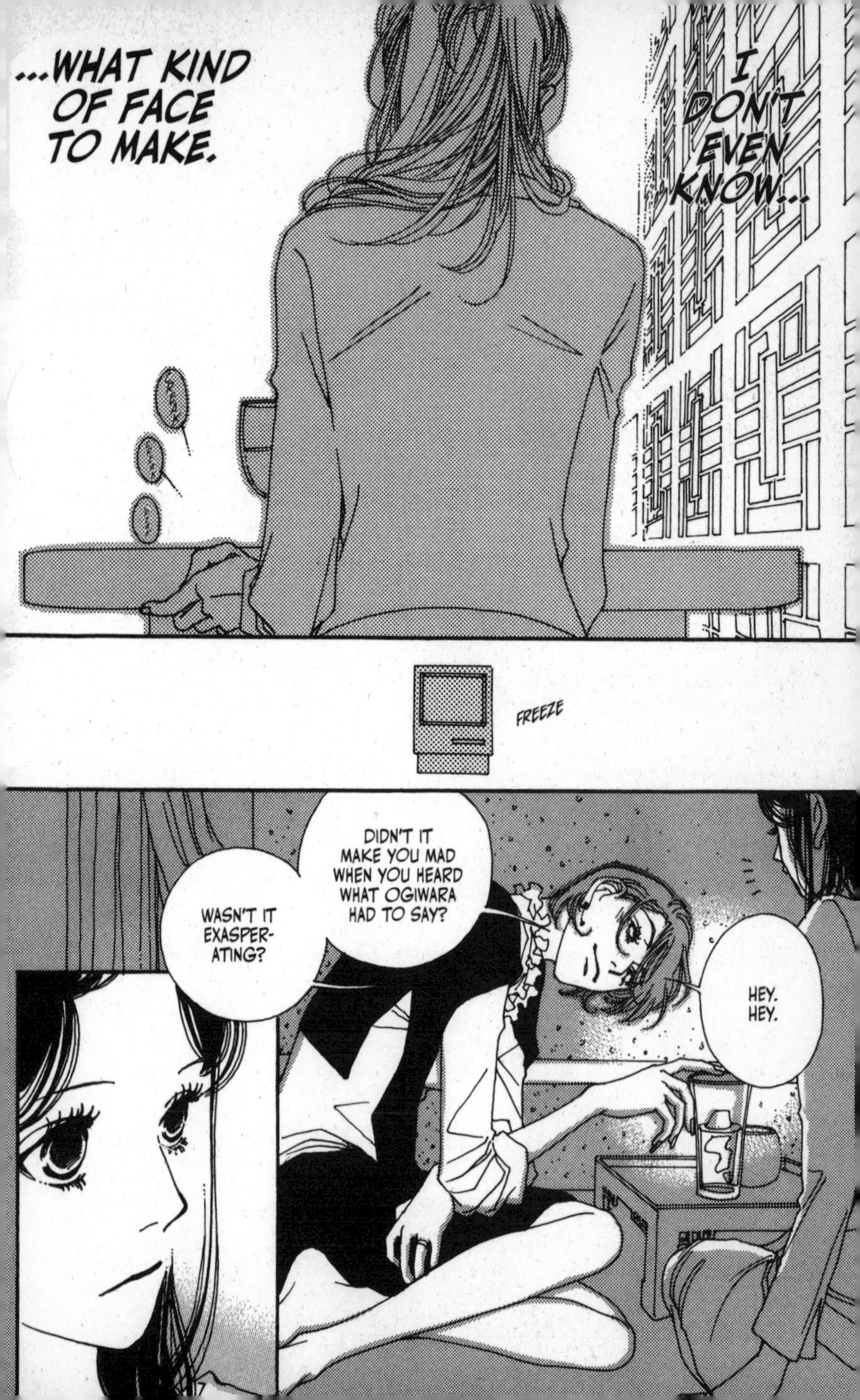
I DON'T EVEN KNOW...
...WHAT KIND OF FACE TO MAKE.
FREEZE
HEY. HEY.
DIDN'T IT MAKE YOU MAD WHEN YOU HEARD WHAT OGIWARA HAD TO SAY?
WASN'T IT EXASPER-ATING?

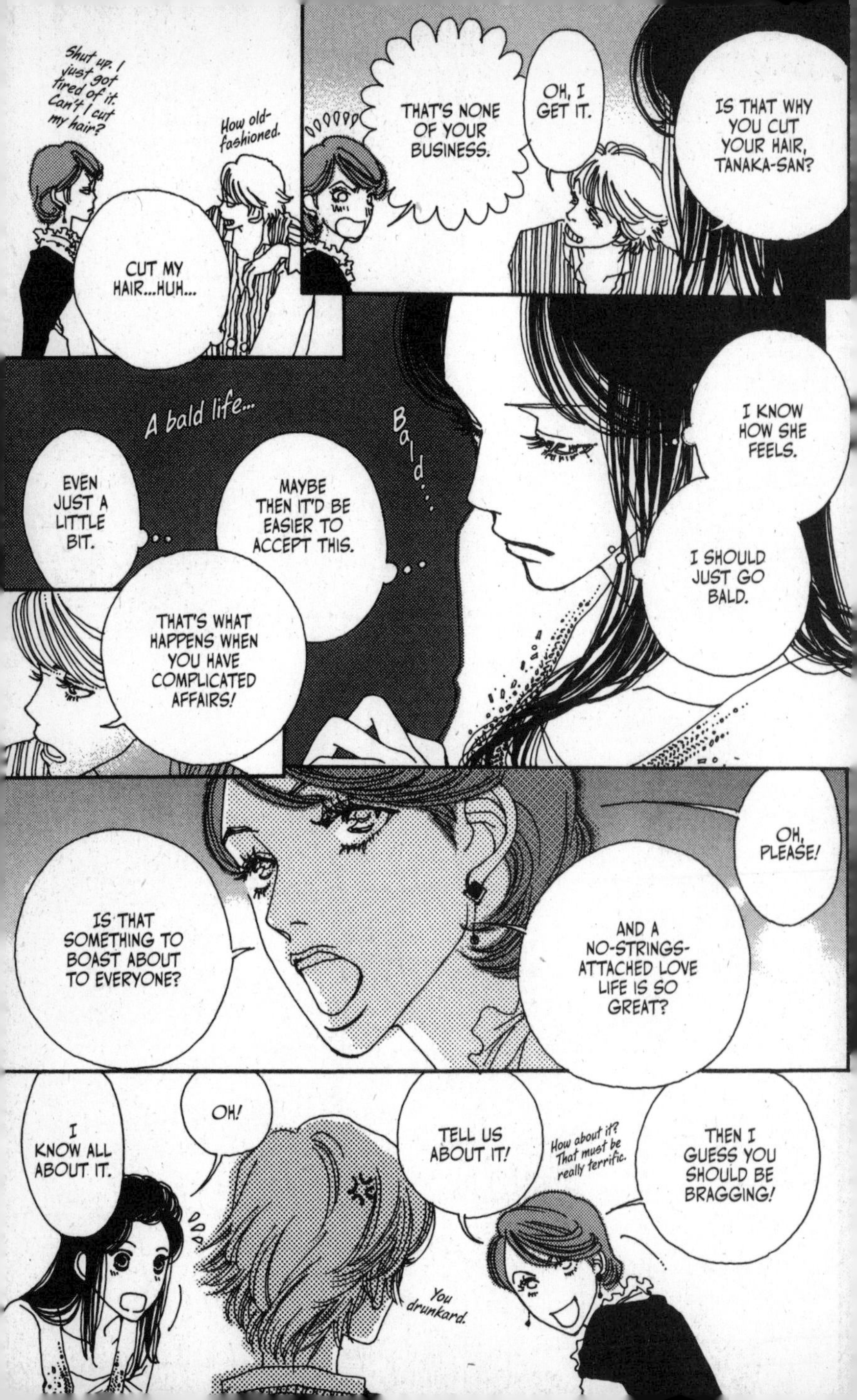
IS THAT WHY YOU CUT YOUR HAIR, TANAKA-SAN?
OH, I GET IT.
THAT'S NONE OF YOUR BUSINESS.
How old-fashioned.
Shut up. I just got tired of it. Can't I cut my hair?
CUT MY HAIR...HUH...
I KNOW HOW SHE FEELS.
I SHOULD JUST GO BALD.
Bald...
MAYBE THEN IT'D BE EASIER TO ACCEPT THIS.
EVEN JUST A LITTLE BIT.
A bald life...
THAT'S WHAT HAPPENS WHEN YOU HAVE COMPLICATED AFFAIRS!
OH, PLEASE!
AND A NO-STRINGS-ATTACHED LOVE LIFE IS SO GREAT?
IS THAT SOMETHING TO BOAST ABOUT TO EVERYONE?
THEN I GUESS YOU SHOULD BE BRAGGING!
How about it? That must be really terrific.
TELL US ABOUT IT!
You drunkard.
OH!
I KNOW ALL ABOUT IT.

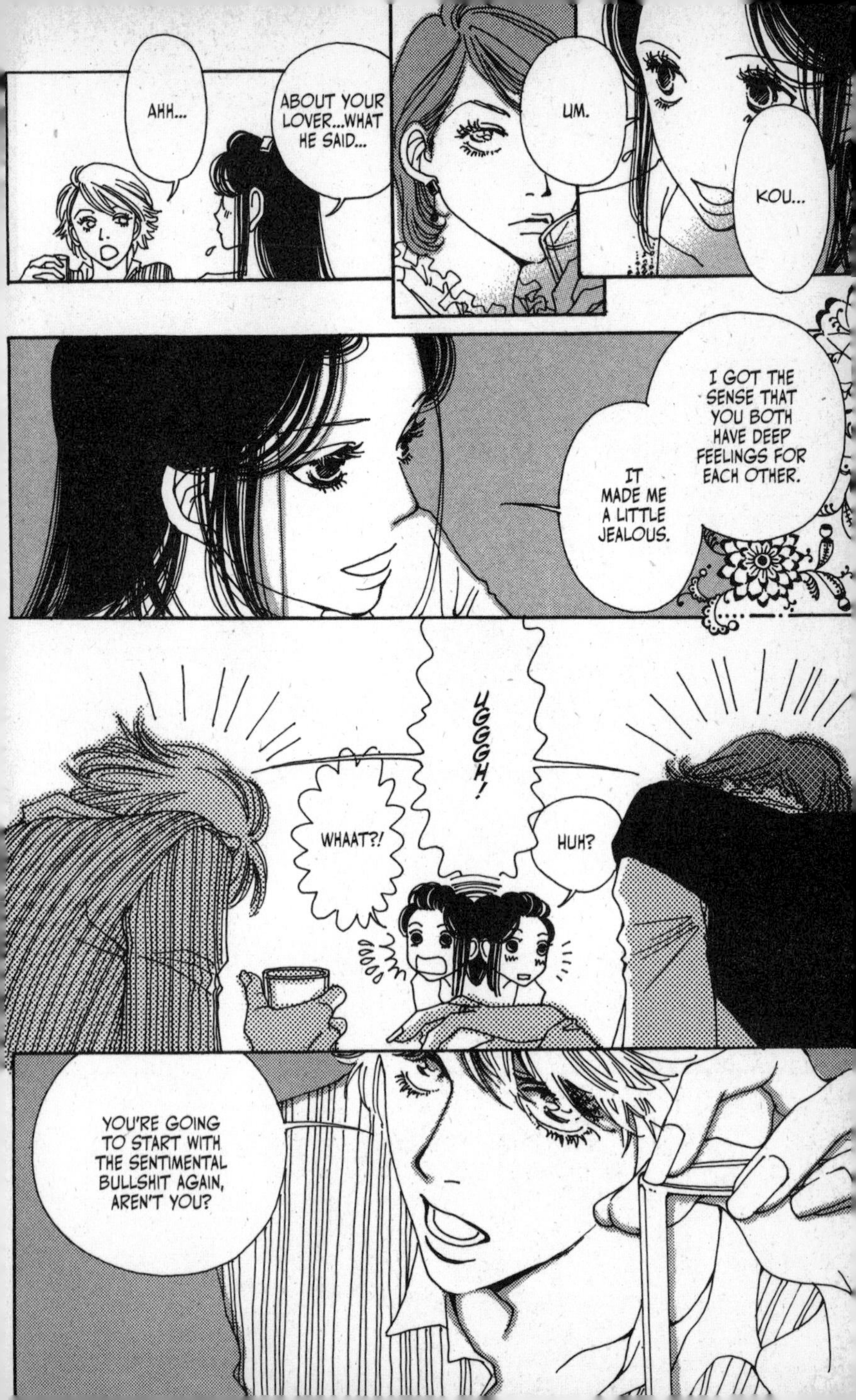
KOU...
UM.
ABOUT YOUR LOVER...WHAT HE SAID...
AHH...
I GOT THE SENSE THAT YOU BOTH HAVE DEEP FEELINGS FOR EACH OTHER.
IT MADE ME A LITTLE JEALOUS.
UGGGH!
HUH?
WHAAT?!
YOU'RE GOING TO START WITH THE SENTIMENTAL BULLSHIT AGAIN, AREN'T YOU?

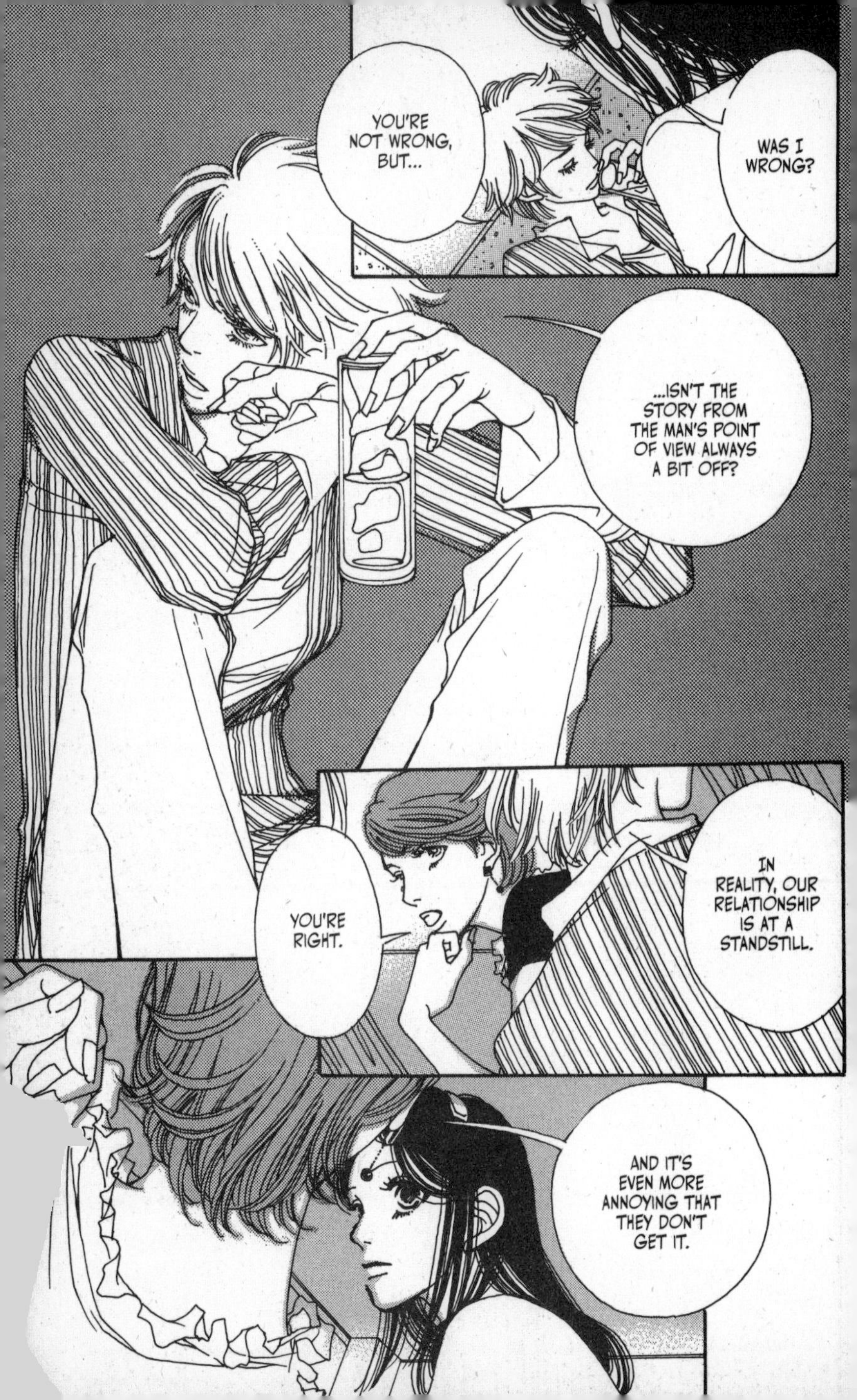
WAS I WRONG?
YOU'RE NOT WRONG, BUT...
...ISN'T THE STORY FROM THE MAN'S POINT OF VIEW ALWAYS A BIT OFF?
IN REALITY, OUR RELATIONSHIP IS AT A STANDSTILL.
YOU'RE RIGHT.
AND IT'S EVEN MORE ANNOYING THAT THEY DON'T GET IT.

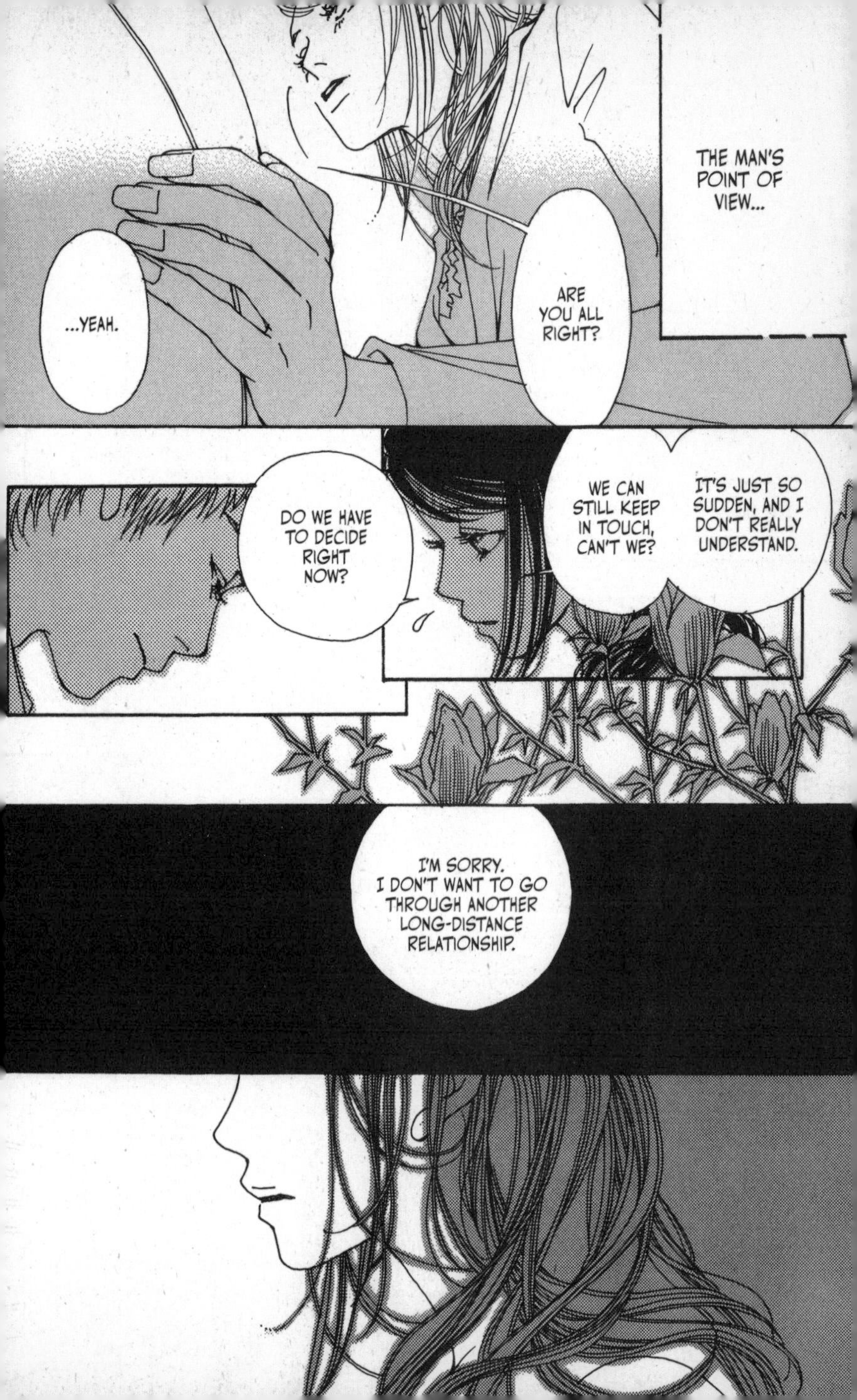
THE MAN'S POINT OF VIEW...
ARE YOU ALL RIGHT?
...YEAH.
IT'S JUST SO SUDDEN, AND I DON'T REALLY UNDERSTAND.
WE CAN STILL KEEP IN TOUCH, CAN'T WE?
DO WE HAVE TO DECIDE RIGHT NOW?
I'M SORRY. I DON'T WANT TO GO THROUGH ANOTHER LONG-DISTANCE RELATIONSHIP.

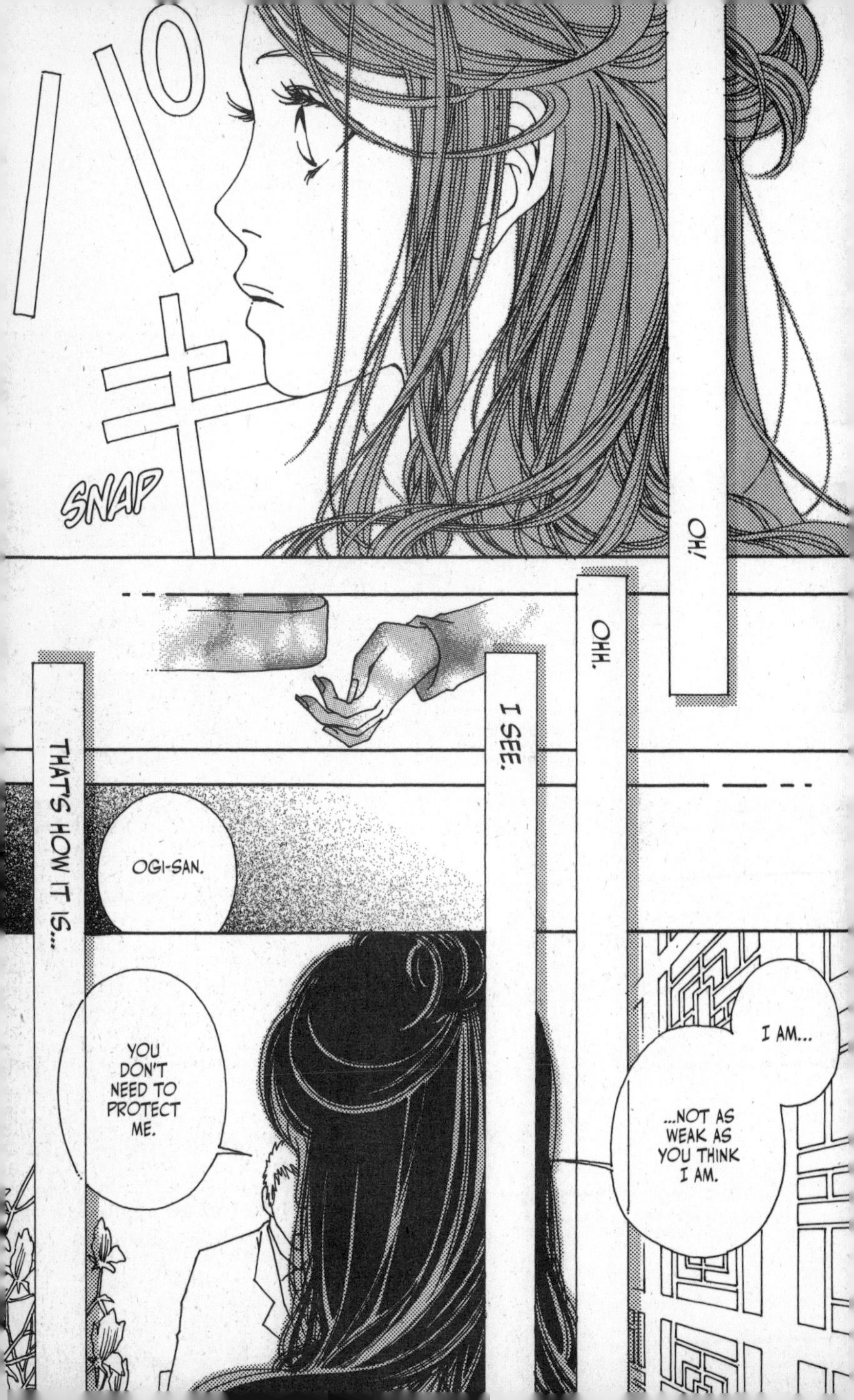
OH!
SNAP
OHH.
I SEE.
THAT'S HOW IT IS...
OGI-SAN.
I AM...
...NOT AS WEAK AS YOU THINK I AM.
YOU DON'T NEED TO PROTECT ME.

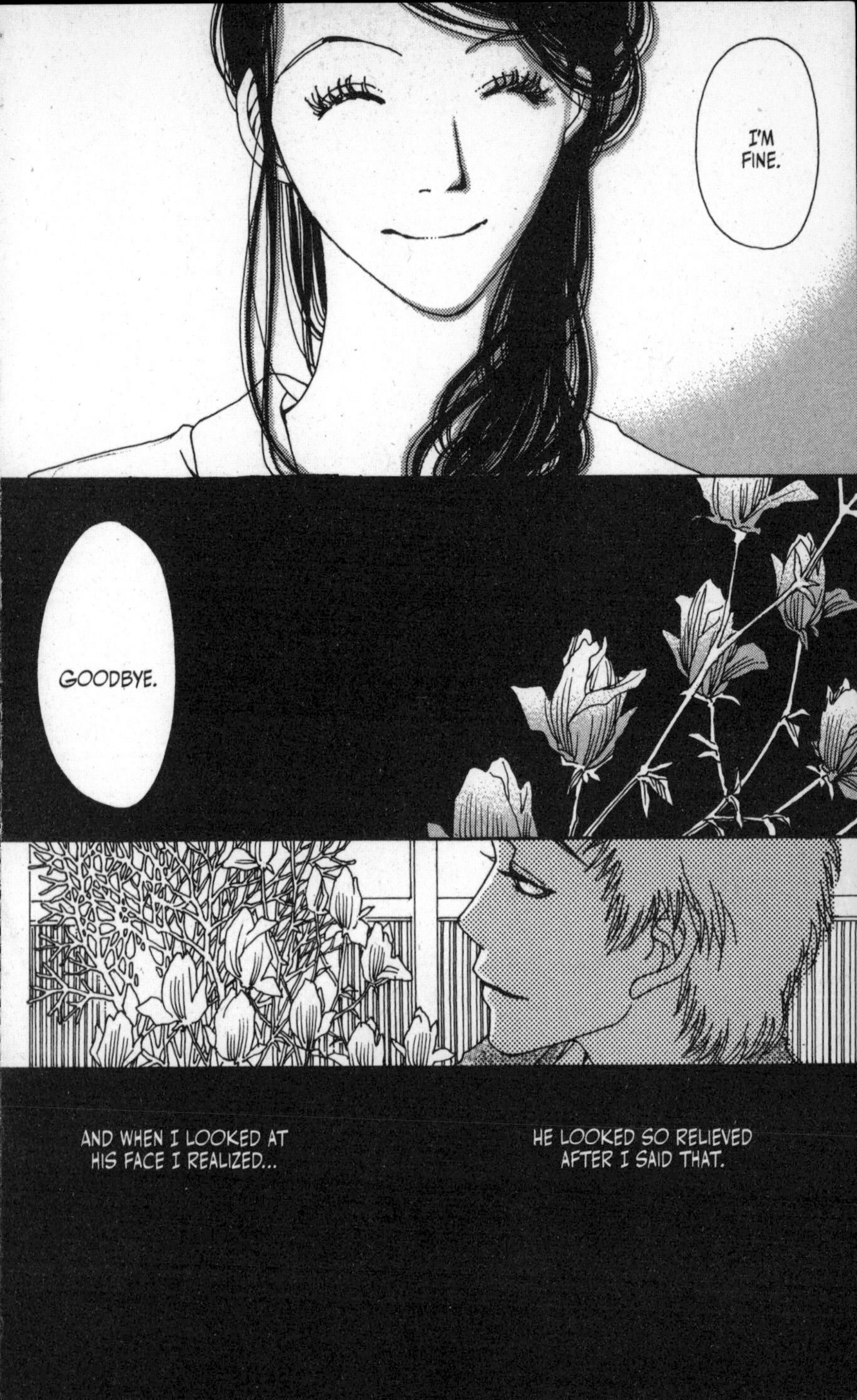
I'M FINE.
GOODBYE.
HE LOOKED SO RELIEVED AFTER I SAID THAT.
AND WHEN I LOOKED AT HIS FACE I REALIZED...

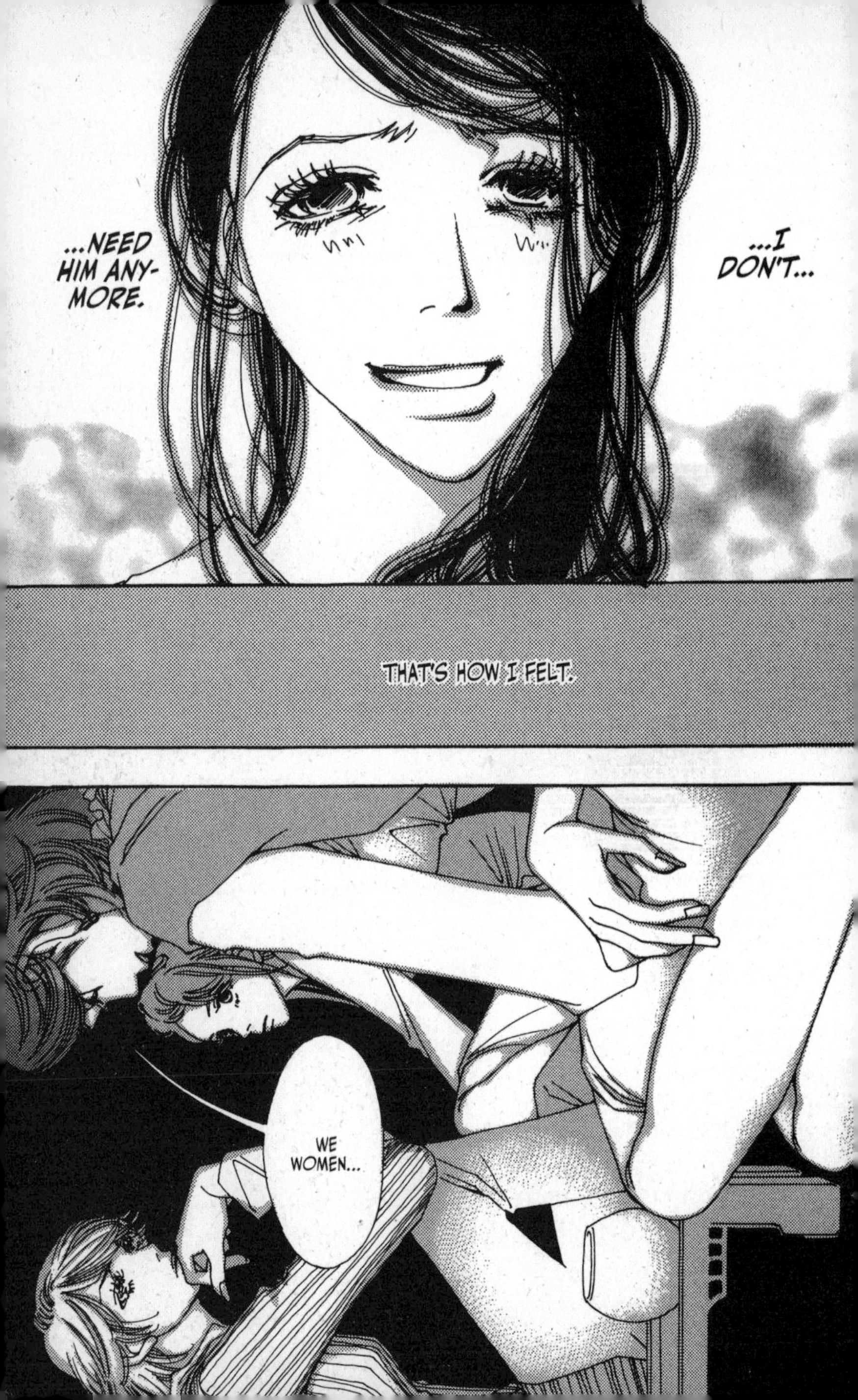
...I DON'T...
...NEED HIM ANY-MORE.
THAT'S HOW I FELT.
WE WOMEN...

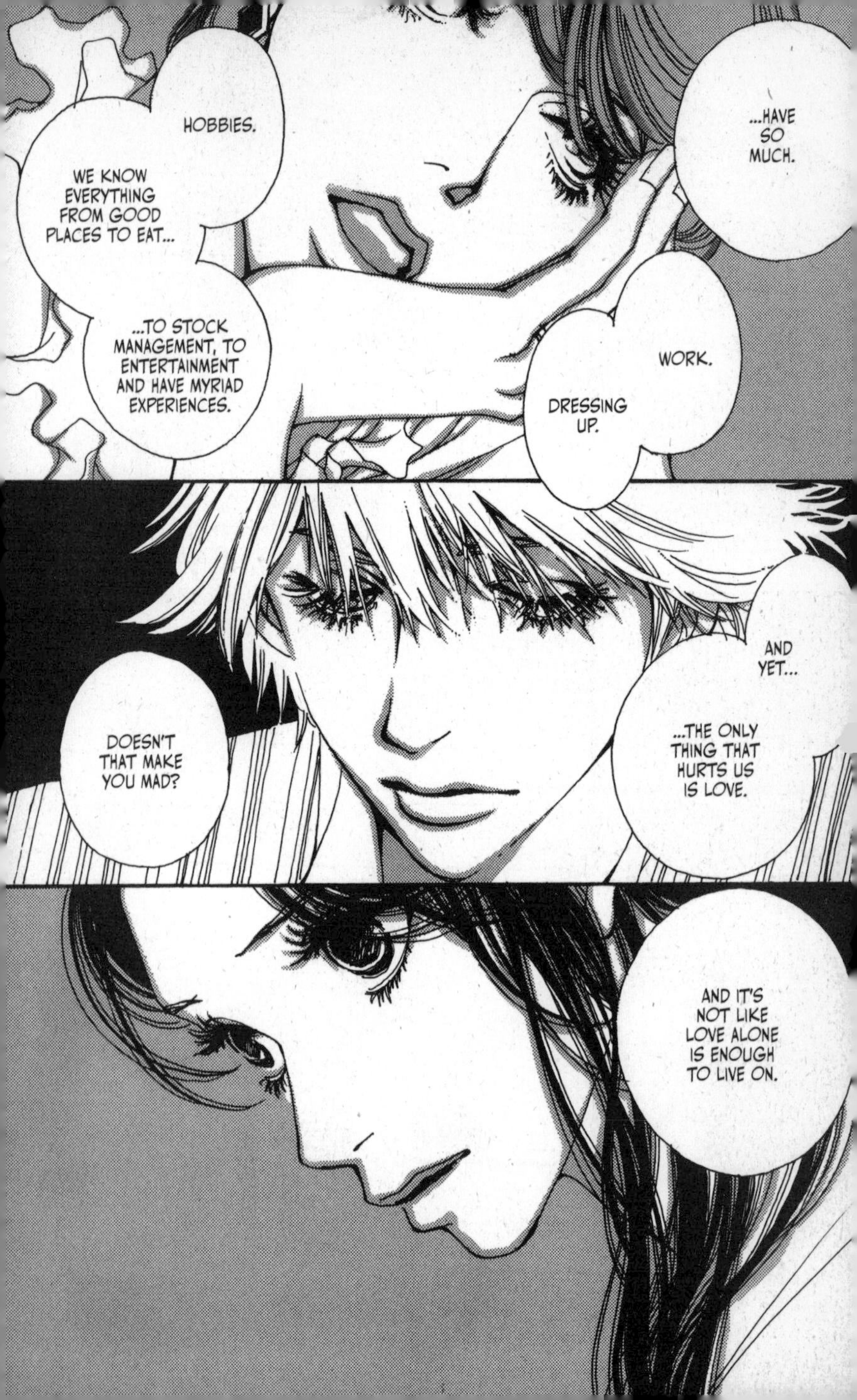
...HAVE SO MUCH.
WORK.
DRESSING UP.
HOBBIES.
WE KNOW EVERYTHING FROM GOOD PLACES TO EAT...
...TO STOCK MANAGEMENT, TO ENTERTAINMENT AND HAVE MYRIAD EXPERIENCES.
AND YET...
...THE ONLY THING THAT HURTS US IS LOVE.
DOESN'T THAT MAKE YOU MAD?
AND IT'S NOT LIKE LOVE ALONE IS ENOUGH TO LIVE ON.

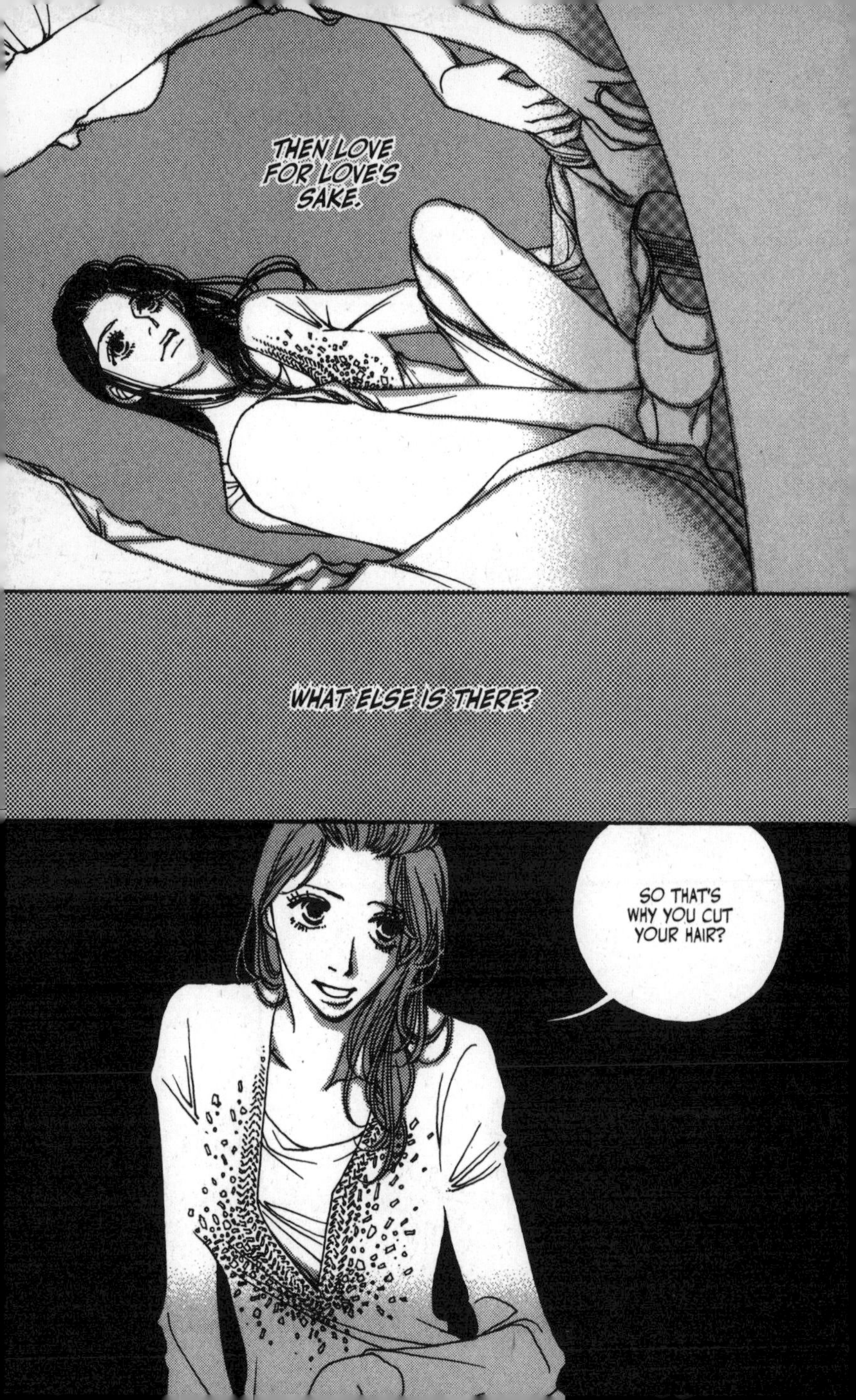
THEN LOVE FOR LOVE'S SAKE.
WHAT ELSE IS THERE?
SO THAT'S WHY YOU CUT YOUR HAIR?

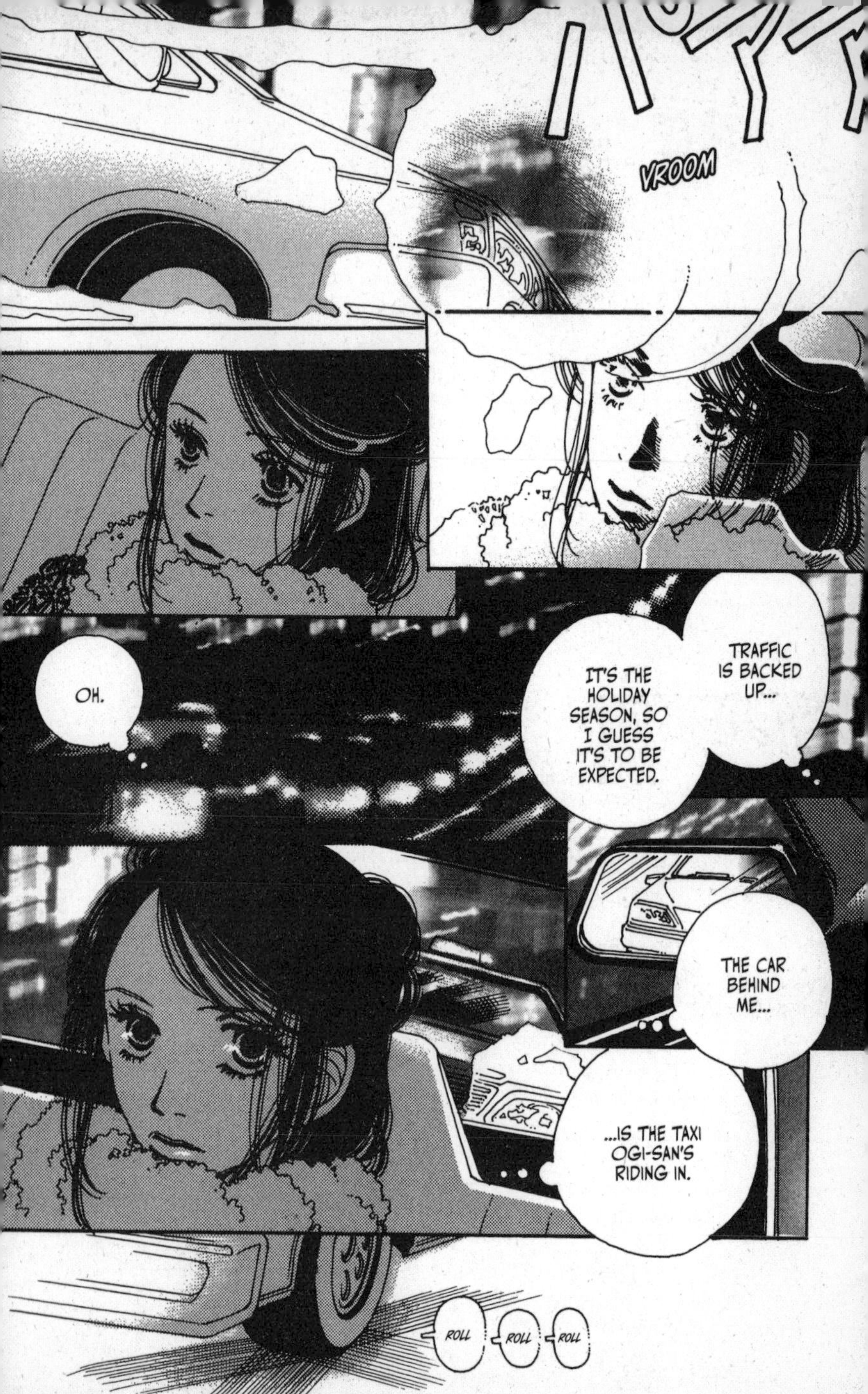
VROOM
TRAFFIC IS BACKED UP...
IT'S THE HOLIDAY SEASON, SO I GUESS IT'S TO BE EXPECTED.
OH.
THE CAR BEHIND ME...
...IS THE TAXI OGI-SAN'S RIDING IN.
ROLL
ROLL
ROLL

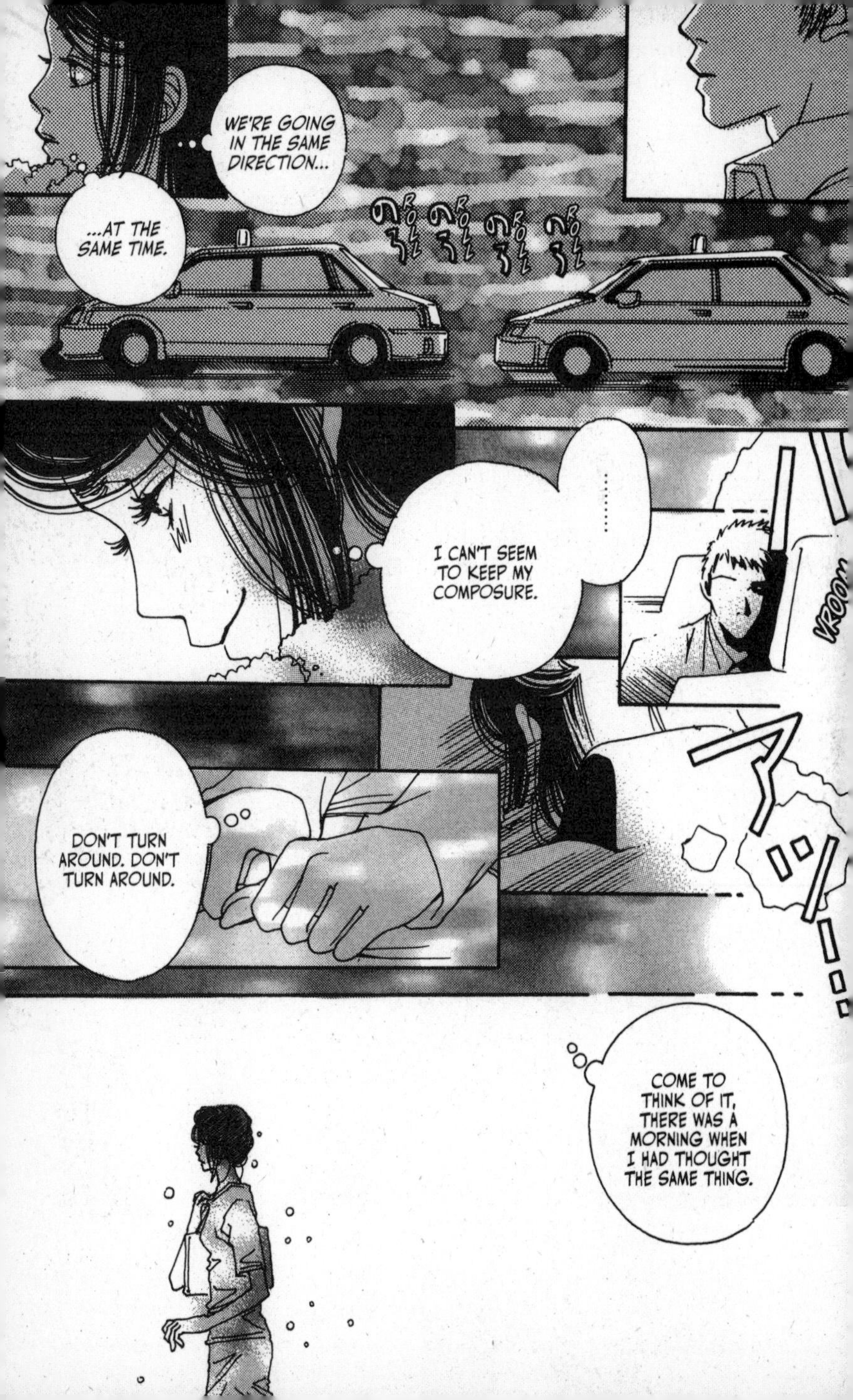
WE'RE GOING IN THE SAME DIRECTION...
...AT THE SAME TIME.
VROOM
......
I CAN'T SEEM TO KEEP MY COMPOSURE.
DON'T TURN AROUND. DON'T TURN AROUND.
COME TO THINK OF IT, THERE WAS A MORNING WHEN I HAD THOUGHT THE SAME THING.

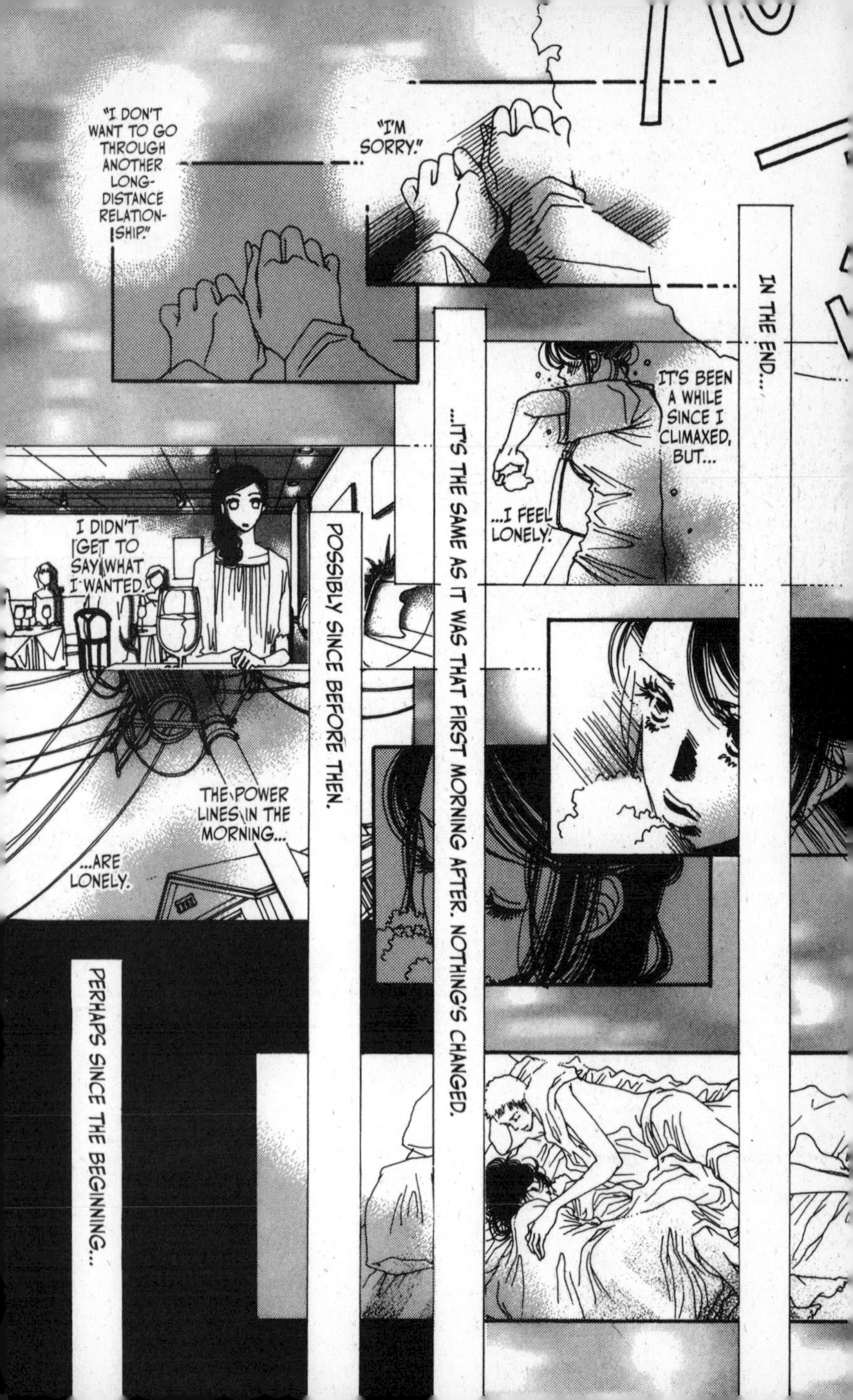
"I'M SORRY."
"I DON'T WANT TO GO THROUGH ANOTHER LONG-DISTANCE RELATIONSHIP."
IN THE END...
IT'S BEEN A WHILE SINCE I CLIMAXED, BUT...
...I FEEL LONELY.
...IT'S THE SAME AS IT WAS THAT FIRST MORNING AFTER. NOTHING'S CHANGED.
I DIDN'T GET TO SAY WHAT I WANTED.
POSSIBLY SINCE BEFORE THEN.
THE POWER LINES IN THE MORNING...
...ARE LONELY.
PERHAPS SINCE THE BEGINNING...

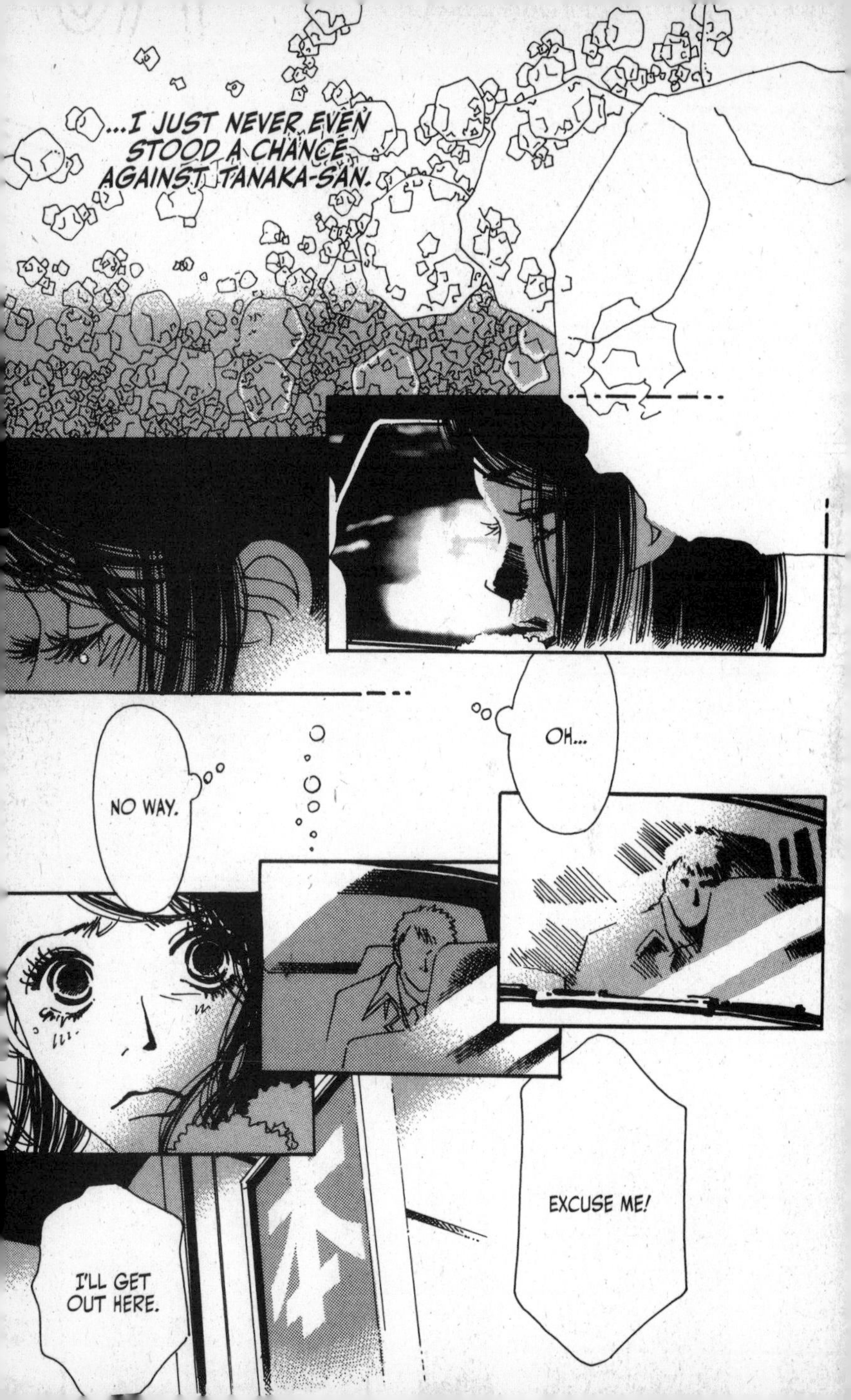
...I JUST NEVER EVEN STOOD A CHANCE AGAINST TANAKA-SAN.
OH...
NO WAY.
EXCUSE ME!
I'LL GET OUT HERE.

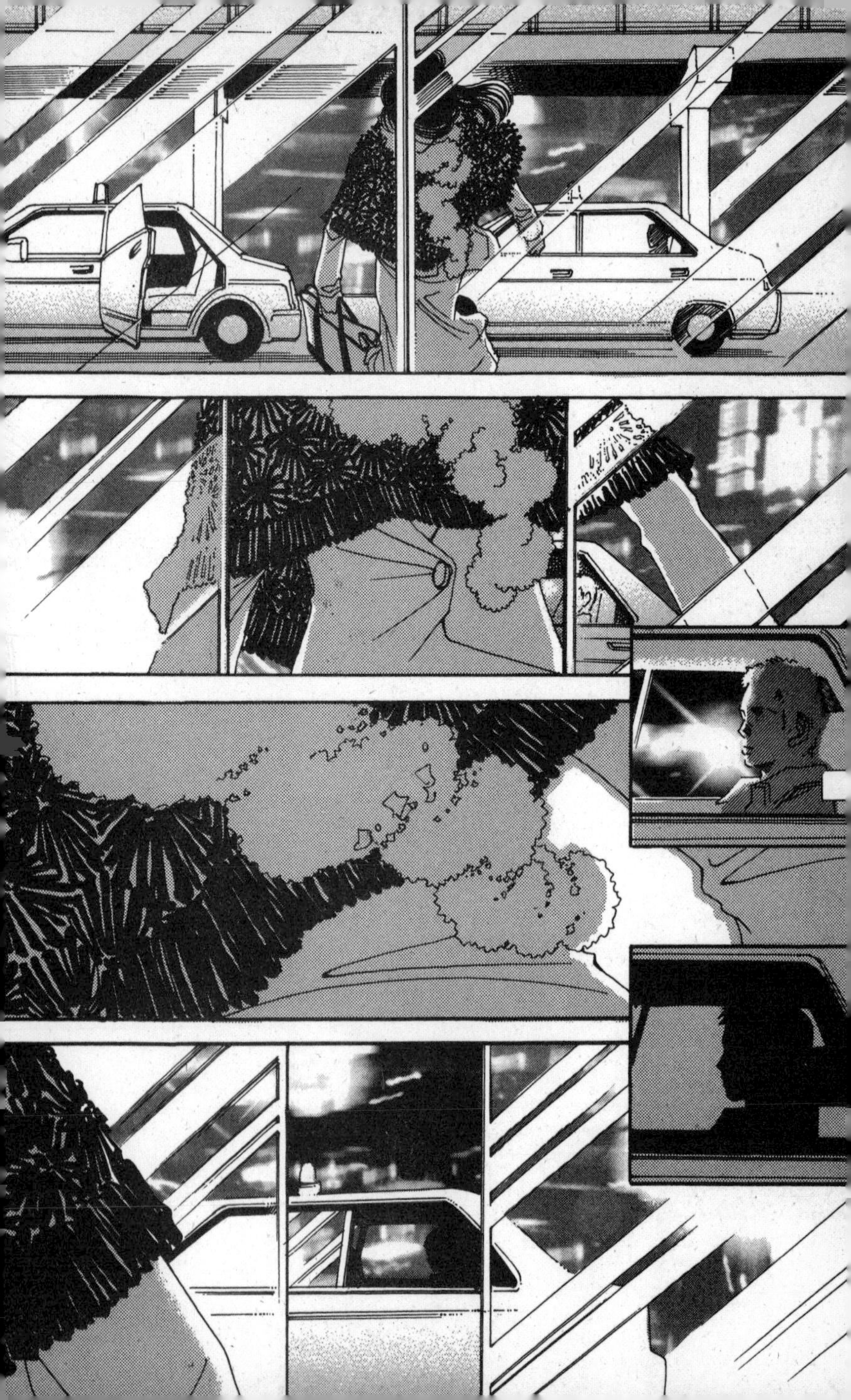

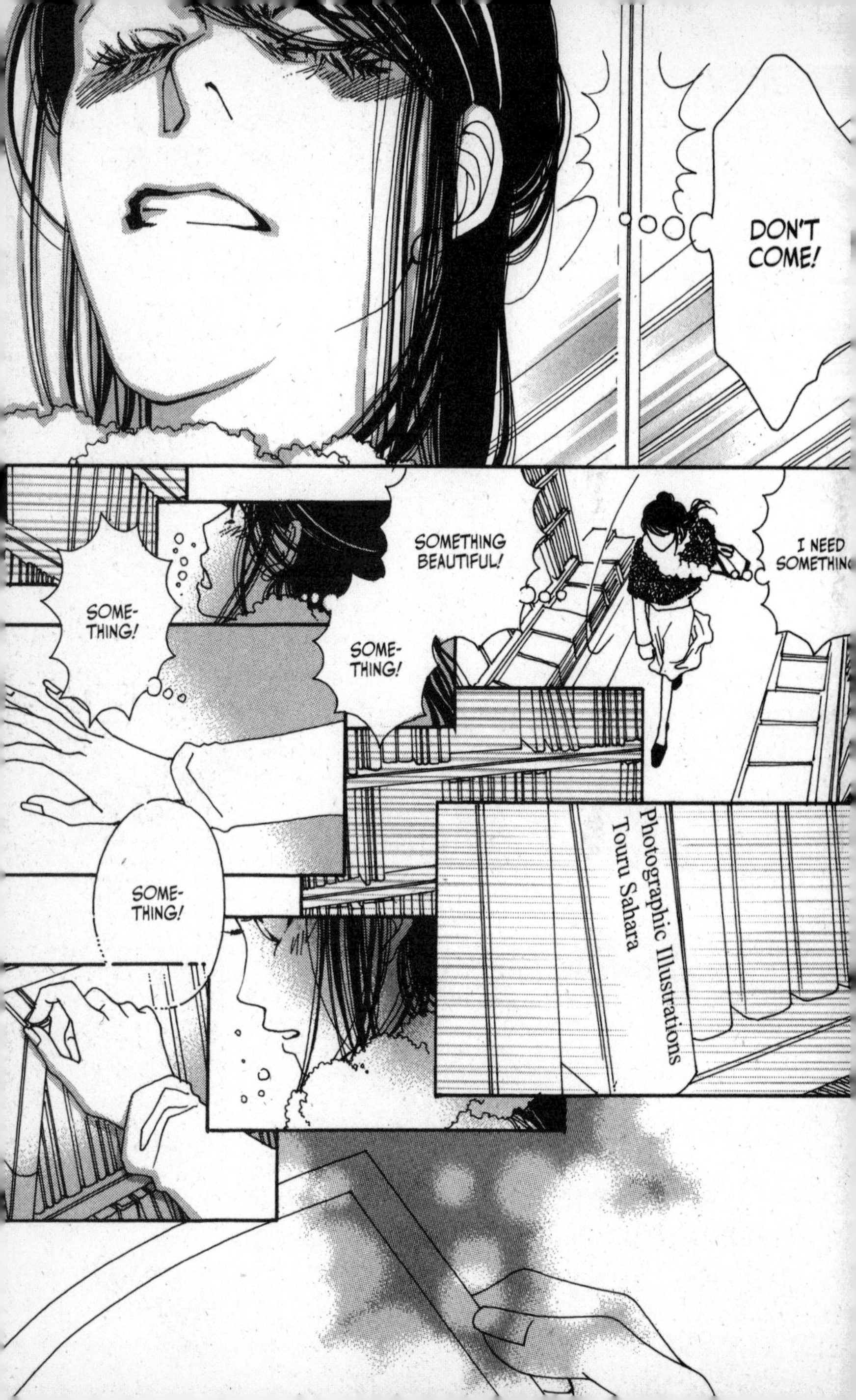
DON'T COME!
I NEED SOMETHIN
SOMETHING BEAUTIFUL!
SOME-THING!
SOME-THING!
Photographic Illustrations
Touru Sahara
SOME-THING!

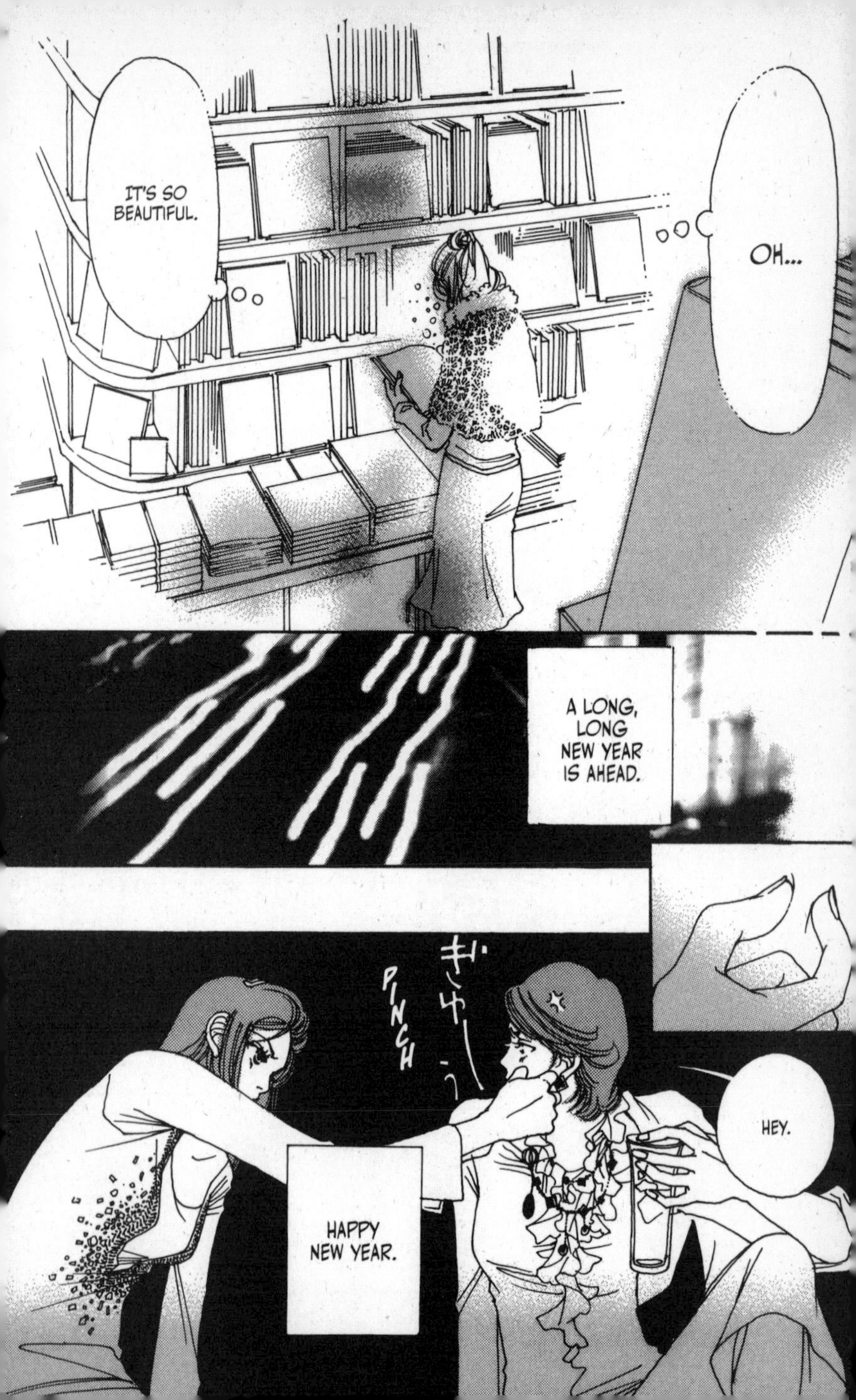
OH...
IT'S SO BEAUTIFUL.
A LONG, LONG NEW YEAR IS AHEAD.
HEY.
PINCH
HAPPY NEW YEAR.

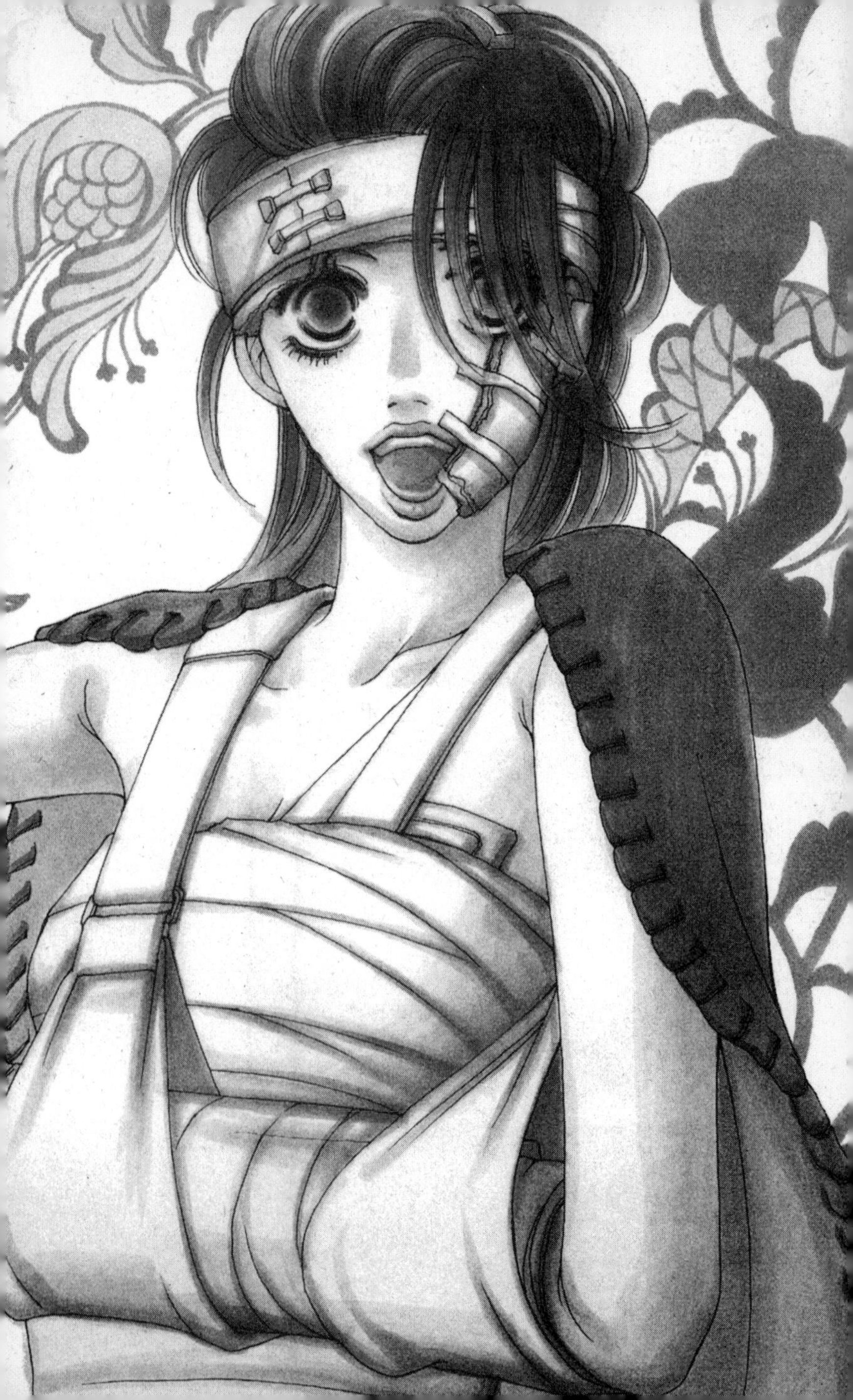

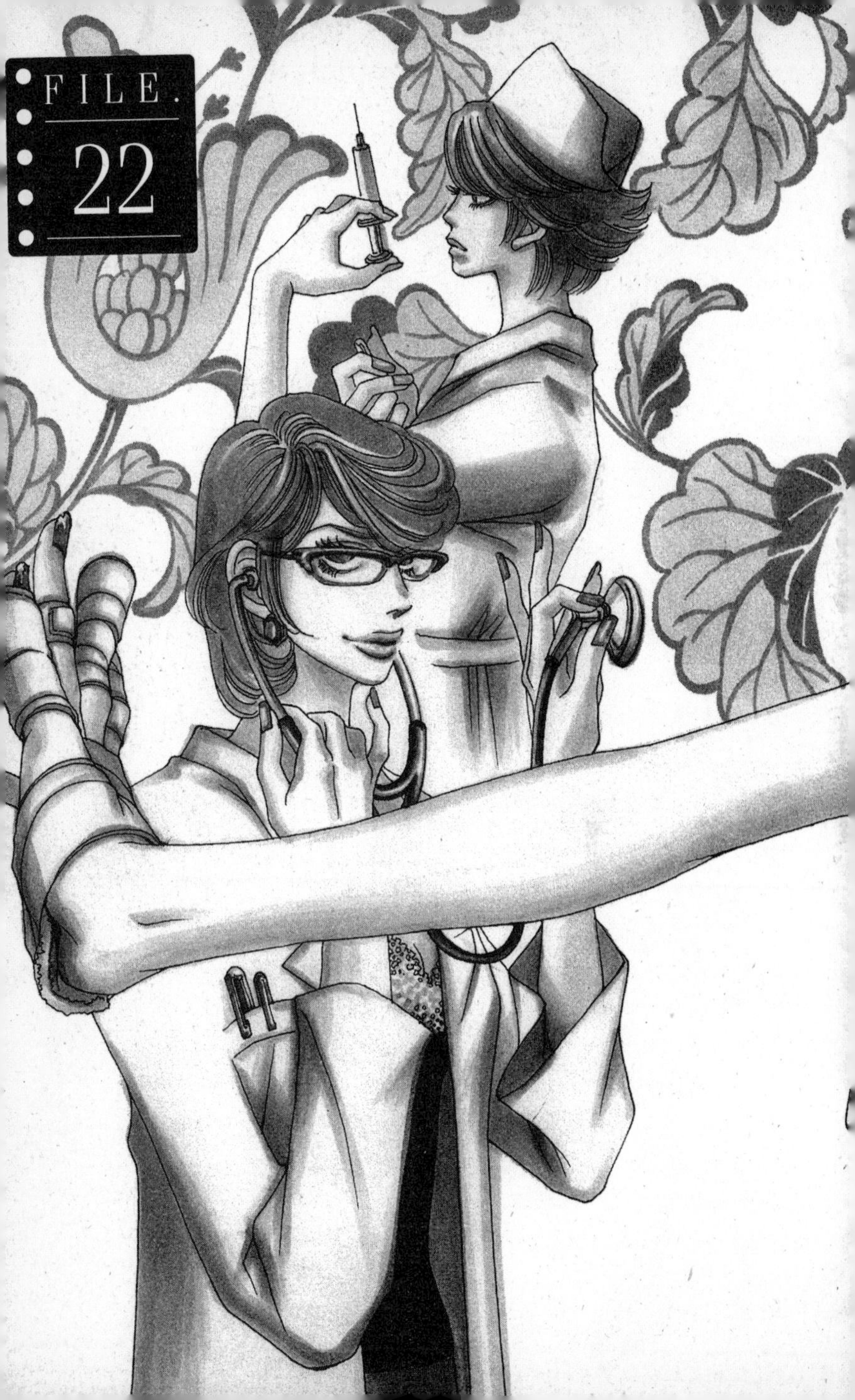
FILE.
22

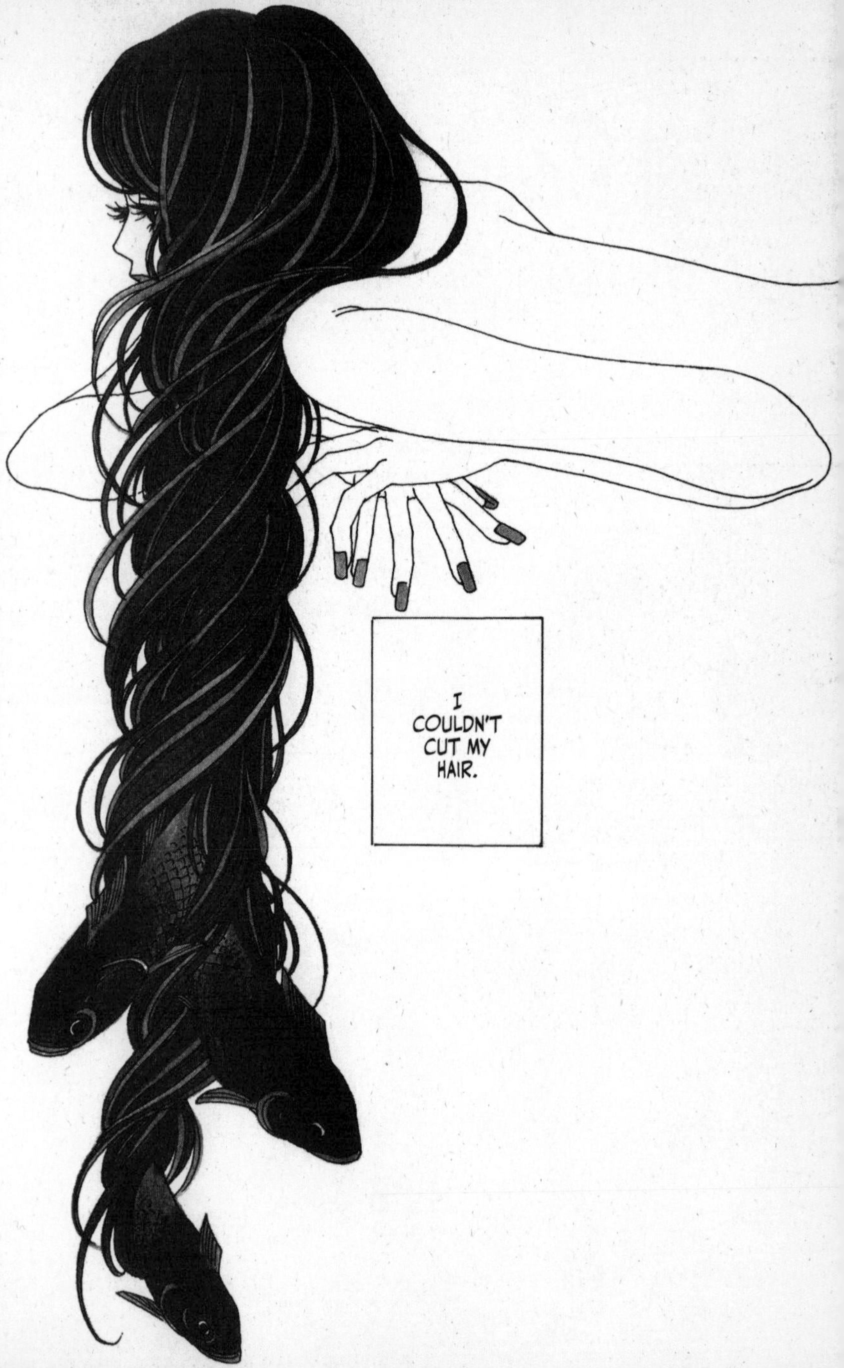
I COULDN'T CUT MY HAIR.

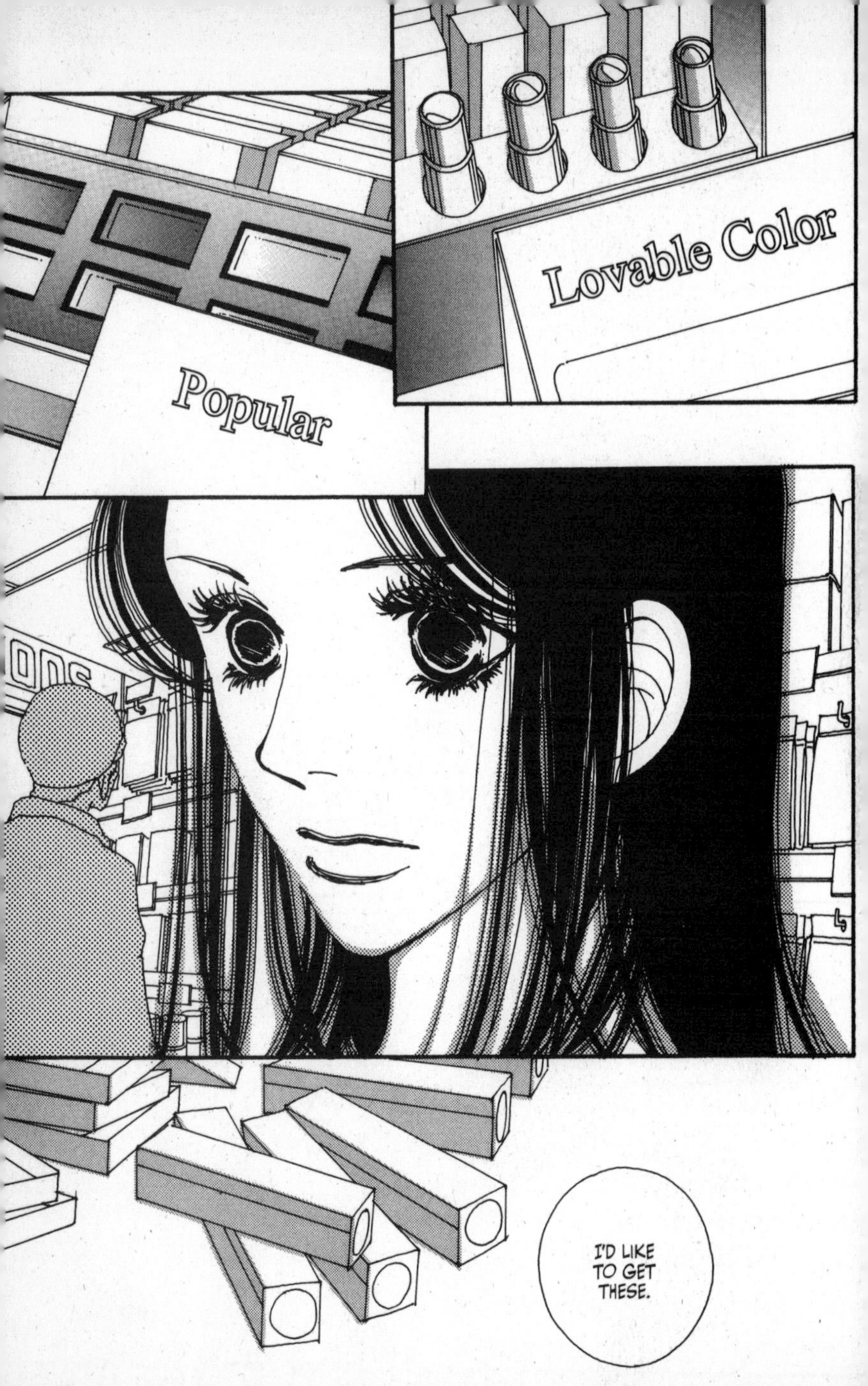
Lovable Color
Popular
I'D LIKE TO GET THESE.

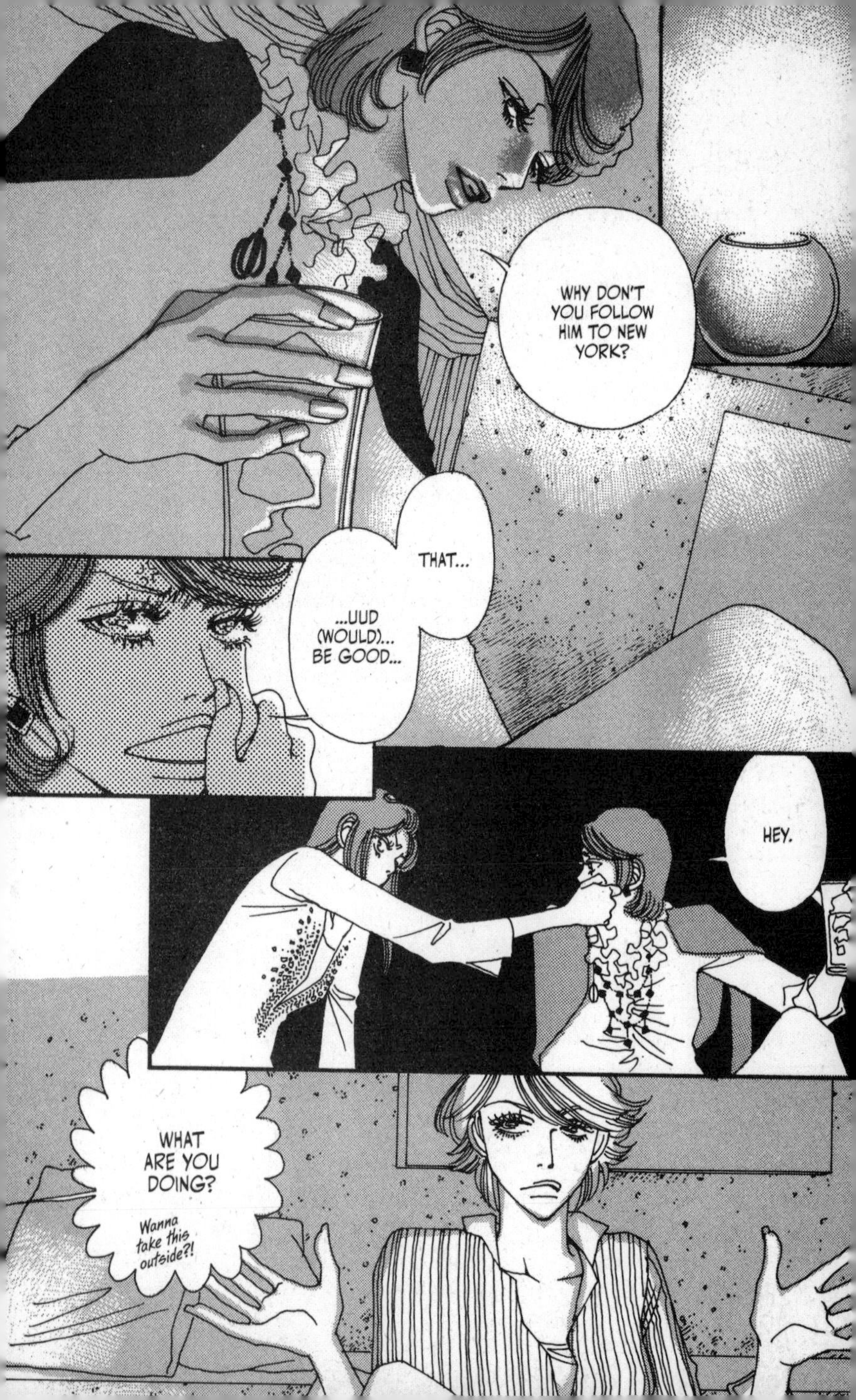
WHY DON'T YOU FOLLOW HIM TO NEW YORK?
THAT...
...UUD (WOULD)... BE GOOD...
HEY.
WHAT ARE YOU DOING?
Wanna take this outside?!

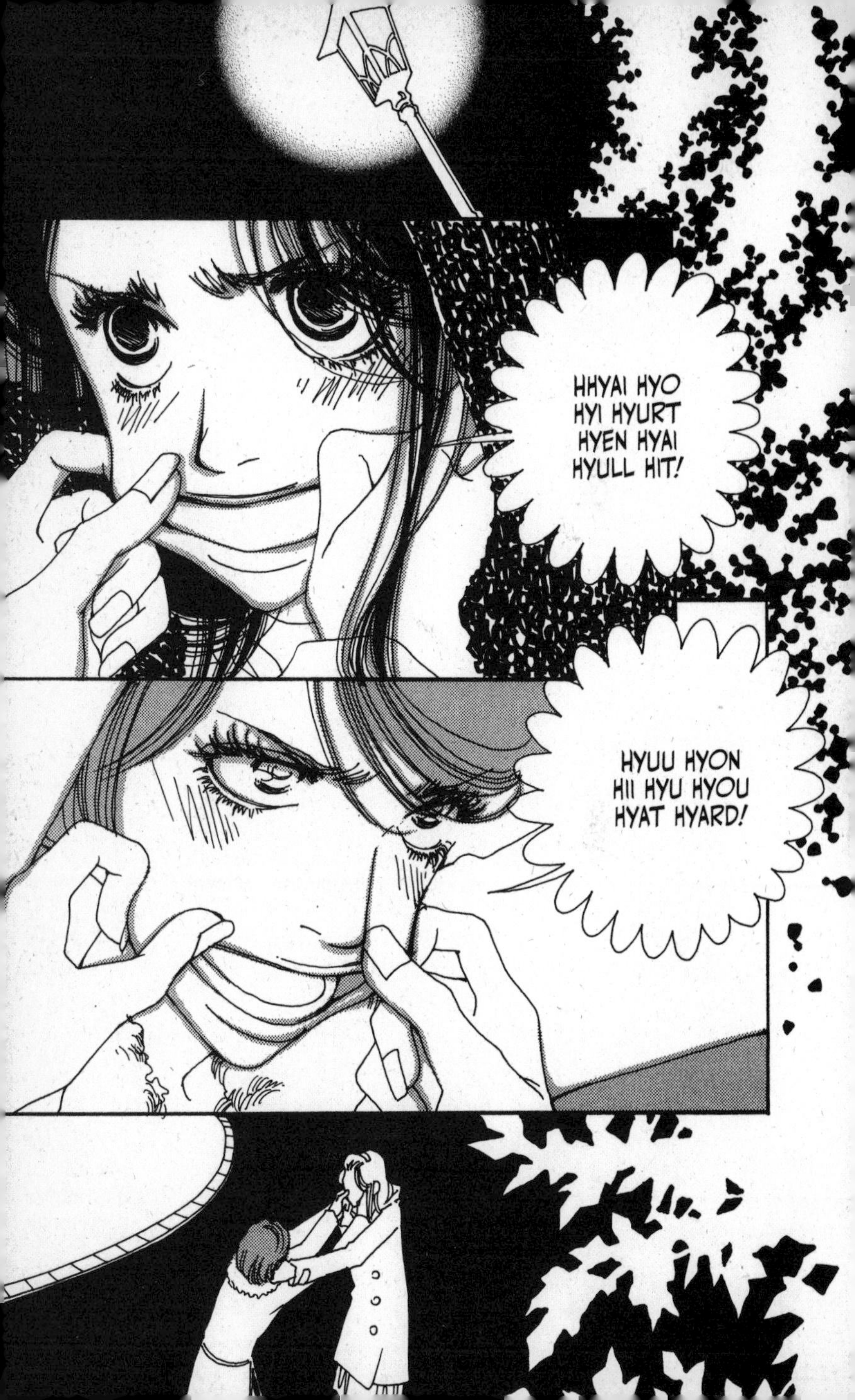
HHYAI HYO HYI HYURT HYEN HYAI HYULL HIT!
HYUU HYON HII HYU HYOU HYAT HYARD!

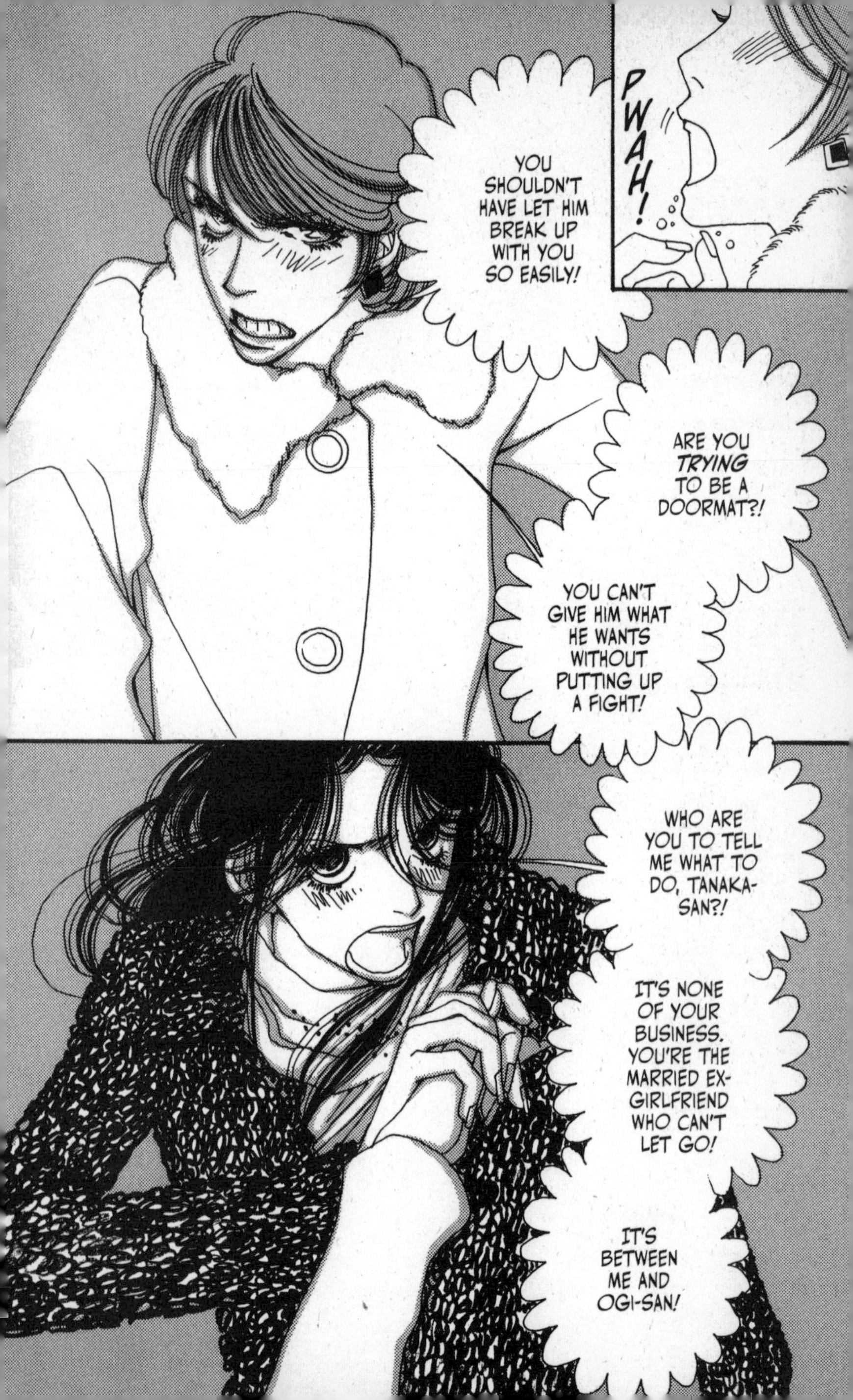
PWAH!
YOU SHOULDN'T HAVE LET HIM BREAK UP WITH YOU SO EASILY!
ARE YOU *TRYING* TO BE A DOORMAT?!
YOU CAN'T GIVE HIM WHAT HE WANTS WITHOUT PUTTING UP A FIGHT!
WHO ARE YOU TO TELL ME WHAT TO DO, TANAKA-SAN?!
IT'S NONE OF YOUR BUSINESS. YOU'RE THE MARRIED EX-GIRLFRIEND WHO CAN'T LET GO!
IT'S BETWEEN ME AND OGI-SAN!

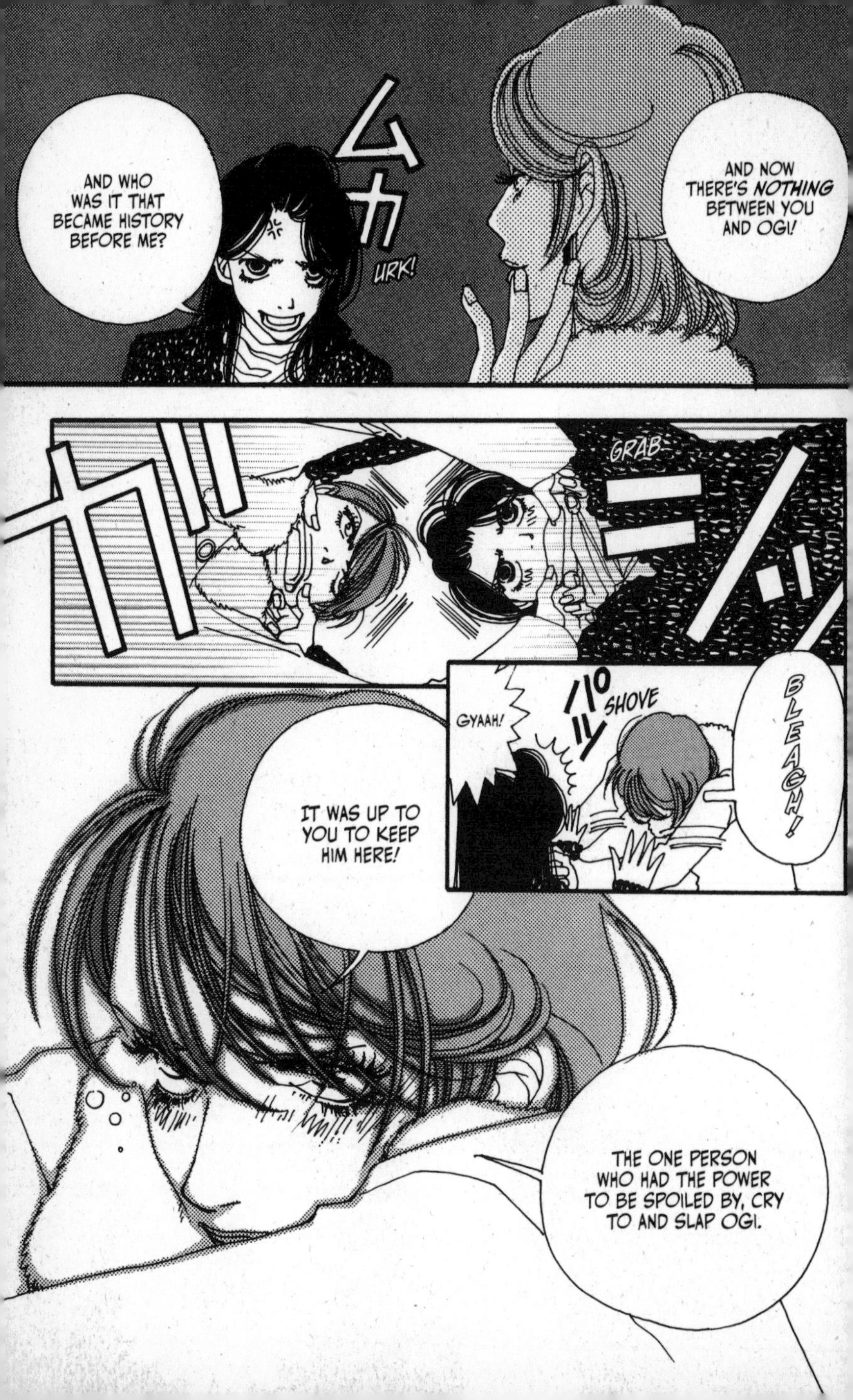
AND NOW THERE'S *NOTHING* BETWEEN YOU AND OGI!
ムカ
URK!
AND WHO WAS IT THAT BECAME HISTORY BEFORE ME?
GRAB
BLEAGH!
SHOVE
GYAAH!
IT WAS UP TO YOU TO KEEP HIM HERE!
THE ONE PERSON WHO HAD THE POWER TO BE SPOILED BY, CRY TO AND SLAP OGI.

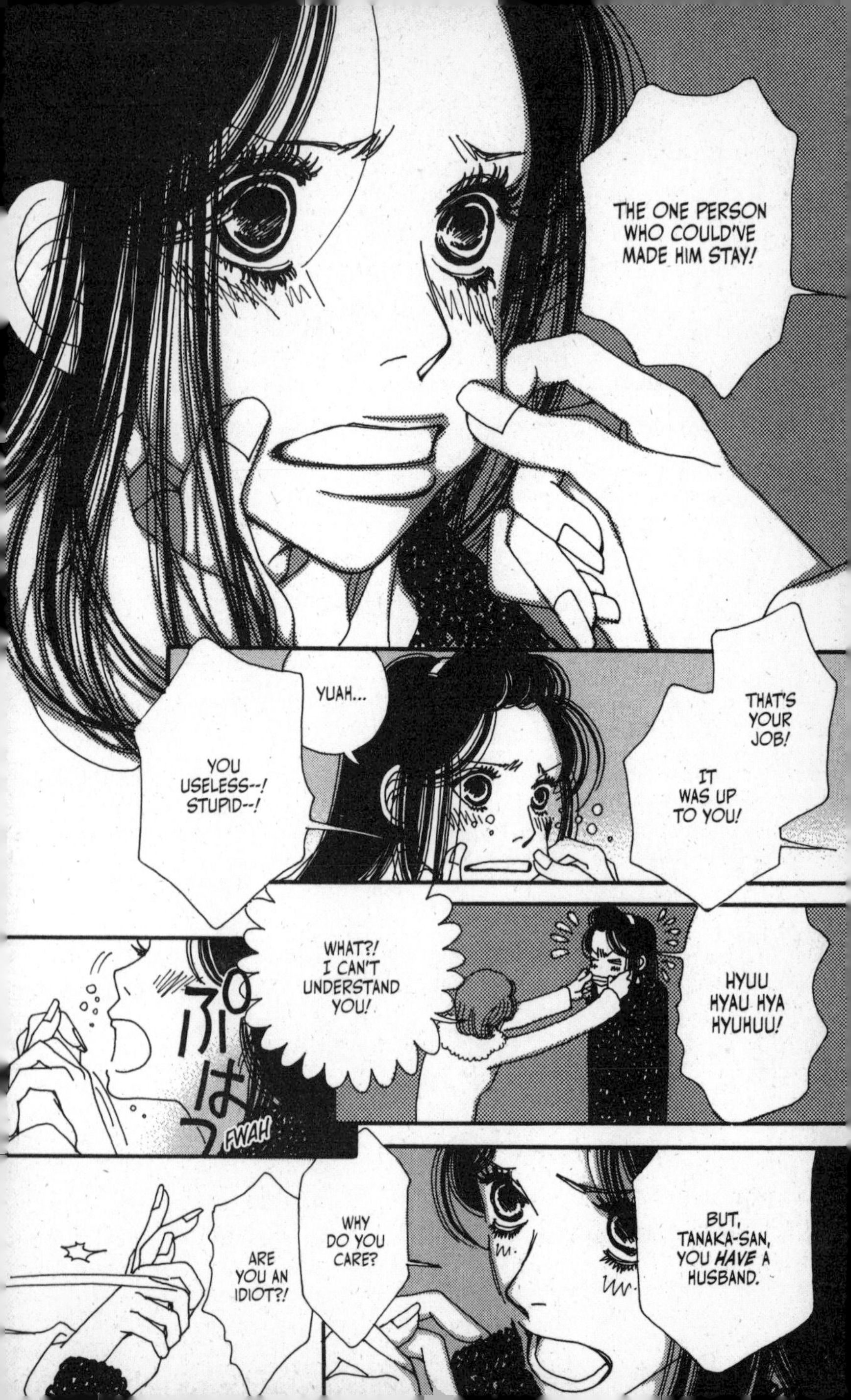
THE ONE PERSON WHO COULD'VE MADE HIM STAY!
THAT'S YOUR JOB!
IT WAS UP TO YOU!
YUAH...
YOU USELESS--! STUPID--!
HYUU HYAU HYA HYUHUU!
WHAT?! I CAN'T UNDERSTAND YOU!
ぷはっ
FWAH
BUT, TANAKA-SAN, YOU *HAVE* A HUSBAND.
WHY DO YOU CARE?
ARE YOU AN IDIOT?!

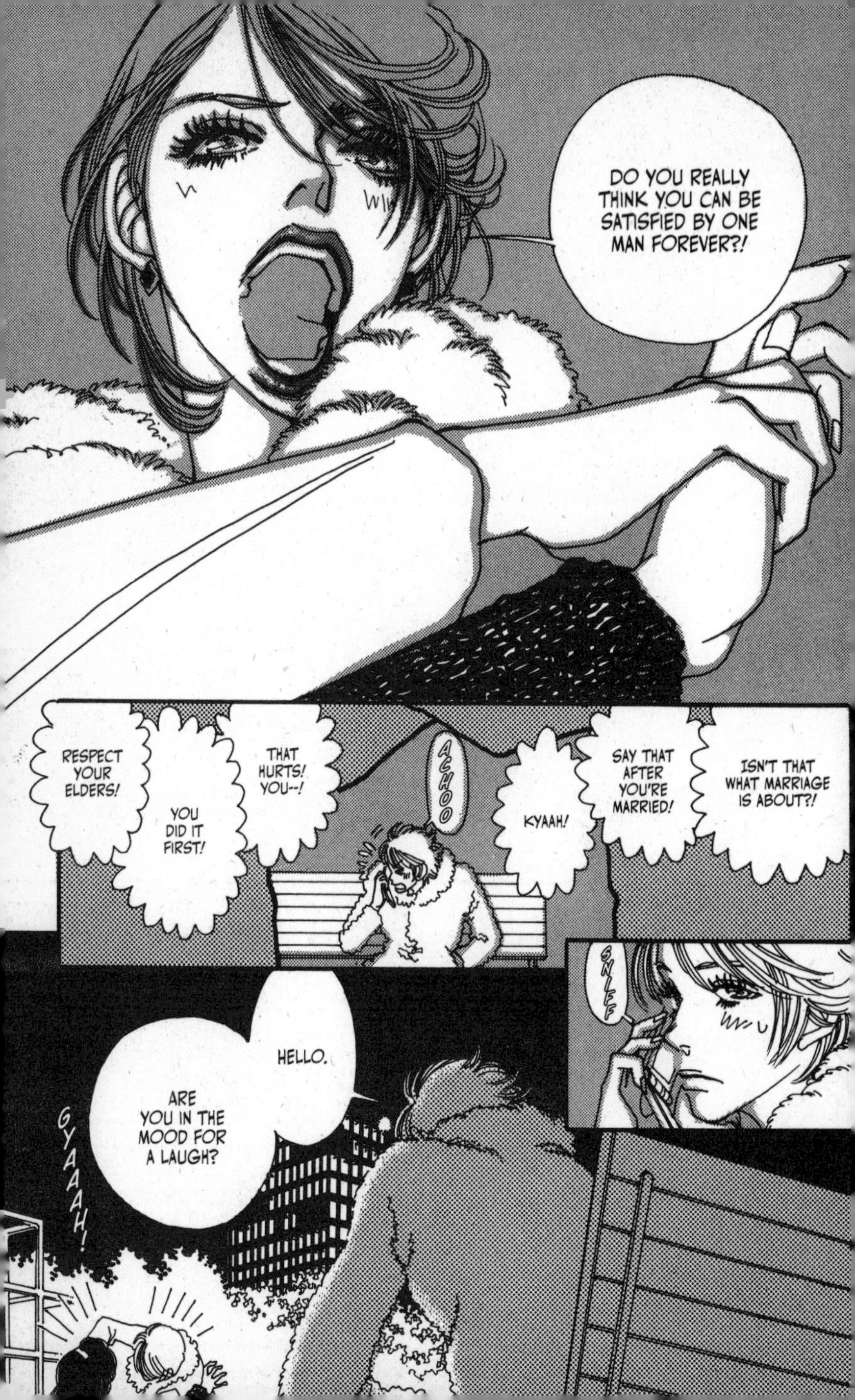
DO YOU REALLY THINK YOU CAN BE SATISFIED BY ONE MAN FOREVER?!
ISN'T THAT WHAT MARRIAGE IS ABOUT?!
SAY THAT AFTER YOU'RE MARRIED!
KYAAH!
ACHOO
THAT HURTS! YOU--!
YOU DID IT FIRST!
RESPECT YOUR ELDERS!
SNIFF
HELLO.
ARE YOU IN THE MOOD FOR A LAUGH?
GYAAAAH!

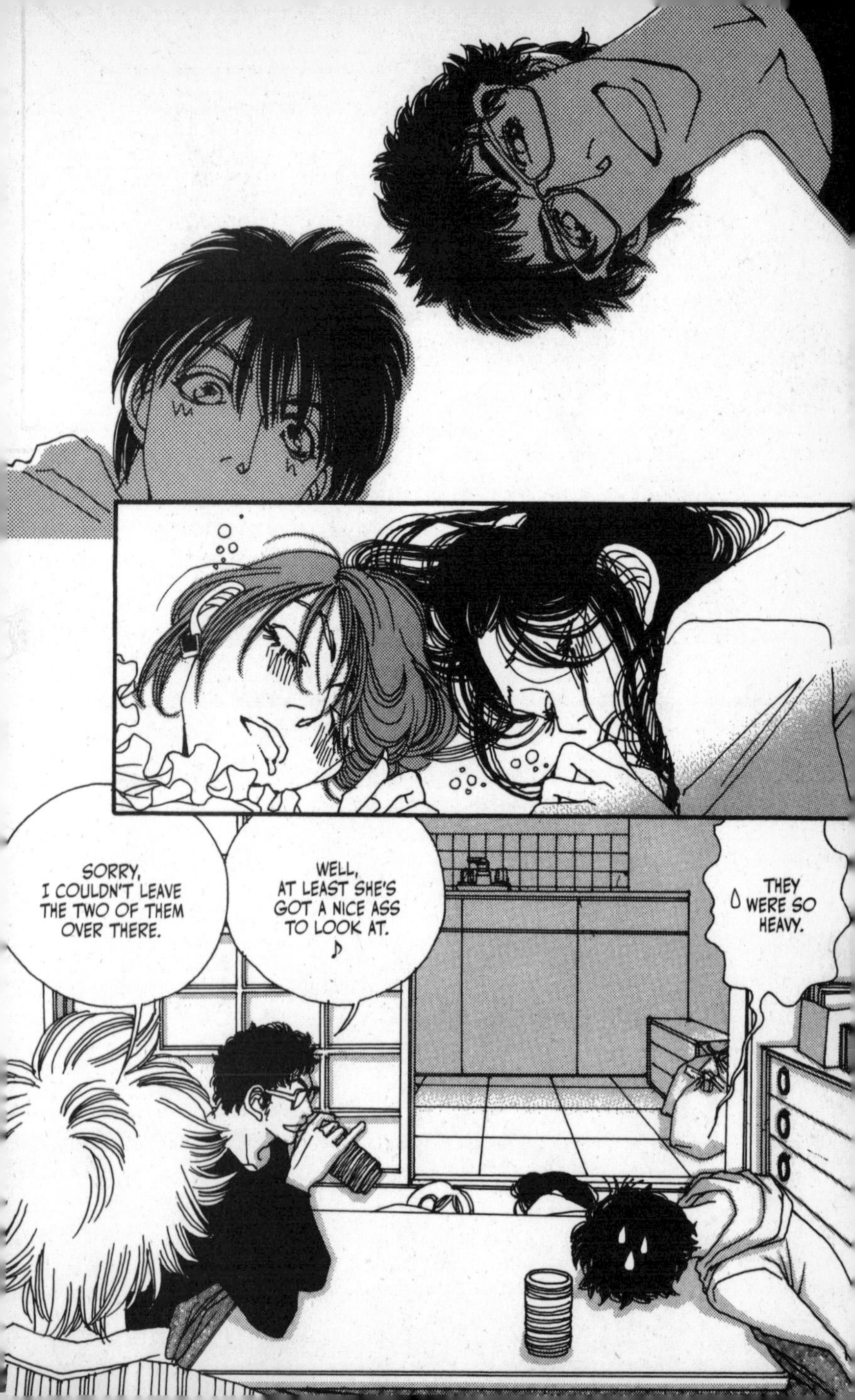
THEY WERE SO HEAVY.
WELL, AT LEAST SHE'S GOT A NICE ASS TO LOOK AT. ♪
SORRY, I COULDN'T LEAVE THE TWO OF THEM OVER THERE.

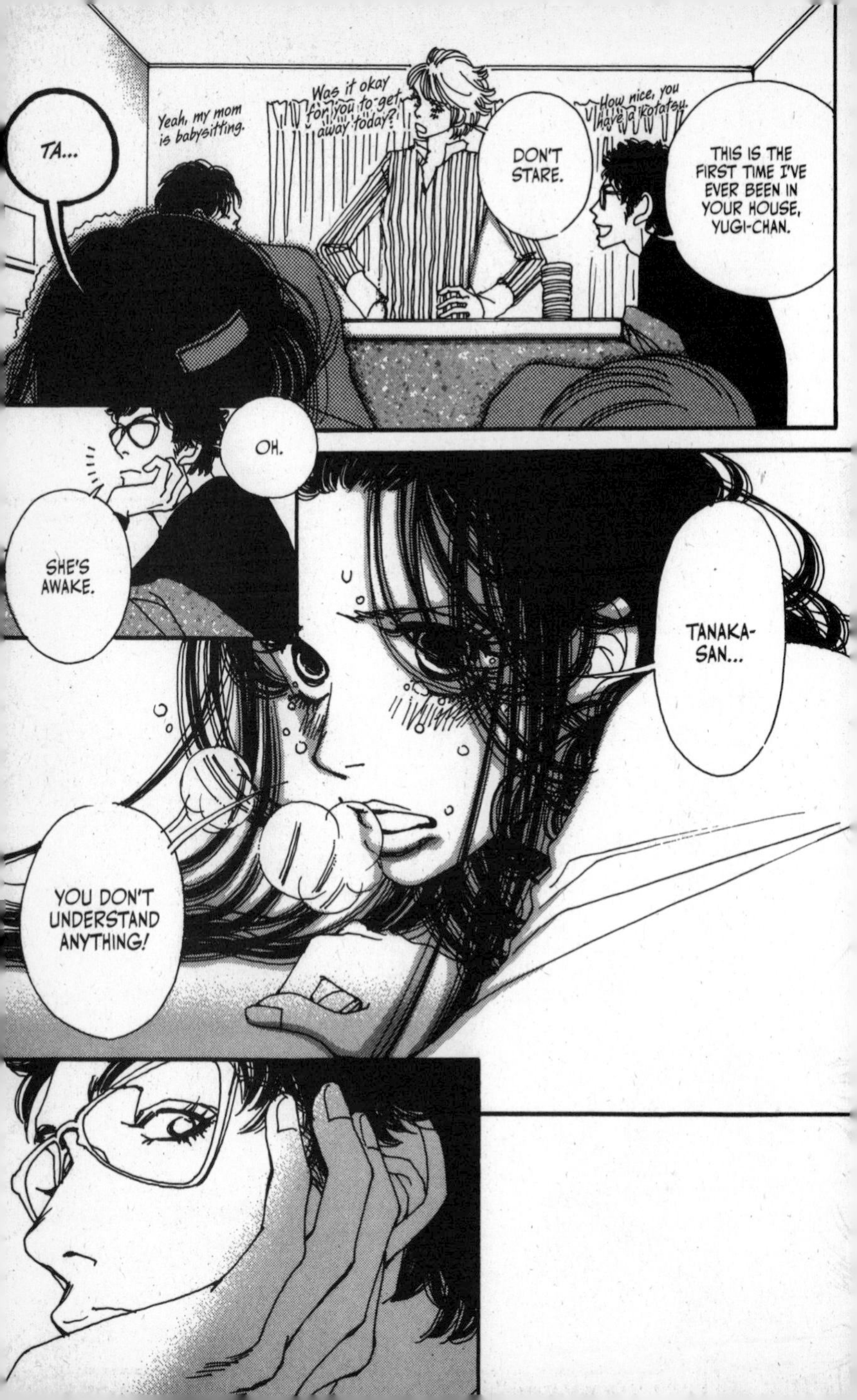
THIS IS THE FIRST TIME I'VE EVER BEEN IN YOUR HOUSE, YUGI-CHAN.
How nice, you have a kotatsu.
DON'T STARE.
Was it okay for you to get away today?
Yeah, my mom is babysitting.
TA...
OH.
SHE'S AWAKE.
TANAKA-SAN...
YOU DON'T UNDERSTAND ANYTHING!

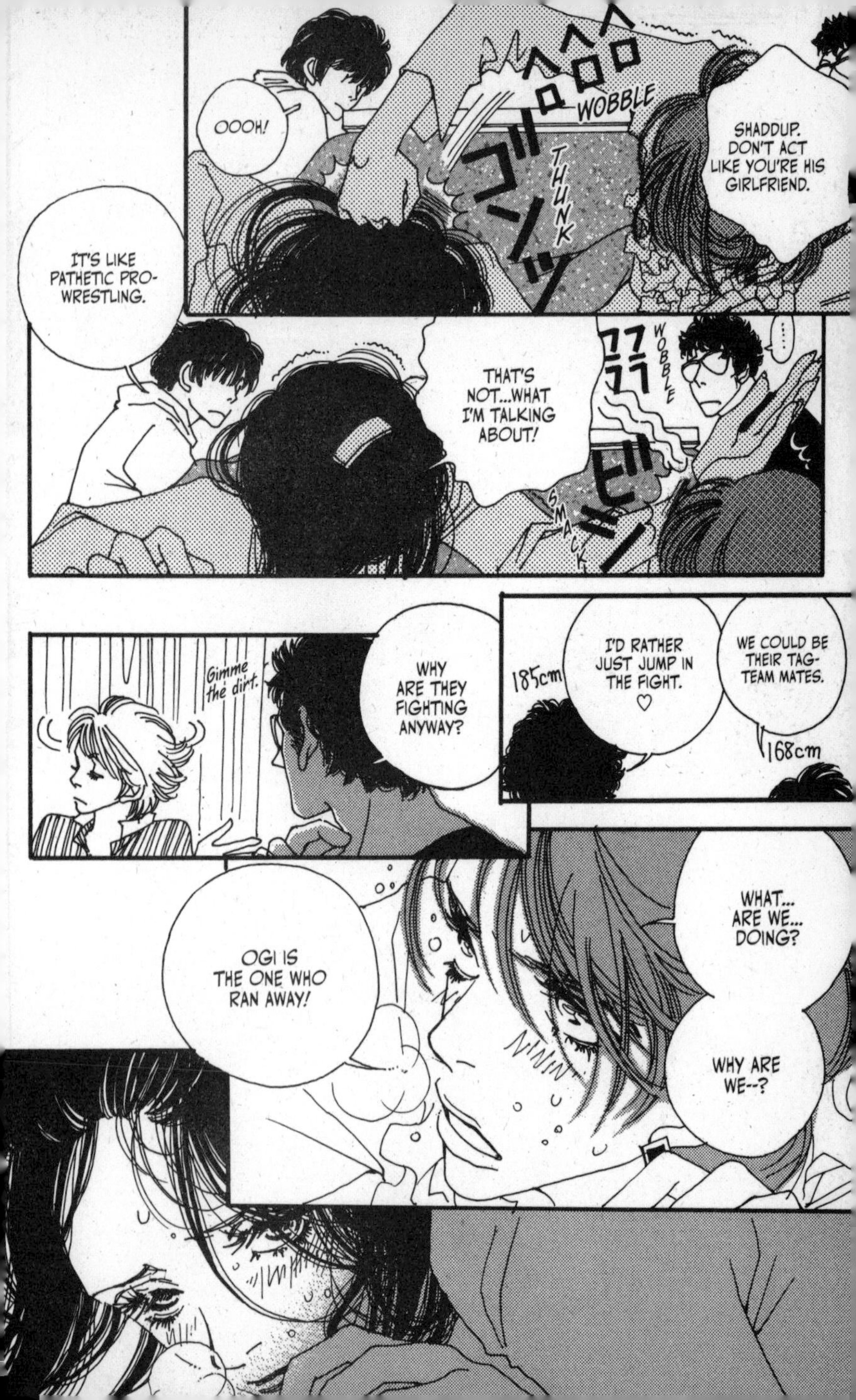
SHADDUP. DON'T ACT LIKE YOU'RE HIS GIRLFRIEND.
WOBBLE
THUNK
OOOH!
...
WOBBLE
THAT'S NOT...WHAT I'M TALKING ABOUT!
SMACK
IT'S LIKE PATHETIC PRO-WRESTLING.
WE COULD BE THEIR TAG-TEAM MATES.
168cm
I'D RATHER JUST JUMP IN THE FIGHT. ♡
185cm
WHY ARE THEY FIGHTING ANYWAY?
Gimme the dirt.
WHAT... ARE WE... DOING?
WHY ARE WE--?
OGI IS THE ONE WHO RAN AWAY!

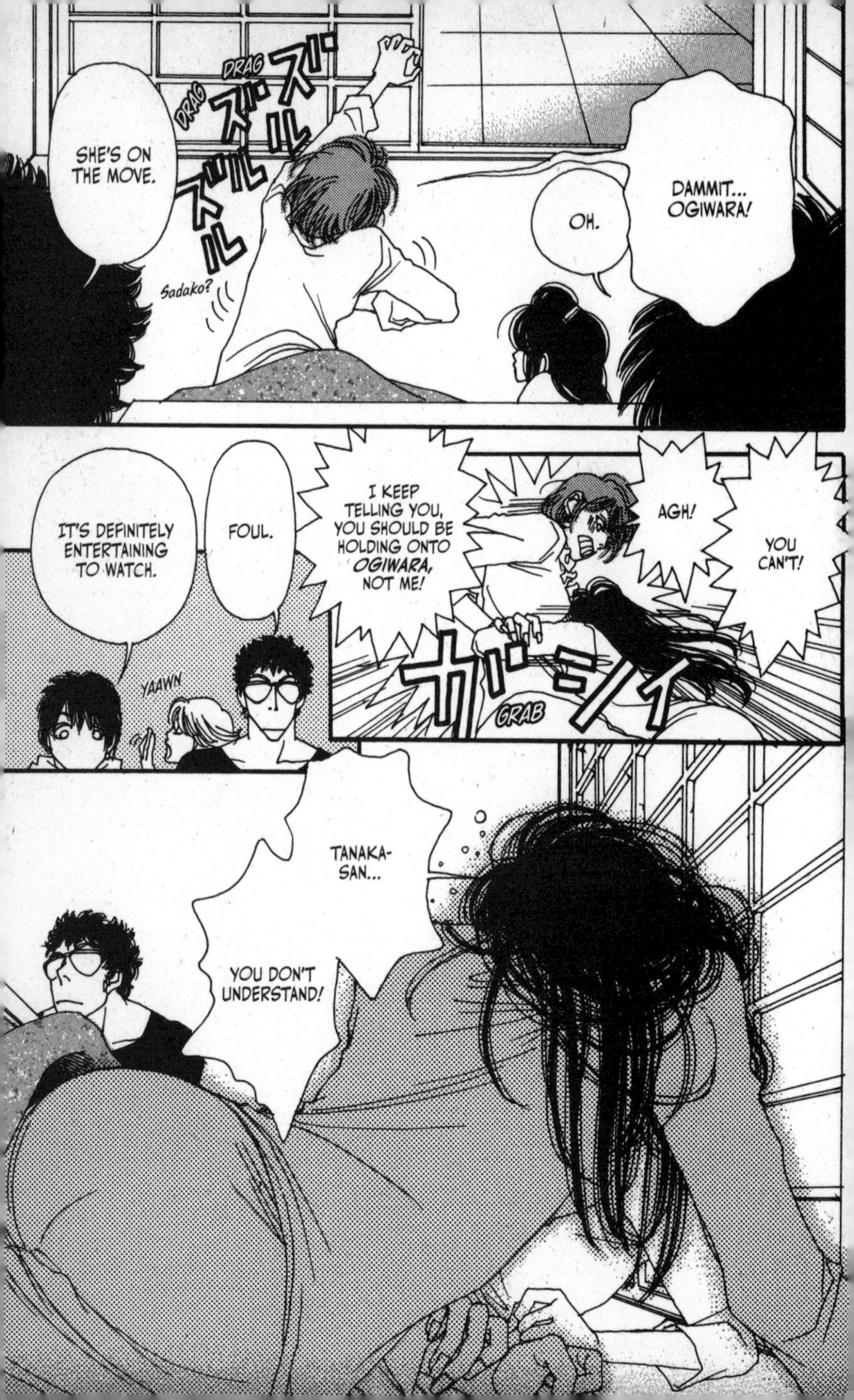
DAMMIT... OGIWARA!
OH.
Sadako?
ズルズル
DRAG
DRAG
SHE'S ON THE MOVE.
YOU CAN'T!
AGH!
I KEEP TELLING YOU, YOU SHOULD BE HOLDING ONTO *OGIWARA,* NOT ME!
ガシィ
GRAB
FOUL.
YAAWN
IT'S DEFINITELY ENTERTAINING TO WATCH.
TANAKA-SAN...
YOU DON'T UNDERSTAND!

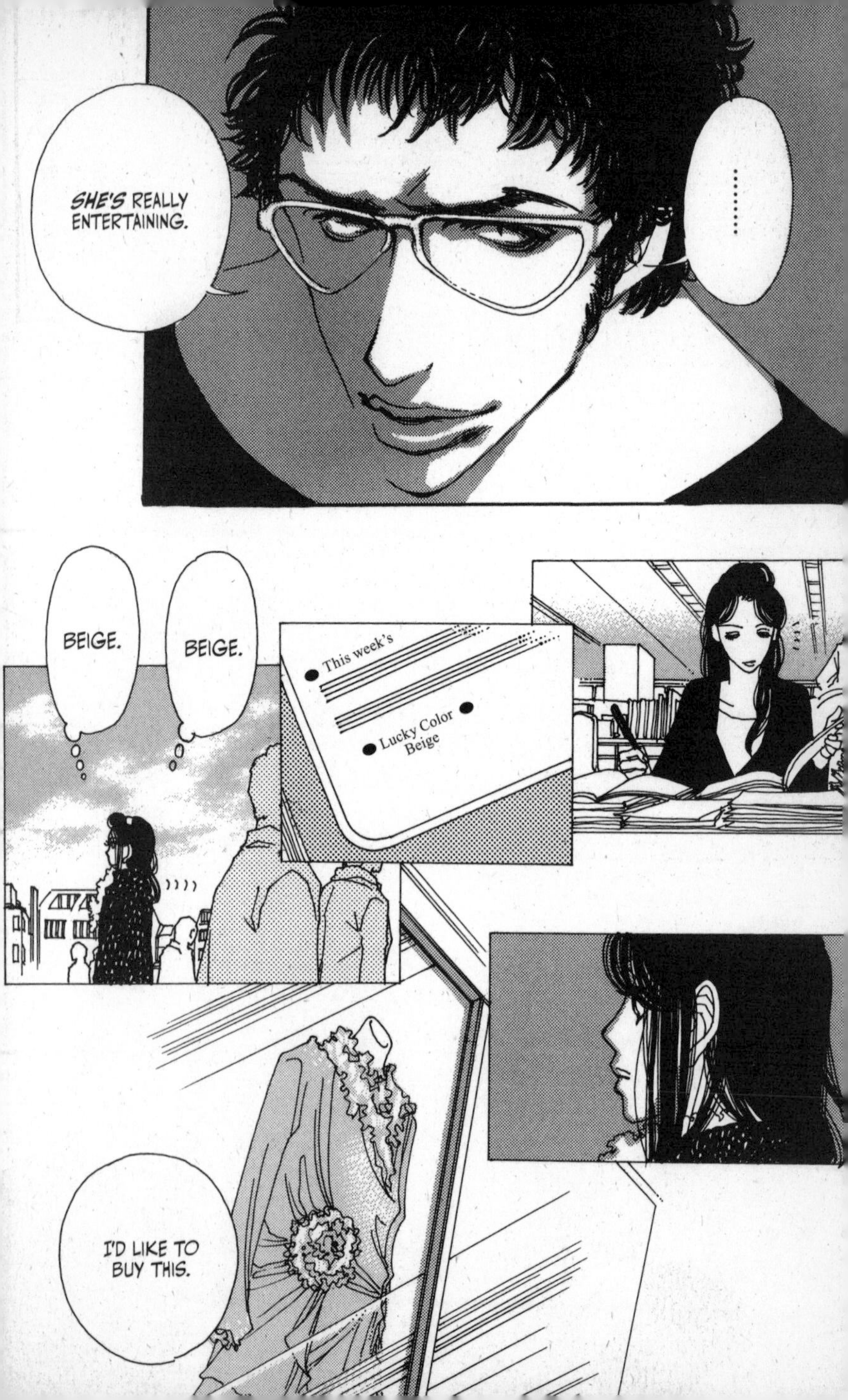
......
SHE'S REALLY ENTERTAINING.
This week's
Lucky Color
Beige
BEIGE.
BEIGE.
I'D LIKE TO BUY THIS.

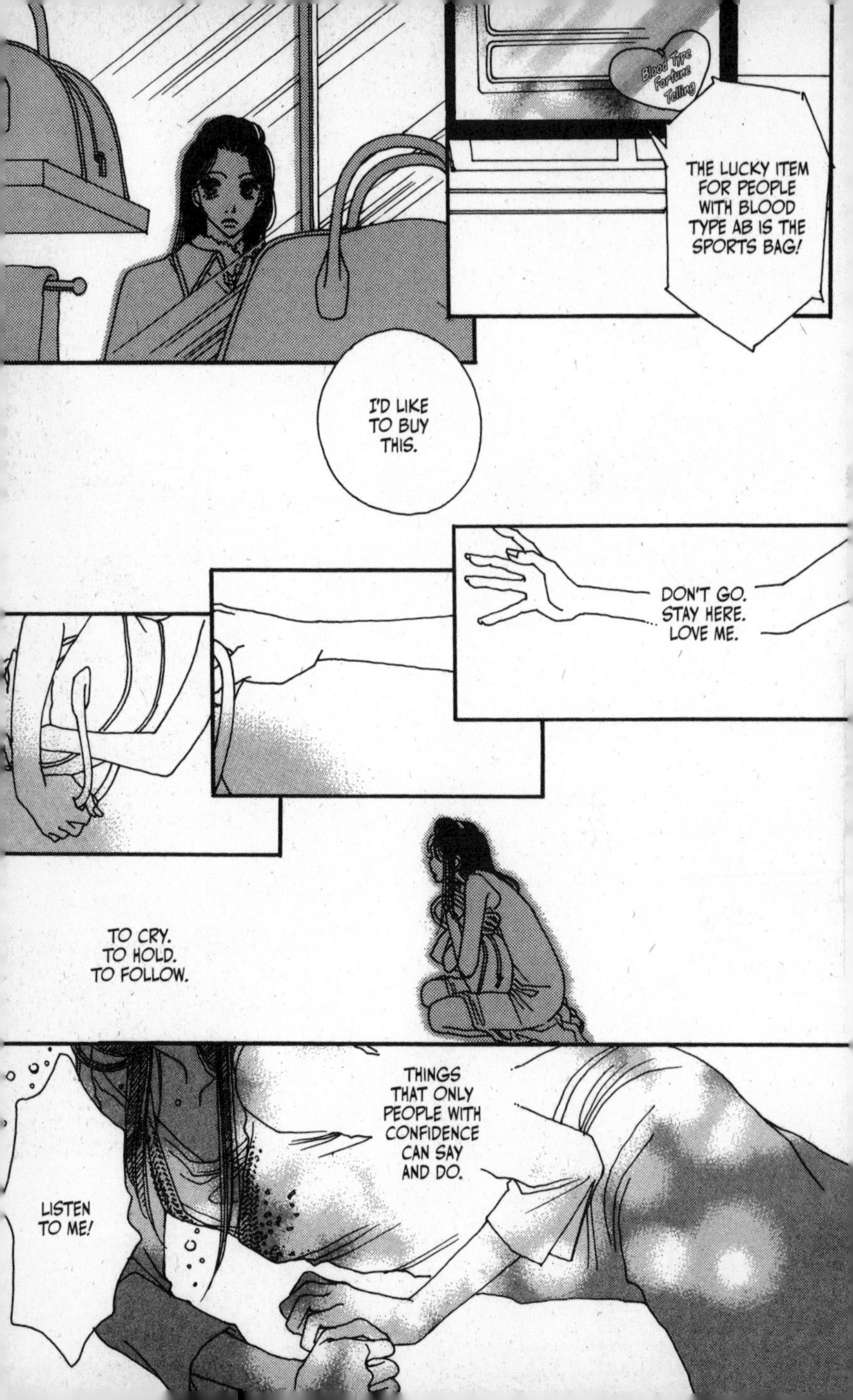
Blood Type Fortune Telling
THE LUCKY ITEM FOR PEOPLE WITH BLOOD TYPE AB IS THE SPORTS BAG!
I'D LIKE TO BUY THIS.
DON'T GO. STAY HERE. LOVE ME.
TO CRY. TO HOLD. TO FOLLOW.
THINGS THAT ONLY PEOPLE WITH CONFIDENCE CAN SAY AND DO.
LISTEN TO ME!

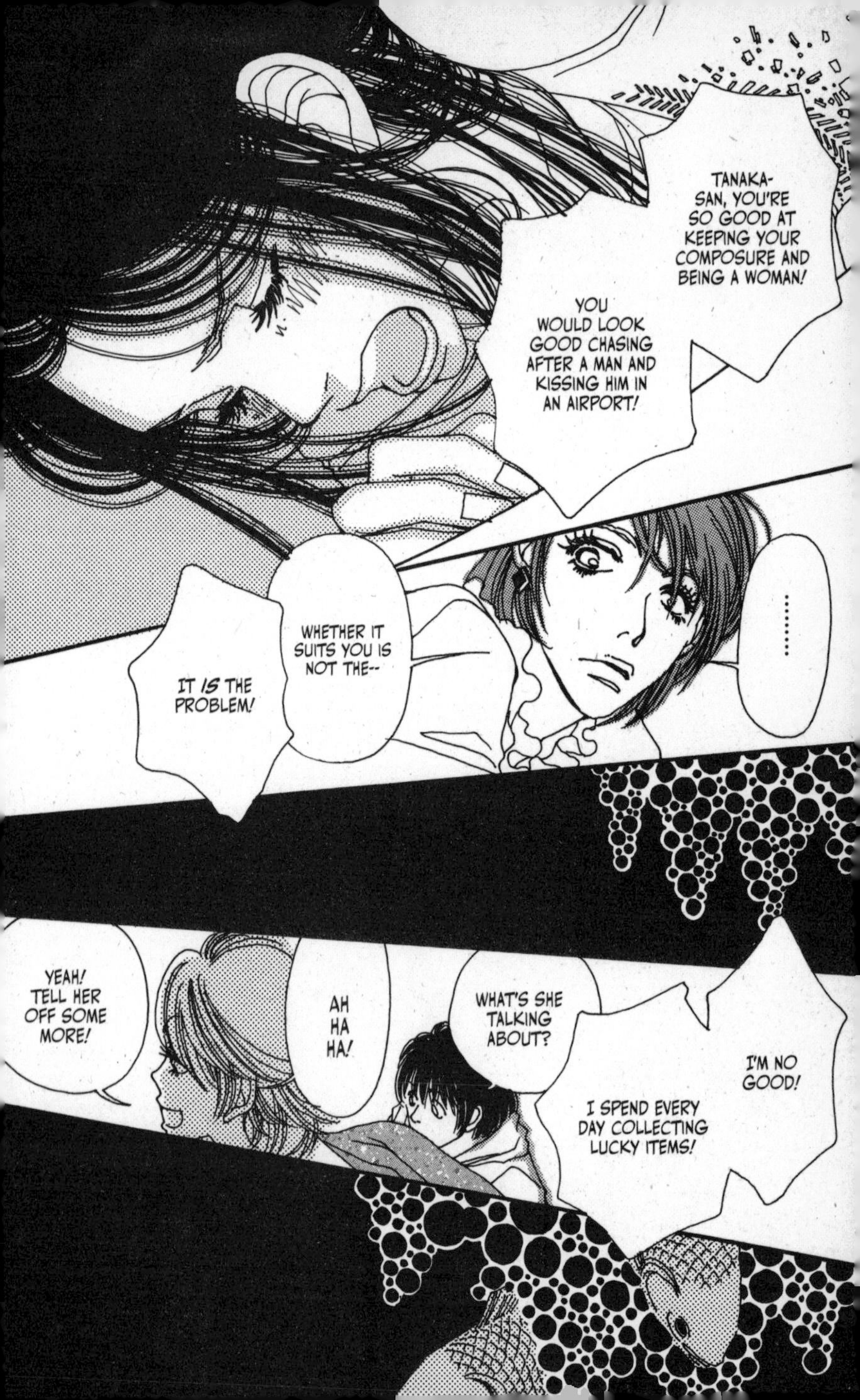
TANAKA-SAN, YOU'RE SO GOOD AT KEEPING YOUR COMPOSURE AND BEING A WOMAN!
YOU WOULD LOOK GOOD CHASING AFTER A MAN AND KISSING HIM IN AN AIRPORT!
......
WHETHER IT SUITS YOU IS NOT THE--
IT *IS* THE PROBLEM!
I'M NO GOOD!
I SPEND EVERY DAY COLLECTING LUCKY ITEMS!
WHAT'S SHE TALKING ABOUT?
AH HA HA!
YEAH! TELL HER OFF SOME MORE!

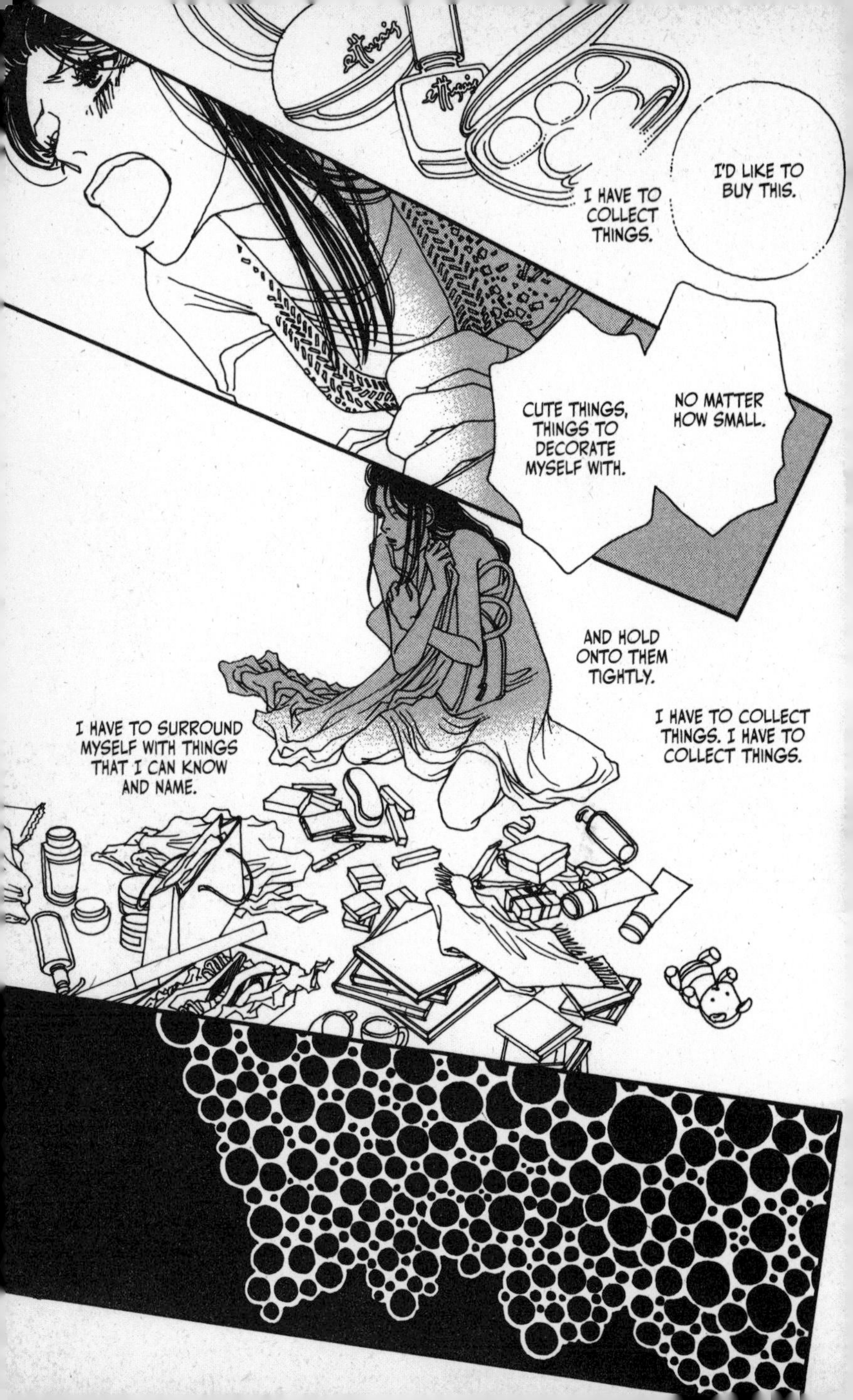
I'D LIKE TO BUY THIS.
I HAVE TO COLLECT THINGS.
NO MATTER HOW SMALL.
CUTE THINGS, THINGS TO DECORATE MYSELF WITH.
AND HOLD ONTO THEM TIGHTLY.
I HAVE TO COLLECT THINGS. I HAVE TO COLLECT THINGS.
I HAVE TO SURROUND MYSELF WITH THINGS THAT I CAN KNOW AND NAME.

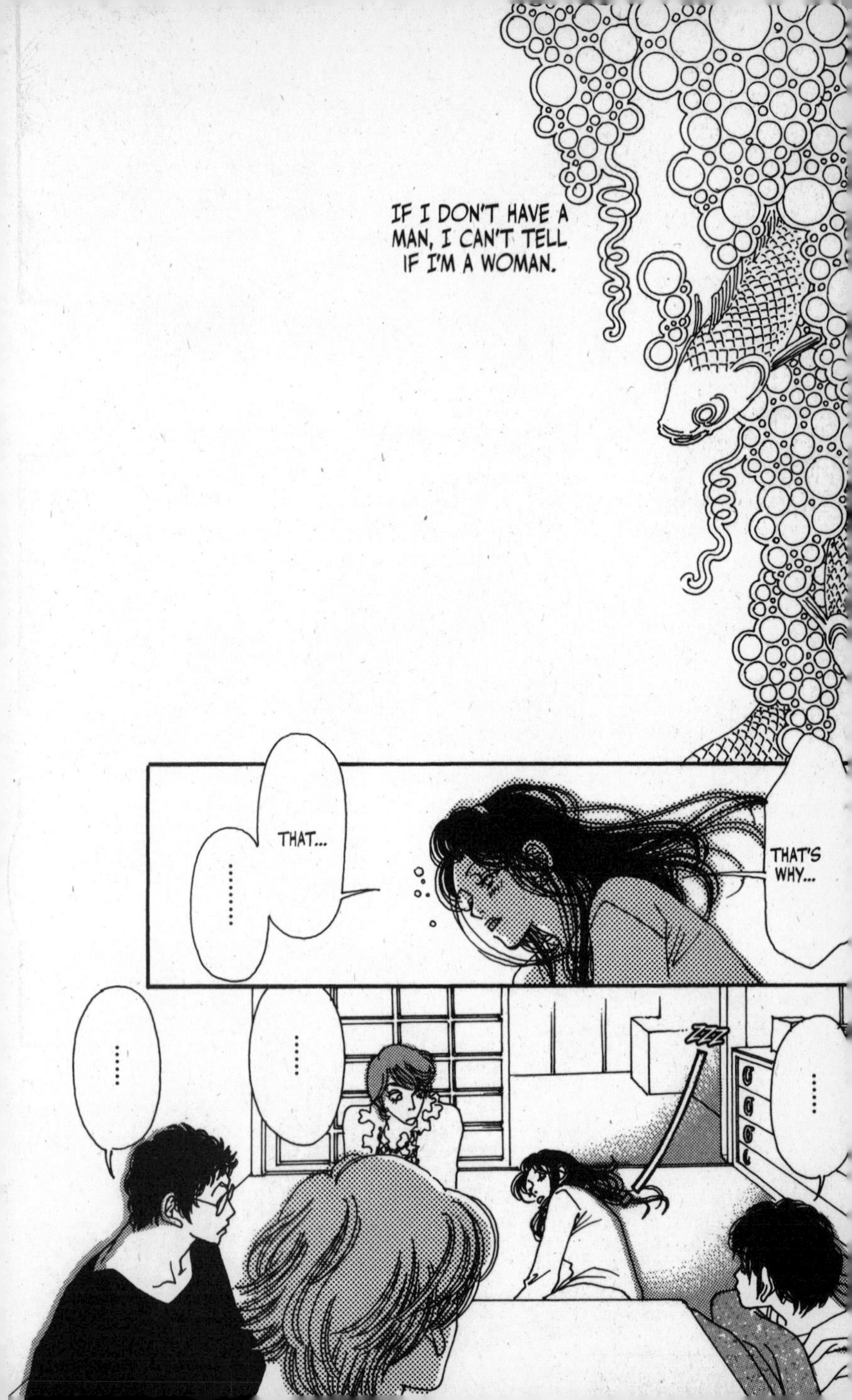
IF I DON'T HAVE A MAN, I CAN'T TELL IF I'M A WOMAN.
THAT'S WHY...
THAT...
......
......
......
......

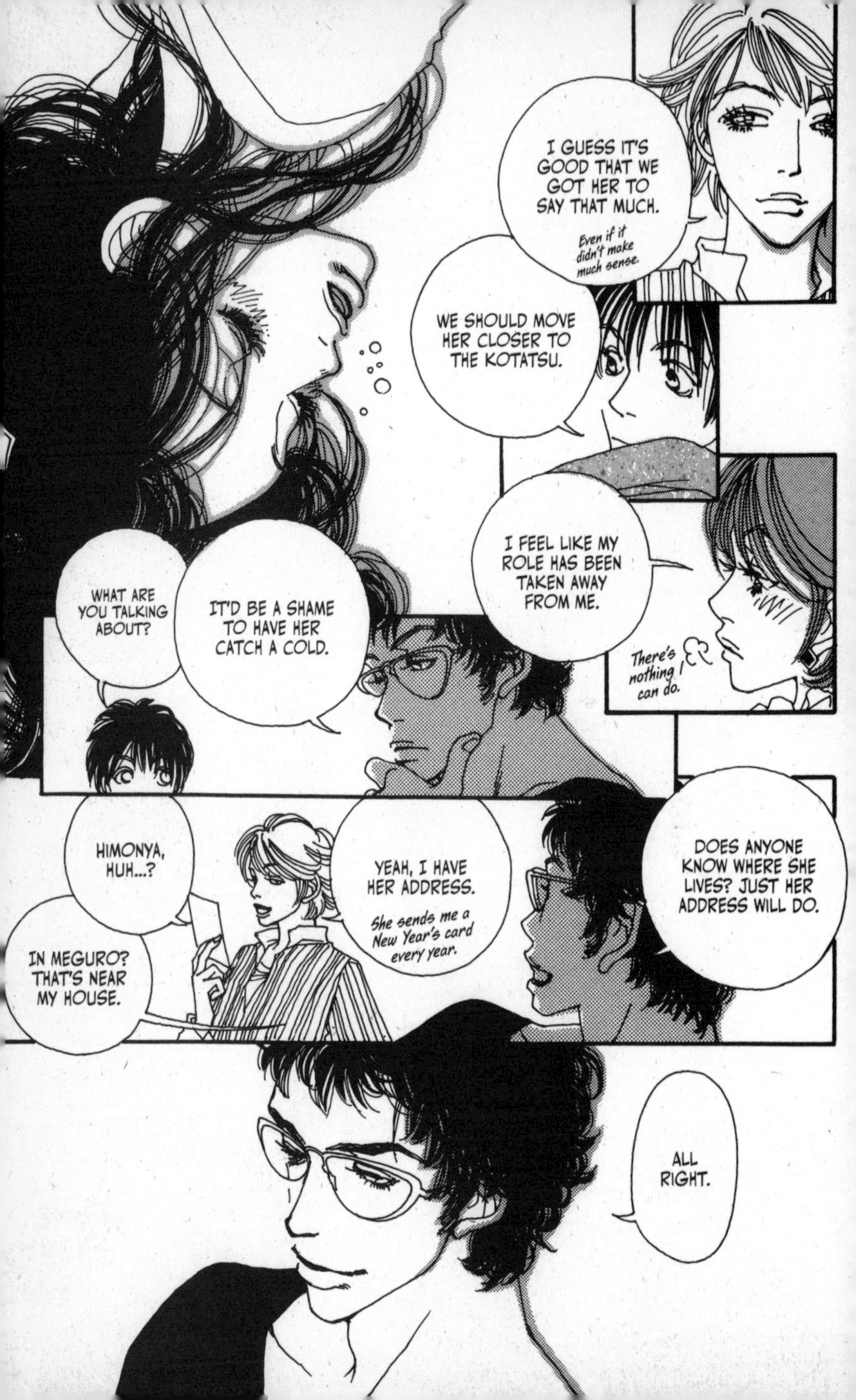
I GUESS IT'S GOOD THAT WE GOT HER TO SAY THAT MUCH.
Even if it didn't make much sense.
WE SHOULD MOVE HER CLOSER TO THE KOTATSU.
I FEEL LIKE MY ROLE HAS BEEN TAKEN AWAY FROM ME.
There's nothing I can do.
IT'D BE A SHAME TO HAVE HER CATCH A COLD.
WHAT ARE YOU TALKING ABOUT?
DOES ANYONE KNOW WHERE SHE LIVES? JUST HER ADDRESS WILL DO.
YEAH, I HAVE HER ADDRESS.
She sends me a New Year's card every year.
HIMONYA, HUH...?
IN MEGURO? THAT'S NEAR MY HOUSE.
ALL RIGHT.

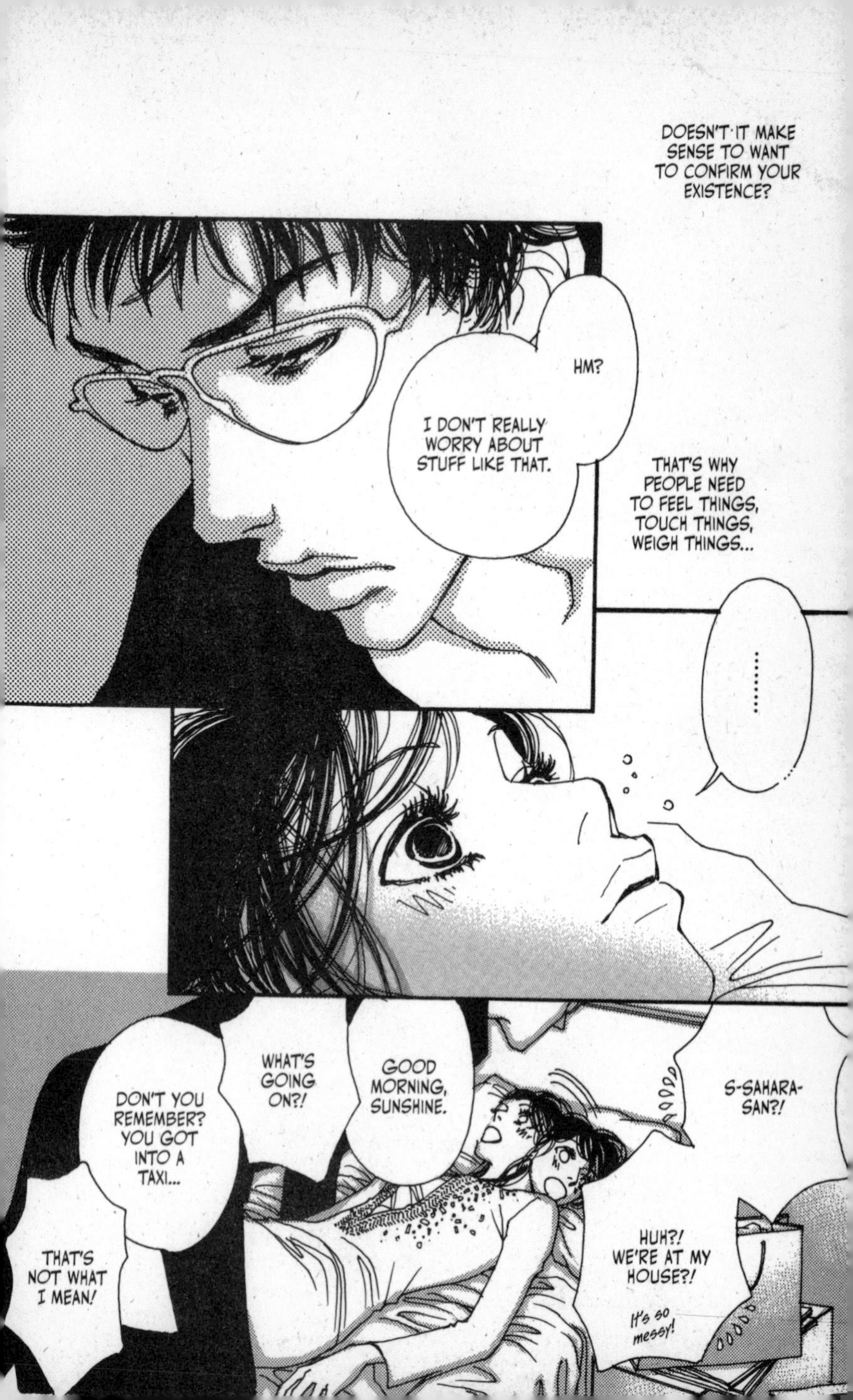
DOESN'T IT MAKE SENSE TO WANT TO CONFIRM YOUR EXISTENCE?
HM?
I DON'T REALLY WORRY ABOUT STUFF LIKE THAT.
THAT'S WHY PEOPLE NEED TO FEEL THINGS, TOUCH THINGS, WEIGH THINGS...
......
S-SAHARA-SAN?!
GOOD MORNING, SUNSHINE.
WHAT'S GOING ON?!
DON'T YOU REMEMBER? YOU GOT INTO A TAXI...
HUH?! WE'RE AT MY HOUSE?!
It's so messy!
THAT'S NOT WHAT I MEAN!

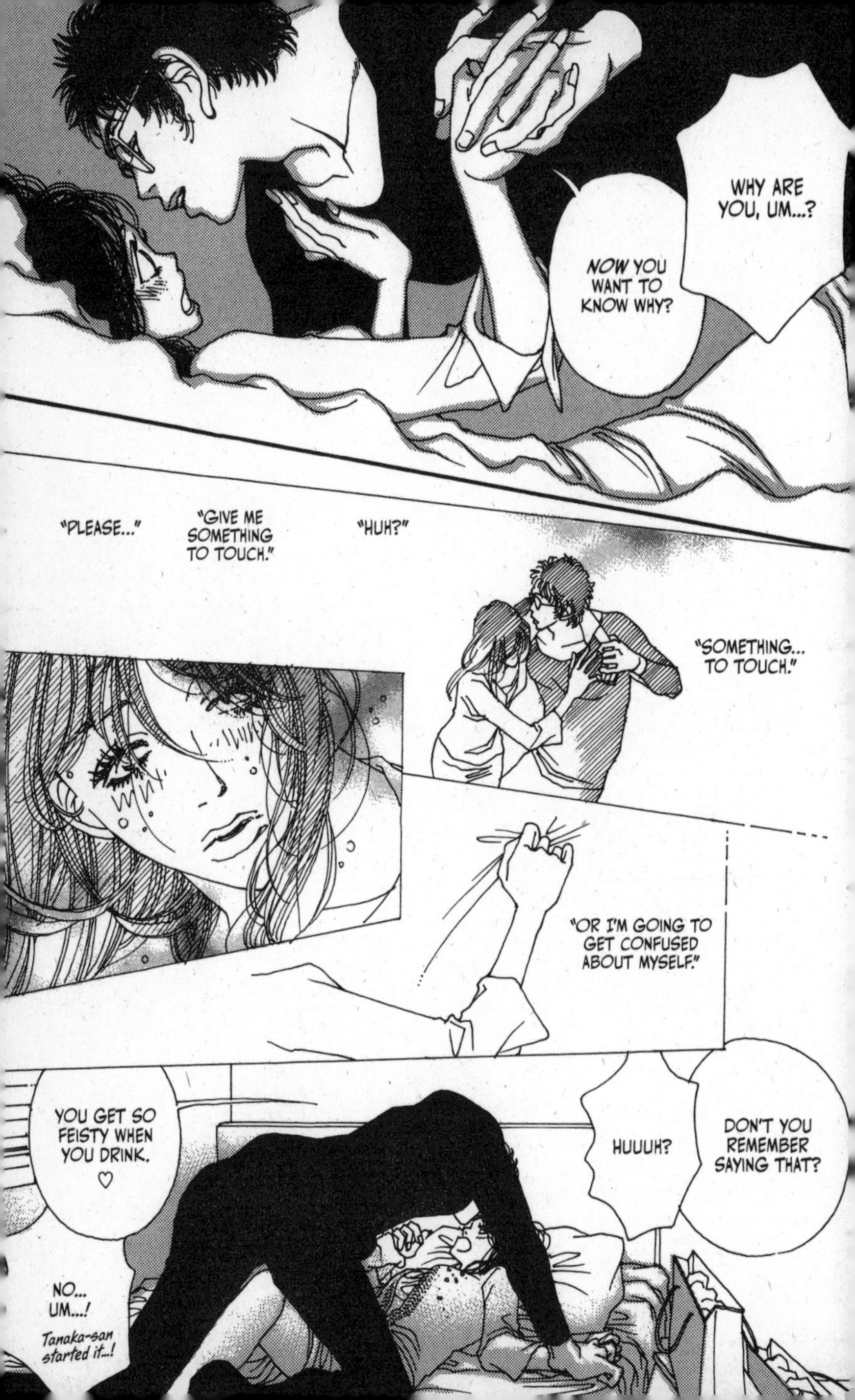
WHY ARE YOU, UM...?
NOW YOU WANT TO KNOW WHY?
"PLEASE..."
"GIVE ME SOMETHING TO TOUCH."
"HUH?"
"SOMETHING... TO TOUCH."
"OR I'M GOING TO GET CONFUSED ABOUT MYSELF."
DON'T YOU REMEMBER SAYING THAT?
HUUUH?
YOU GET SO FEISTY WHEN YOU DRINK. ♡
NO... UM...!
Tanaka-san started it...!

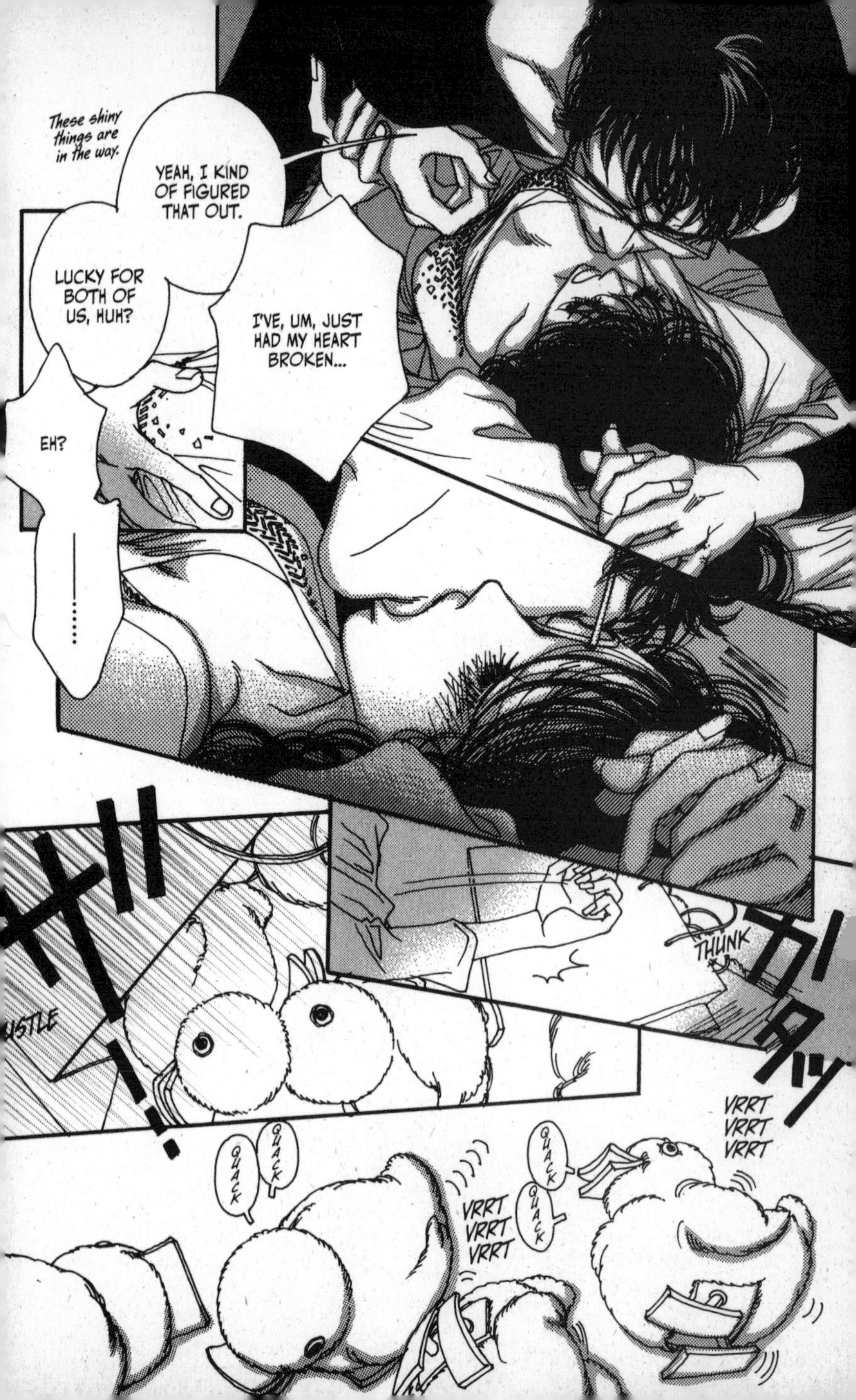

YEAH, I KIND OF FIGURED THAT OUT.
These shiny things are in the way.
I'VE, UM, JUST HAD MY HEART BROKEN...
LUCKY FOR BOTH OF US, HUH?
EH?
......
THUNK
USTLE
VRRT VRRT VRRT
QUACK
QUACK
VRRT VRRT VRRT
QUACK
QUACK

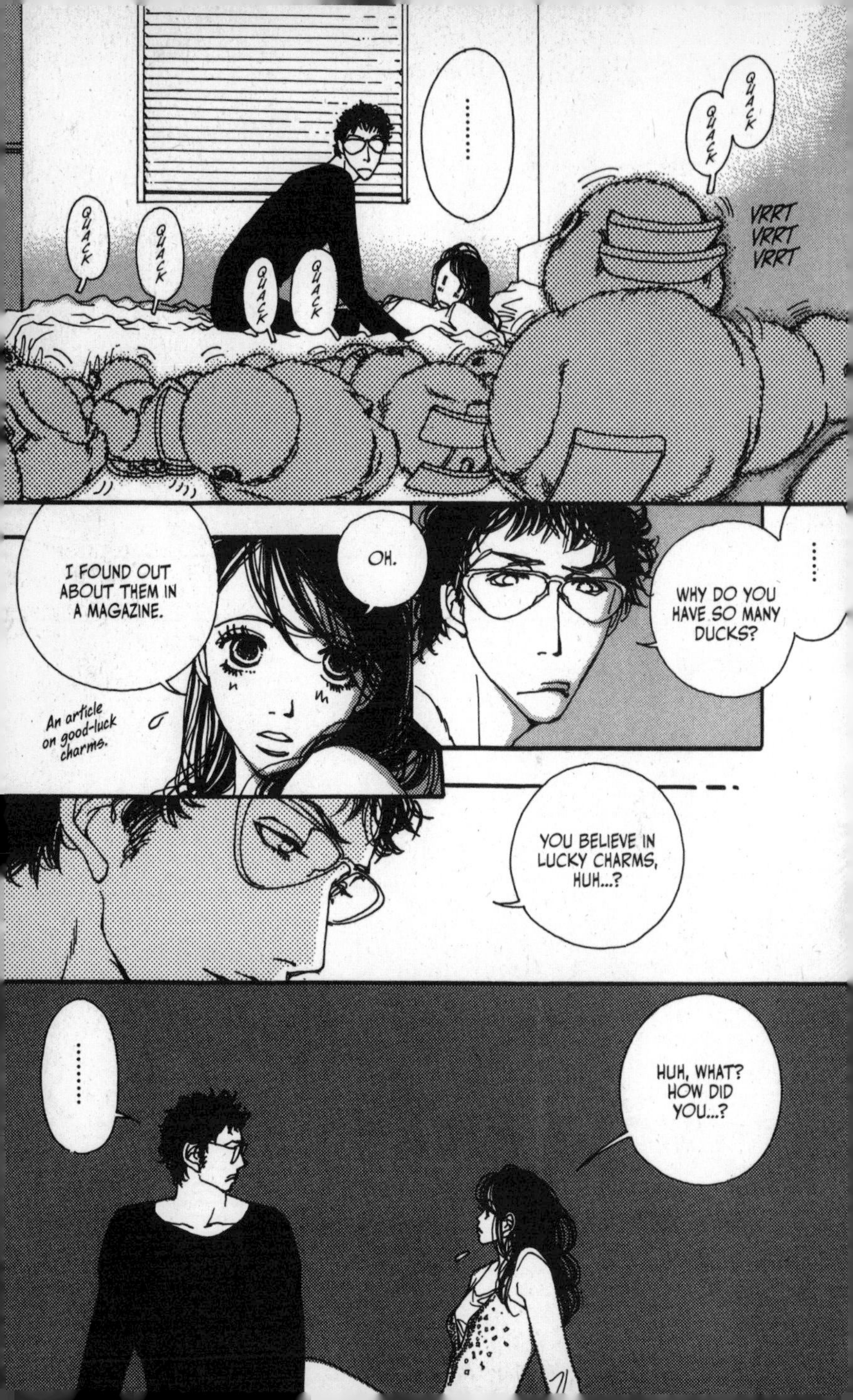
QUACK QUACK
VRRT VRRT VRRT
......
QUACK QUACK
QUACK QUACK
......
WHY DO YOU HAVE SO MANY DUCKS?
OH.
I FOUND OUT ABOUT THEM IN A MAGAZINE.
An article on good-luck charms.
YOU BELIEVE IN LUCKY CHARMS, HUH...?
HUH, WHAT? HOW DID YOU...?
......

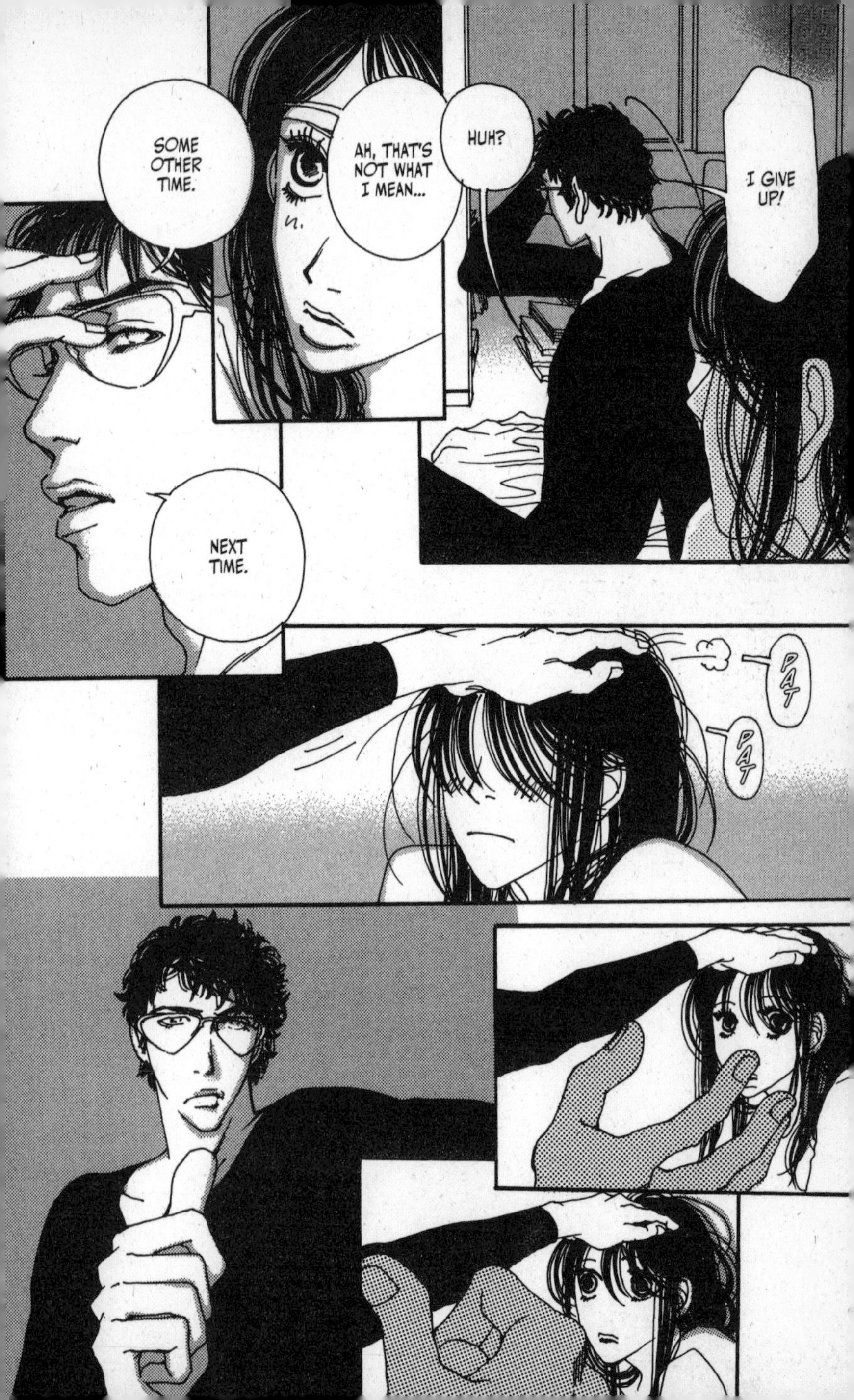
I GIVE UP!
HUH?
AH, THAT'S NOT WHAT I MEAN...
SOME OTHER TIME.
NEXT TIME.
PAT
PAT

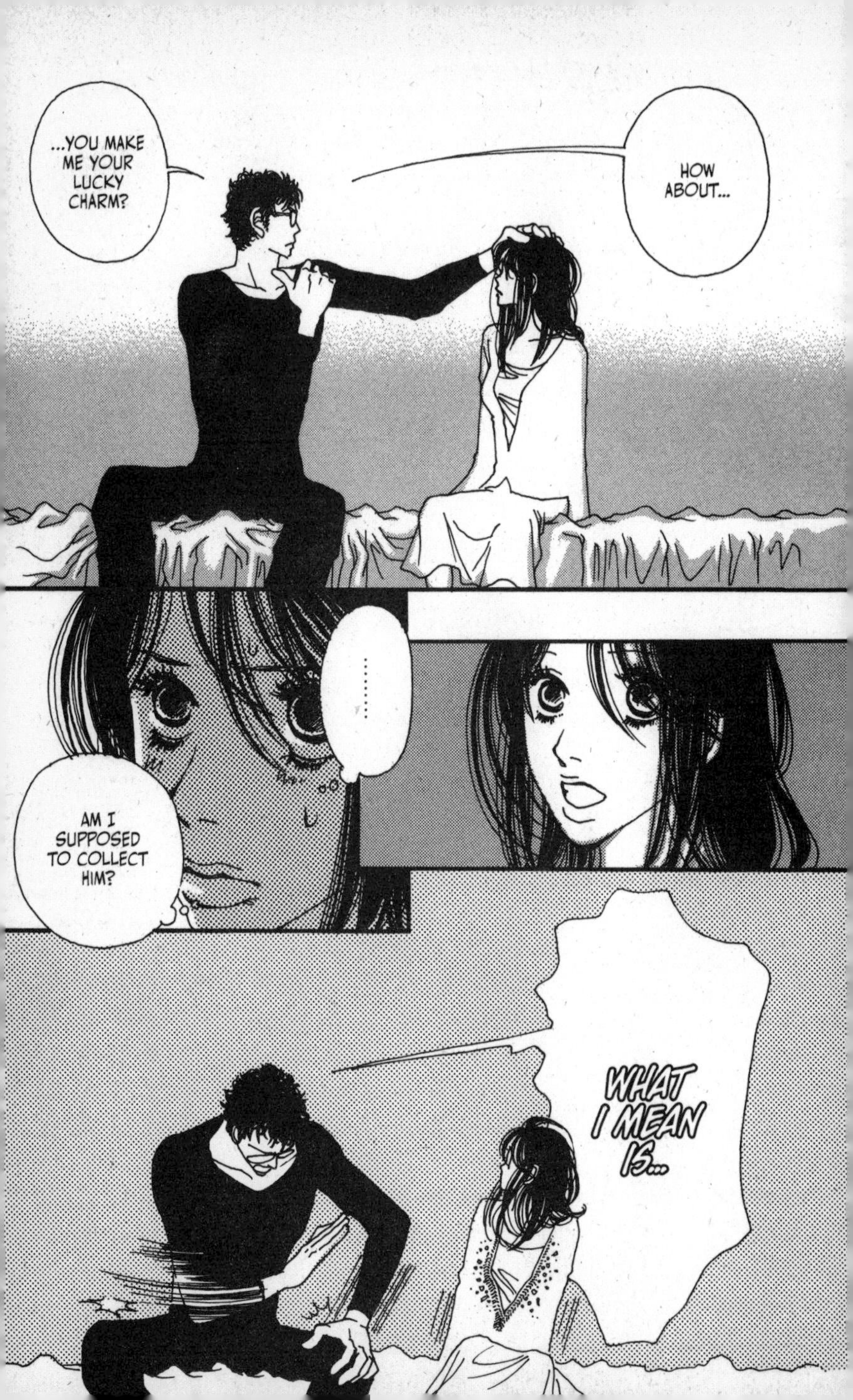
HOW ABOUT...
...YOU MAKE ME YOUR LUCKY CHARM?
......
AM I SUPPOSED TO COLLECT HIM?
WHAT I MEAN IS...

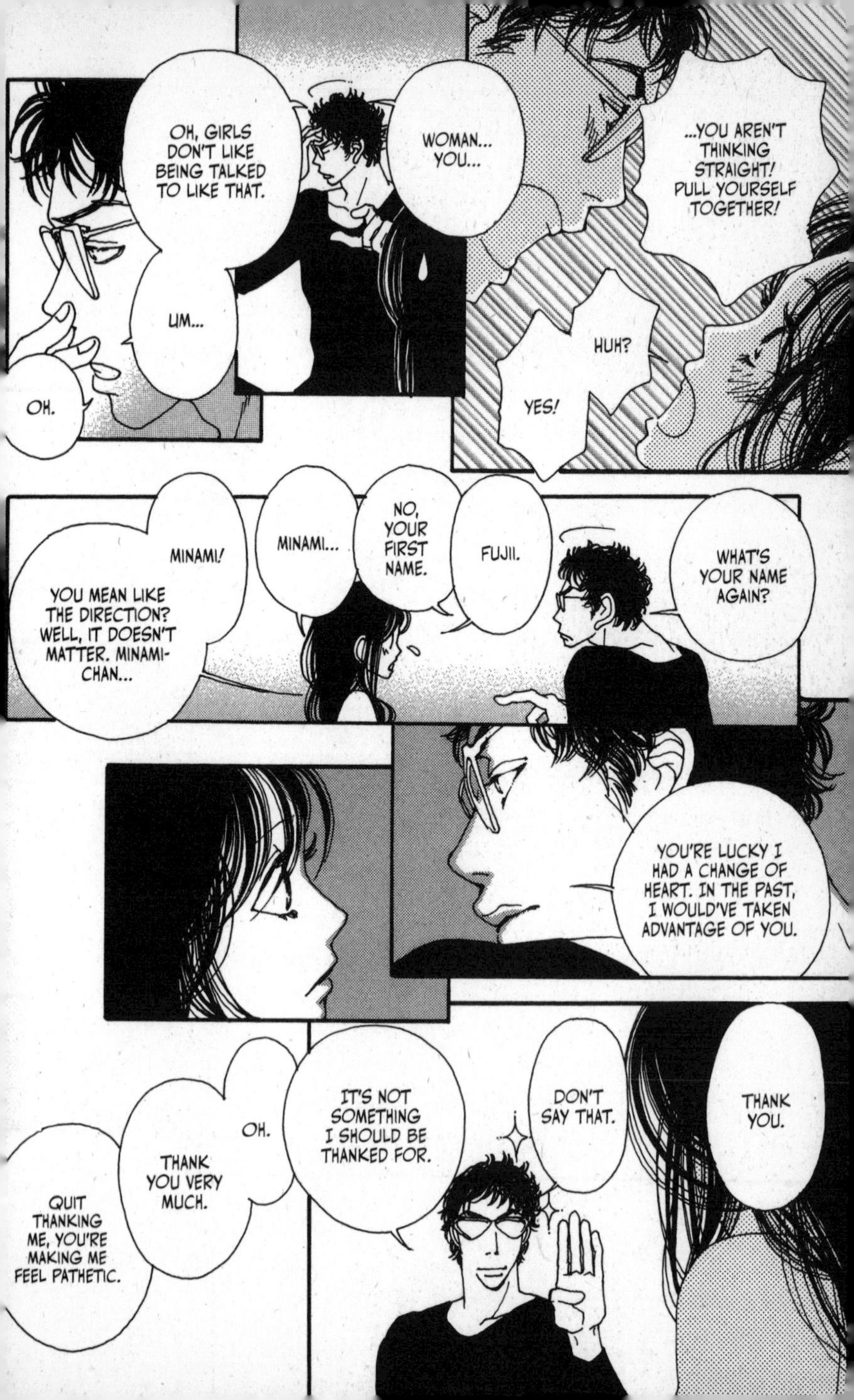
...YOU AREN'T THINKING STRAIGHT! PULL YOURSELF TOGETHER!
HUH?
YES!
WOMAN... YOU...
OH, GIRLS DON'T LIKE BEING TALKED TO LIKE THAT.
UM...
OH.
WHAT'S YOUR NAME AGAIN?
FUJII.
NO, YOUR FIRST NAME.
MINAMI...
MINAMI!
YOU MEAN LIKE THE DIRECTION? WELL, IT DOESN'T MATTER. MINAMI-CHAN...
YOU'RE LUCKY I HAD A CHANGE OF HEART. IN THE PAST, I WOULD'VE TAKEN ADVANTAGE OF YOU.
THANK YOU.
DON'T SAY THAT.
IT'S NOT SOMETHING I SHOULD BE THANKED FOR.
OH.
THANK YOU VERY MUCH.
QUIT THANKING ME, YOU'RE MAKING ME FEEL PATHETIC.

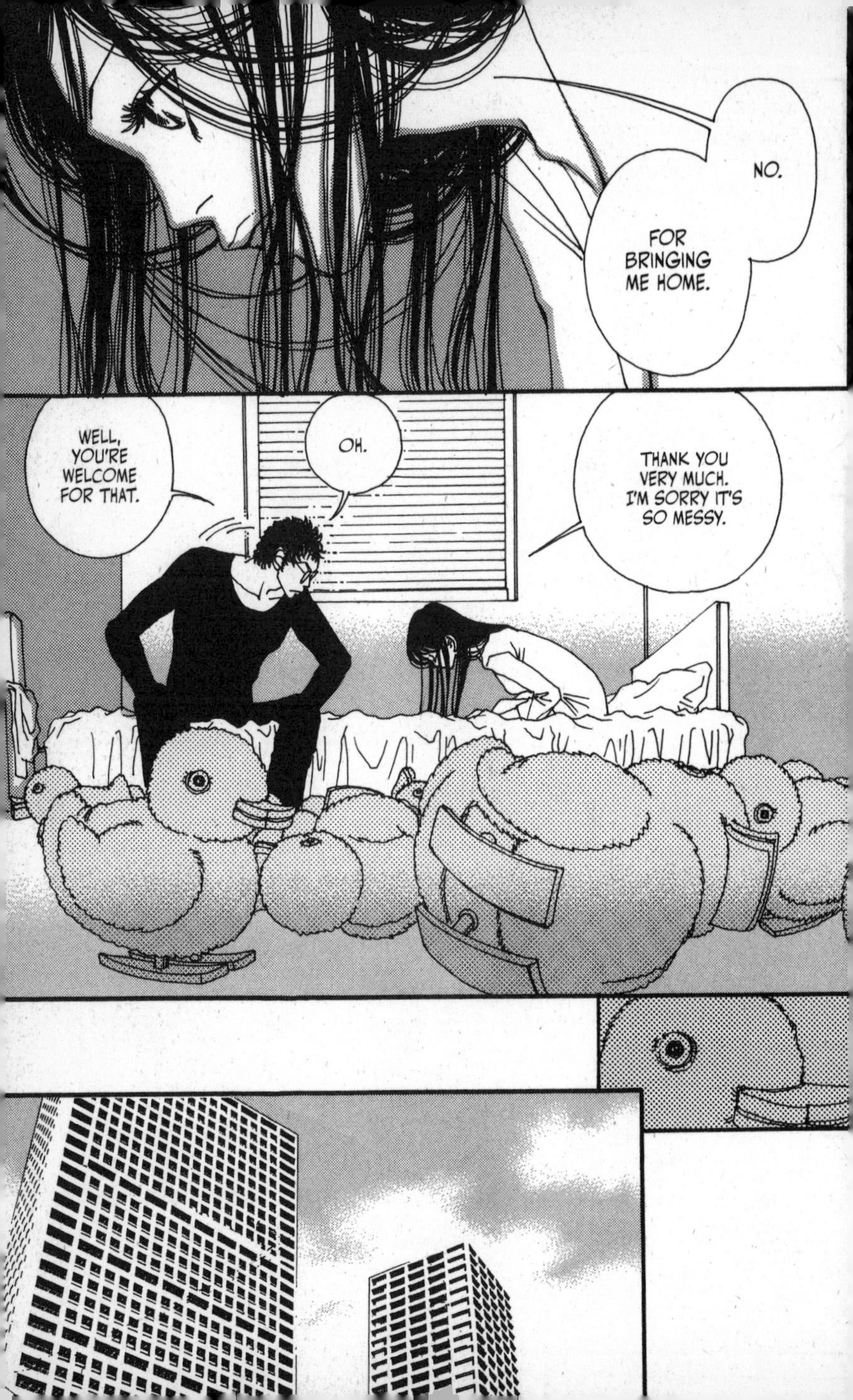
NO.
FOR BRINGING ME HOME.
THANK YOU VERY MUCH. I'M SORRY IT'S SO MESSY.
OH.
WELL, YOU'RE WELCOME FOR THAT.

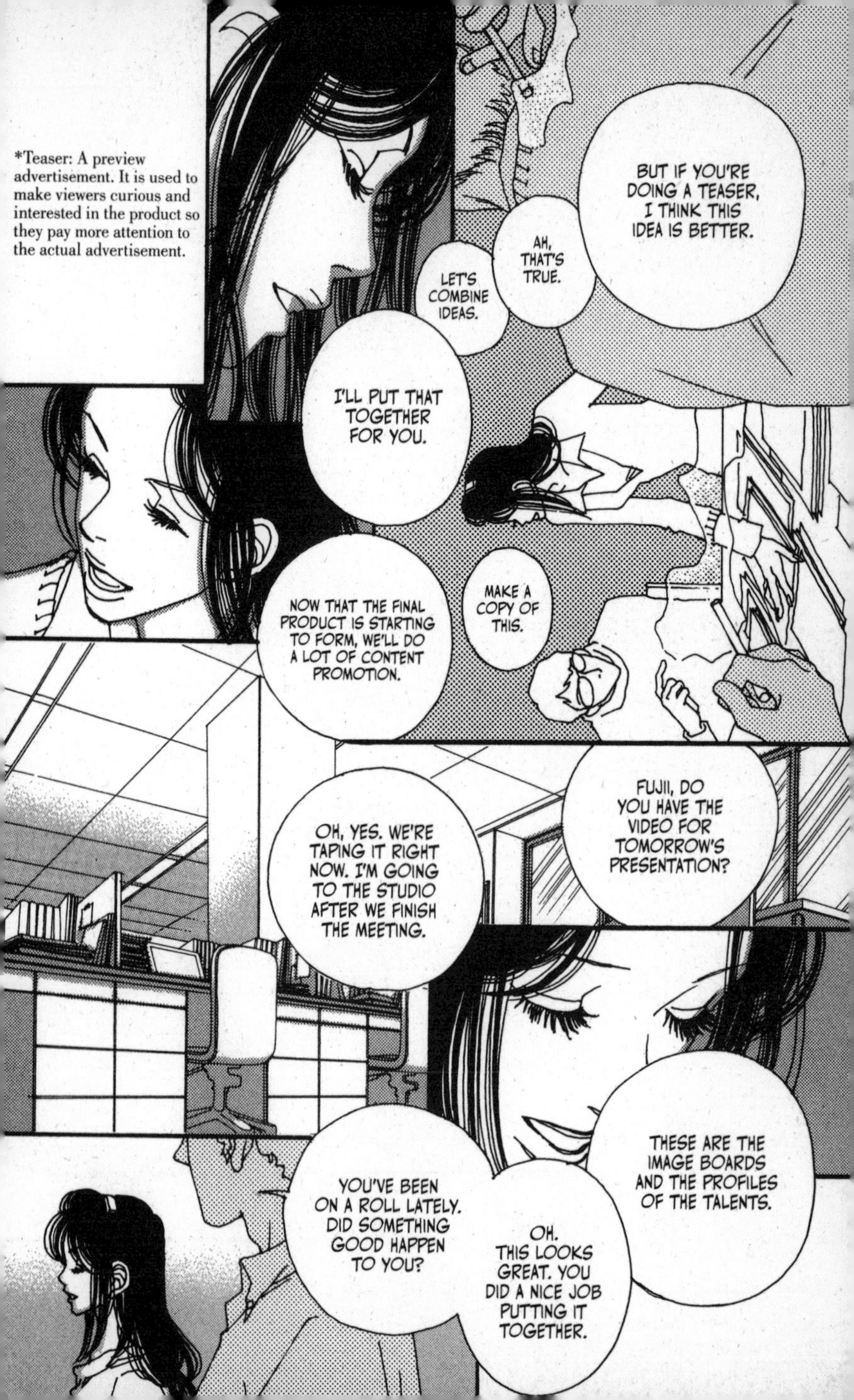
BUT IF YOU'RE DOING A TEASER, I THINK THIS IDEA IS BETTER.
AH, THAT'S TRUE.
LET'S COMBINE IDEAS.
I'LL PUT THAT TOGETHER FOR YOU.
MAKE A COPY OF THIS.
NOW THAT THE FINAL PRODUCT IS STARTING TO FORM, WE'LL DO A LOT OF CONTENT PROMOTION.
FUJII, DO YOU HAVE THE VIDEO FOR TOMORROW'S PRESENTATION?
OH, YES. WE'RE TAPING IT RIGHT NOW. I'M GOING TO THE STUDIO AFTER WE FINISH THE MEETING.
THESE ARE THE IMAGE BOARDS AND THE PROFILES OF THE TALENTS.
OH. THIS LOOKS GREAT. YOU DID A NICE JOB PUTTING IT TOGETHER.
YOU'VE BEEN ON A ROLL LATELY. DID SOMETHING GOOD HAPPEN TO YOU?

*Teaser: A preview advertisement. It is used to make viewers curious and interested in the product so they pay more attention to the actual advertisement.

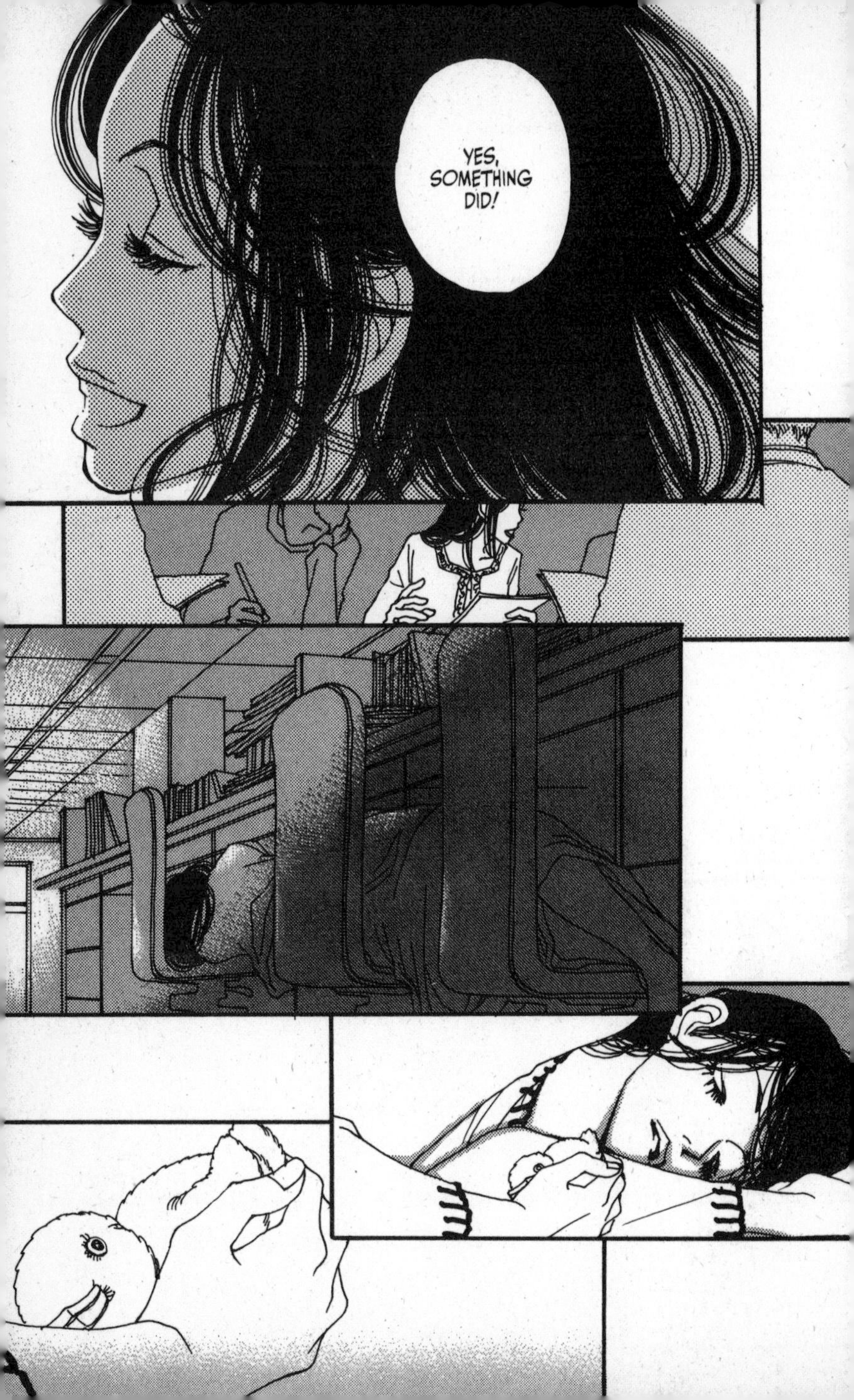
YES, SOMETHING DID!

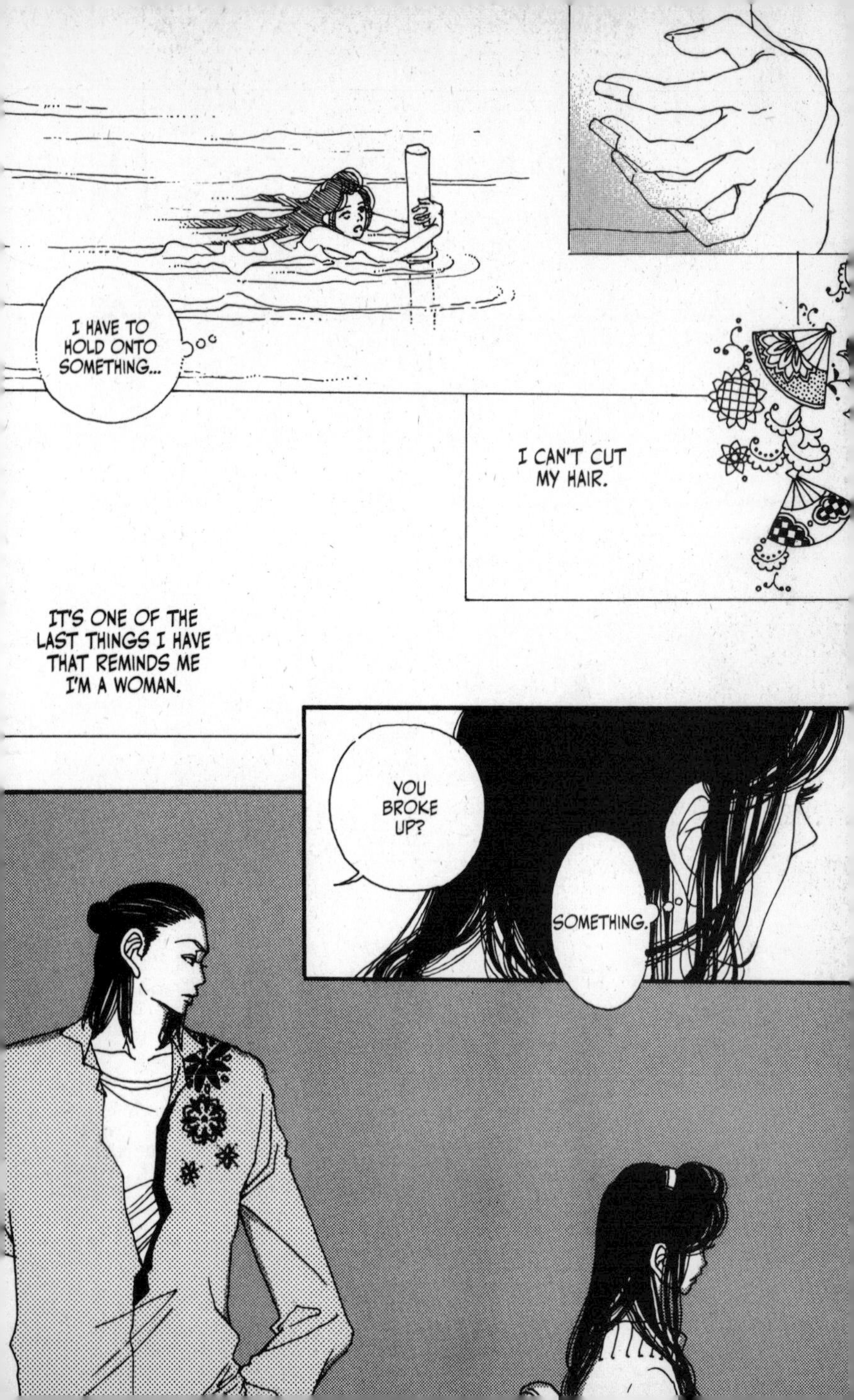
I HAVE TO HOLD ONTO SOMETHING...
I CAN'T CUT MY HAIR.
IT'S ONE OF THE LAST THINGS I HAVE THAT REMINDS ME I'M A WOMAN.
YOU BROKE UP?
SOMETHING.

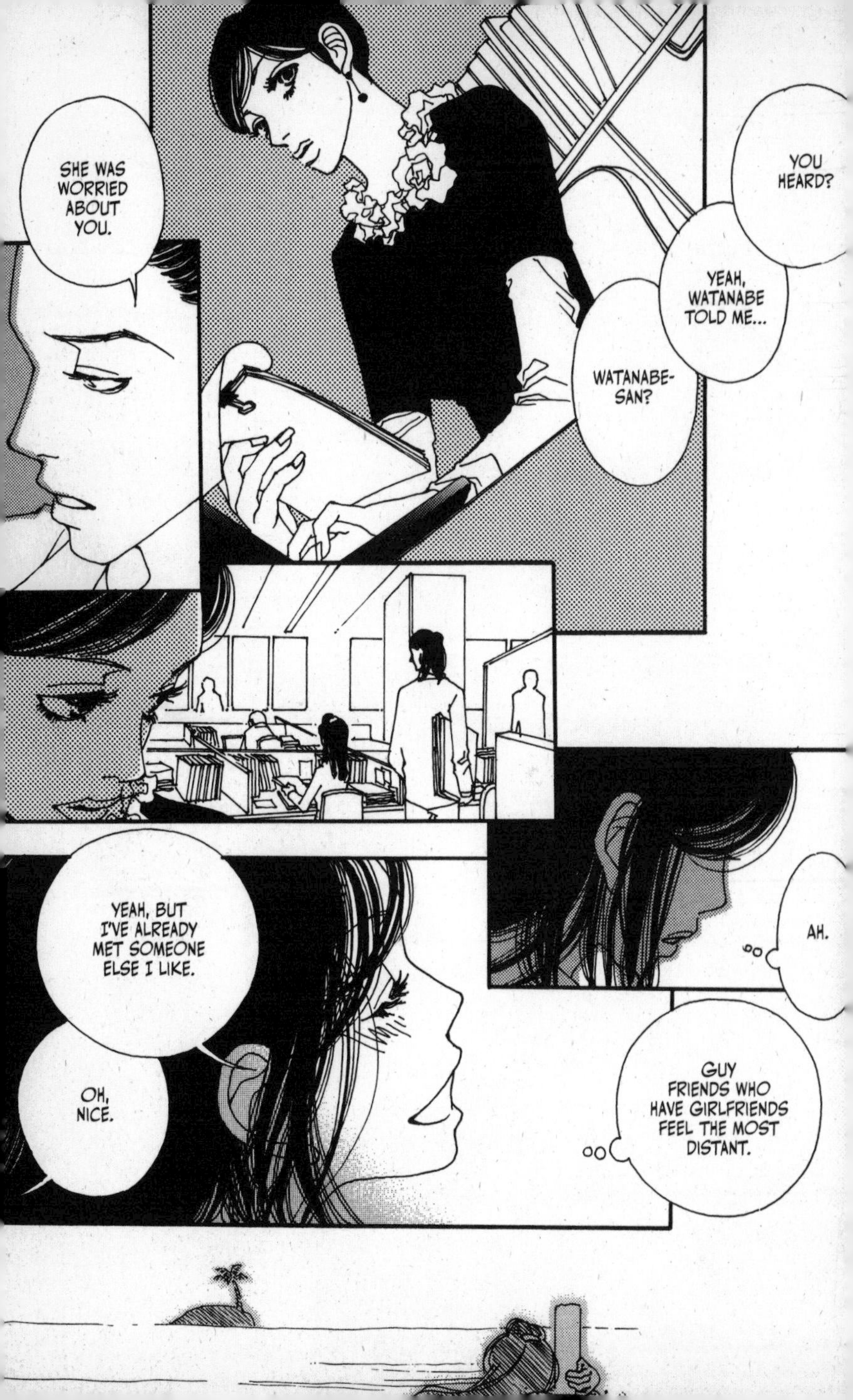
YOU HEARD?
YEAH, WATANABE TOLD ME...
WATANABE-SAN?
SHE WAS WORRIED ABOUT YOU.
AH.
YEAH, BUT I'VE ALREADY MET SOMEONE ELSE I LIKE.
OH, NICE.
GUY FRIENDS WHO HAVE GIRLFRIENDS FEEL THE MOST DISTANT.

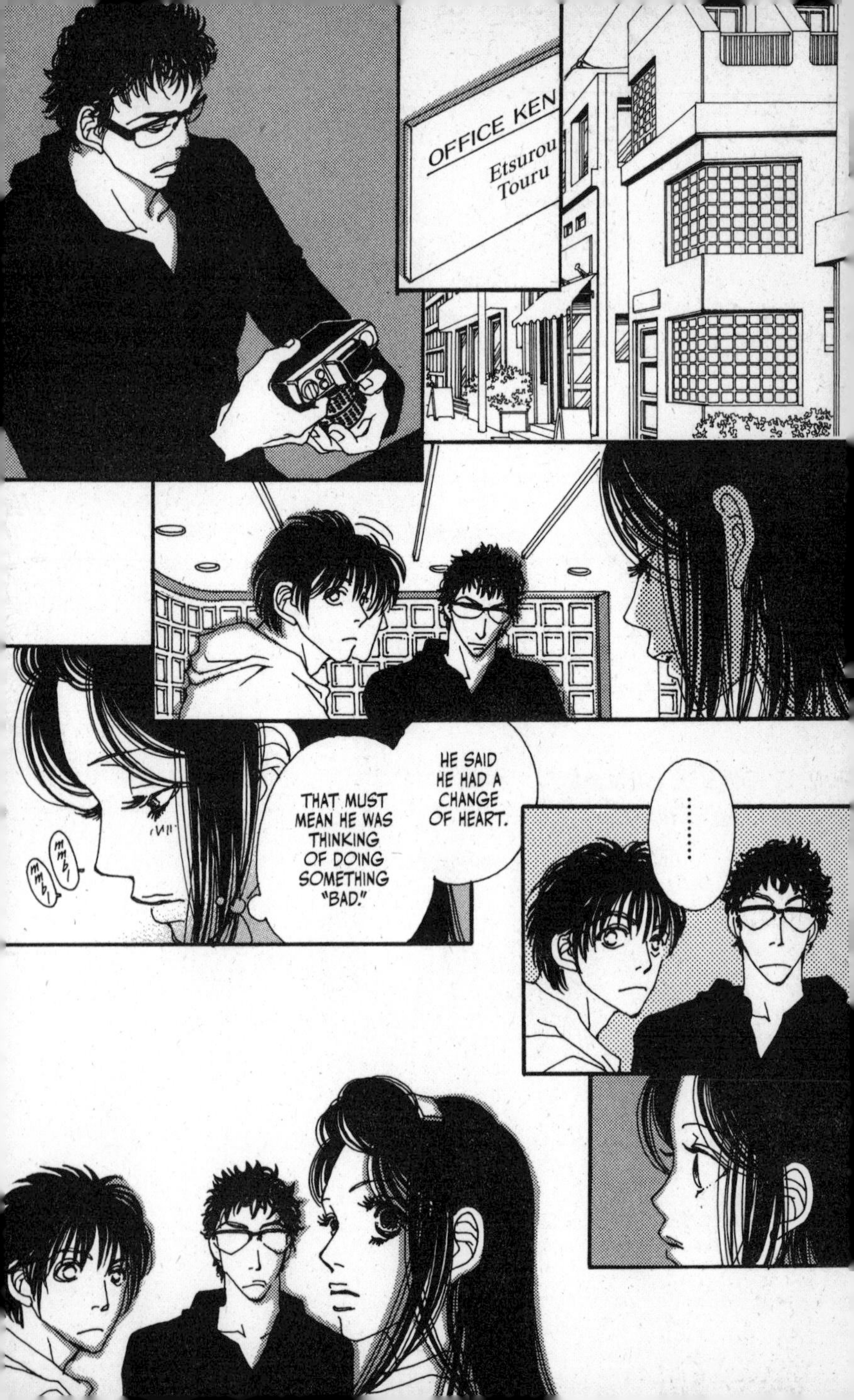
OFFICE KEN
Etsurou
Touru
HE SAID HE HAD A CHANGE OF HEART.
THAT MUST MEAN HE WAS THINKING OF DOING SOMETHING "BAD."
mmb!
mmb!
......

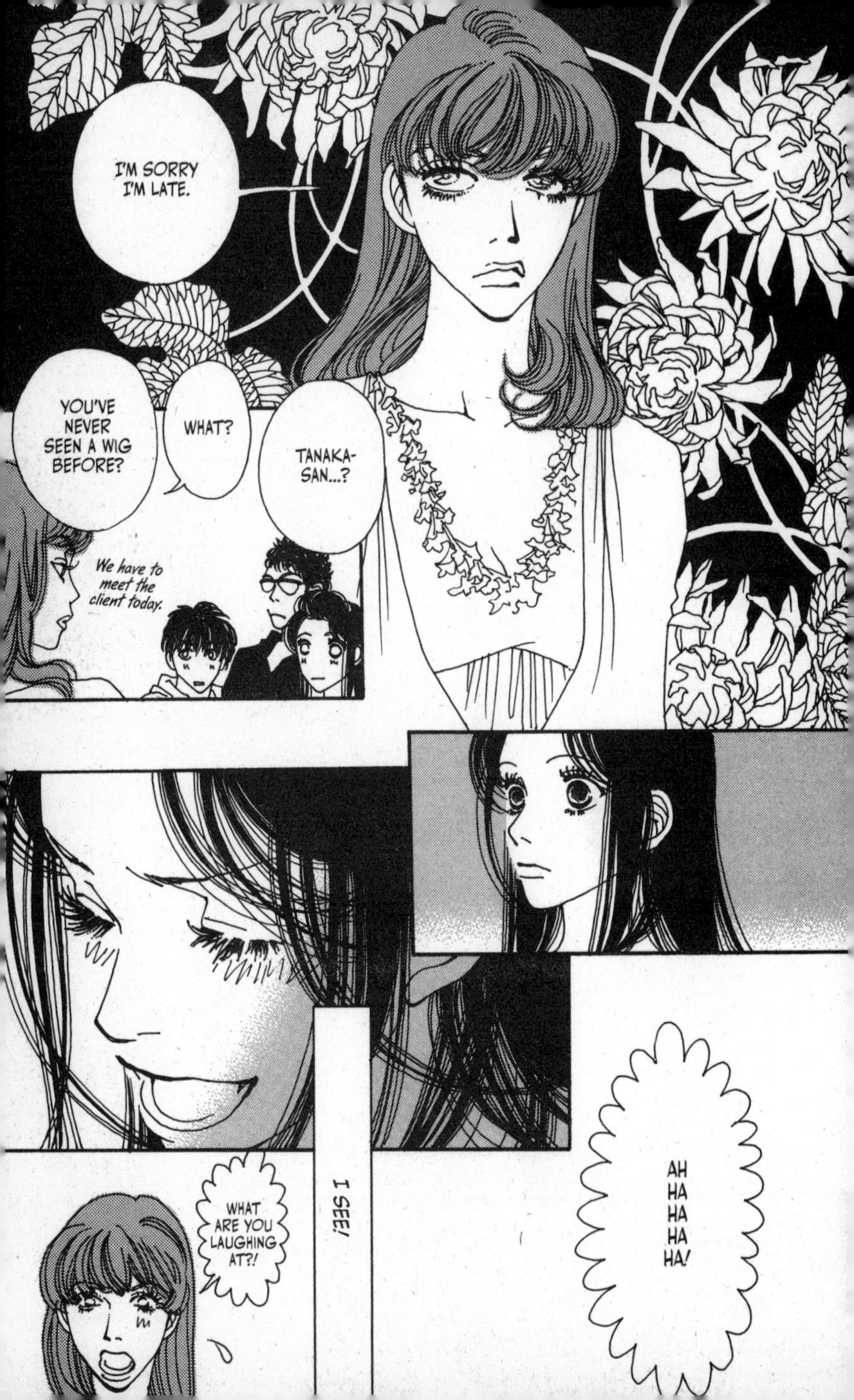

I'M SORRY I'M LATE.
TANAKA-SAN...?
WHAT?
YOU'VE NEVER SEEN A WIG BEFORE?
We have to meet the client today.
AH HA HA HA HA!
I SEE!
WHAT ARE YOU LAUGHING AT?!

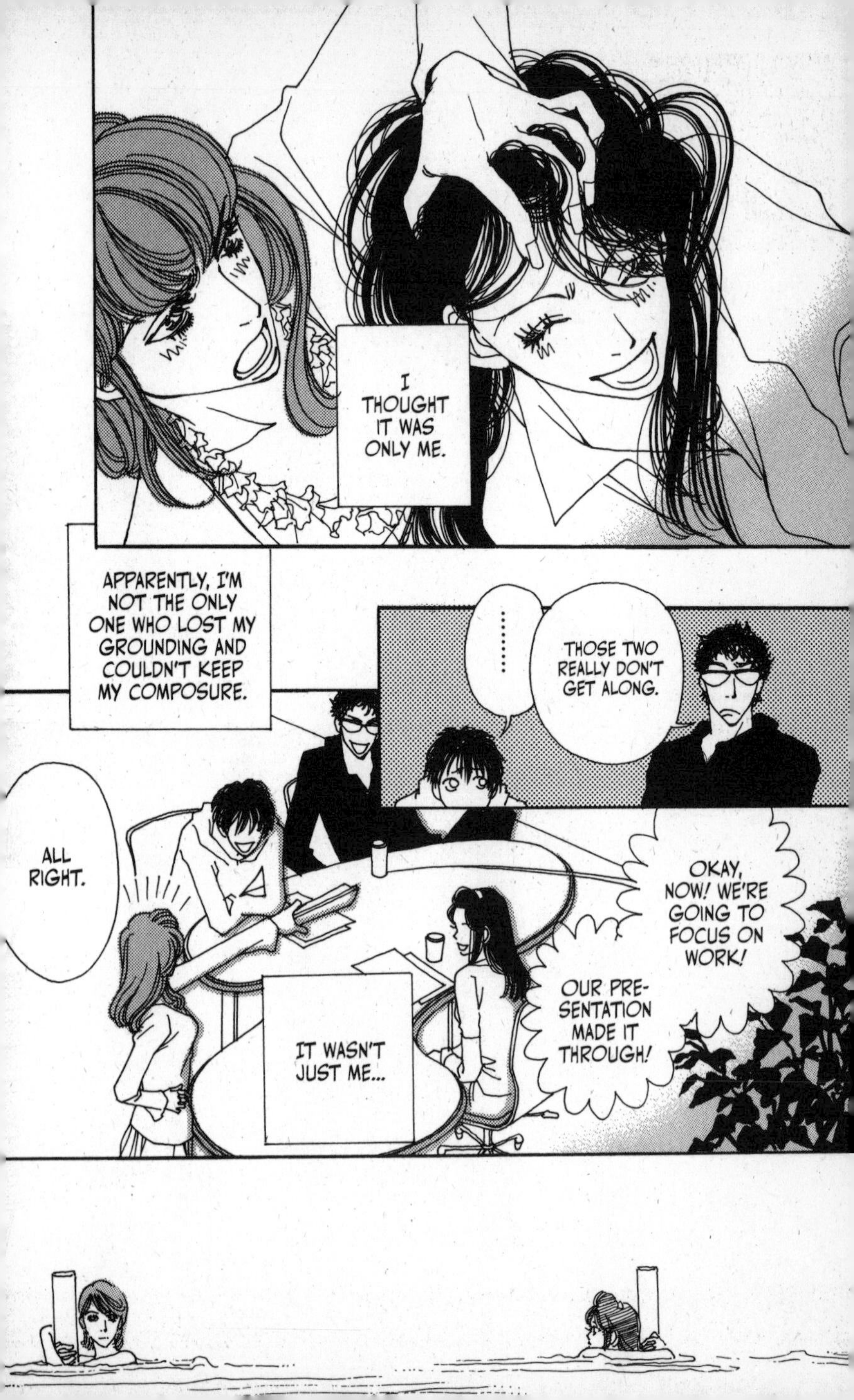
I THOUGHT IT WAS ONLY ME.
THOSE TWO REALLY DON'T GET ALONG.
......
APPARENTLY, I'M NOT THE ONLY ONE WHO LOST MY GROUNDING AND COULDN'T KEEP MY COMPOSURE.
OKAY, NOW! WE'RE GOING TO FOCUS ON WORK!
OUR PRE-SENTATION MADE IT THROUGH!
ALL RIGHT.
IT WASN'T JUST ME...

FILE. 23

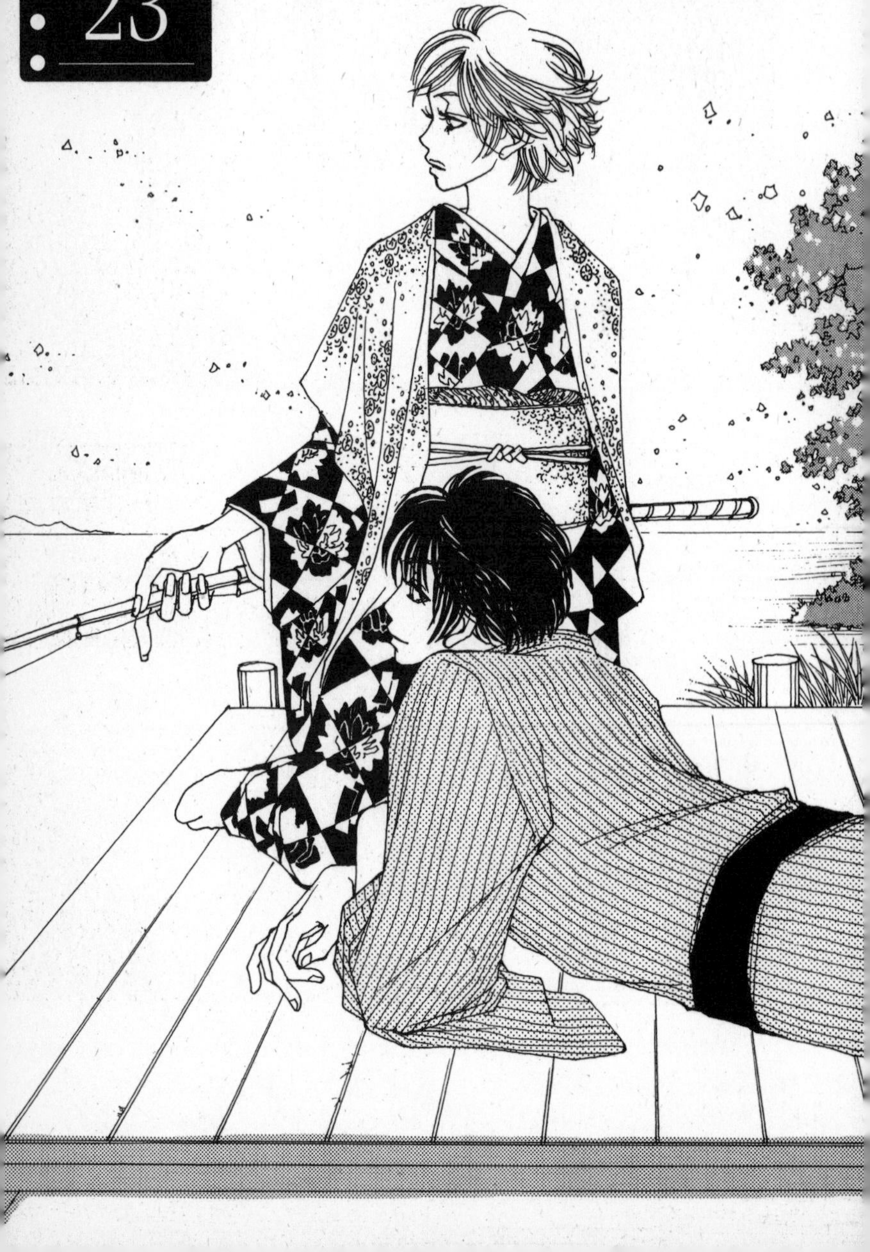

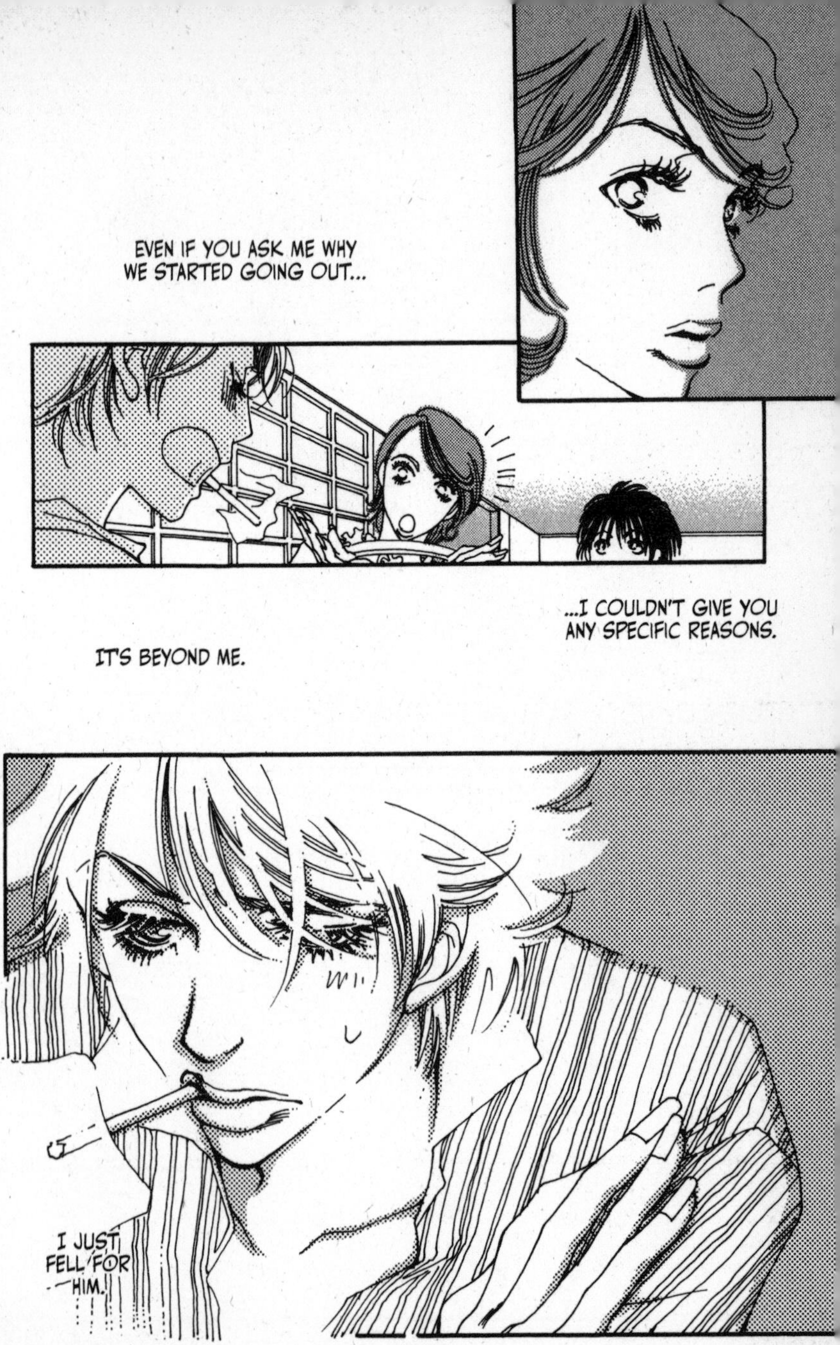
EVEN IF YOU ASK ME WHY WE STARTED GOING OUT...
...I COULDN'T GIVE YOU ANY SPECIFIC REASONS.
IT'S BEYOND ME.
I JUST FELL FOR HIM.

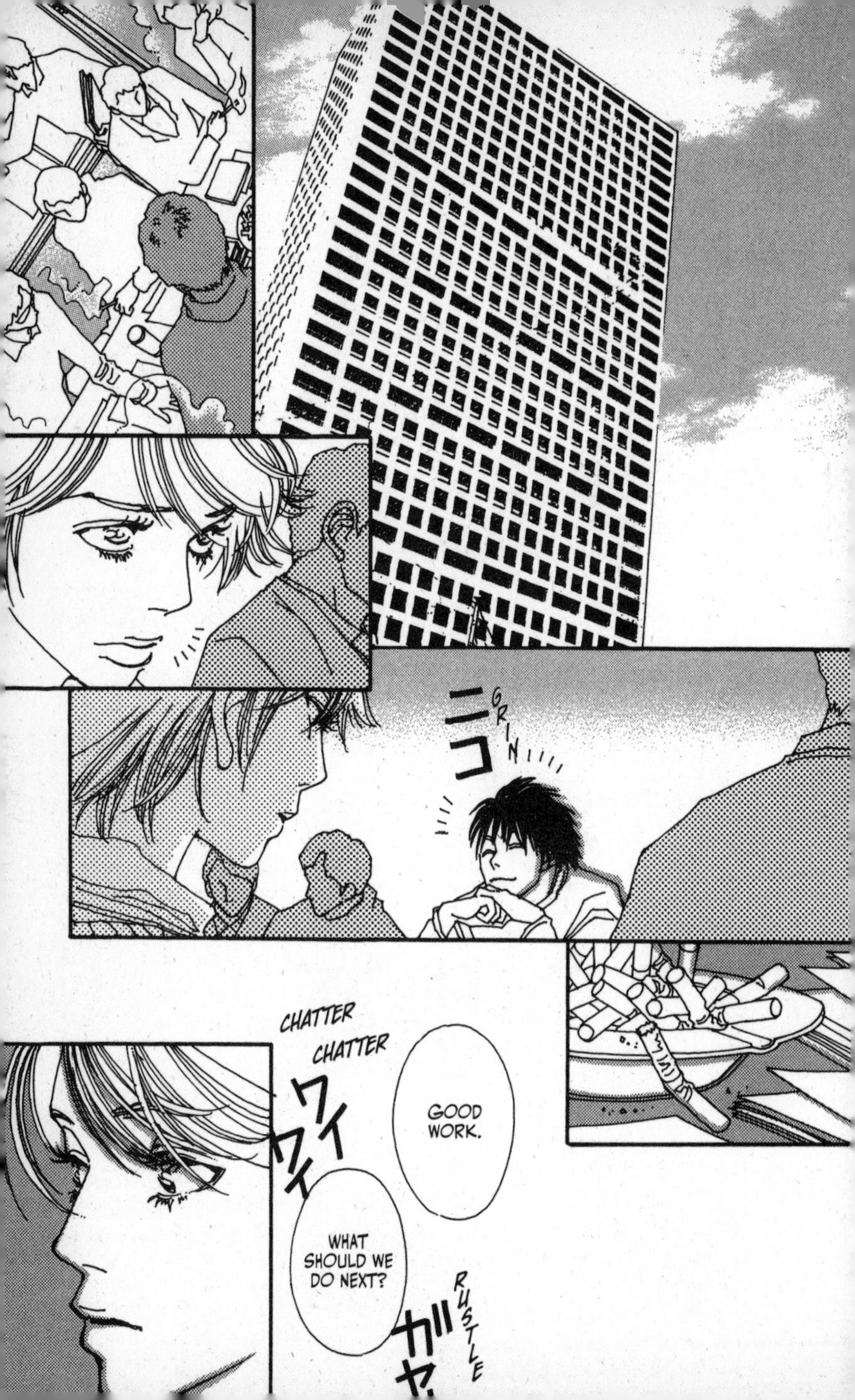
ニコ
GRIN
ワイワイ
CHATTER
CHATTER
GOOD WORK.
WHAT SHOULD WE DO NEXT?
ガヤ
RUSTLE

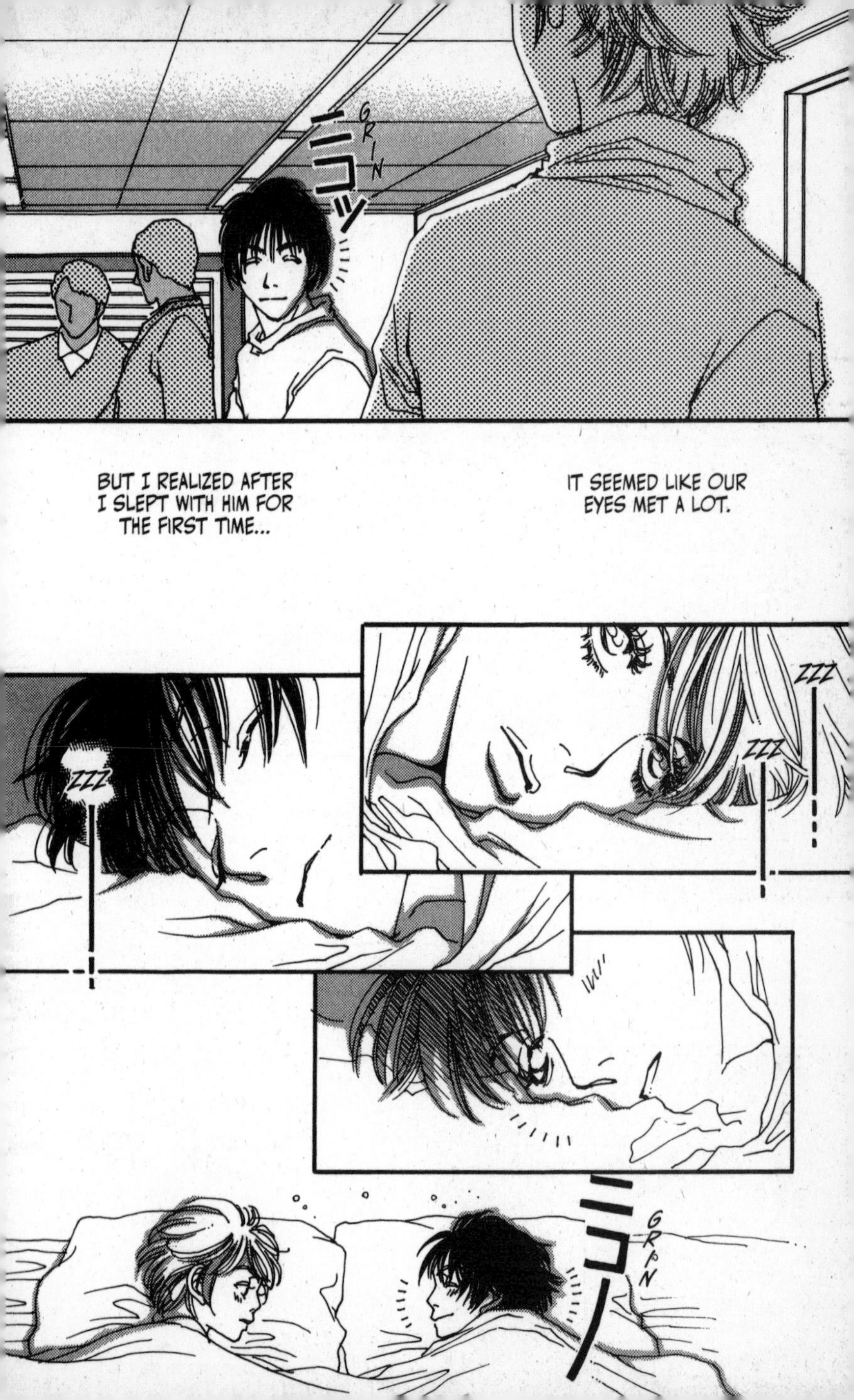
GRIN
IT SEEMED LIKE OUR EYES MET A LOT.
BUT I REALIZED AFTER I SLEPT WITH HIM FOR THE FIRST TIME...
ZZZ
ZZZ
ZZZ
GRIN

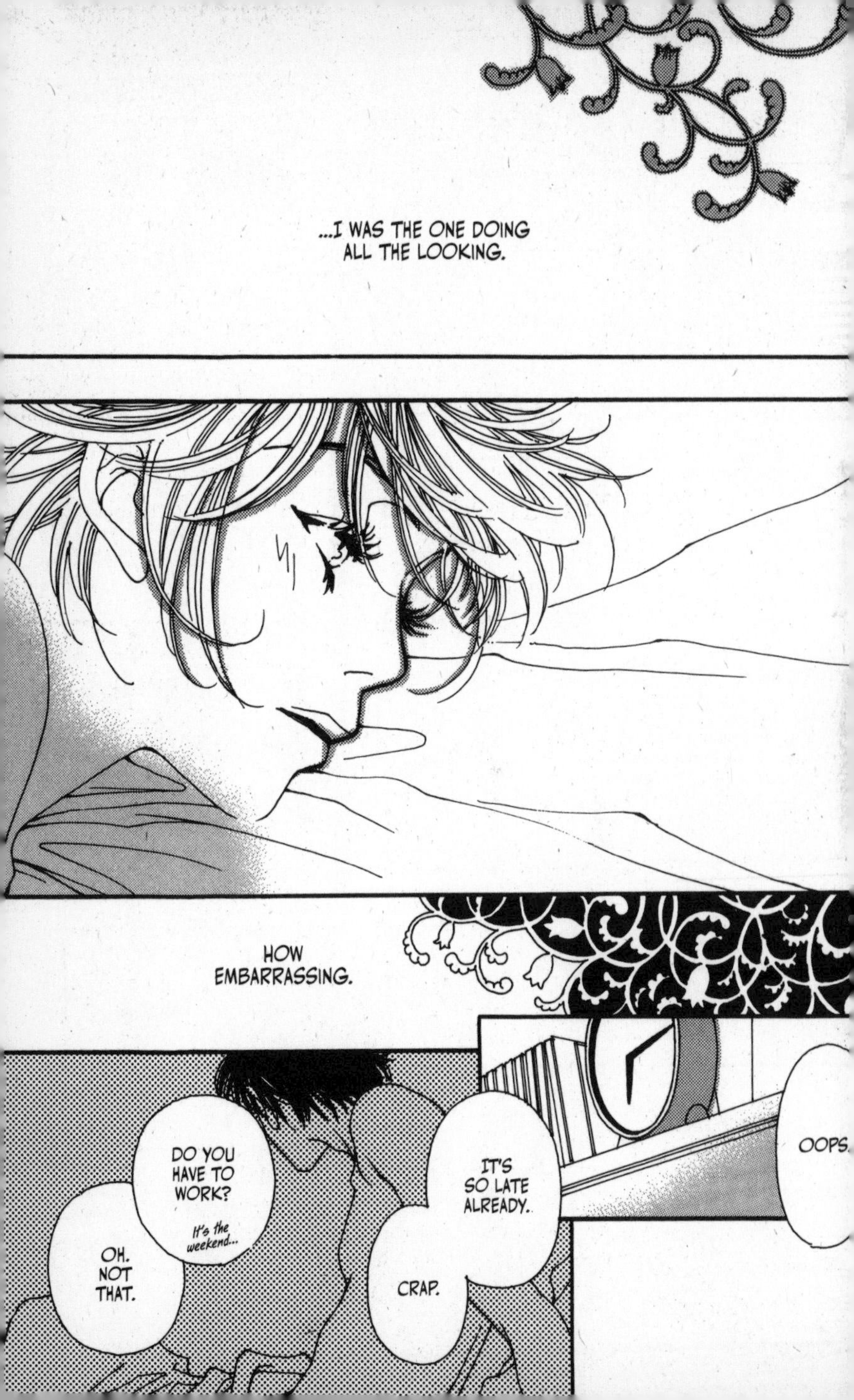
...I WAS THE ONE DOING ALL THE LOOKING.
HOW EMBARRASSING.
OOPS.
IT'S SO LATE ALREADY.
CRAP.
DO YOU HAVE TO WORK?
It's the weekend...
OH. NOT THAT.

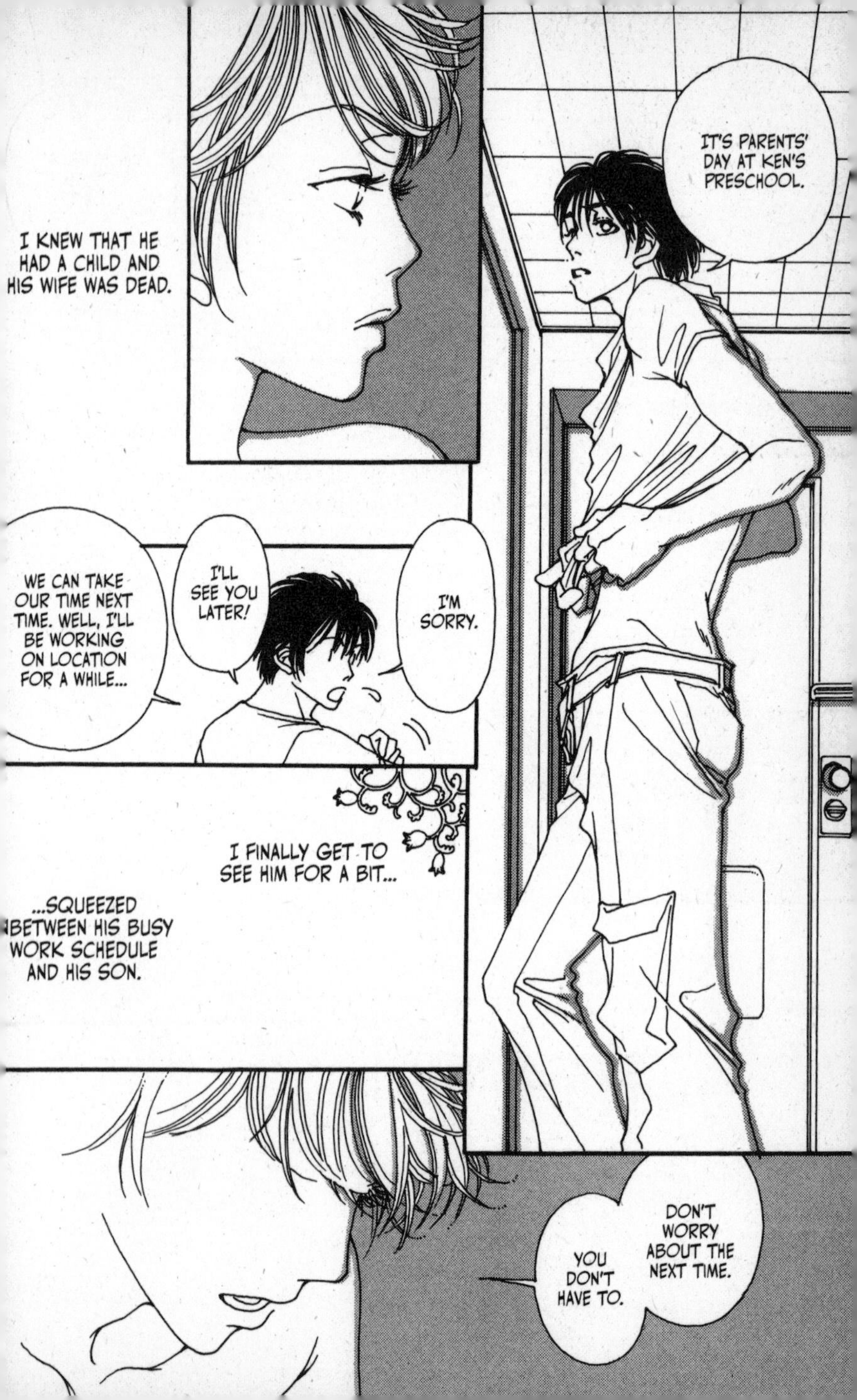
IT'S PARENTS' DAY AT KEN'S PRESCHOOL.
I KNEW THAT HE HAD A CHILD AND HIS WIFE WAS DEAD.
I'M SORRY.
I'LL SEE YOU LATER!
WE CAN TAKE OUR TIME NEXT TIME. WELL, I'LL BE WORKING ON LOCATION FOR A WHILE...
I FINALLY GET TO SEE HIM FOR A BIT...
...SQUEEZED BETWEEN HIS BUSY WORK SCHEDULE AND HIS SON.
DON'T WORRY ABOUT THE NEXT TIME.
YOU DON'T HAVE TO.

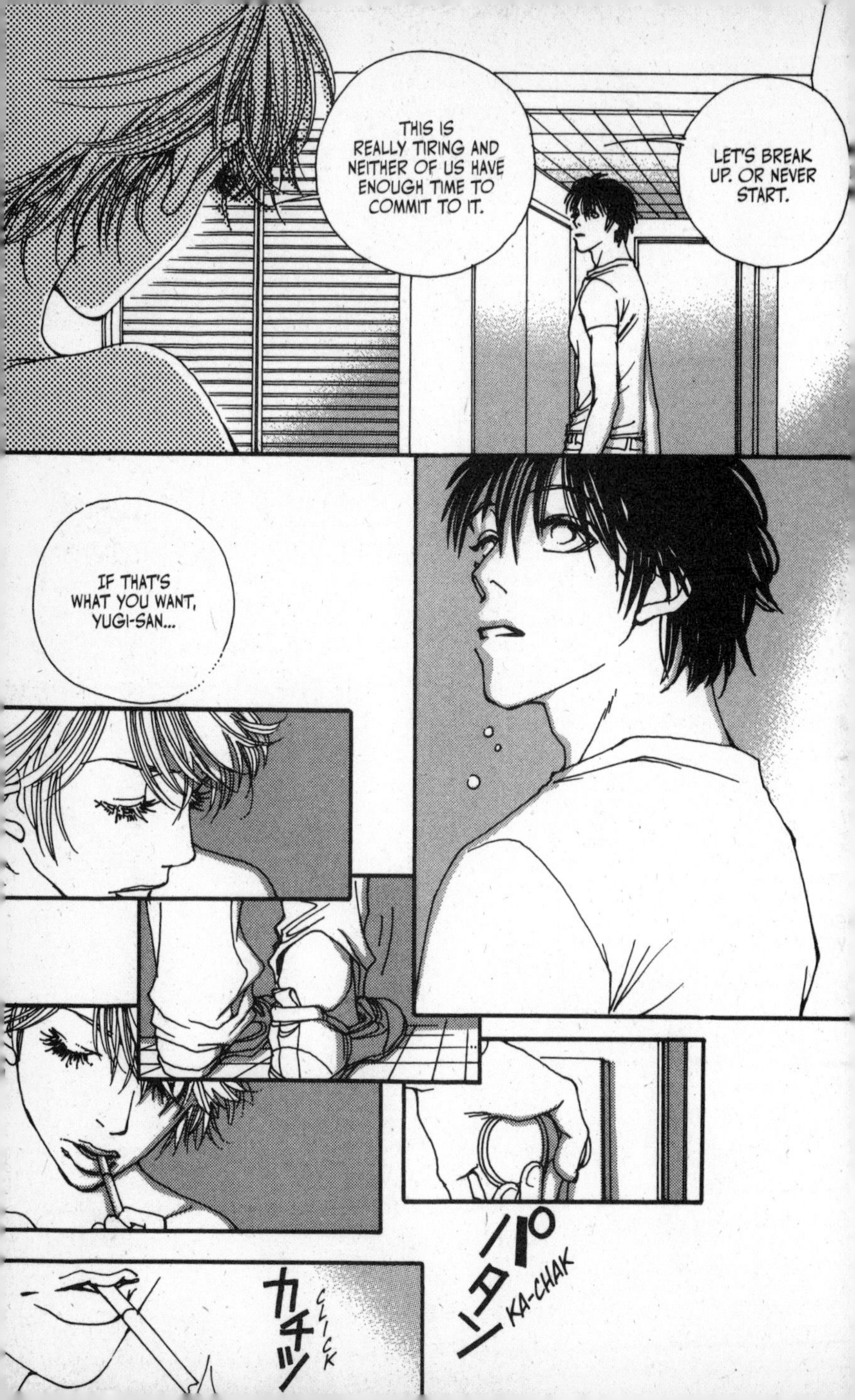
LET'S BREAK UP. OR NEVER START.
THIS IS REALLY TIRING AND NEITHER OF US HAVE ENOUGH TIME TO COMMIT TO IT.
IF THAT'S WHAT YOU WANT, YUGI-SAN...
パタン KA-CHAK
カチッ CLICK

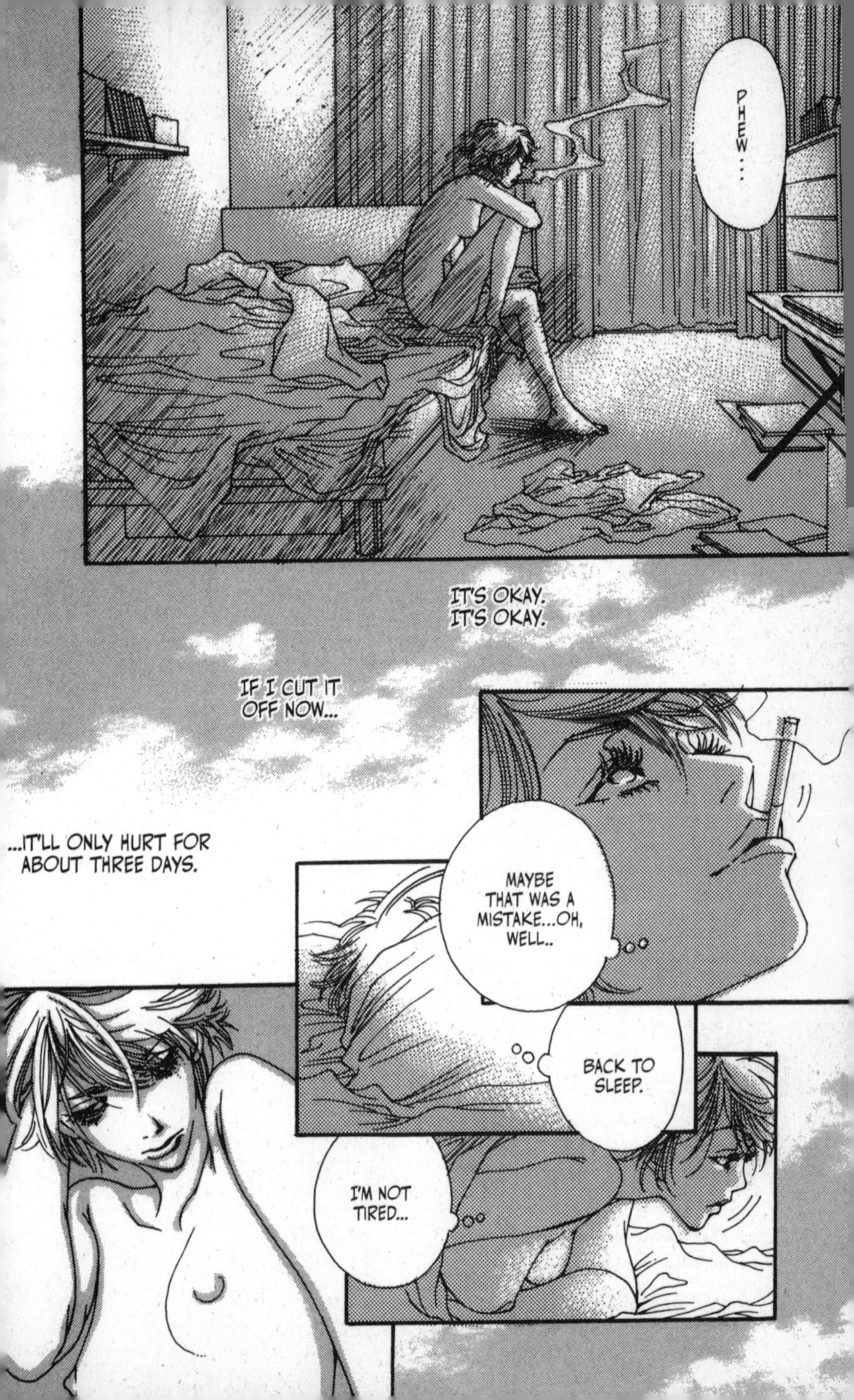
PHEW...
IT'S OKAY. IT'S OKAY.
IF I CUT IT OFF NOW...
MAYBE THAT WAS A MISTAKE...OH, WELL..
...IT'LL ONLY HURT FOR ABOUT THREE DAYS.
BACK TO SLEEP.
I'M NOT TIRED...

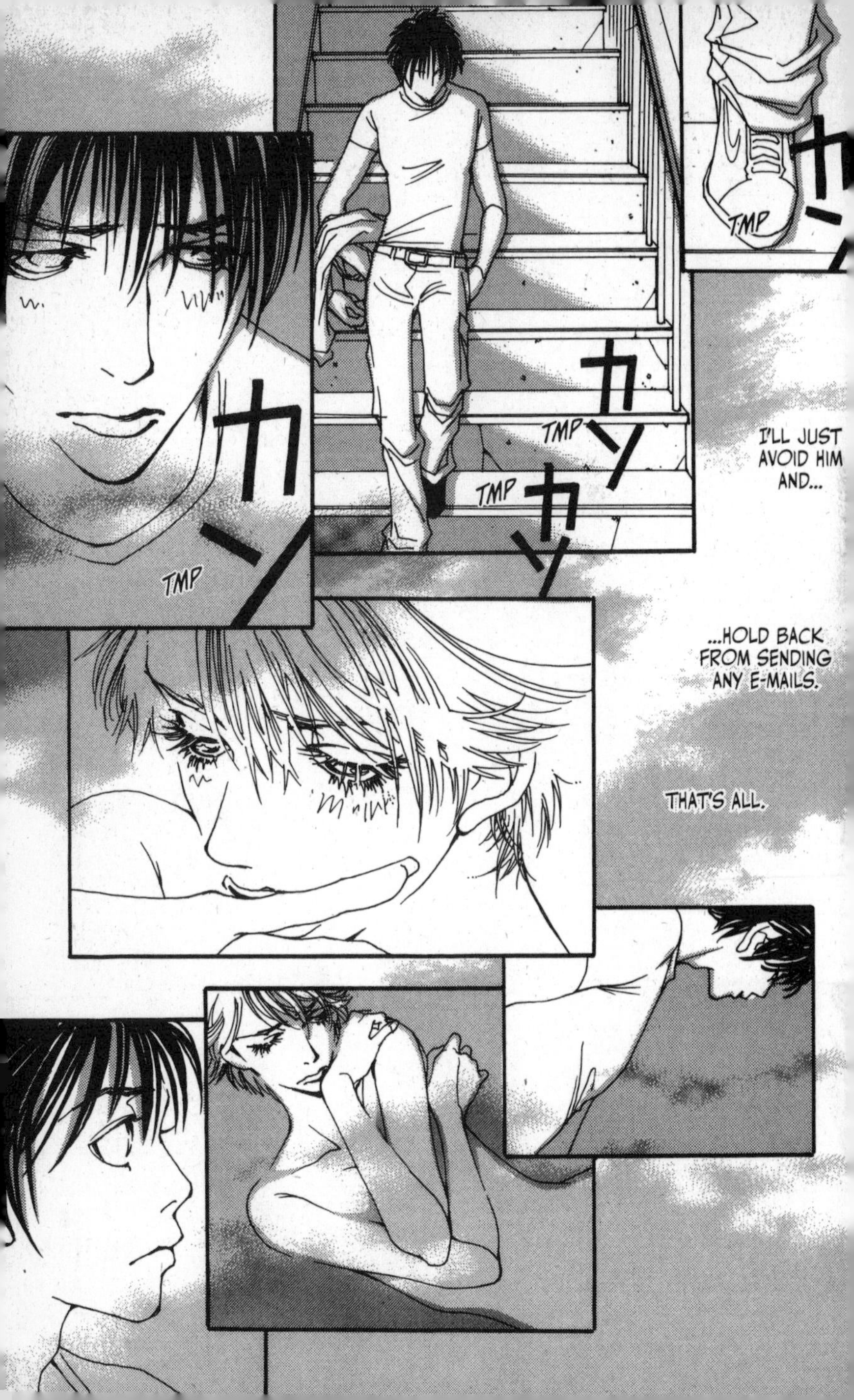
TMP
TMP
TMP
TMP
I'LL JUST AVOID HIM AND...
...HOLD BACK FROM SENDING ANY E-MAILS.
THAT'S ALL.

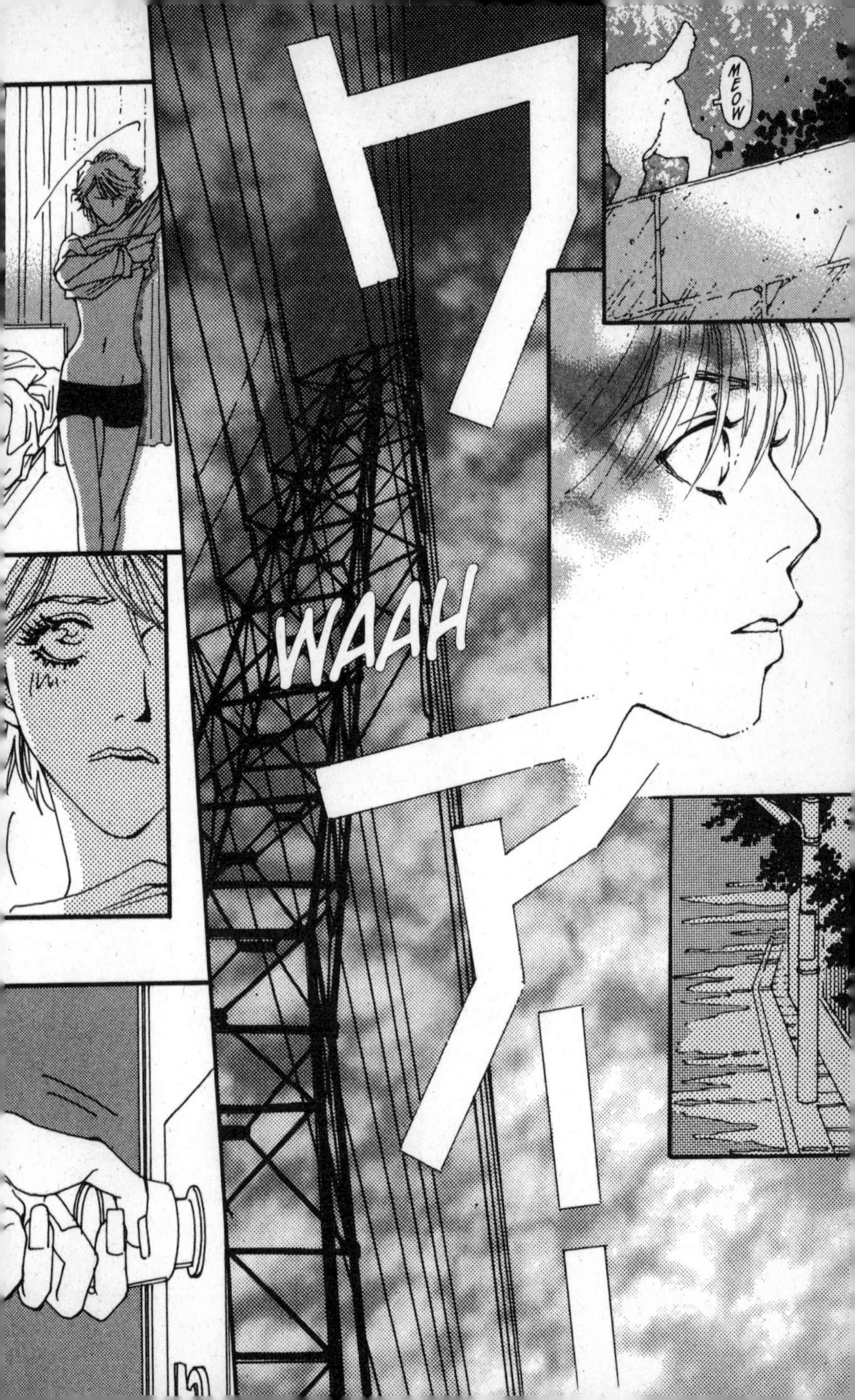
MEOW
WAAH

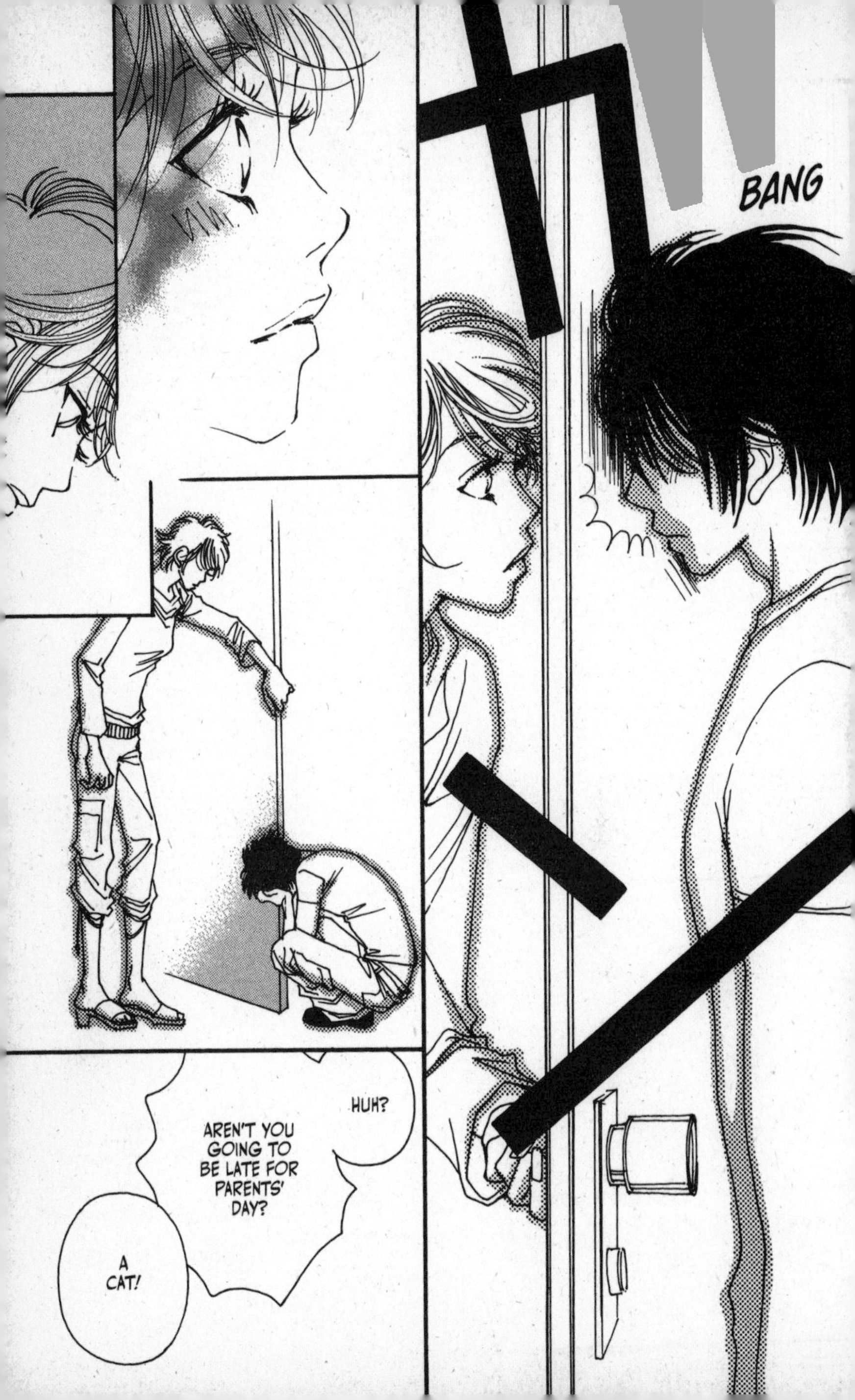
BANG
HUH?
AREN'T YOU GOING TO BE LATE FOR PARENTS' DAY?
A CAT!

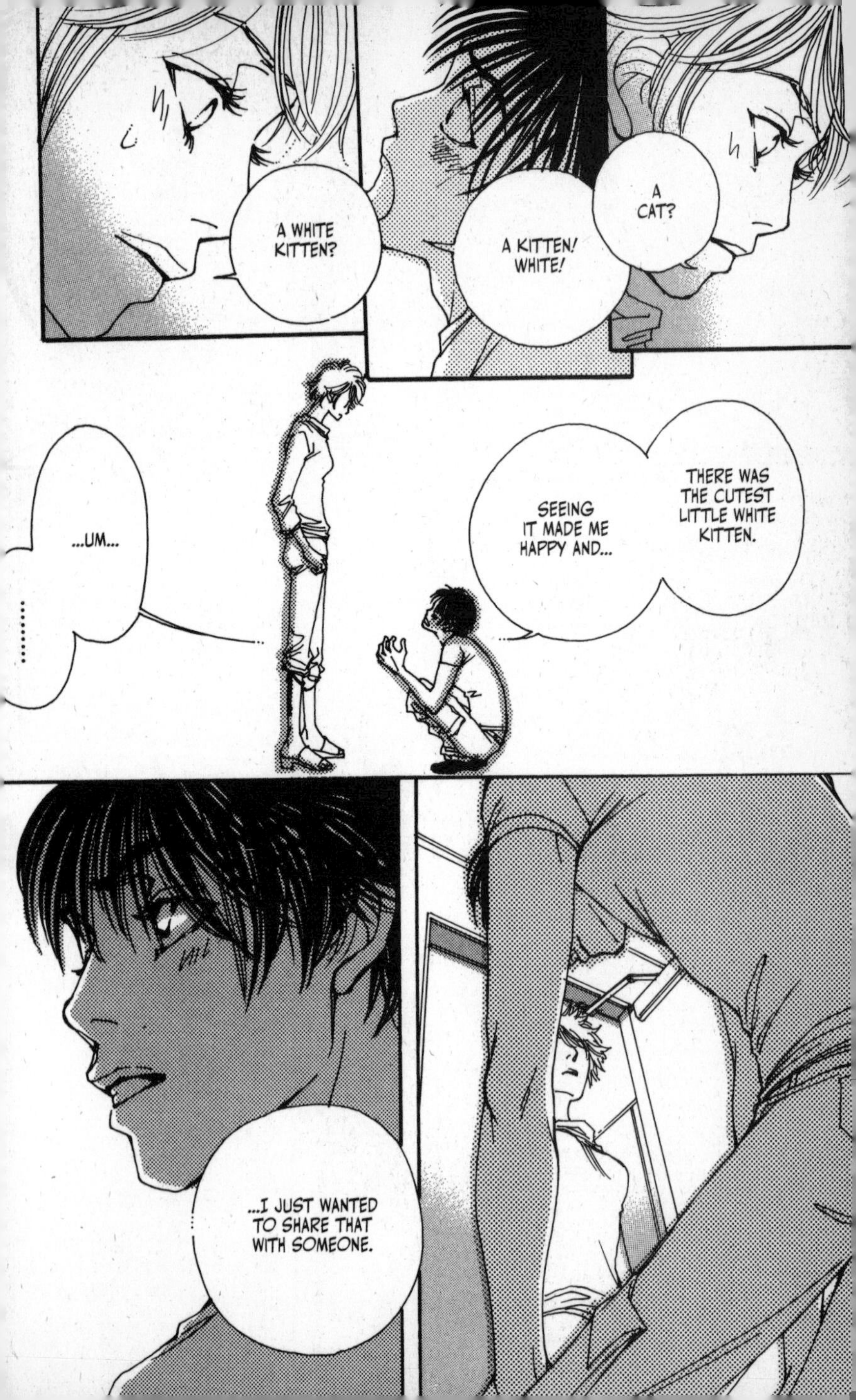
A CAT?
A KITTEN! WHITE!
A WHITE KITTEN?
THERE WAS THE CUTEST LITTLE WHITE KITTEN.
SEEING IT MADE ME HAPPY AND...
...UM...
......
...I JUST WANTED TO SHARE THAT WITH SOMEONE.

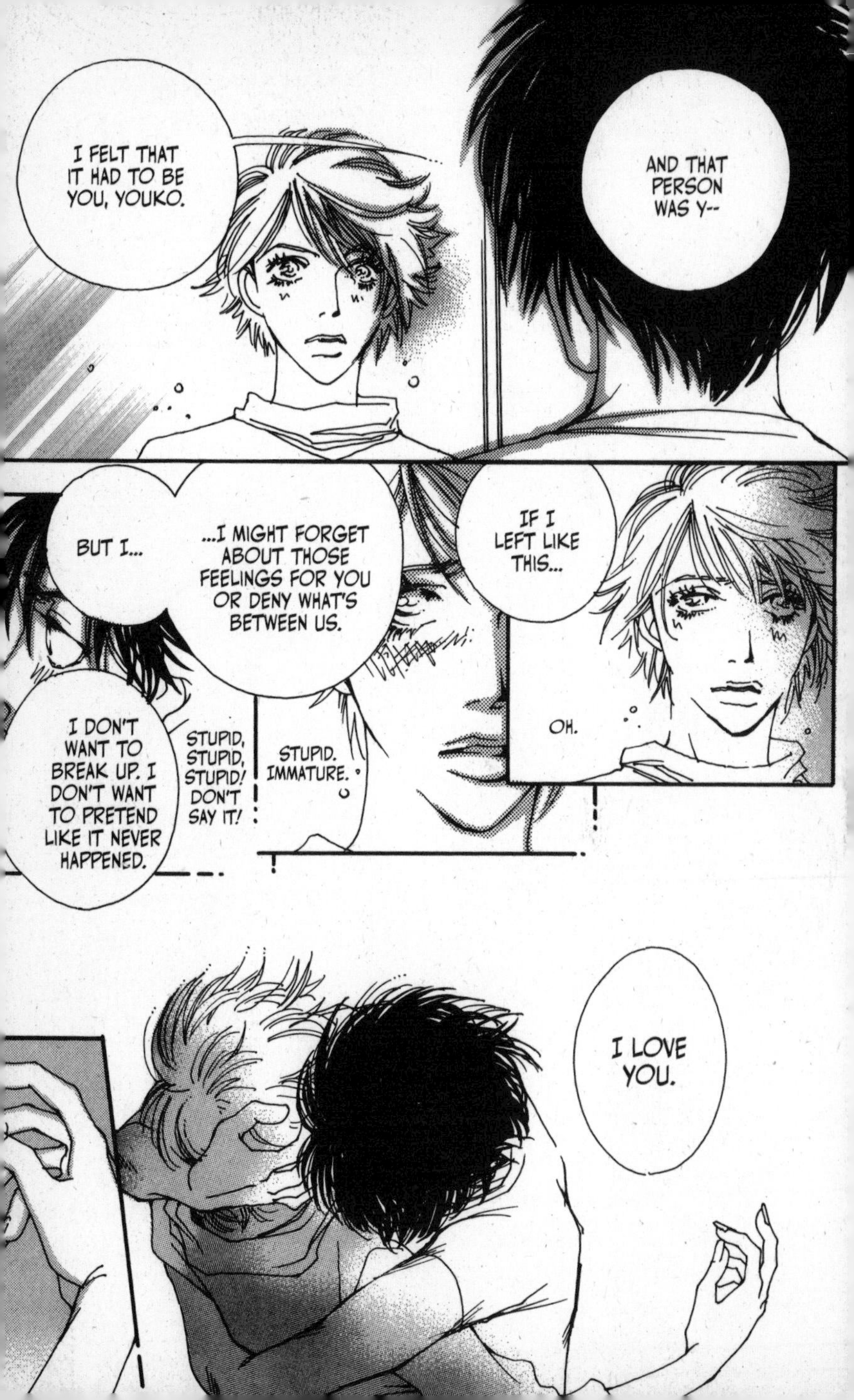
AND THAT PERSON WAS Y--
I FELT THAT IT HAD TO BE YOU, YOUKO.
IF I LEFT LIKE THIS...
OH.
...I MIGHT FORGET ABOUT THOSE FEELINGS FOR YOU OR DENY WHAT'S BETWEEN US.
STUPID. IMMATURE.
BUT I...
STUPID, STUPID, STUPID! DON'T SAY IT!
I DON'T WANT TO BREAK UP. I DON'T WANT TO PRETEND LIKE IT NEVER HAPPENED.
I LOVE YOU.

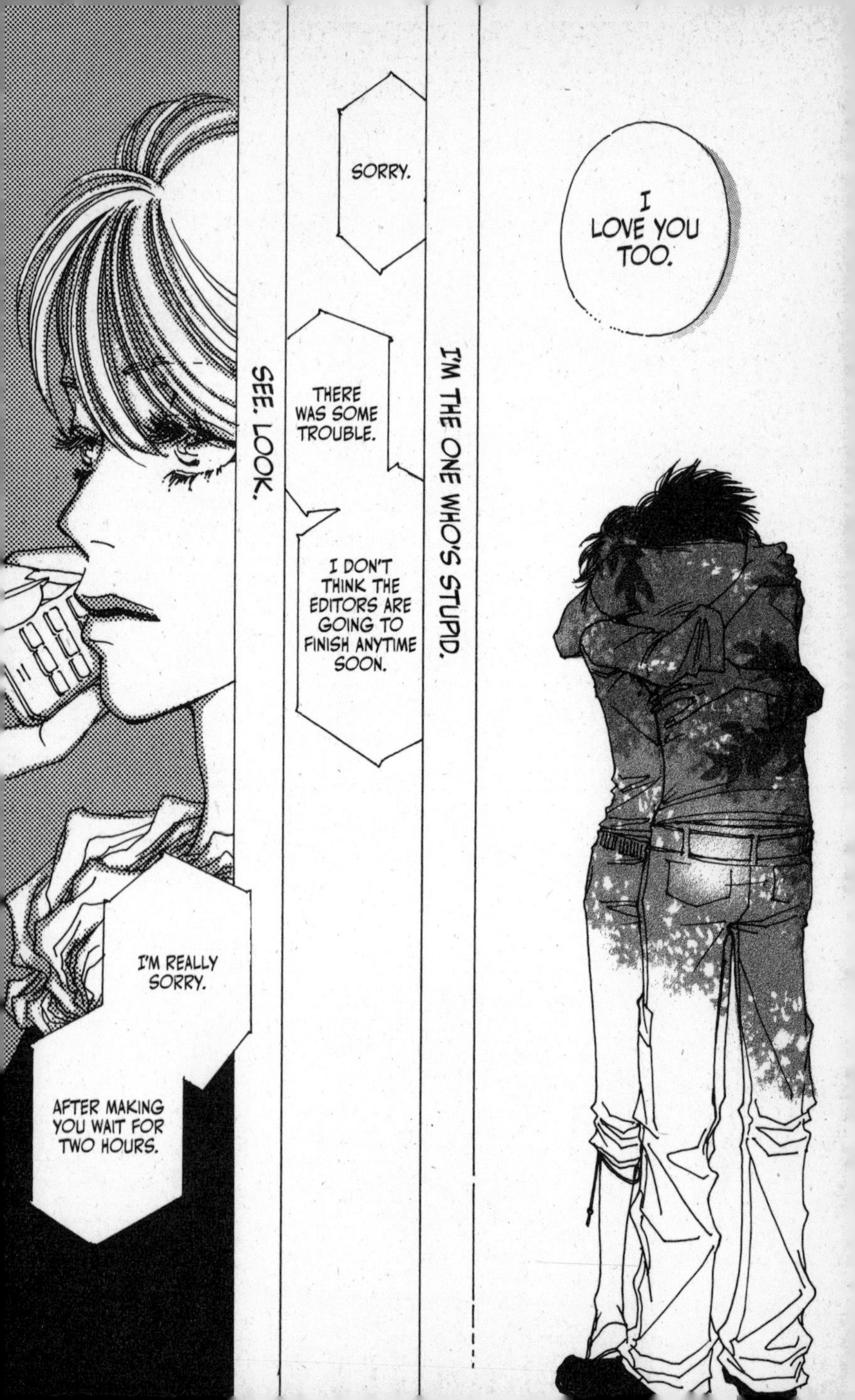
I LOVE YOU TOO.
I'M THE ONE WHO'S STUPID.
SORRY.
THERE WAS SOME TROUBLE.
I DON'T THINK THE EDITORS ARE GOING TO FINISH ANYTIME SOON.
SEE. LOOK.
I'M REALLY SORRY.
AFTER MAKING YOU WAIT FOR TWO HOURS.

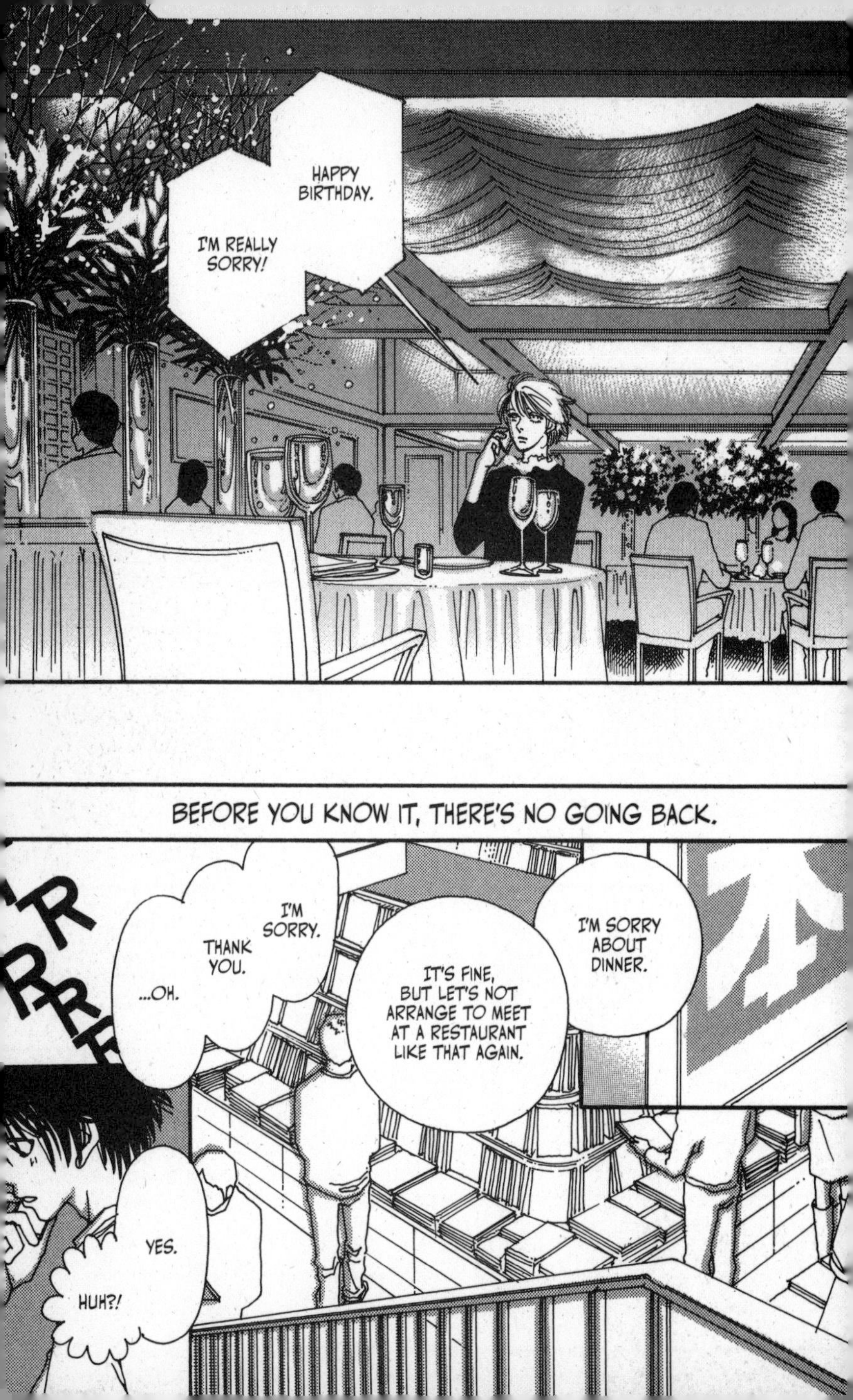
HAPPY BIRTHDAY.
I'M REALLY SORRY!
BEFORE YOU KNOW IT, THERE'S NO GOING BACK.
I'M SORRY ABOUT DINNER.
IT'S FINE, BUT LET'S NOT ARRANGE TO MEET AT A RESTAURANT LIKE THAT AGAIN.
I'M SORRY.
THANK YOU.
...OH.
RRRR
YES.
HUH?!

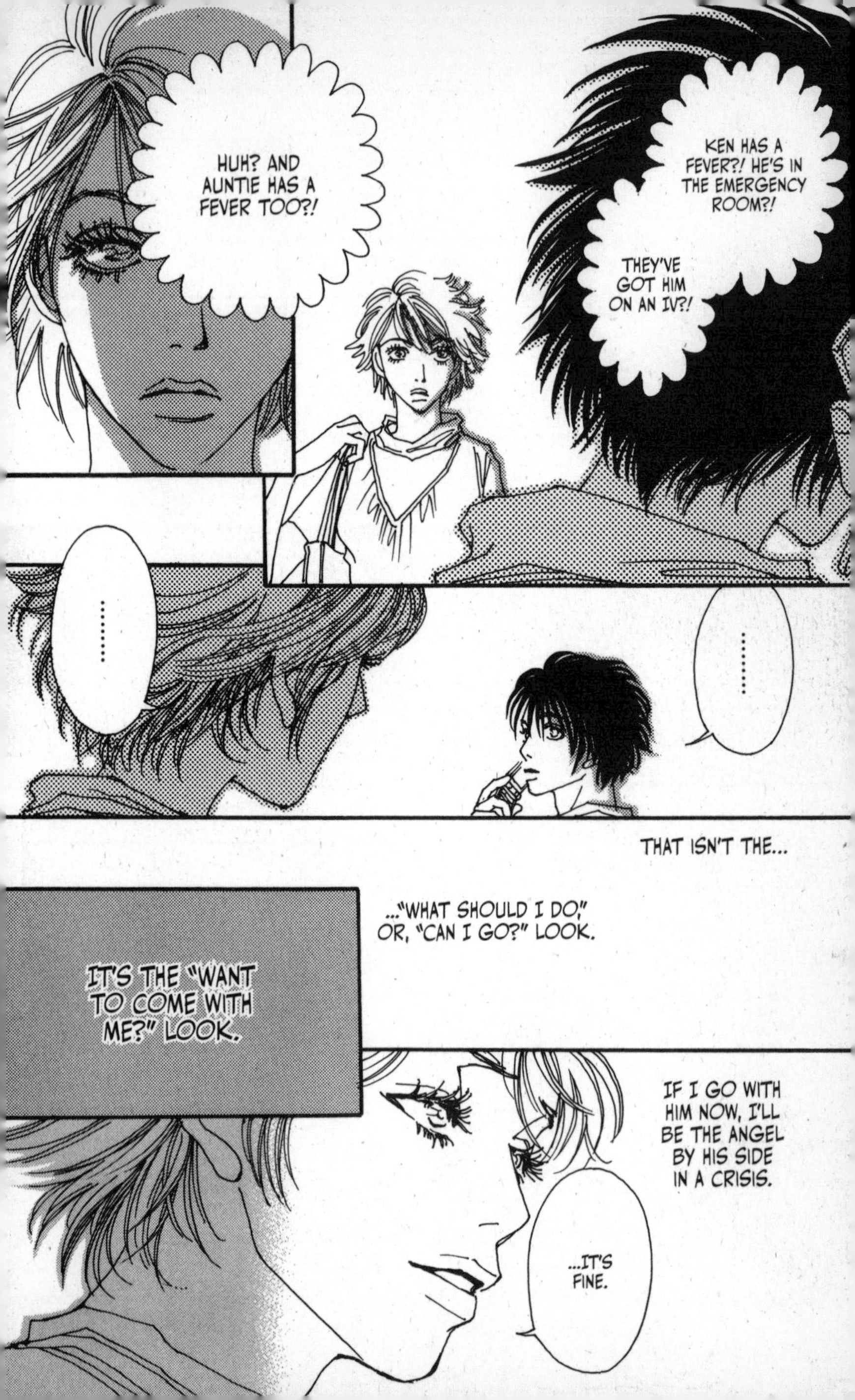
KEN HAS A FEVER?! HE'S IN THE EMERGENCY ROOM?!
THEY'VE GOT HIM ON AN IV?!
HUH? AND AUNTIE HAS A FEVER TOO?!
......
......
THAT ISN'T THE...
..."WHAT SHOULD I DO," OR, "CAN I GO?" LOOK.
IT'S THE "WANT TO COME WITH ME?" LOOK.
IF I GO WITH HIM NOW, I'LL BE THE ANGEL BY HIS SIDE IN A CRISIS.
...IT'S FINE.

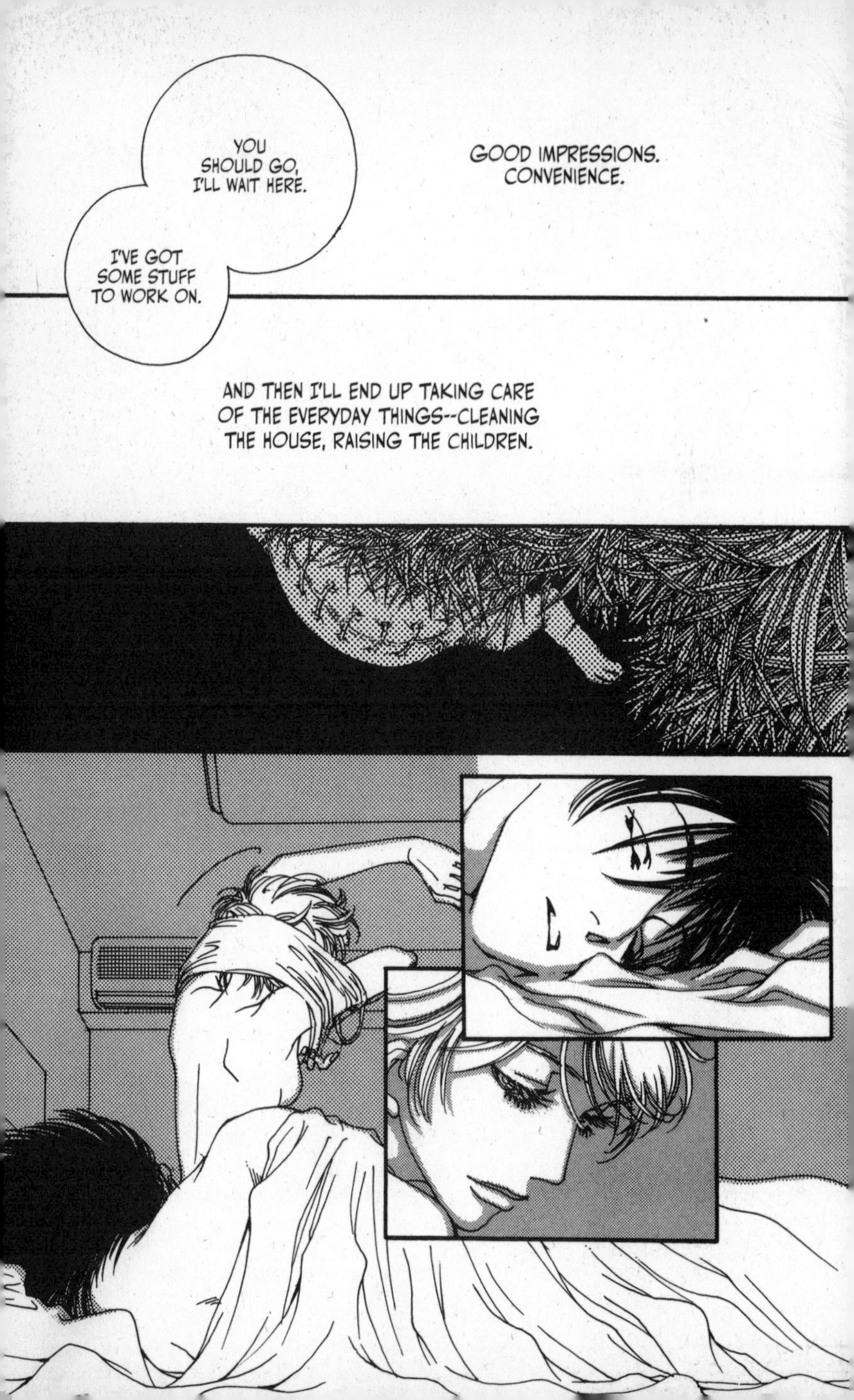
GOOD IMPRESSIONS. CONVENIENCE.
YOU SHOULD GO, I'LL WAIT HERE.
I'VE GOT SOME STUFF TO WORK ON.
AND THEN I'LL END UP TAKING CARE OF THE EVERYDAY THINGS--CLEANING THE HOUSE, RAISING THE CHILDREN.

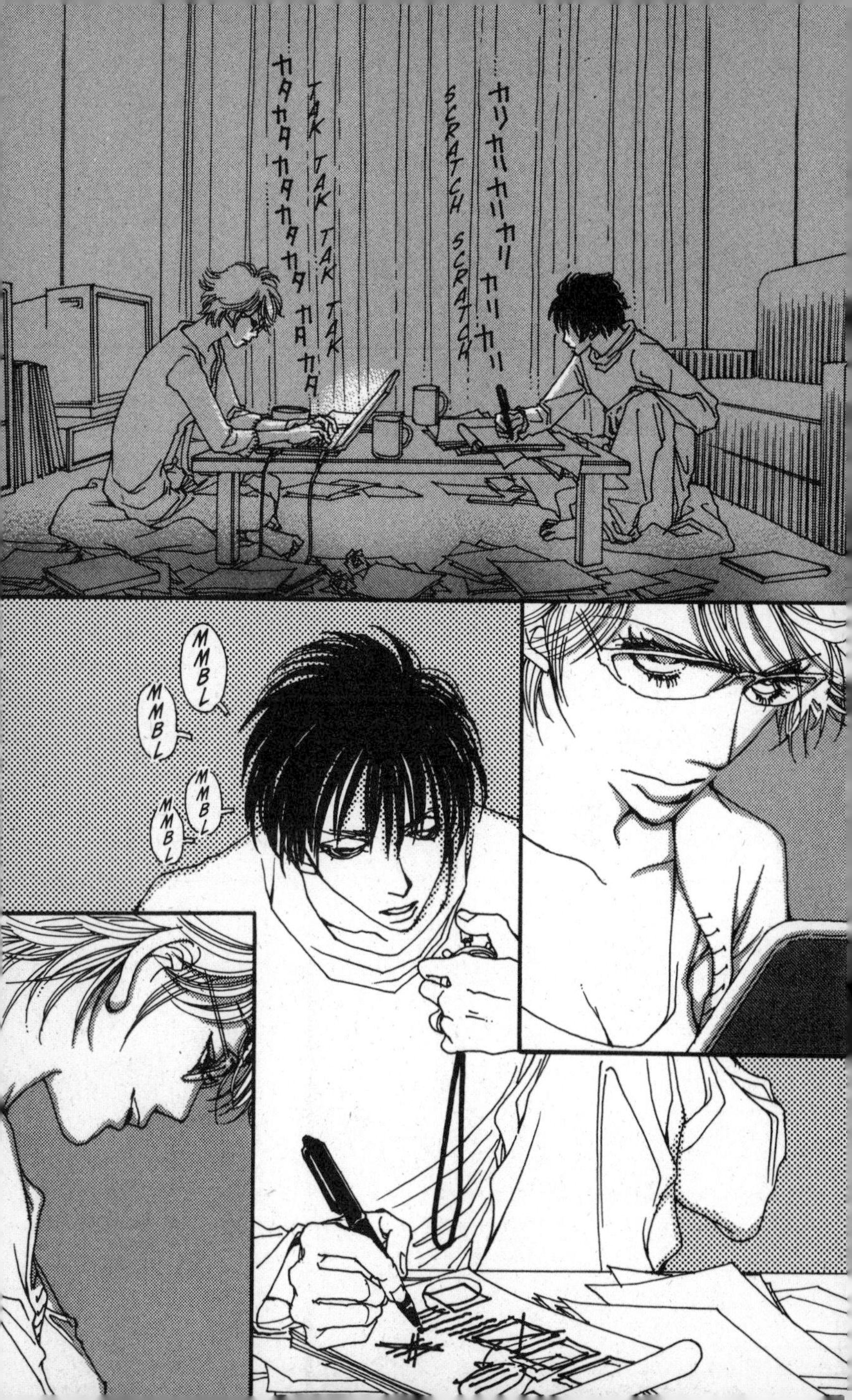

カリカリカリカリ カリカリ
SCRATCH SCRATCH
TAK TAK TAK TAK
カタカタカタカタカタ カタカタ
MMBL
MMBL
MMBL
MMBL

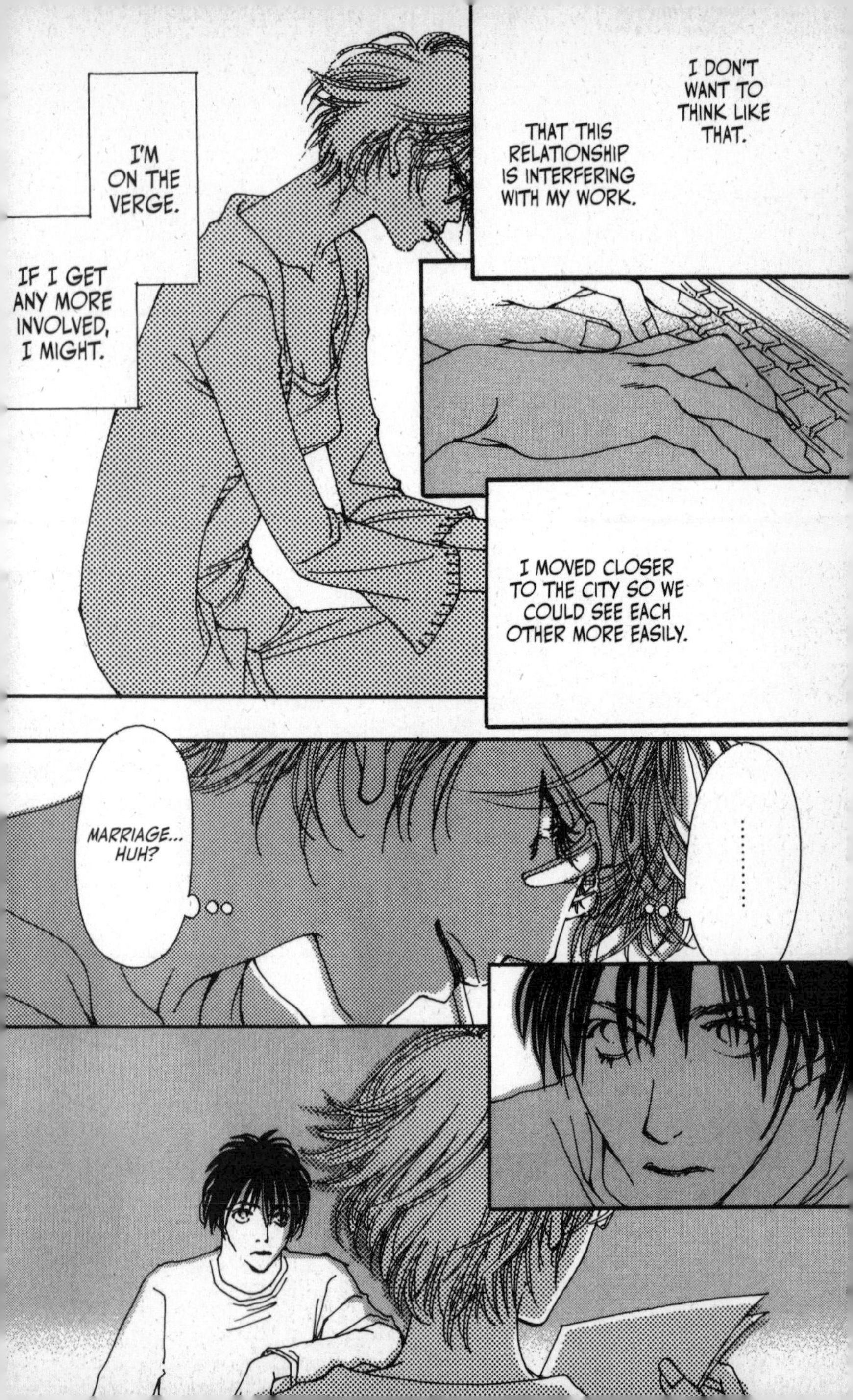
I DON'T WANT TO THINK LIKE THAT.
THAT THIS RELATIONSHIP IS INTERFERING WITH MY WORK.
I MOVED CLOSER TO THE CITY SO WE COULD SEE EACH OTHER MORE EASILY.
I'M ON THE VERGE.
IF I GET ANY MORE INVOLVED, I MIGHT.
......
MARRIAGE... HUH?

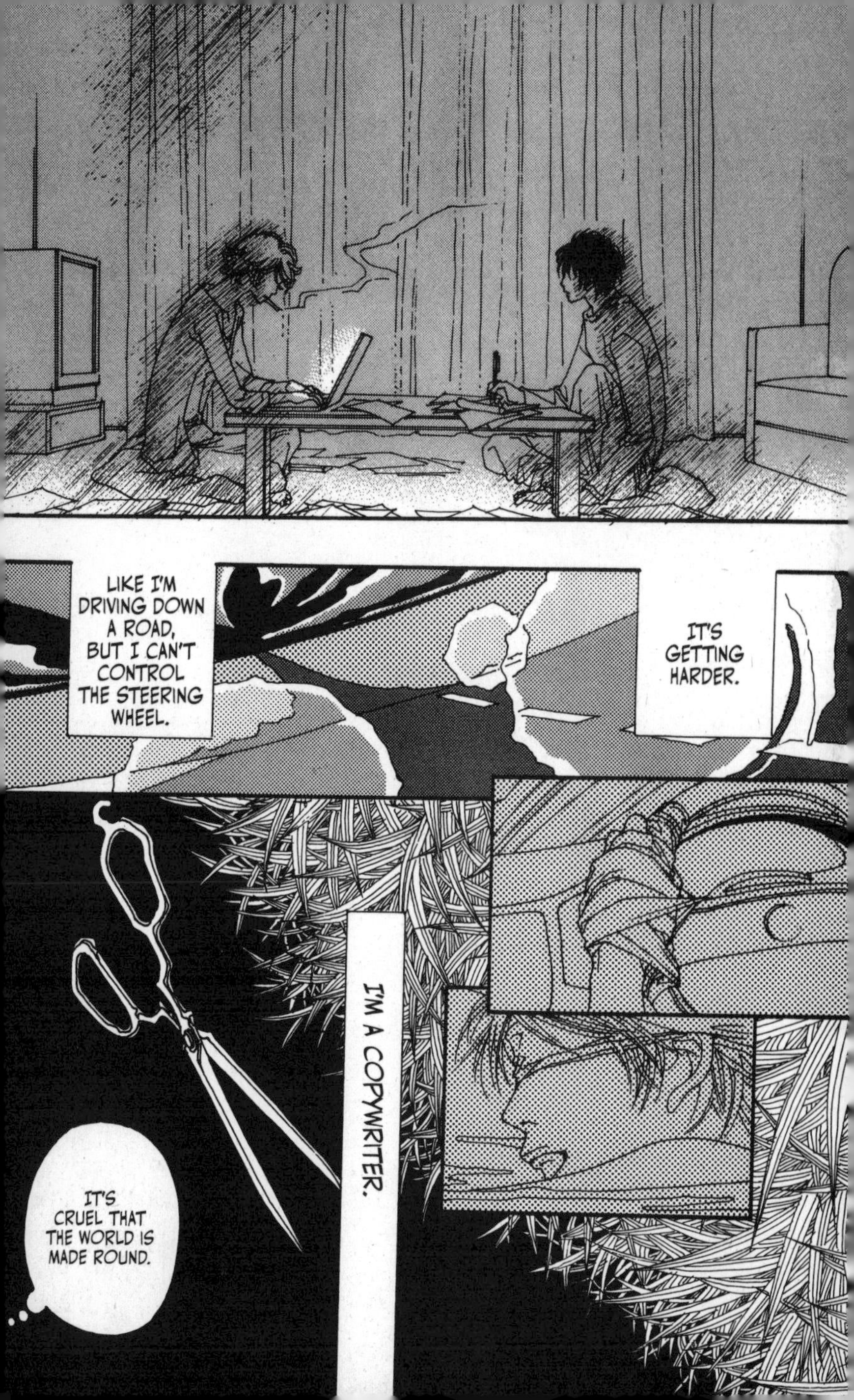

IT'S GETTING HARDER.
LIKE I'M DRIVING DOWN A ROAD, BUT I CAN'T CONTROL THE STEERING WHEEL.
I'M A COPYWRITER.
IT'S CRUEL THAT THE WORLD IS MADE ROUND.

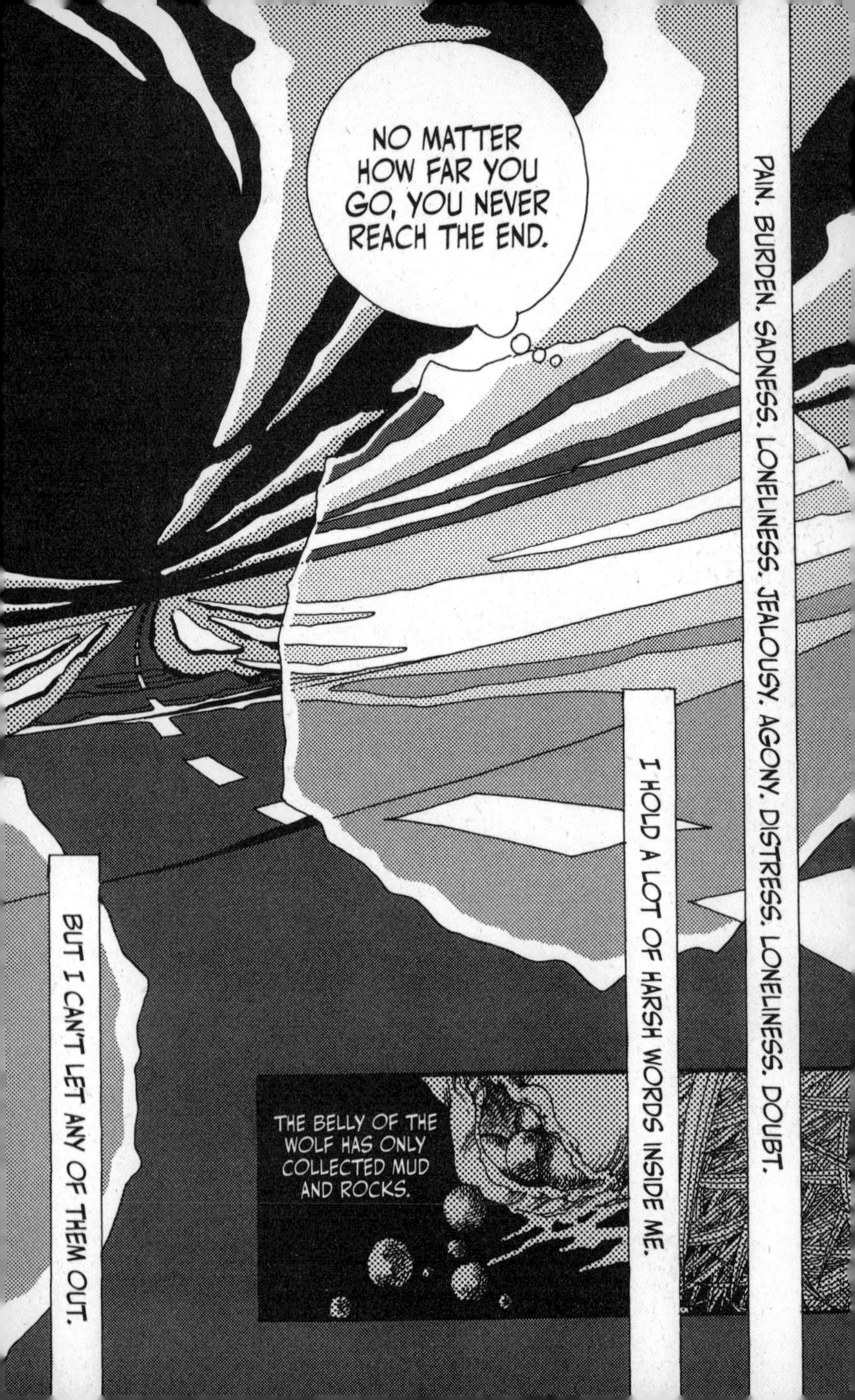
PAIN. BURDEN. SADNESS. LONELINESS. JEALOUSY. AGONY. DISTRESS. LONELINESS. DOUBT.
NO MATTER HOW FAR YOU GO, YOU NEVER REACH THE END.
I HOLD A LOT OF HARSH WORDS INSIDE ME.
THE BELLY OF THE WOLF HAS ONLY COLLECTED MUD AND ROCKS.
BUT I CAN'T LET ANY OF THEM OUT.

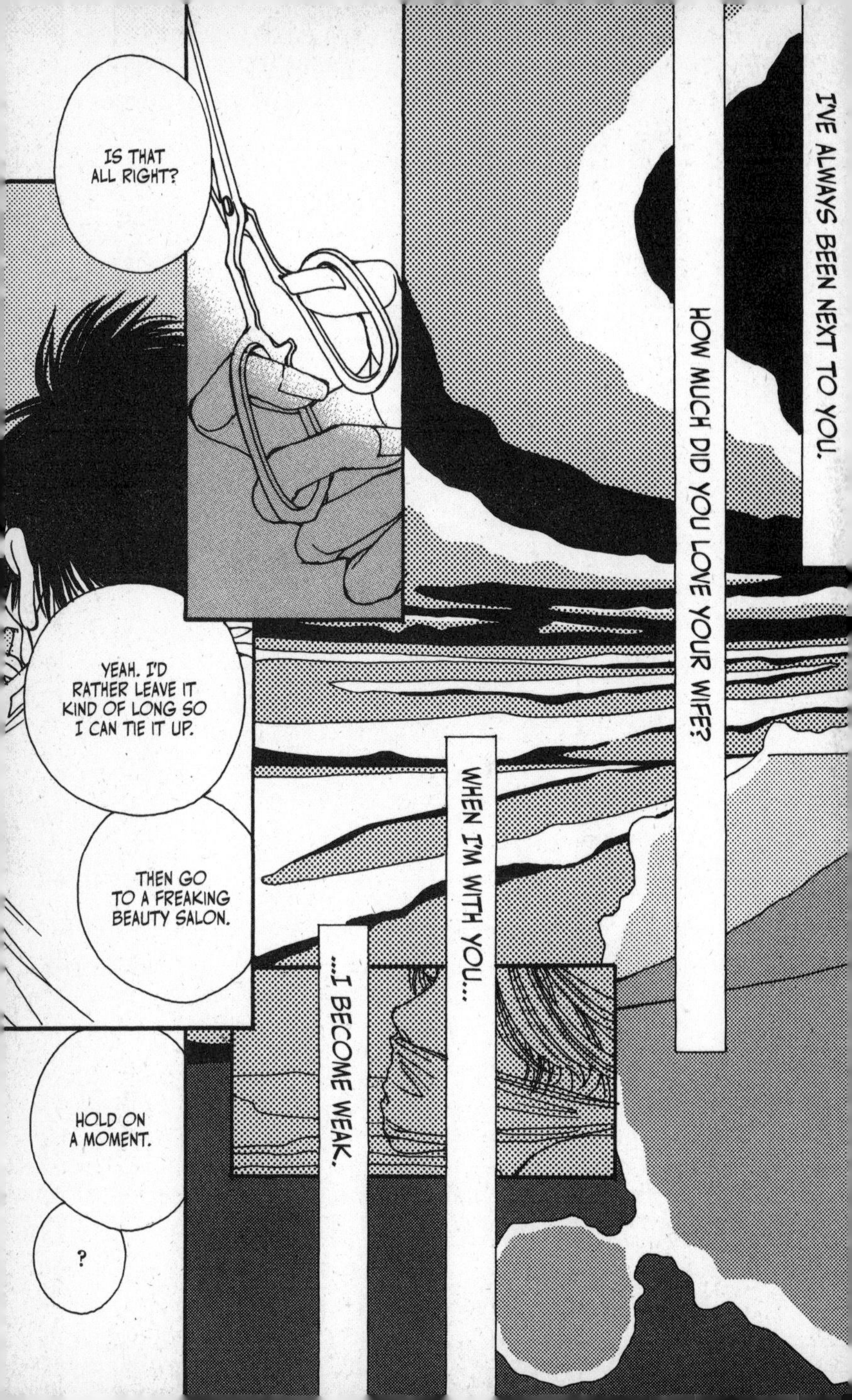
I'VE ALWAYS BEEN NEXT TO YOU.
HOW MUCH DID YOU LOVE YOUR WIFE?
IS THAT ALL RIGHT?
YEAH. I'D RATHER LEAVE IT KIND OF LONG SO I CAN TIE IT UP.
THEN GO TO A FREAKING BEAUTY SALON.
WHEN I'M WITH YOU...
...I BECOME WEAK.
HOLD ON A MOMENT.
?

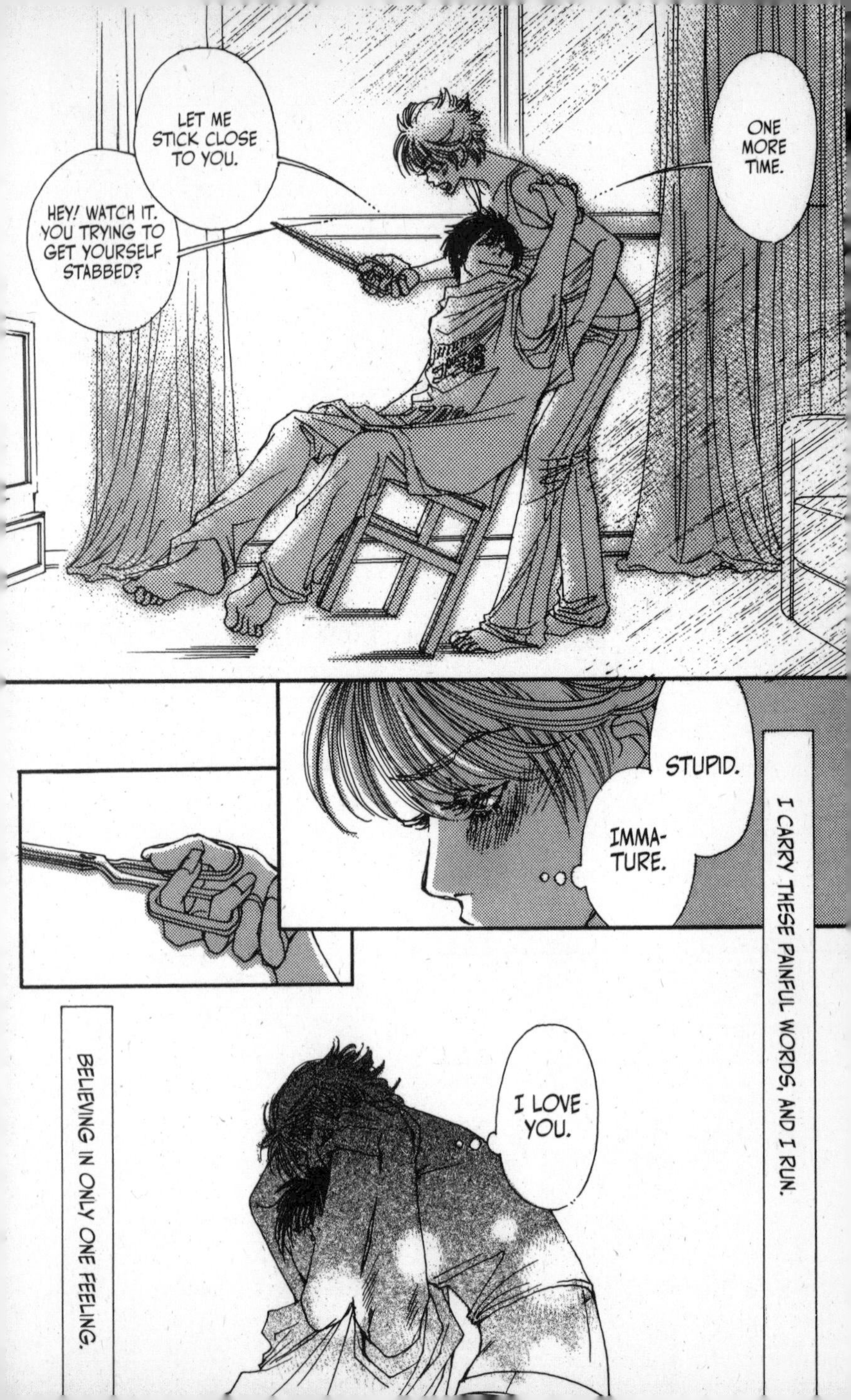
ONE MORE TIME.
LET ME STICK CLOSE TO YOU.
HEY! WATCH IT. YOU TRYING TO GET YOURSELF STABBED?
I CARRY THESE PAINFUL WORDS, AND I RUN.
STUPID.
IMMA-TURE.
I LOVE YOU.
BELIEVING IN ONLY ONE FEELING.

Suppli 4

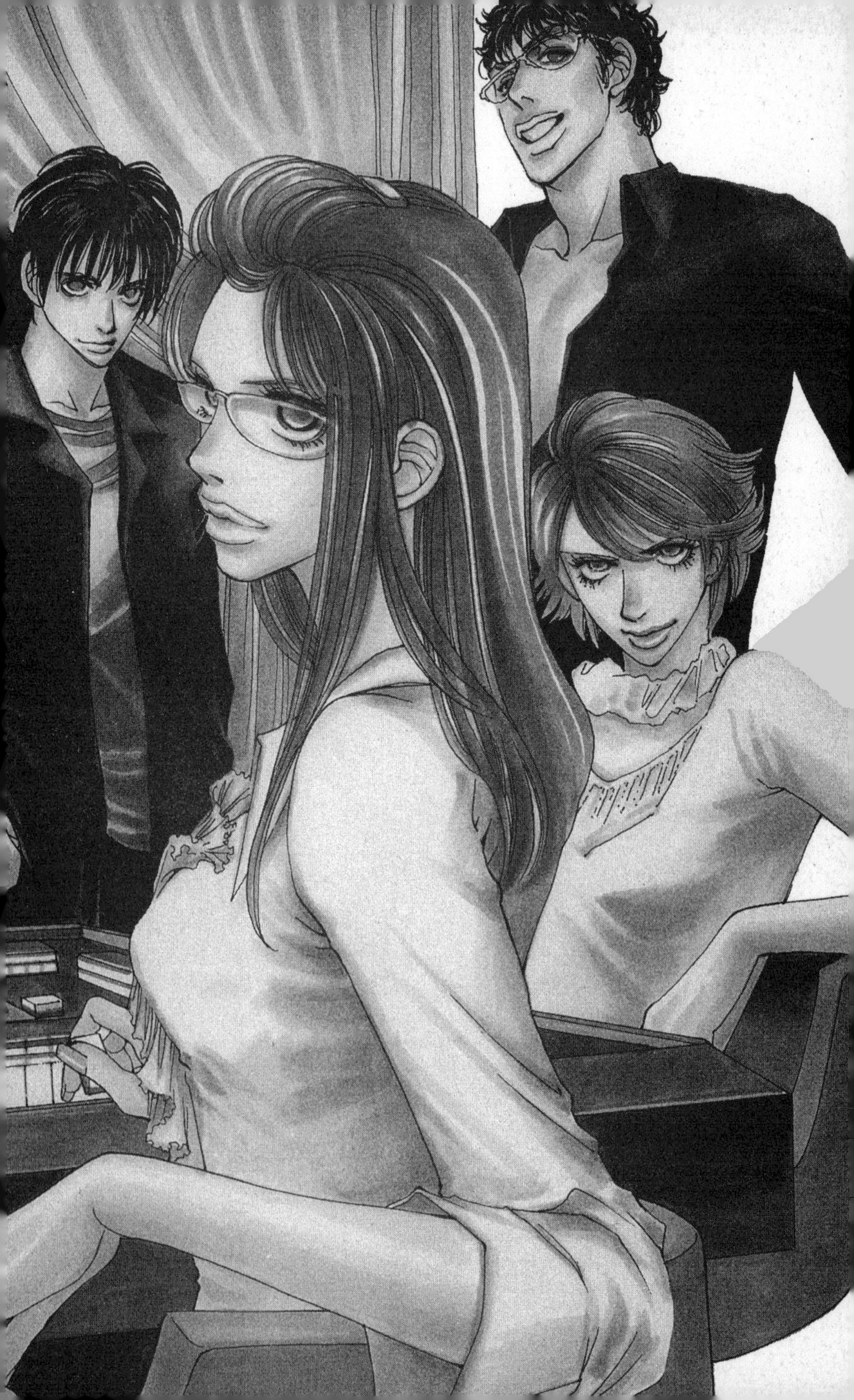

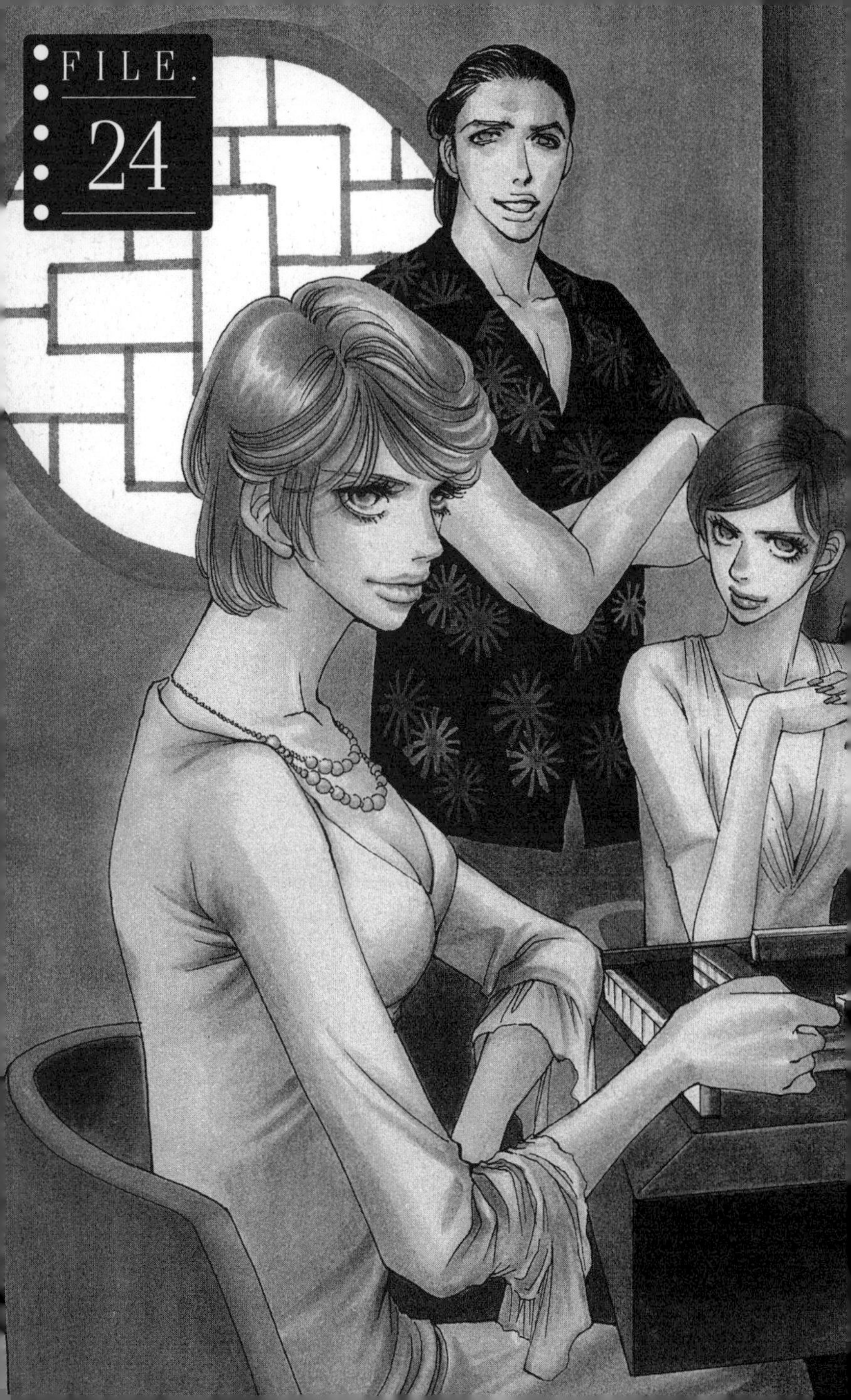
FILE.
24

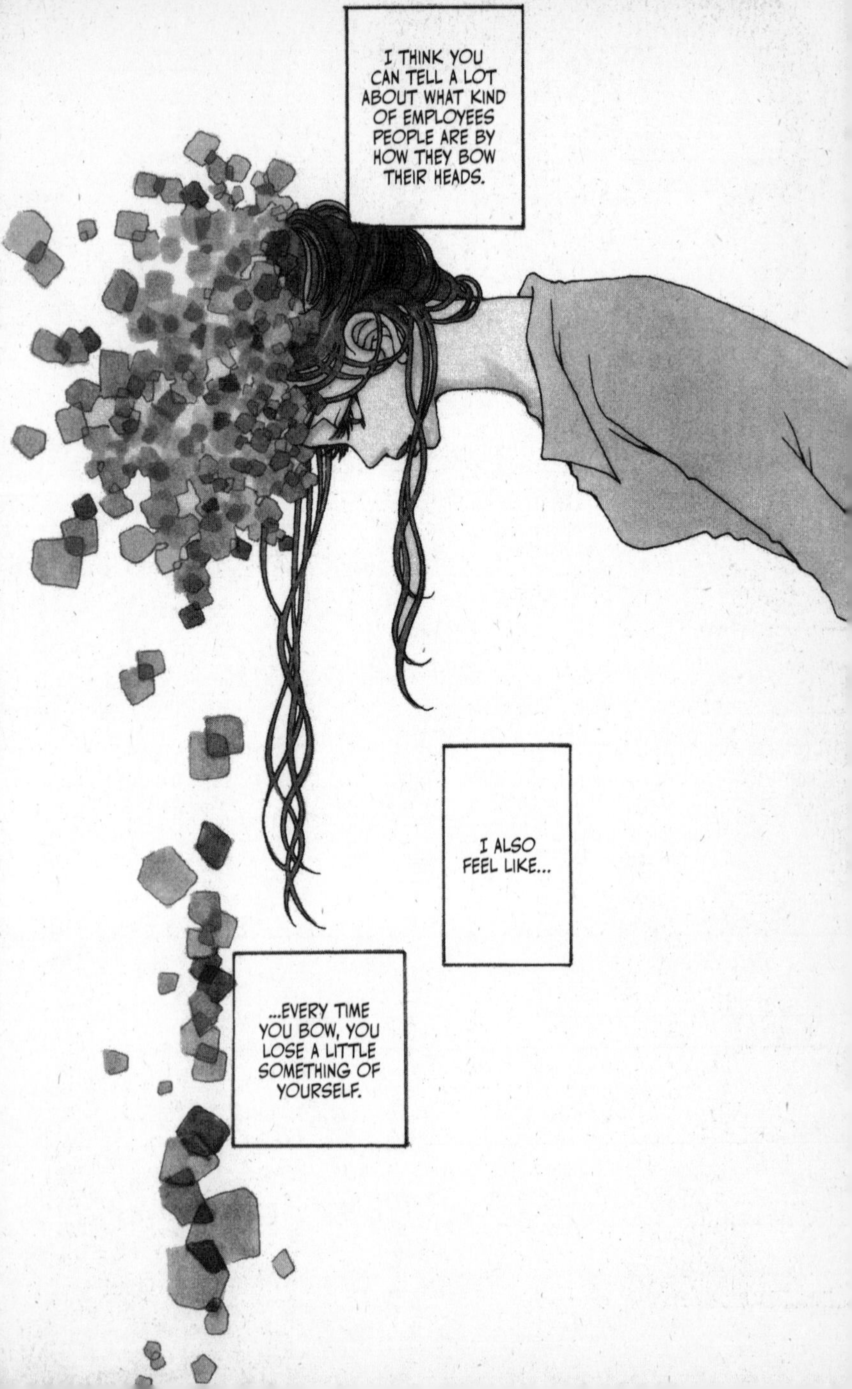
I THINK YOU CAN TELL A LOT ABOUT WHAT KIND OF EMPLOYEES PEOPLE ARE BY HOW THEY BOW THEIR HEADS.
I ALSO FEEL LIKE...
...EVERY TIME YOU BOW, YOU LOSE A LITTLE SOMETHING OF YOURSELF.

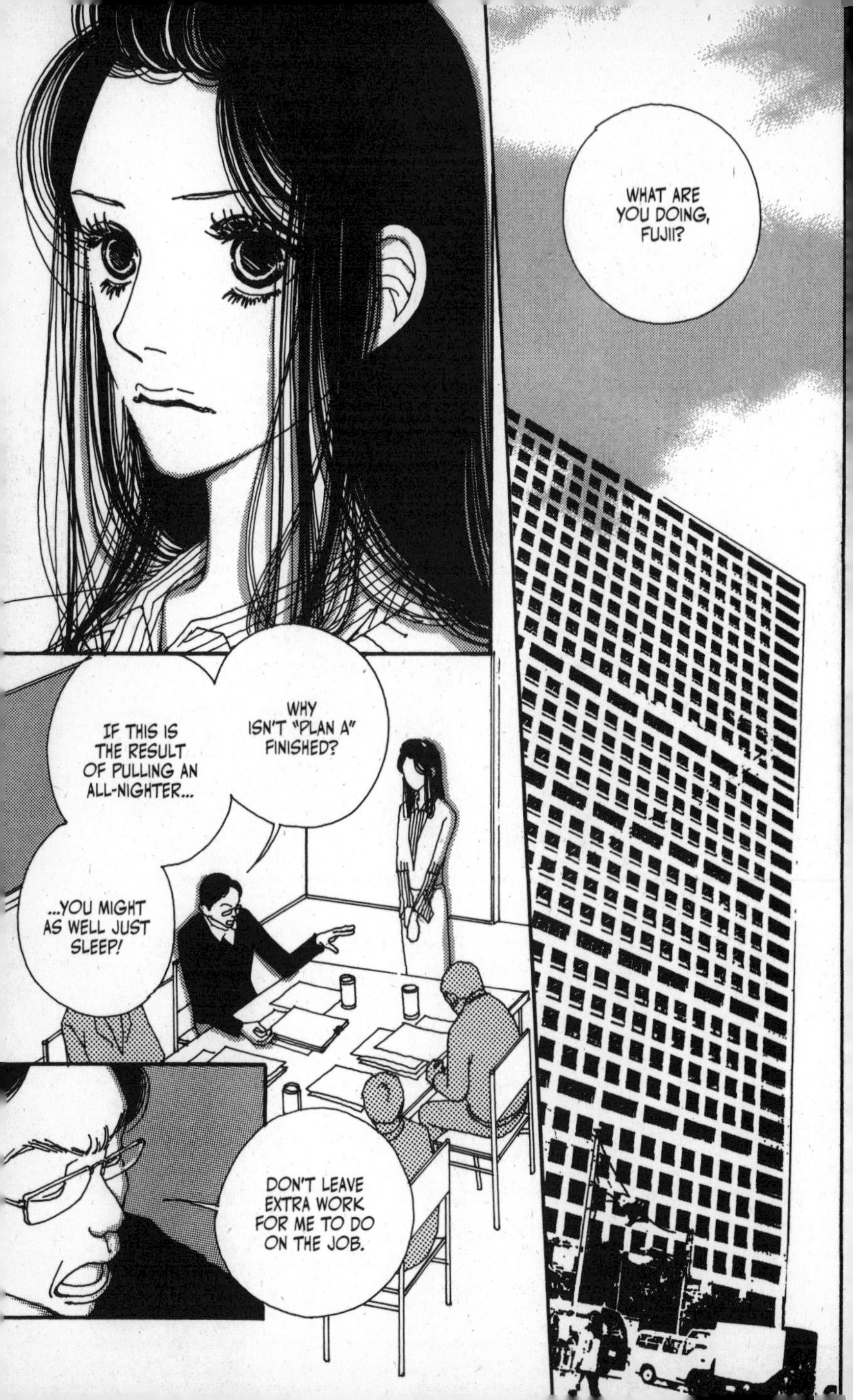
WHAT ARE YOU DOING, FUJII?
WHY ISN'T "PLAN A" FINISHED?
IF THIS IS THE RESULT OF PULLING AN ALL-NIGHTER...
...YOU MIGHT AS WELL JUST SLEEP!
DON'T LEAVE EXTRA WORK FOR ME TO DO ON THE JOB.

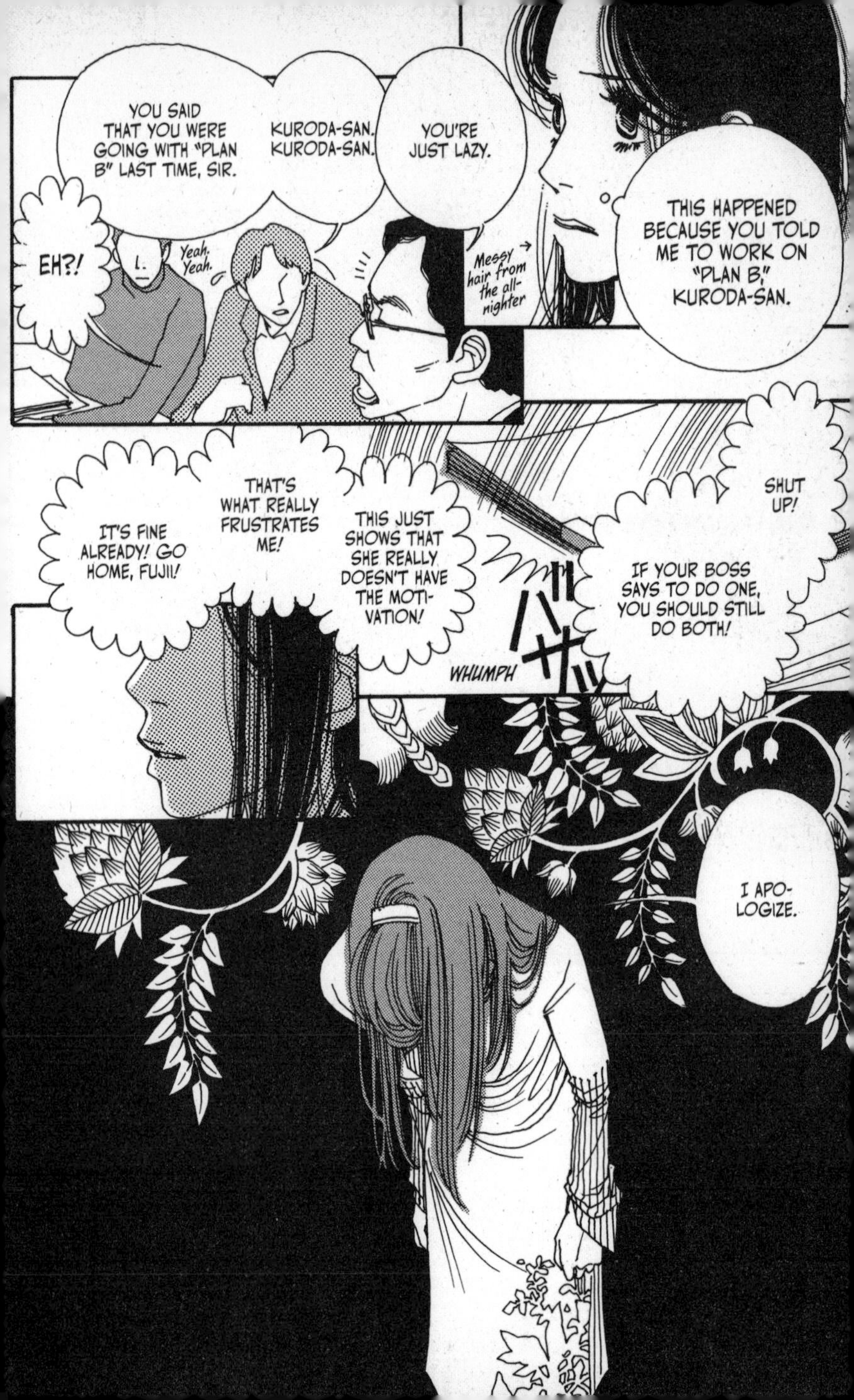
THIS HAPPENED BECAUSE YOU TOLD ME TO WORK ON "PLAN B," KURODA-SAN.
YOU'RE JUST LAZY.
Messy hair from the all-nighter
KURODA-SAN. KURODA-SAN.
YOU SAID THAT YOU WERE GOING WITH "PLAN B" LAST TIME, SIR.
Yeah. Yeah.
EH?!
SHUT UP!
IF YOUR BOSS SAYS TO DO ONE, YOU SHOULD STILL DO BOTH!
バサッ
WHUMPH
THIS JUST SHOWS THAT SHE REALLY DOESN'T HAVE THE MOTI-VATION!
THAT'S WHAT REALLY FRUSTRATES ME!
IT'S FINE ALREADY! GO HOME, FUJII!
I APO-LOGIZE.

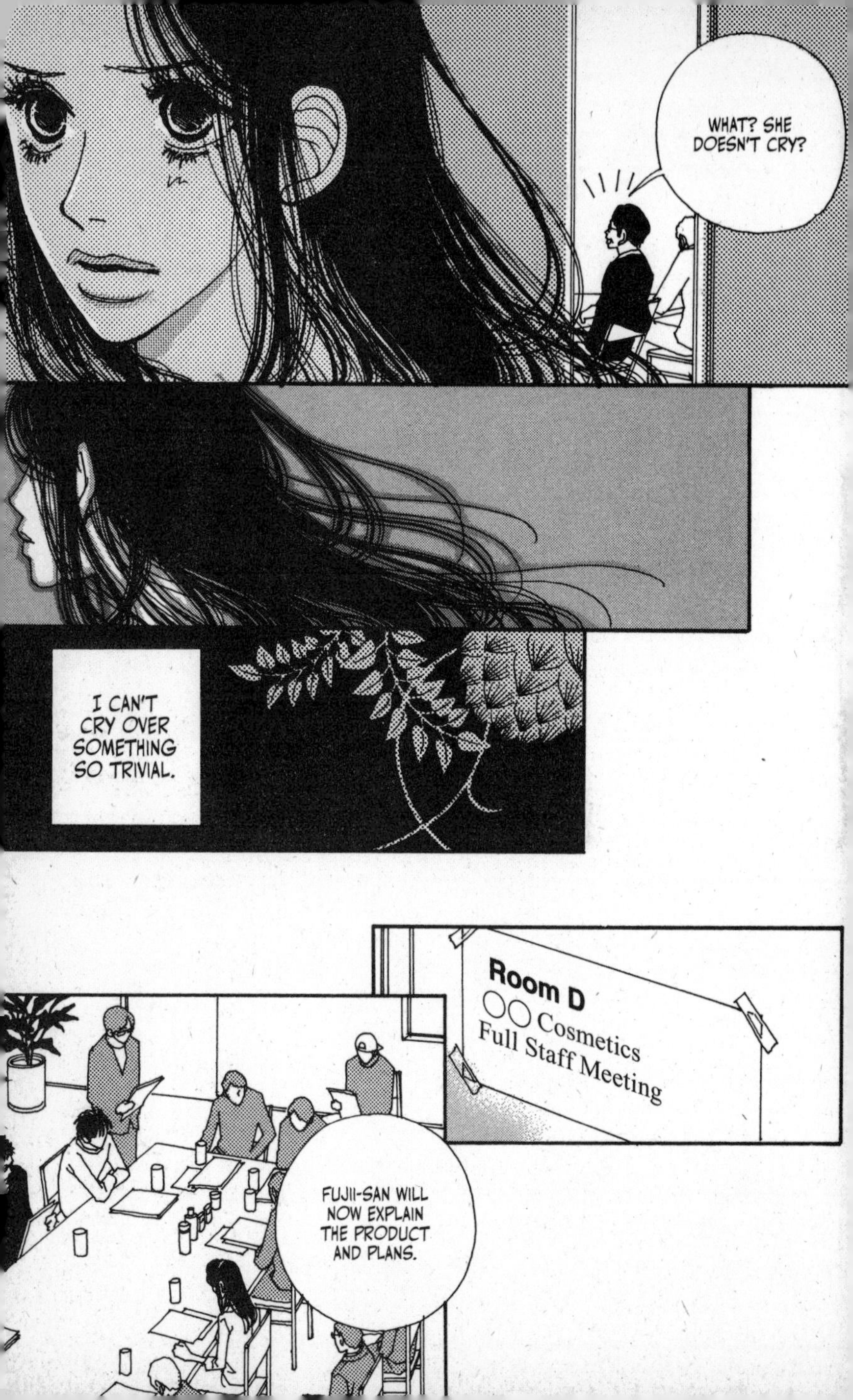
WHAT? SHE DOESN'T CRY?
I CAN'T CRY OVER SOMETHING SO TRIVIAL.
Room D
○○ Cosmetics
Full Staff Meeting
FUJII-SAN WILL NOW EXPLAIN THE PRODUCT AND PLANS.

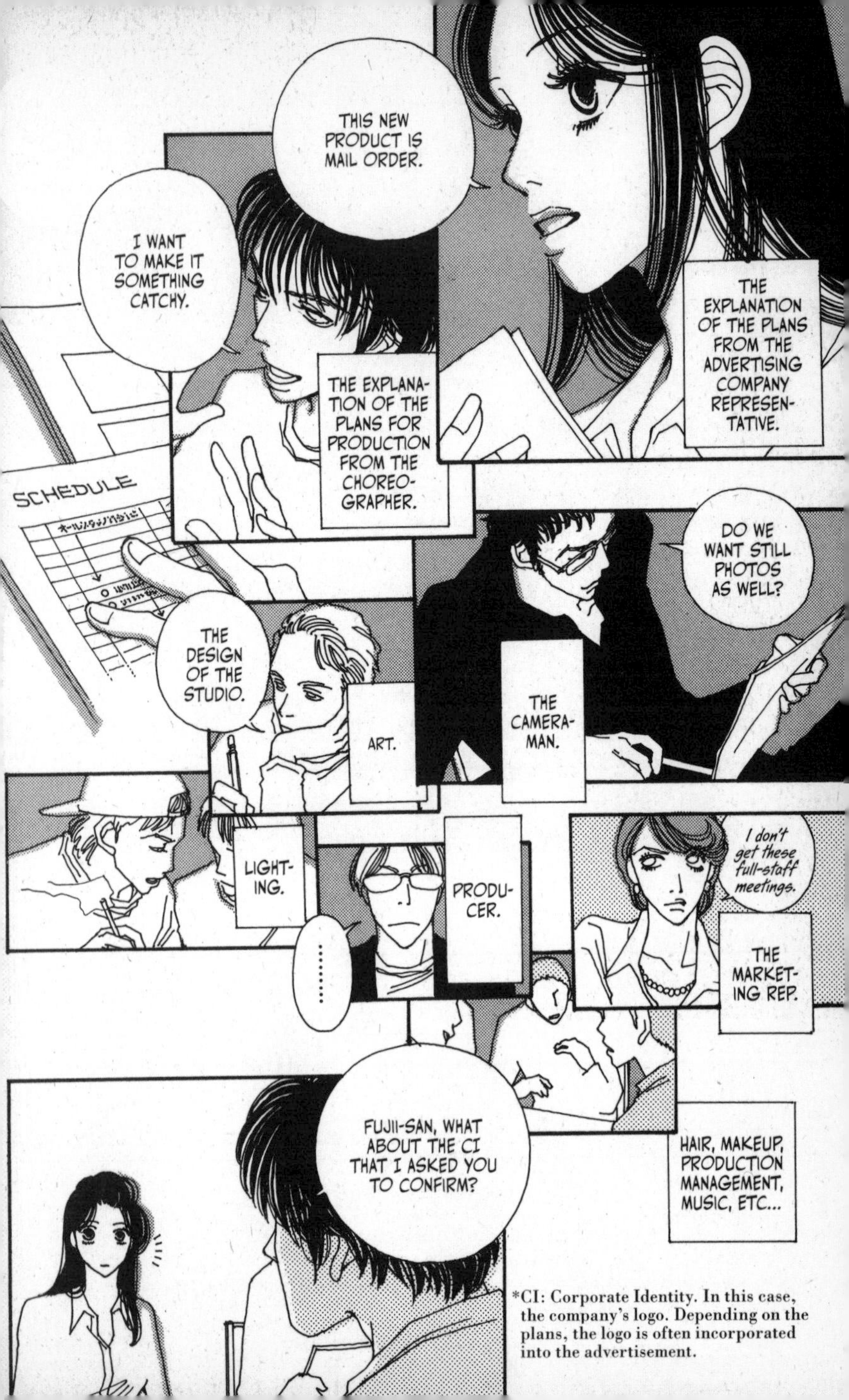
THIS NEW PRODUCT IS MAIL ORDER.
THE EXPLANATION OF THE PLANS FROM THE ADVERTISING COMPANY REPRESENTATIVE.
I WANT TO MAKE IT SOMETHING CATCHY.
THE EXPLANATION OF THE PLANS FOR PRODUCTION FROM THE CHOREOGRAPHER.
SCHEDULE
DO WE WANT STILL PHOTOS AS WELL?
THE CAMERAMAN.
THE DESIGN OF THE STUDIO.
ART.
I don't get these full-staff meetings.
THE MARKETING REP.
PRODUCER.
......
LIGHTING.
HAIR, MAKEUP, PRODUCTION MANAGEMENT, MUSIC, ETC...
FUJII-SAN, WHAT ABOUT THE CI THAT I ASKED YOU TO CONFIRM?

*CI: Corporate Identity. In this case, the company's logo. Depending on the plans, the logo is often incorporated into the advertisement.

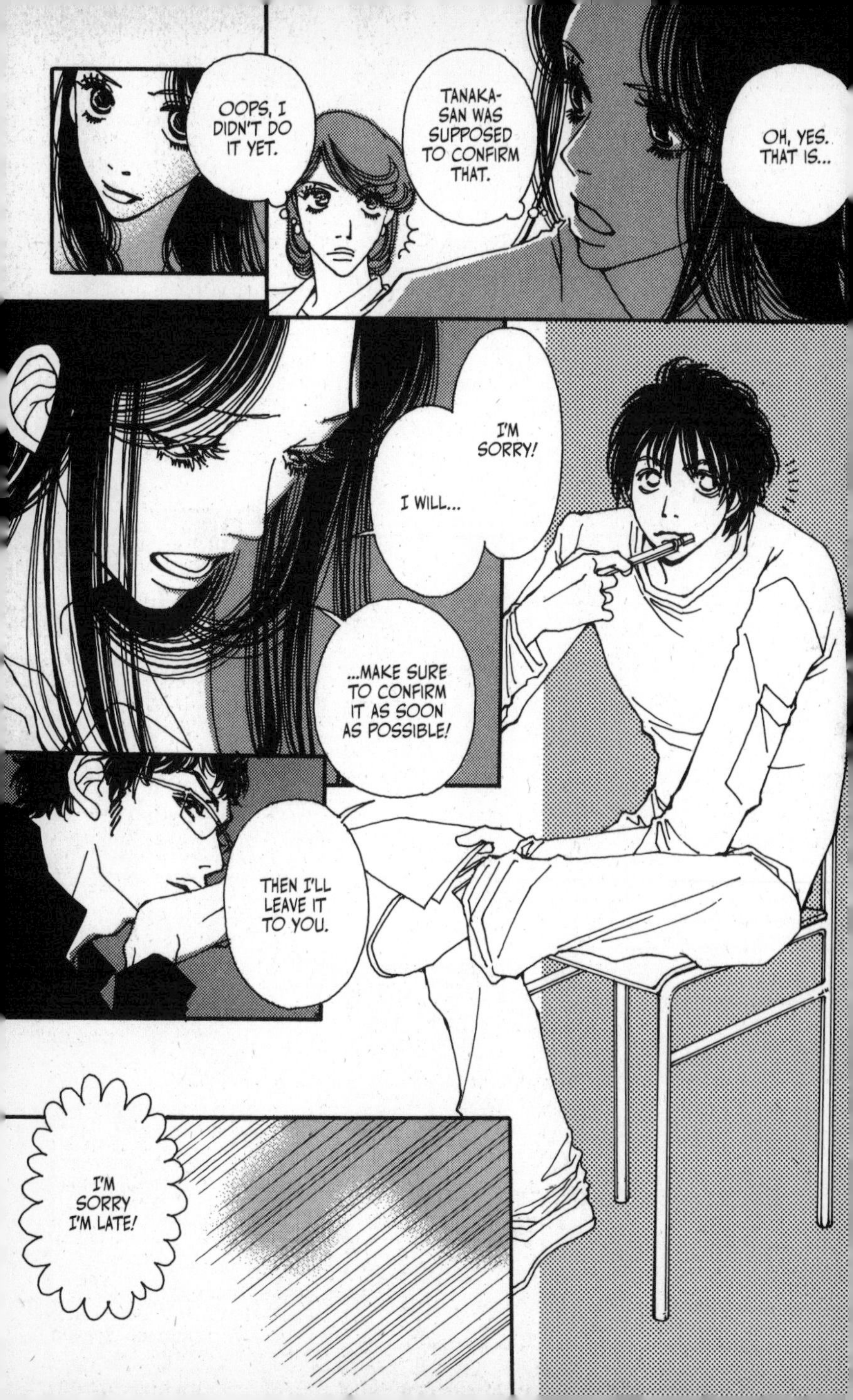
OH, YES. THAT IS...
TANAKA-SAN WAS SUPPOSED TO CONFIRM THAT.
OOPS, I DIDN'T DO IT YET.
I'M SORRY!
I WILL...
...MAKE SURE TO CONFIRM IT AS SOON AS POSSIBLE!
THEN I'LL LEAVE IT TO YOU.
I'M SORRY I'M LATE!

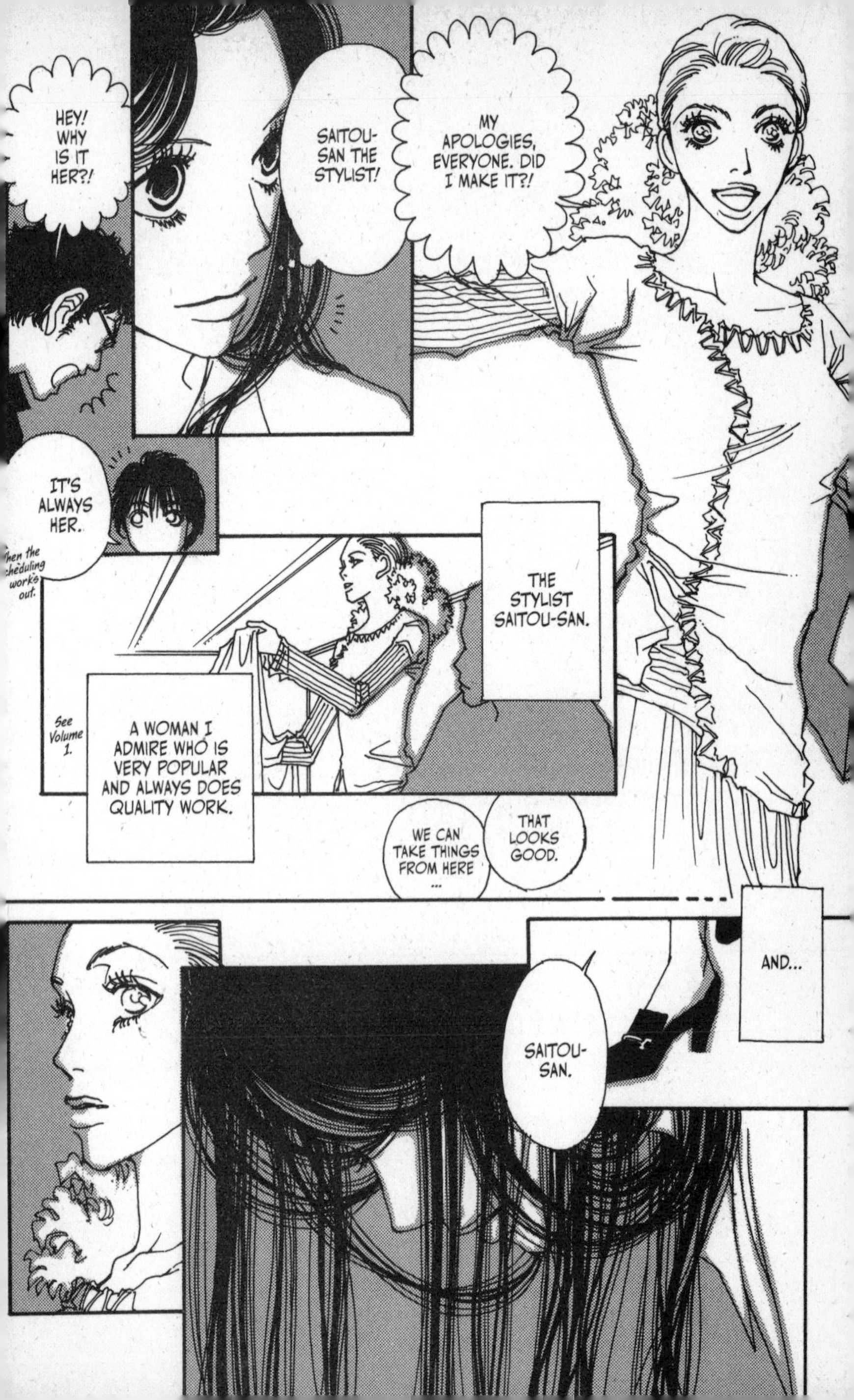
MY APOLOGIES, EVERYONE. DID I MAKE IT?!
SAITOU-SAN THE STYLIST!
HEY! WHY IS IT HER?!
IT'S ALWAYS HER.
hen the scheduling works out.
THE STYLIST SAITOU-SAN.
A WOMAN I ADMIRE WHO IS VERY POPULAR AND ALWAYS DOES QUALITY WORK.
See Volume 1.
THAT LOOKS GOOD.
WE CAN TAKE THINGS FROM HERE ...
AND...
SAITOU-SAN.

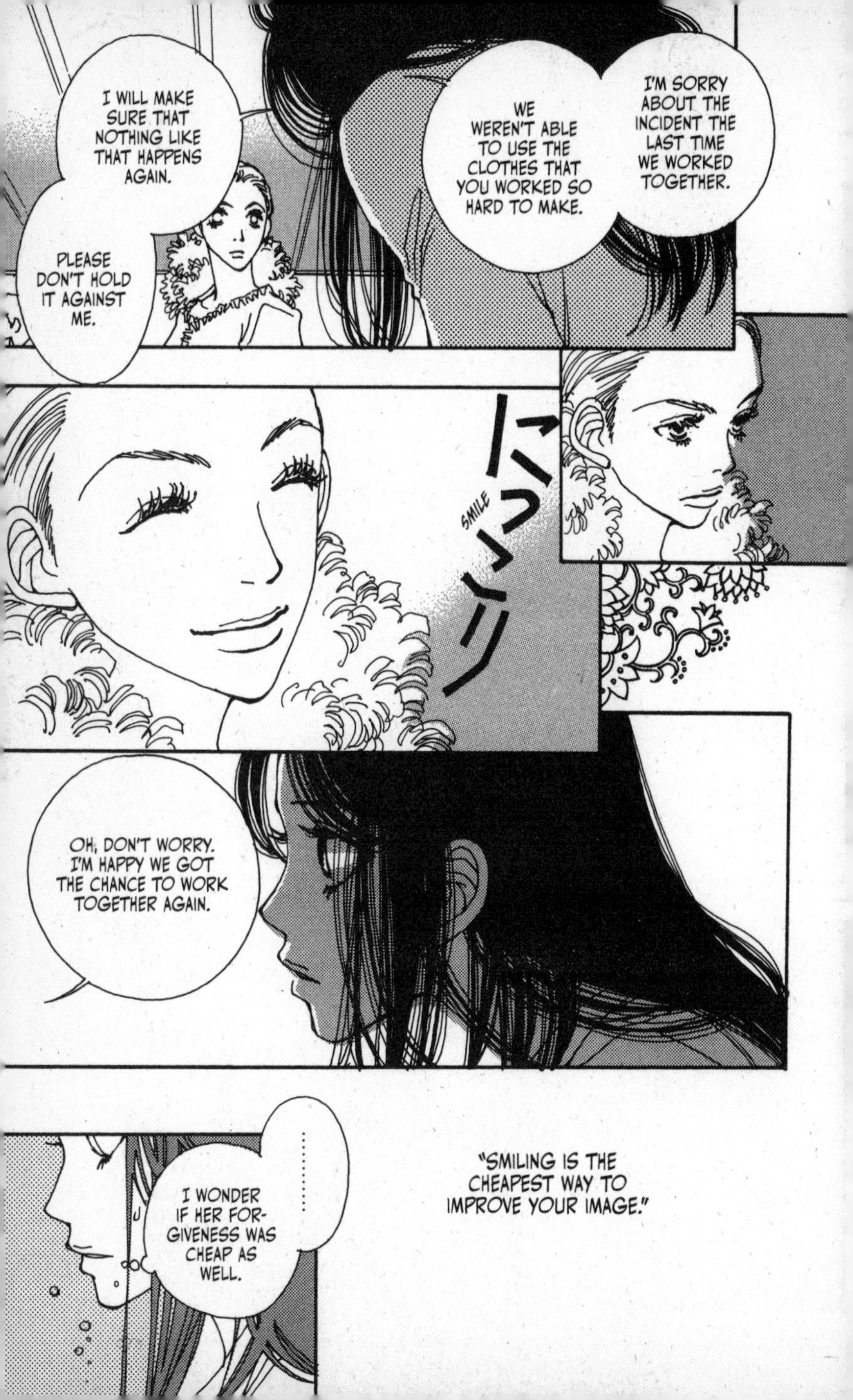
I'M SORRY ABOUT THE INCIDENT THE LAST TIME WE WORKED TOGETHER.
WE WEREN'T ABLE TO USE THE CLOTHES THAT YOU WORKED SO HARD TO MAKE.
I WILL MAKE SURE THAT NOTHING LIKE THAT HAPPENS AGAIN.
PLEASE DON'T HOLD IT AGAINST ME.
ニッコリ
SMILE
OH, DON'T WORRY. I'M HAPPY WE GOT THE CHANCE TO WORK TOGETHER AGAIN.
"SMILING IS THE CHEAPEST WAY TO IMPROVE YOUR IMAGE."
......
I WONDER IF HER FOR-GIVENESS WAS CHEAP AS WELL.

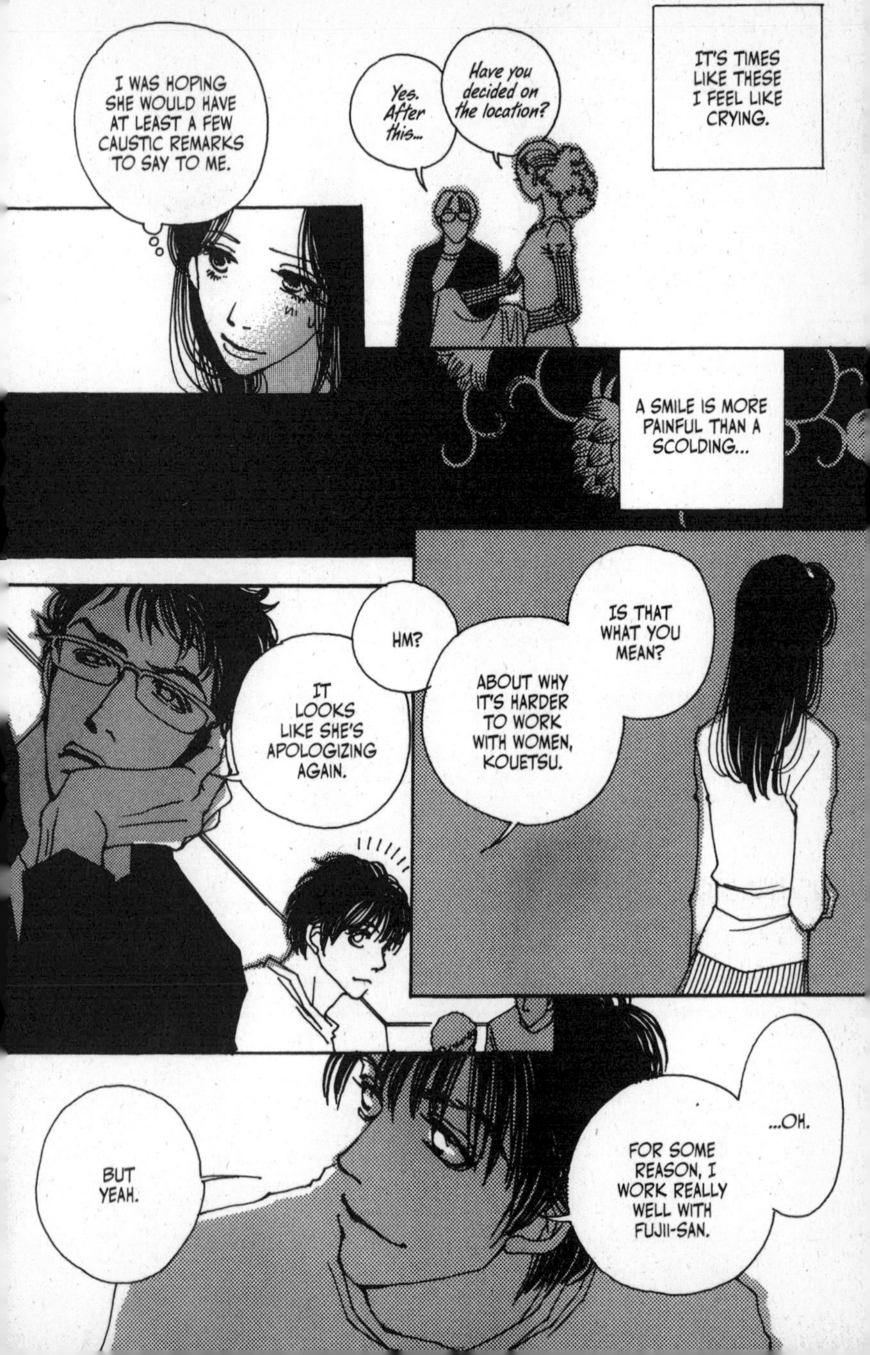
IT'S TIMES LIKE THESE I FEEL LIKE CRYING.
Have you decided on the location?
Yes. After this...
I WAS HOPING SHE WOULD HAVE AT LEAST A FEW CAUSTIC REMARKS TO SAY TO ME.
A SMILE IS MORE PAINFUL THAN A SCOLDING...
IT LOOKS LIKE SHE'S APOLOGIZING AGAIN.
HM?
IS THAT WHAT YOU MEAN?
ABOUT WHY IT'S HARDER TO WORK WITH WOMEN, KOUETSU.
...OH.
FOR SOME REASON, I WORK REALLY WELL WITH FUJII-SAN.
BUT YEAH.

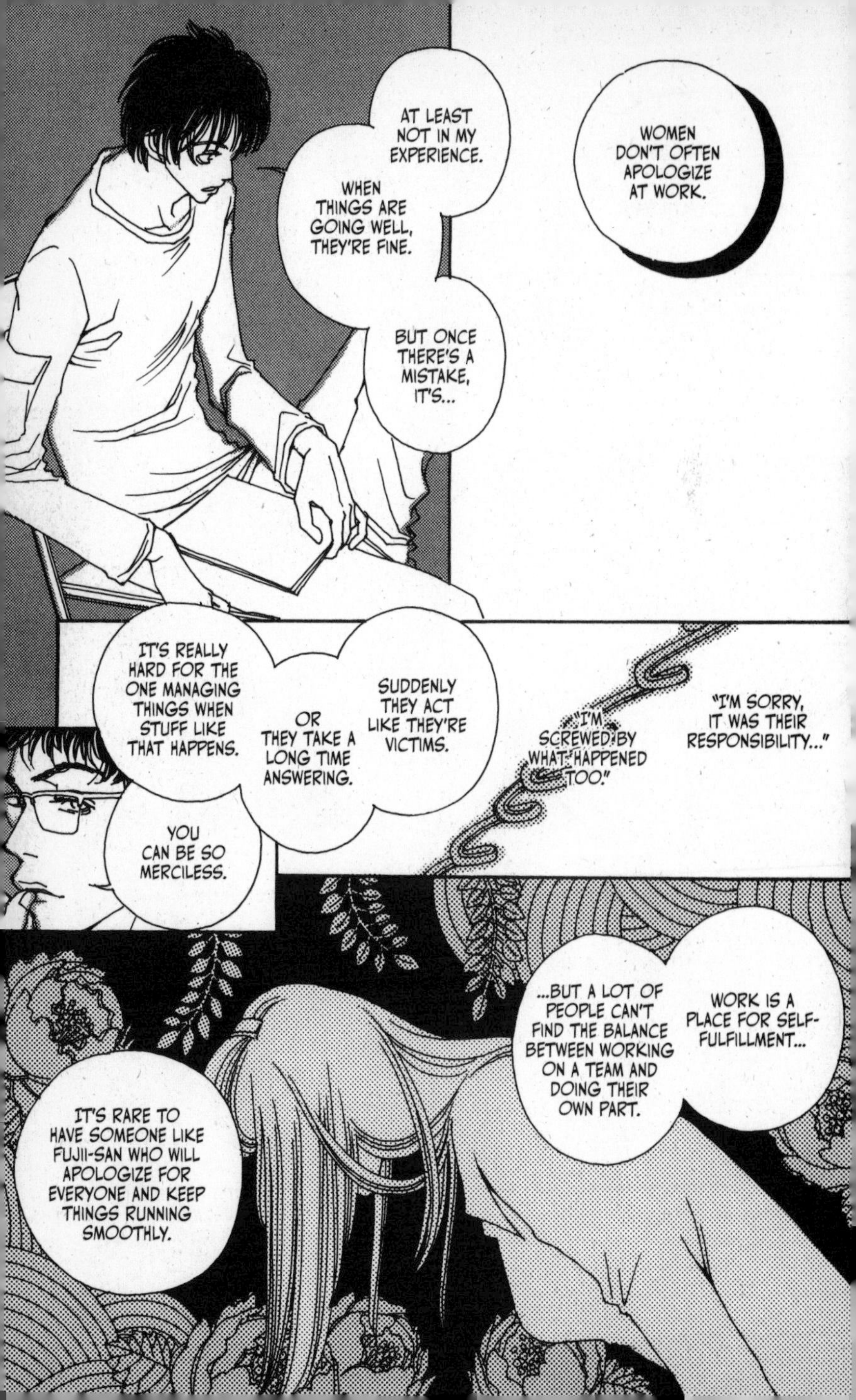
WOMEN DON'T OFTEN APOLOGIZE AT WORK.
AT LEAST NOT IN MY EXPERIENCE.
WHEN THINGS ARE GOING WELL, THEY'RE FINE.
BUT ONCE THERE'S A MISTAKE, IT'S...
"I'M SORRY, IT WAS THEIR RESPONSIBILITY..."
"I'M SCREWED BY WHAT HAPPENED TOO."
SUDDENLY THEY ACT LIKE THEY'RE VICTIMS.
OR THEY TAKE A LONG TIME ANSWERING.
IT'S REALLY HARD FOR THE ONE MANAGING THINGS WHEN STUFF LIKE THAT HAPPENS.
YOU CAN BE SO MERCILESS.
WORK IS A PLACE FOR SELF-FULFILLMENT...
...BUT A LOT OF PEOPLE CAN'T FIND THE BALANCE BETWEEN WORKING ON A TEAM AND DOING THEIR OWN PART.
IT'S RARE TO HAVE SOMEONE LIKE FUJII-SAN WHO WILL APOLOGIZE FOR EVERYONE AND KEEP THINGS RUNNING SMOOTHLY.

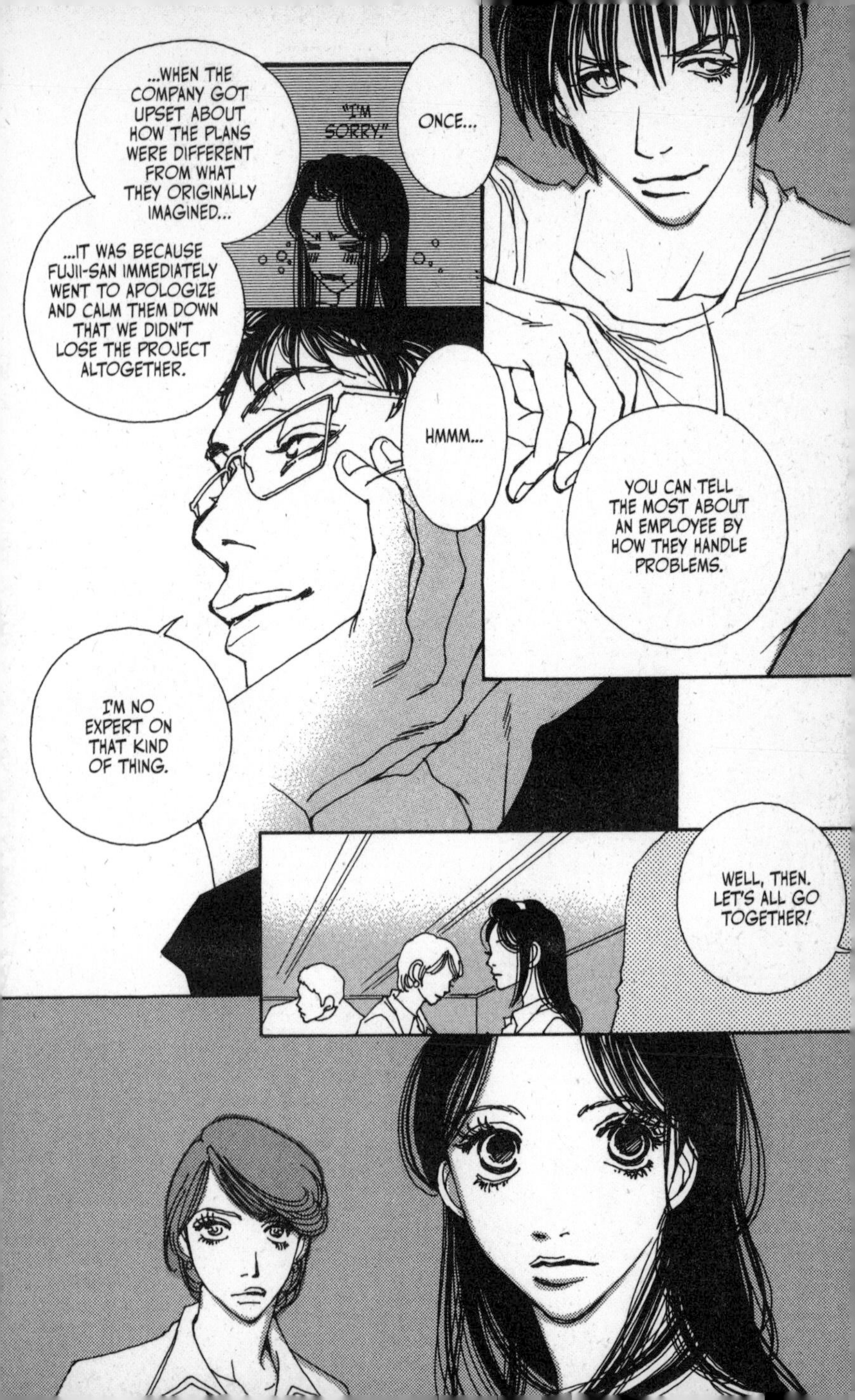
ONCE...
"I'M SORRY."
...WHEN THE COMPANY GOT UPSET ABOUT HOW THE PLANS WERE DIFFERENT FROM WHAT THEY ORIGINALLY IMAGINED...
...IT WAS BECAUSE FUJII-SAN IMMEDIATELY WENT TO APOLOGIZE AND CALM THEM DOWN THAT WE DIDN'T LOSE THE PROJECT ALTOGETHER.
HMMM...
YOU CAN TELL THE MOST ABOUT AN EMPLOYEE BY HOW THEY HANDLE PROBLEMS.
I'M NO EXPERT ON THAT KIND OF THING.
WELL, THEN. LET'S ALL GO TOGETHER!

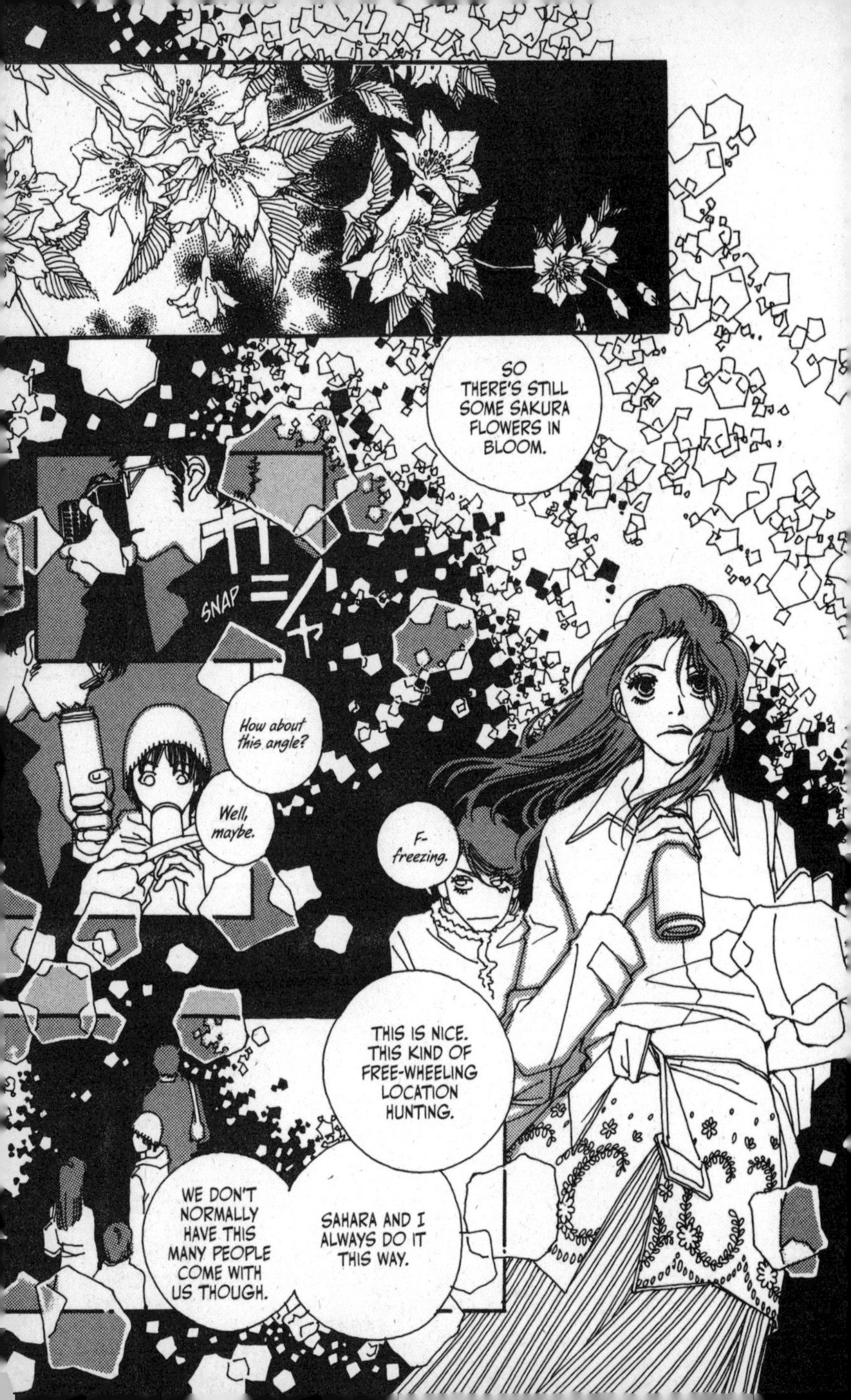
SO THERE'S STILL SOME SAKURA FLOWERS IN BLOOM.
F-freezing.
THIS IS NICE. THIS KIND OF FREE-WHEELING LOCATION HUNTING.
SAHARA AND I ALWAYS DO IT THIS WAY.
WE DON'T NORMALLY HAVE THIS MANY PEOPLE COME WITH US THOUGH.
SNAP
How about this angle?
Well, maybe.

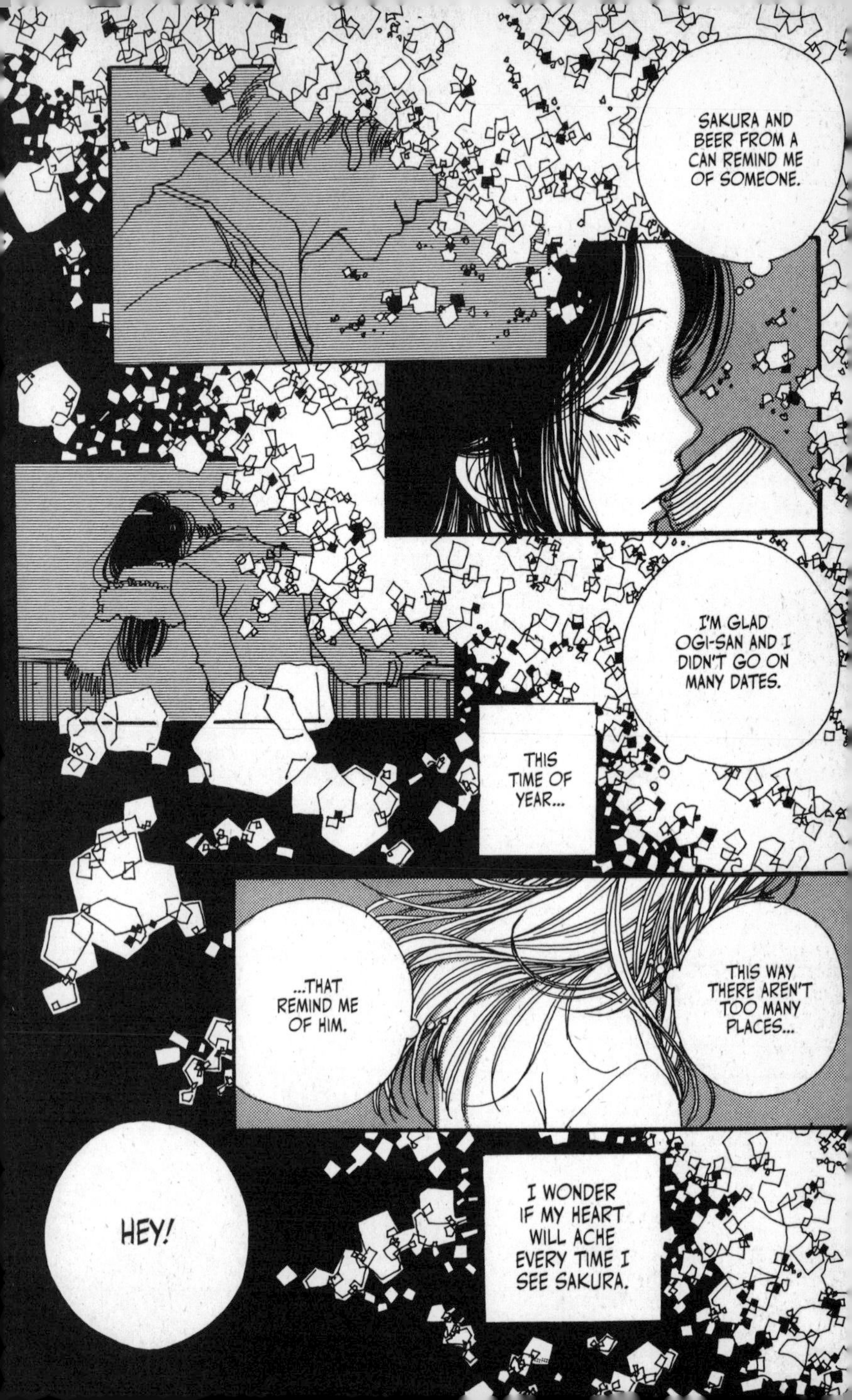
SAKURA AND BEER FROM A CAN REMIND ME OF SOMEONE.
I'M GLAD OGI-SAN AND I DIDN'T GO ON MANY DATES.
THIS TIME OF YEAR...
THIS WAY THERE AREN'T TOO MANY PLACES...
...THAT REMIND ME OF HIM.
I WONDER IF MY HEART WILL ACHE EVERY TIME I SEE SAKURA.
HEY!

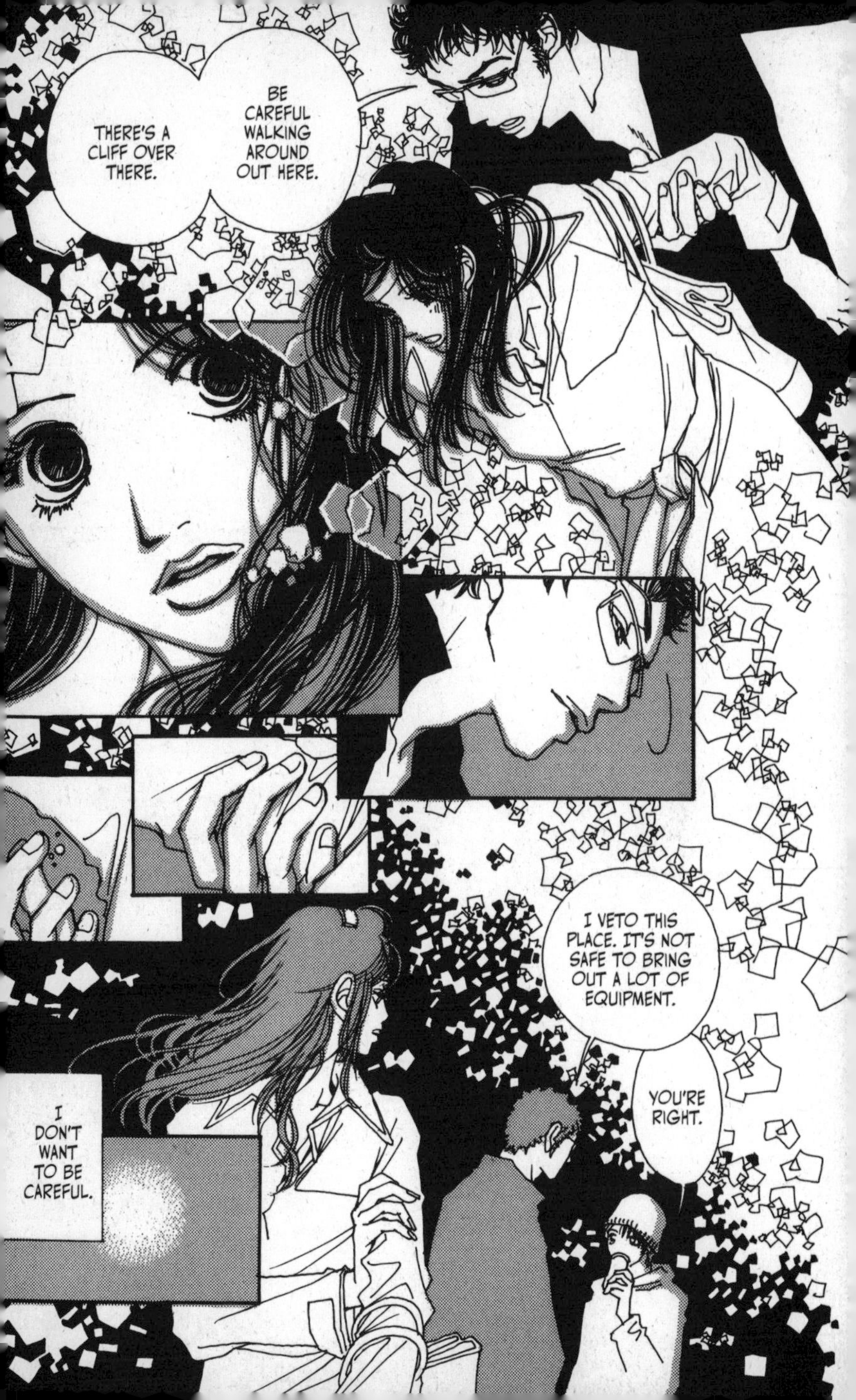
BE CAREFUL WALKING AROUND OUT HERE.
THERE'S A CLIFF OVER THERE.
I VETO THIS PLACE. IT'S NOT SAFE TO BRING OUT A LOT OF EQUIPMENT.
YOU'RE RIGHT.
I DON'T WANT TO BE CAREFUL.

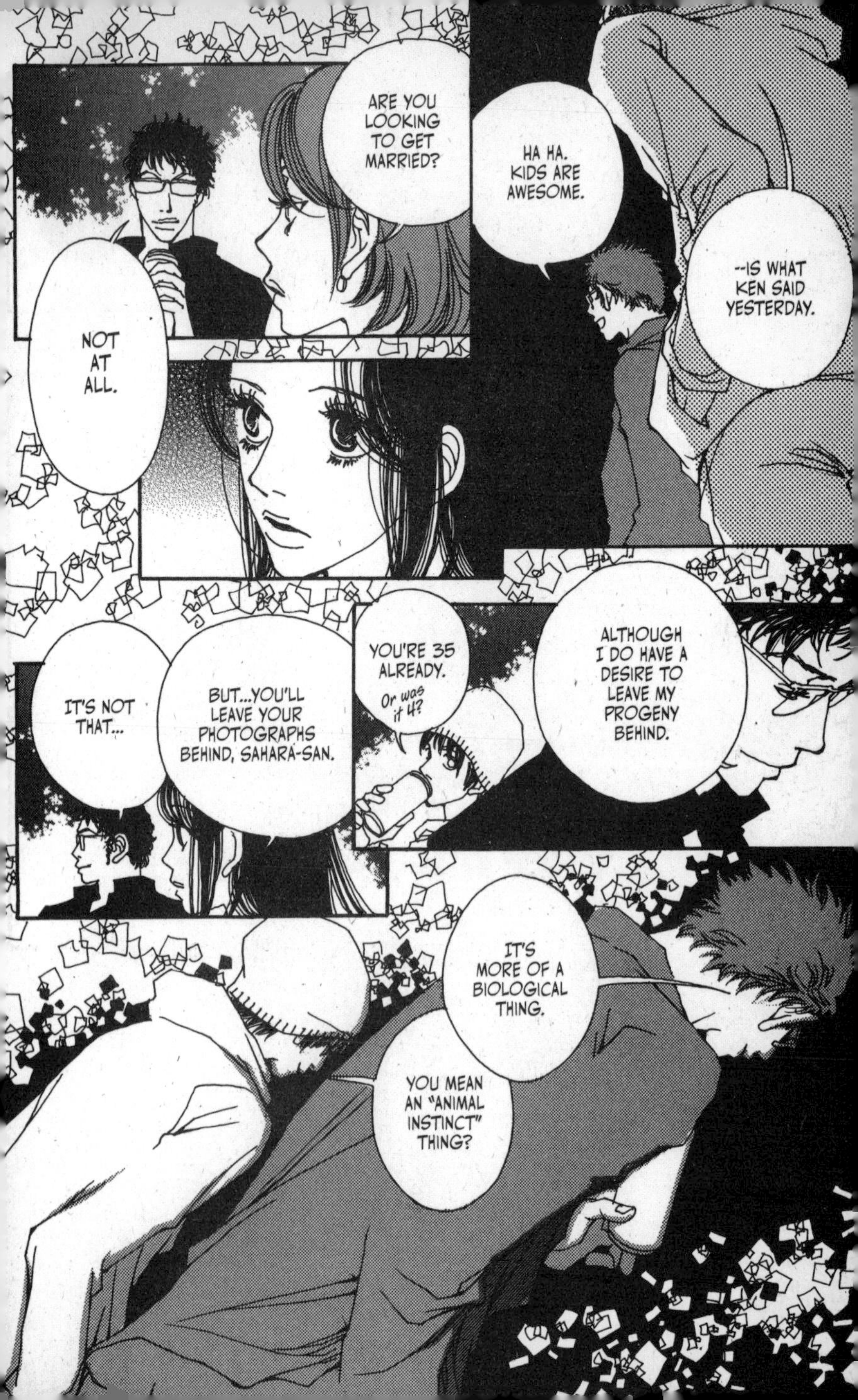
HA HA. KIDS ARE AWESOME.
--IS WHAT KEN SAID YESTERDAY.
ARE YOU LOOKING TO GET MARRIED?
NOT AT ALL.
ALTHOUGH I DO HAVE A DESIRE TO LEAVE MY PROGENY BEHIND.
YOU'RE 35 ALREADY.
Or was it 4?
BUT...YOU'LL LEAVE YOUR PHOTOGRAPHS BEHIND, SAHARA-SAN.
IT'S NOT THAT...
IT'S MORE OF A BIOLOGICAL THING.
YOU MEAN AN "ANIMAL INSTINCT" THING?

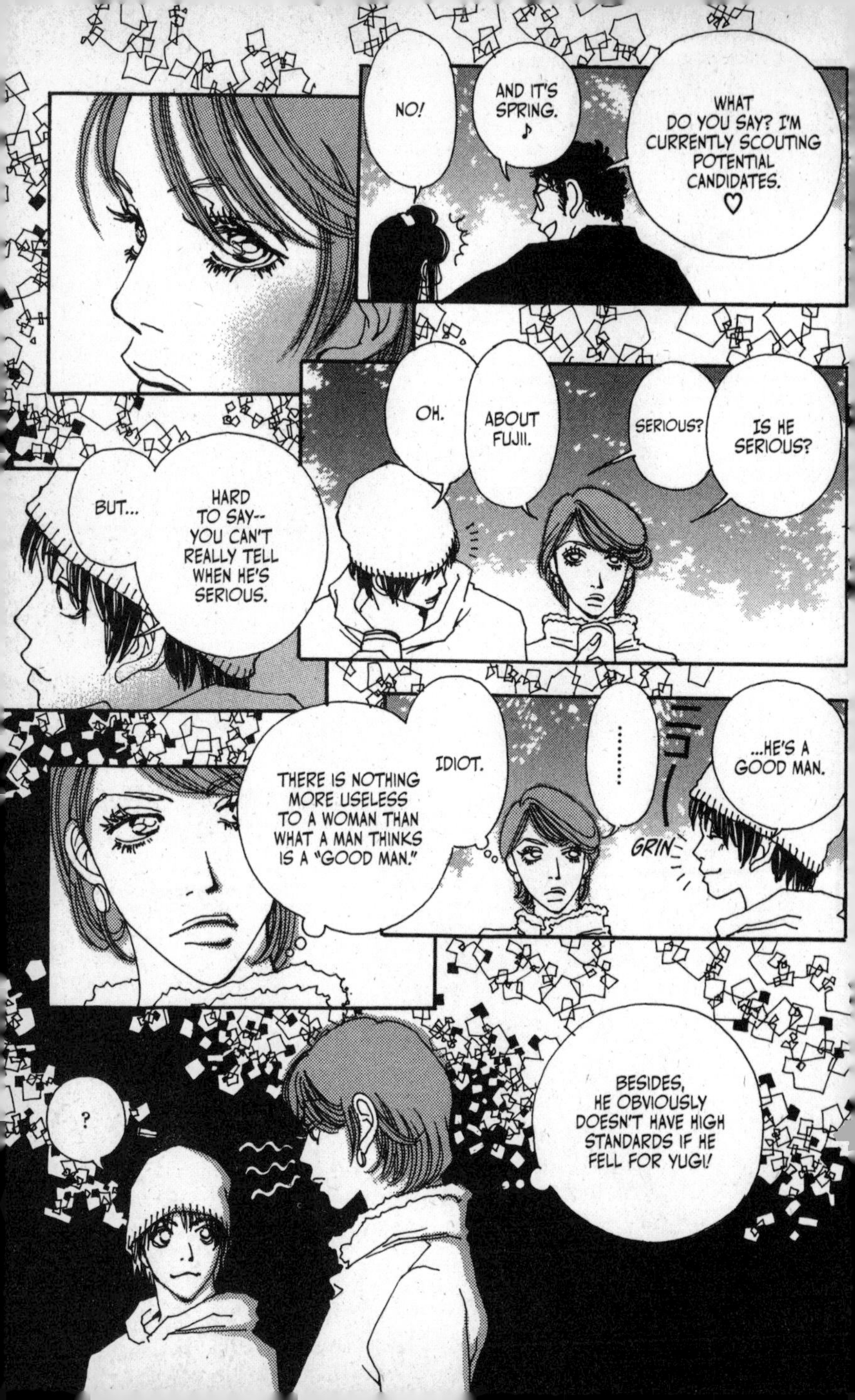
WHAT DO YOU SAY? I'M CURRENTLY SCOUTING POTENTIAL CANDIDATES. ♡
AND IT'S SPRING. ♪
NO!
IS HE SERIOUS?
SERIOUS?
ABOUT FUJII.
OH.
HARD TO SAY-- YOU CAN'T REALLY TELL WHEN HE'S SERIOUS.
BUT...
...HE'S A GOOD MAN.
GRIN
......
IDIOT.
THERE IS NOTHING MORE USELESS TO A WOMAN THAN WHAT A MAN THINKS IS A "GOOD MAN."
BESIDES, HE OBVIOUSLY DOESN'T HAVE HIGH STANDARDS IF HE FELL FOR YUGI!
?

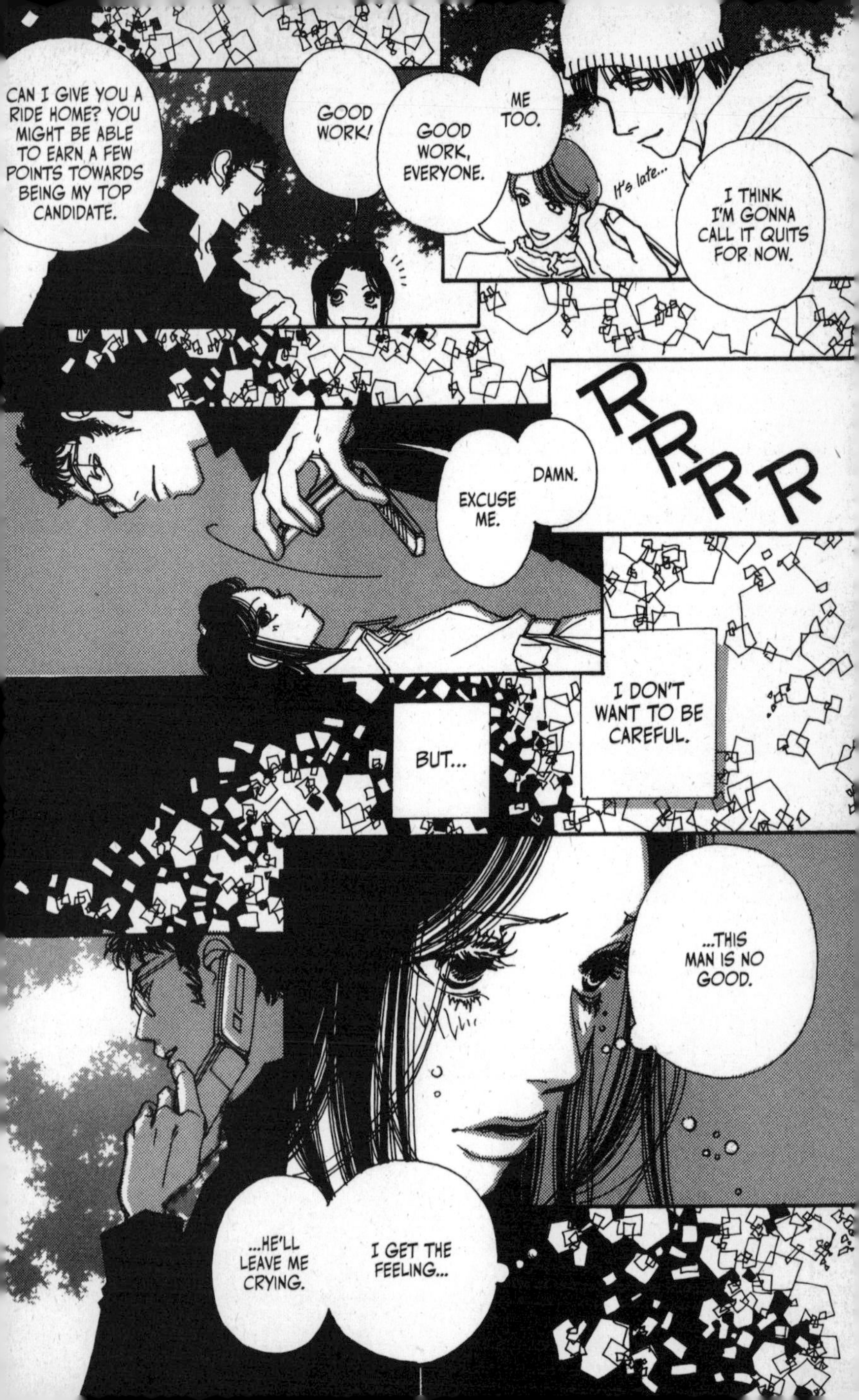
I THINK I'M GONNA CALL IT QUITS FOR NOW.
It's late...
ME TOO.
GOOD WORK, EVERYONE.
GOOD WORK!
CAN I GIVE YOU A RIDE HOME? YOU MIGHT BE ABLE TO EARN A FEW POINTS TOWARDS BEING MY TOP CANDIDATE.
RRRR
DAMN.
EXCUSE ME.
I DON'T WANT TO BE CAREFUL.
BUT...
...THIS MAN IS NO GOOD.
I GET THE FEELING...
...HE'LL LEAVE ME CRYING.

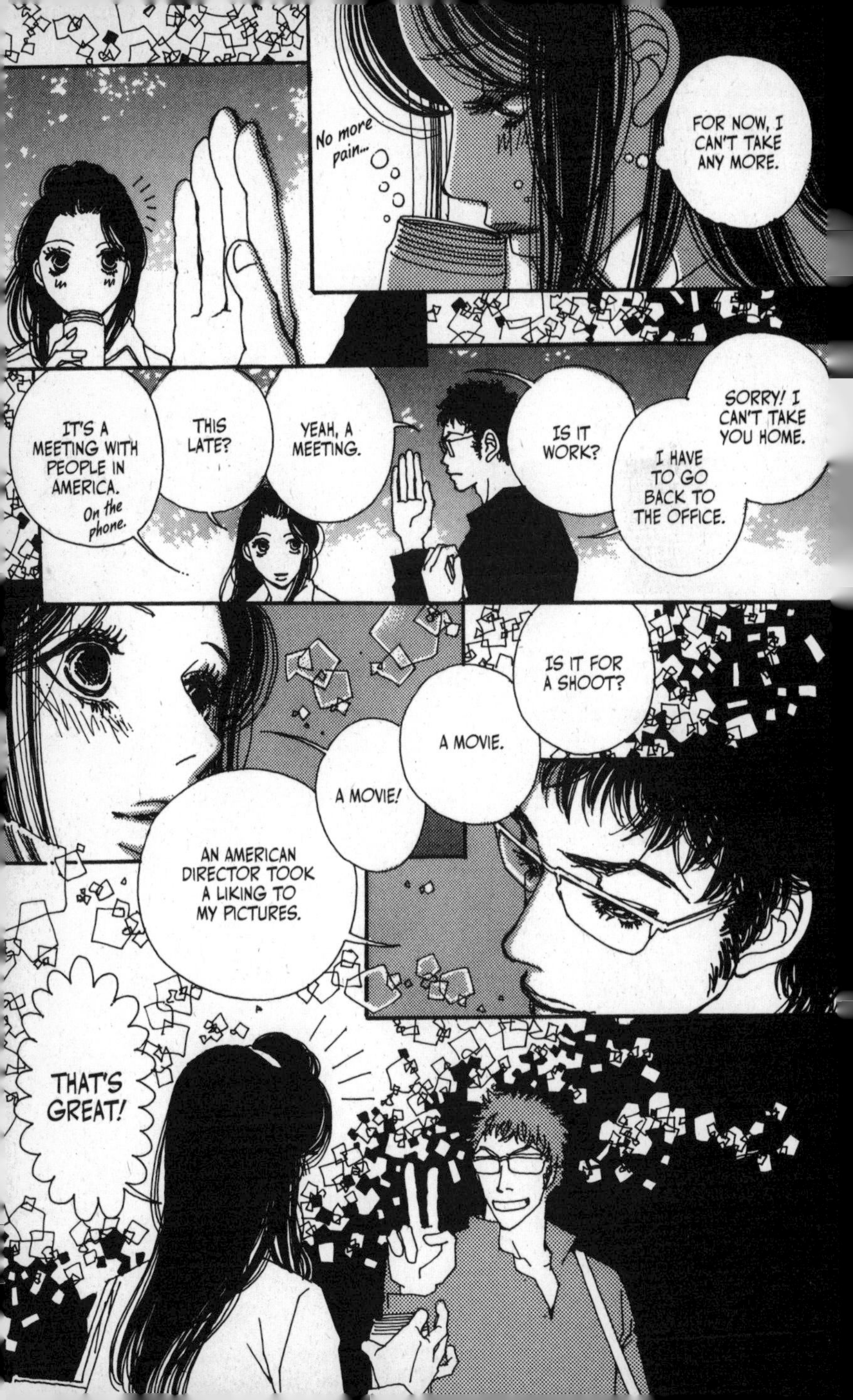
FOR NOW, I CAN'T TAKE ANY MORE.
No more pain...
SORRY! I CAN'T TAKE YOU HOME.
I HAVE TO GO BACK TO THE OFFICE.
IS IT WORK?
YEAH, A MEETING.
THIS LATE?
IT'S A MEETING WITH PEOPLE IN AMERICA.
On the phone.
IS IT FOR A SHOOT?
A MOVIE.
A MOVIE!
AN AMERICAN DIRECTOR TOOK A LIKING TO MY PICTURES.
THAT'S GREAT!

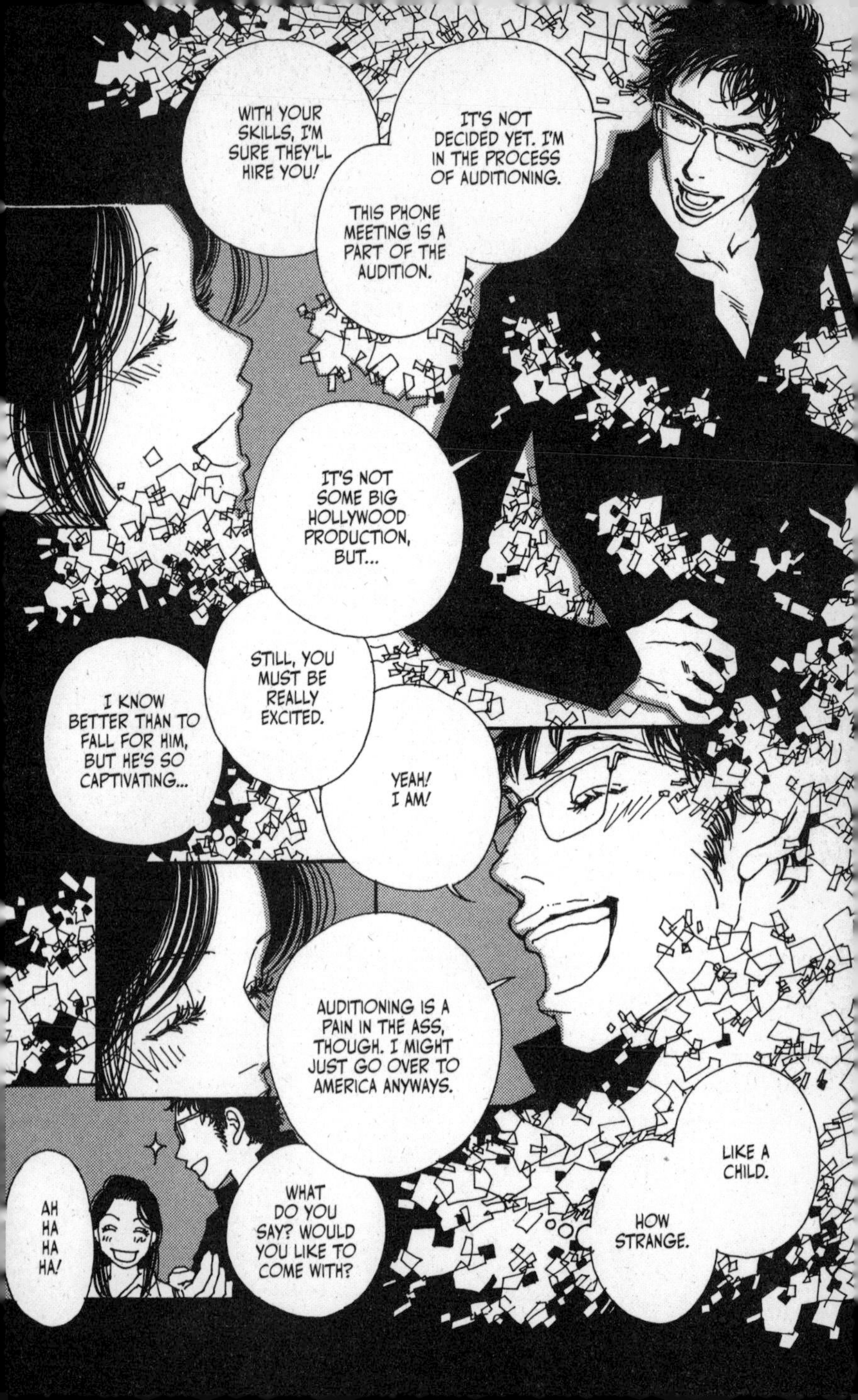

WITH YOUR SKILLS, I'M SURE THEY'LL HIRE YOU!
IT'S NOT DECIDED YET. I'M IN THE PROCESS OF AUDITIONING.
THIS PHONE MEETING IS A PART OF THE AUDITION.
IT'S NOT SOME BIG HOLLYWOOD PRODUCTION, BUT...
STILL, YOU MUST BE REALLY EXCITED.
YEAH! I AM!
I KNOW BETTER THAN TO FALL FOR HIM, BUT HE'S SO CAPTIVATING...
AUDITIONING IS A PAIN IN THE ASS, THOUGH. I MIGHT JUST GO OVER TO AMERICA ANYWAYS.
LIKE A CHILD.
HOW STRANGE.
WHAT DO YOU SAY? WOULD YOU LIKE TO COME WITH?
AH HA HA HA!

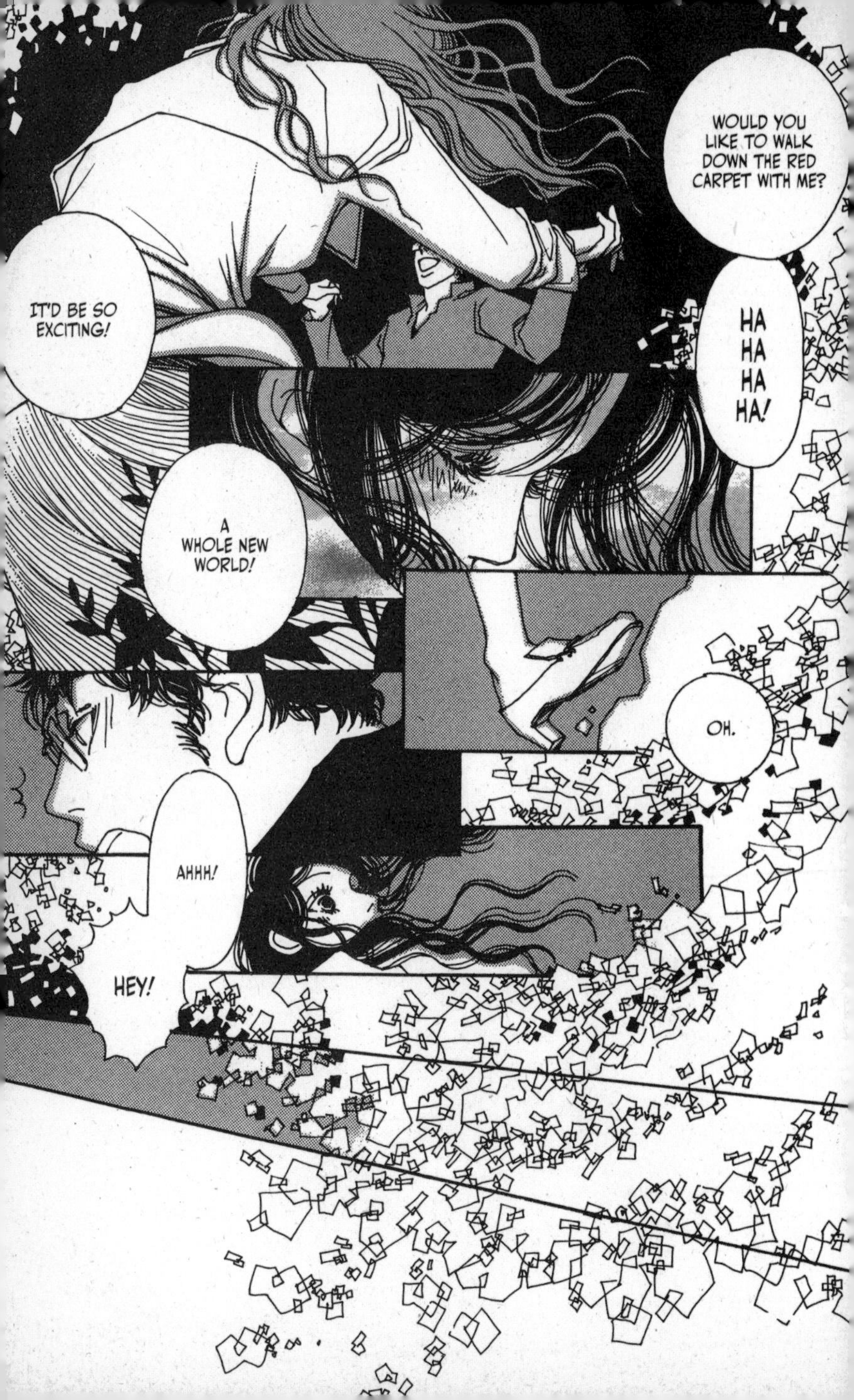
WOULD YOU LIKE TO WALK DOWN THE RED CARPET WITH ME?
IT'D BE SO EXCITING!
HA HA HA HA!
A WHOLE NEW WORLD!
OH.
AHHH!
HEY!

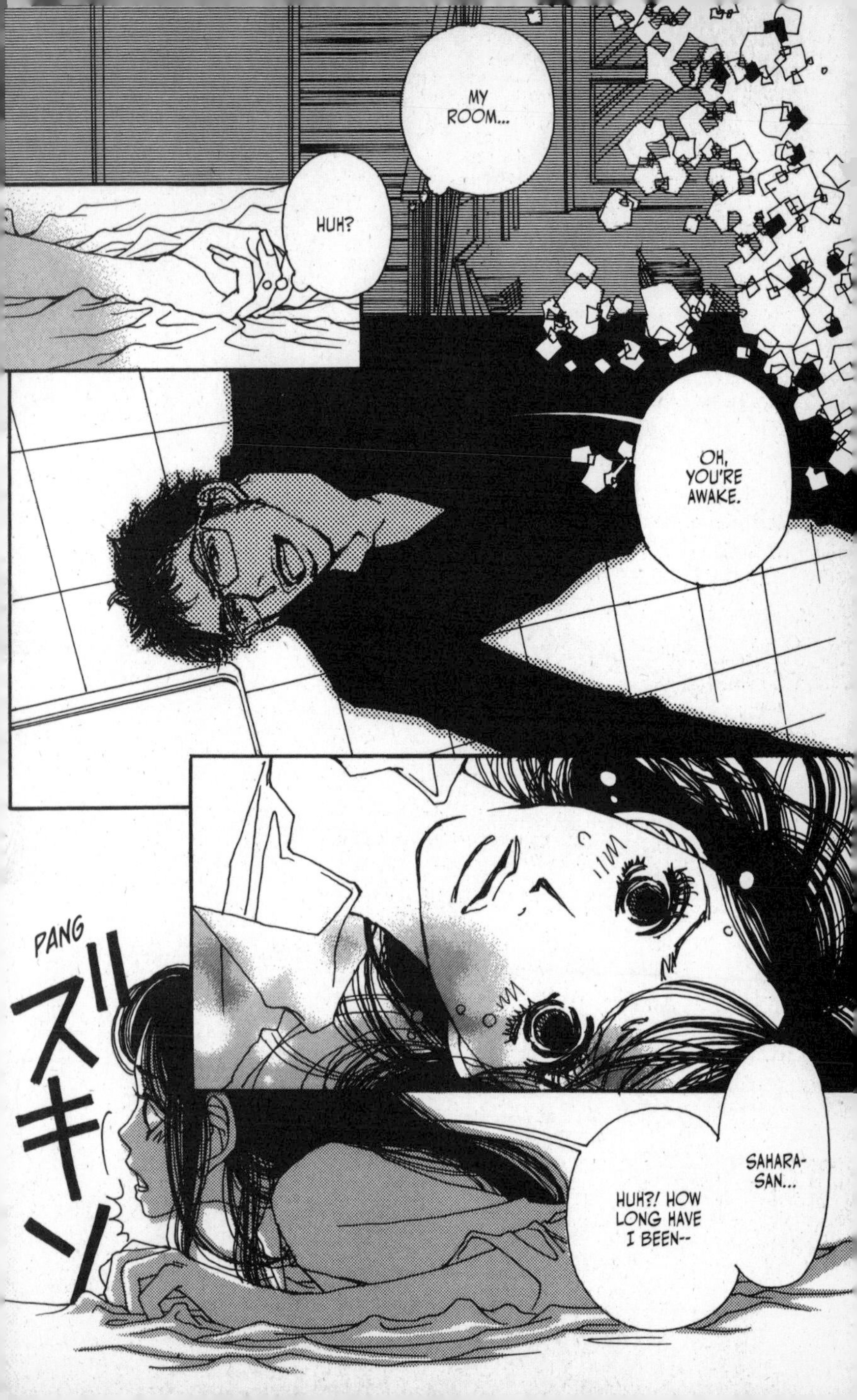
MY ROOM...
HUH?
OH, YOU'RE AWAKE.
SAHARA-SAN...
HUH?! HOW LONG HAVE I BEEN--
PANG
ズキン

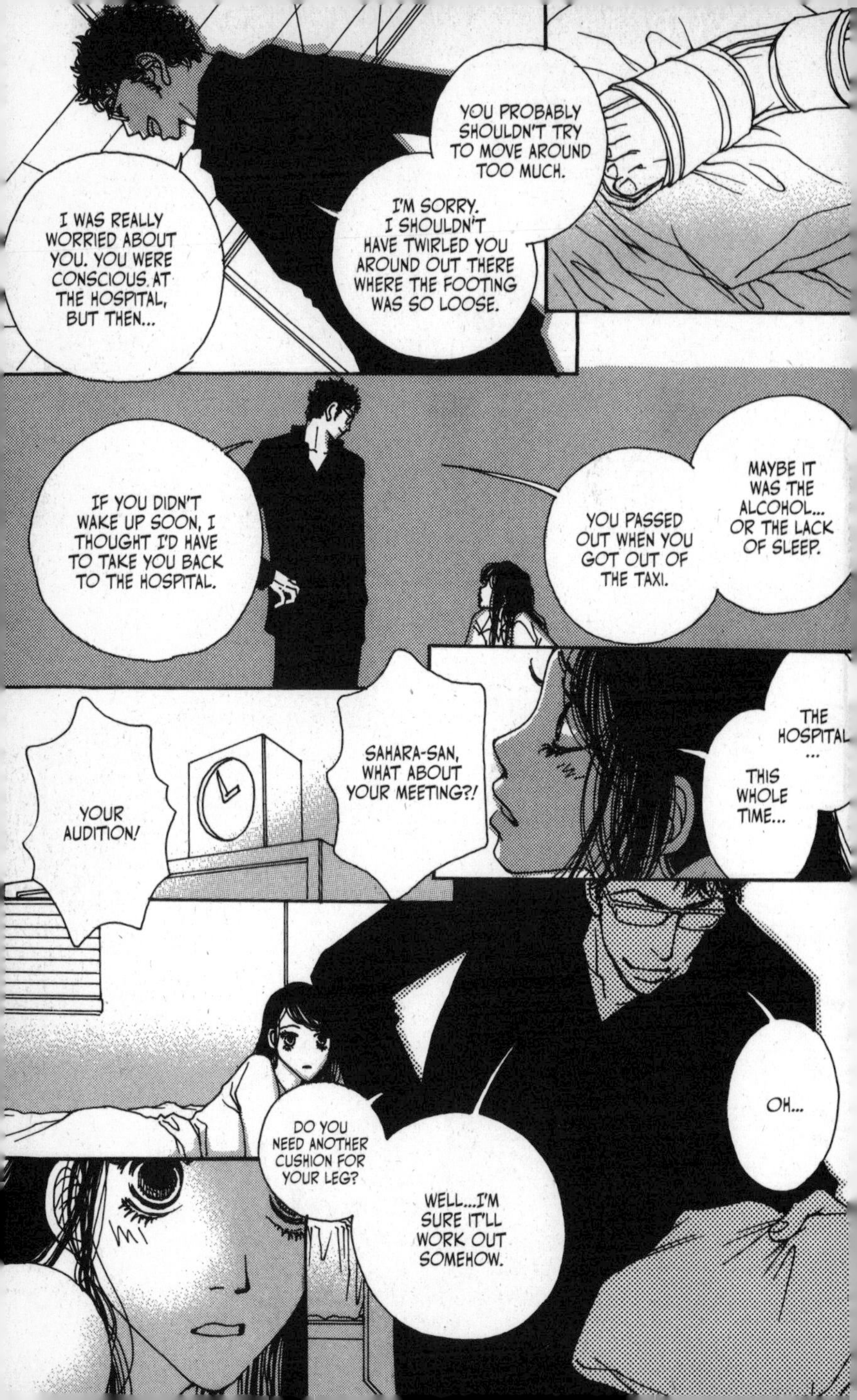
YOU PROBABLY SHOULDN'T TRY TO MOVE AROUND TOO MUCH.
I'M SORRY. I SHOULDN'T HAVE TWIRLED YOU AROUND OUT THERE WHERE THE FOOTING WAS SO LOOSE.
I WAS REALLY WORRIED ABOUT YOU. YOU WERE CONSCIOUS AT THE HOSPITAL, BUT THEN...
MAYBE IT WAS THE ALCOHOL... OR THE LACK OF SLEEP.
YOU PASSED OUT WHEN YOU GOT OUT OF THE TAXI.
IF YOU DIDN'T WAKE UP SOON, I THOUGHT I'D HAVE TO TAKE YOU BACK TO THE HOSPITAL.
THE HOSPITAL...
THIS WHOLE TIME...
SAHARA-SAN, WHAT ABOUT YOUR MEETING?!
YOUR AUDITION!
OH...
DO YOU NEED ANOTHER CUSHION FOR YOUR LEG?
WELL...I'M SURE IT'LL WORK OUT SOMEHOW.

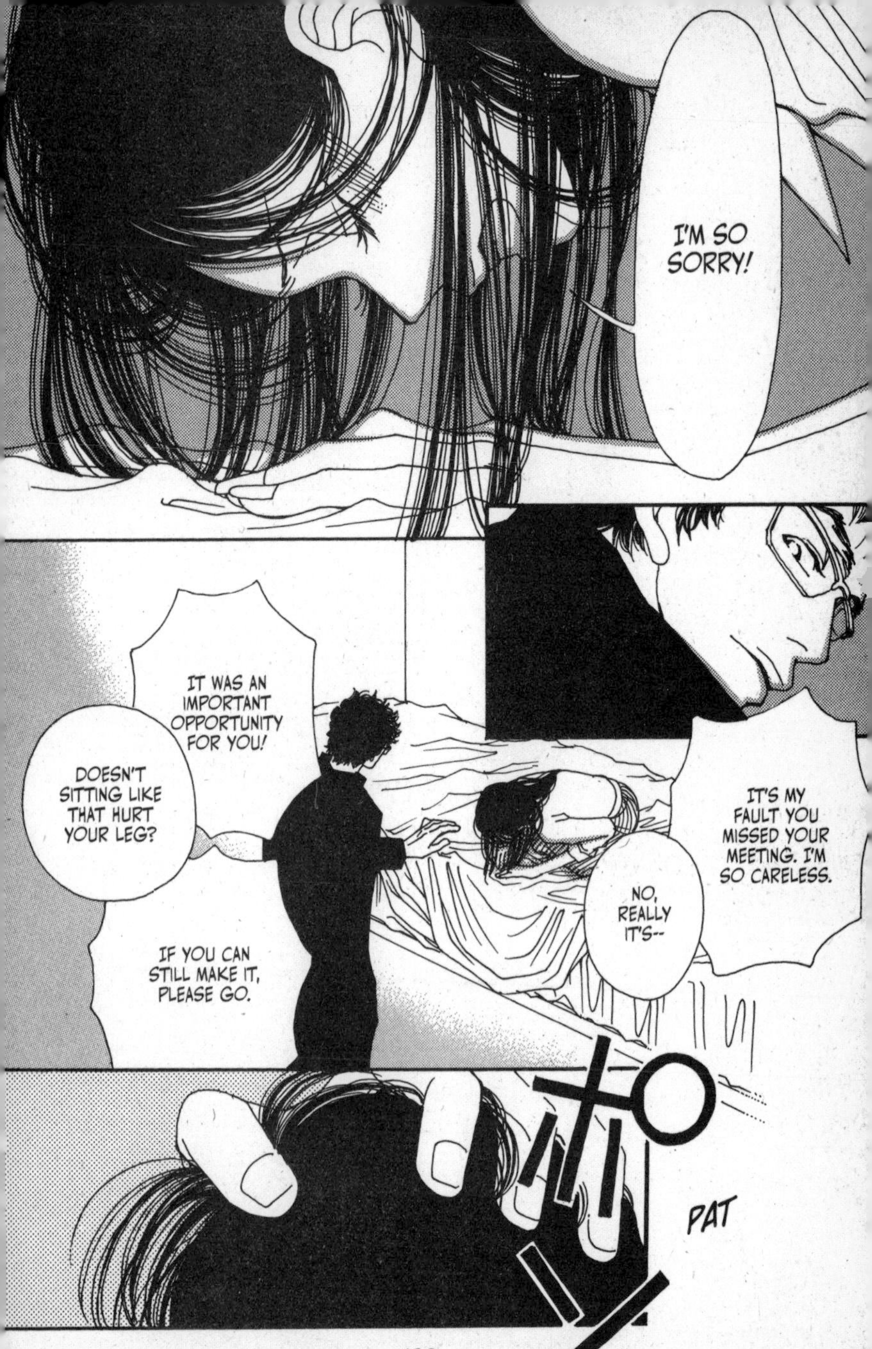
I'M SO SORRY!
IT'S MY FAULT YOU MISSED YOUR MEETING. I'M SO CARELESS.
NO, REALLY IT'S--
IT WAS AN IMPORTANT OPPORTUNITY FOR YOU!
DOESN'T SITTING LIKE THAT HURT YOUR LEG?
IF YOU CAN STILL MAKE IT, PLEASE GO.
PAT

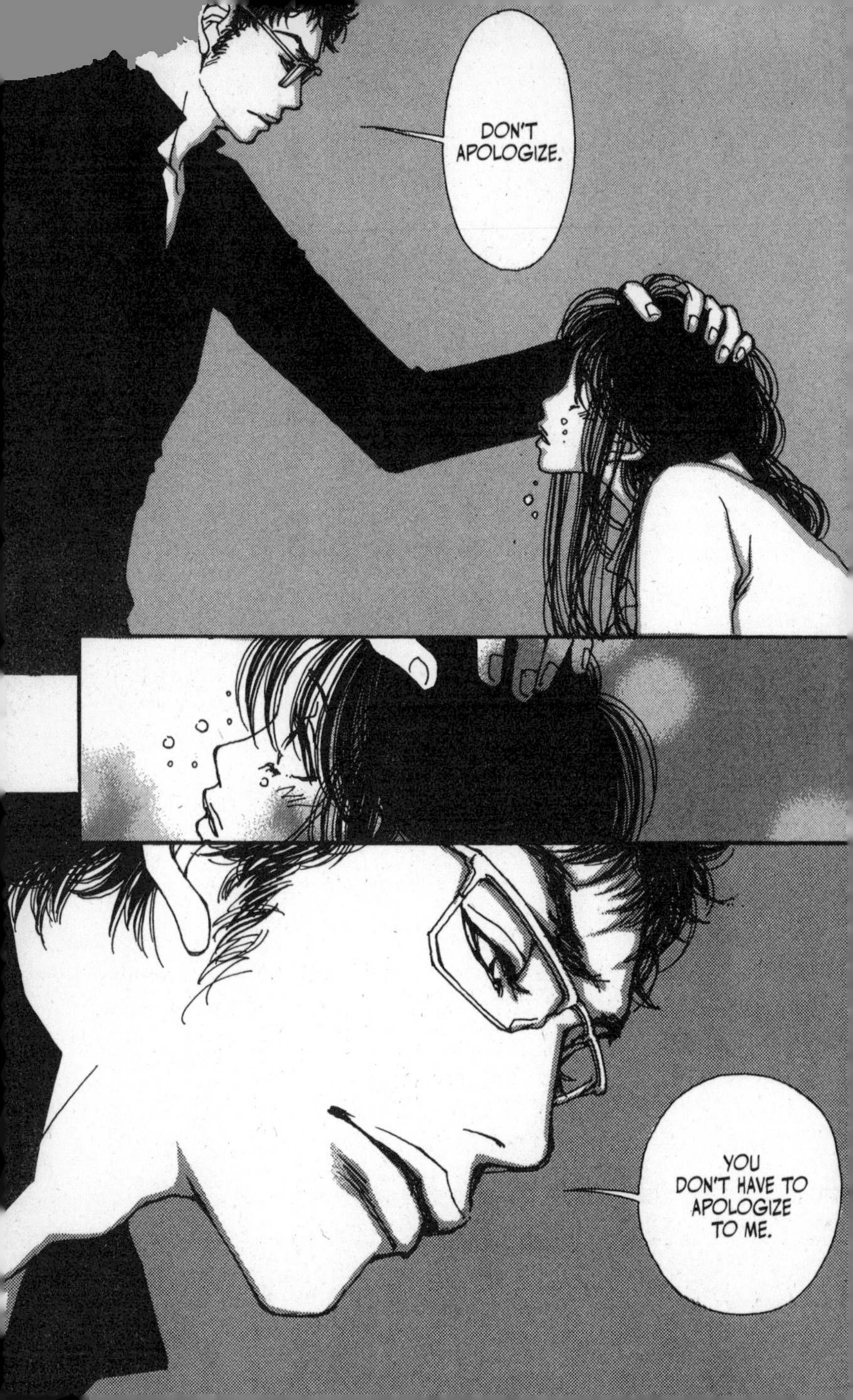
DON'T APOLOGIZE.
YOU DON'T HAVE TO APOLOGIZE TO ME.

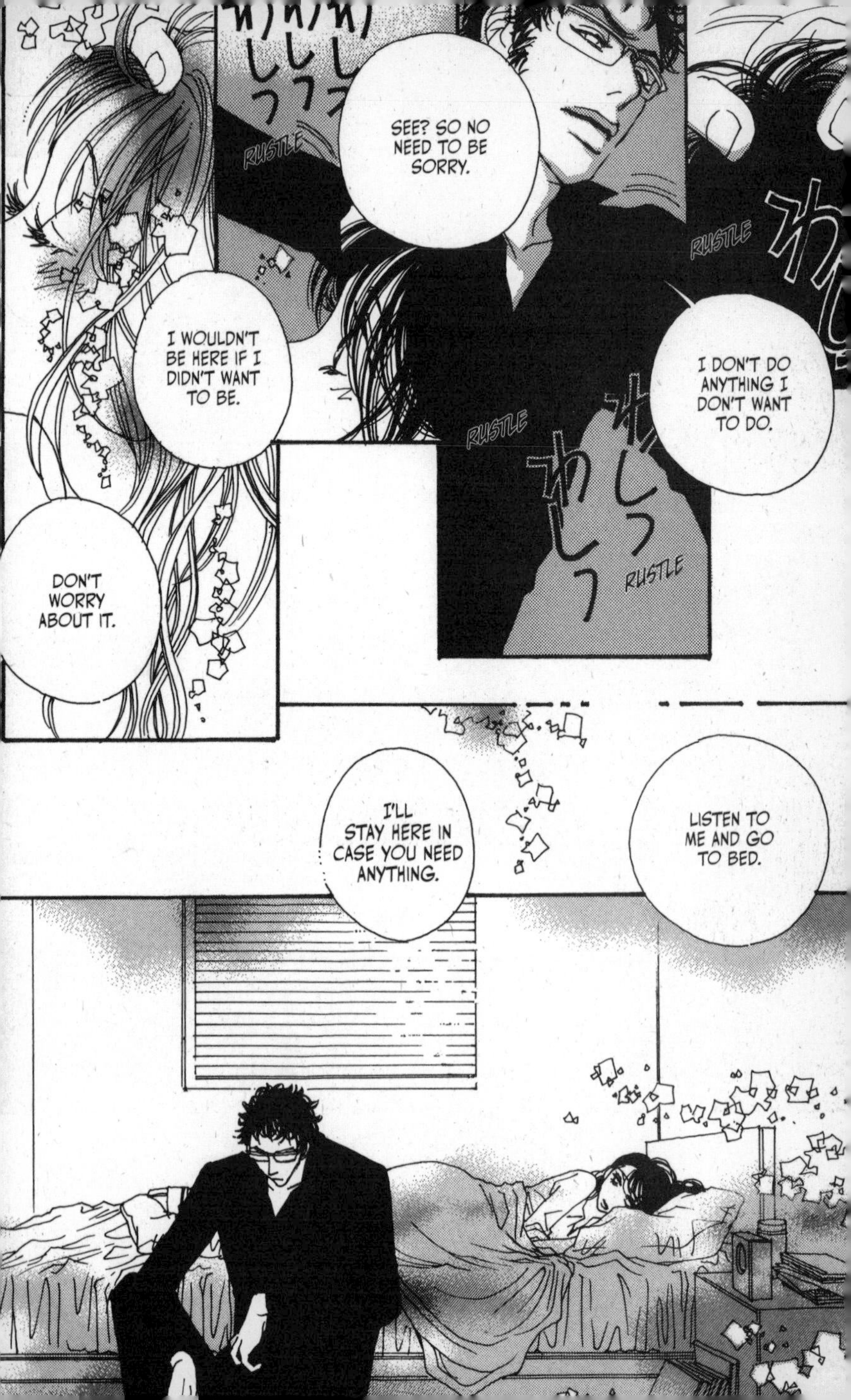
RUSTLE
I DON'T DO ANYTHING I DON'T WANT TO DO.
SEE? SO NO NEED TO BE SORRY.
RUSTLE
RUSTLE
RUSTLE
I WOULDN'T BE HERE IF I DIDN'T WANT TO BE.
DON'T WORRY ABOUT IT.
LISTEN TO ME AND GO TO BED.
I'LL STAY HERE IN CASE YOU NEED ANYTHING.

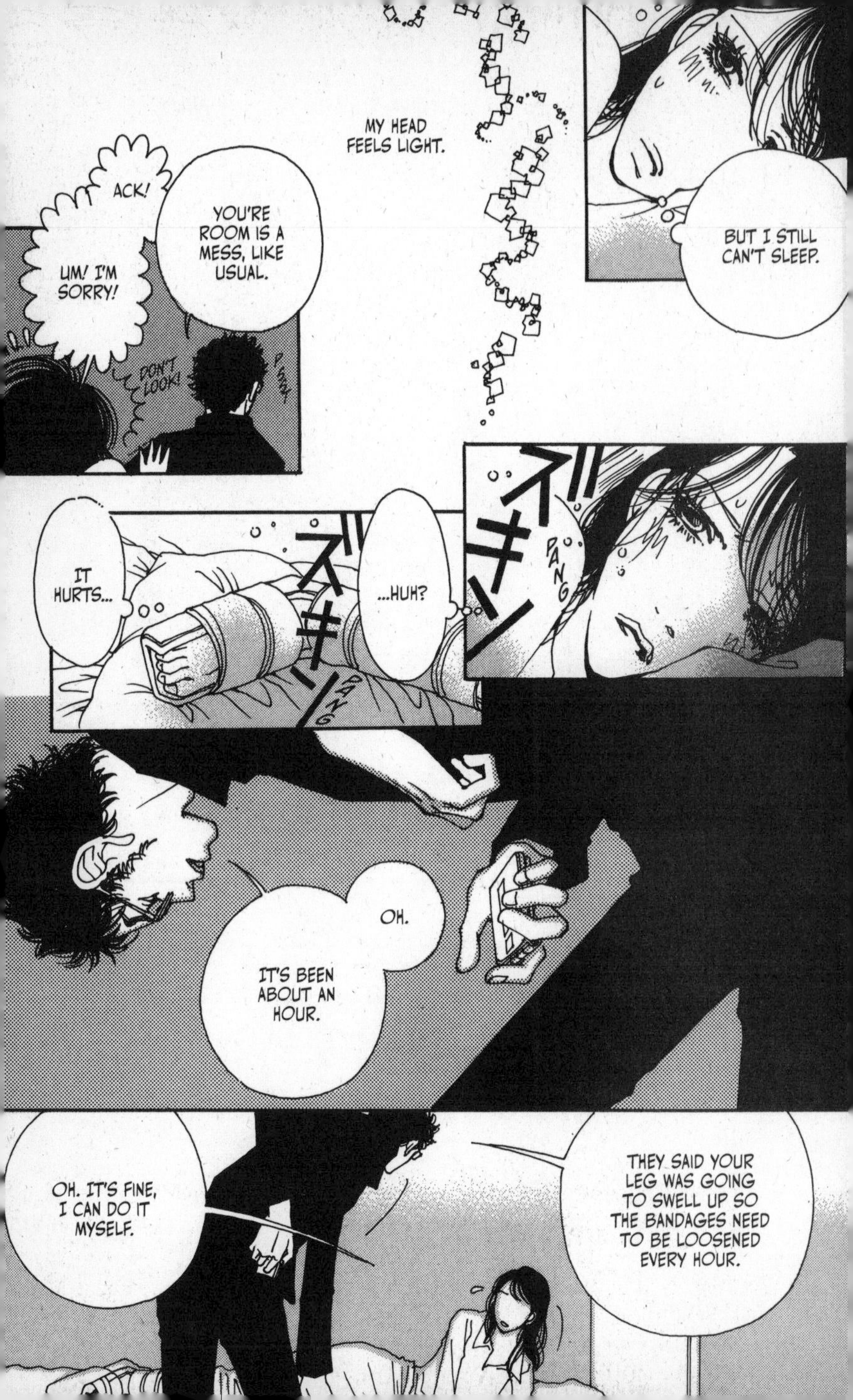
MY HEAD FEELS LIGHT.
BUT I STILL CAN'T SLEEP.
YOU'RE ROOM IS A MESS, LIKE USUAL.
ACK!
UM! I'M SORRY!
DON'T LOOK!
PANG
...HUH?
IT HURTS...
PANG
OH.
IT'S BEEN ABOUT AN HOUR.
THEY SAID YOUR LEG WAS GOING TO SWELL UP SO THE BANDAGES NEED TO BE LOOSENED EVERY HOUR.
OH. IT'S FINE, I CAN DO IT MYSELF.

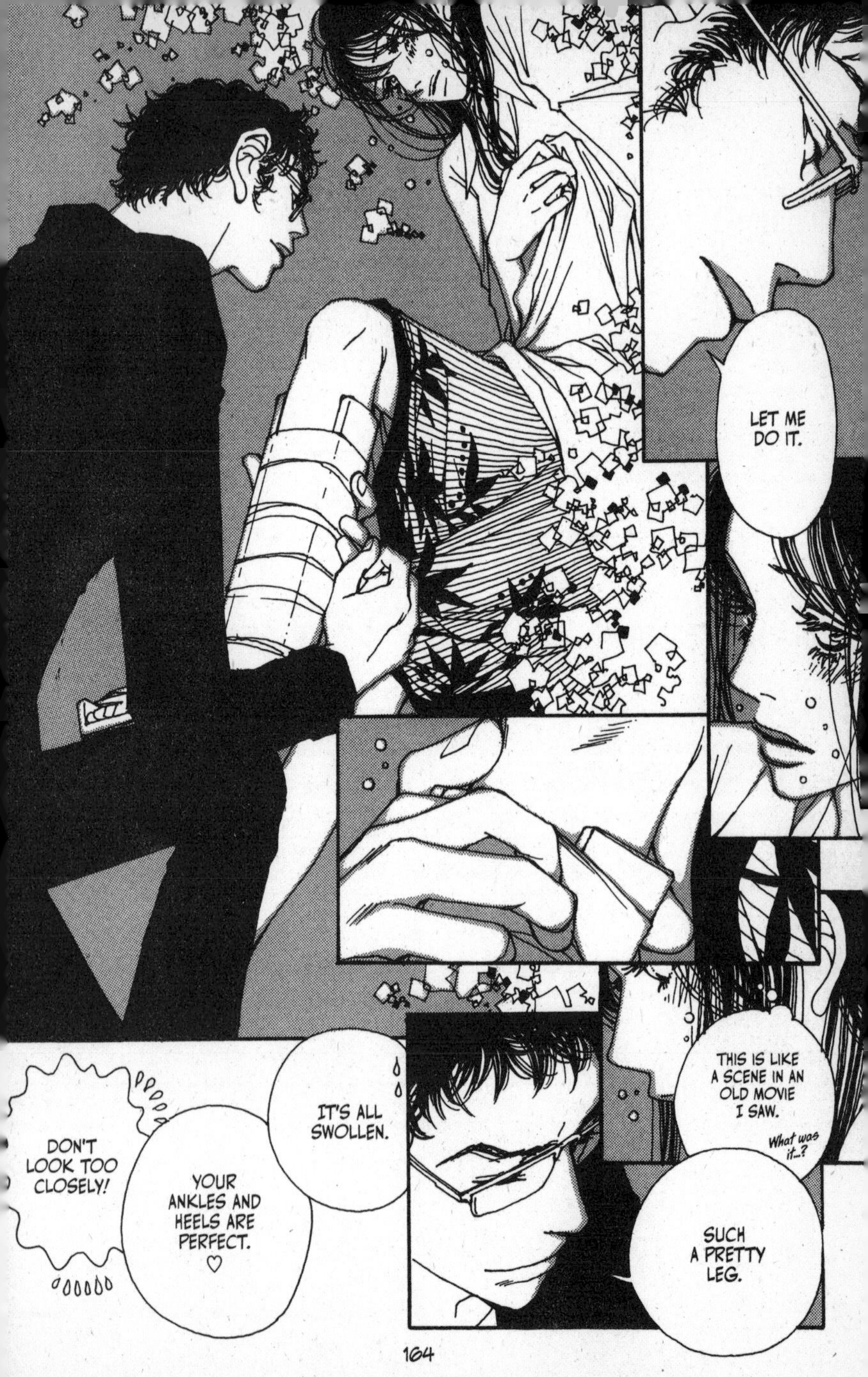
LET ME DO IT.
THIS IS LIKE A SCENE IN AN OLD MOVIE I SAW.
What was it...?
SUCH A PRETTY LEG.
IT'S ALL SWOLLEN.
YOUR ANKLES AND HEELS ARE PERFECT. ♡
DON'T LOOK TOO CLOSELY!

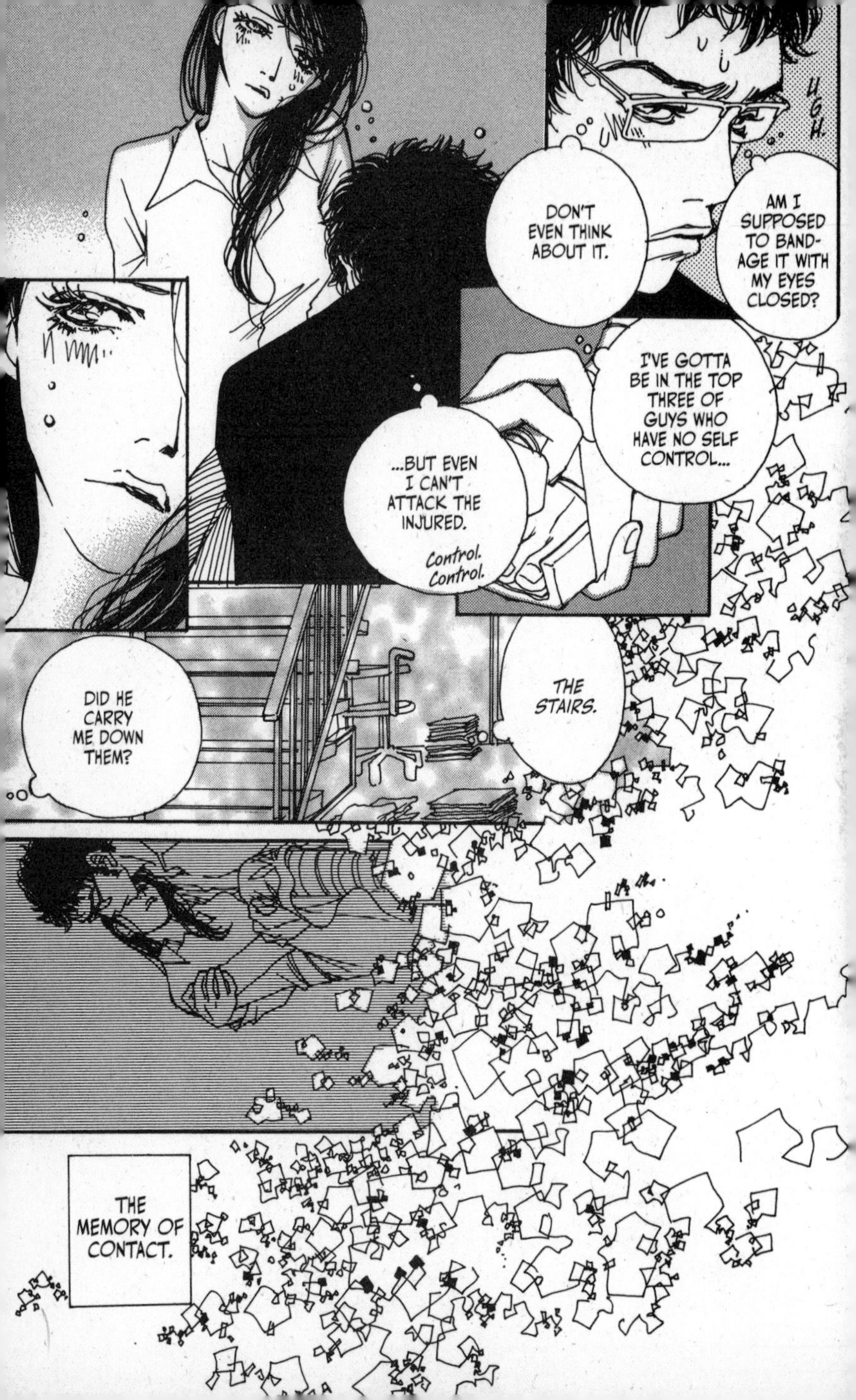
UGH.
AM I SUPPOSED TO BAND-AGE IT WITH MY EYES CLOSED?
DON'T EVEN THINK ABOUT IT.
I'VE GOTTA BE IN THE TOP THREE OF GUYS WHO HAVE NO SELF CONTROL...
...BUT EVEN I CAN'T ATTACK THE INJURED.
Control. Control.
THE STAIRS.
DID HE CARRY ME DOWN THEM?
THE MEMORY OF CONTACT.

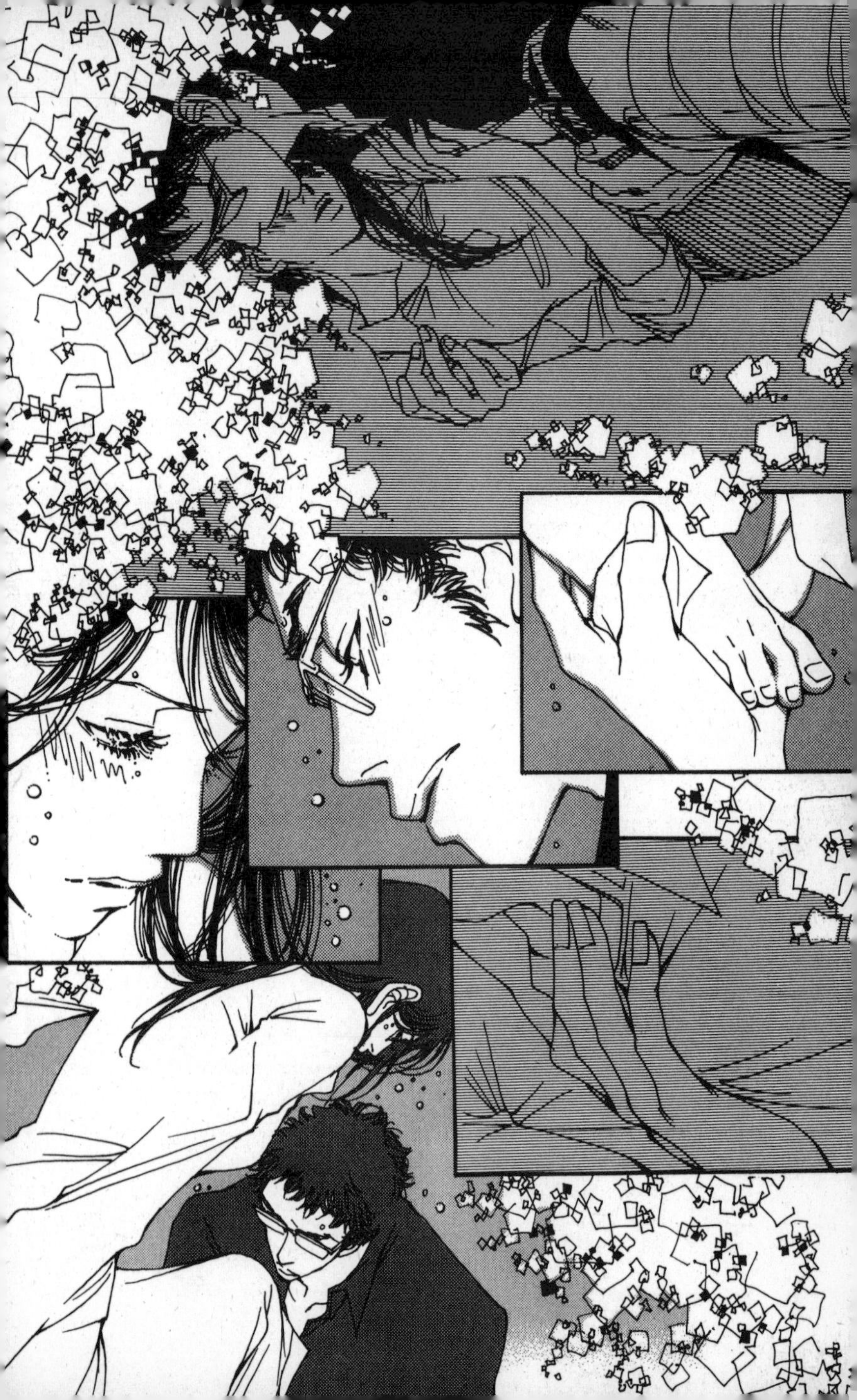

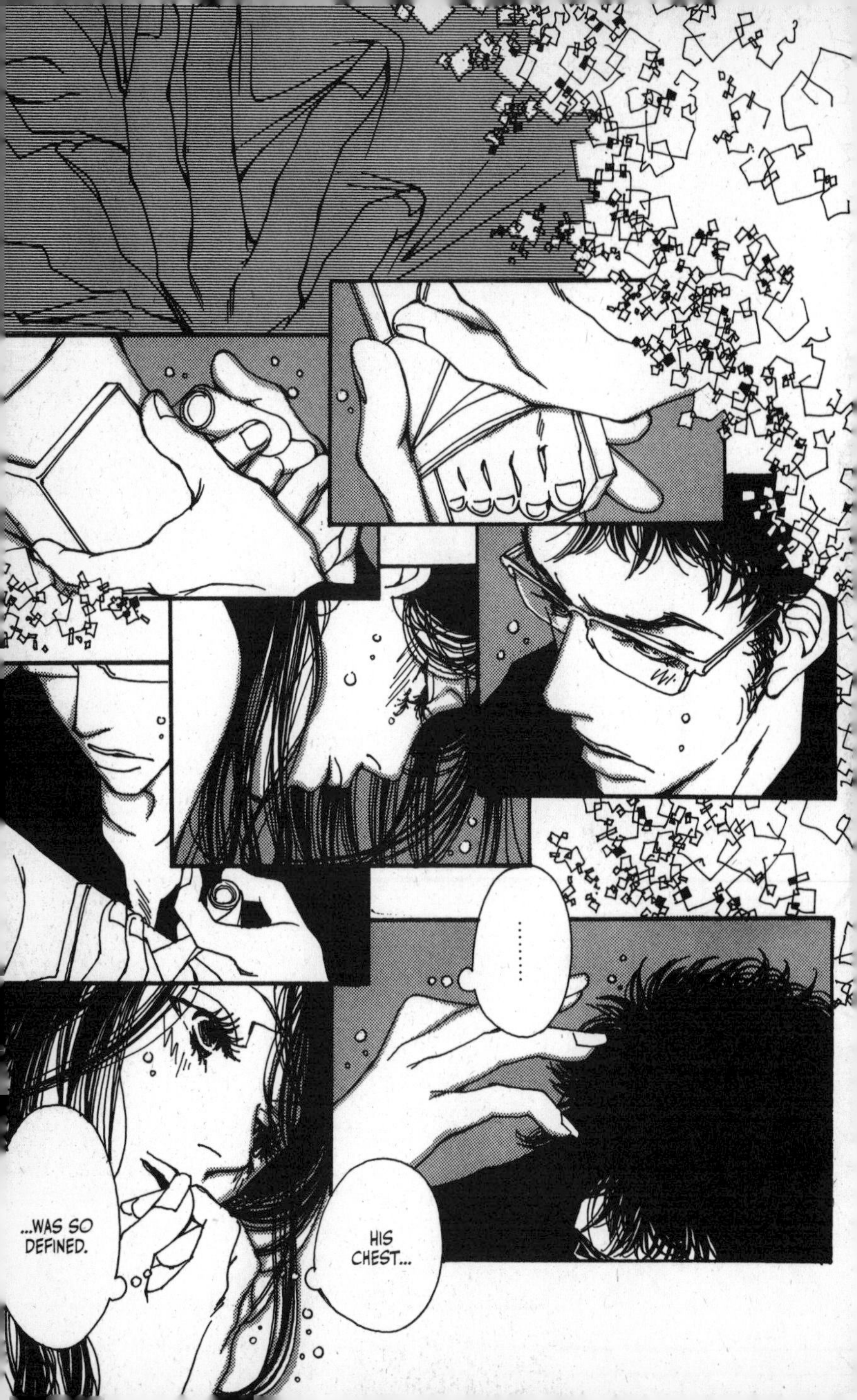
......
HIS CHEST...
...WAS SO DEFINED.

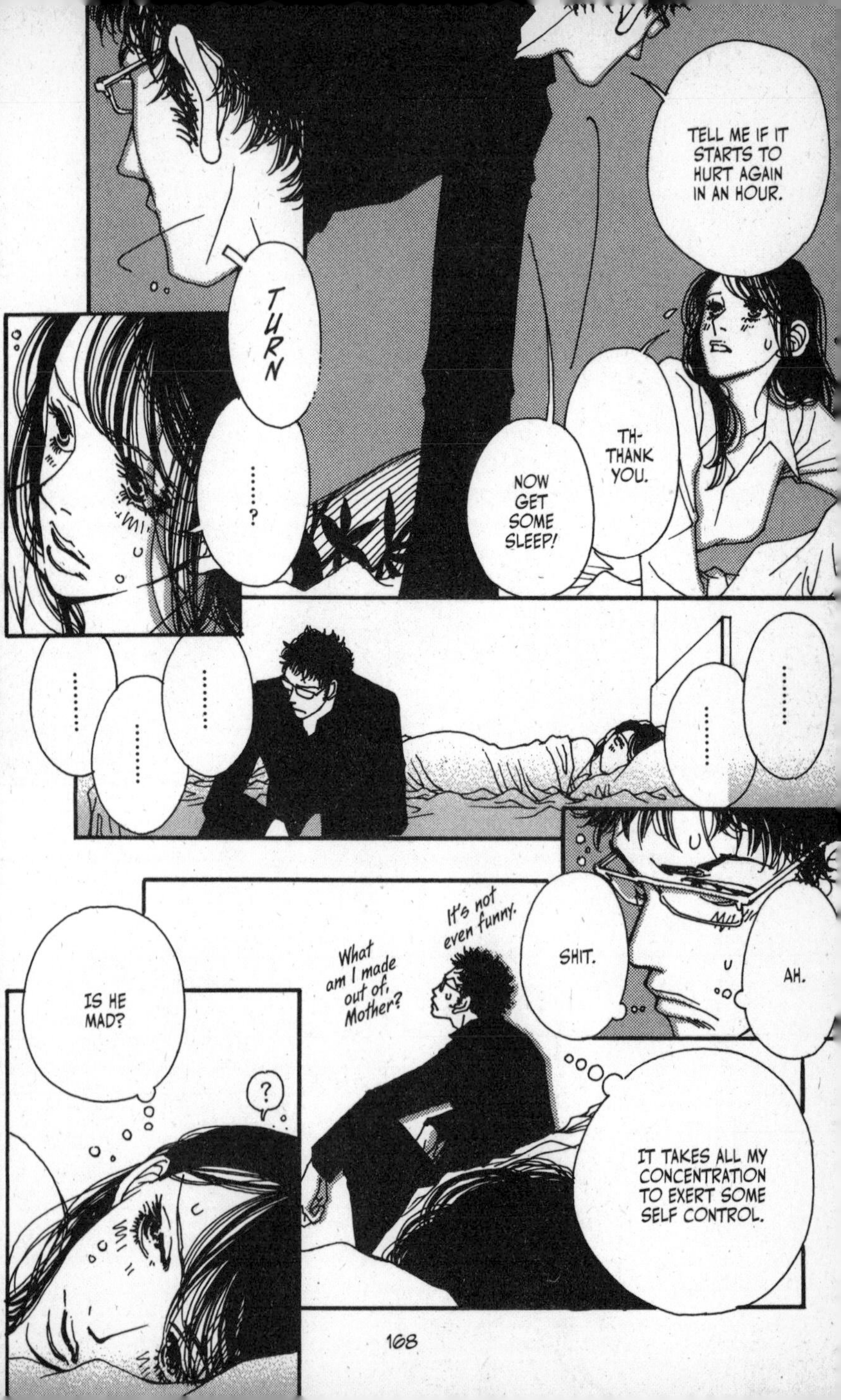
TELL ME IF IT STARTS TO HURT AGAIN IN AN HOUR.
TH- THANK YOU.
NOW GET SOME SLEEP!
TURN
......?
....
....
....
....
....
AH.
SHIT.
IT TAKES ALL MY CONCENTRATION TO EXERT SOME SELF CONTROL.
It's not even funny.
What am I made out of, Mother?
IS HE MAD?
?

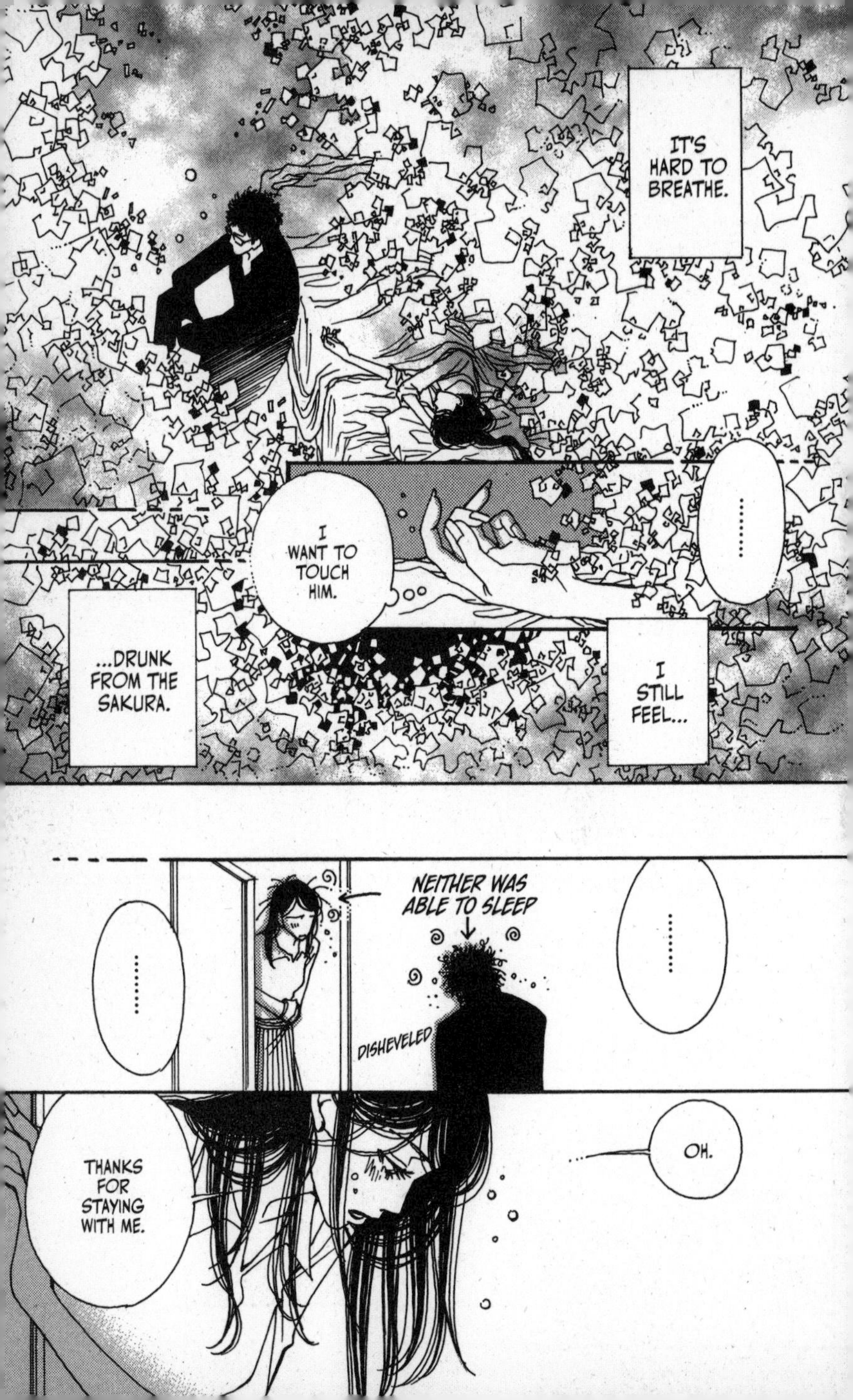
IT'S HARD TO BREATHE.
......
I WANT TO TOUCH HIM.
I STILL FEEL...
...DRUNK FROM THE SAKURA.
......
NEITHER WAS ABLE TO SLEEP
DISHEVELED
......
...OH.
THANKS FOR STAYING WITH ME.

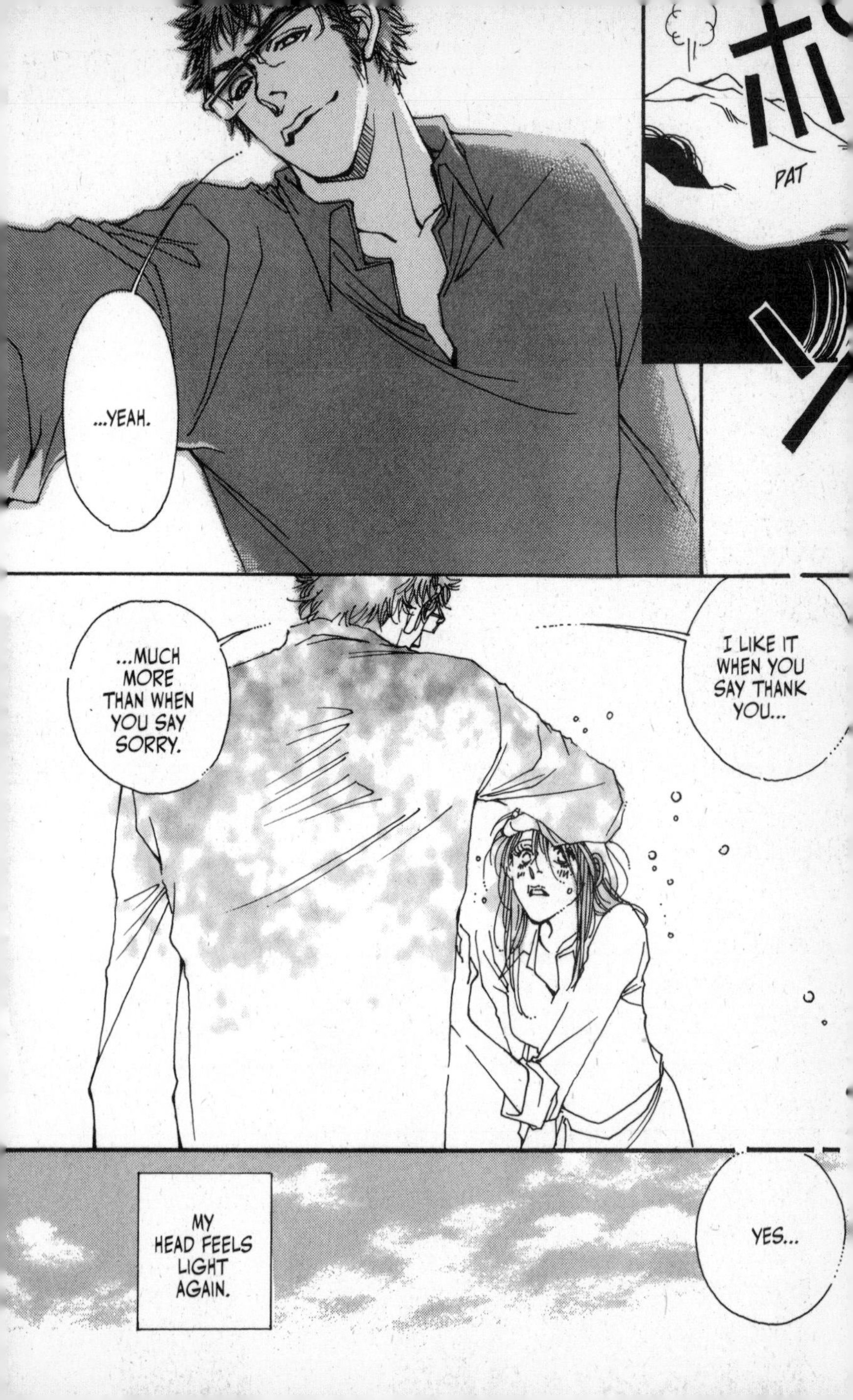
ポン
PAT
...YEAH.
I LIKE IT WHEN YOU SAY THANK YOU...
...MUCH MORE THAN WHEN YOU SAY SORRY.
YES...
MY HEAD FEELS LIGHT AGAIN.

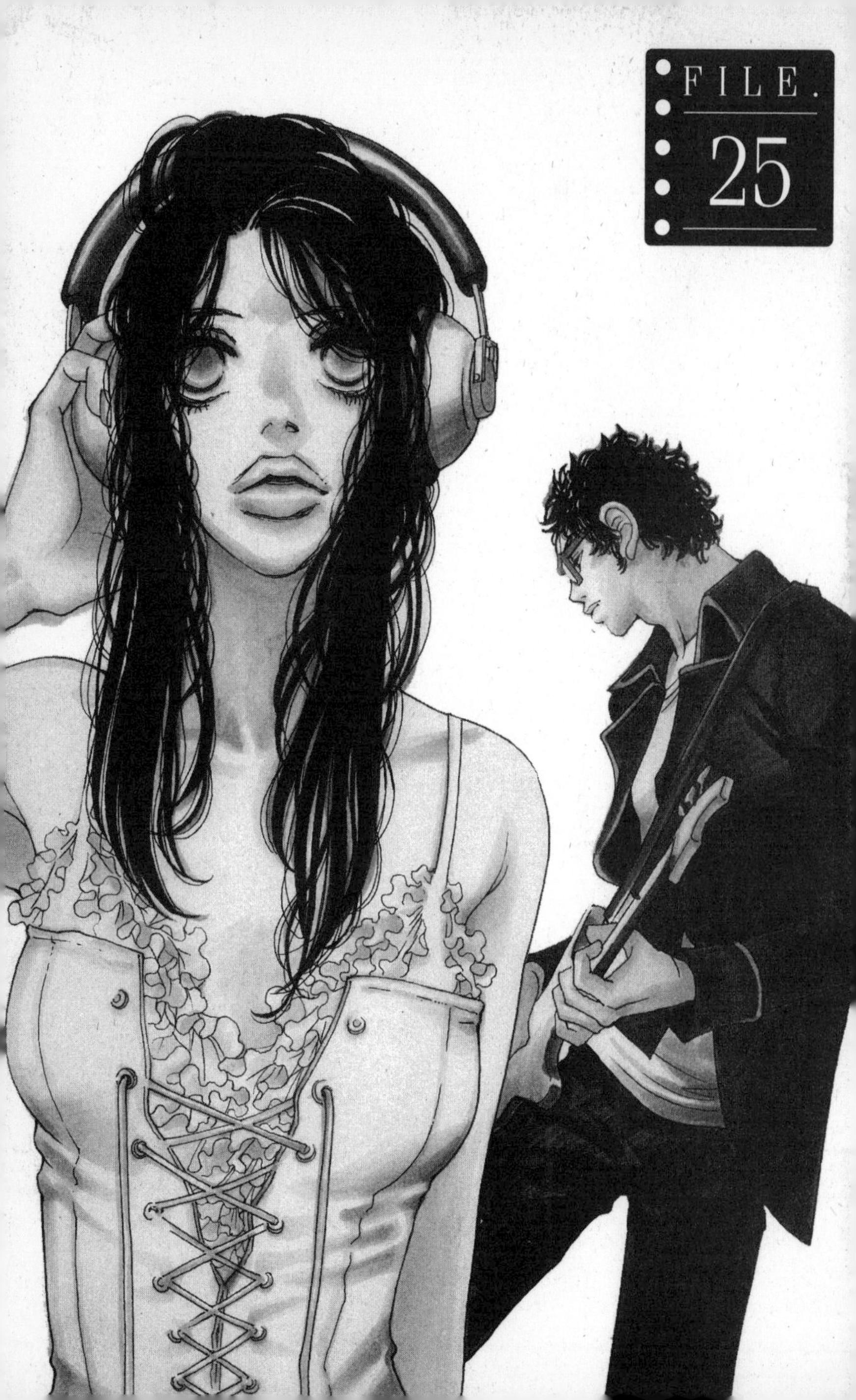
FILE. 25

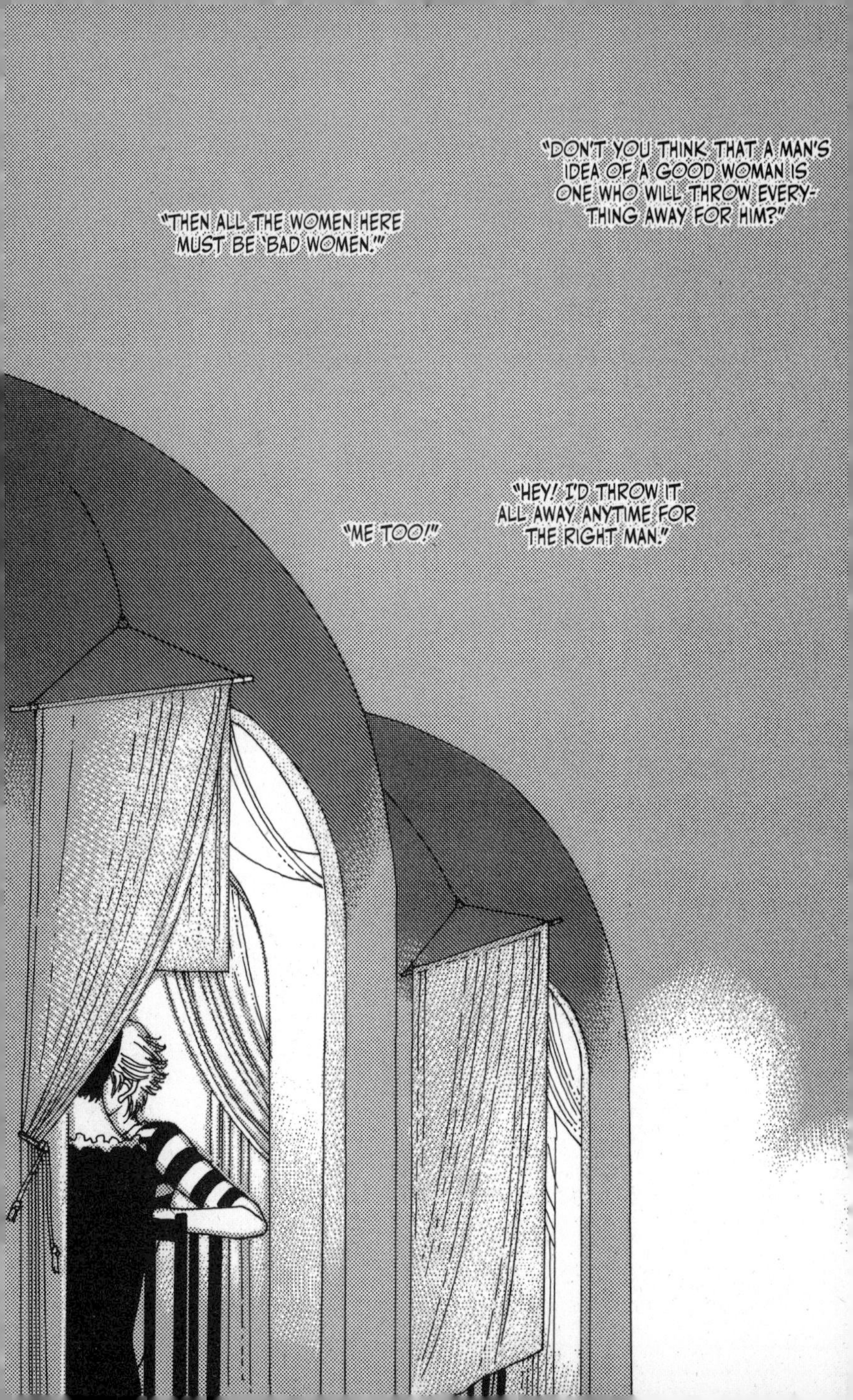
"DON'T YOU THINK THAT A MAN'S IDEA OF A GOOD WOMAN IS ONE WHO WILL THROW EVERY-THING AWAY FOR HIM?"
"THEN ALL THE WOMEN HERE MUST BE 'BAD WOMEN.'"
"HEY! I'D THROW IT ALL AWAY ANYTIME FOR THE RIGHT MAN."
"ME TOO!"

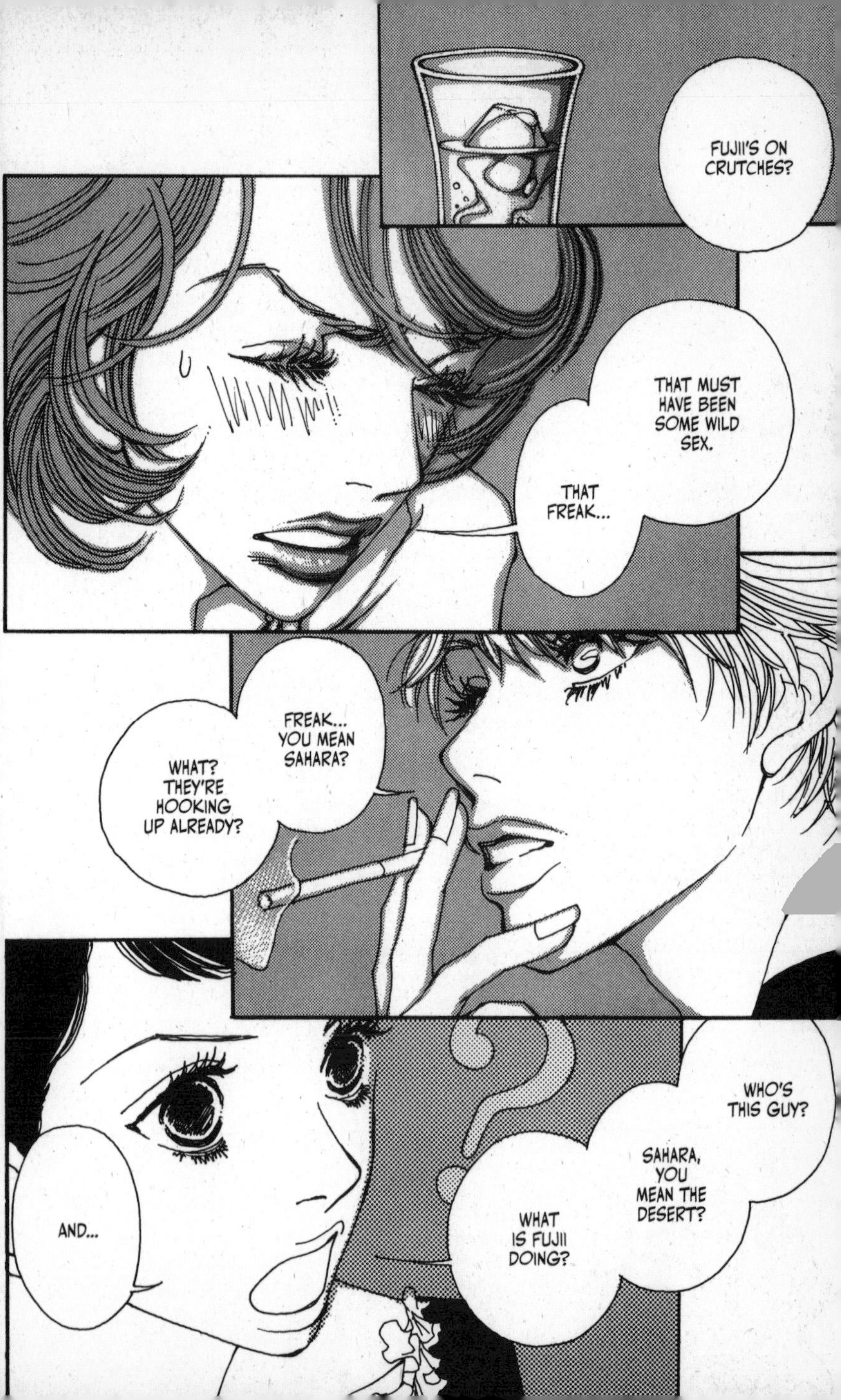
FUJII'S ON CRUTCHES?
THAT MUST HAVE BEEN SOME WILD SEX.
THAT FREAK...
FREAK... YOU MEAN SAHARA?
WHAT? THEY'RE HOOKING UP ALREADY?
WHO'S THIS GUY?
SAHARA, YOU MEAN THE DESERT?
WHAT IS FUJII DOING?
AND...

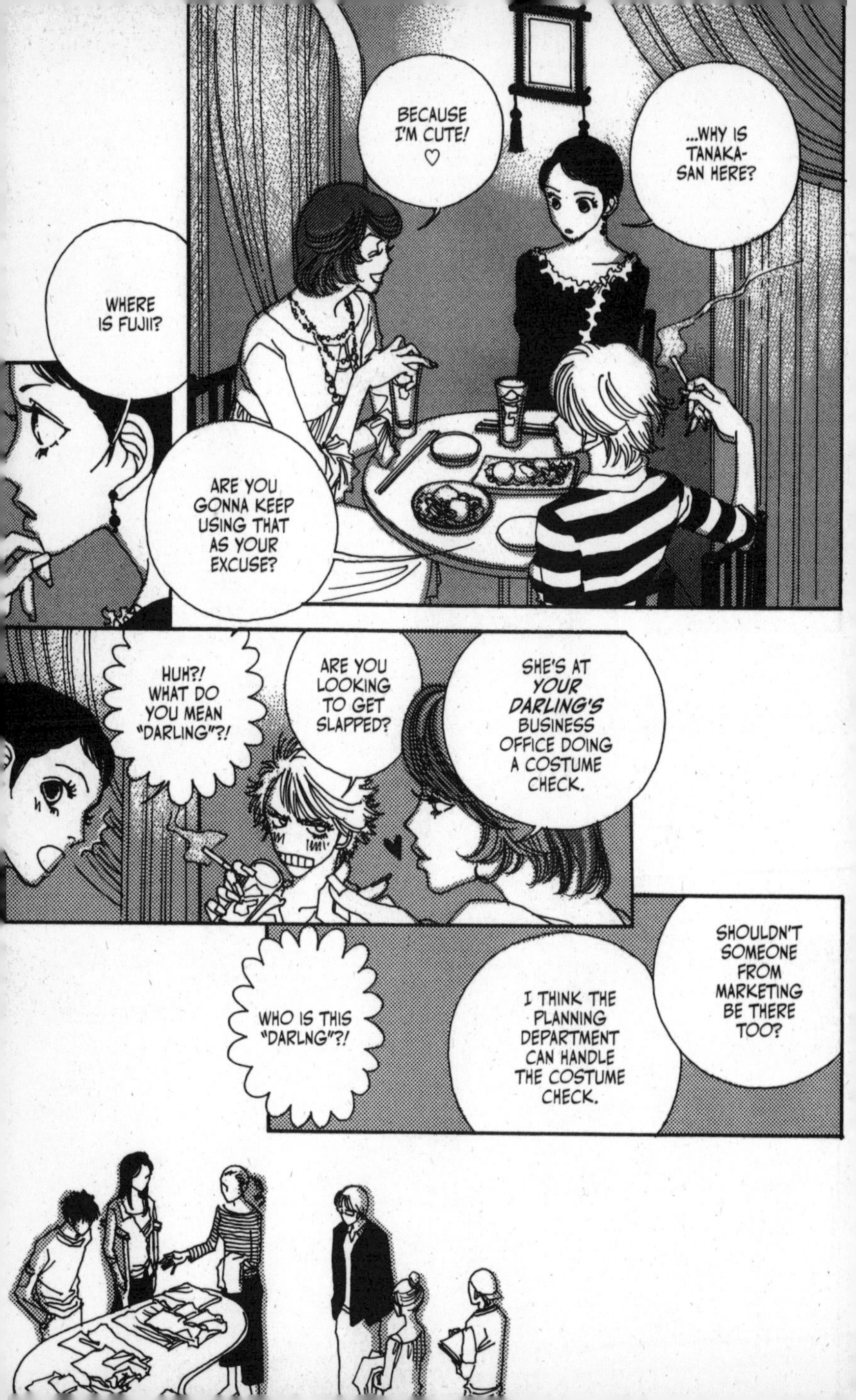
...WHY IS TANAKA-SAN HERE?
BECAUSE I'M CUTE! ♡
WHERE IS FUJII?
ARE YOU GONNA KEEP USING THAT AS YOUR EXCUSE?
SHE'S AT *YOUR DARLING'S* BUSINESS OFFICE DOING A COSTUME CHECK.
ARE YOU LOOKING TO GET SLAPPED?
HUH?! WHAT DO YOU MEAN "DARLING"?!
SHOULDN'T SOMEONE FROM MARKETING BE THERE TOO?
I THINK THE PLANNING DEPARTMENT CAN HANDLE THE COSTUME CHECK.
WHO IS THIS "DARLNG"?!

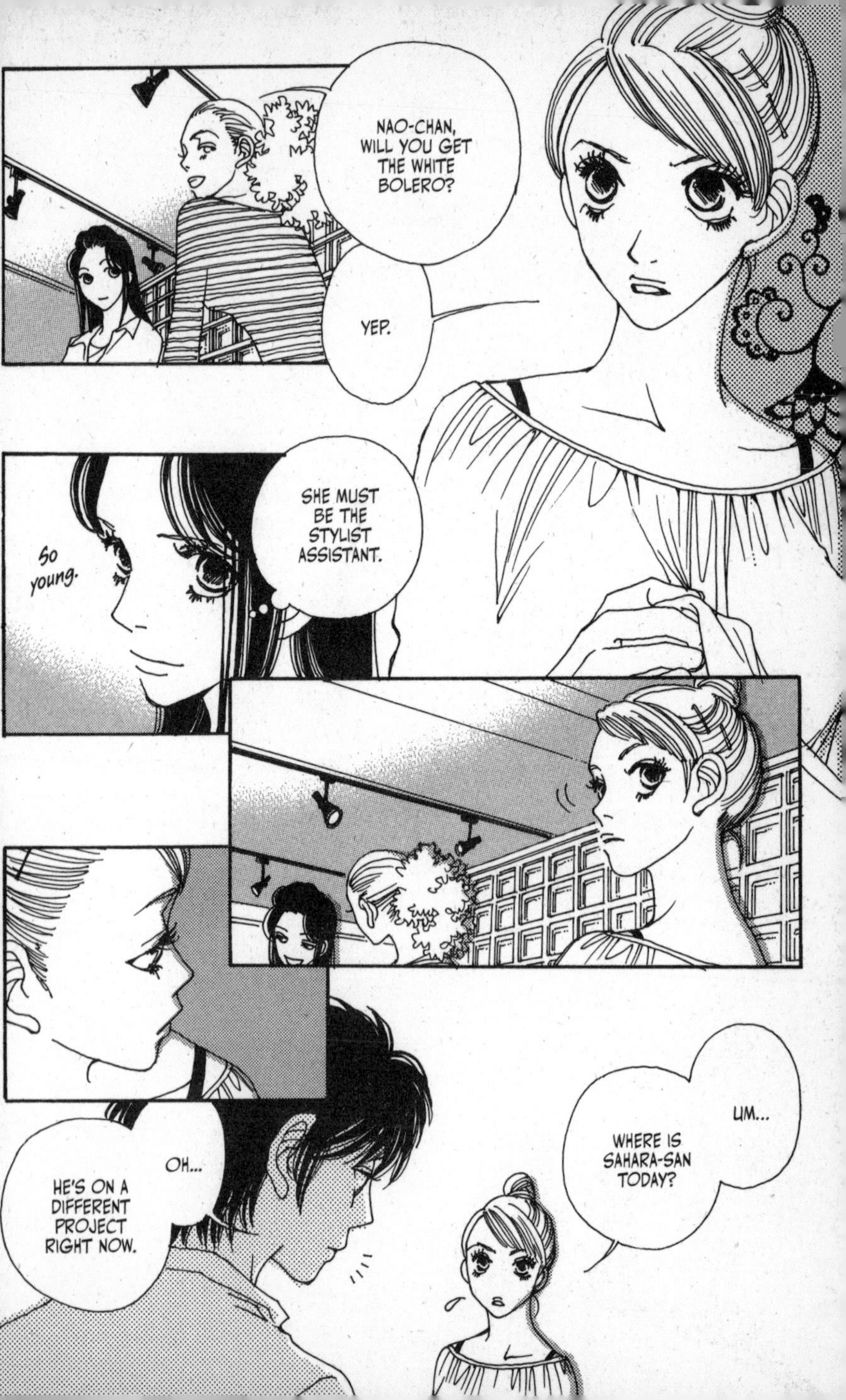
NAO-CHAN, WILL YOU GET THE WHITE BOLERO?
YEP.
SHE MUST BE THE STYLIST ASSISTANT.
So young.
UM...
WHERE IS SAHARA-SAN TODAY?
OH...
HE'S ON A DIFFERENT PROJECT RIGHT NOW.

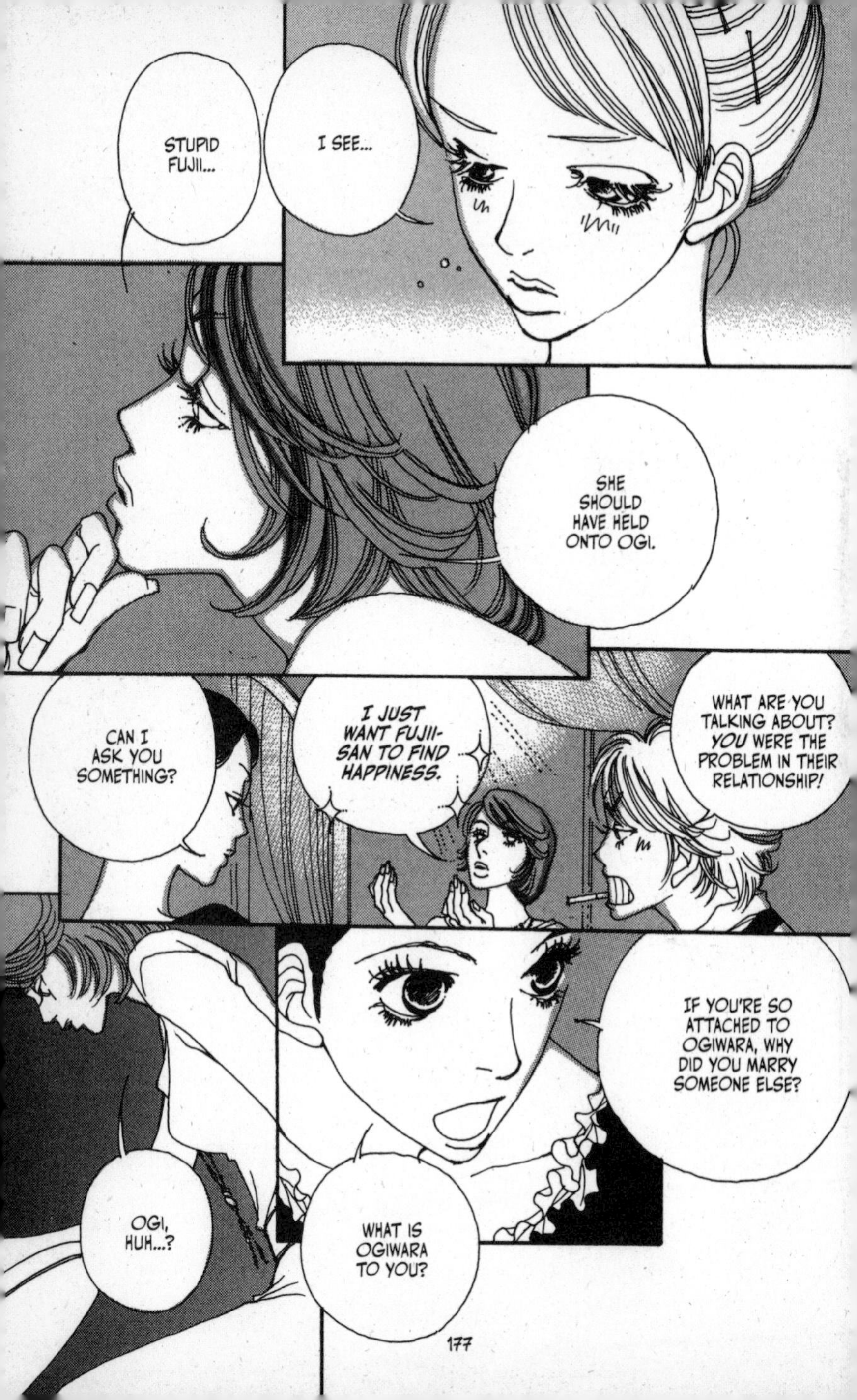
I SEE...
STUPID FUJII...
SHE SHOULD HAVE HELD ONTO OGI.
WHAT ARE YOU TALKING ABOUT? *YOU* WERE THE PROBLEM IN THEIR RELATIONSHIP!
I JUST WANT FUJII-SAN TO FIND HAPPINESS.
CAN I ASK YOU SOMETHING?
IF YOU'RE SO ATTACHED TO OGIWARA, WHY DID YOU MARRY SOMEONE ELSE?
WHAT IS OGIWARA TO YOU?
OGI, HUH...?

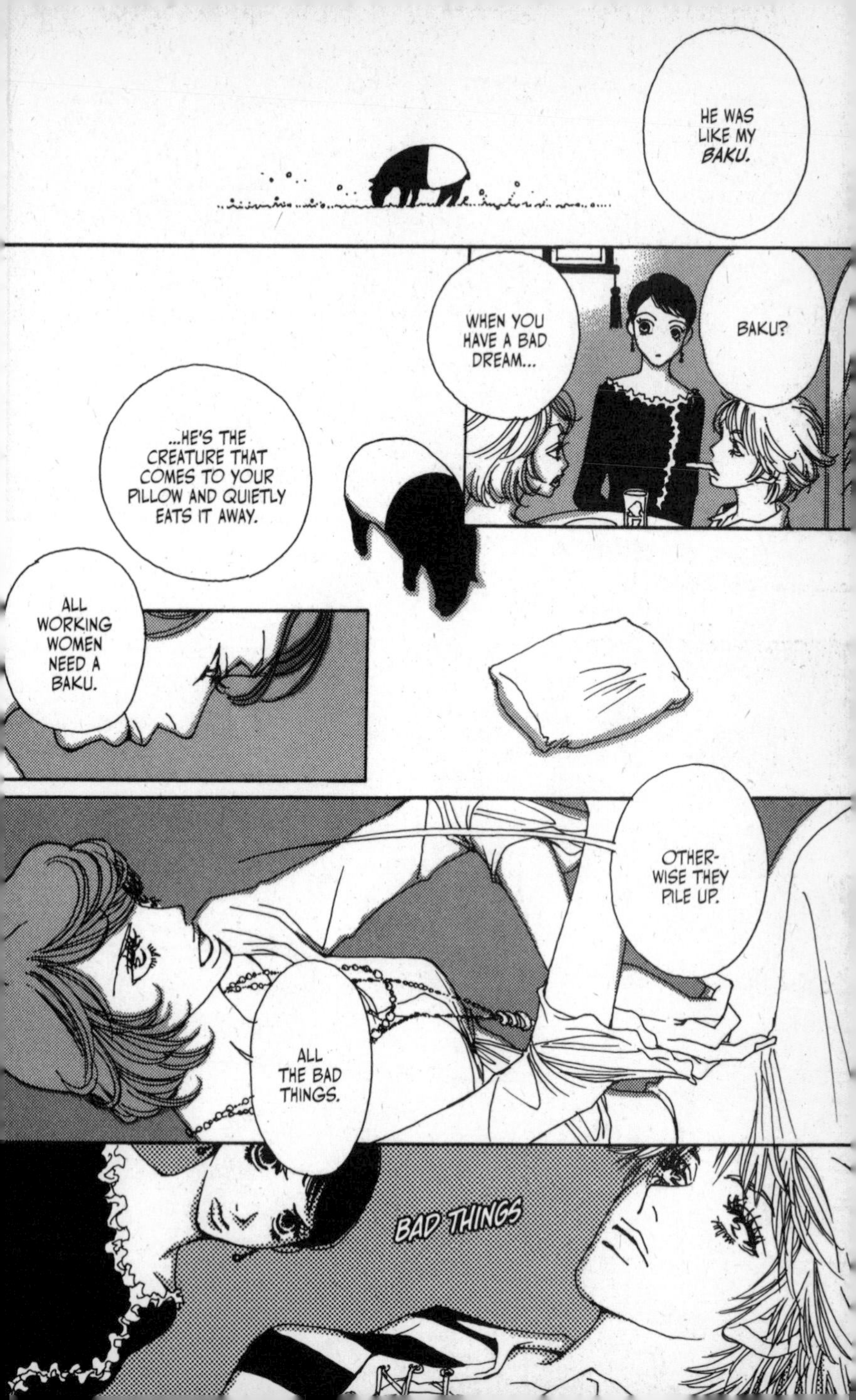
HE WAS LIKE MY BAKU.
BAKU?
WHEN YOU HAVE A BAD DREAM...
...HE'S THE CREATURE THAT COMES TO YOUR PILLOW AND QUIETLY EATS IT AWAY.
ALL WORKING WOMEN NEED A BAKU.
OTHER-WISE THEY PILE UP.
ALL THE BAD THINGS.
BAD THINGS

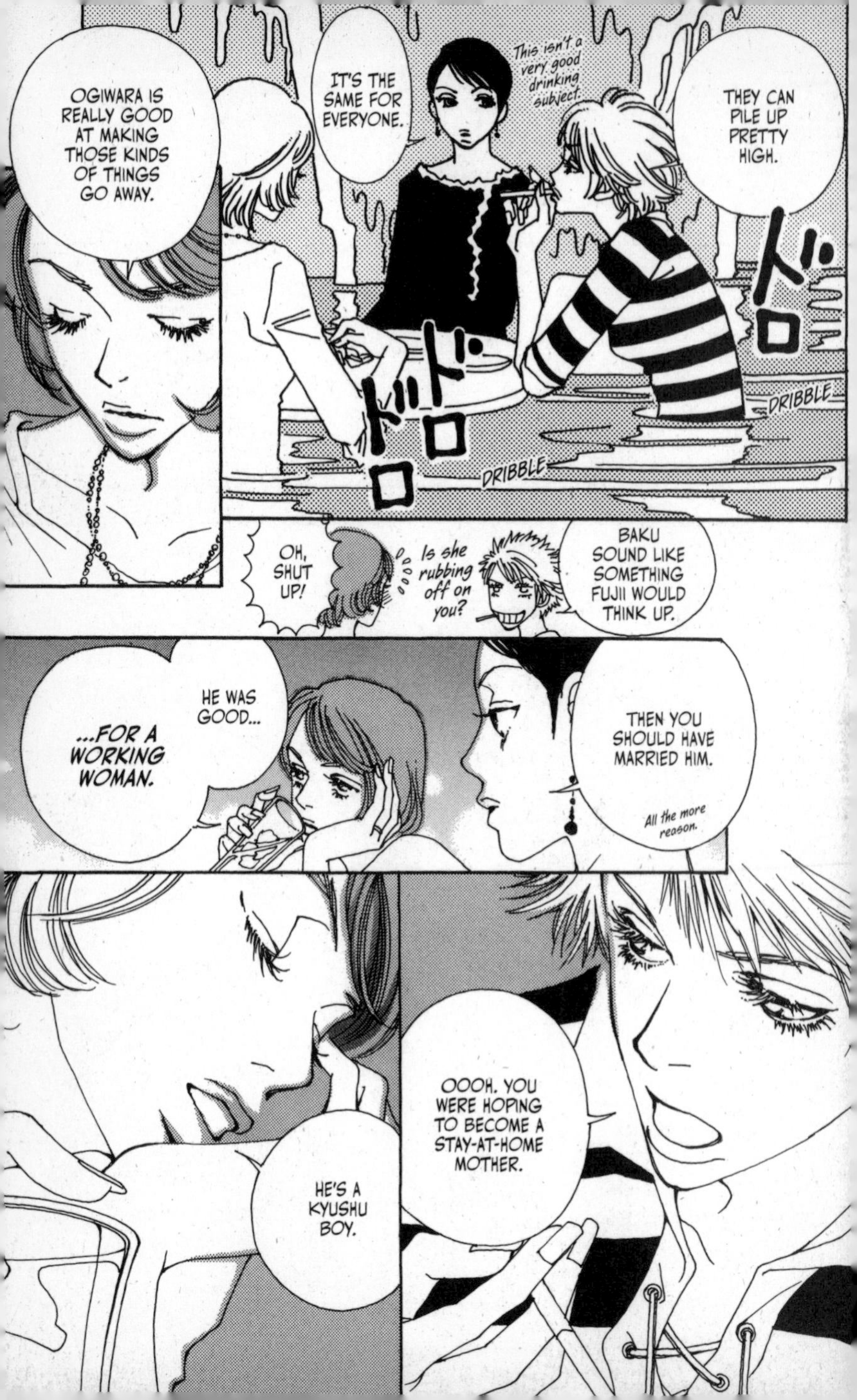
THEY CAN PILE UP PRETTY HIGH.
ドロ
This isn't a very good drinking subject.
IT'S THE SAME FOR EVERYONE.
ドロドロ
DRIBBLE
DRIBBLE
BAKU SOUND LIKE SOMETHING FUJII WOULD THINK UP.
Is she rubbing off on you?
OH, SHUT UP!
OGIWARA IS REALLY GOOD AT MAKING THOSE KINDS OF THINGS GO AWAY.
THEN YOU SHOULD HAVE MARRIED HIM.
All the more reason.
HE WAS GOOD...
...FOR A WORKING WOMAN.
OOOH. YOU WERE HOPING TO BECOME A STAY-AT-HOME MOTHER.
HE'S A KYUSHU BOY.

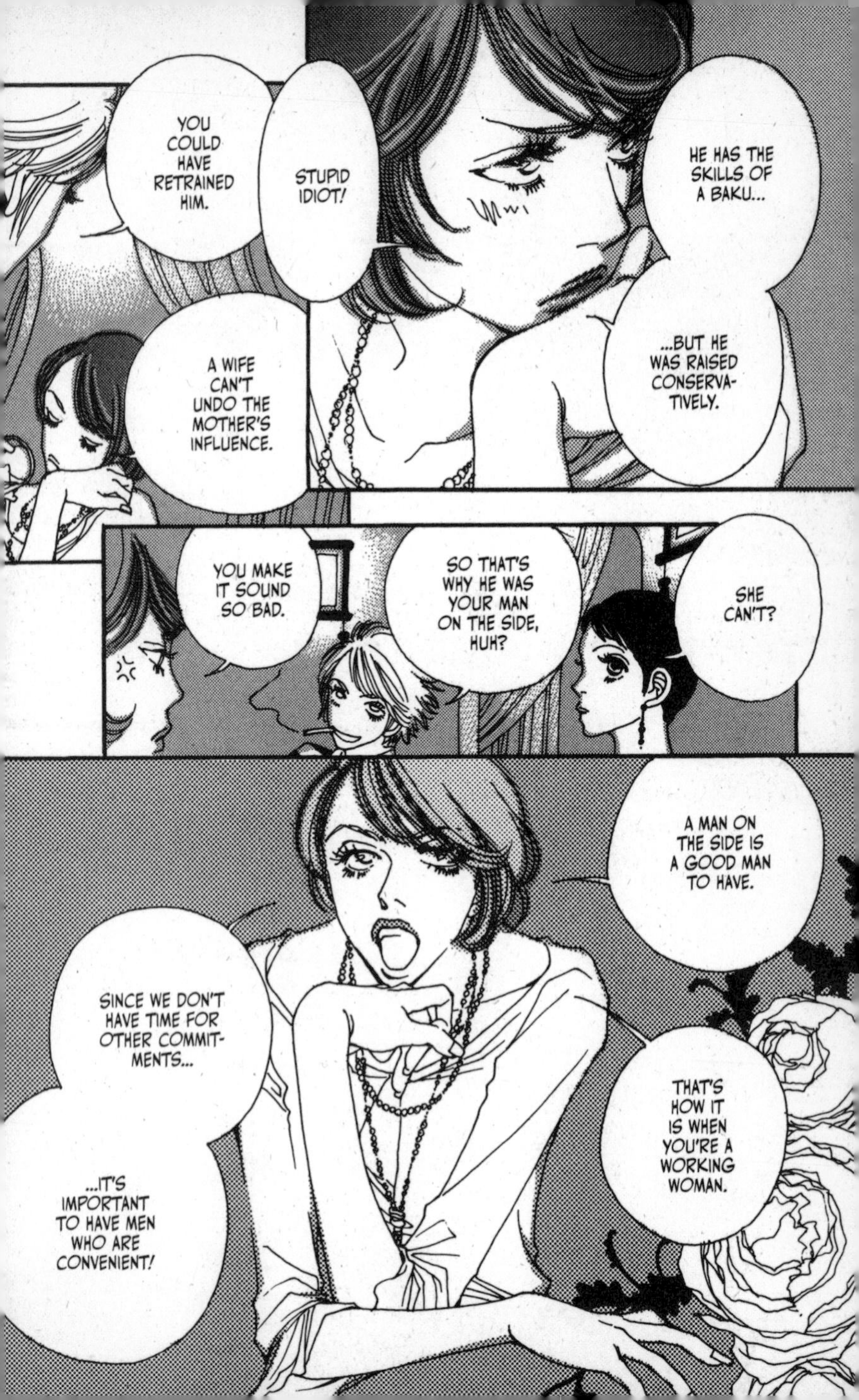
HE HAS THE SKILLS OF A BAKU...
...BUT HE WAS RAISED CONSERVATIVELY.
STUPID IDIOT!
YOU COULD HAVE RETRAINED HIM.
A WIFE CAN'T UNDO THE MOTHER'S INFLUENCE.
SHE CAN'T?
SO THAT'S WHY HE WAS YOUR MAN ON THE SIDE, HUH?
YOU MAKE IT SOUND SO BAD.
A MAN ON THE SIDE IS A GOOD MAN TO HAVE.
THAT'S HOW IT IS WHEN YOU'RE A WORKING WOMAN.
SINCE WE DON'T HAVE TIME FOR OTHER COMMITMENTS...
...IT'S IMPORTANT TO HAVE MEN WHO ARE CONVENIENT!

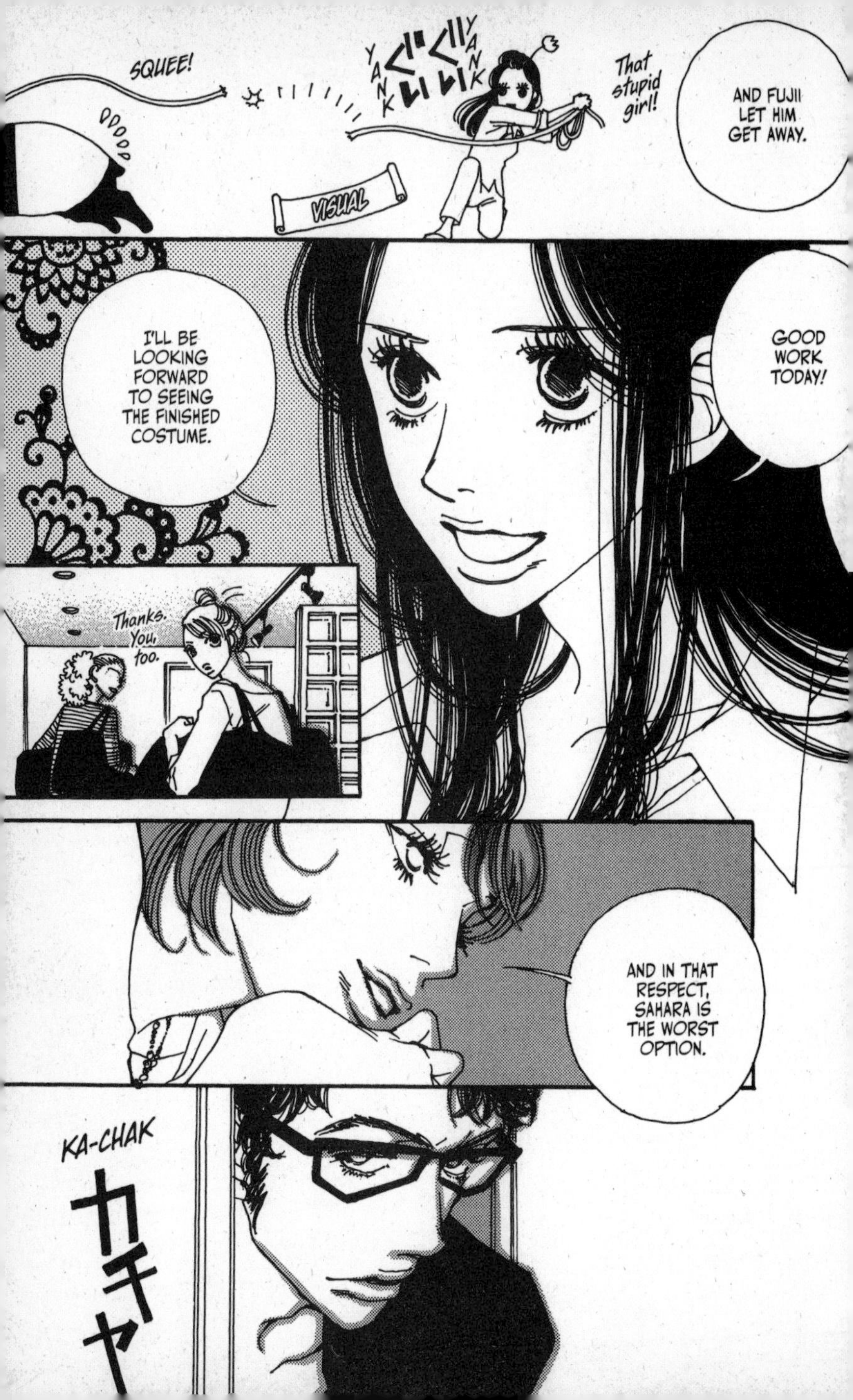

AND FUJII LET HIM GET AWAY.
That stupid girl!
YANK YANK
VISUAL
SQUEE!
GOOD WORK TODAY!
I'LL BE LOOKING FORWARD TO SEEING THE FINISHED COSTUME.
Thanks. You, too.
AND IN THAT RESPECT, SAHARA IS THE WORST OPTION.
KA-CHAK
カチャ

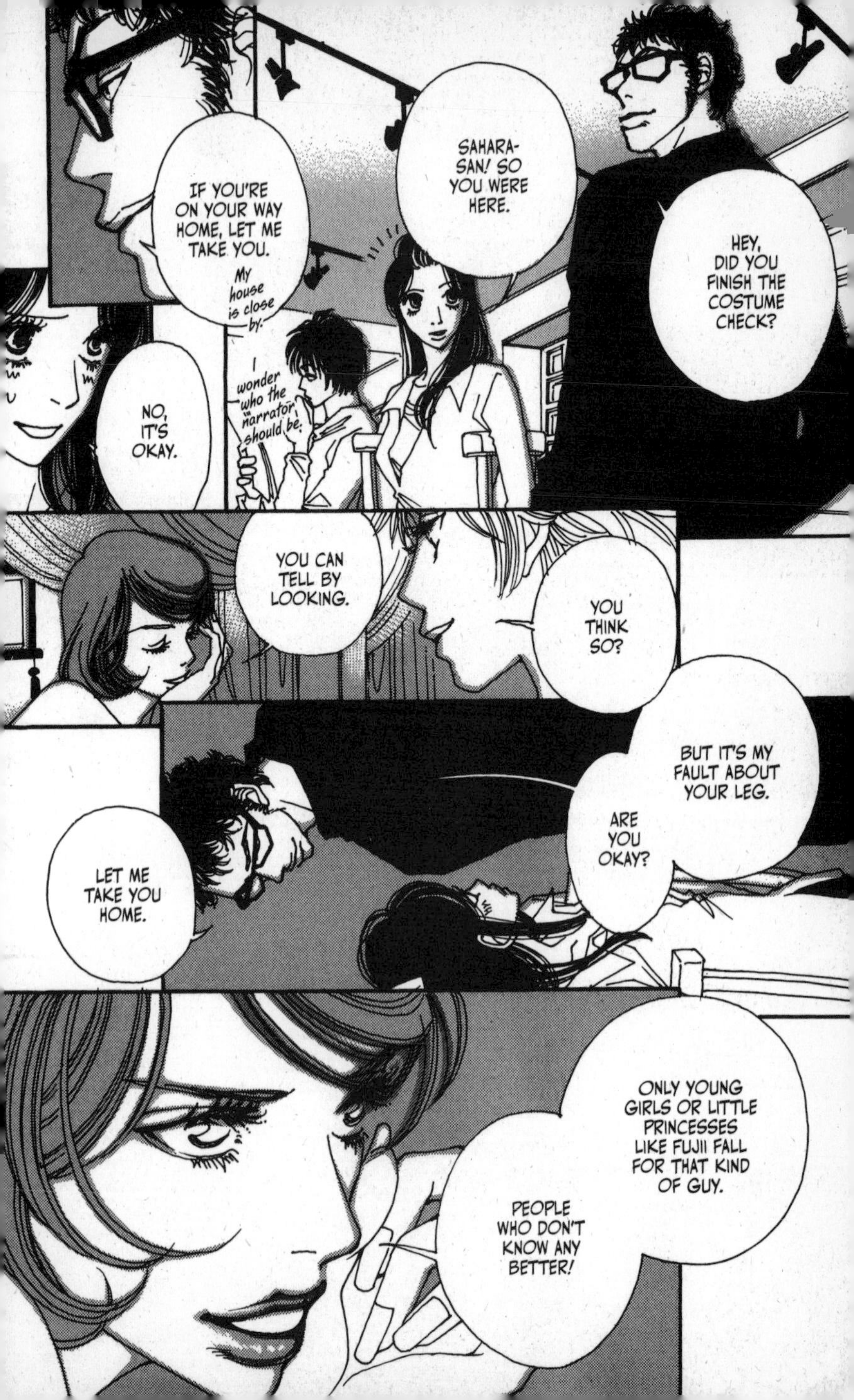
HEY, DID YOU FINISH THE COSTUME CHECK?
SAHARA-SAN! SO YOU WERE HERE.
IF YOU'RE ON YOUR WAY HOME, LET ME TAKE YOU.
My house is close by.
I wonder who the narrator should be.
NO, IT'S OKAY.
YOU THINK SO?
YOU CAN TELL BY LOOKING.
BUT IT'S MY FAULT ABOUT YOUR LEG.
ARE YOU OKAY?
LET ME TAKE YOU HOME.
ONLY YOUNG GIRLS OR LITTLE PRINCESSES LIKE FUJII FALL FOR THAT KIND OF GUY.
PEOPLE WHO DON'T KNOW ANY BETTER!

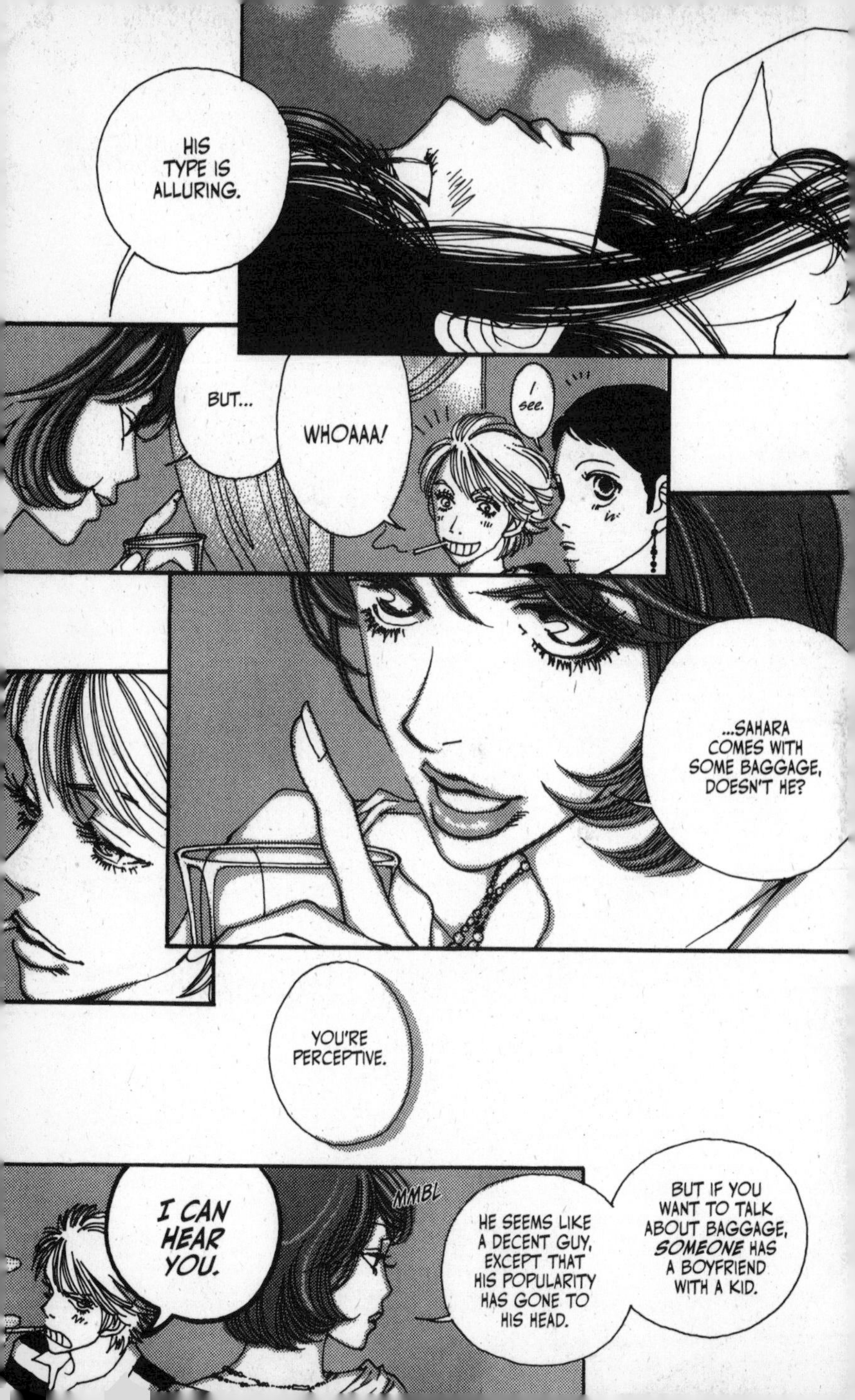
HIS TYPE IS ALLURING.
I see.
WHOAAA!
BUT...
...SAHARA COMES WITH SOME BAGGAGE, DOESN'T HE?
YOU'RE PERCEPTIVE.
BUT IF YOU WANT TO TALK ABOUT BAGGAGE, *SOMEONE* HAS A BOYFRIEND WITH A KID.
HE SEEMS LIKE A DECENT GUY, EXCEPT THAT HIS POPULARITY HAS GONE TO HIS HEAD.
MMBL
I CAN HEAR YOU.

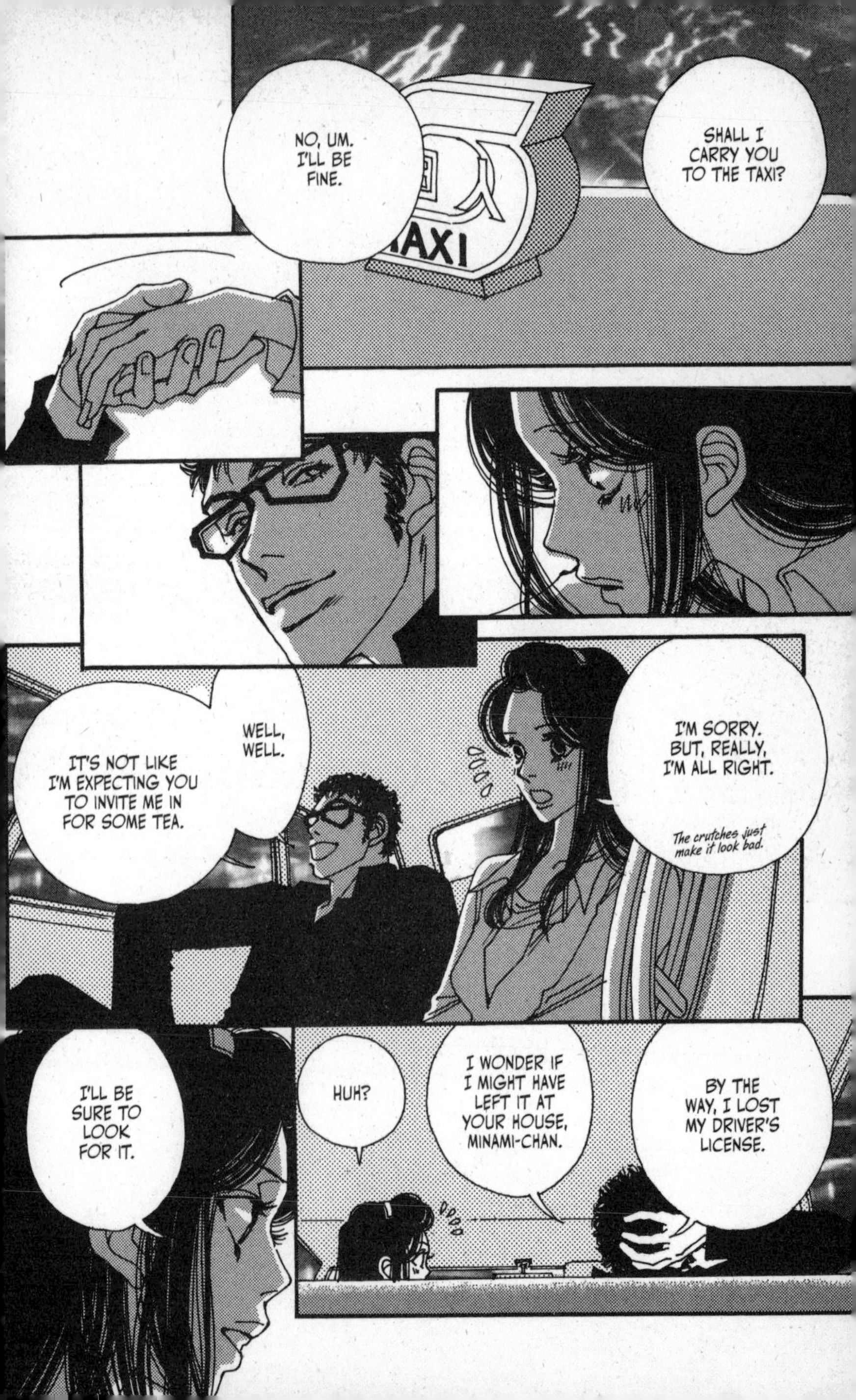
SHALL I CARRY YOU TO THE TAXI?
NO, UM. I'LL BE FINE.
TAXI
I'M SORRY. BUT, REALLY, I'M ALL RIGHT.
The crutches just make it look bad.
WELL, WELL.
IT'S NOT LIKE I'M EXPECTING YOU TO INVITE ME IN FOR SOME TEA.
BY THE WAY, I LOST MY DRIVER'S LICENSE.
I WONDER IF I MIGHT HAVE LEFT IT AT YOUR HOUSE, MINAMI-CHAN.
HUH?
I'LL BE SURE TO LOOK FOR IT.

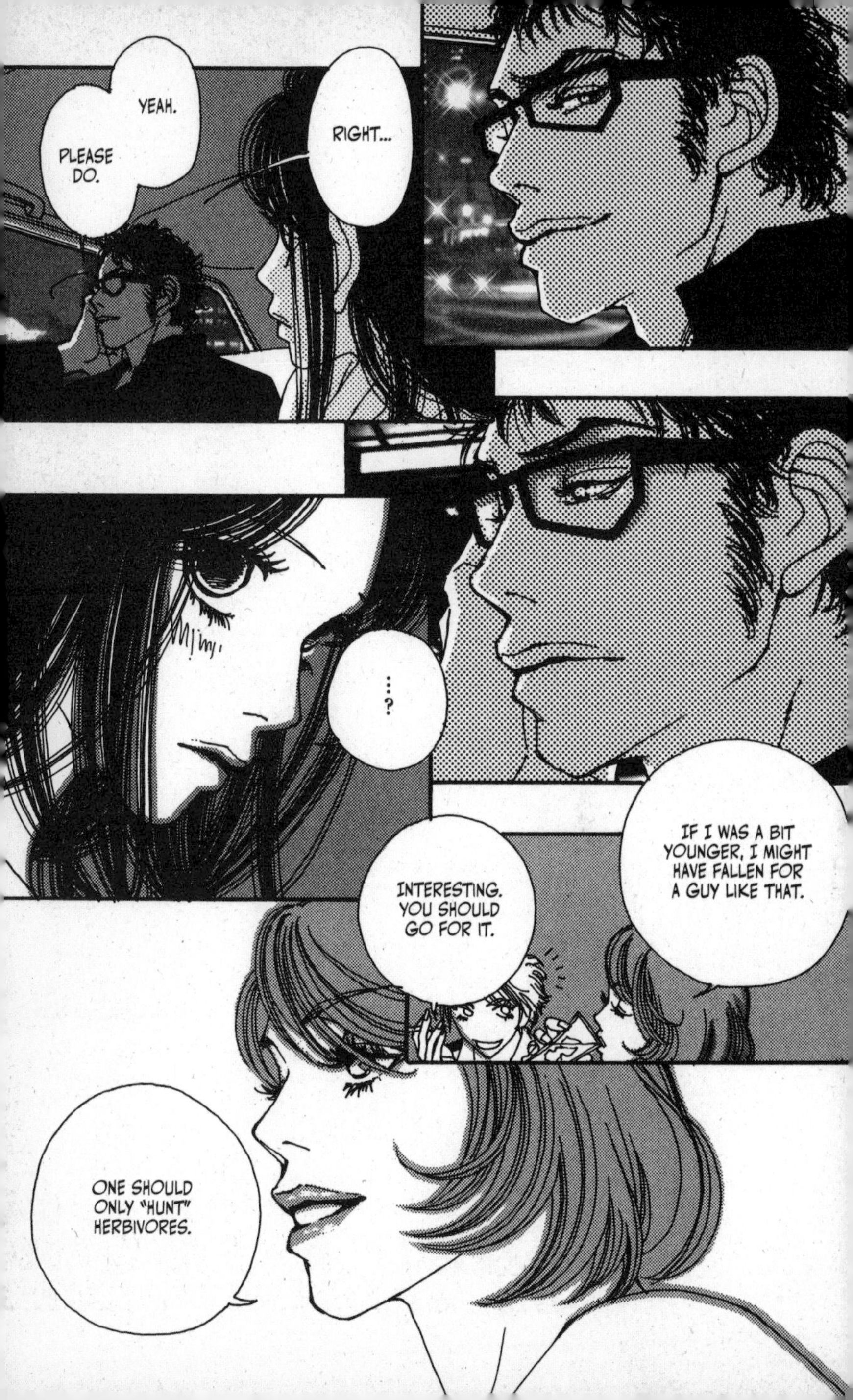
RIGHT...
YEAH. PLEASE DO.
...?
IF I WAS A BIT YOUNGER, I MIGHT HAVE FALLEN FOR A GUY LIKE THAT.
INTERESTING. YOU SHOULD GO FOR IT.
ONE SHOULD ONLY "HUNT" HERBIVORES.

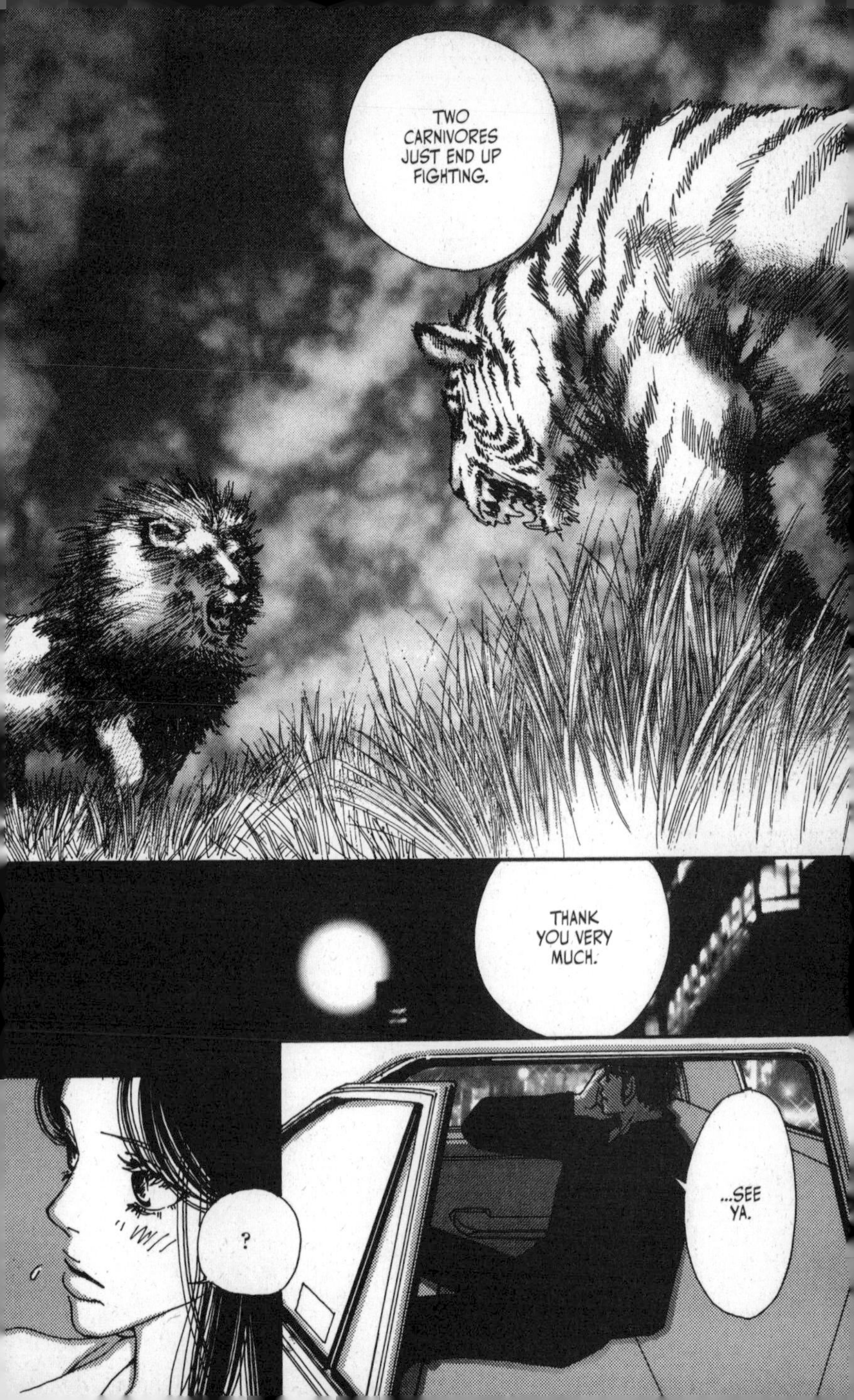
TWO CARNIVORES JUST END UP FIGHTING.
THANK YOU VERY MUCH.
...SEE YA.
?

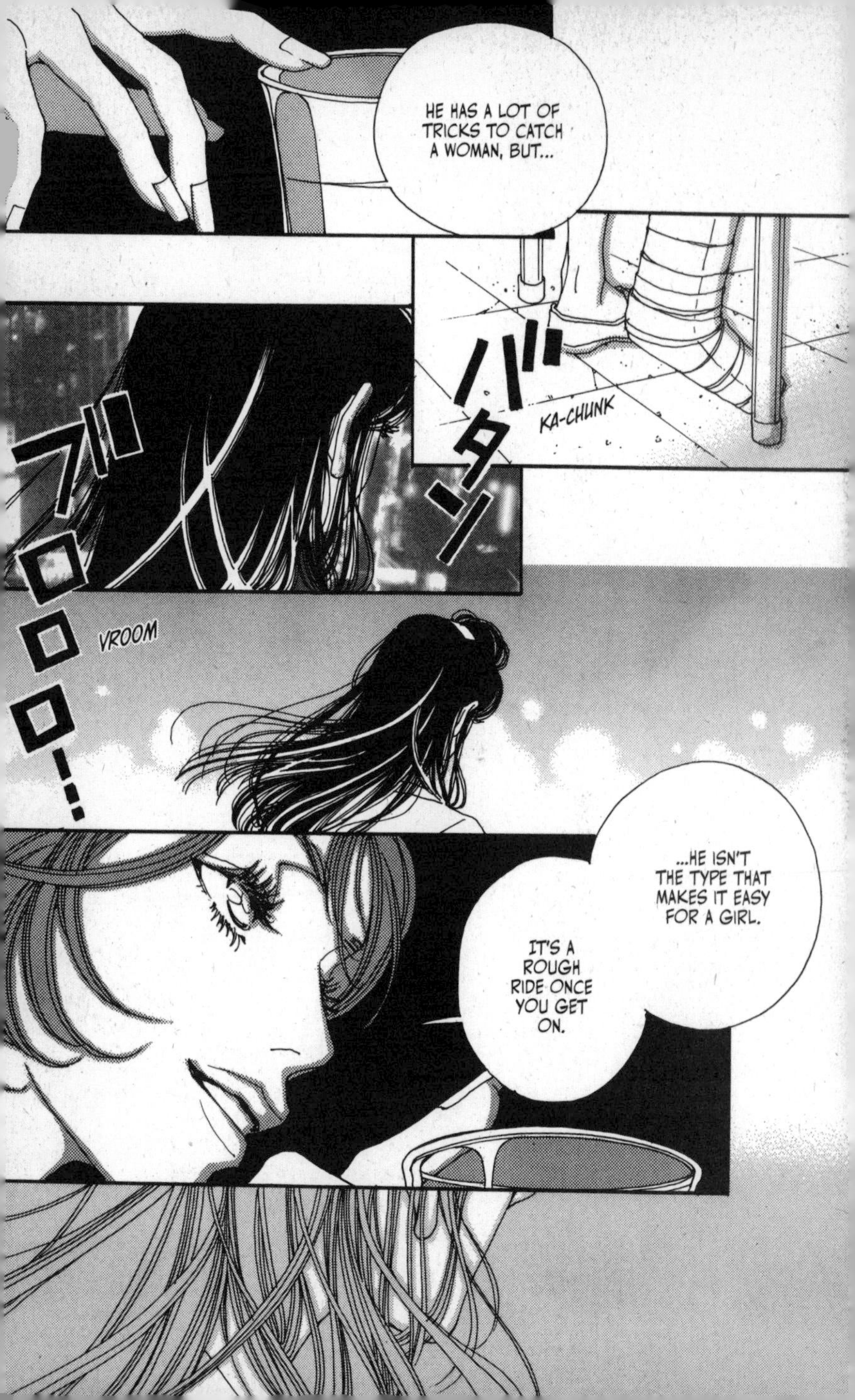

HE HAS A LOT OF TRICKS TO CATCH A WOMAN, BUT...
バタン
KA-CHUNK
ブロロロー!!
VROOM
...HE ISN'T THE TYPE THAT MAKES IT EASY FOR A GIRL.
IT'S A ROUGH RIDE ONCE YOU GET ON.

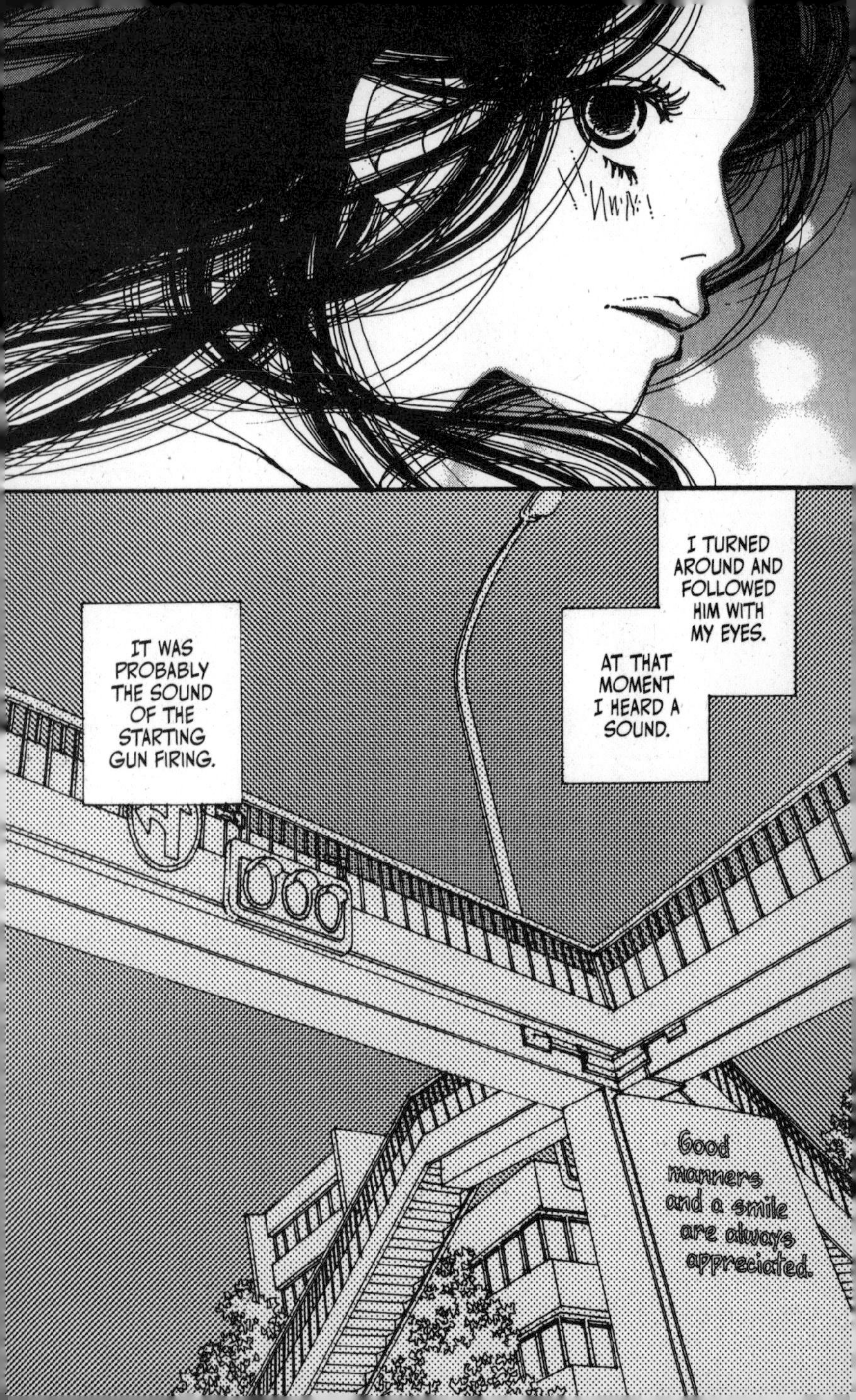
I TURNED AROUND AND FOLLOWED HIM WITH MY EYES.
AT THAT MOMENT I HEARD A SOUND.
IT WAS PROBABLY THE SOUND OF THE STARTING GUN FIRING.
Good manners and a smile are always appreciated.

To Be Continued

Suppli™

BY MARI OKAZAKI

5

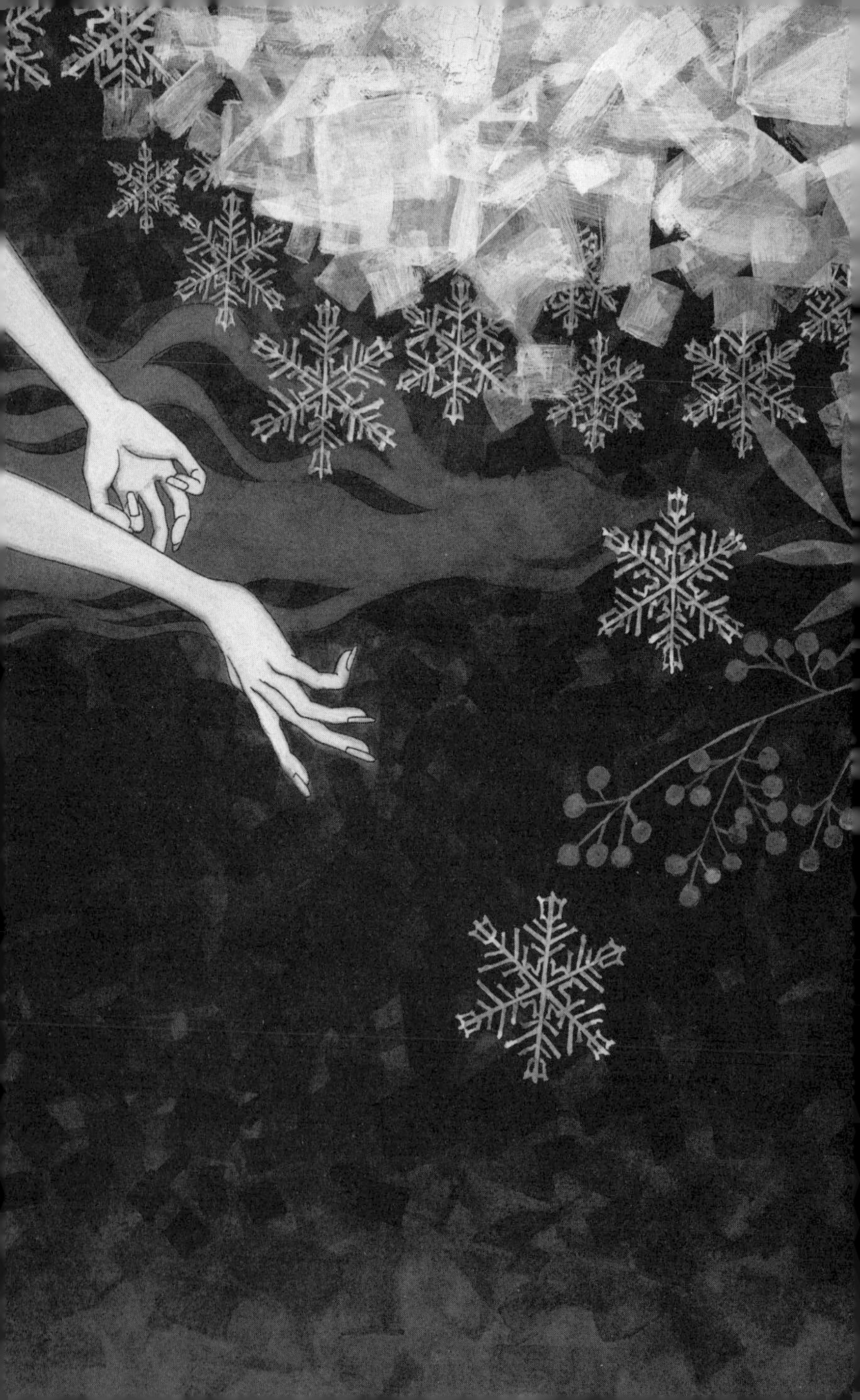

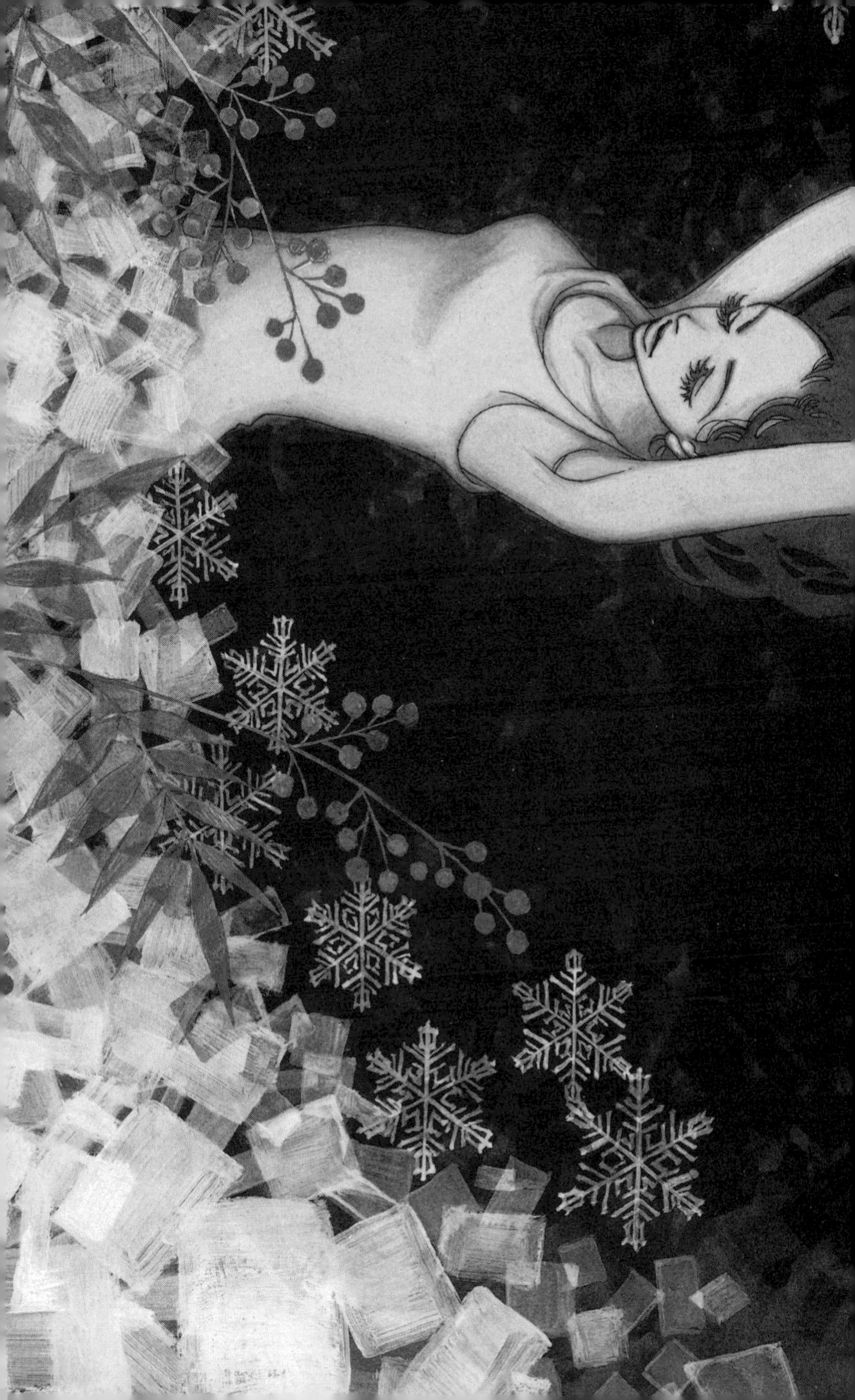

CONTENTS ❄

FILE. 26

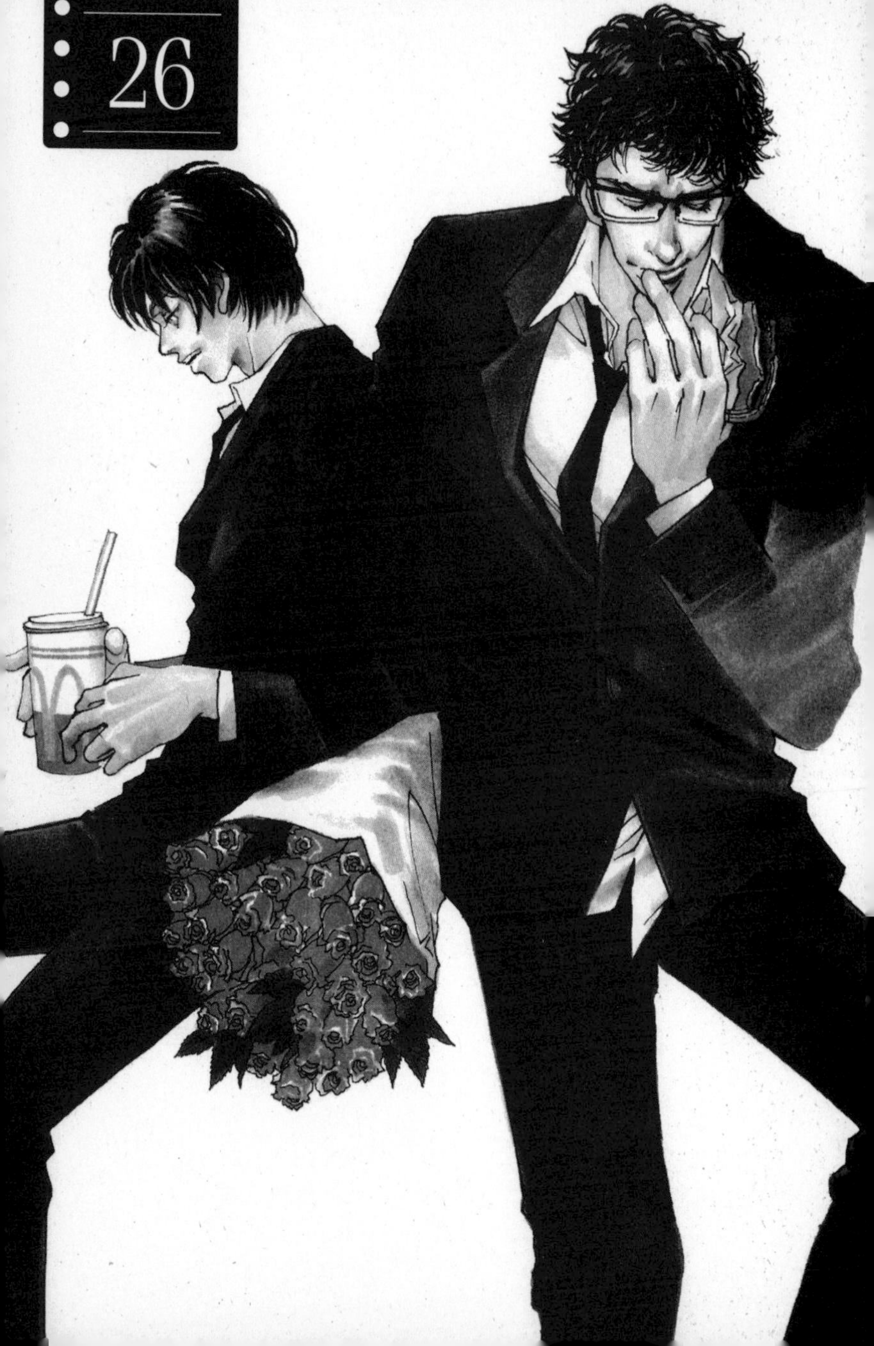

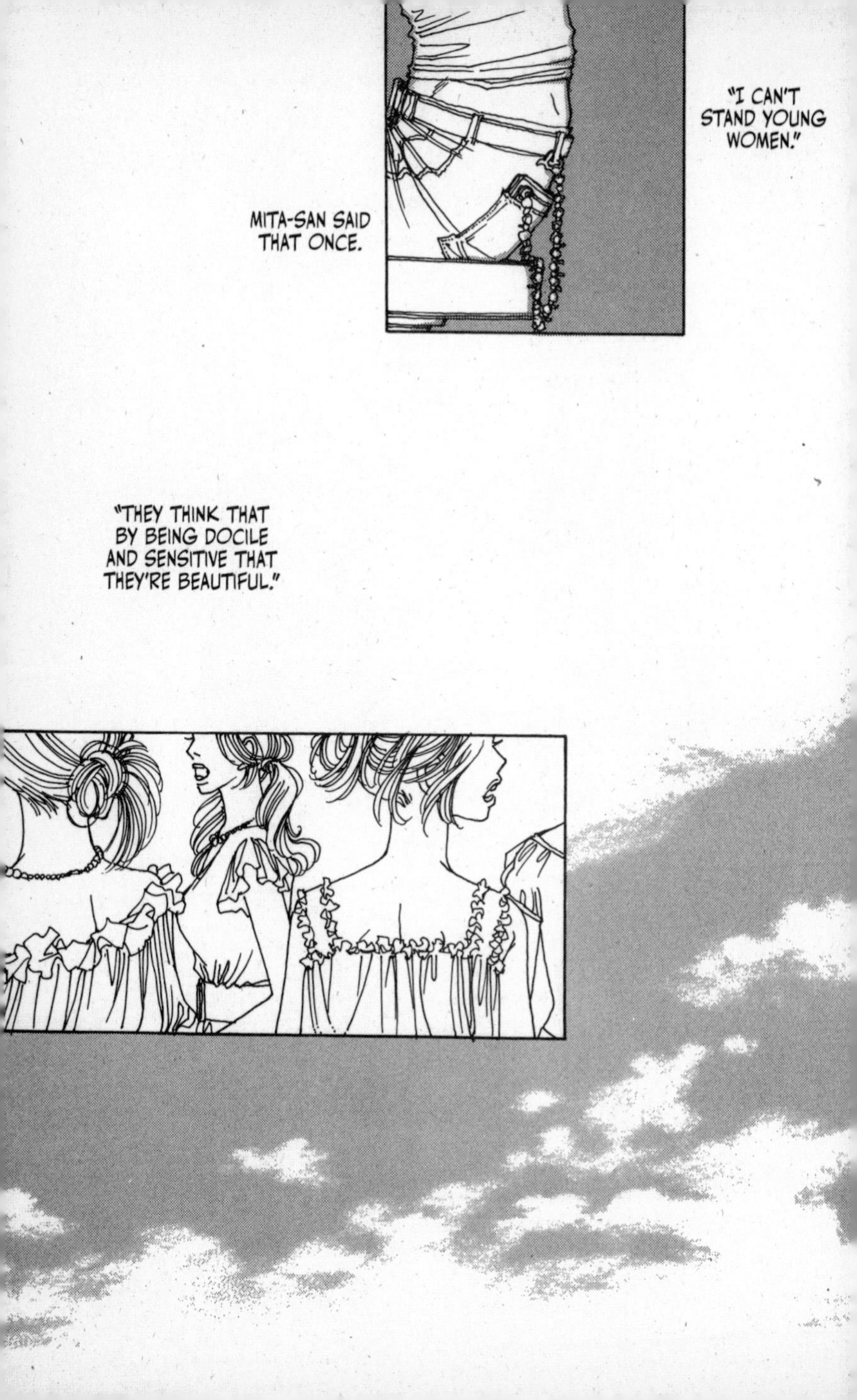
"I CAN'T STAND YOUNG WOMEN."
MITA-SAN SAID THAT ONCE.
"THEY THINK THAT BY BEING DOCILE AND SENSITIVE THAT THEY'RE BEAUTIFUL."

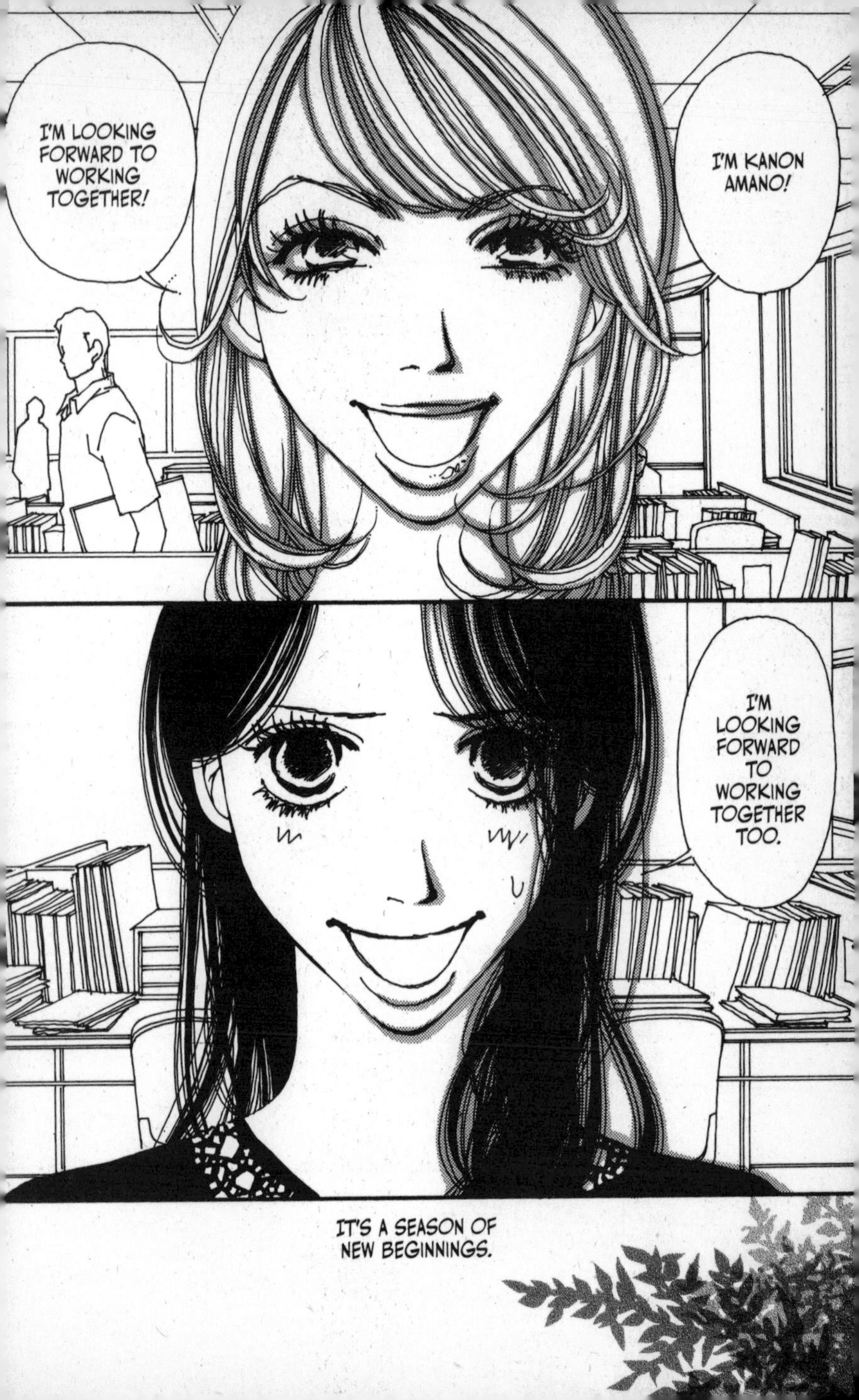
I'M KANON AMANO!
I'M LOOKING FORWARD TO WORKING TOGETHER!
I'M LOOKING FORWARD TO WORKING TOGETHER TOO.
IT'S A SEASON OF NEW BEGINNINGS.

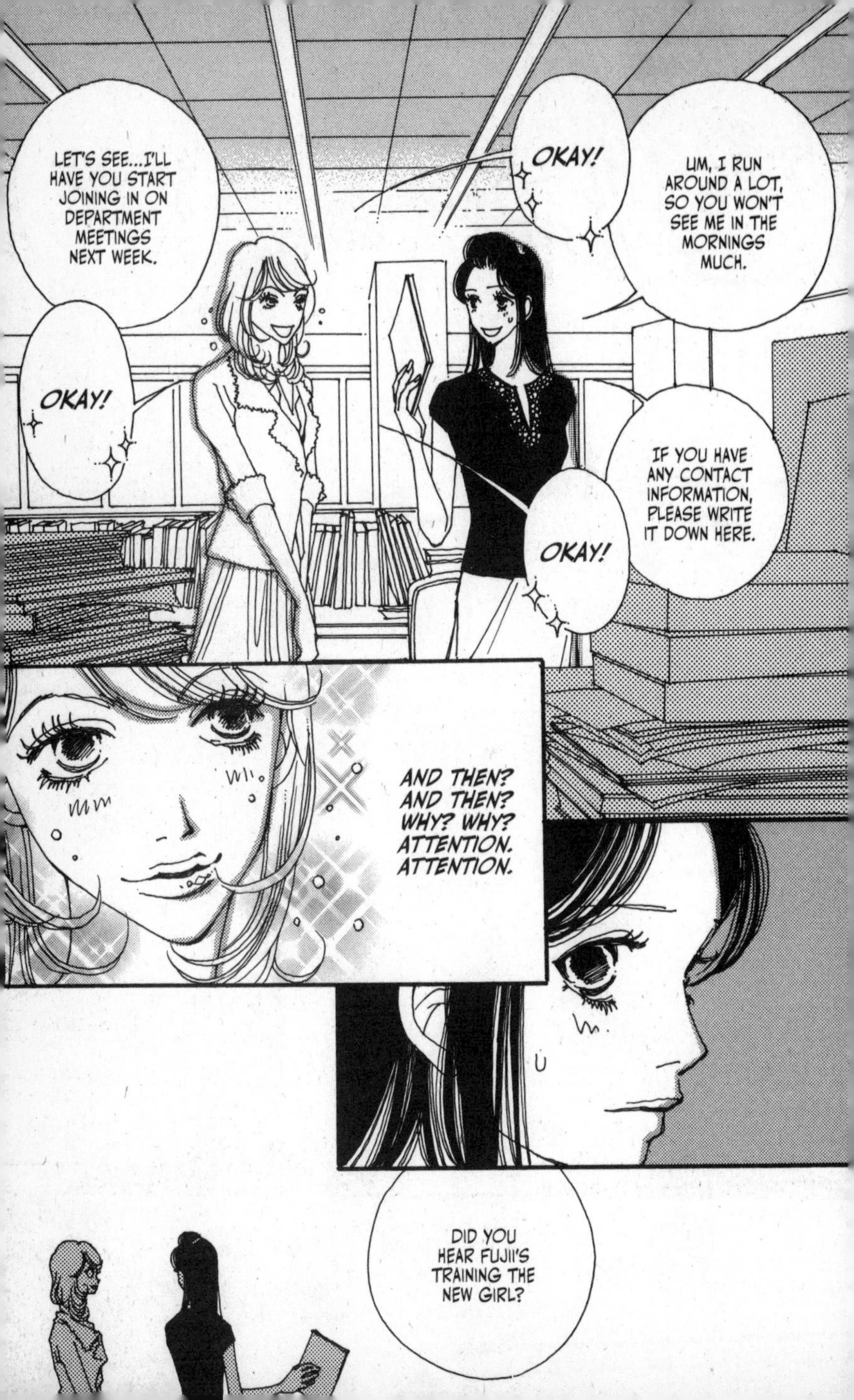

UM, I RUN AROUND A LOT, SO YOU WON'T SEE ME IN THE MORNINGS MUCH.
OKAY!
LET'S SEE...I'LL HAVE YOU START JOINING IN ON DEPARTMENT MEETINGS NEXT WEEK.
OKAY!
IF YOU HAVE ANY CONTACT INFORMATION, PLEASE WRITE IT DOWN HERE.
OKAY!
AND THEN? AND THEN? WHY? WHY? ATTENTION. ATTENTION.
DID YOU HEAR FUJII'S TRAINING THE NEW GIRL?

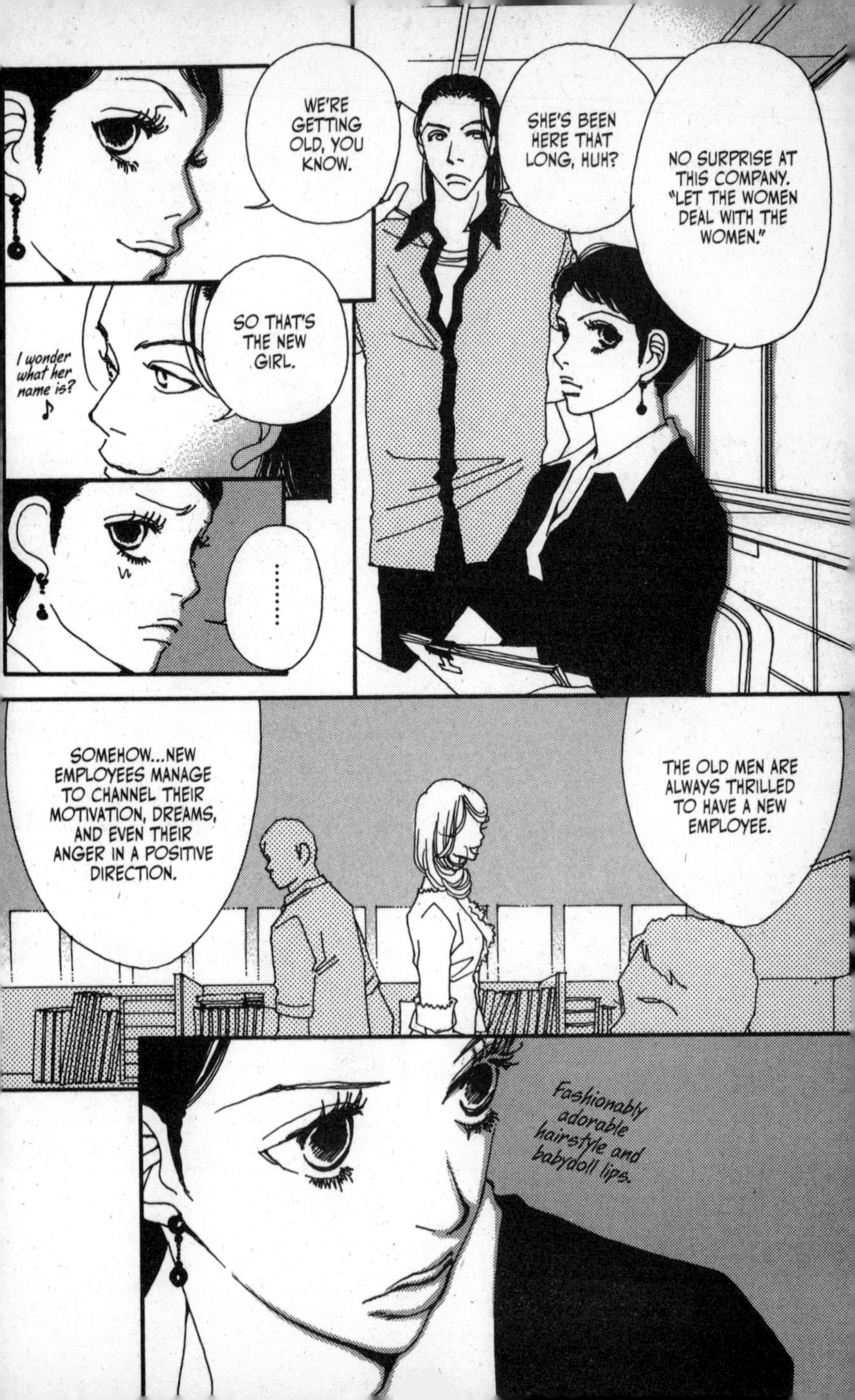
NO SURPRISE AT THIS COMPANY. "LET THE WOMEN DEAL WITH THE WOMEN."
SHE'S BEEN HERE THAT LONG, HUH?
WE'RE GETTING OLD, YOU KNOW.
SO THAT'S THE NEW GIRL.
I wonder what her name is? ♪
……
THE OLD MEN ARE ALWAYS THRILLED TO HAVE A NEW EMPLOYEE.
SOMEHOW...NEW EMPLOYEES MANAGE TO CHANNEL THEIR MOTIVATION, DREAMS, AND EVEN THEIR ANGER IN A POSITIVE DIRECTION.
Fashionably adorable hairstyle and babydoll lips.

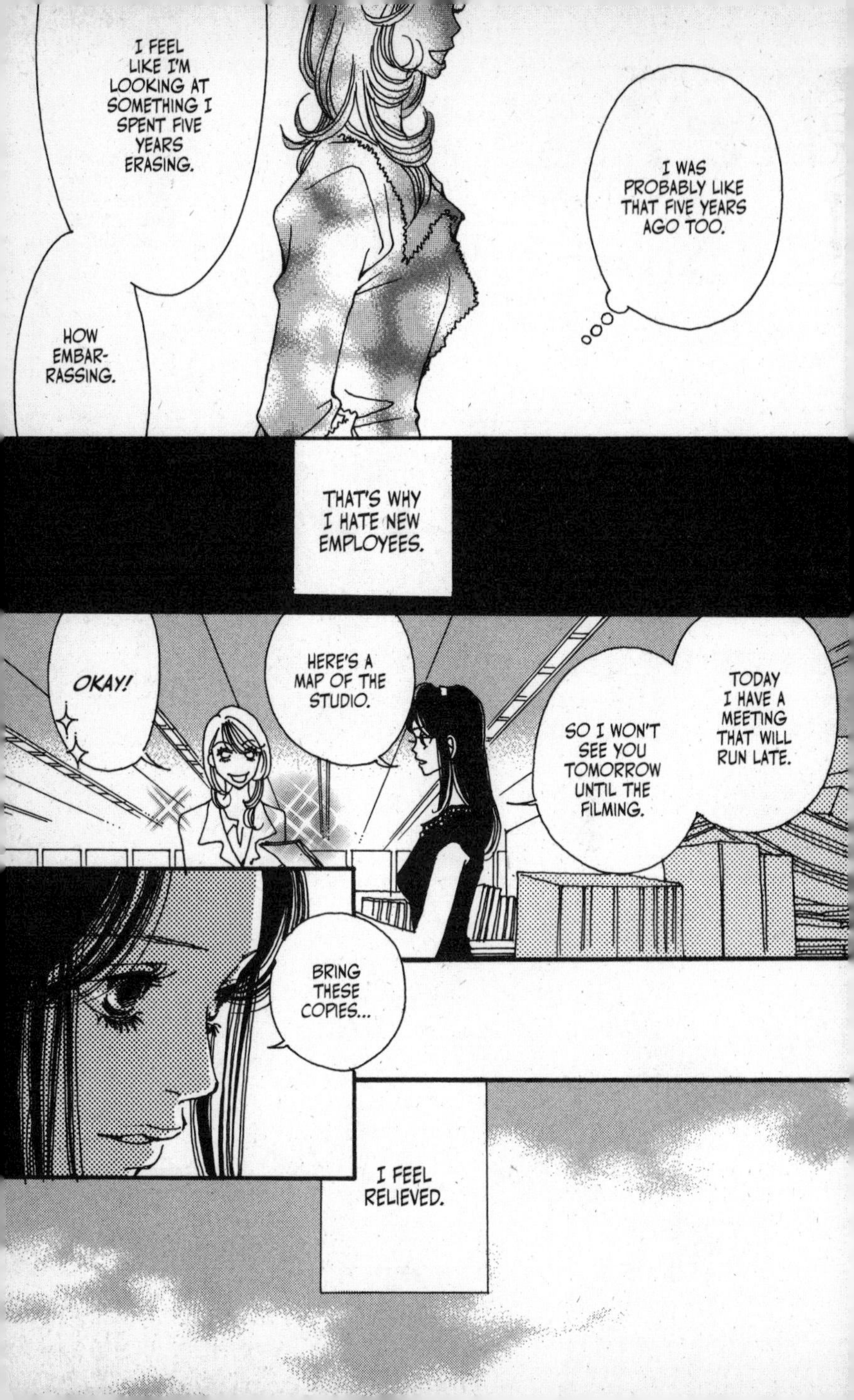
I WAS PROBABLY LIKE THAT FIVE YEARS AGO TOO.
I FEEL LIKE I'M LOOKING AT SOMETHING I SPENT FIVE YEARS ERASING.
HOW EMBAR-RASSING.
THAT'S WHY I HATE NEW EMPLOYEES.
TODAY I HAVE A MEETING THAT WILL RUN LATE.
SO I WON'T SEE YOU TOMORROW UNTIL THE FILMING.
HERE'S A MAP OF THE STUDIO.
OKAY!
BRING THESE COPIES...
I FEEL RELIEVED.

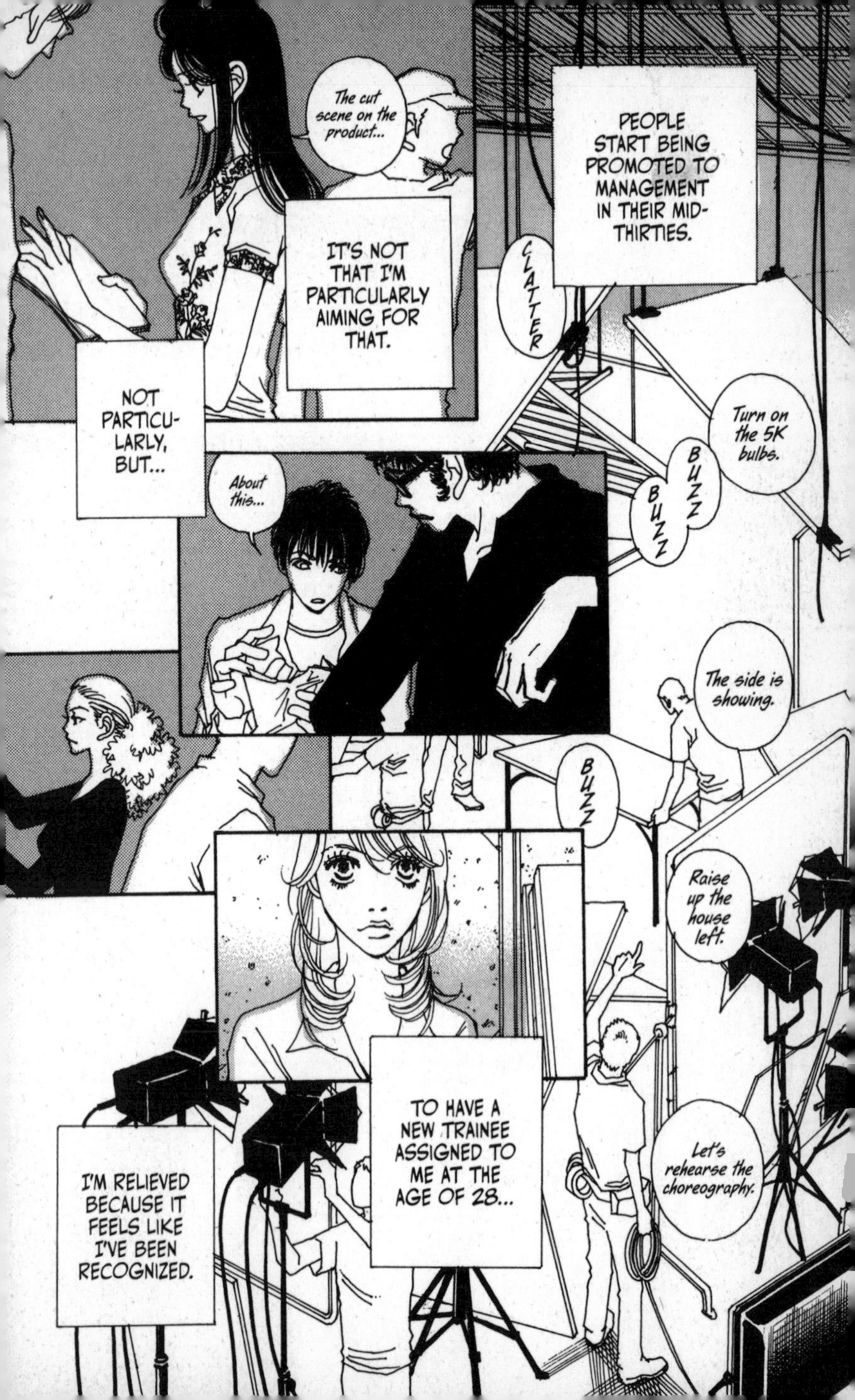
PEOPLE START BEING PROMOTED TO MANAGEMENT IN THEIR MID-THIRTIES.
CLATTER
The cut scene on the product...
IT'S NOT THAT I'M PARTICULARLY AIMING FOR THAT.
NOT PARTICULARLY, BUT...
Turn on the 5K bulbs.
BUZZ
BUZZ
About this...
The side is showing.
BUZZ
Raise up the house left.
Let's rehearse the choreography.
TO HAVE A NEW TRAINEE ASSIGNED TO ME AT THE AGE OF 28...
I'M RELIEVED BECAUSE IT FEELS LIKE I'VE BEEN RECOGNIZED.

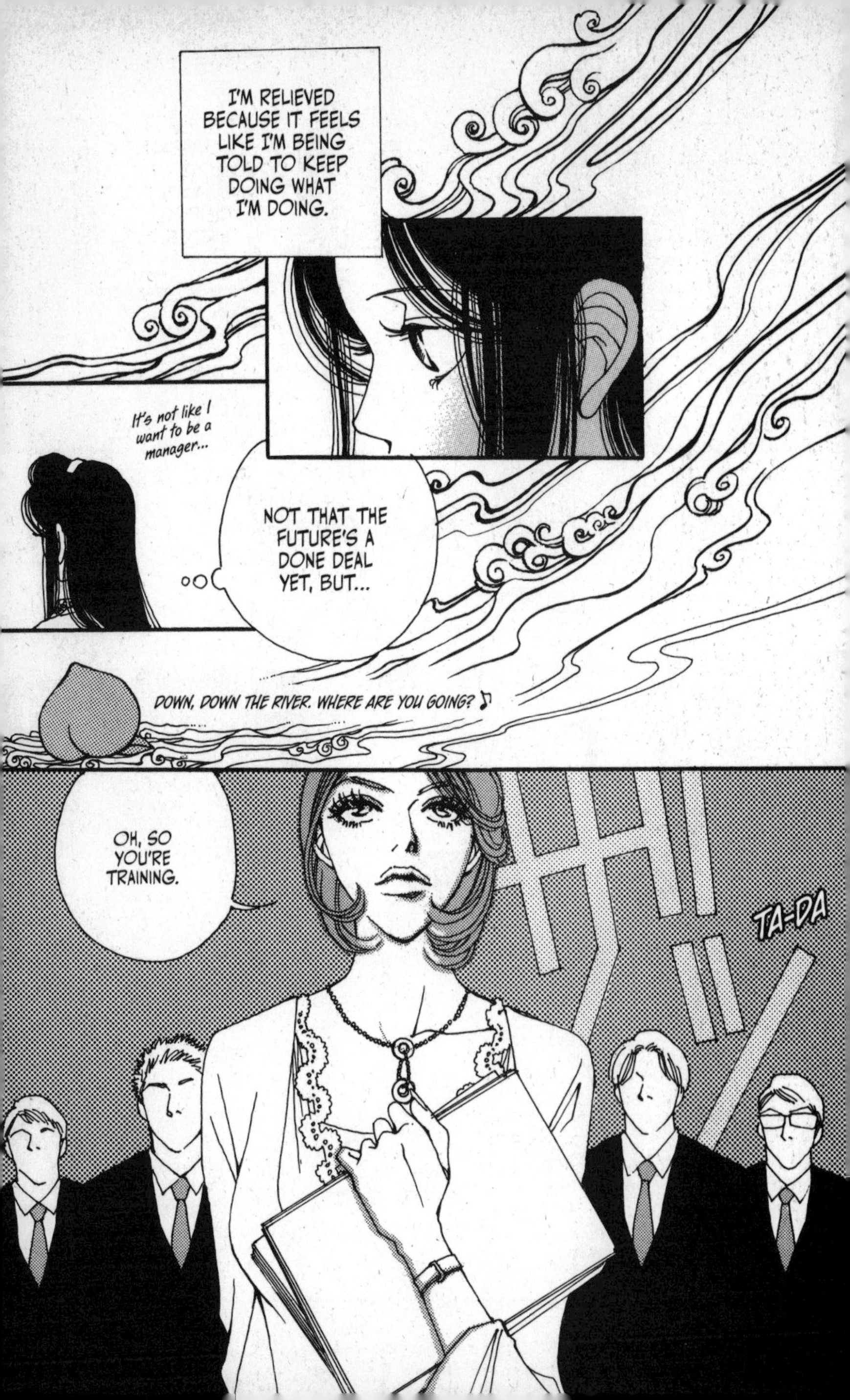
I'M RELIEVED BECAUSE IT FEELS LIKE I'M BEING TOLD TO KEEP DOING WHAT I'M DOING.
It's not like I want to be a manager...
NOT THAT THE FUTURE'S A DONE DEAL YET, BUT...
DOWN, DOWN THE RIVER. WHERE ARE YOU GOING? ♪
OH, SO YOU'RE TRAINING.
TA-DA

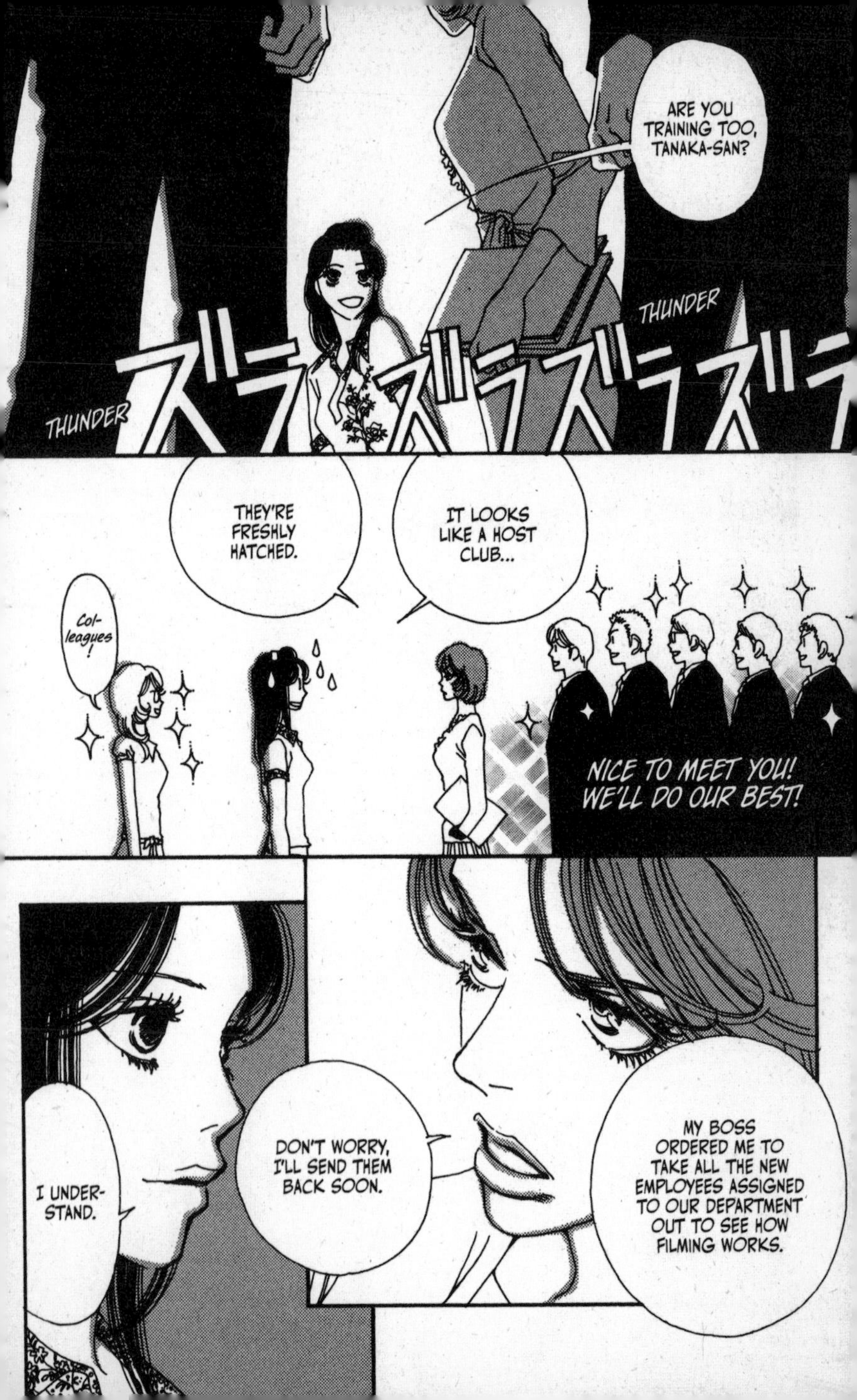
ARE YOU TRAINING TOO, TANAKA-SAN?
THUNDER
ズラズラズラズラ
THUNDER
NICE TO MEET YOU! WE'LL DO OUR BEST!
IT LOOKS LIKE A HOST CLUB...
THEY'RE FRESHLY HATCHED.
Col-leagues!
MY BOSS ORDERED ME TO TAKE ALL THE NEW EMPLOYEES ASSIGNED TO OUR DEPARTMENT OUT TO SEE HOW FILMING WORKS.
DON'T WORRY, I'LL SEND THEM BACK SOON.
I UNDER-STAND.

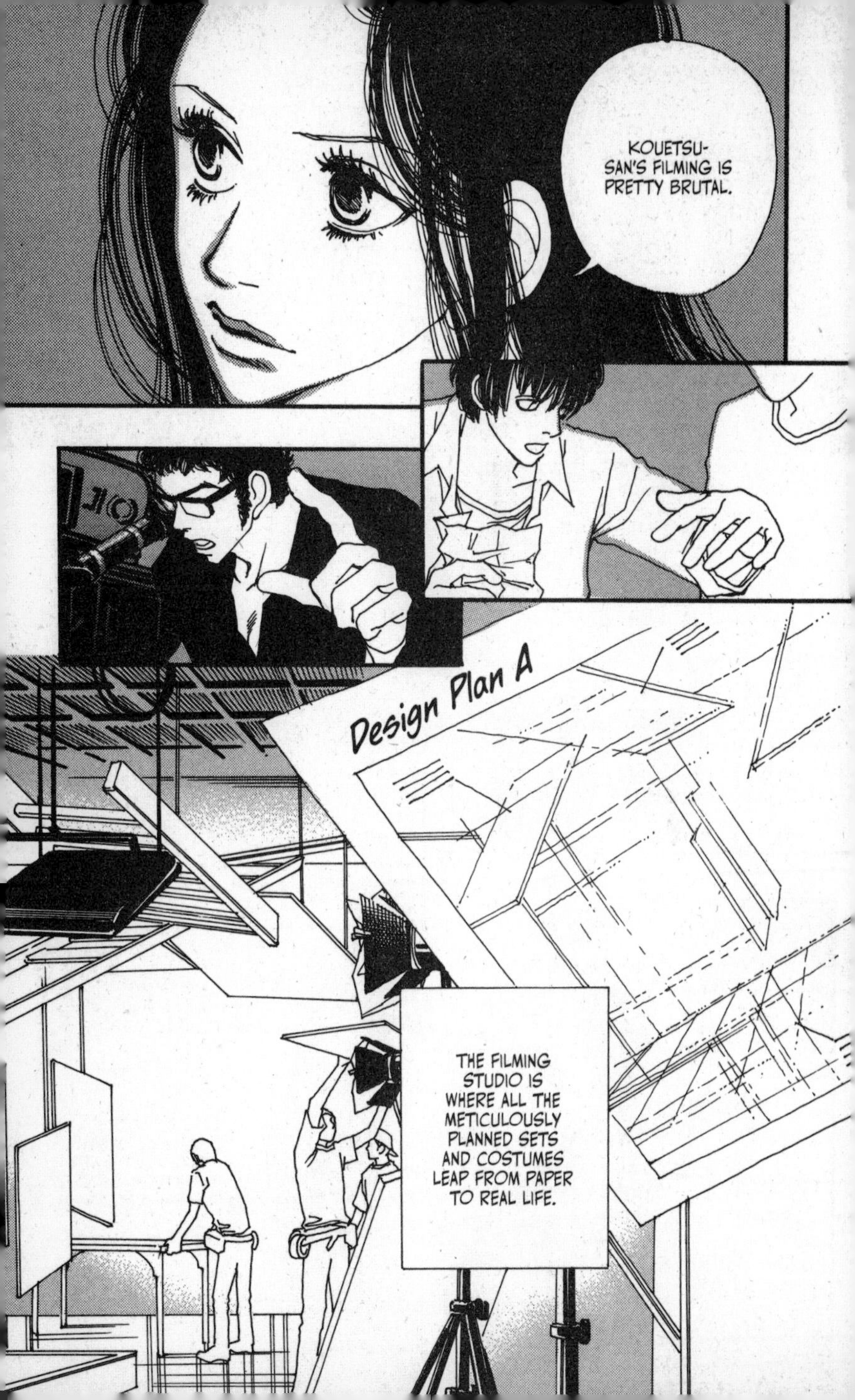
KOUETSU-SAN'S FILMING IS PRETTY BRUTAL.
Design Plan A
THE FILMING STUDIO IS WHERE ALL THE METICULOUSLY PLANNED SETS AND COSTUMES LEAP FROM PAPER TO REAL LIFE.

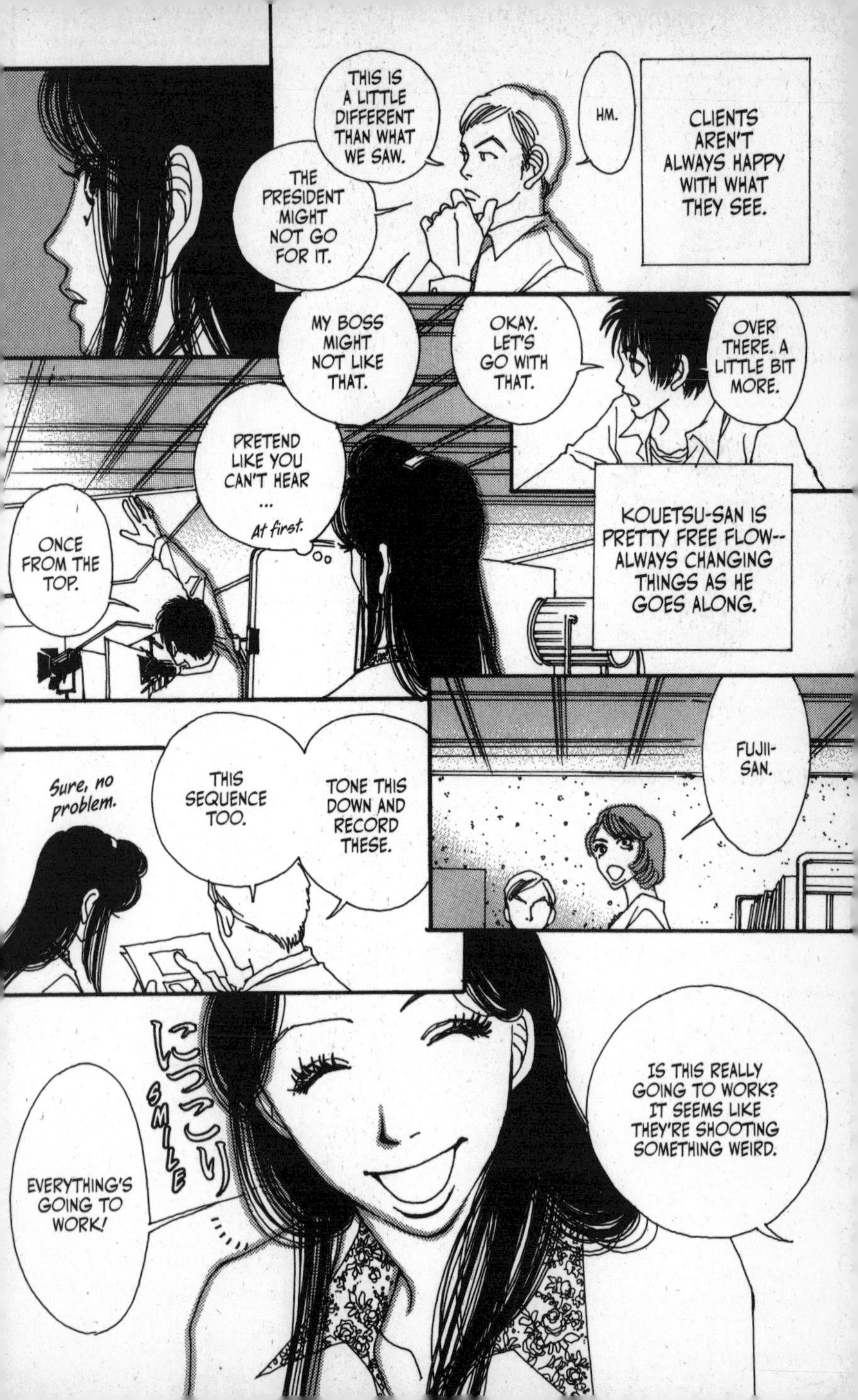
CLIENTS AREN'T ALWAYS HAPPY WITH WHAT THEY SEE.
HM.
THIS IS A LITTLE DIFFERENT THAN WHAT WE SAW.
THE PRESIDENT MIGHT NOT GO FOR IT.
OVER THERE. A LITTLE BIT MORE.
OKAY. LET'S GO WITH THAT.
MY BOSS MIGHT NOT LIKE THAT.
KOUETSU-SAN IS PRETTY FREE FLOW-- ALWAYS CHANGING THINGS AS HE GOES ALONG.
PRETEND LIKE YOU CAN'T HEAR ...
At first.
ONCE FROM THE TOP.
FUJII-SAN.
TONE THIS DOWN AND RECORD THESE.
THIS SEQUENCE TOO.
Sure, no problem.
IS THIS REALLY GOING TO WORK? IT SEEMS LIKE THEY'RE SHOOTING SOMETHING WEIRD.
にっこり
SMILE
EVERYTHING'S GOING TO WORK!

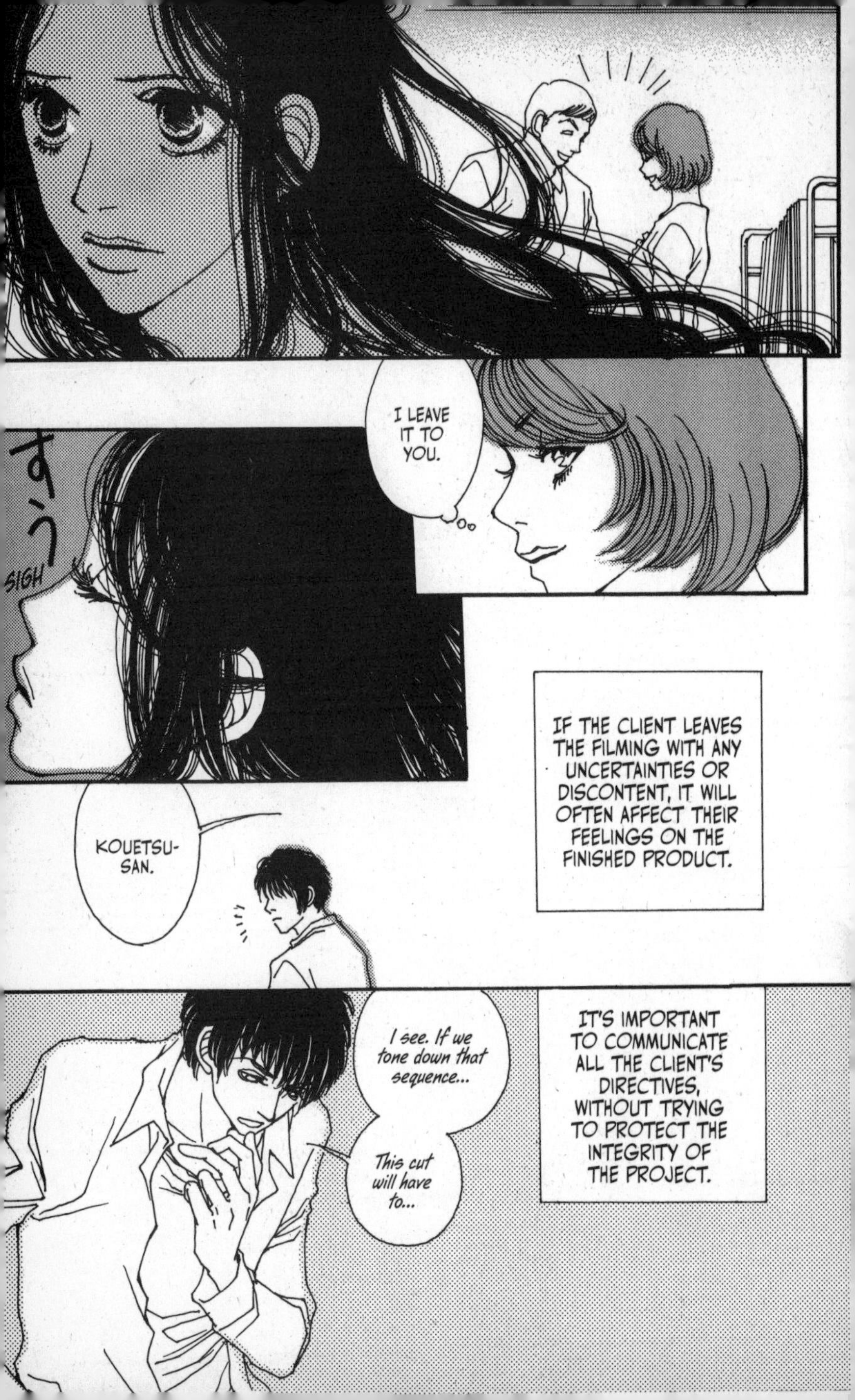
I LEAVE IT TO YOU.
すう
SIGH
IF THE CLIENT LEAVES THE FILMING WITH ANY UNCERTAINTIES OR DISCONTENT, IT WILL OFTEN AFFECT THEIR FEELINGS ON THE FINISHED PRODUCT.
KOUETSU-SAN.
IT'S IMPORTANT TO COMMUNICATE ALL THE CLIENT'S DIRECTIVES, WITHOUT TRYING TO PROTECT THE INTEGRITY OF THE PROJECT.
I see. If we tone down that sequence...
This cut will have to...

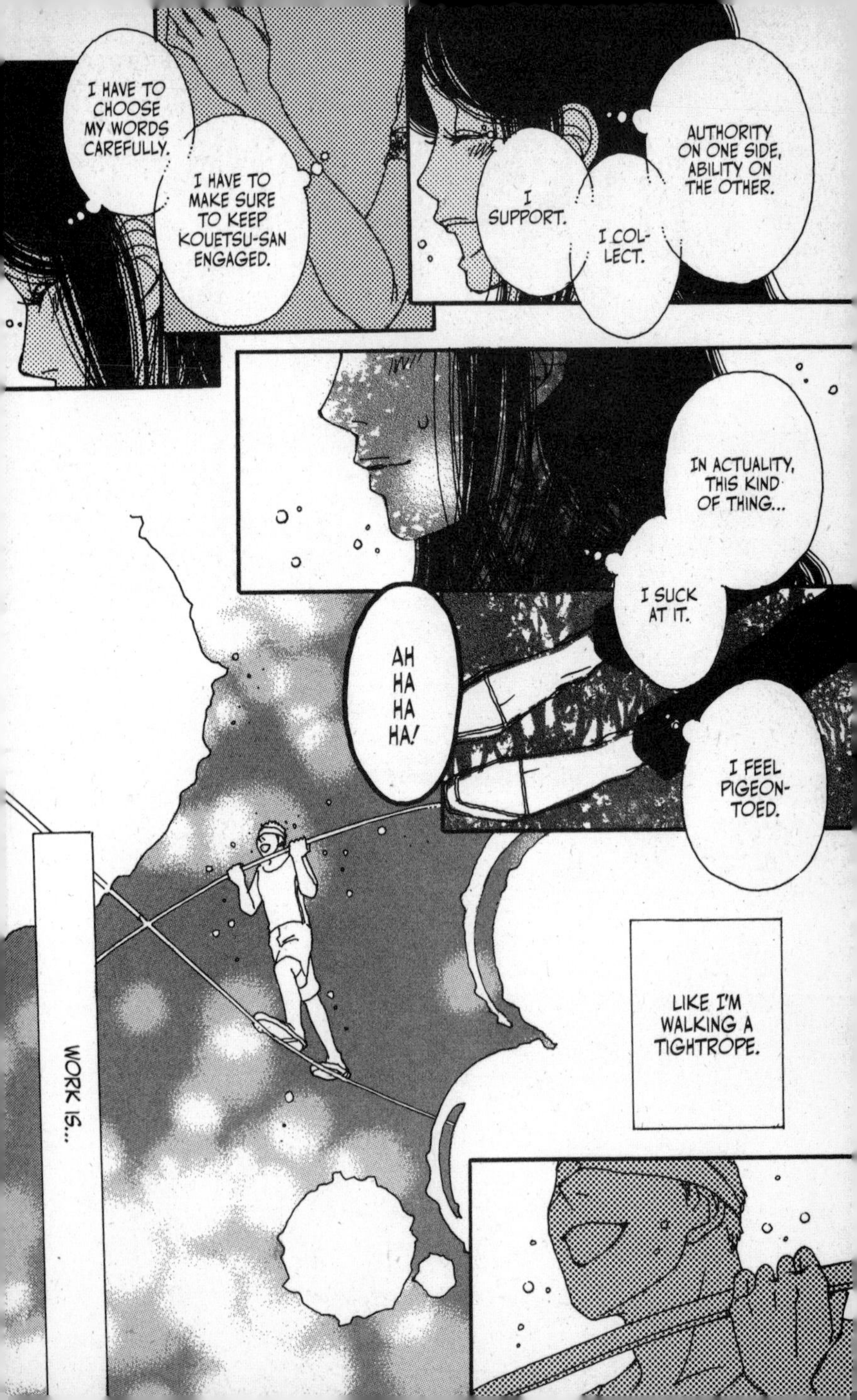
AUTHORITY ON ONE SIDE, ABILITY ON THE OTHER.
I COL-LECT.
I SUPPORT.
I HAVE TO MAKE SURE TO KEEP KOUETSU-SAN ENGAGED.
I HAVE TO CHOOSE MY WORDS CAREFULLY.
IN ACTUALITY, THIS KIND OF THING...
I SUCK AT IT.
I FEEL PIGEON-TOED.
AH HA HA HA!
LIKE I'M WALKING A TIGHTROPE.
WORK IS...

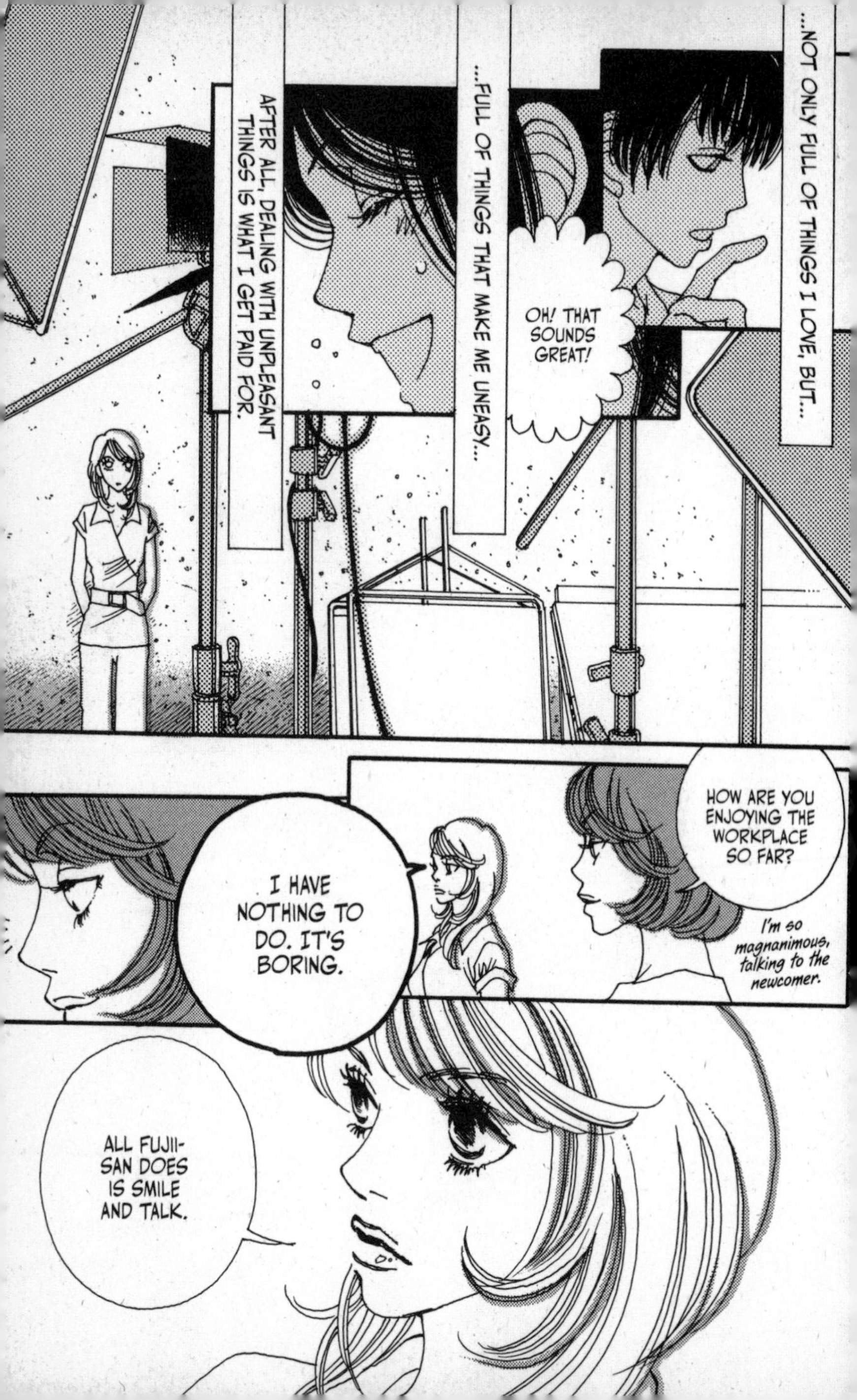
...NOT ONLY FULL OF THINGS I LOVE, BUT...
OH! THAT SOUNDS GREAT!
...FULL OF THINGS THAT MAKE ME UNEASY...
AFTER ALL, DEALING WITH UNPLEASANT THINGS IS WHAT I GET PAID FOR.
HOW ARE YOU ENJOYING THE WORKPLACE SO FAR?
I'm so magnanimous, talking to the newcomer.
I HAVE NOTHING TO DO. IT'S BORING.
ALL FUJII-SAN DOES IS SMILE AND TALK.

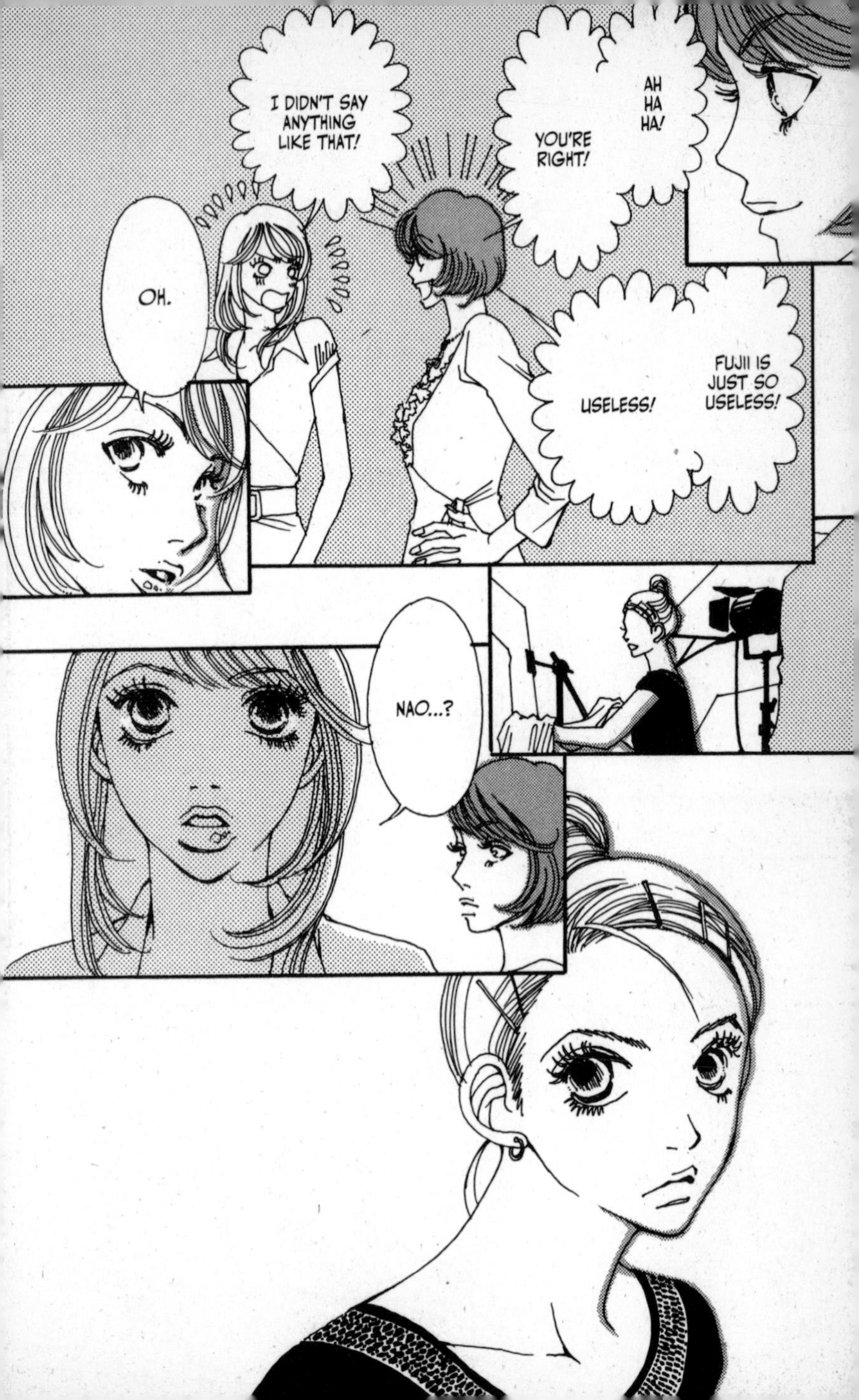
AH HA HA!
YOU'RE RIGHT!
I DIDN'T SAY ANYTHING LIKE THAT!
FUJII IS JUST SO USELESS!
USELESS!
OH.
NAO...?

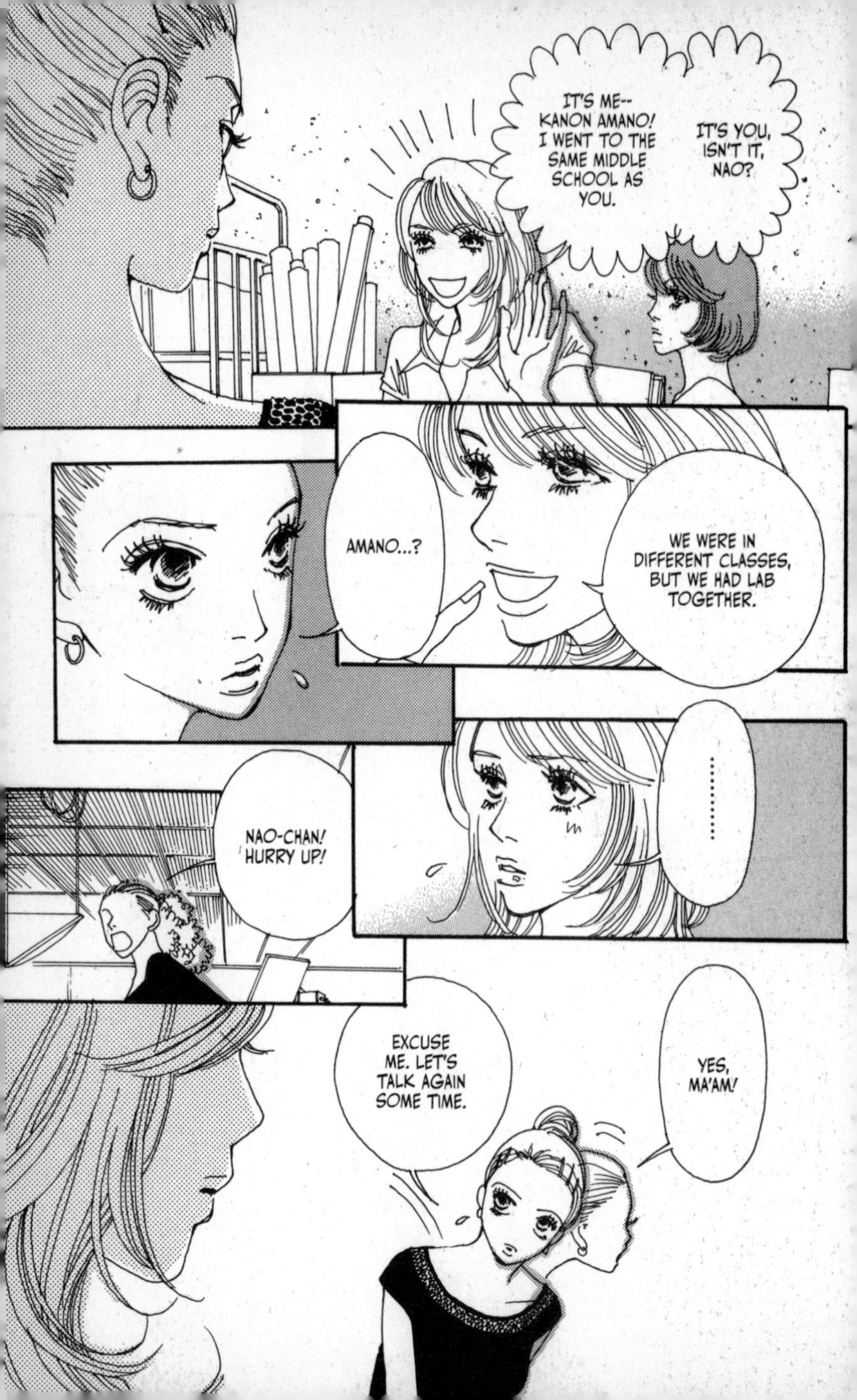
IT'S YOU, ISN'T IT, NAO?
IT'S ME-- KANON AMANO! I WENT TO THE SAME MIDDLE SCHOOL AS YOU.
WE WERE IN DIFFERENT CLASSES, BUT WE HAD LAB TOGETHER.
AMANO...?
......
NAO-CHAN! HURRY UP!
YES, MA'AM!
EXCUSE ME. LET'S TALK AGAIN SOME TIME.

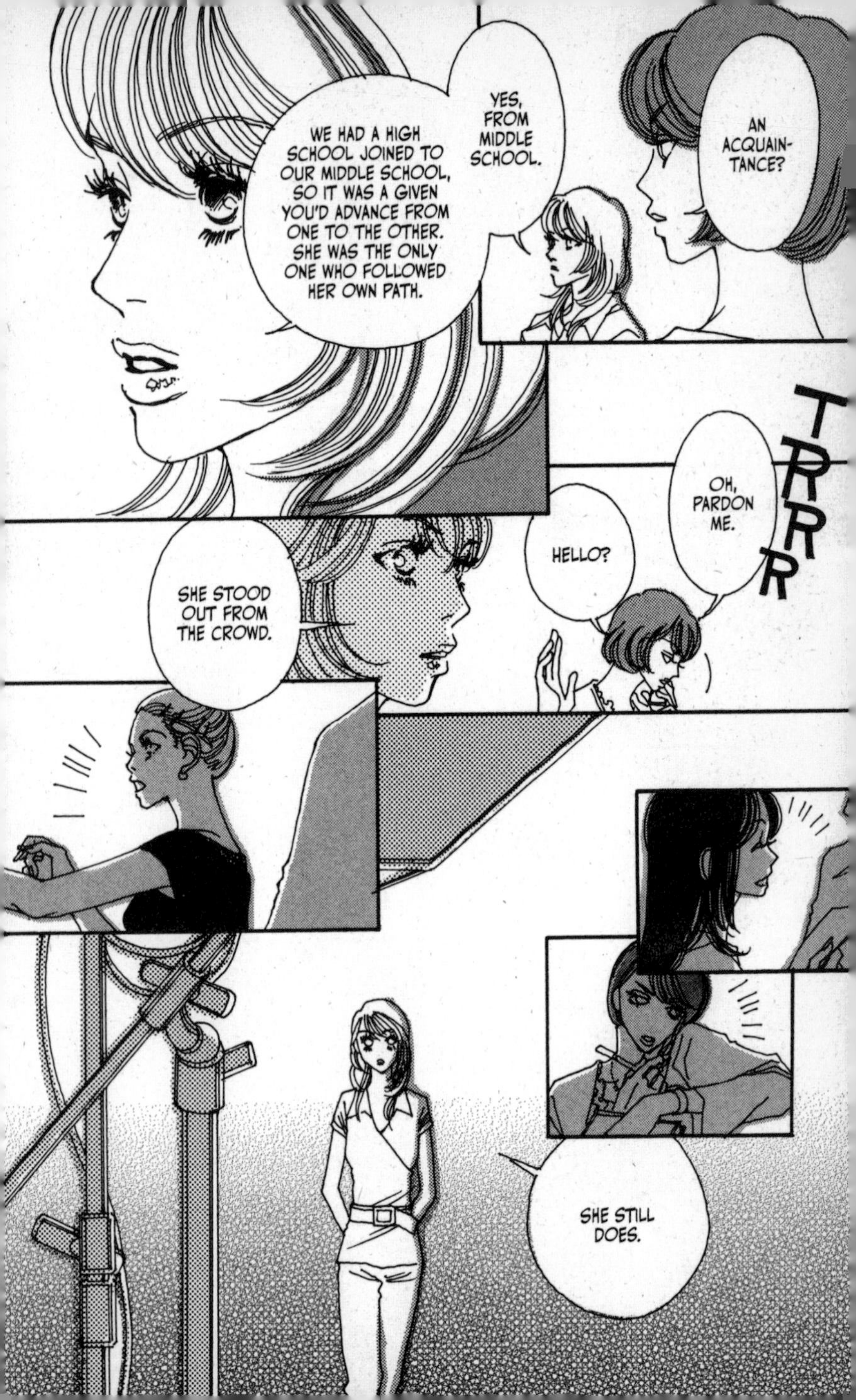
AN ACQUAINTANCE?
YES, FROM MIDDLE SCHOOL.
WE HAD A HIGH SCHOOL JOINED TO OUR MIDDLE SCHOOL, SO IT WAS A GIVEN YOU'D ADVANCE FROM ONE TO THE OTHER. SHE WAS THE ONLY ONE WHO FOLLOWED HER OWN PATH.
TRRR
OH, PARDON ME.
HELLO?
SHE STOOD OUT FROM THE CROWD.
SHE STILL DOES.

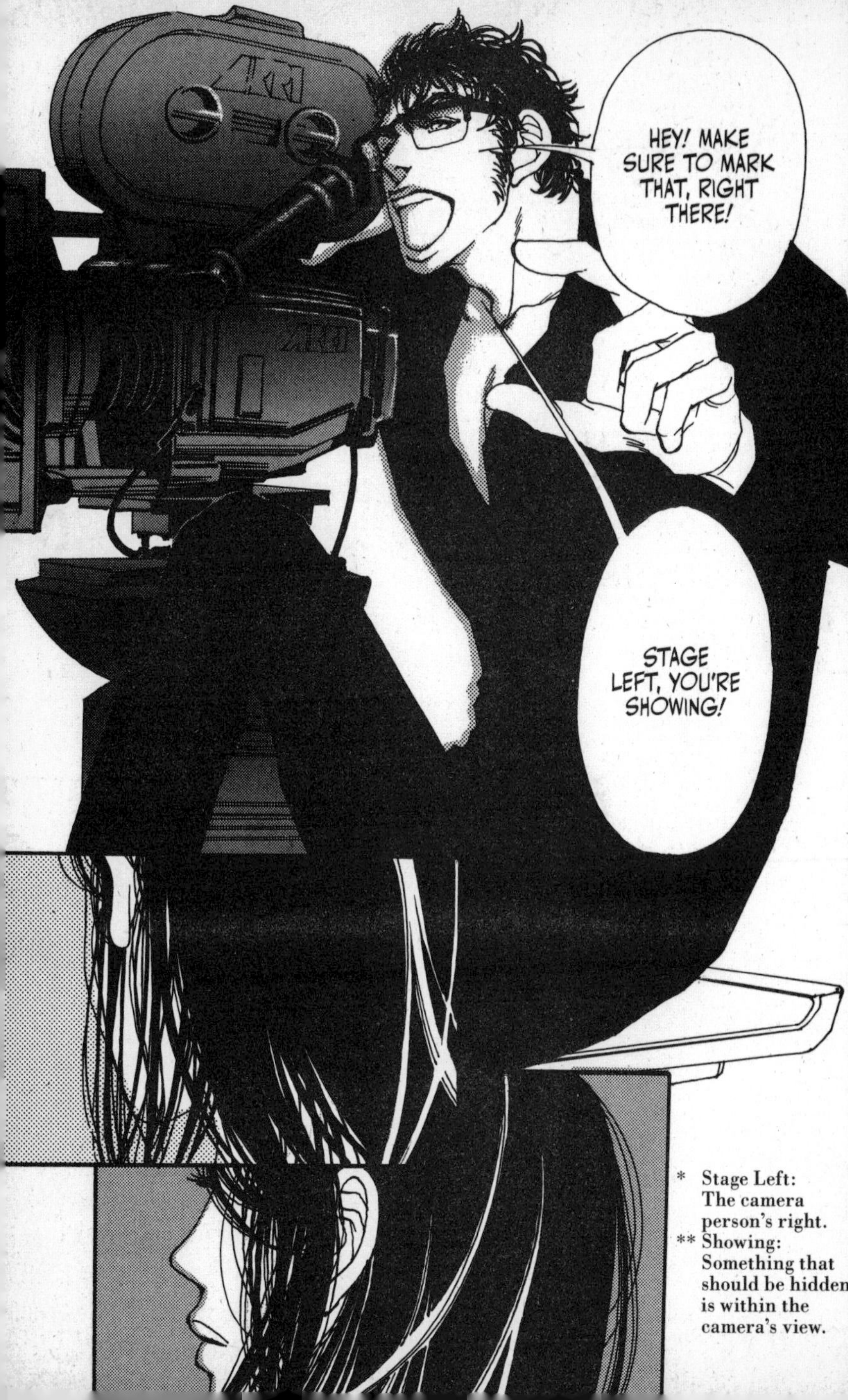
HEY! MAKE SURE TO MARK THAT, RIGHT THERE!
STAGE LEFT, YOU'RE SHOWING!

* Stage Left: The camera person's right.
** Showing: Something that should be hidden is within the camera's view.

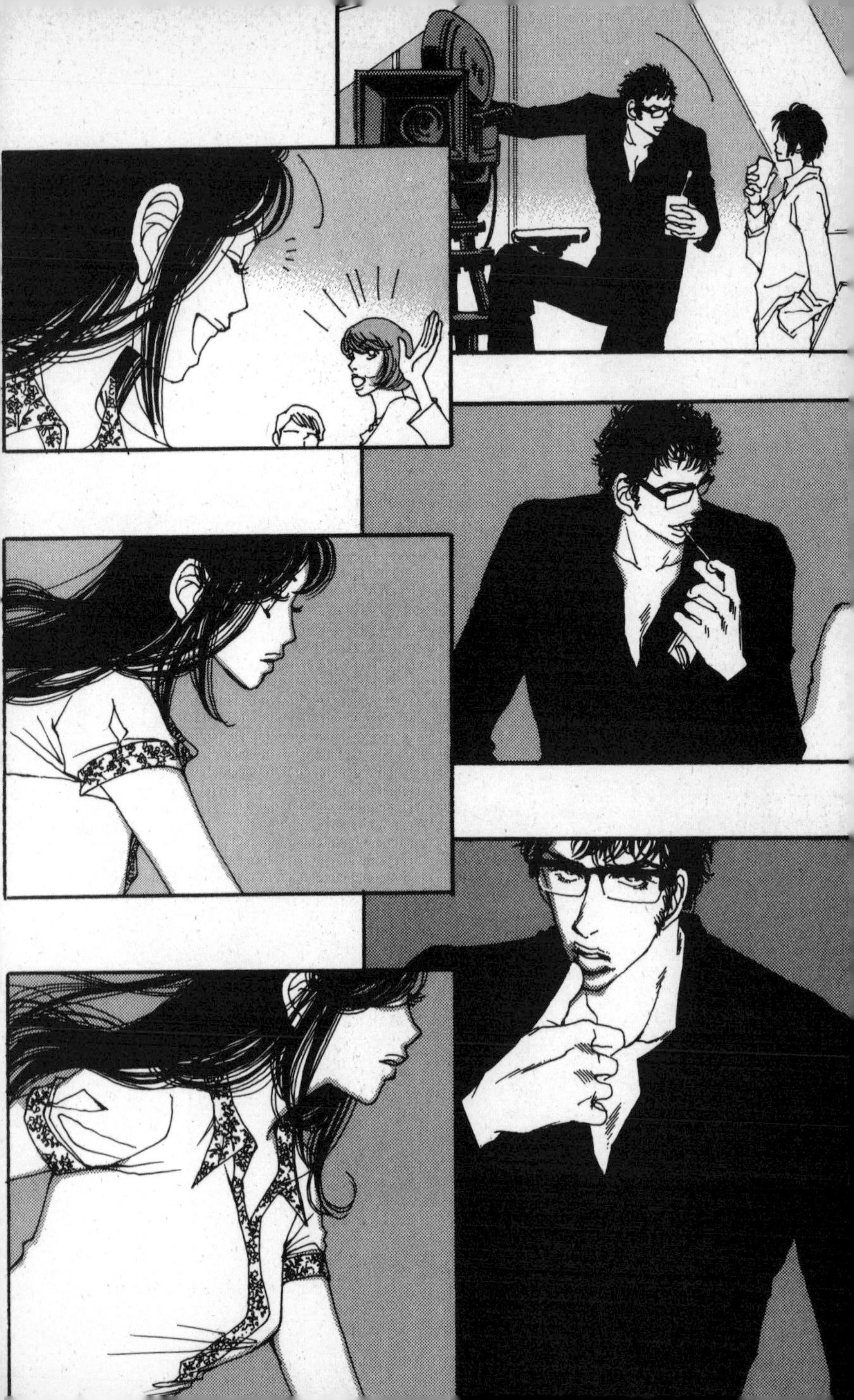

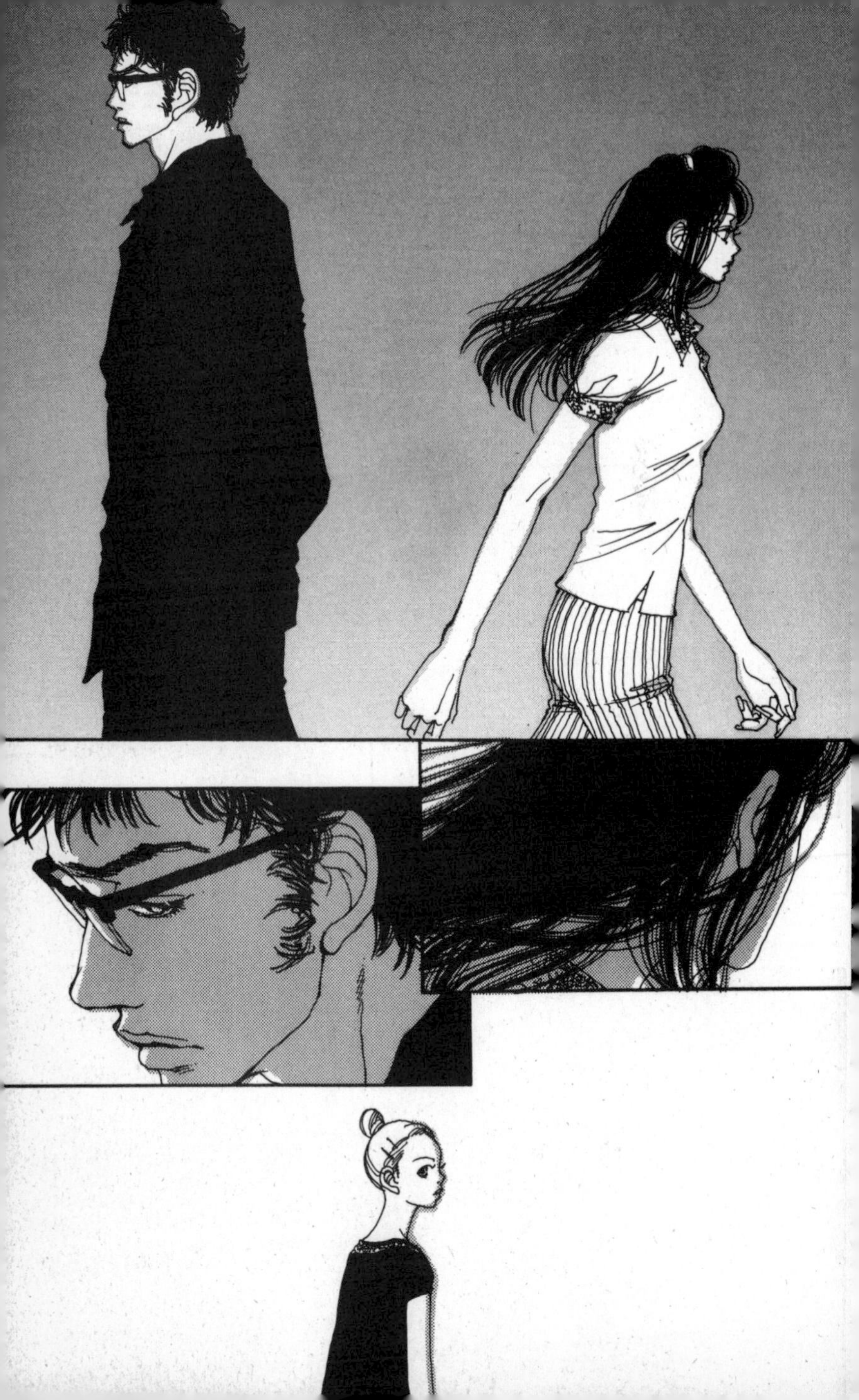

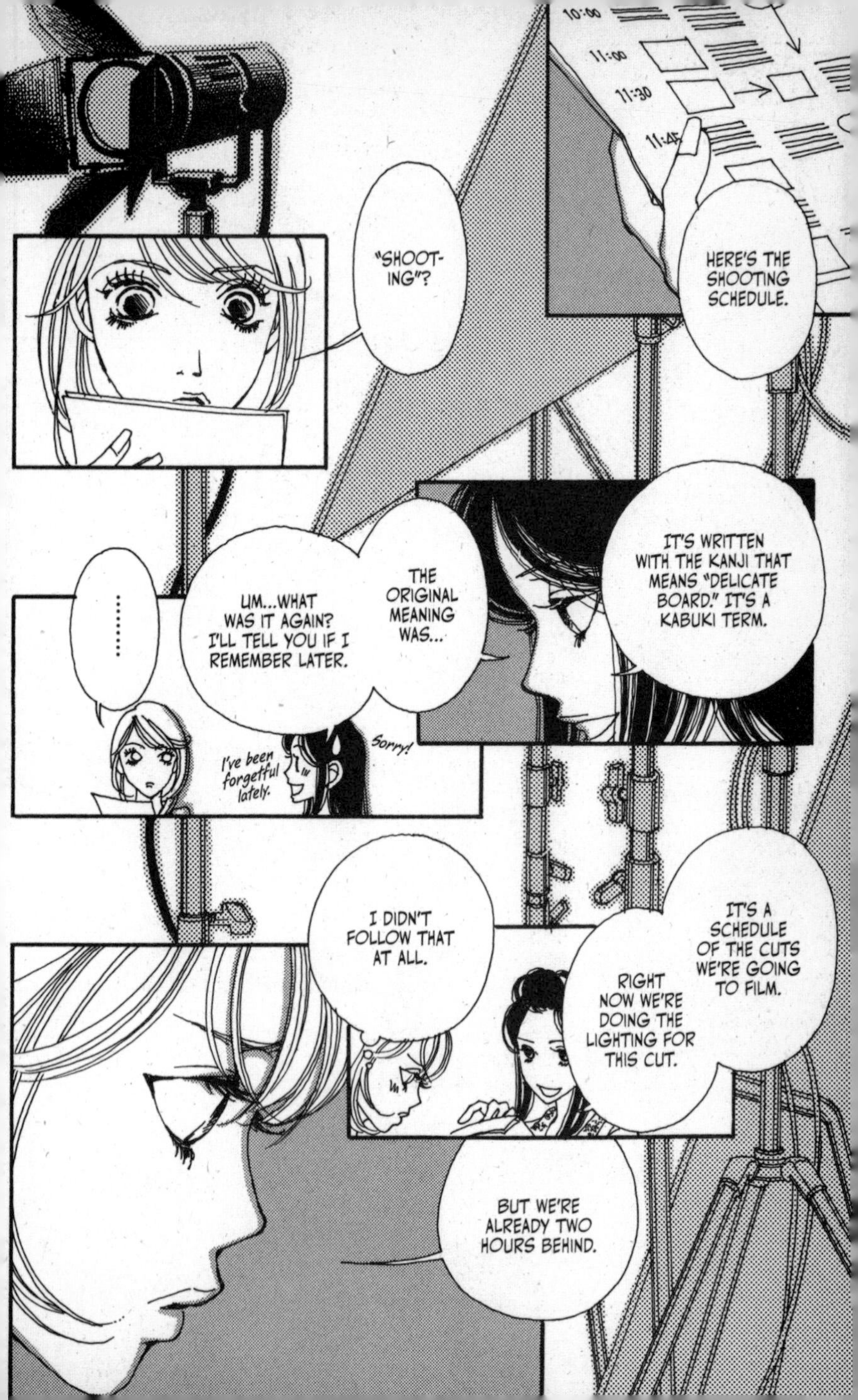
HERE'S THE SHOOTING SCHEDULE.
"SHOOT-ING"?
IT'S WRITTEN WITH THE KANJI THAT MEANS "DELICATE BOARD." IT'S A KABUKI TERM.
THE ORIGINAL MEANING WAS...
UM...WHAT WAS IT AGAIN? I'LL TELL YOU IF I REMEMBER LATER.
......
Sorry!
I've been forgetful lately.
IT'S A SCHEDULE OF THE CUTS WE'RE GOING TO FILM.
RIGHT NOW WE'RE DOING THE LIGHTING FOR THIS CUT.
I DIDN'T FOLLOW THAT AT ALL.
BUT WE'RE ALREADY TWO HOURS BEHIND.

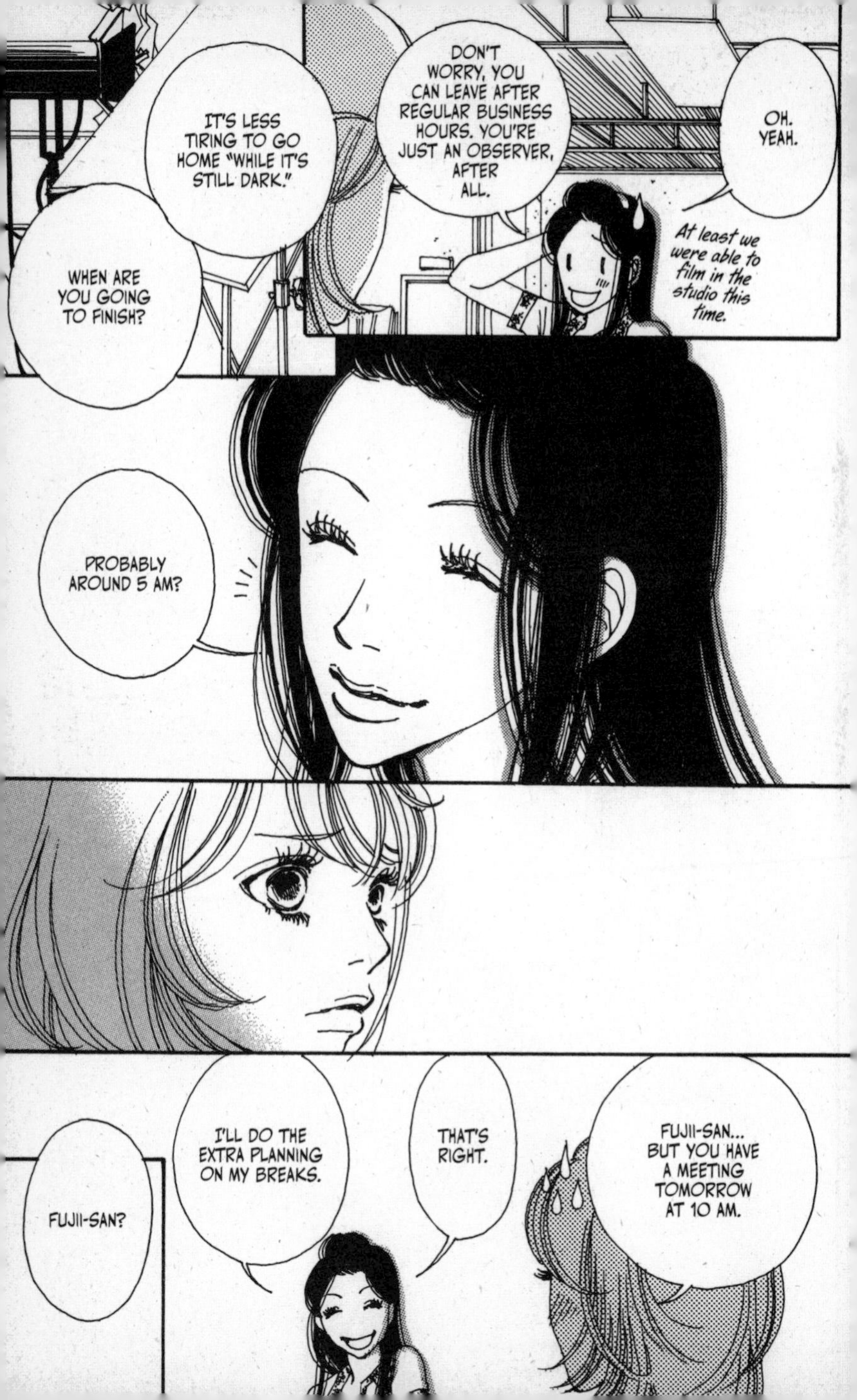
OH. YEAH.
At least we were able to film in the studio this time.
DON'T WORRY, YOU CAN LEAVE AFTER REGULAR BUSINESS HOURS. YOU'RE JUST AN OBSERVER, AFTER ALL.
IT'S LESS TIRING TO GO HOME "WHILE IT'S STILL DARK."
WHEN ARE YOU GOING TO FINISH?
PROBABLY AROUND 5 AM?
FUJII-SAN... BUT YOU HAVE A MEETING TOMORROW AT 10 AM.
THAT'S RIGHT.
I'LL DO THE EXTRA PLANNING ON MY BREAKS.
FUJII-SAN?

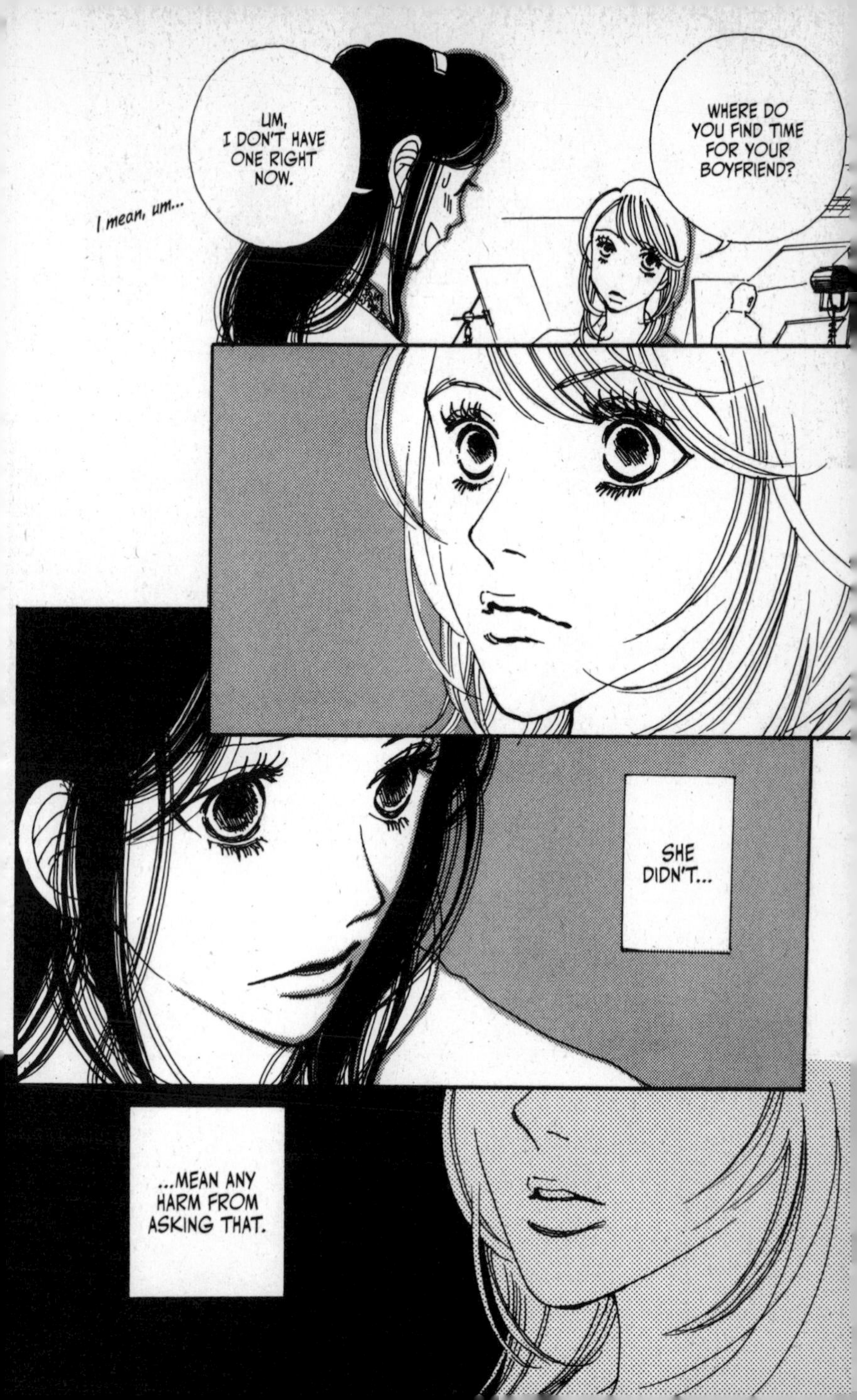
WHERE DO YOU FIND TIME FOR YOUR BOYFRIEND?
UM, I DON'T HAVE ONE RIGHT NOW.
I mean, um...
SHE DIDN'T...
...MEAN ANY HARM FROM ASKING THAT.

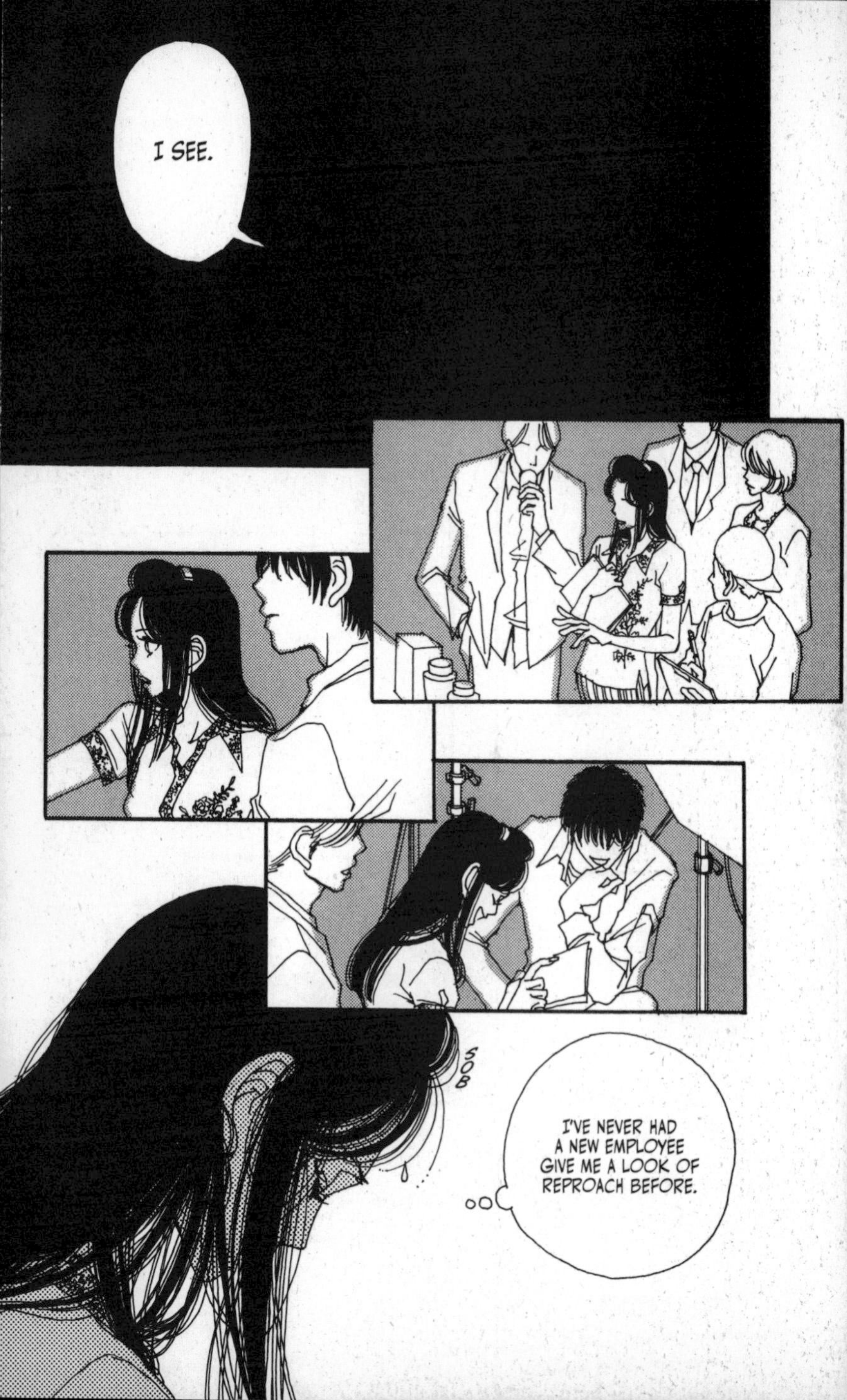
I SEE.
SOB
I'VE NEVER HAD A NEW EMPLOYEE GIVE ME A LOOK OF REPROACH BEFORE.

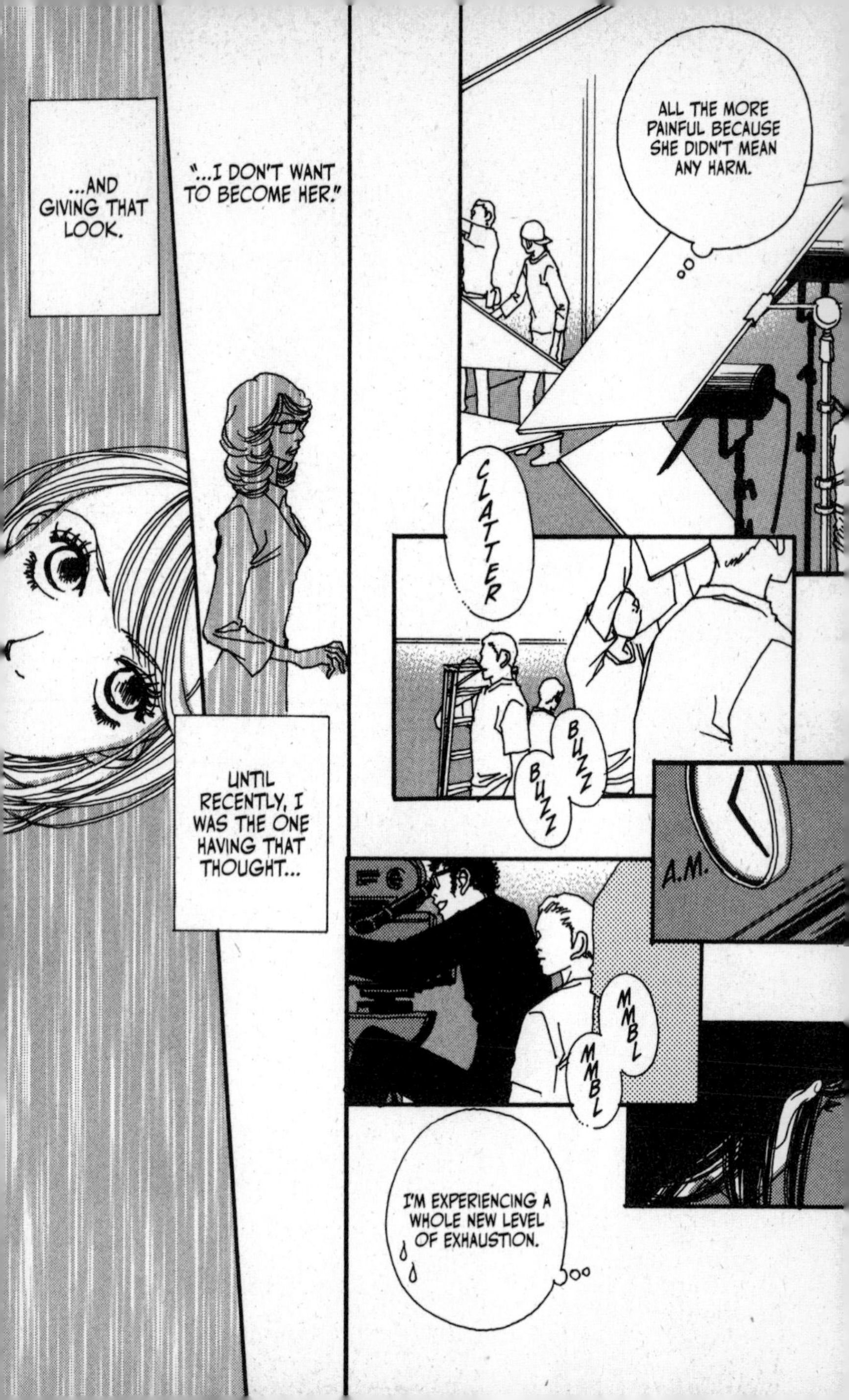
ALL THE MORE PAINFUL BECAUSE SHE DIDN'T MEAN ANY HARM.
CLATTER
BUZZ BUZZ
A.M.
MMBL MMBL
I'M EXPERIENCING A WHOLE NEW LEVEL OF EXHAUSTION.
"...I DON'T WANT TO BECOME HER."
UNTIL RECENTLY, I WAS THE ONE HAVING THAT THOUGHT...
...AND GIVING THAT LOOK.

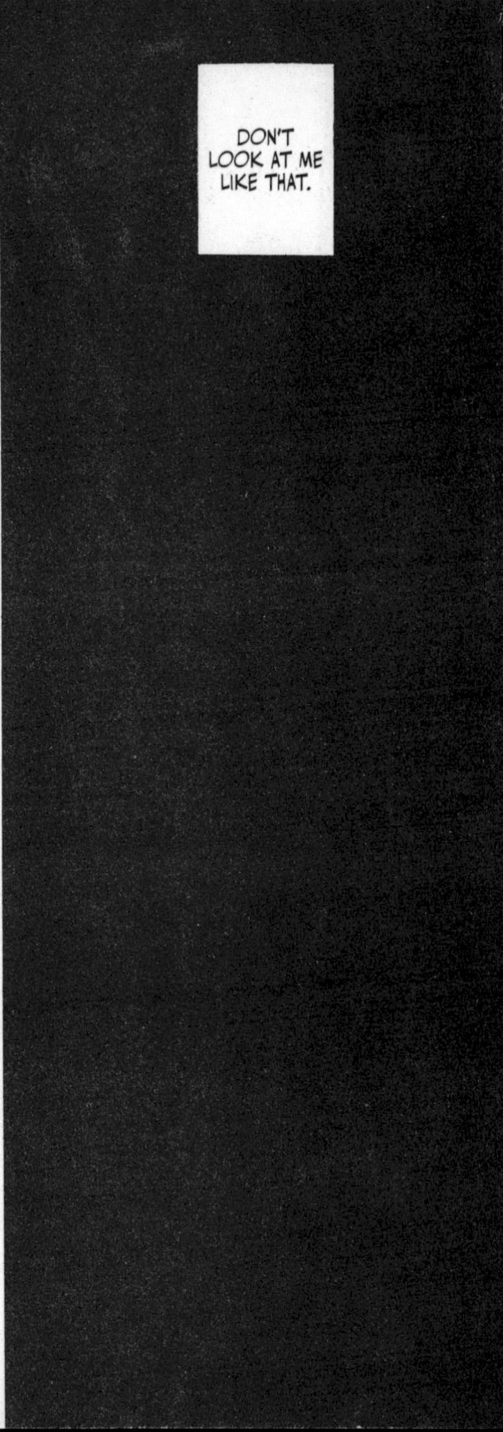
DON'T LOOK AT ME LIKE THAT.

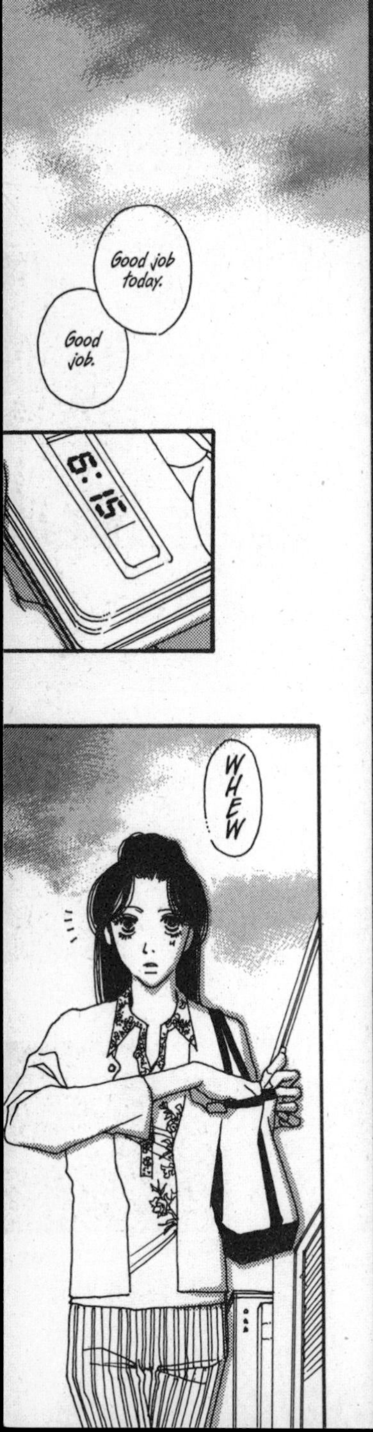
Good job today.
Good job.
6:15
WHEW

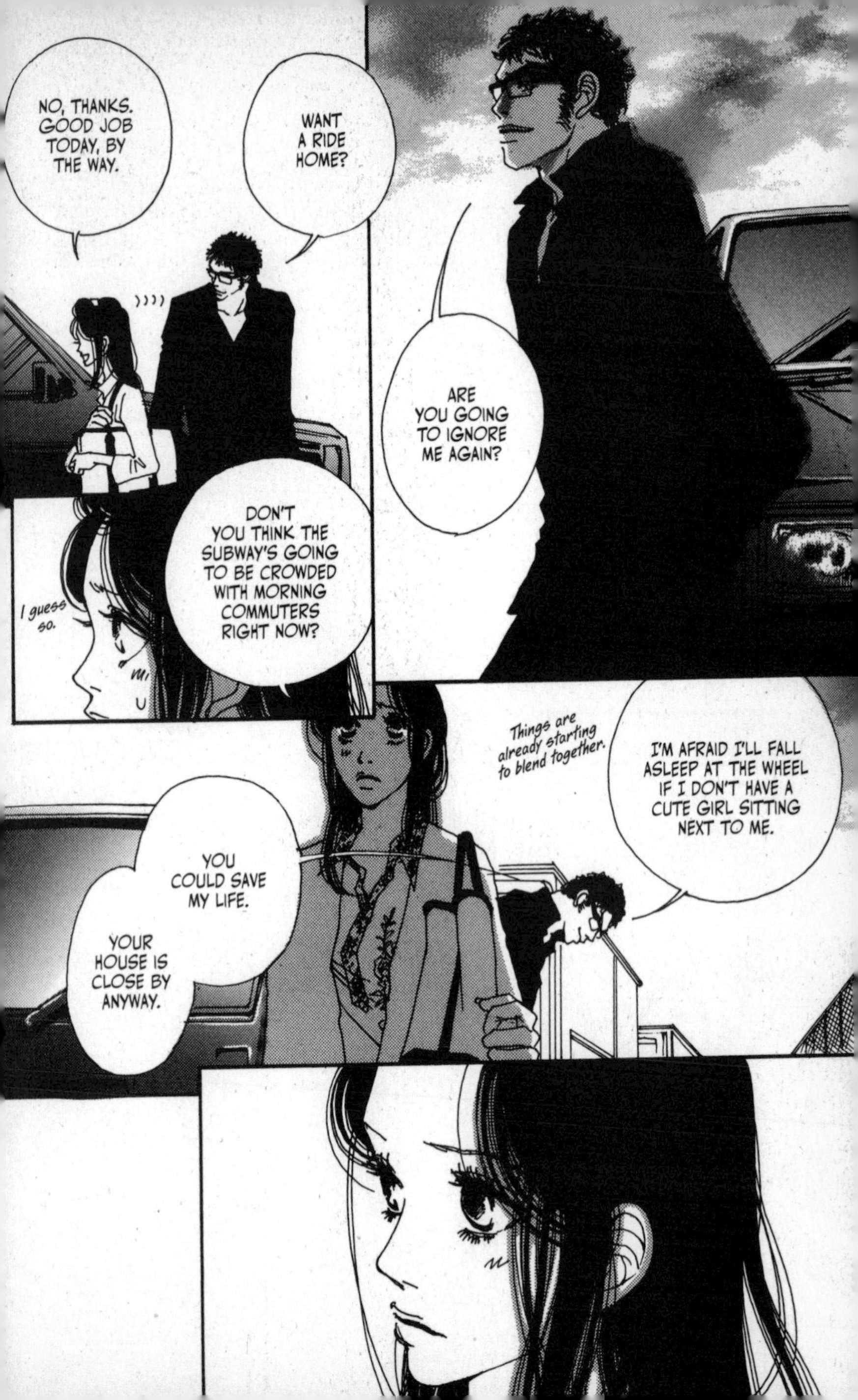
ARE YOU GOING TO IGNORE ME AGAIN?
WANT A RIDE HOME?
NO, THANKS. GOOD JOB TODAY, BY THE WAY.
DON'T YOU THINK THE SUBWAY'S GOING TO BE CROWDED WITH MORNING COMMUTERS RIGHT NOW?
I guess so.
I'M AFRAID I'LL FALL ASLEEP AT THE WHEEL IF I DON'T HAVE A CUTE GIRL SITTING NEXT TO ME.
Things are already starting to blend together.
YOU COULD SAVE MY LIFE.
YOUR HOUSE IS CLOSE BY ANYWAY.

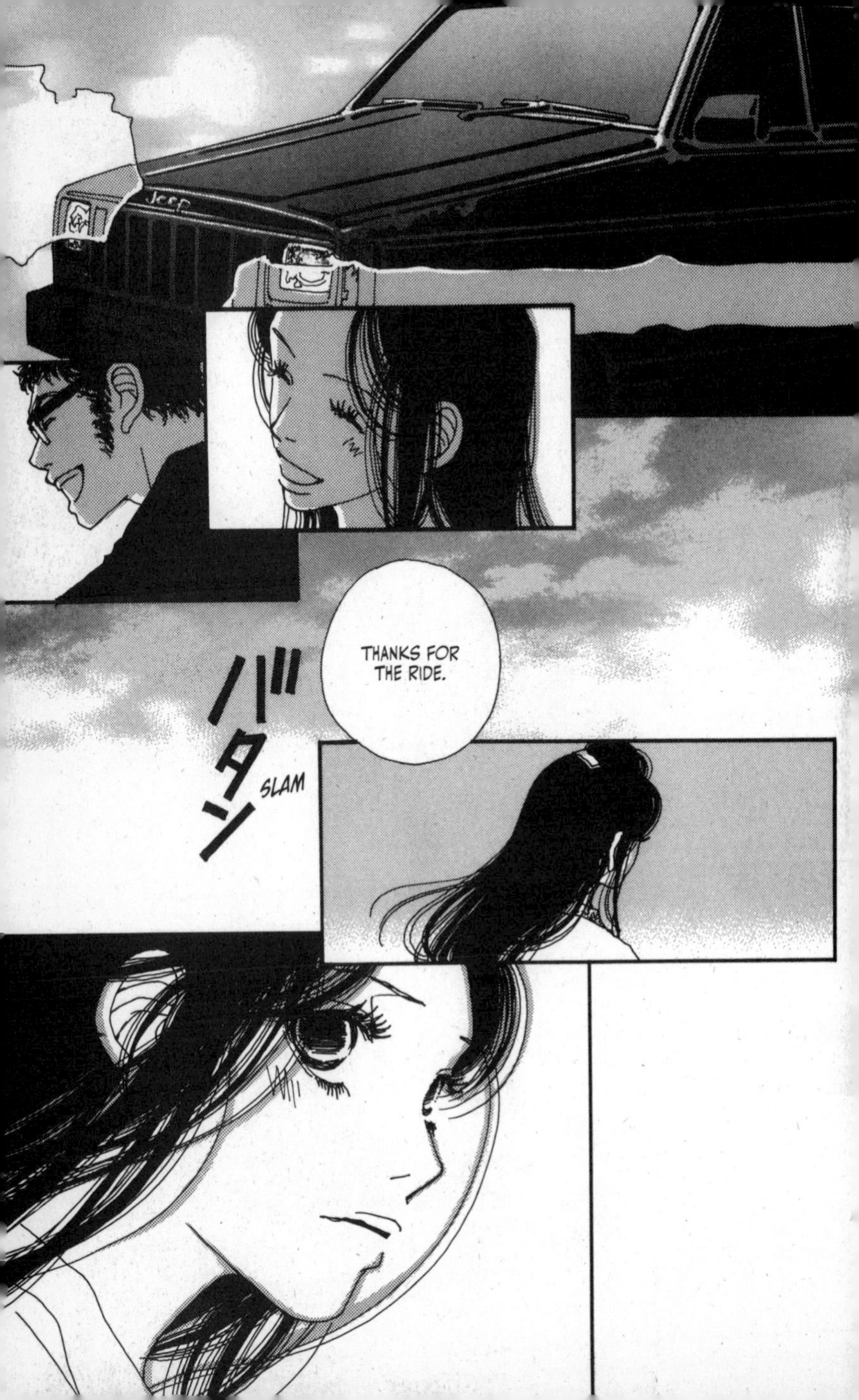
THANKS FOR THE RIDE.
バタン
SLAM

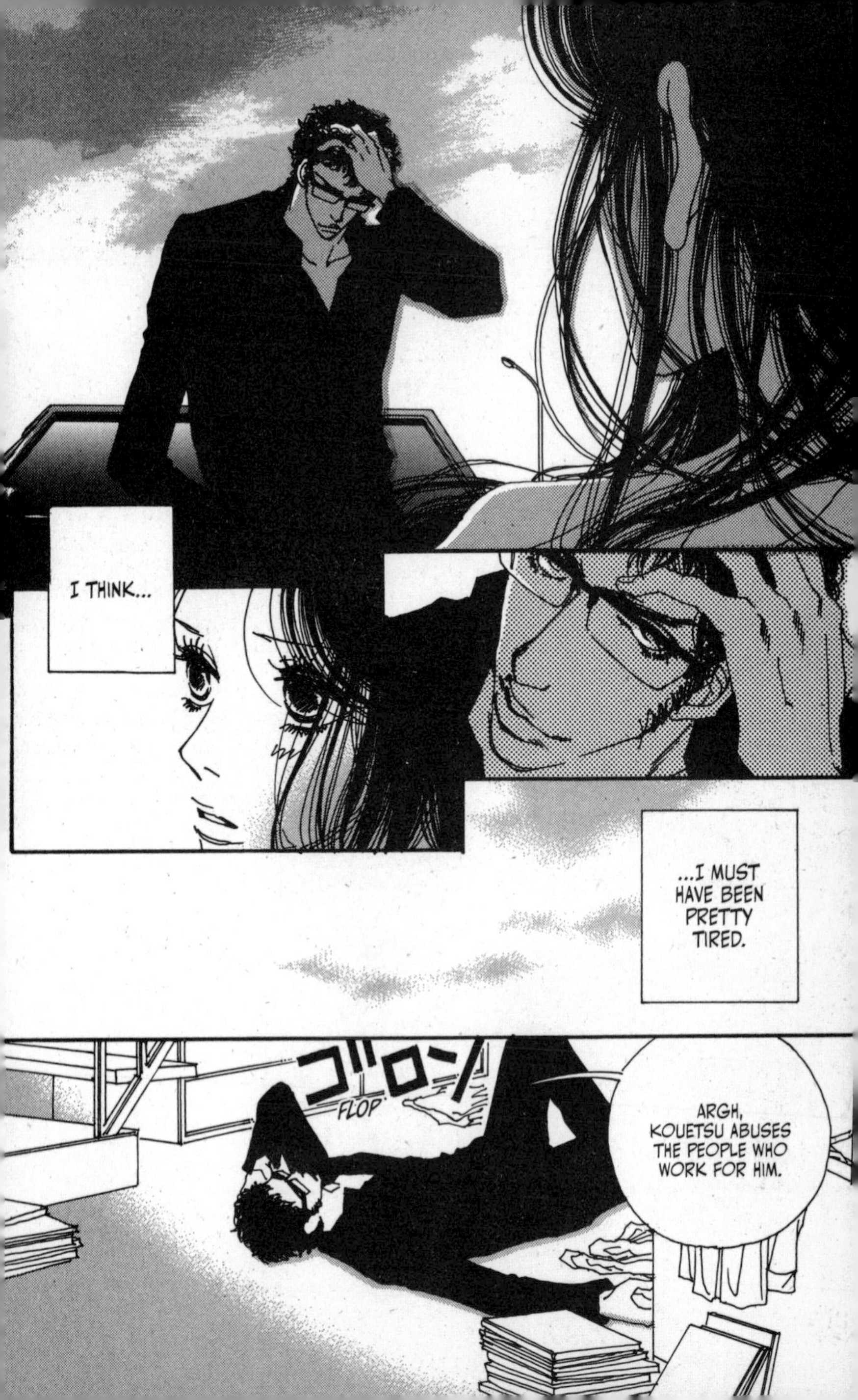
I THINK...
...I MUST HAVE BEEN PRETTY TIRED.
ARGH, KOUETSU ABUSES THE PEOPLE WHO WORK FOR HIM.
ゴロン
FLOP

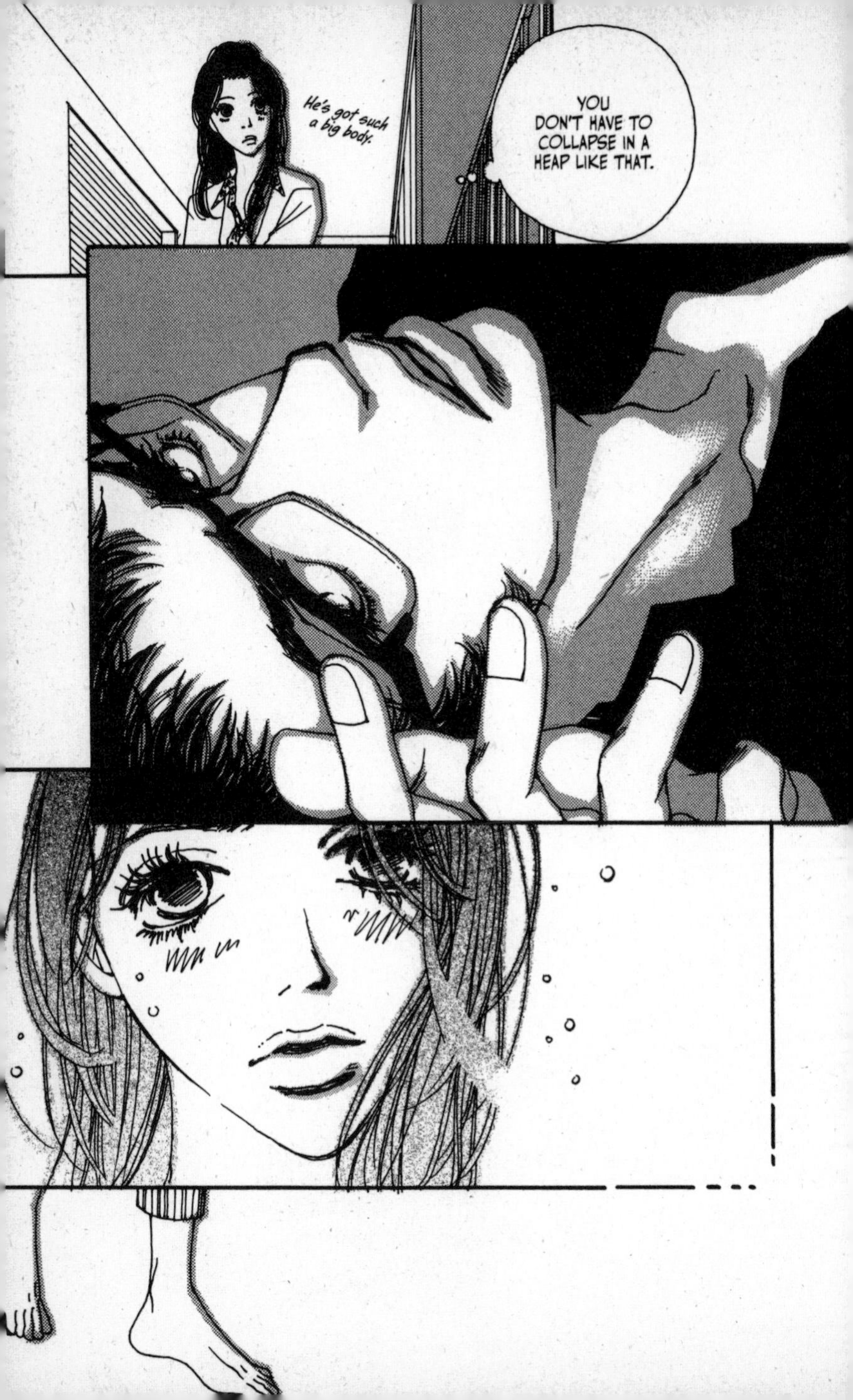
YOU DON'T HAVE TO COLLAPSE IN A HEAP LIKE THAT.
He's got such a big body.

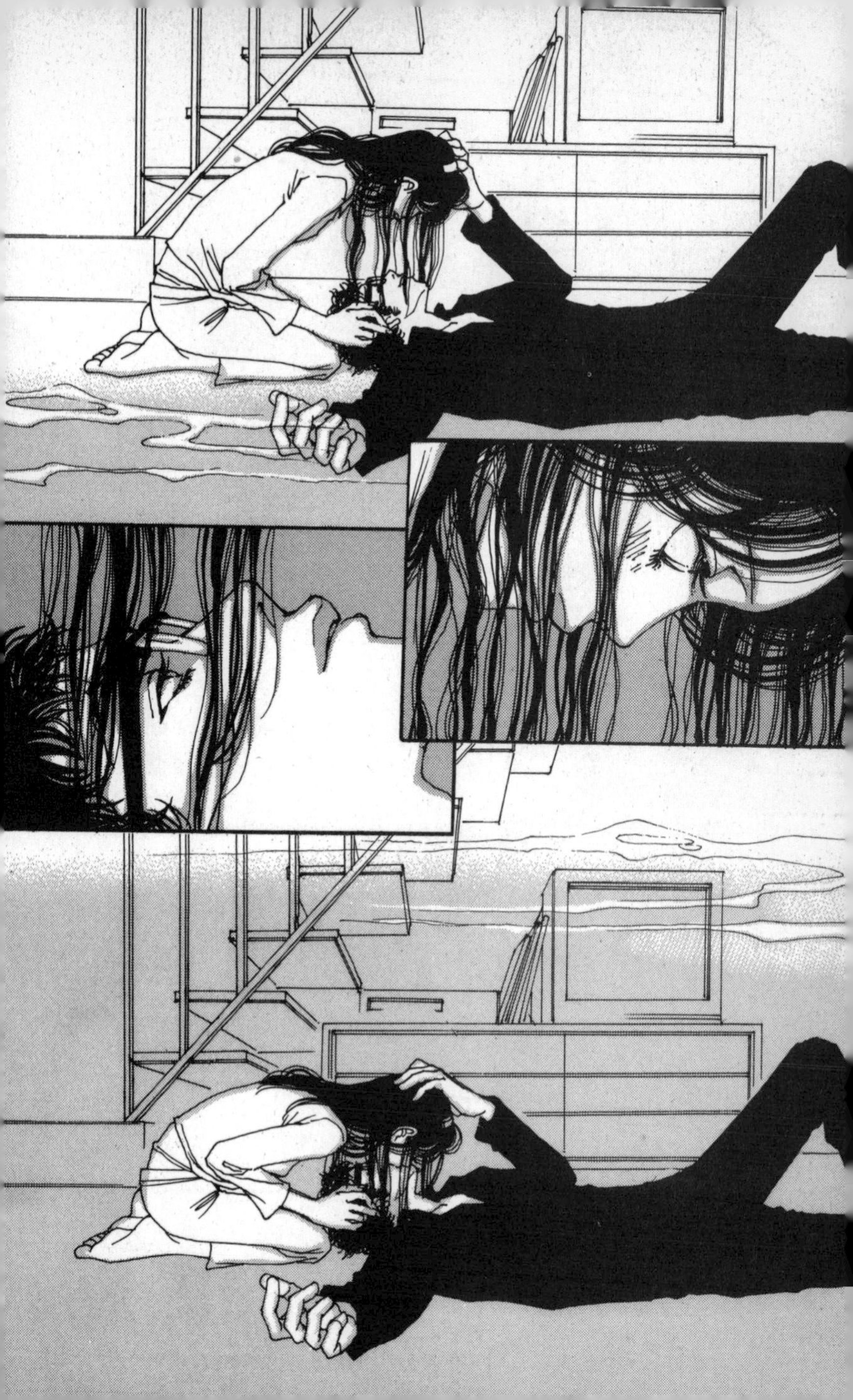

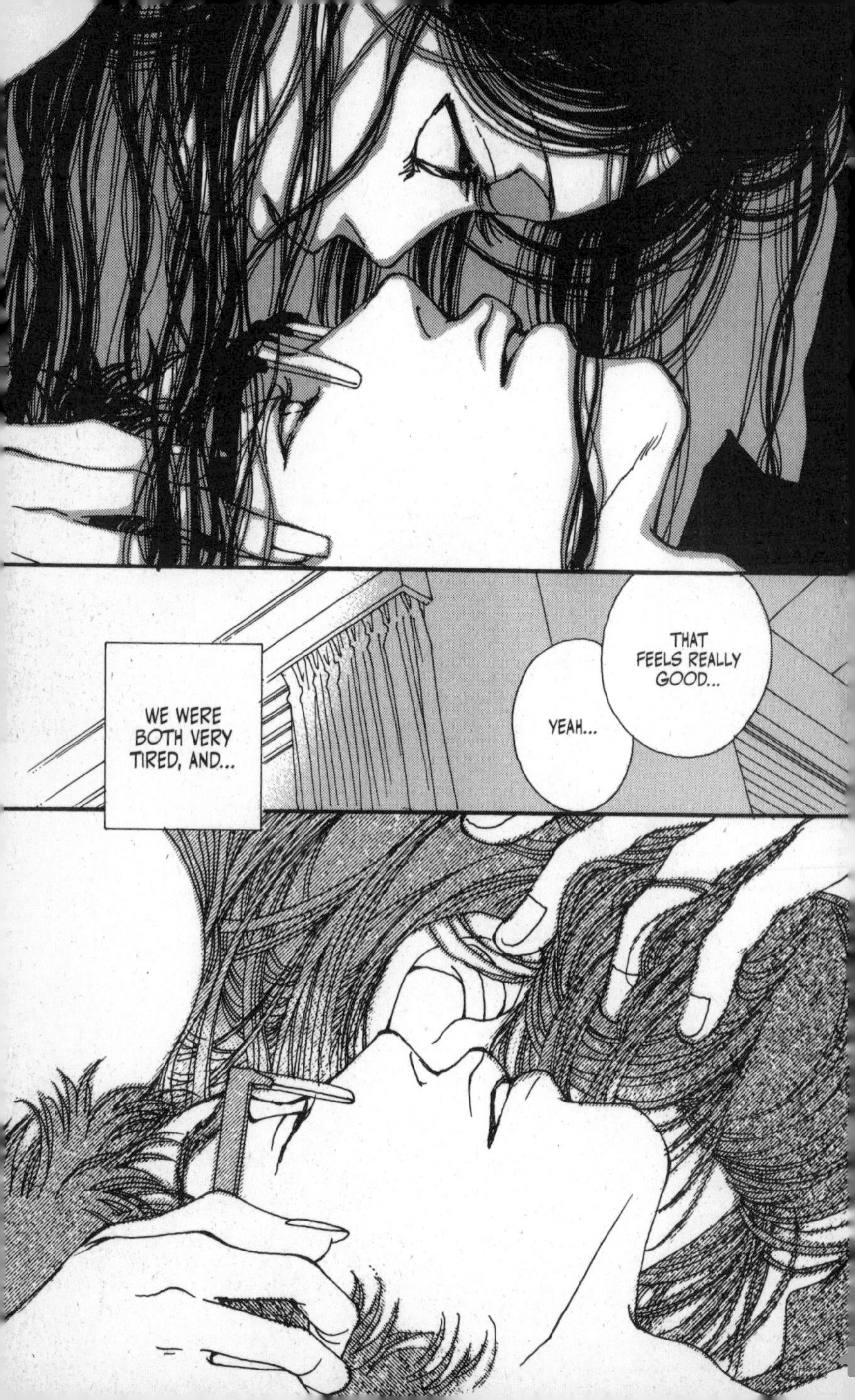
THAT FEELS REALLY GOOD...
YEAH...
WE WERE BOTH VERY TIRED, AND...

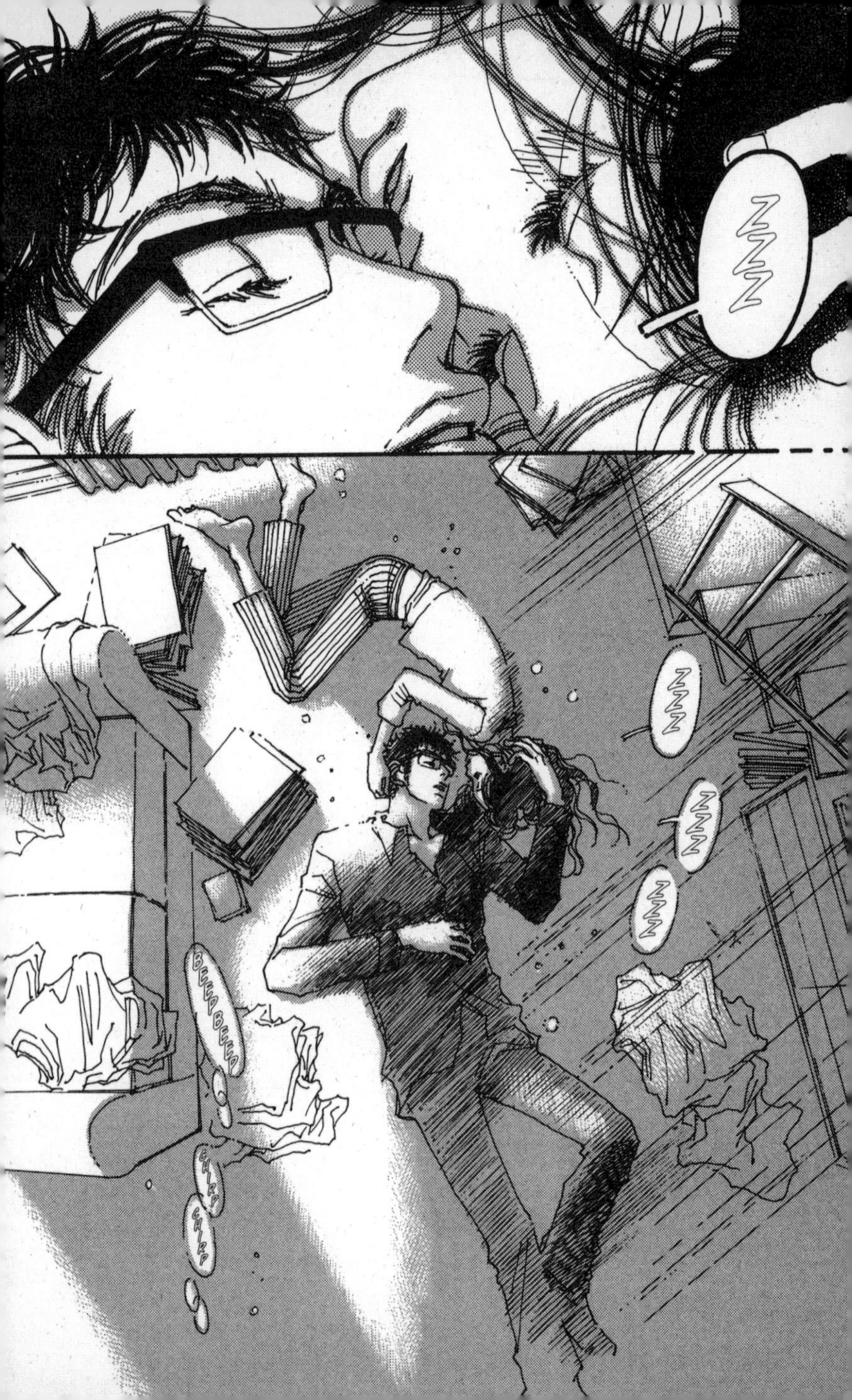
ZZZ
ZZZ
ZZZ
ZZZ
BEEP BEEP
CHIRP
CHIRP

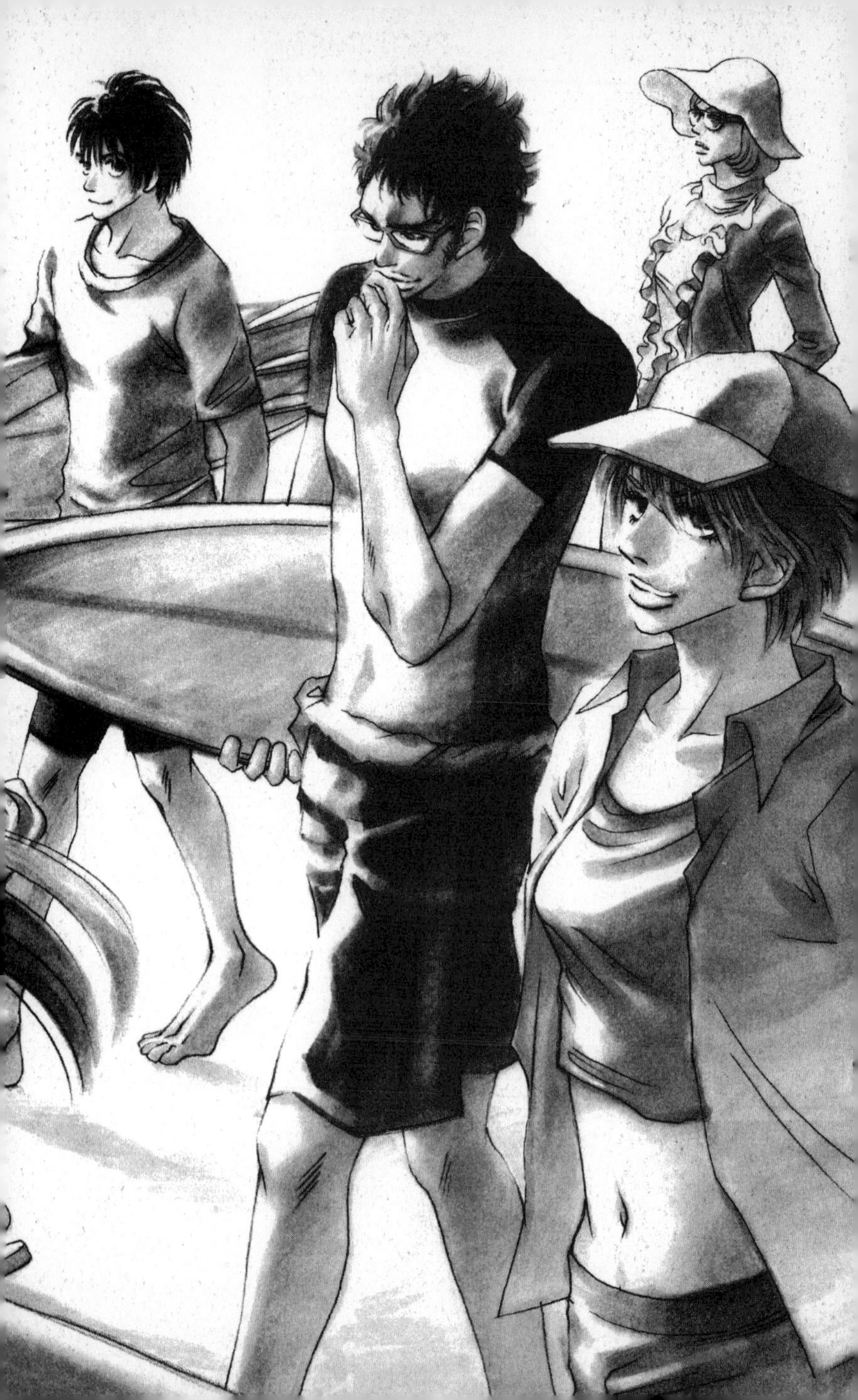

FILE. 27

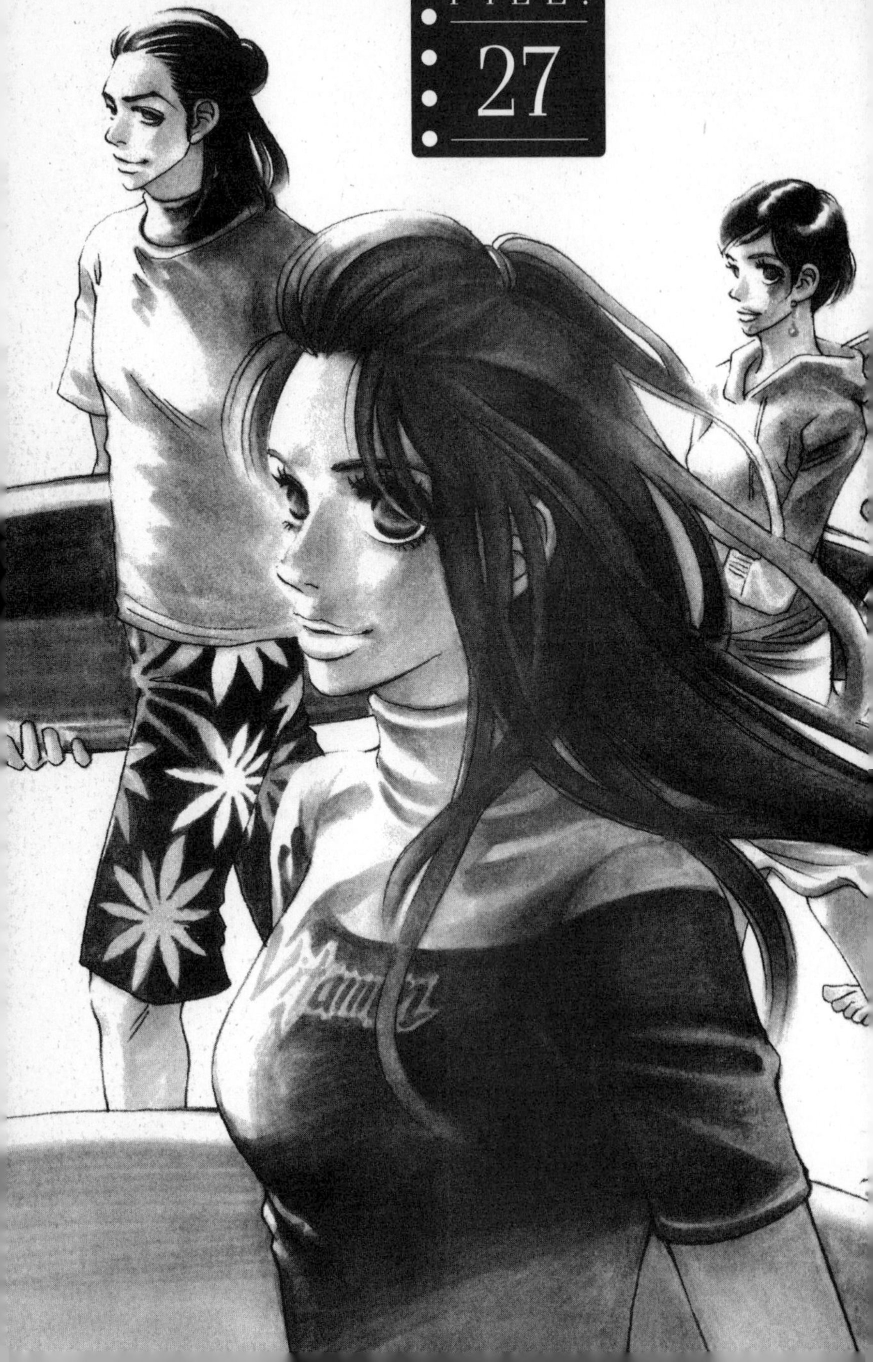

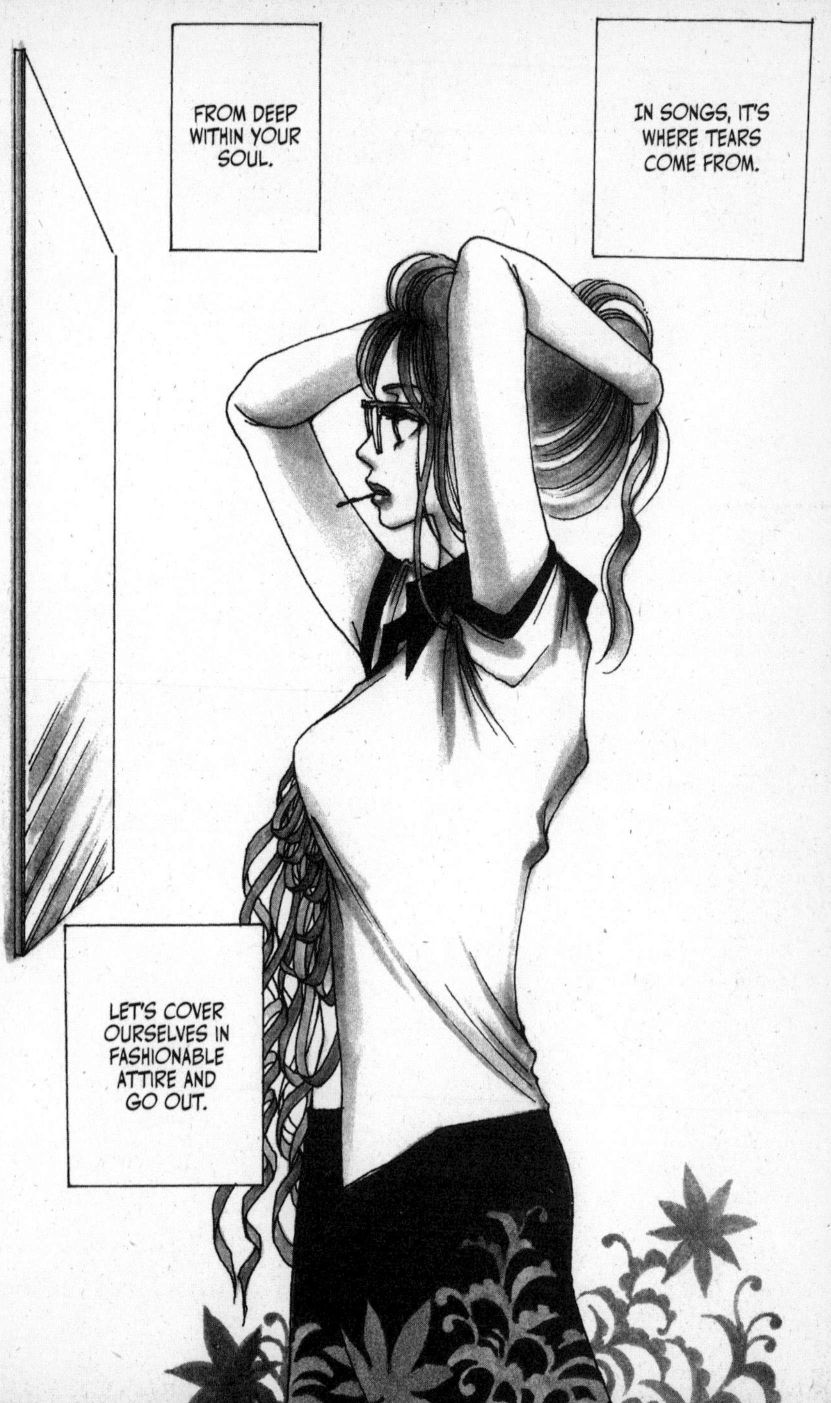
IN SONGS, IT'S WHERE TEARS COME FROM.
FROM DEEP WITHIN YOUR SOUL.
LET'S COVER OURSELVES IN FASHIONABLE ATTIRE AND GO OUT.

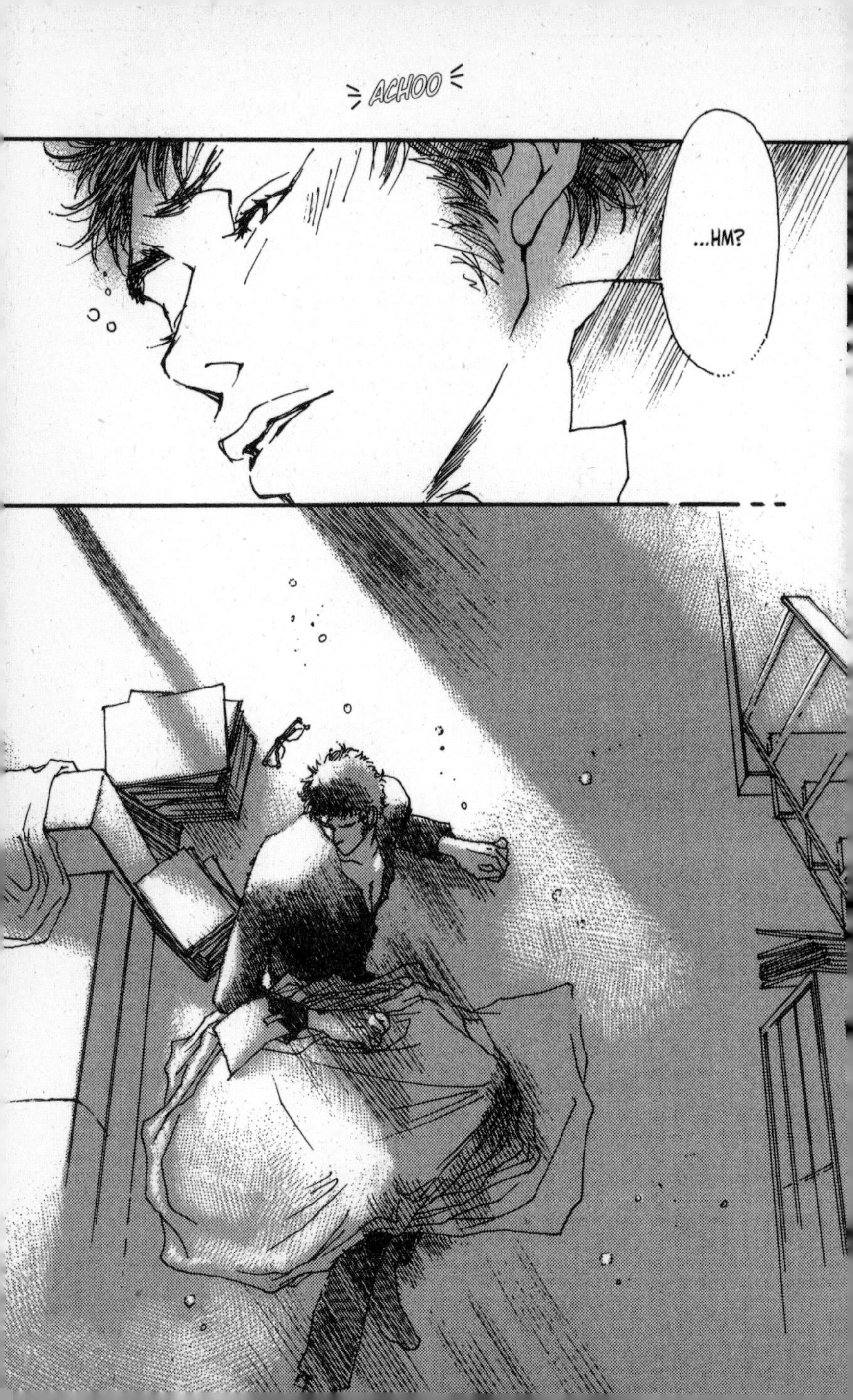
ACHOO
...HM?

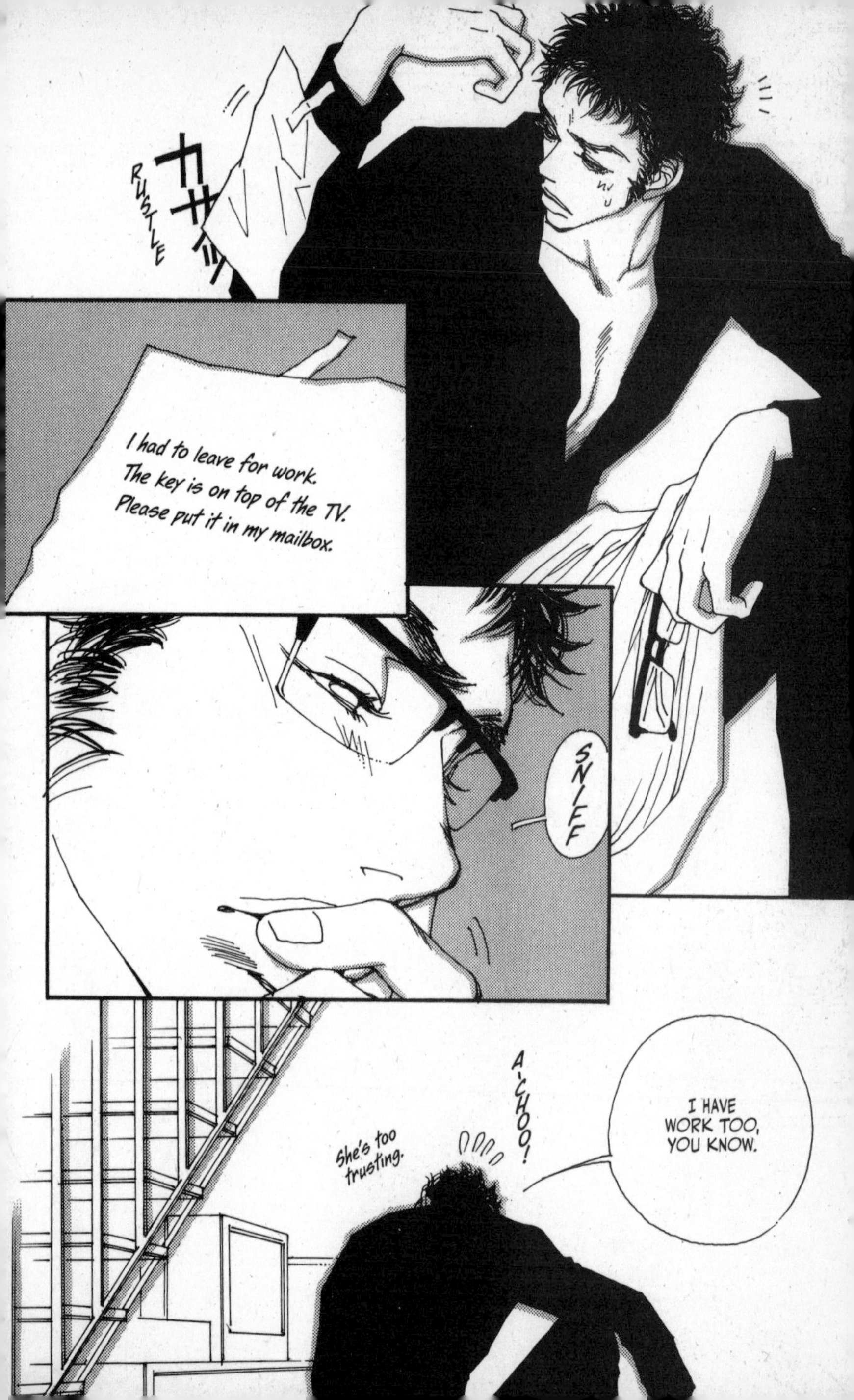
カサッ
RUSTLE
I had to leave for work. The key is on top of the TV. Please put it in my mailbox.
SNIFF
I HAVE WORK TOO, YOU KNOW.
A-CHOO!
She's too trusting.

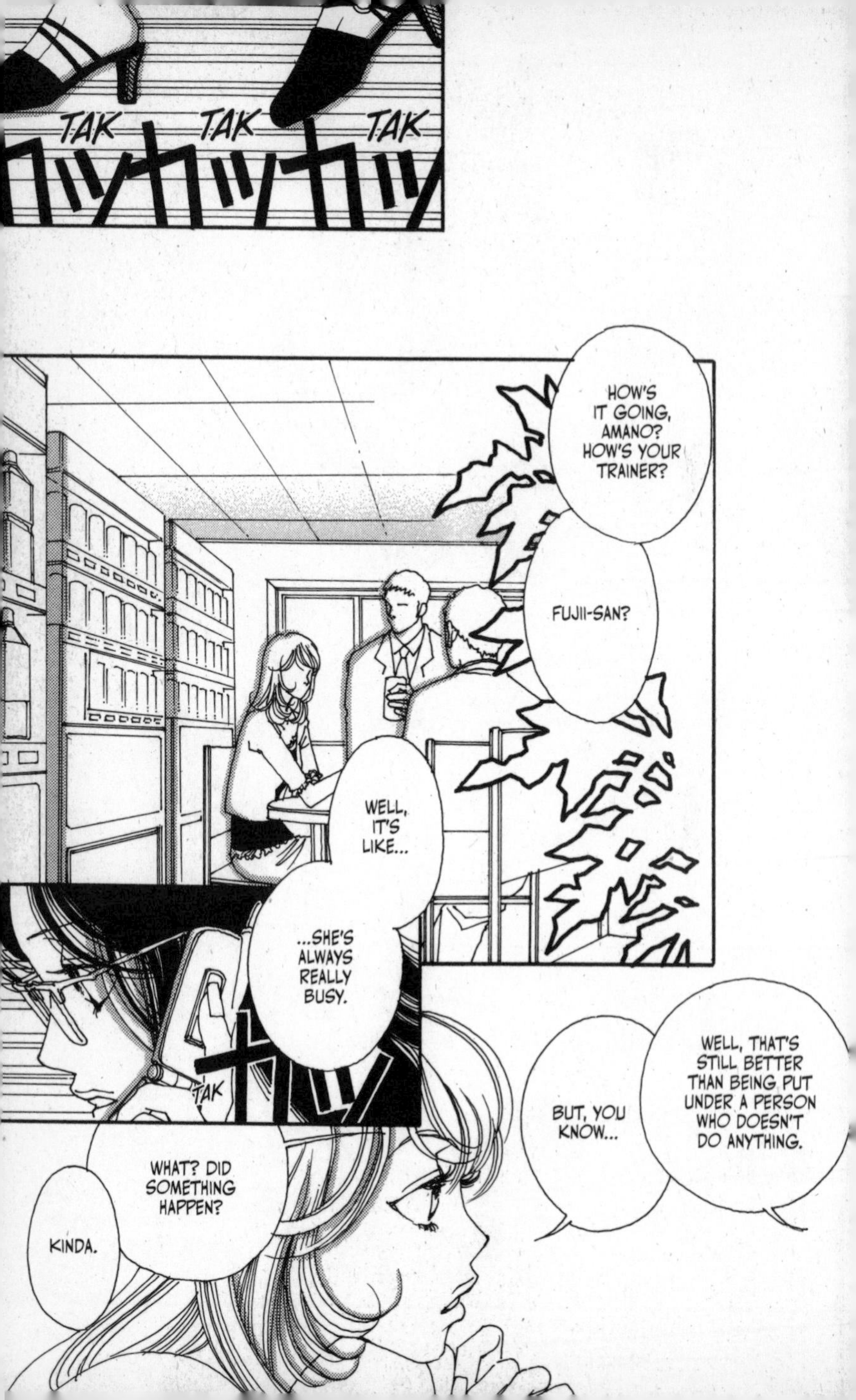
TAK TAK TAK
カッカッカッ
HOW'S IT GOING, AMANO? HOW'S YOUR TRAINER?
FUJII-SAN?
WELL, IT'S LIKE...
...SHE'S ALWAYS REALLY BUSY.
TAK
WELL, THAT'S STILL BETTER THAN BEING PUT UNDER A PERSON WHO DOESN'T DO ANYTHING.
BUT, YOU KNOW...
WHAT? DID SOMETHING HAPPEN?
KINDA.

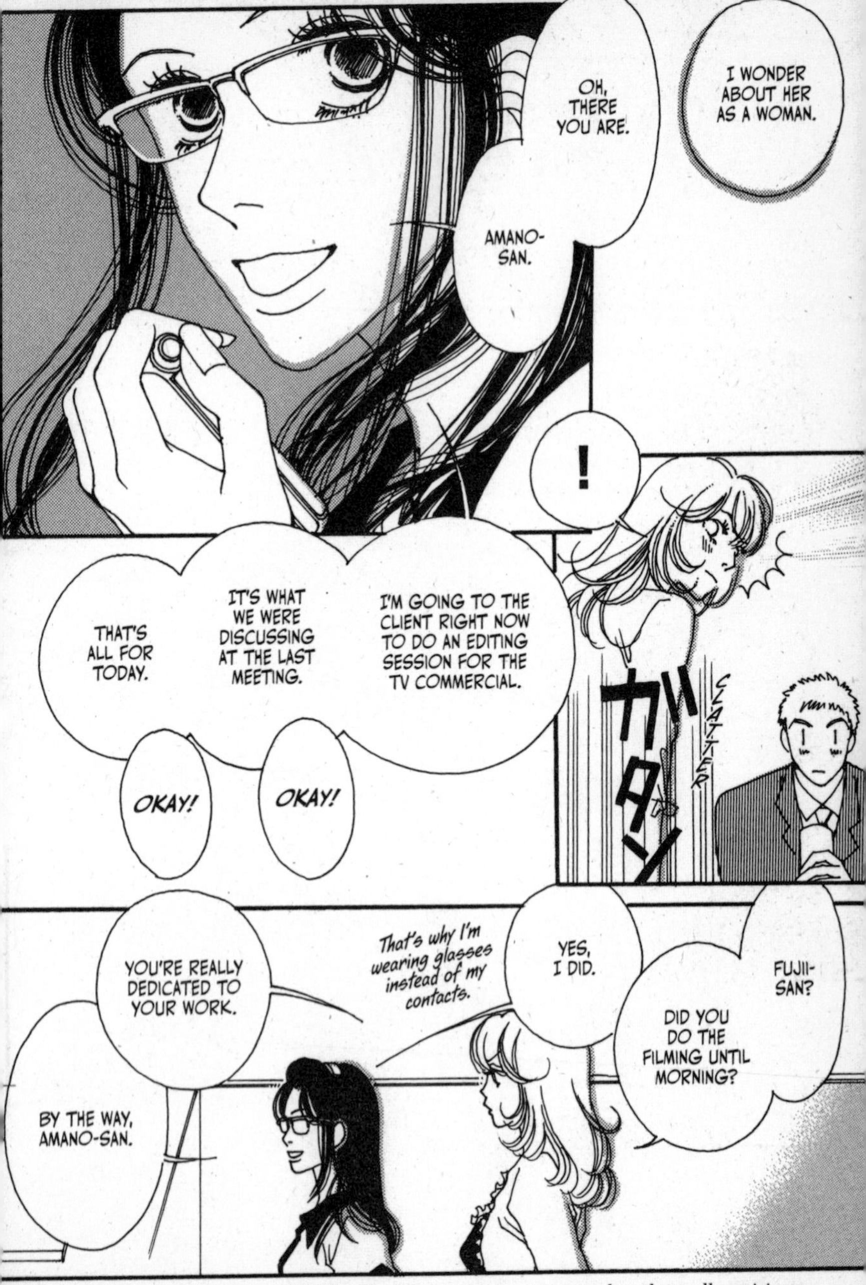
I WONDER ABOUT HER AS A WOMAN.
OH, THERE YOU ARE.
AMANO-SAN.
!
カタン
CLATTER
I'M GOING TO THE CLIENT RIGHT NOW TO DO AN EDITING SESSION FOR THE TV COMMERCIAL.
IT'S WHAT WE WERE DISCUSSING AT THE LAST MEETING.
THAT'S ALL FOR TODAY.
OKAY!
OKAY!
FUJII-SAN?
DID YOU DO THE FILMING UNTIL MORNING?
YES, I DID.
That's why I'm wearing glasses instead of my contacts.
YOU'RE REALLY DEDICATED TO YOUR WORK.
BY THE WAY, AMANO-SAN.

*Editing Session: The film is edited digitally. The colorist, camera person and producer all participate.

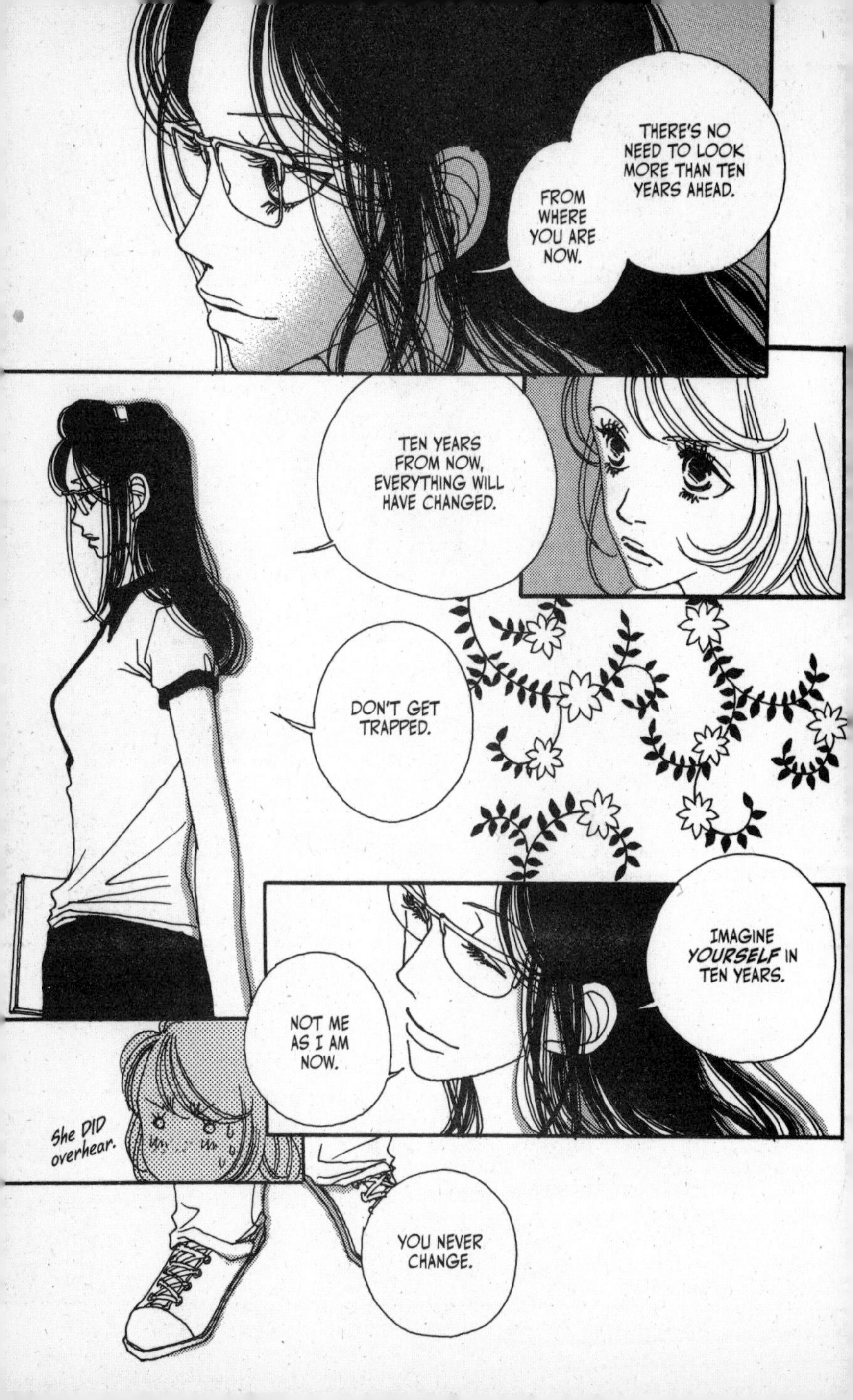
THERE'S NO NEED TO LOOK MORE THAN TEN YEARS AHEAD.
FROM WHERE YOU ARE NOW.
TEN YEARS FROM NOW, EVERYTHING WILL HAVE CHANGED.
DON'T GET TRAPPED.
IMAGINE *YOURSELF* IN TEN YEARS.
NOT ME AS I AM NOW.
She DID overhear.
YOU NEVER CHANGE.

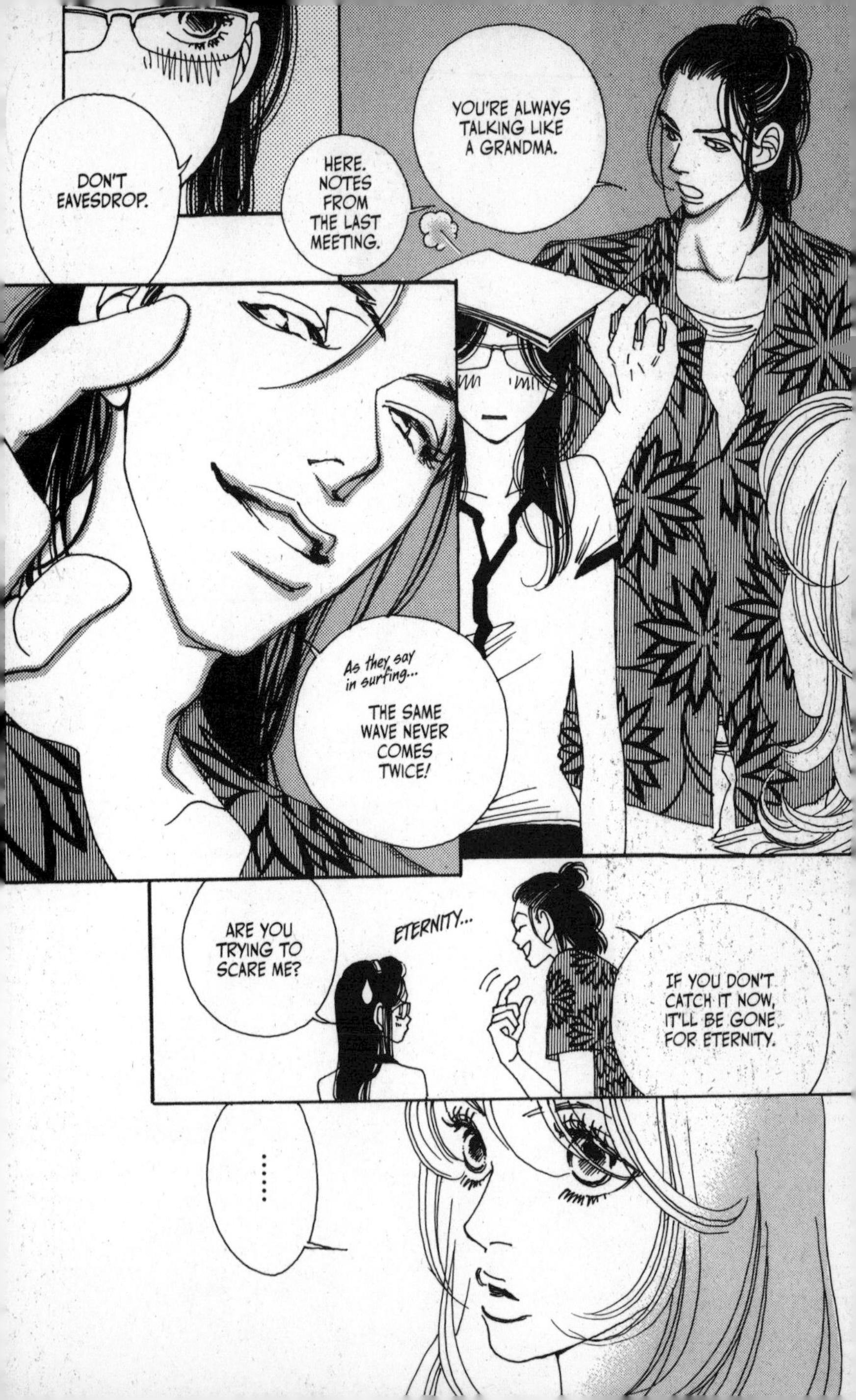
YOU'RE ALWAYS TALKING LIKE A GRANDMA.
HERE. NOTES FROM THE LAST MEETING.
DON'T EAVESDROP.
As they say in surfing... THE SAME WAVE NEVER COMES TWICE!
IF YOU DON'T CATCH IT NOW, IT'LL BE GONE FOR ETERNITY.
ETERNITY...
ARE YOU TRYING TO SCARE ME?
......

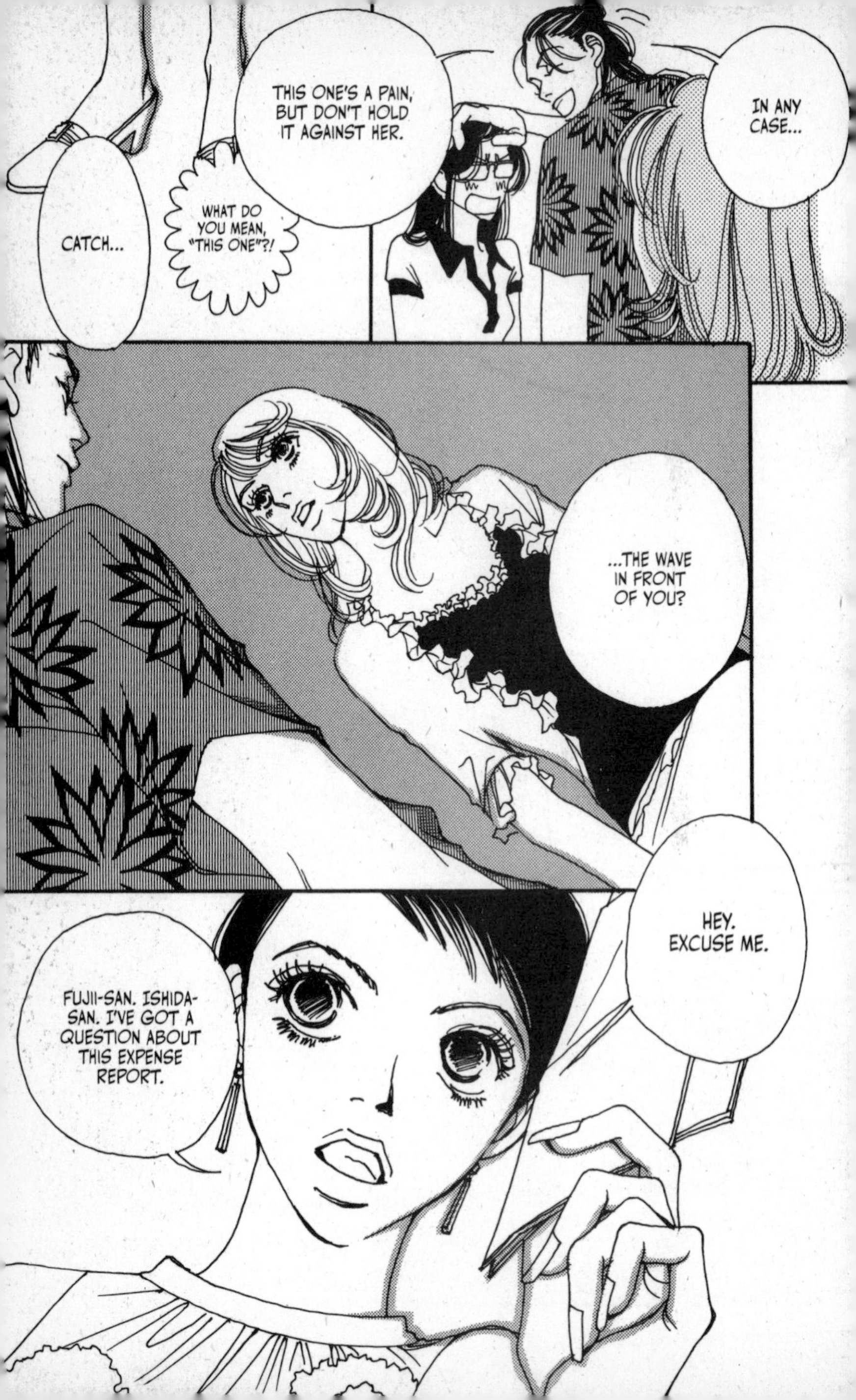
THIS ONE'S A PAIN, BUT DON'T HOLD IT AGAINST HER.
WHAT DO YOU MEAN, "THIS ONE"?!
IN ANY CASE...
CATCH...
...THE WAVE IN FRONT OF YOU?
HEY. EXCUSE ME.
FUJII-SAN. ISHIDA-SAN. I'VE GOT A QUESTION ABOUT THIS EXPENSE REPORT.

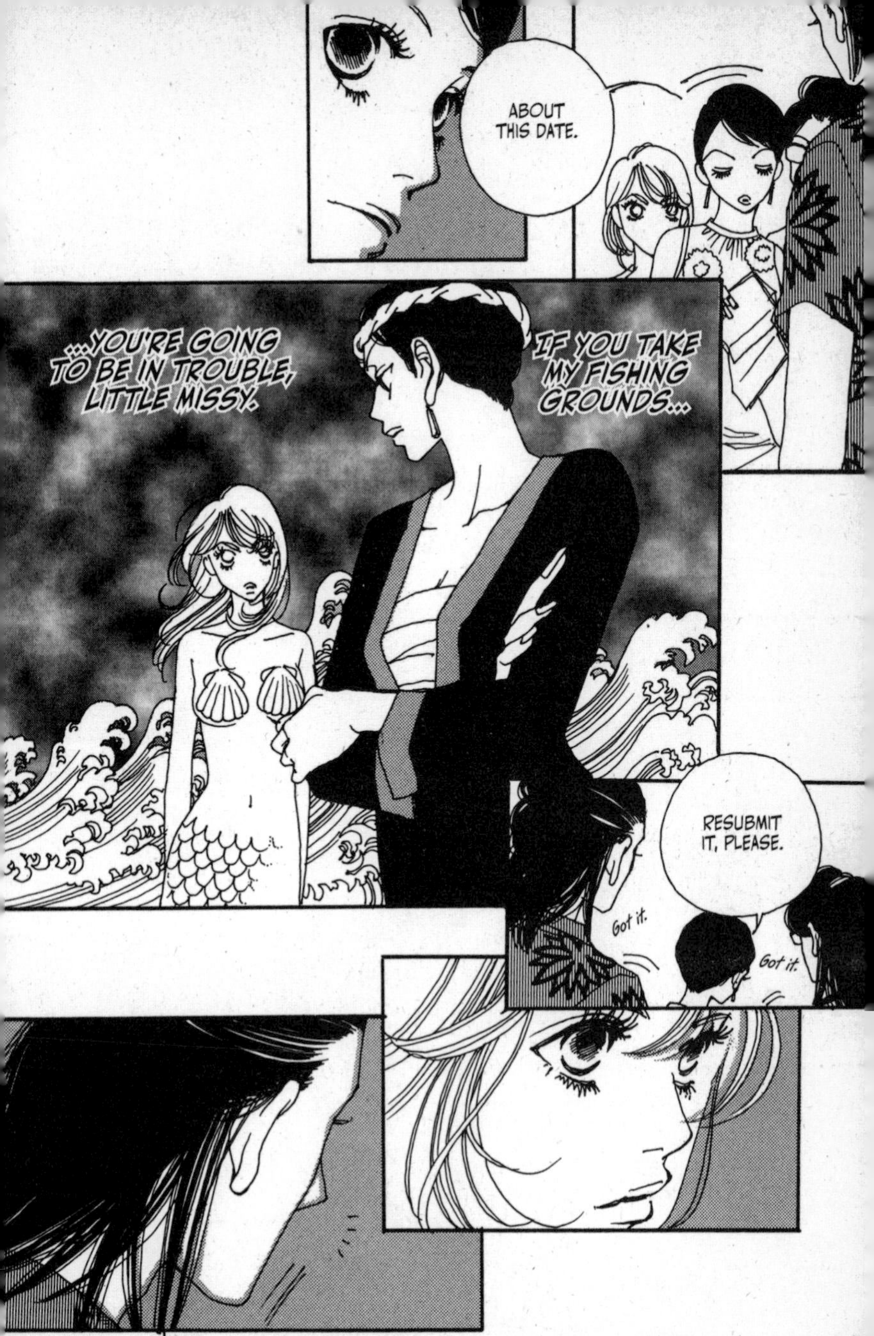
ABOUT THIS DATE.
IF YOU TAKE MY FISHING GROUNDS...
...YOU'RE GOING TO BE IN TROUBLE, LITTLE MISSY.
RESUBMIT IT, PLEASE.
Got it.
Got it.

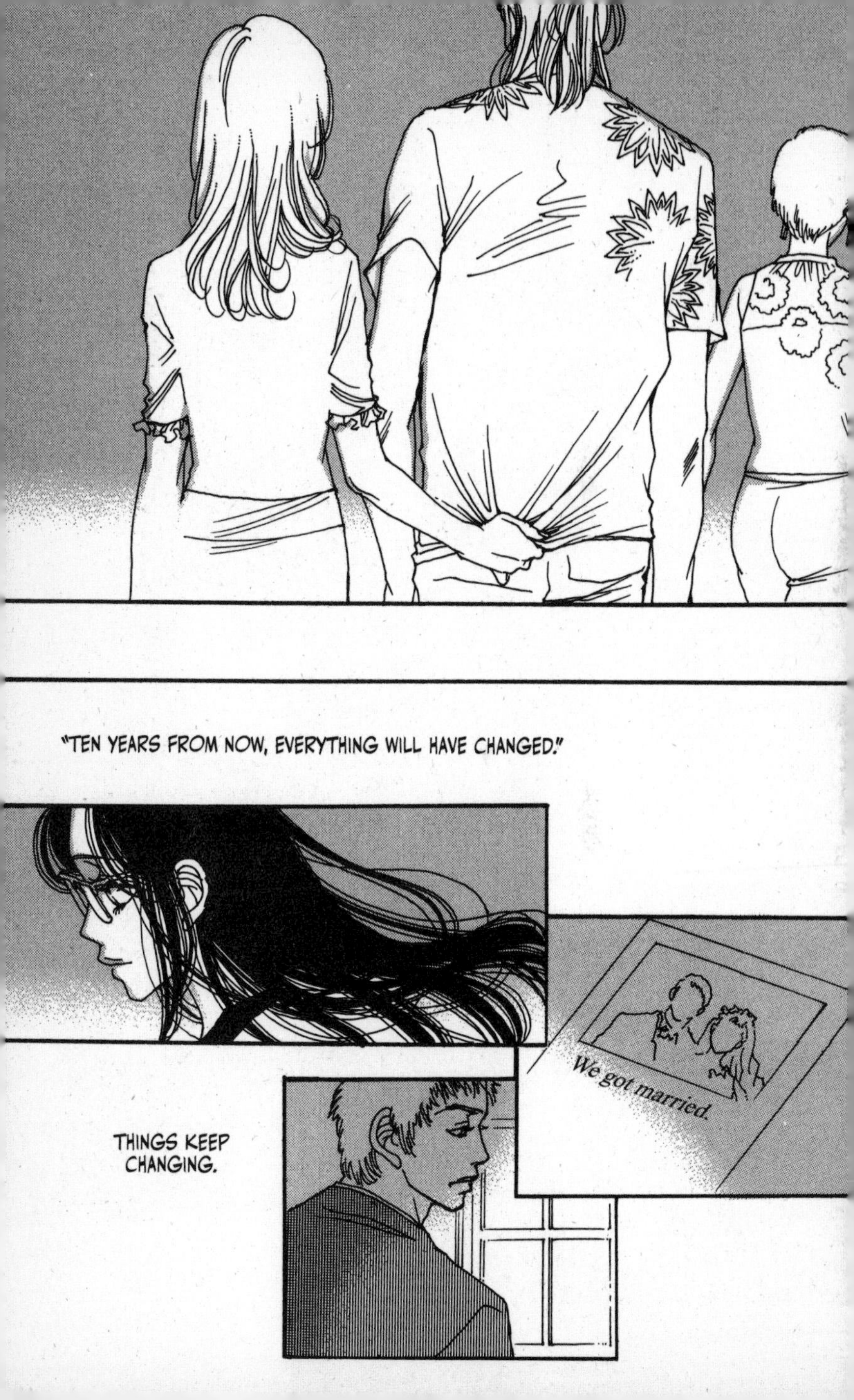
"TEN YEARS FROM NOW, EVERYTHING WILL HAVE CHANGED."
We got married.
THINGS KEEP
CHANGING.

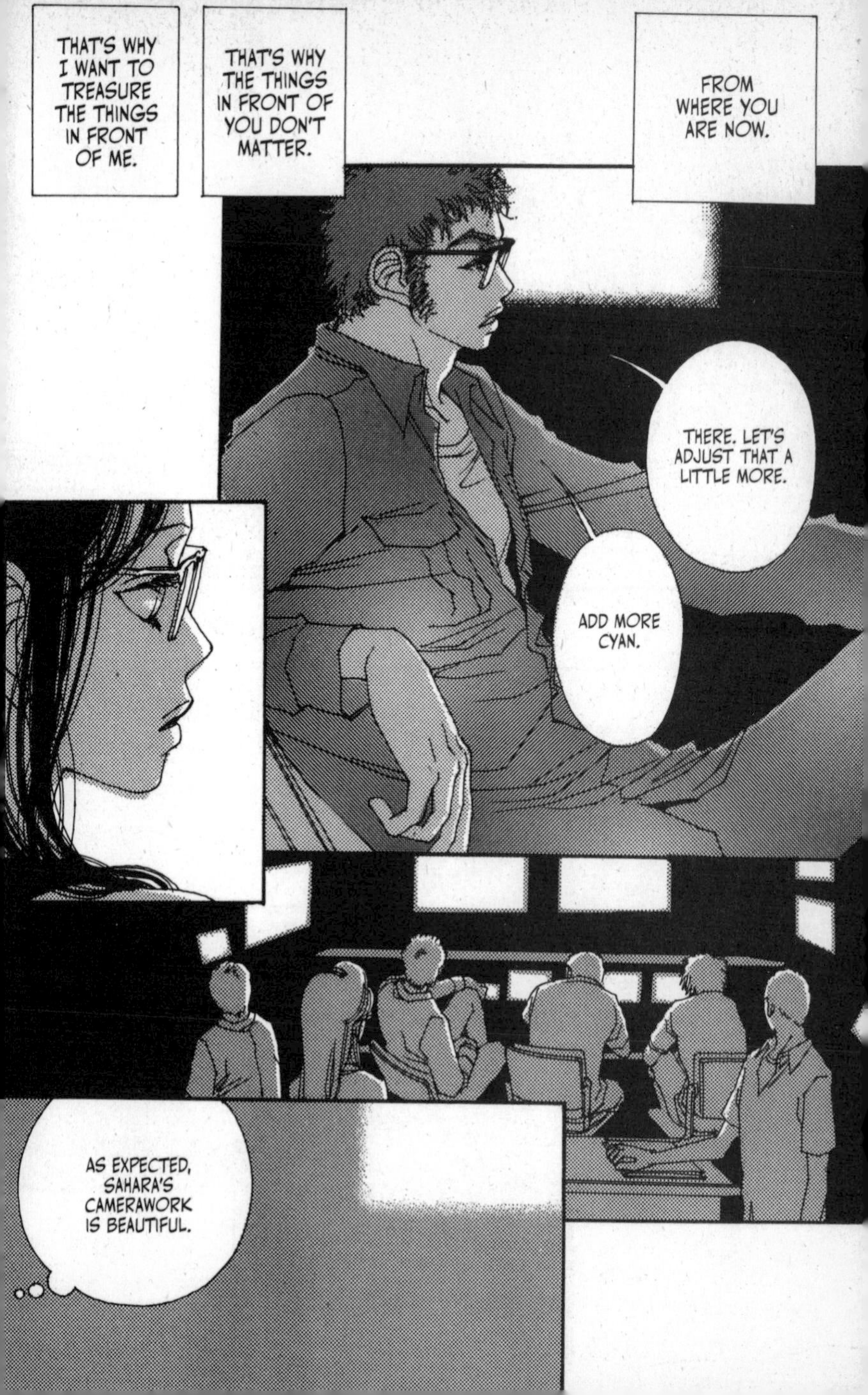
FROM WHERE YOU ARE NOW.
THAT'S WHY THE THINGS IN FRONT OF YOU DON'T MATTER.
THAT'S WHY I WANT TO TREASURE THE THINGS IN FRONT OF ME.
THERE. LET'S ADJUST THAT A LITTLE MORE.
ADD MORE CYAN.
AS EXPECTED, SAHARA'S CAMERAWORK IS BEAUTIFUL.

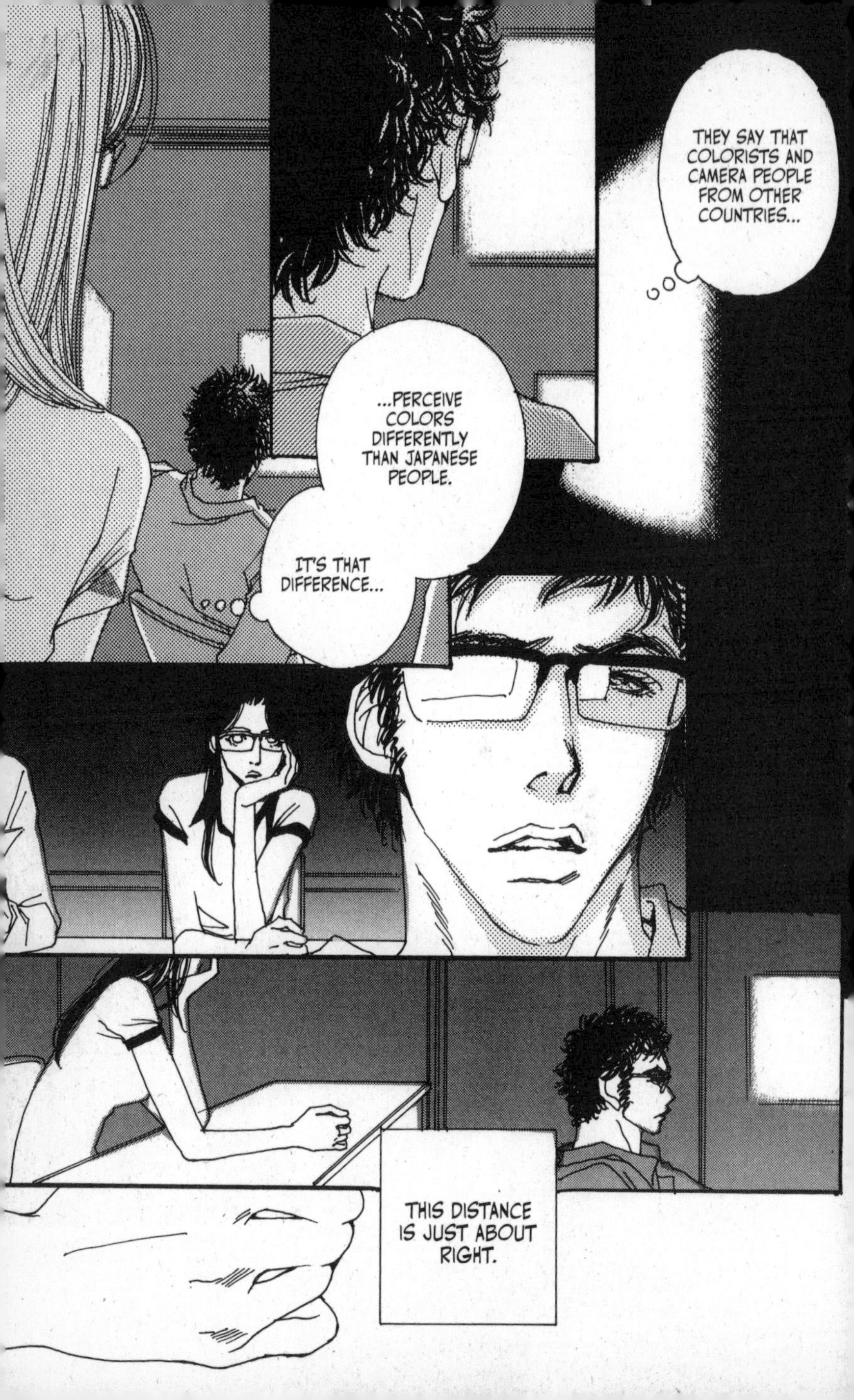
THEY SAY THAT COLORISTS AND CAMERA PEOPLE FROM OTHER COUNTRIES...
...PERCEIVE COLORS DIFFERENTLY THAN JAPANESE PEOPLE.
IT'S THAT DIFFERENCE...
THIS DISTANCE IS JUST ABOUT RIGHT.

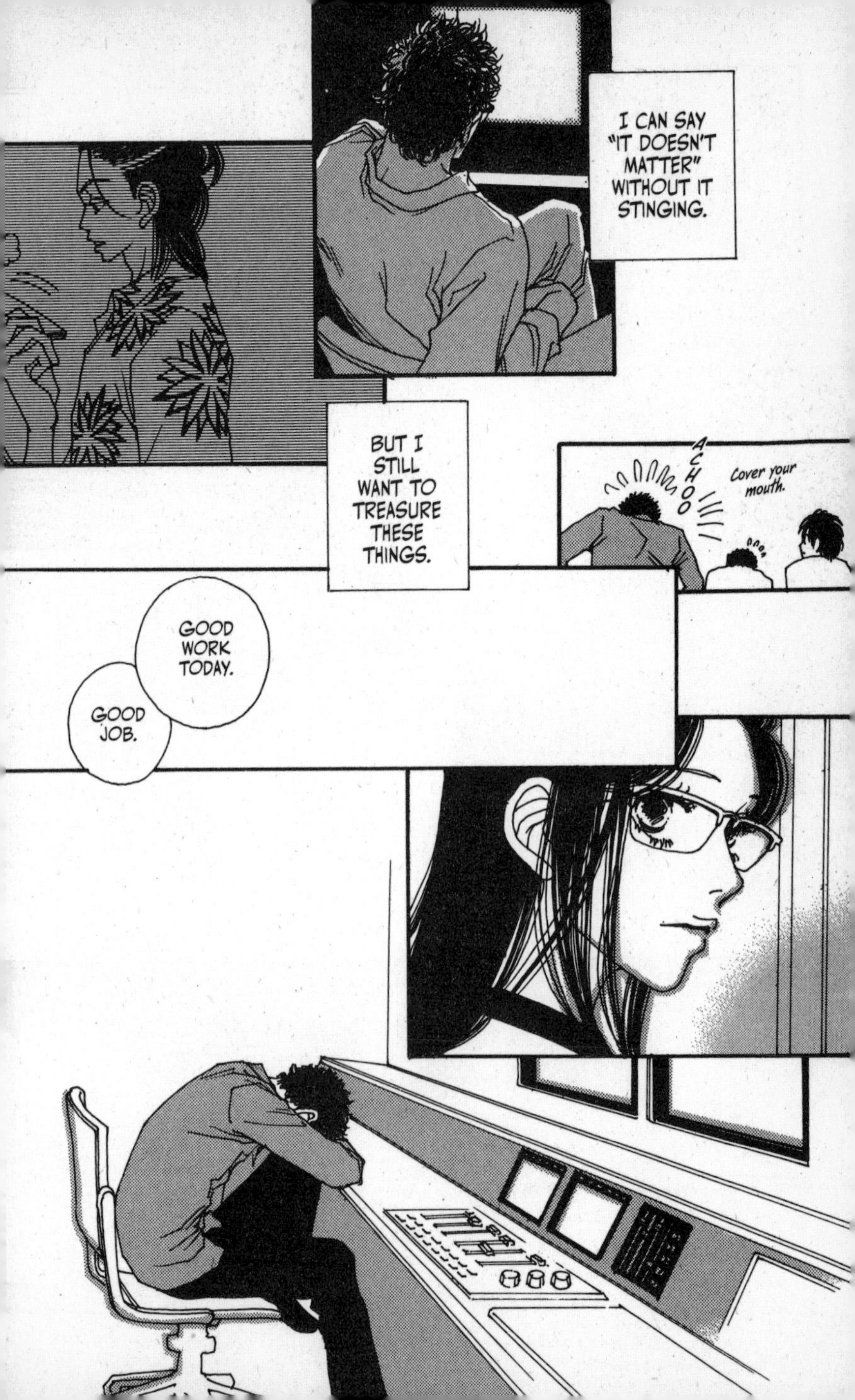
I CAN SAY "IT DOESN'T MATTER" WITHOUT IT STINGING.
BUT I STILL WANT TO TREASURE THESE THINGS.
ACHOO
Cover your mouth.
GOOD WORK TODAY.
GOOD JOB.

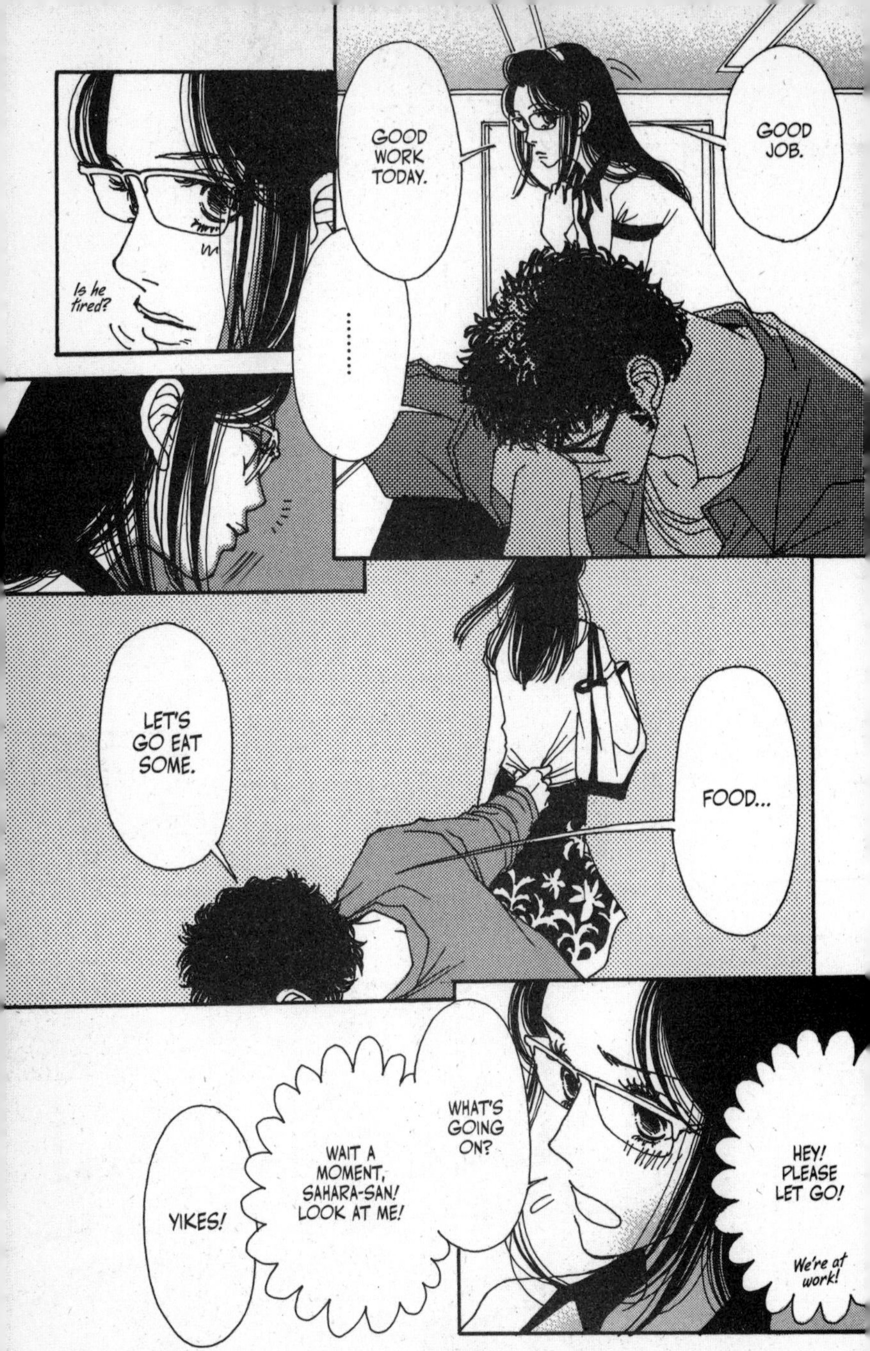
GOOD JOB.
GOOD WORK TODAY.
......
Is he tired?
FOOD...
LET'S GO EAT SOME.
HEY! PLEASE LET GO!
We're at work!
WHAT'S GOING ON?
WAIT A MOMENT, SAHARA-SAN! LOOK AT ME!
YIKES!

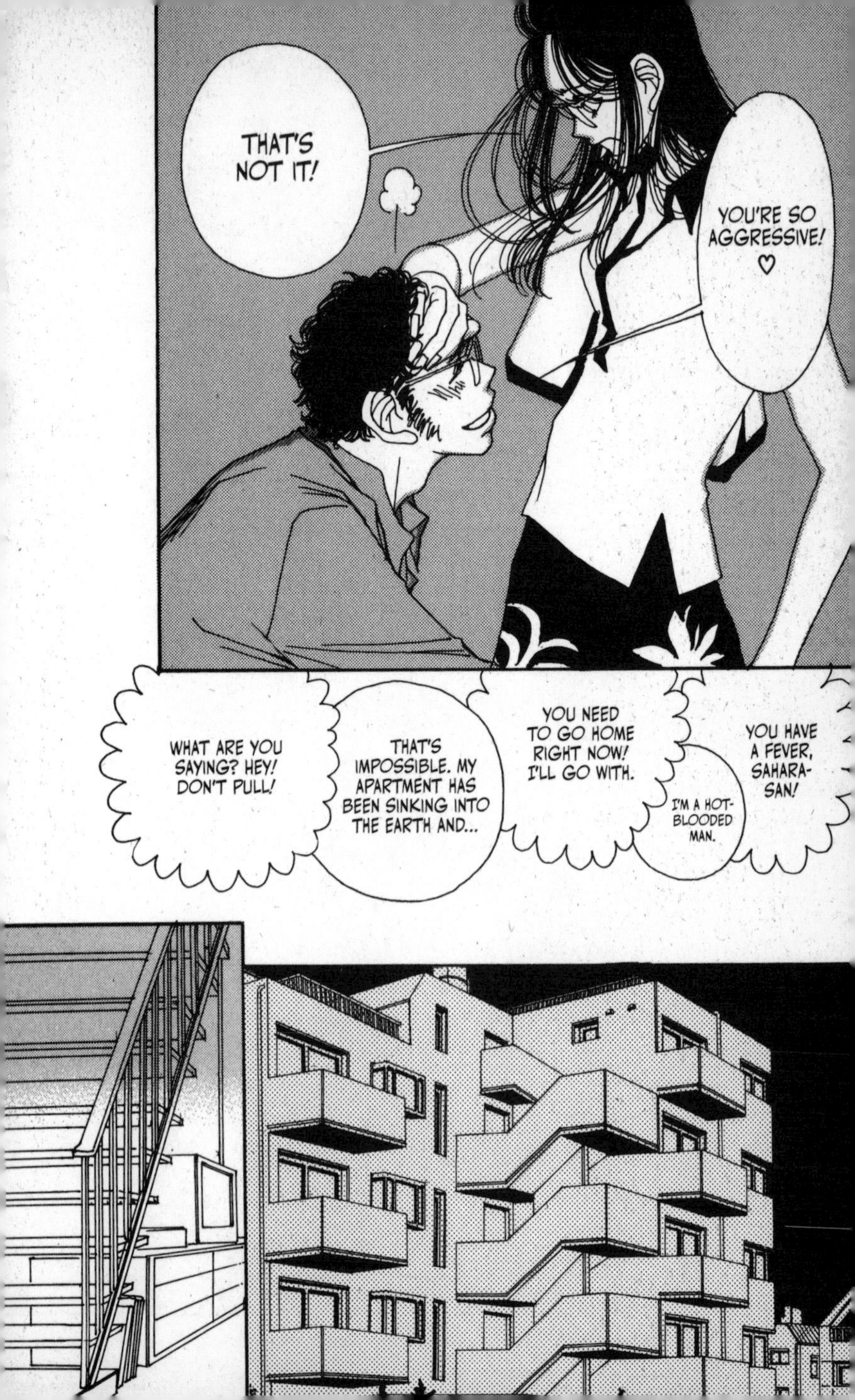
YOU'RE SO AGGRESSIVE! ♡
THAT'S NOT IT!
YOU HAVE A FEVER, SAHARA-SAN!
I'M A HOT-BLOODED MAN.
YOU NEED TO GO HOME RIGHT NOW! I'LL GO WITH.
THAT'S IMPOSSIBLE. MY APARTMENT HAS BEEN SINKING INTO THE EARTH AND...
WHAT ARE YOU SAYING? HEY! DON'T PULL!

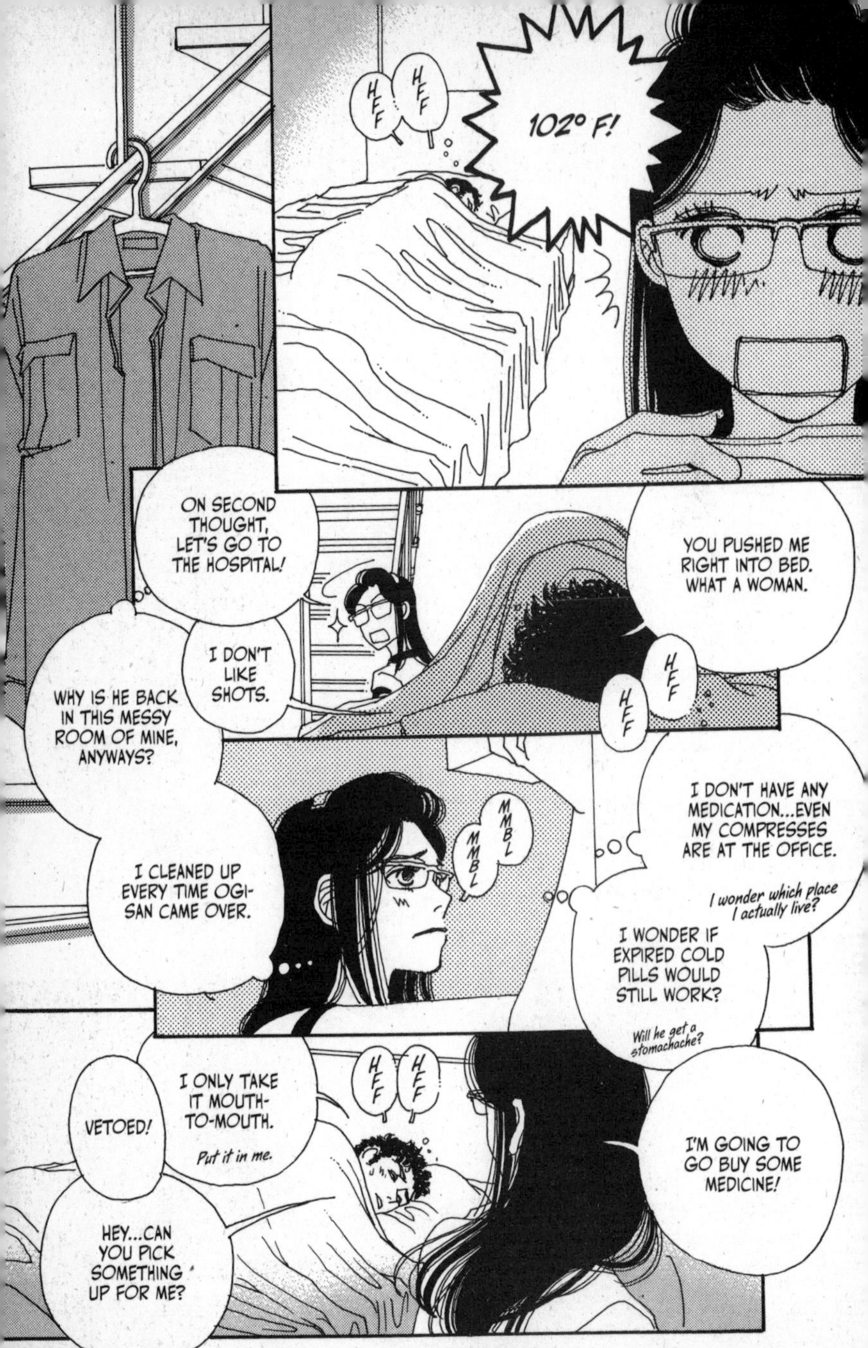
102° F!
HFF HFF
YOU PUSHED ME RIGHT INTO BED. WHAT A WOMAN.
HFF HFF
ON SECOND THOUGHT, LET'S GO TO THE HOSPITAL!
I DON'T LIKE SHOTS.
WHY IS HE BACK IN THIS MESSY ROOM OF MINE, ANYWAYS?
I DON'T HAVE ANY MEDICATION...EVEN MY COMPRESSES ARE AT THE OFFICE.
MMBL MMBL
I wonder which place I actually live?
I WONDER IF EXPIRED COLD PILLS WOULD STILL WORK?
Will he get a stomachache?
I CLEANED UP EVERY TIME OGI-SAN CAME OVER.
I'M GOING TO GO BUY SOME MEDICINE!
HFF HFF
I ONLY TAKE IT MOUTH-TO-MOUTH.
Put it in me.
VETOED!
HEY...CAN YOU PICK SOMETHING UP FOR ME?

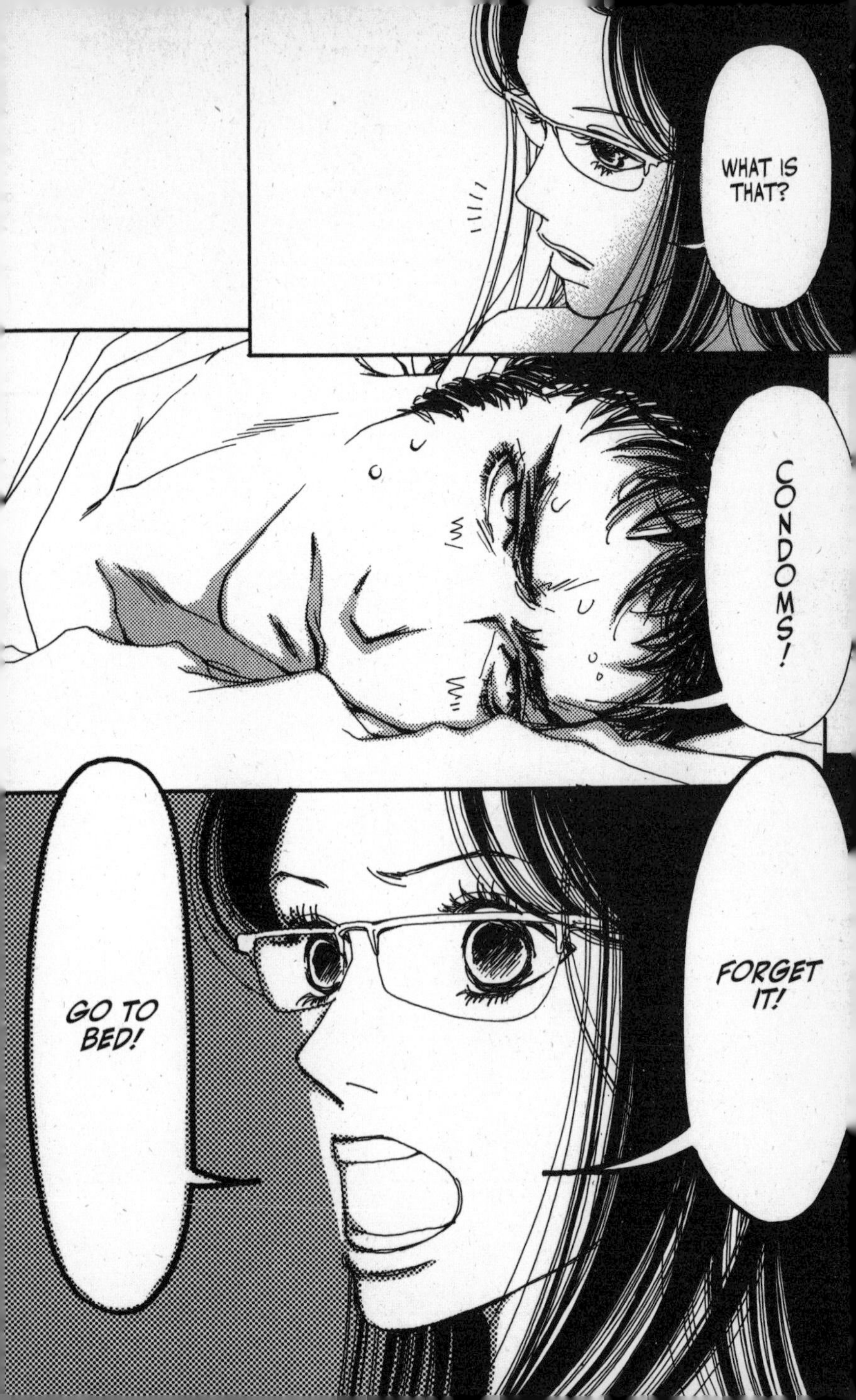
WHAT IS THAT?
CONDOMS!
FORGET IT!
GO TO BED!

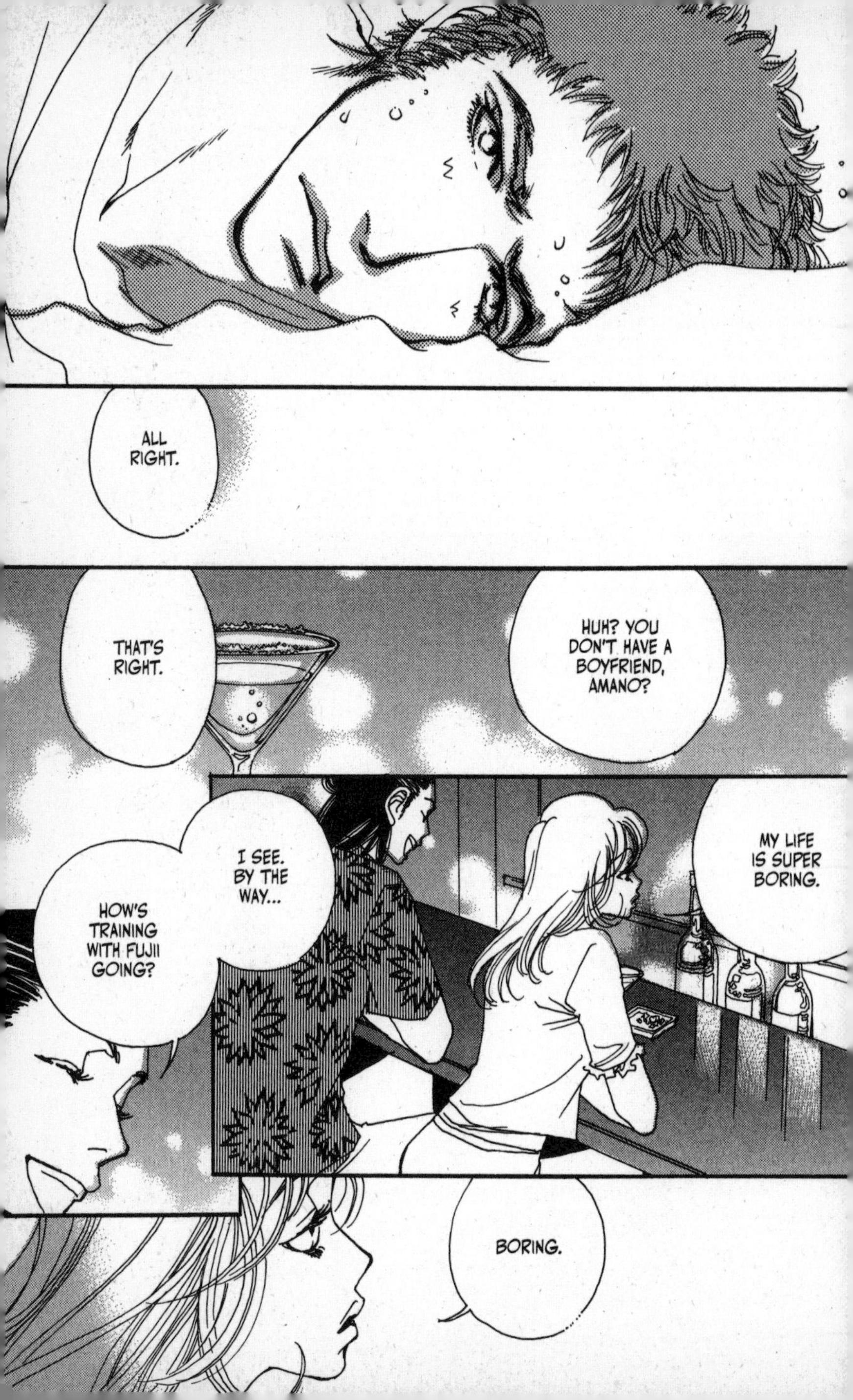
ALL RIGHT.
HUH? YOU DON'T HAVE A BOYFRIEND, AMANO?
THAT'S RIGHT.
MY LIFE IS SUPER BORING.
I SEE. BY THE WAY...
HOW'S TRAINING WITH FUJII GOING?
BORING.

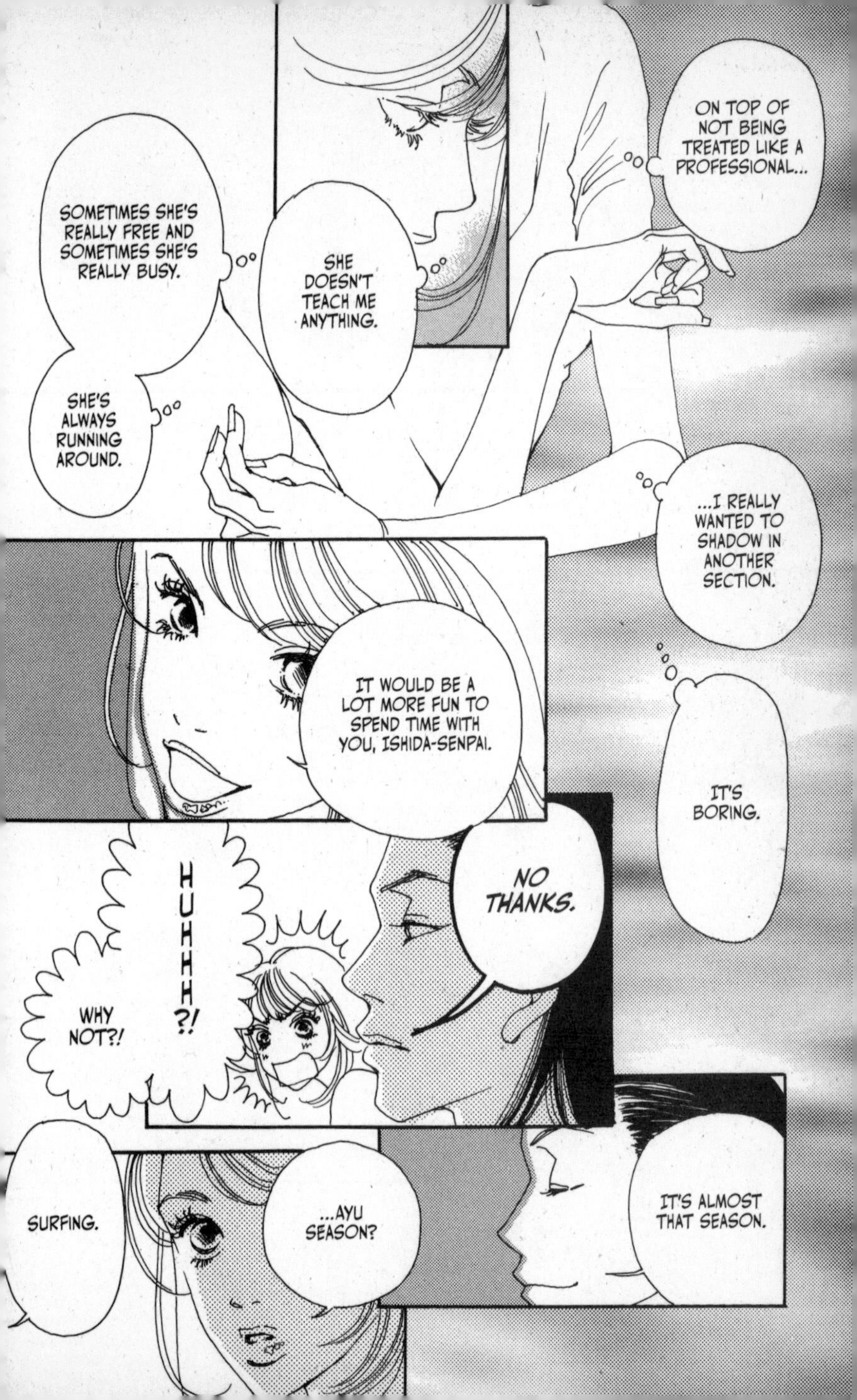
ON TOP OF NOT BEING TREATED LIKE A PROFESSIONAL...
SHE DOESN'T TEACH ME ANYTHING.
SOMETIMES SHE'S REALLY FREE AND SOMETIMES SHE'S REALLY BUSY.
SHE'S ALWAYS RUNNING AROUND.
...I REALLY WANTED TO SHADOW IN ANOTHER SECTION.
IT'S BORING.
IT WOULD BE A LOT MORE FUN TO SPEND TIME WITH YOU, ISHIDA-SENPAI.
NO THANKS.
HUHHH?!
WHY NOT?!
IT'S ALMOST THAT SEASON.
...AYU SEASON?
SURFING.

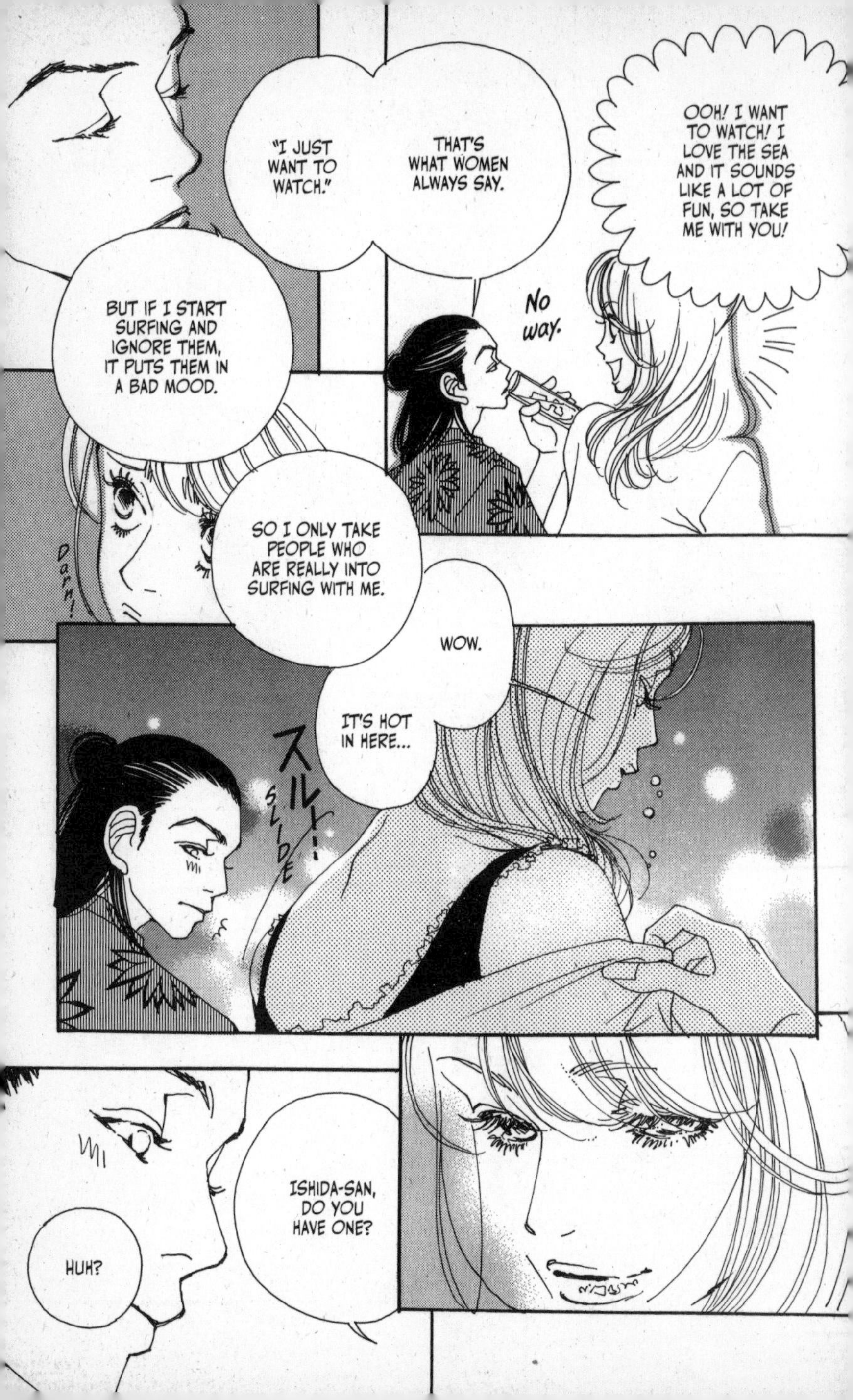
OOH! I WANT TO WATCH! I LOVE THE SEA AND IT SOUNDS LIKE A LOT OF FUN, SO TAKE ME WITH YOU!
No way.
"I JUST WANT TO WATCH."
THAT'S WHAT WOMEN ALWAYS SAY.
BUT IF I START SURFING AND IGNORE THEM, IT PUTS THEM IN A BAD MOOD.
SO I ONLY TAKE PEOPLE WHO ARE REALLY INTO SURFING WITH ME.
Darn!
WOW.
IT'S HOT IN HERE...
スルー
SLIDE
ISHIDA-SAN, DO YOU HAVE ONE?
HUH?

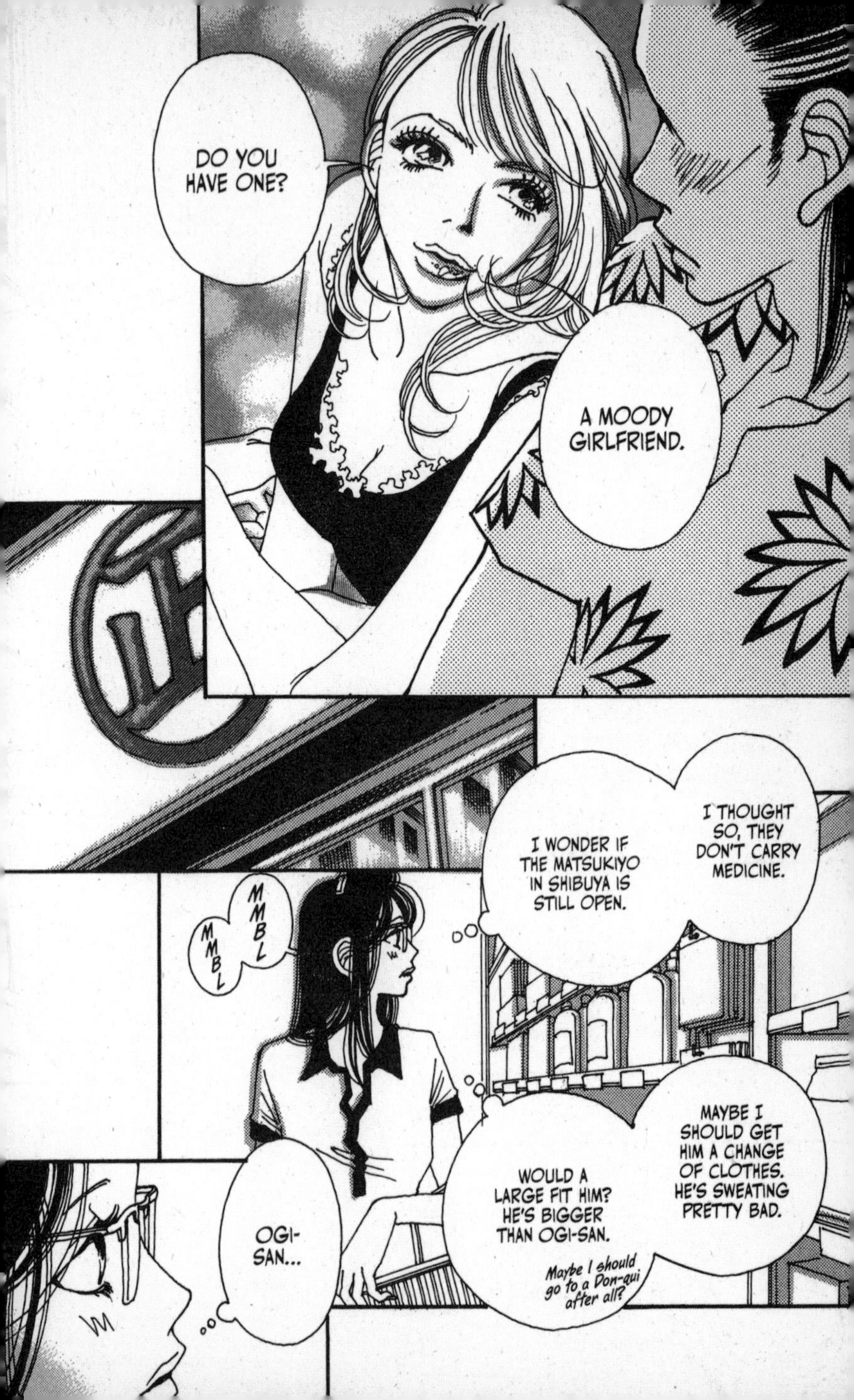
DO YOU HAVE ONE?
A MOODY GIRLFRIEND.
I THOUGHT SO, THEY DON'T CARRY MEDICINE.
I WONDER IF THE MATSUKIYO IN SHIBUYA IS STILL OPEN.
MMBL MMBL
MAYBE I SHOULD GET HIM A CHANGE OF CLOTHES. HE'S SWEATING PRETTY BAD.
WOULD A LARGE FIT HIM? HE'S BIGGER THAN OGI-SAN.
Maybe I should go to a Don-qui after all?
OGI-SAN...

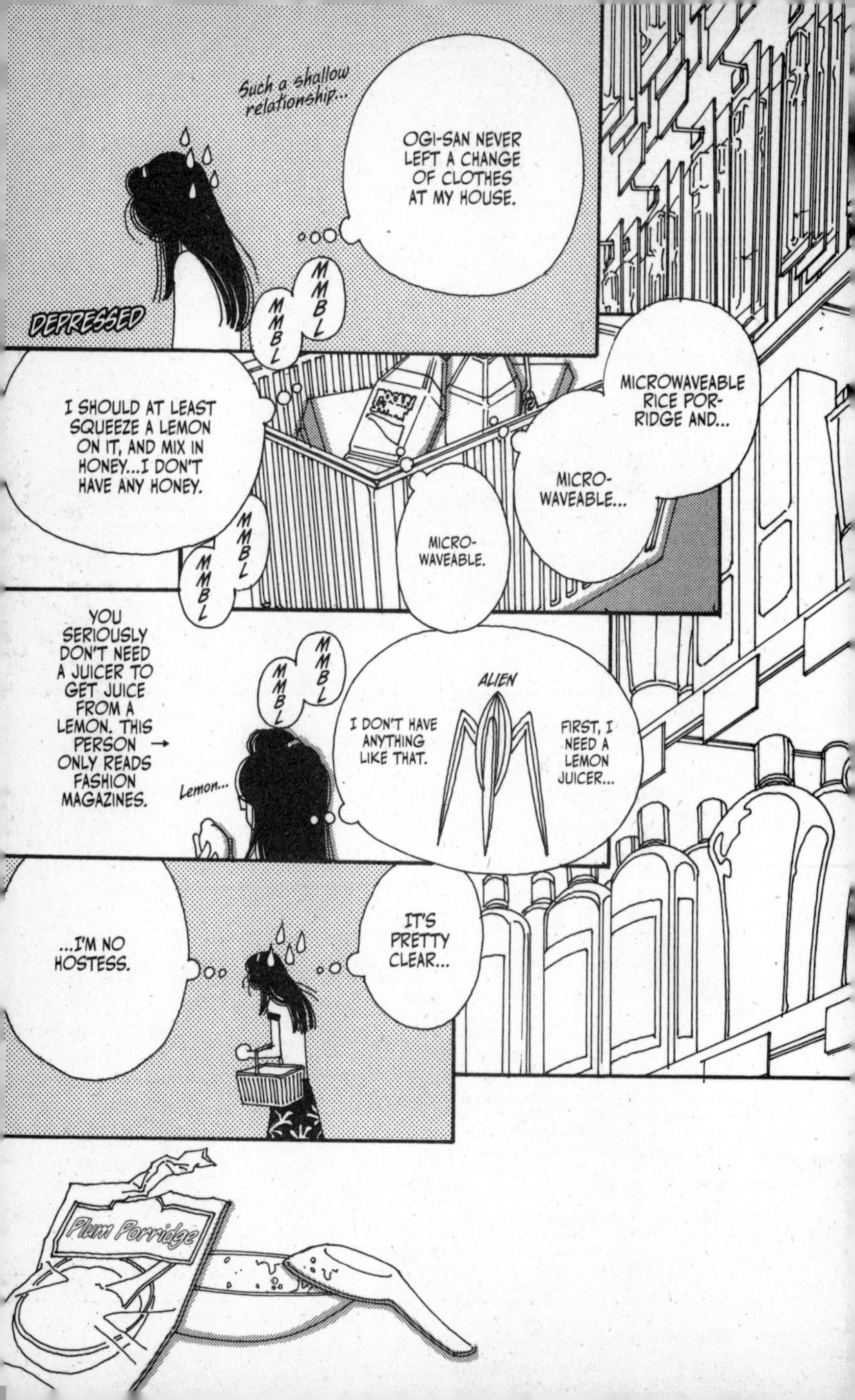

OGI-SAN NEVER LEFT A CHANGE OF CLOTHES AT MY HOUSE.
Such a shallow relationship...
MMBL MMBL
DEPRESSED
MICROWAVEABLE RICE POR-RIDGE AND...
MICRO-WAVEABLE...
MICRO-WAVEABLE.
I SHOULD AT LEAST SQUEEZE A LEMON ON IT, AND MIX IN HONEY...I DON'T HAVE ANY HONEY.
MMBL MMBL
FIRST, I NEED A LEMON JUICER...
ALIEN
I DON'T HAVE ANYTHING LIKE THAT.
MMBL MMBL
Lemon...
YOU SERIOUSLY DON'T NEED A JUICER TO GET JUICE FROM A LEMON. THIS PERSON → ONLY READS FASHION MAGAZINES.
IT'S PRETTY CLEAR...
...I'M NO HOSTESS.
Plum Porridge

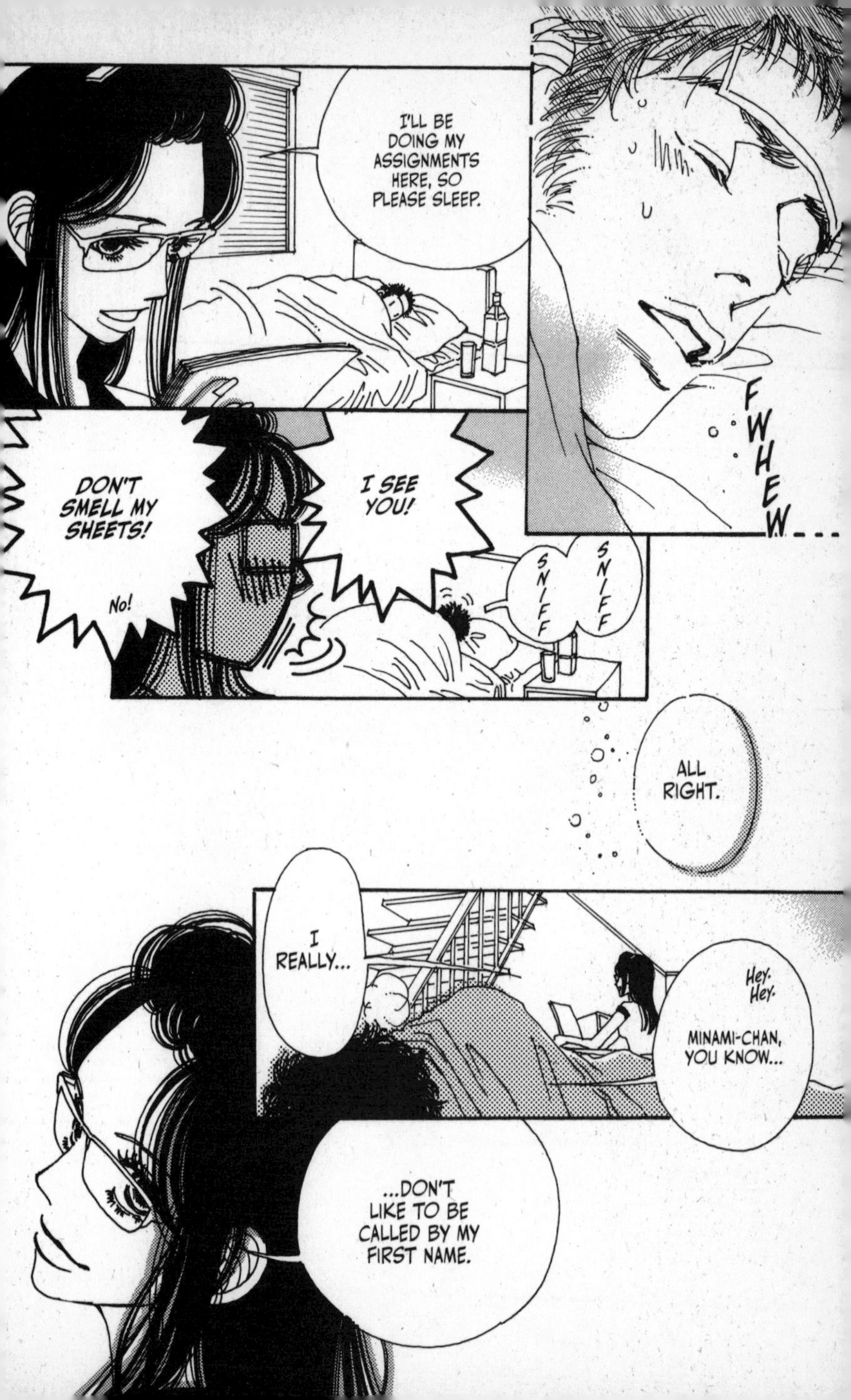

FWHEW...
I'LL BE DOING MY ASSIGNMENTS HERE, SO PLEASE SLEEP.
SNIFF SNIFF
I SEE YOU!
DON'T SMELL MY SHEETS!
No!
ALL RIGHT.
Hey. Hey.
MINAMI-CHAN, YOU KNOW...
I REALLY...
...DON'T LIKE TO BE CALLED BY MY FIRST NAME.

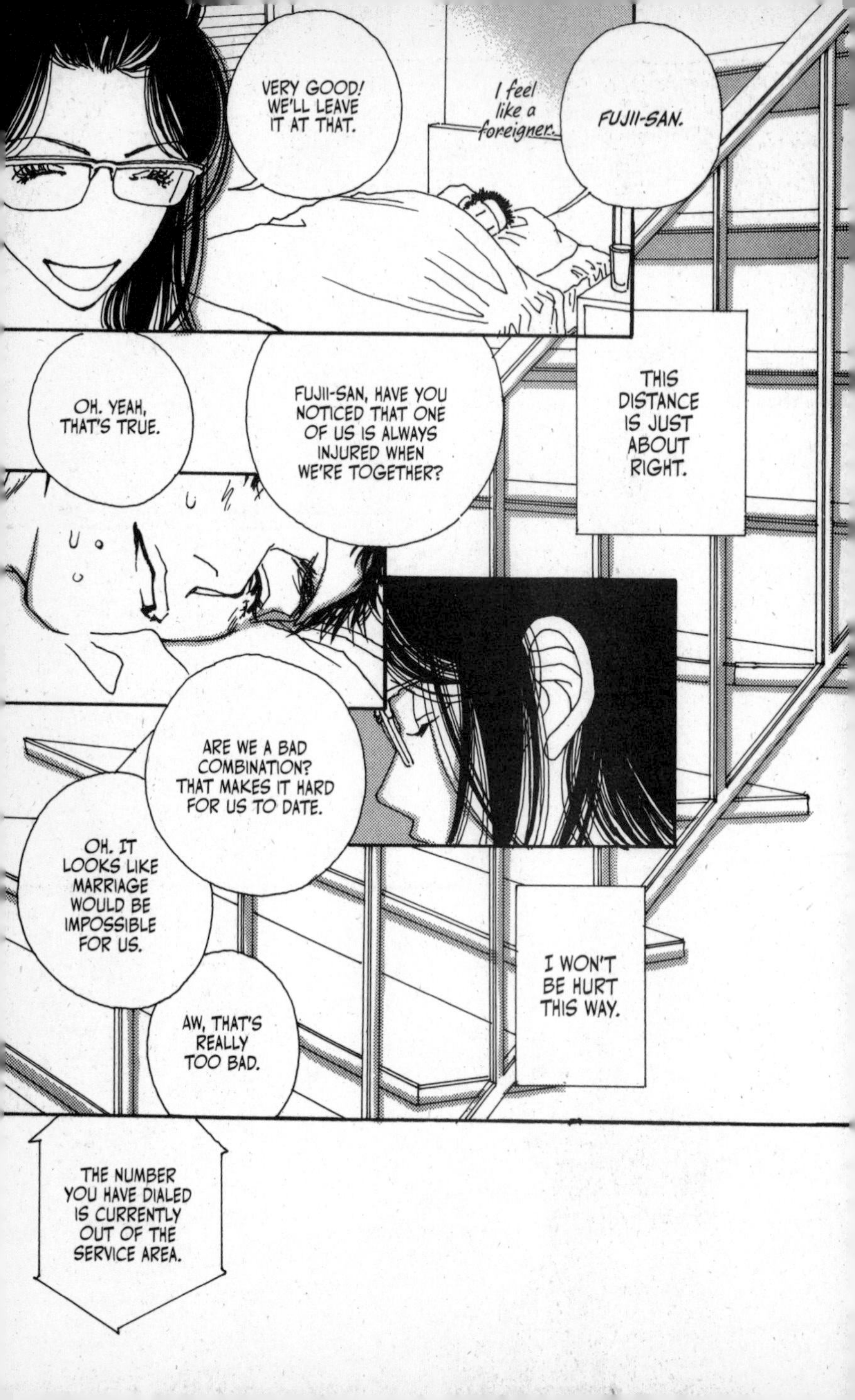
FUJII-SAN.
I feel like a foreigner.
VERY GOOD! WE'LL LEAVE IT AT THAT.
THIS DISTANCE IS JUST ABOUT RIGHT.
FUJII-SAN, HAVE YOU NOTICED THAT ONE OF US IS ALWAYS INJURED WHEN WE'RE TOGETHER?
OH. YEAH, THAT'S TRUE.
ARE WE A BAD COMBINATION? THAT MAKES IT HARD FOR US TO DATE.
OH. IT LOOKS LIKE MARRIAGE WOULD BE IMPOSSIBLE FOR US.
I WON'T BE HURT THIS WAY.
AW, THAT'S REALLY TOO BAD.
THE NUMBER YOU HAVE DIALED IS CURRENTLY OUT OF THE SERVICE AREA.

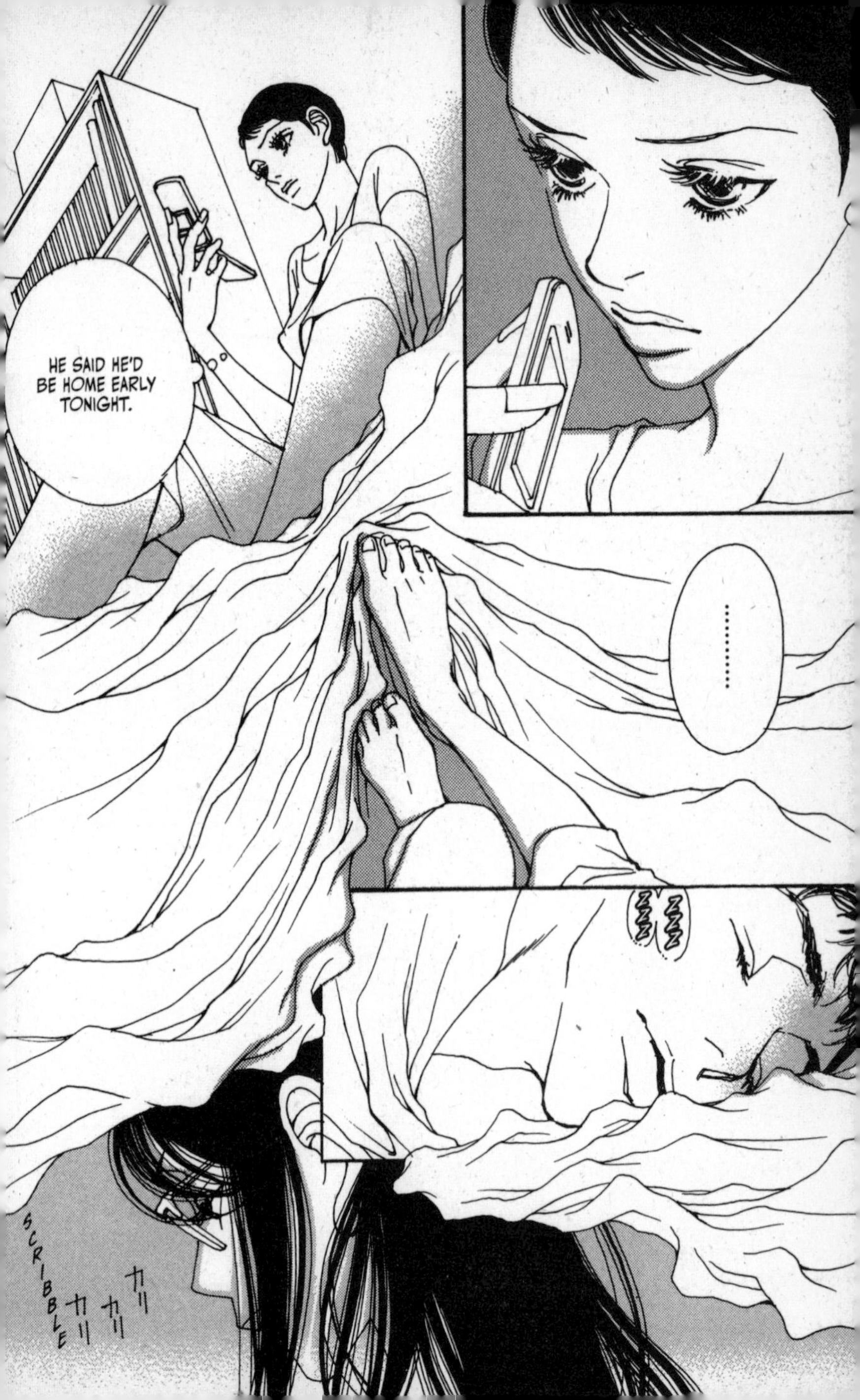
HE SAID HE'D BE HOME EARLY TONIGHT.
......
ZZZ
ZZZ
SCRIBBLE
カリ
カリ
カリ

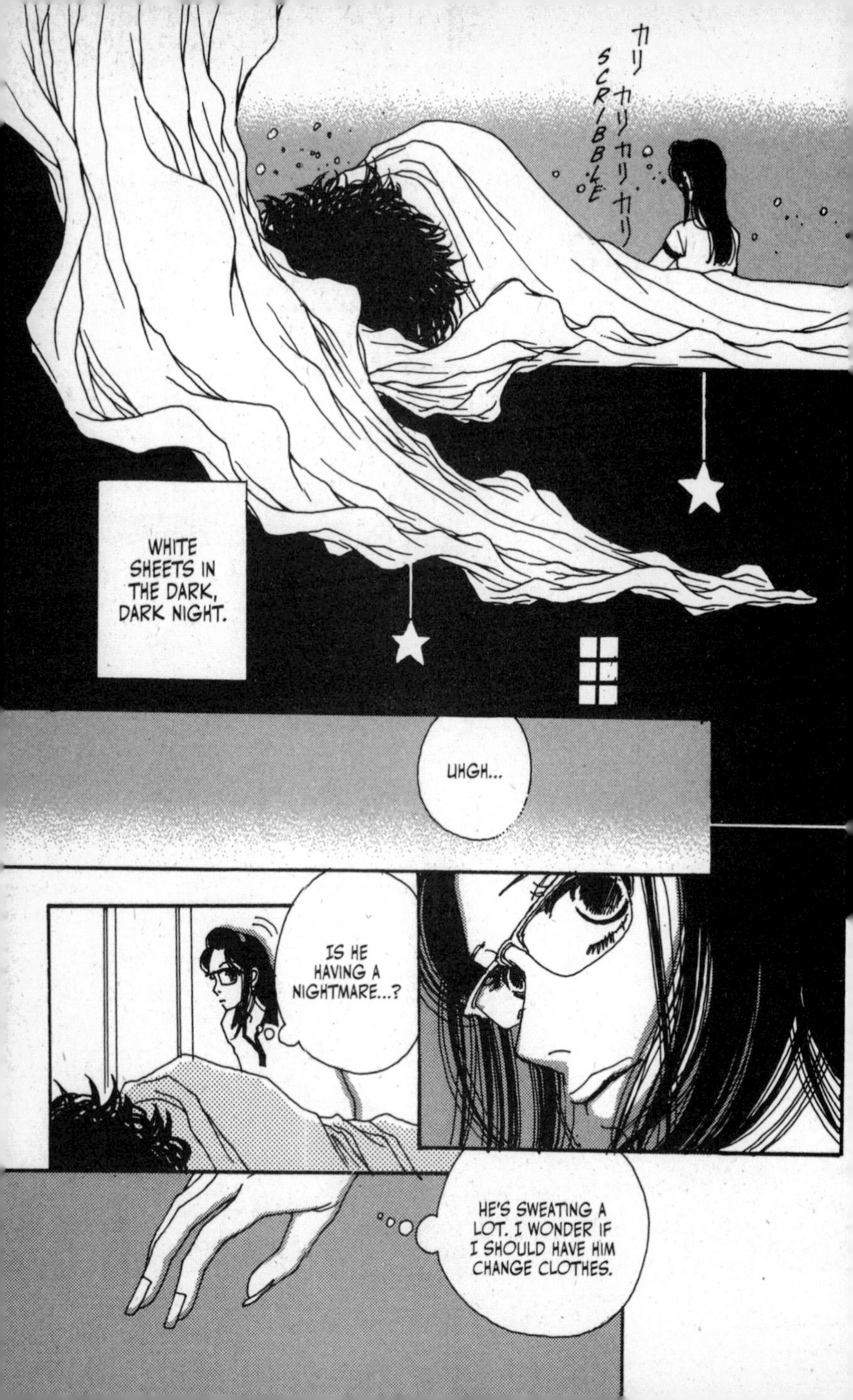
カリカリカリカリ
SCRIBBLE
WHITE SHEETS IN THE DARK, DARK NIGHT.
UHGH...
IS HE HAVING A NIGHTMARE...?
HE'S SWEATING A LOT. I WONDER IF I SHOULD HAVE HIM CHANGE CLOTHES.

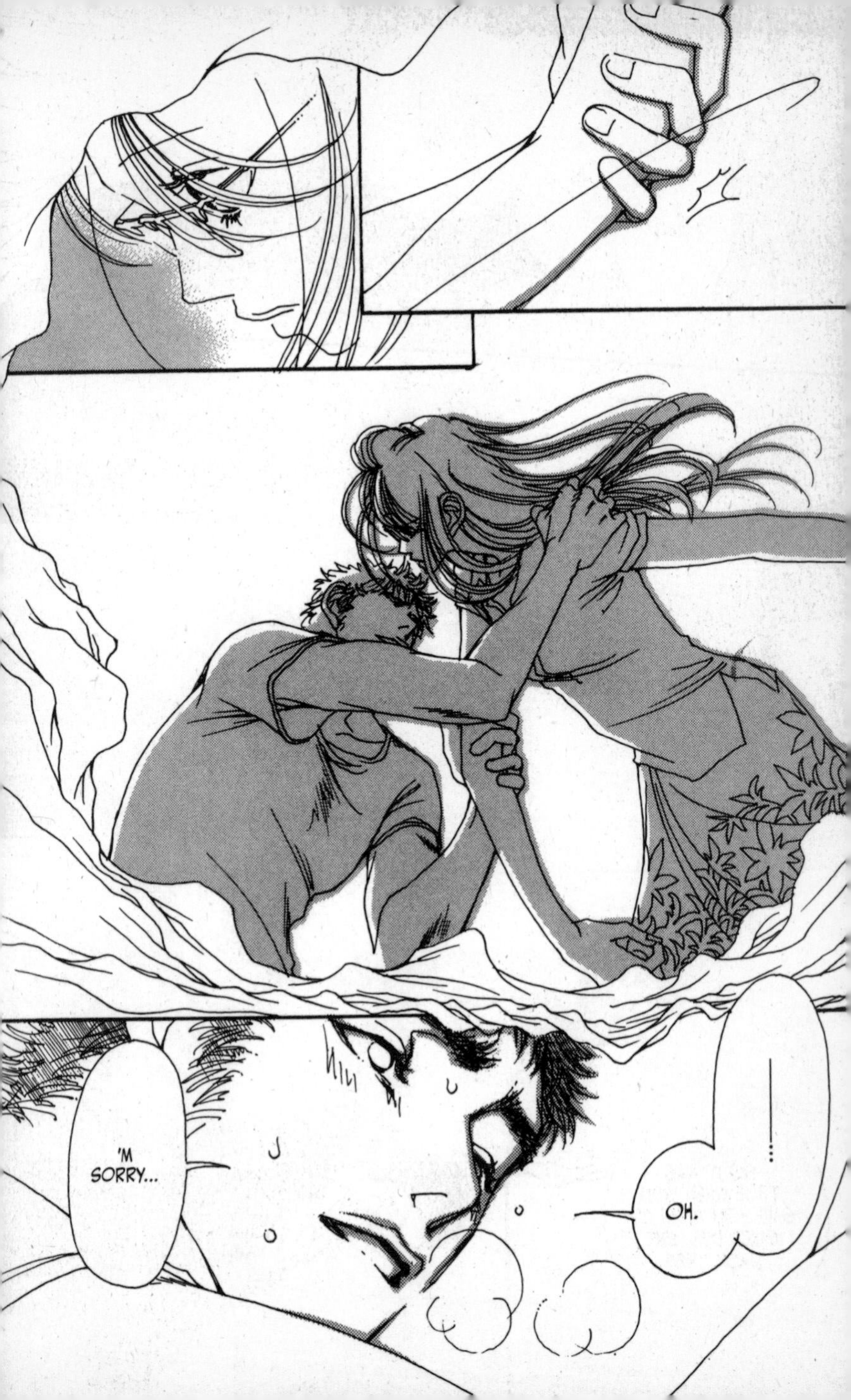

......!
OH.
'M SORRY...

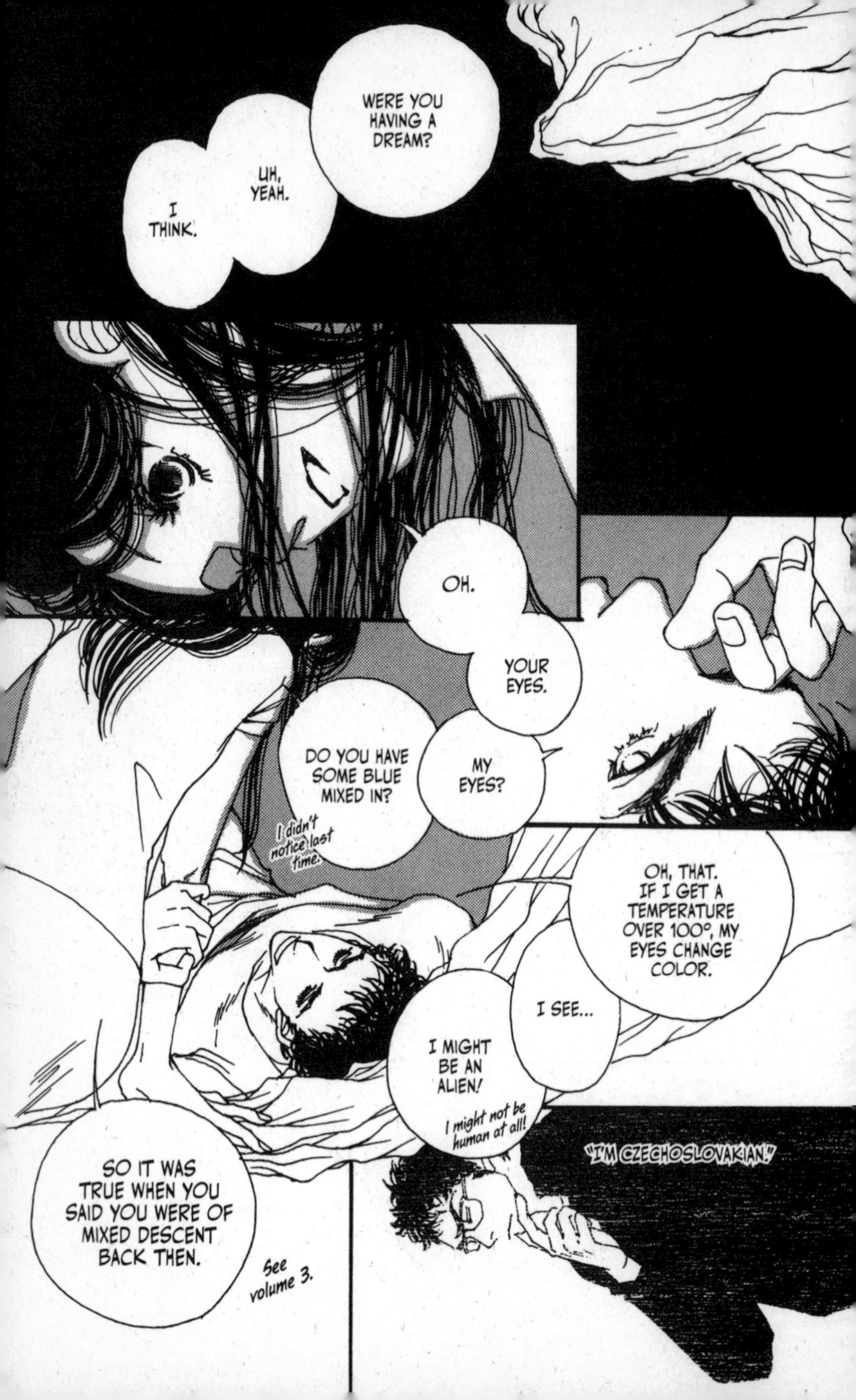
WERE YOU HAVING A DREAM?
UH, YEAH.
I THINK.
OH.
YOUR EYES.
MY EYES?
DO YOU HAVE SOME BLUE MIXED IN?
I didn't notice last time.
OH, THAT. IF I GET A TEMPERATURE OVER 100°, MY EYES CHANGE COLOR.
I SEE...
I MIGHT BE AN ALIEN!
I might not be human at all!
"I'M CZECHOSLOVAKIAN."
SO IT WAS TRUE WHEN YOU SAID YOU WERE OF MIXED DESCENT BACK THEN.
See volume 3.

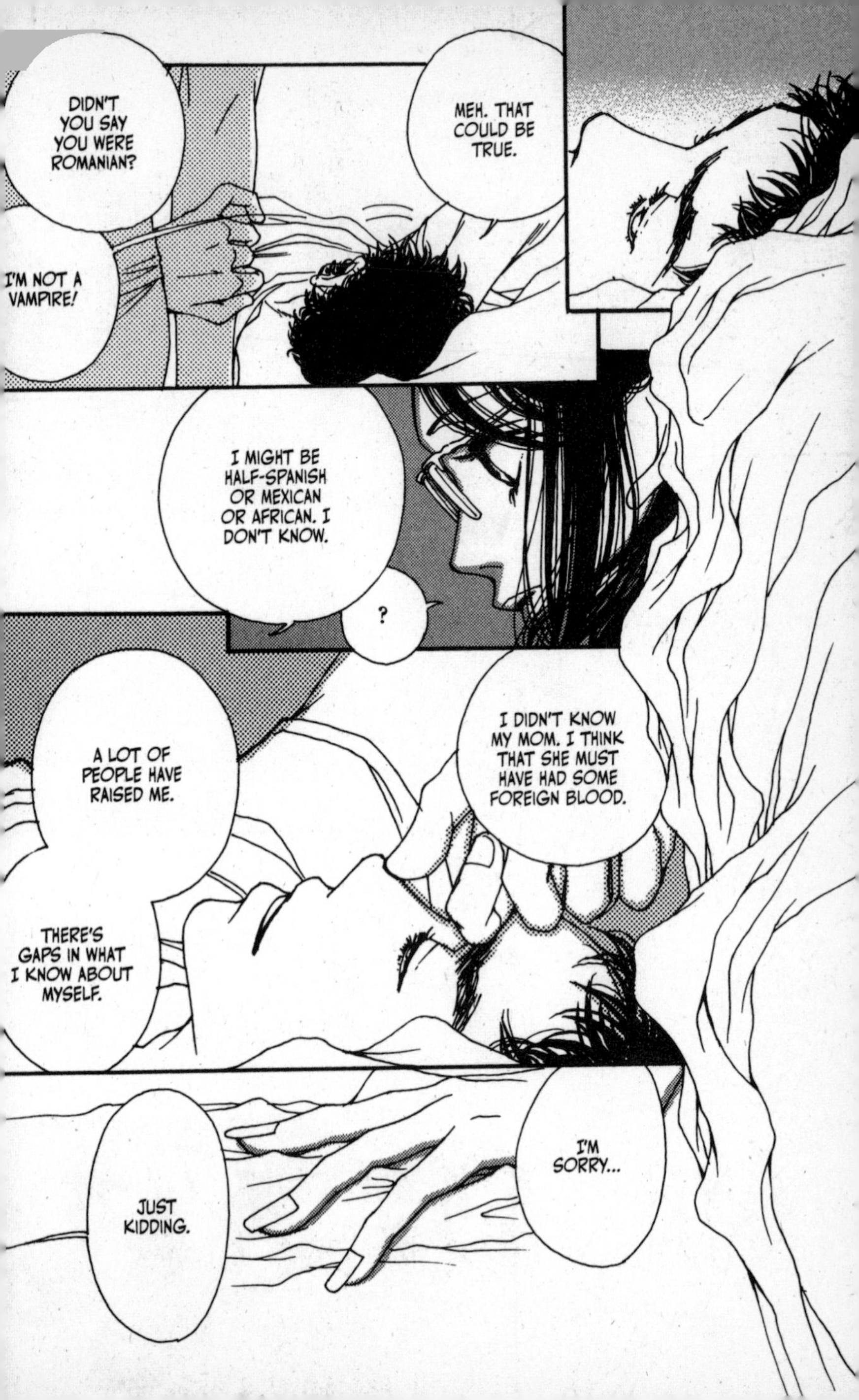
MEH. THAT COULD BE TRUE.
DIDN'T YOU SAY YOU WERE ROMANIAN?
I'M NOT A VAMPIRE!
I MIGHT BE HALF-SPANISH OR MEXICAN OR AFRICAN. I DON'T KNOW.
?
I DIDN'T KNOW MY MOM. I THINK THAT SHE MUST HAVE HAD SOME FOREIGN BLOOD.
A LOT OF PEOPLE HAVE RAISED ME.
THERE'S GAPS IN WHAT I KNOW ABOUT MYSELF.
I'M SORRY...
JUST KIDDING.

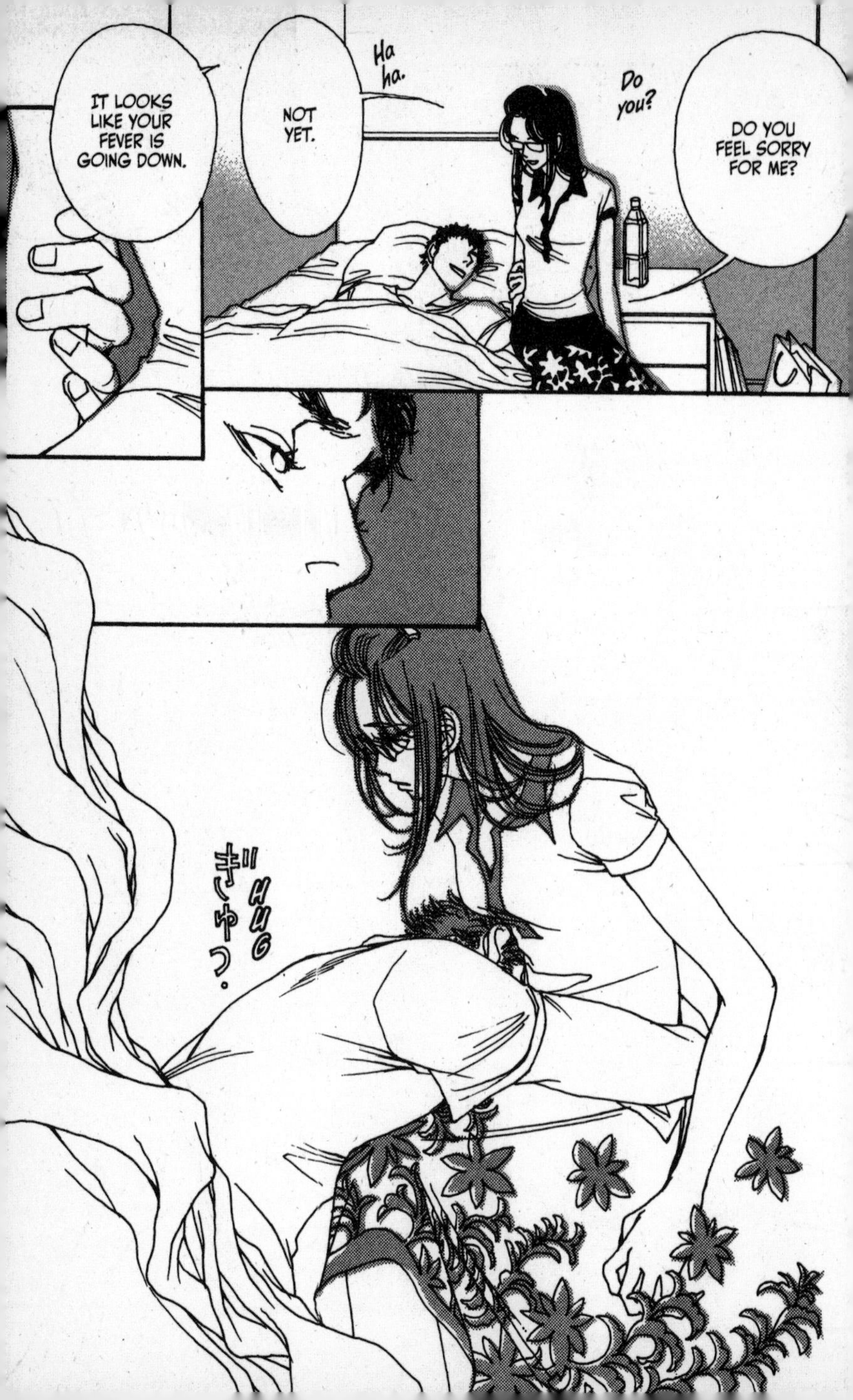
DO YOU FEEL SORRY FOR ME?
Do you?
Ha ha.
NOT YET.
IT LOOKS LIKE YOUR FEVER IS GOING DOWN.
HUG
ぎゅっ。

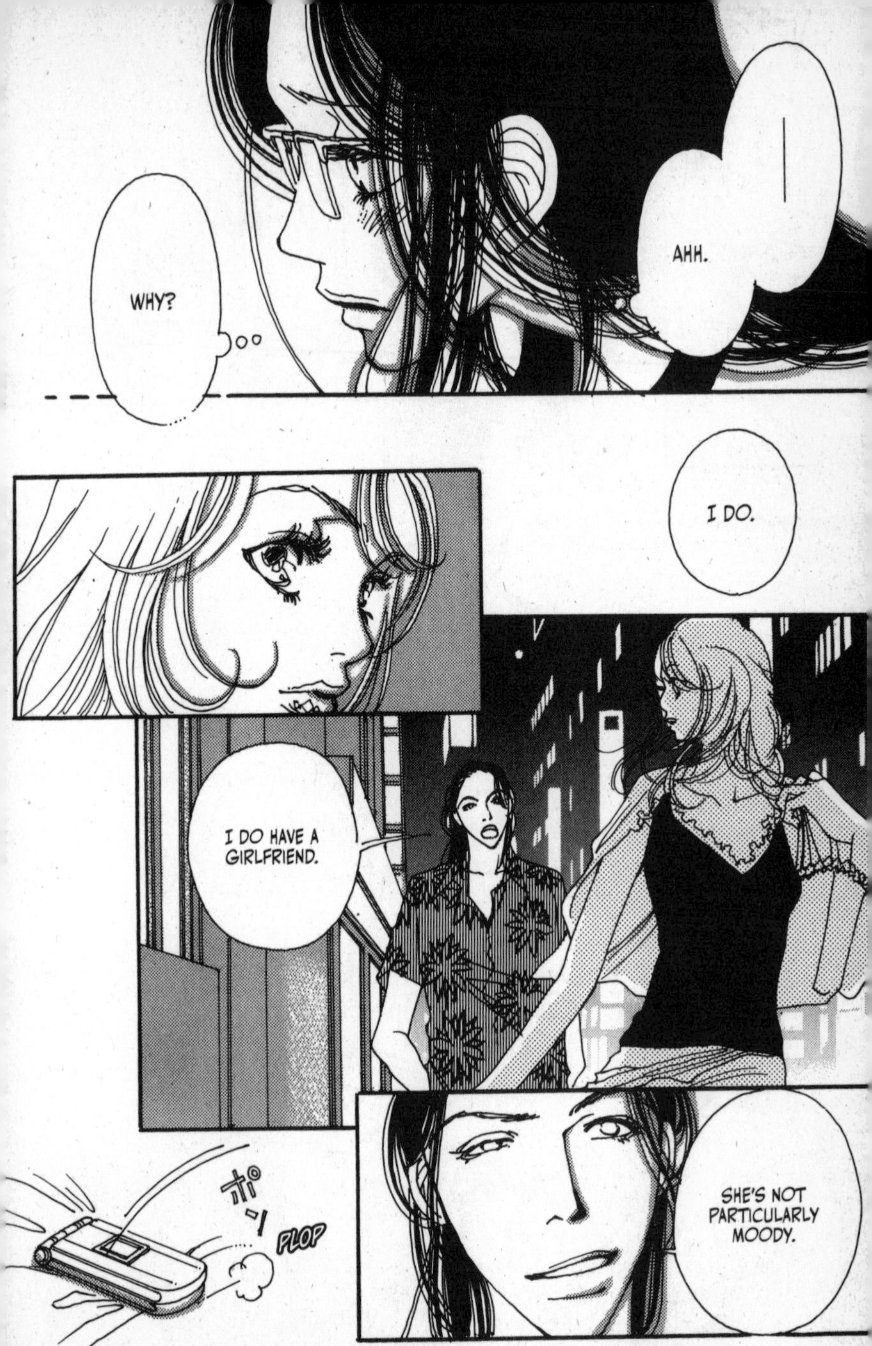
AHH.
WHY?
I DO.
I DO HAVE A GIRLFRIEND.
SHE'S NOT PARTICULARLY MOODY.
PLOP

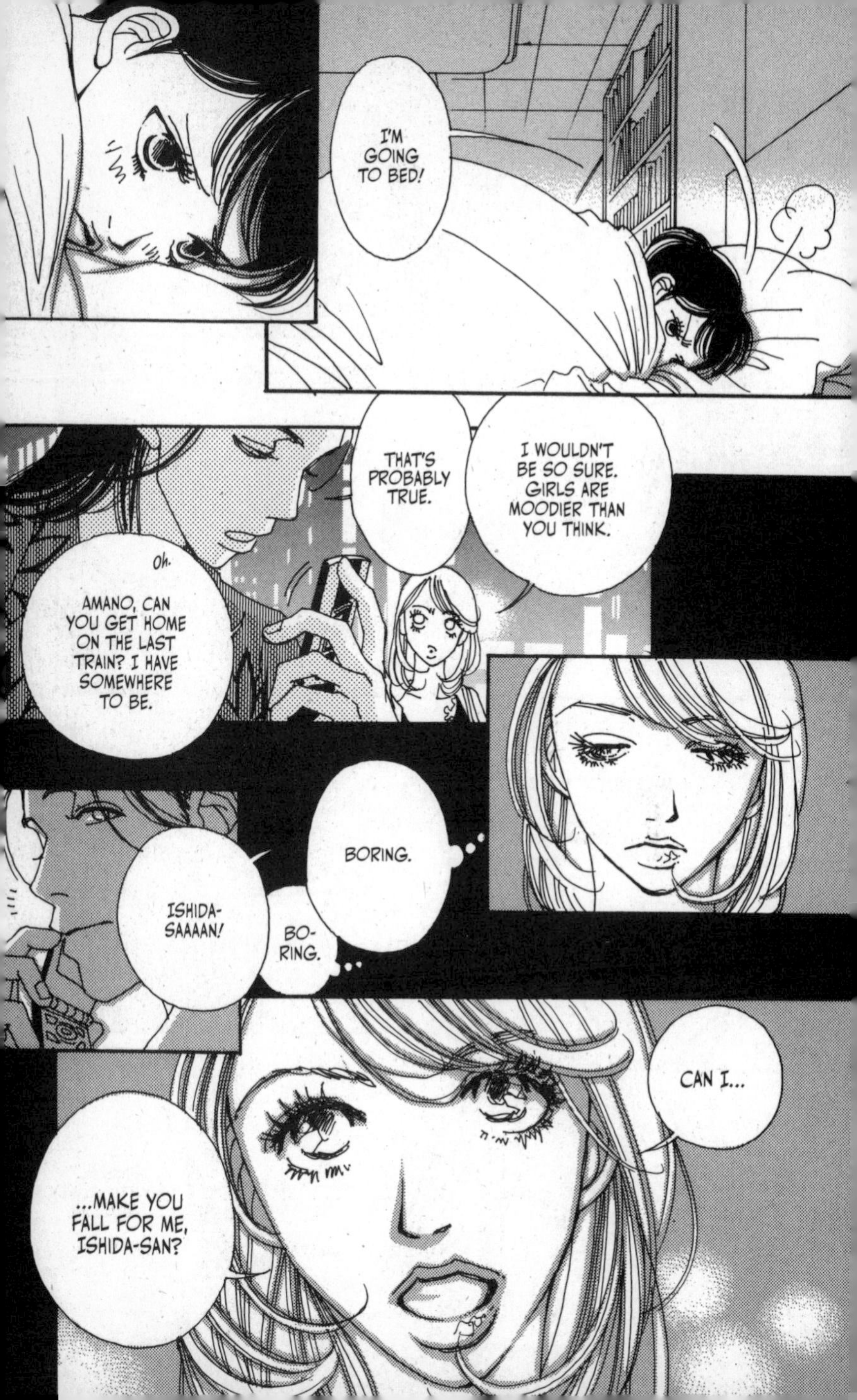
I'M GOING TO BED!
I WOULDN'T BE SO SURE. GIRLS ARE MOODIER THAN YOU THINK.
THAT'S PROBABLY TRUE.
Oh.
AMANO, CAN YOU GET HOME ON THE LAST TRAIN? I HAVE SOMEWHERE TO BE.
BORING.
BO-RING.
ISHIDA-SAAAAN!
CAN I...
...MAKE YOU FALL FOR ME, ISHIDA-SAN?

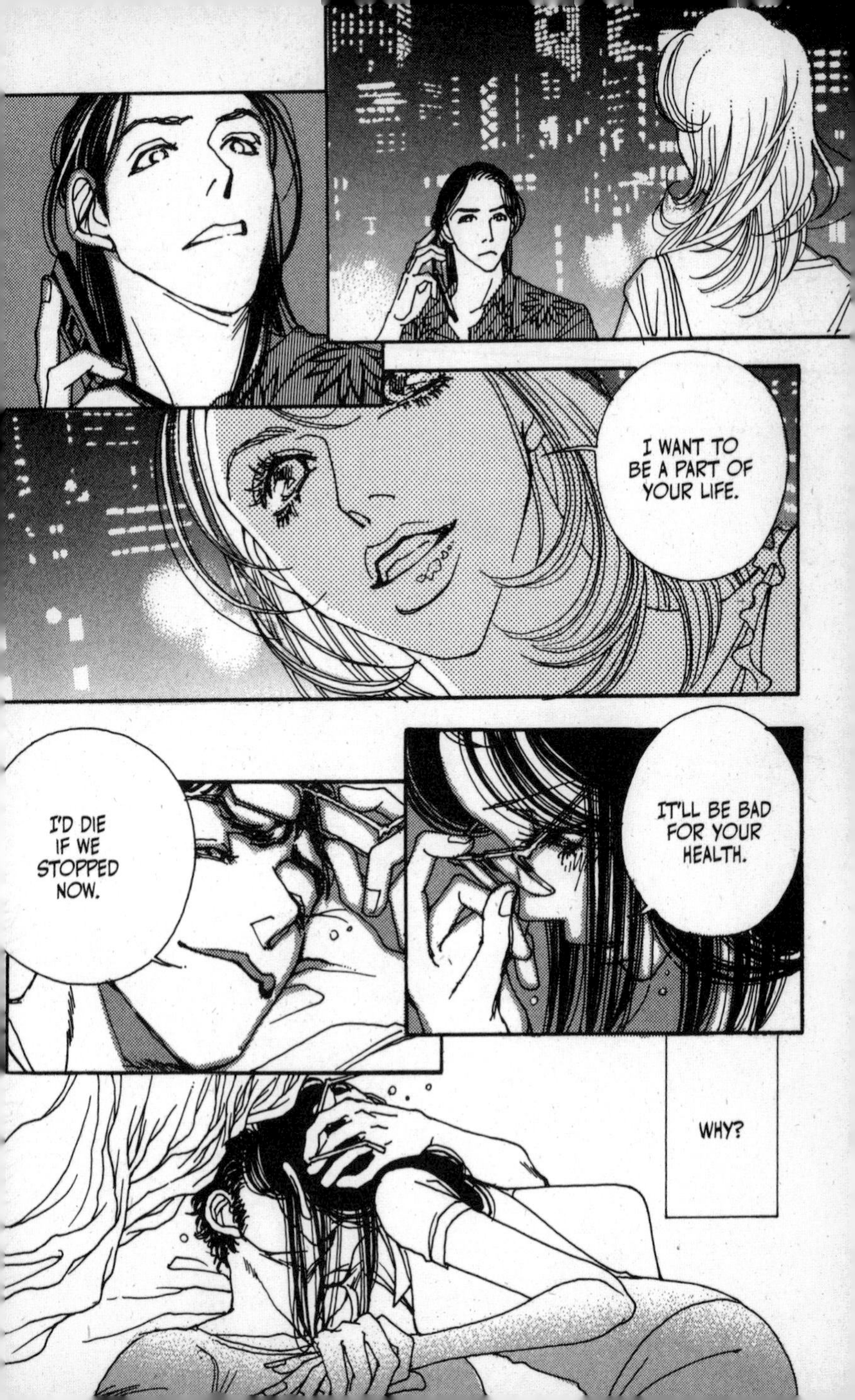
I WANT TO BE A PART OF YOUR LIFE.
IT'LL BE BAD FOR YOUR HEALTH.
I'D DIE IF WE STOPPED NOW.
WHY?

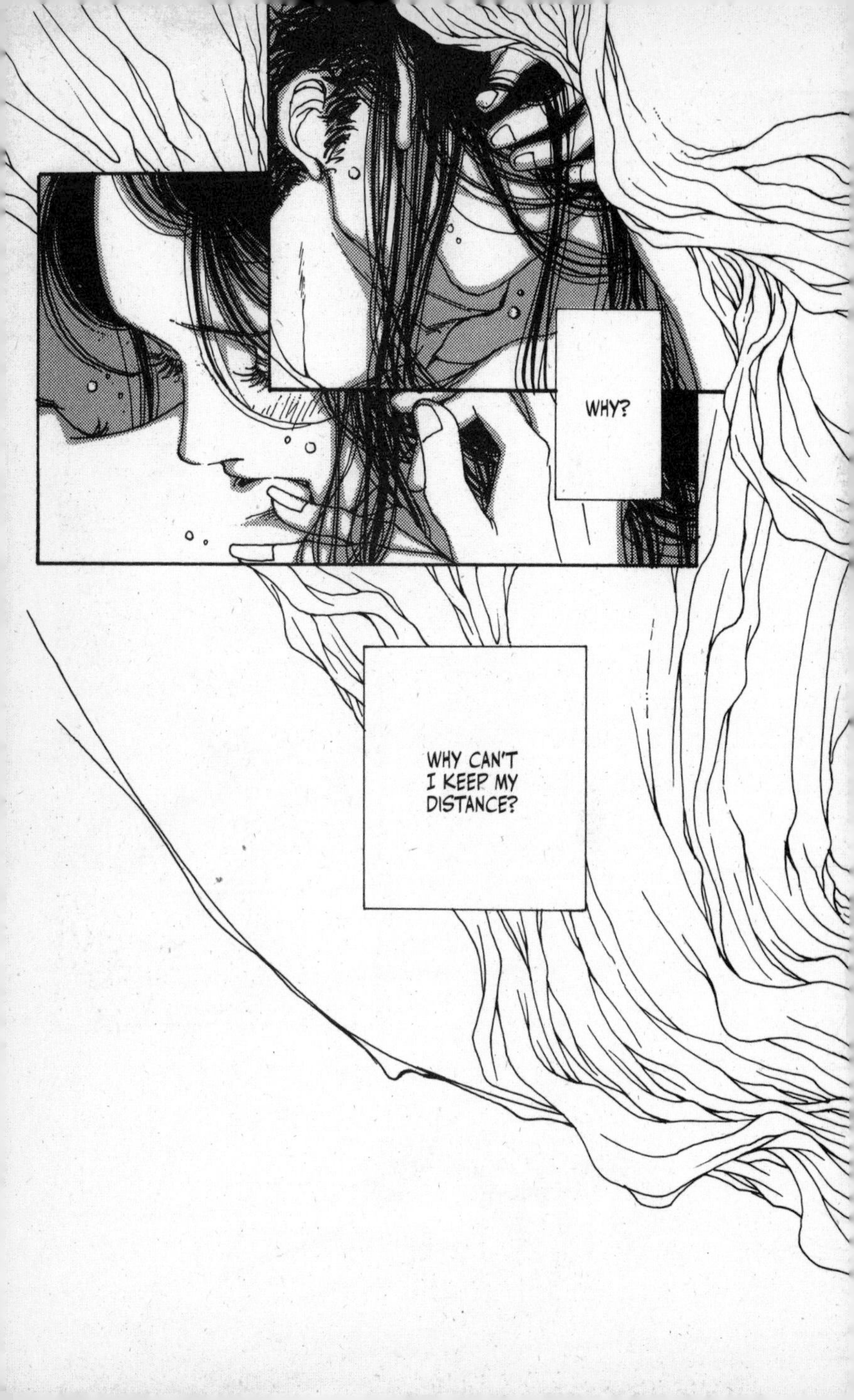
WHY?
WHY CAN'T I KEEP MY DISTANCE?

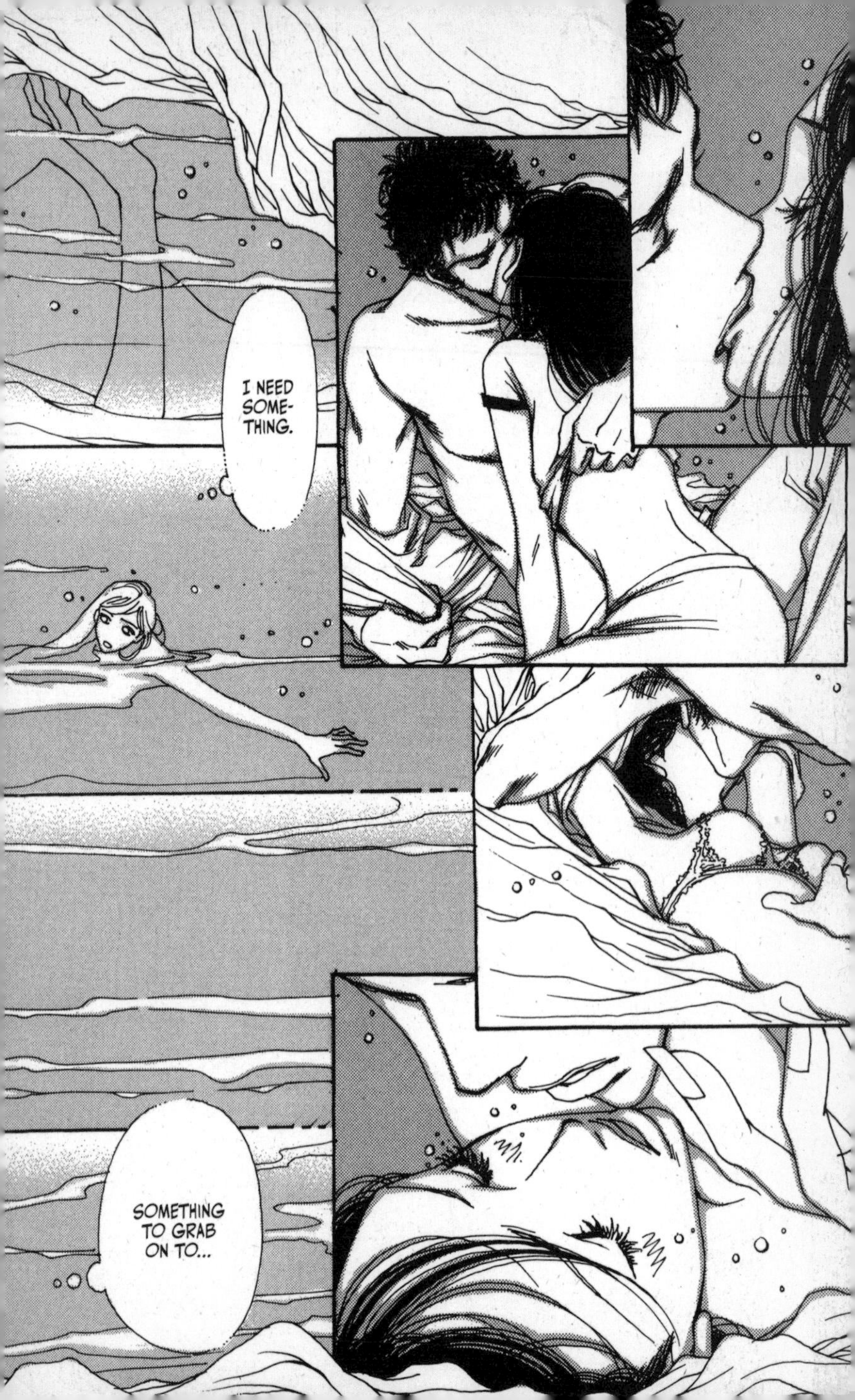
I NEED SOME-THING.
SOMETHING TO GRAB ON TO...

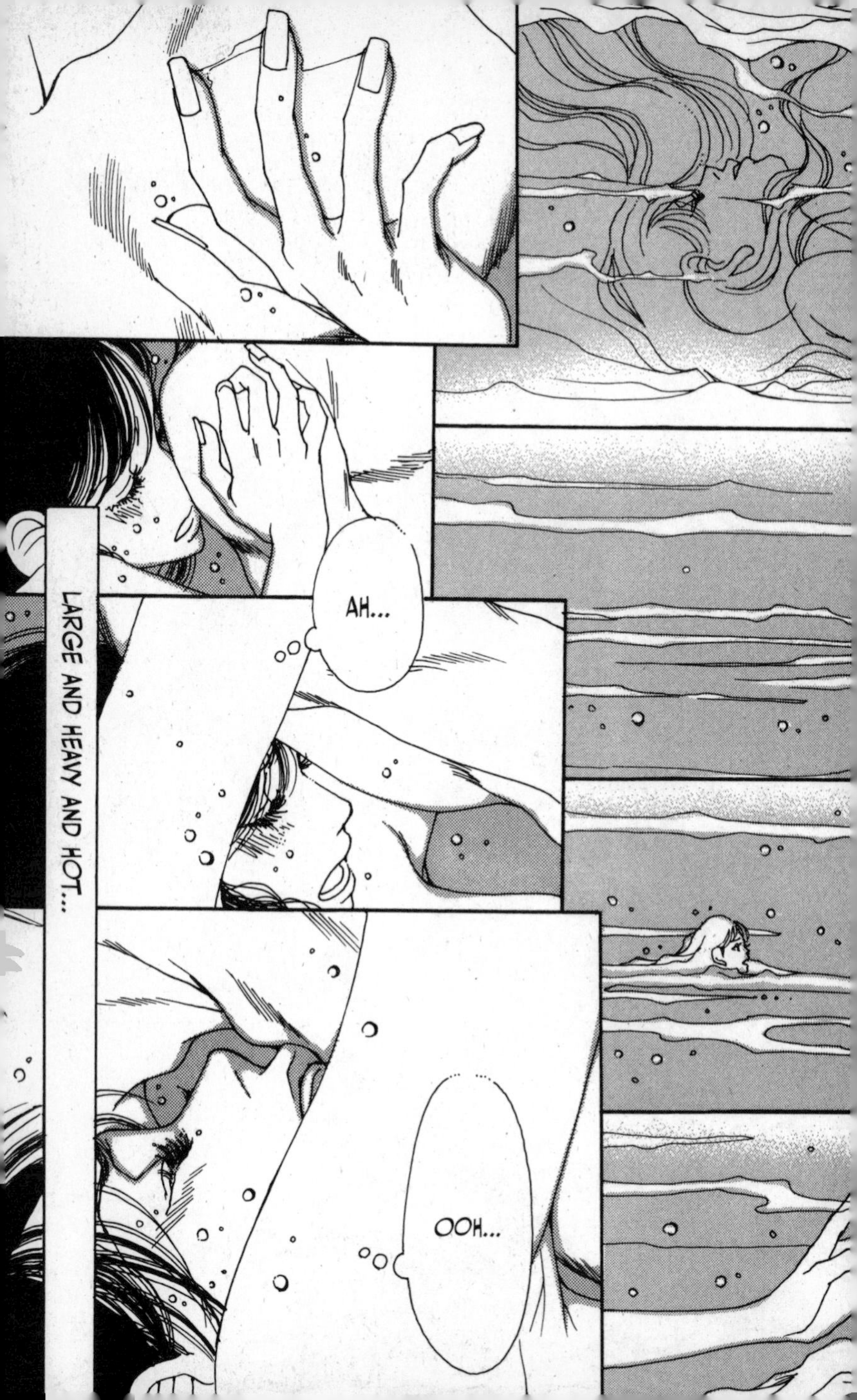
AH...
LARGE AND HEAVY AND HOT...
OOH...

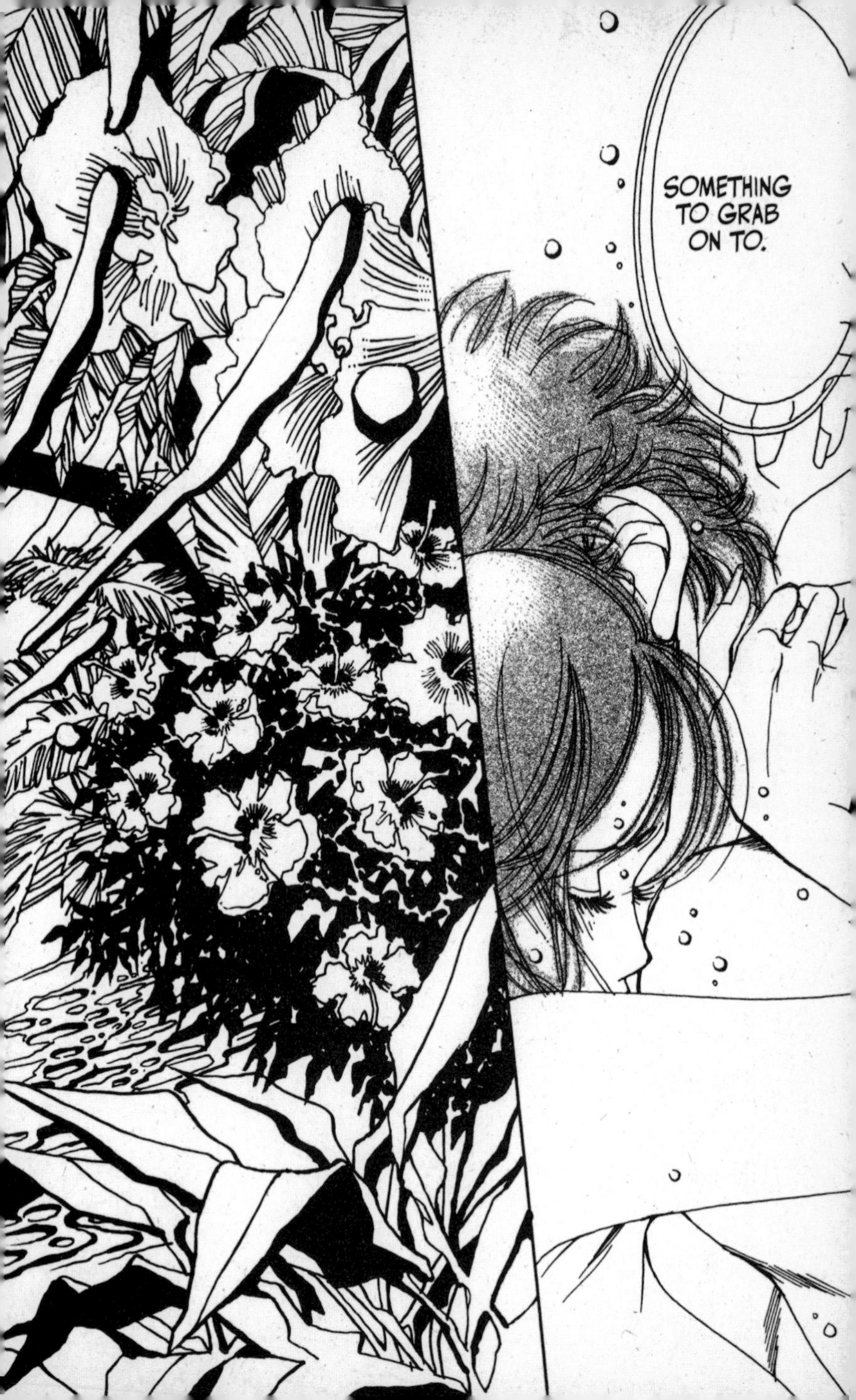
SOMETHING TO GRAB ON TO.

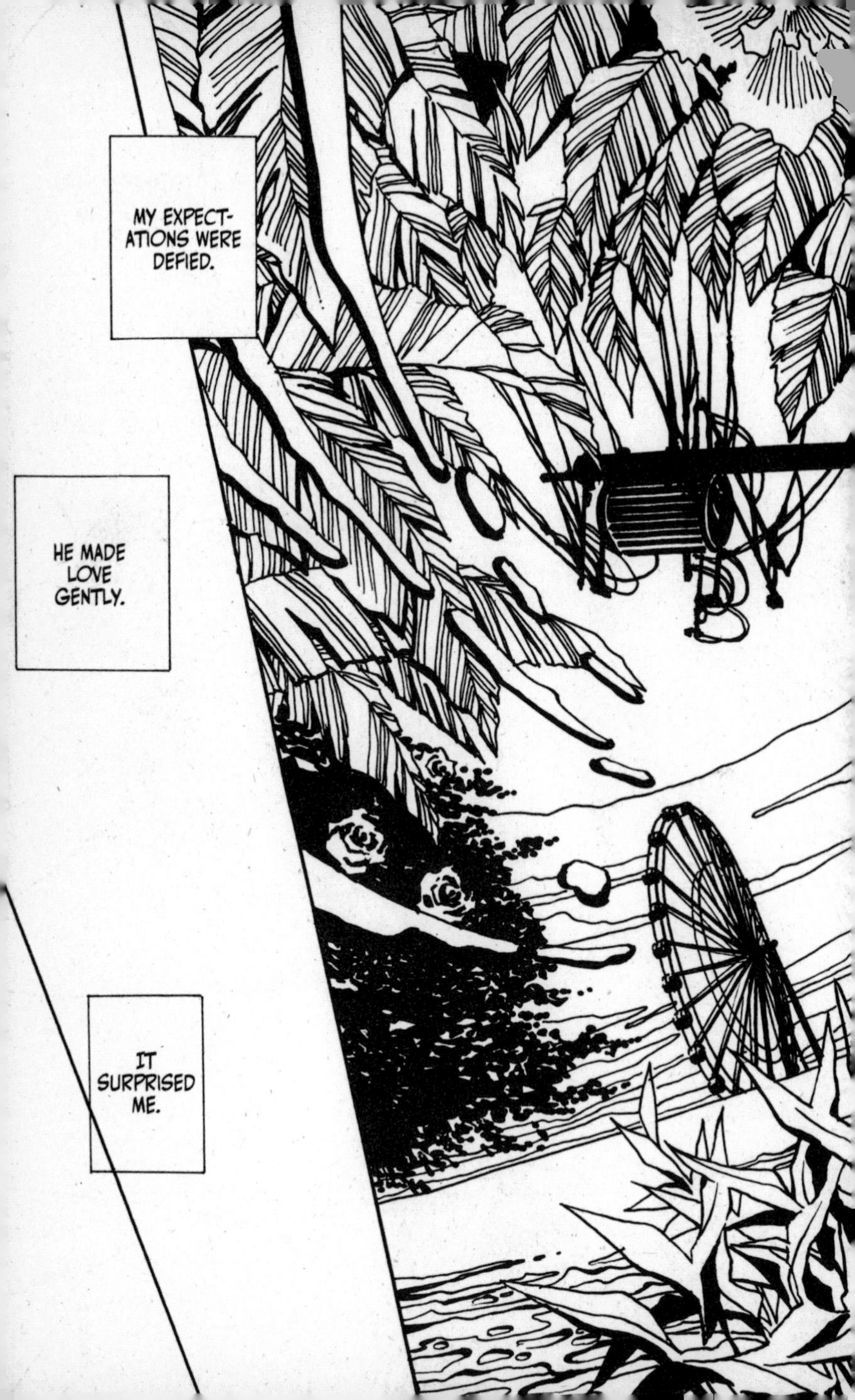
MY EXPECTATIONS WERE DEFIED.
HE MADE LOVE GENTLY.
IT SURPRISED ME.

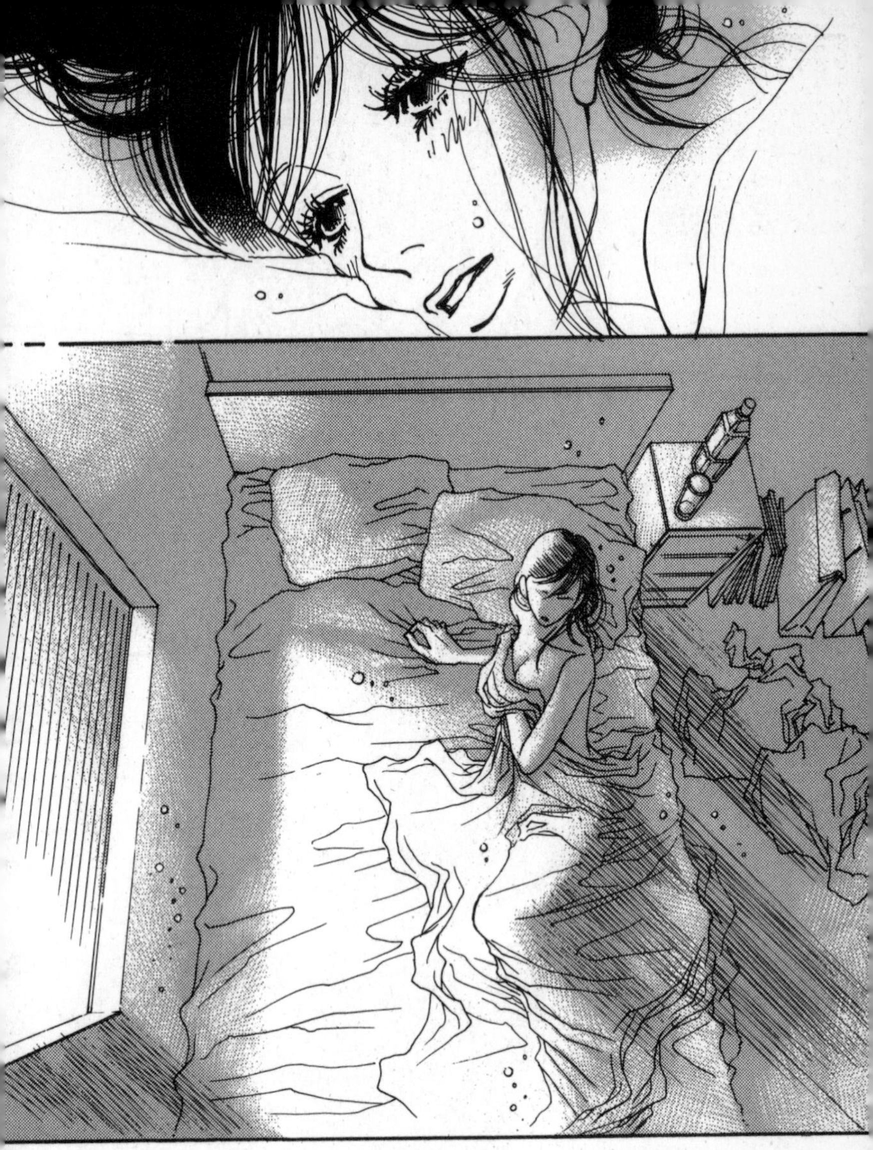

"SAHARA'S FILMING ON LOCATION IN AMERICA FOR TWO WEEKS."

THAT'S WHAT KOUETSU-SAN TOLD ME WHEN I ASKED HIM.

FILE. 28

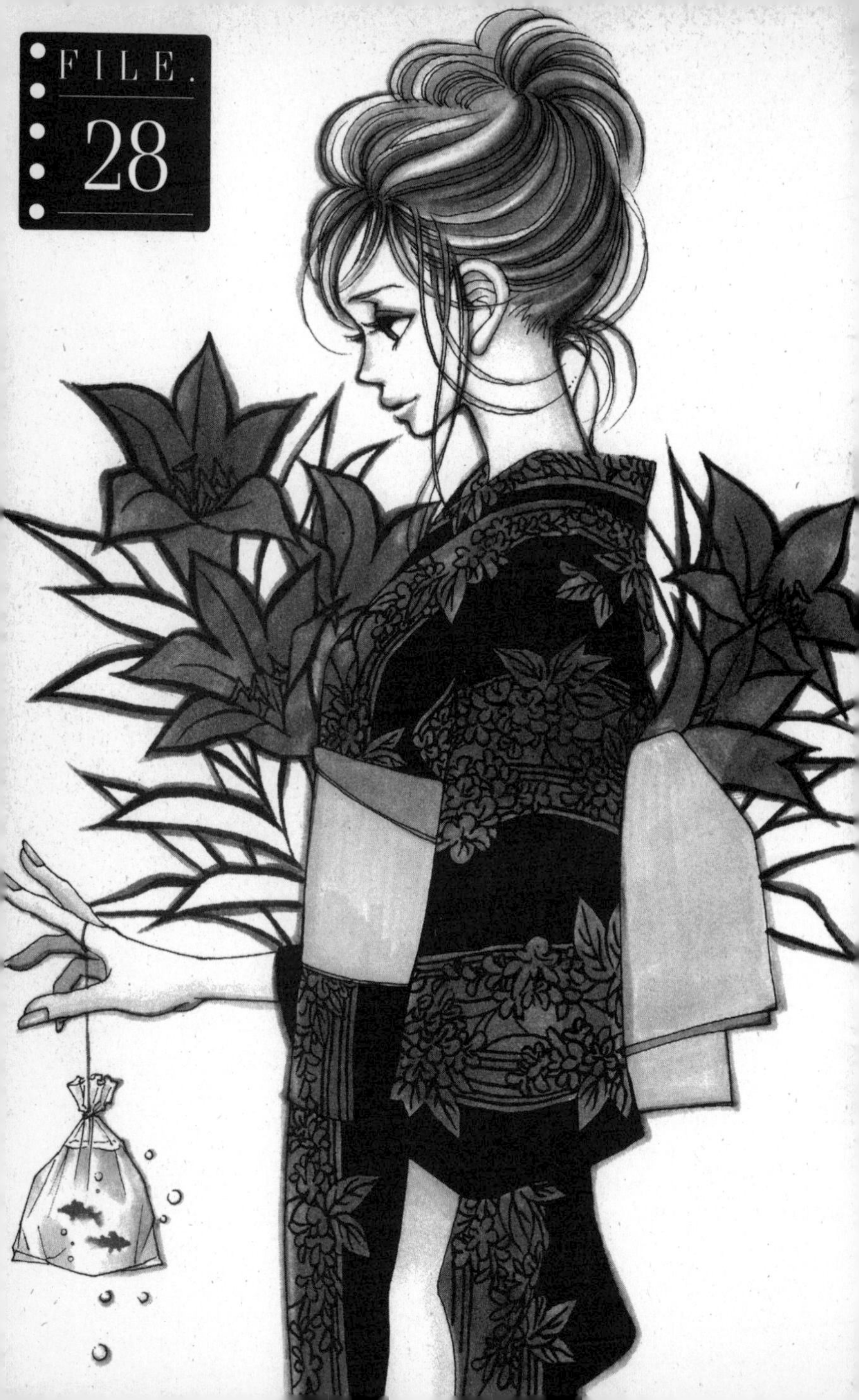

S u p p l i 5

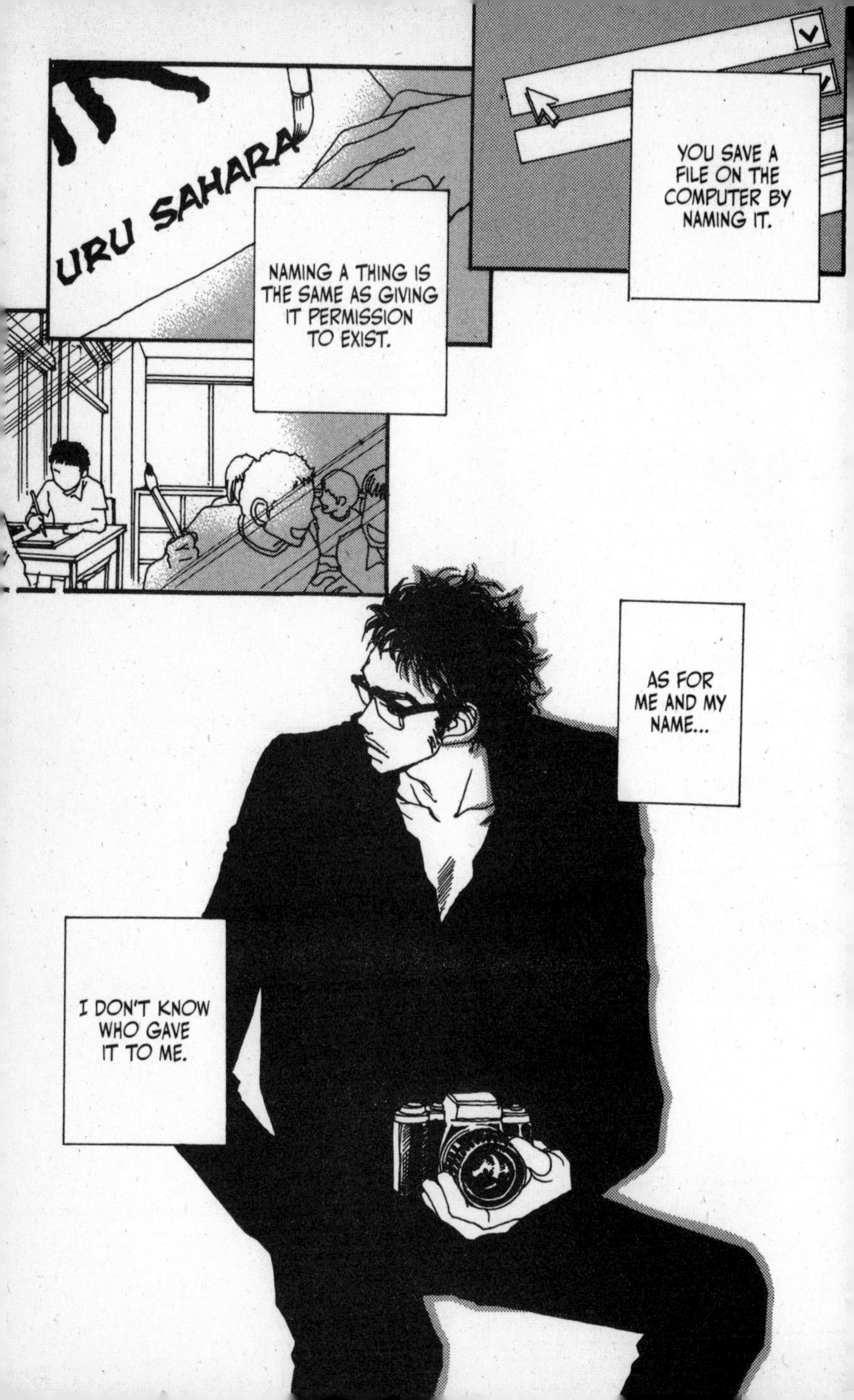
YOU SAVE A FILE ON THE COMPUTER BY NAMING IT.
URU SAHARA
NAMING A THING IS THE SAME AS GIVING IT PERMISSION TO EXIST.
AS FOR ME AND MY NAME...
I DON'T KNOW WHO GAVE IT TO ME.

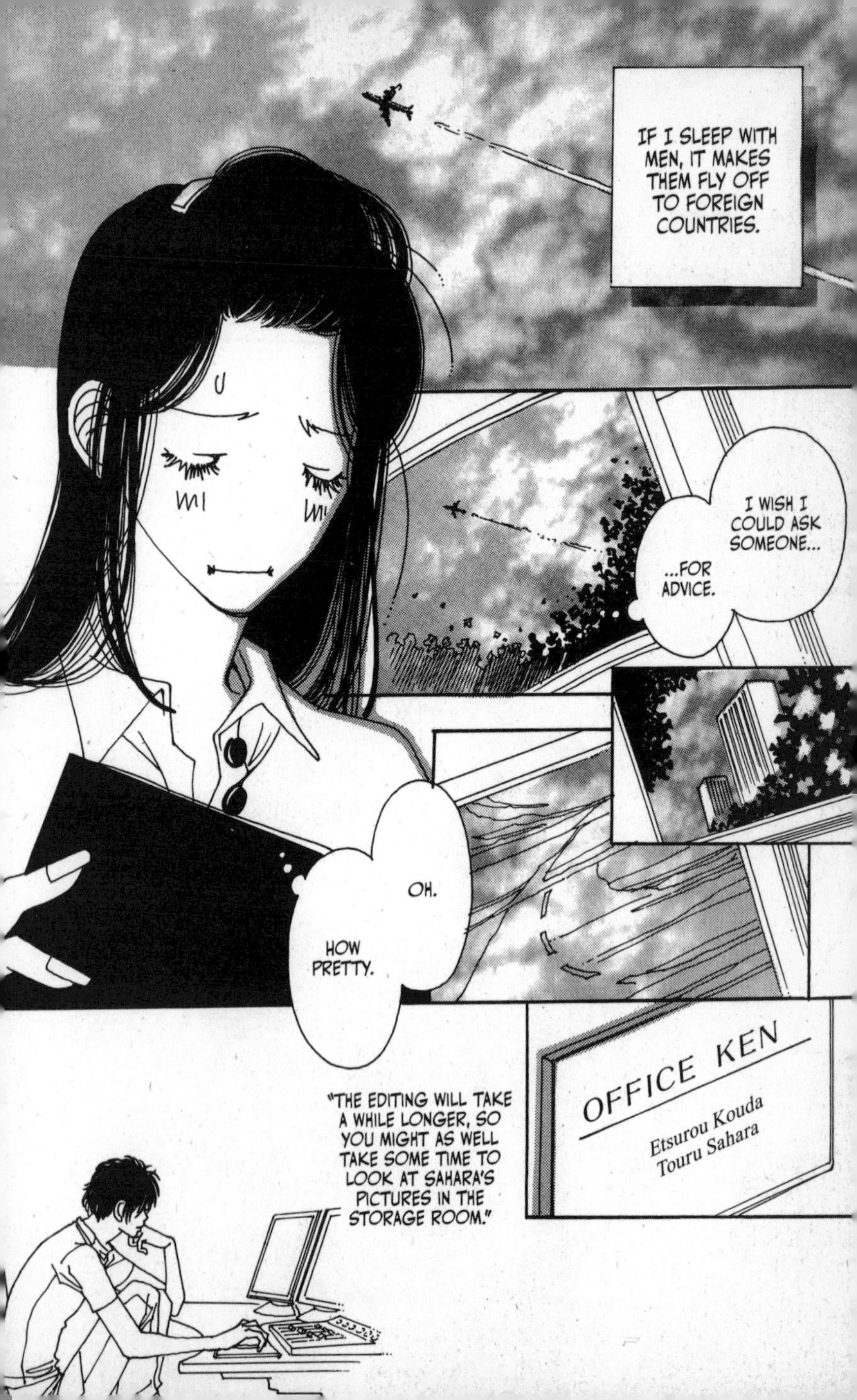
IF I SLEEP WITH MEN, IT MAKES THEM FLY OFF TO FOREIGN COUNTRIES.
I WISH I COULD ASK SOMEONE...
...FOR ADVICE.
OH.
HOW PRETTY.
OFFICE KEN
Etsurou Kouda
Touru Sahara
"THE EDITING WILL TAKE A WHILE LONGER, SO YOU MIGHT AS WELL TAKE SOME TIME TO LOOK AT SAHARA'S PICTURES IN THE STORAGE ROOM."

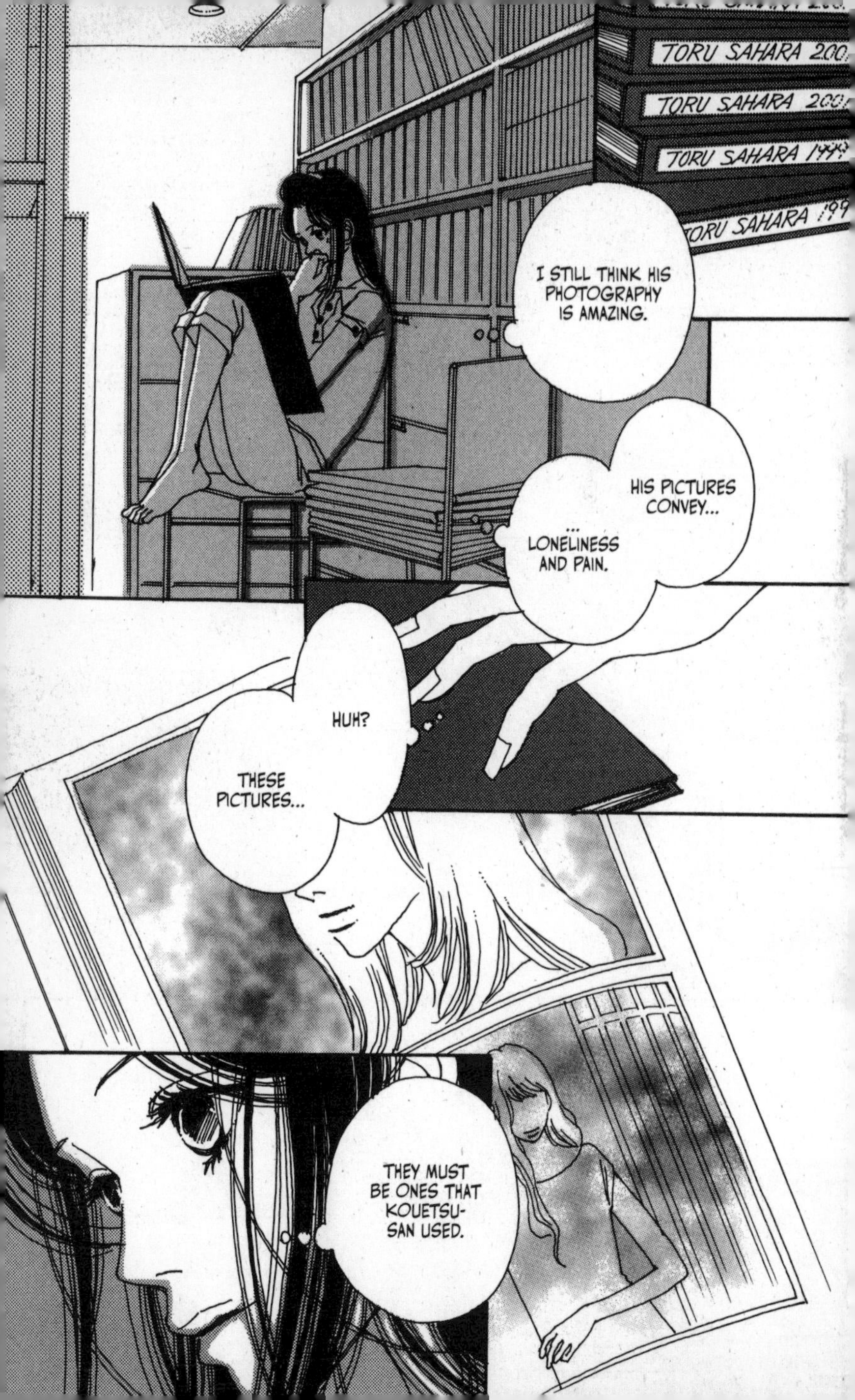
TORU SAHARA 200
TORU SAHARA 200
TORU SAHARA 199
TORU SAHARA 199
I STILL THINK HIS PHOTOGRAPHY IS AMAZING.
HIS PICTURES CONVEY...
...LONELINESS AND PAIN.
HUH?
THESE PICTURES...
THEY MUST BE ONES THAT KOUETSU-SAN USED.

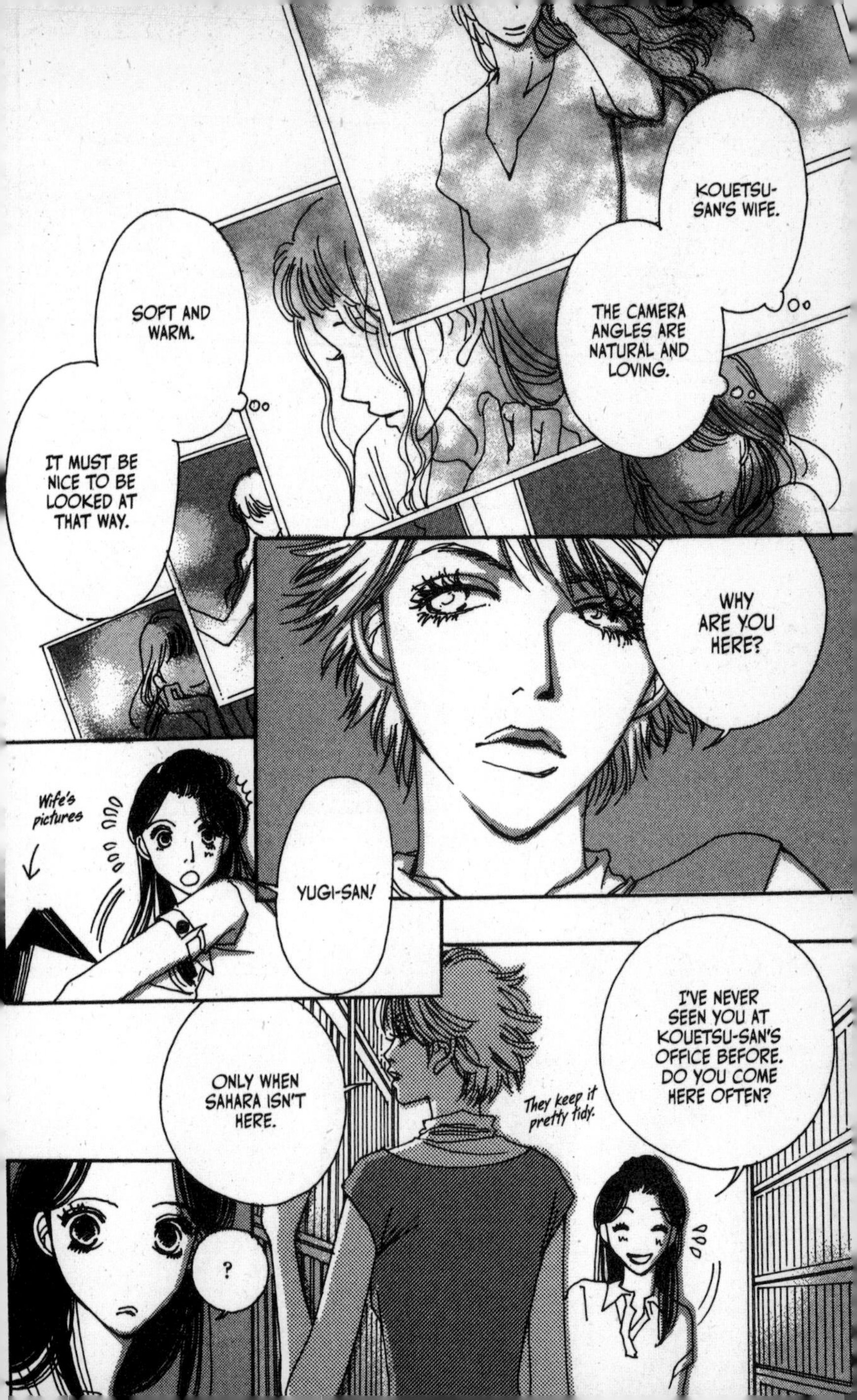
KOUETSU-SAN'S WIFE.
THE CAMERA ANGLES ARE NATURAL AND LOVING.
SOFT AND WARM.
IT MUST BE NICE TO BE LOOKED AT THAT WAY.
WHY ARE YOU HERE?
Wife's pictures
YUGI-SAN!
I'VE NEVER SEEN YOU AT KOUETSU-SAN'S OFFICE BEFORE. DO YOU COME HERE OFTEN?
They keep it pretty tidy.
ONLY WHEN SAHARA ISN'T HERE.
?

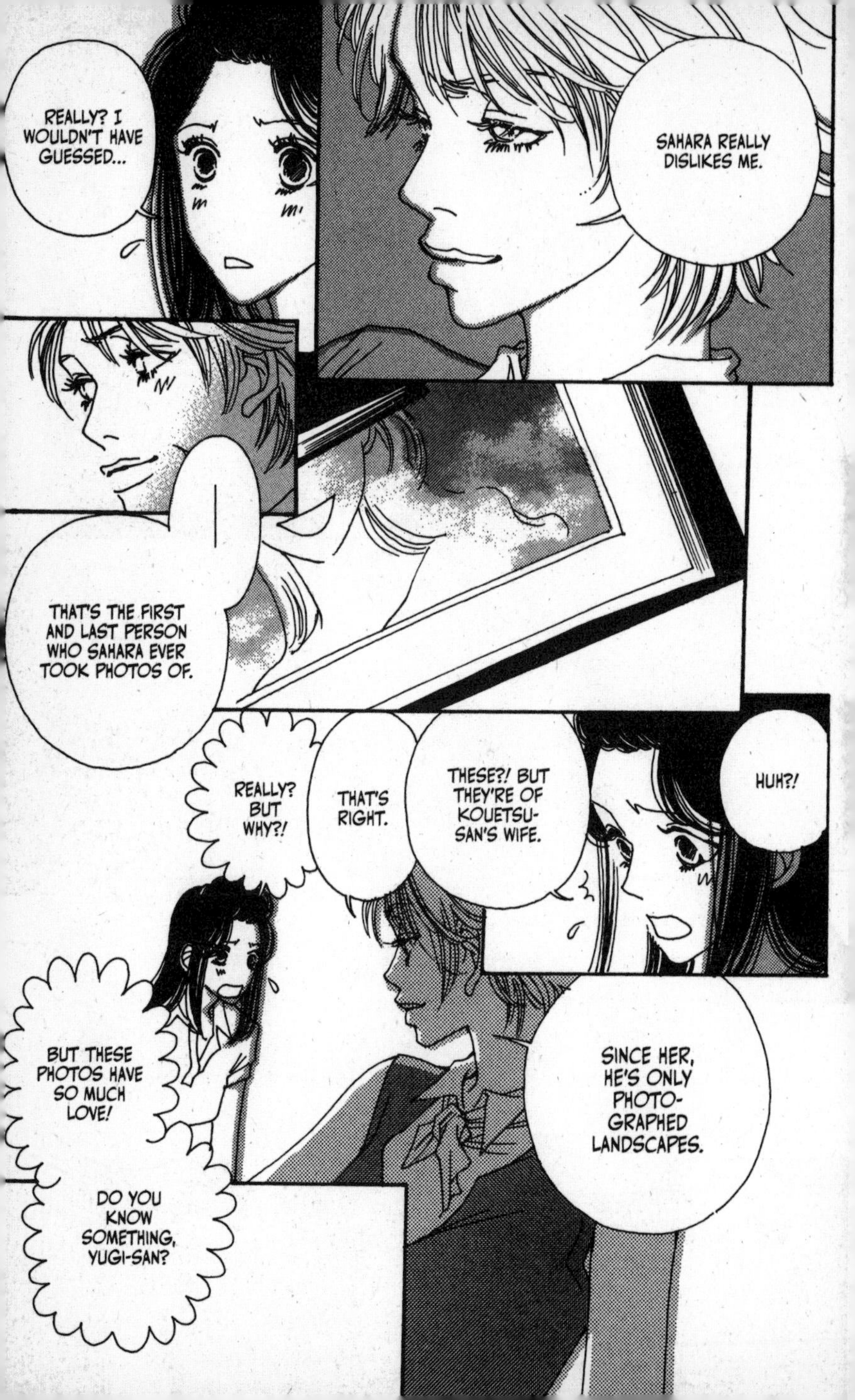
SAHARA REALLY DISLIKES ME.
REALLY? I WOULDN'T HAVE GUESSED...
THAT'S THE FIRST AND LAST PERSON WHO SAHARA EVER TOOK PHOTOS OF.
HUH?!
THESE?! BUT THEY'RE OF KOUETSU-SAN'S WIFE.
THAT'S RIGHT.
REALLY? BUT WHY?!
SINCE HER, HE'S ONLY PHOTO-GRAPHED LANDSCAPES.
BUT THESE PHOTOS HAVE SO MUCH LOVE!
DO YOU KNOW SOMETHING, YUGI-SAN?

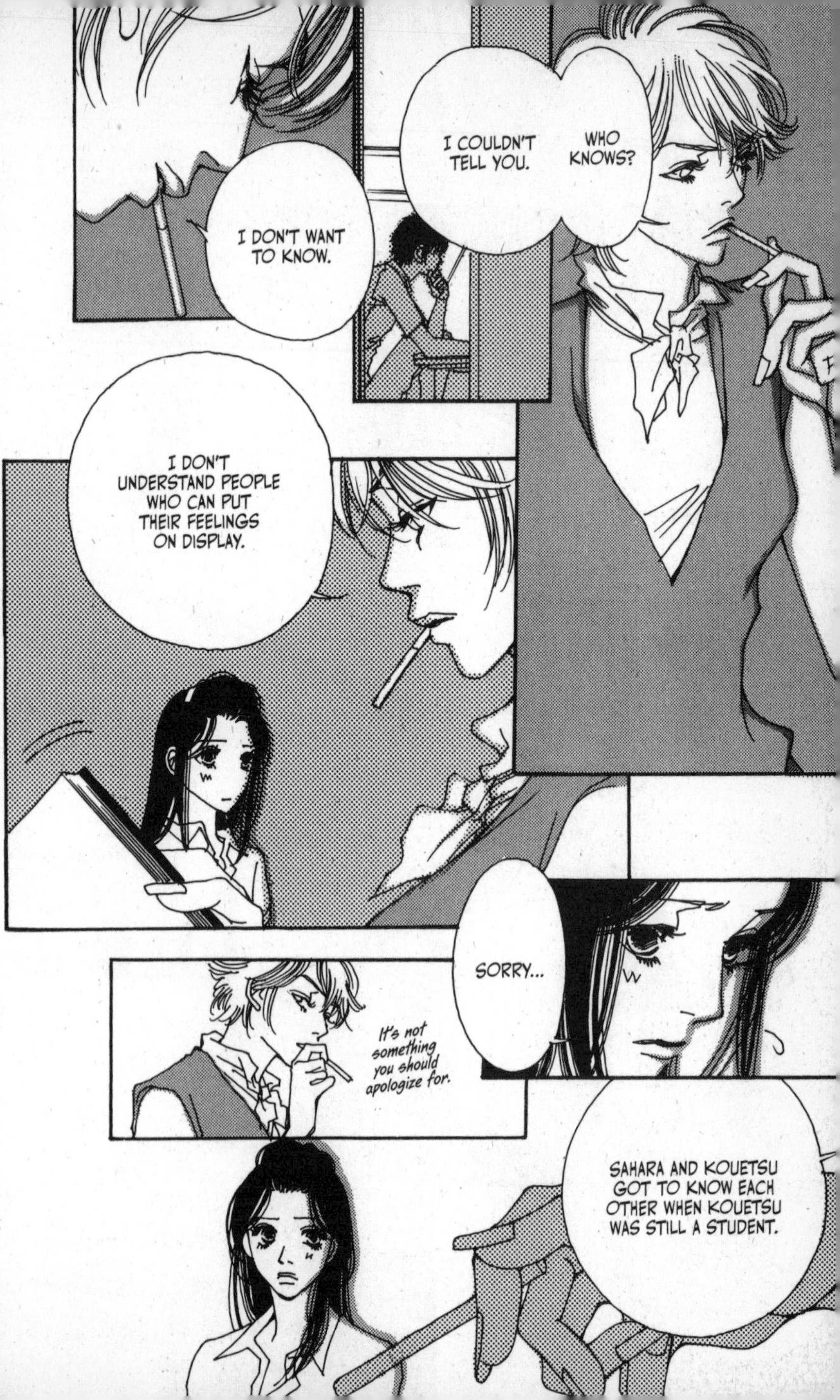
WHO KNOWS?
I COULDN'T TELL YOU.
I DON'T WANT TO KNOW.
I DON'T UNDERSTAND PEOPLE WHO CAN PUT THEIR FEELINGS ON DISPLAY.
SORRY...
It's not something you should apologize for.
SAHARA AND KOUETSU GOT TO KNOW EACH OTHER WHEN KOUETSU WAS STILL A STUDENT.

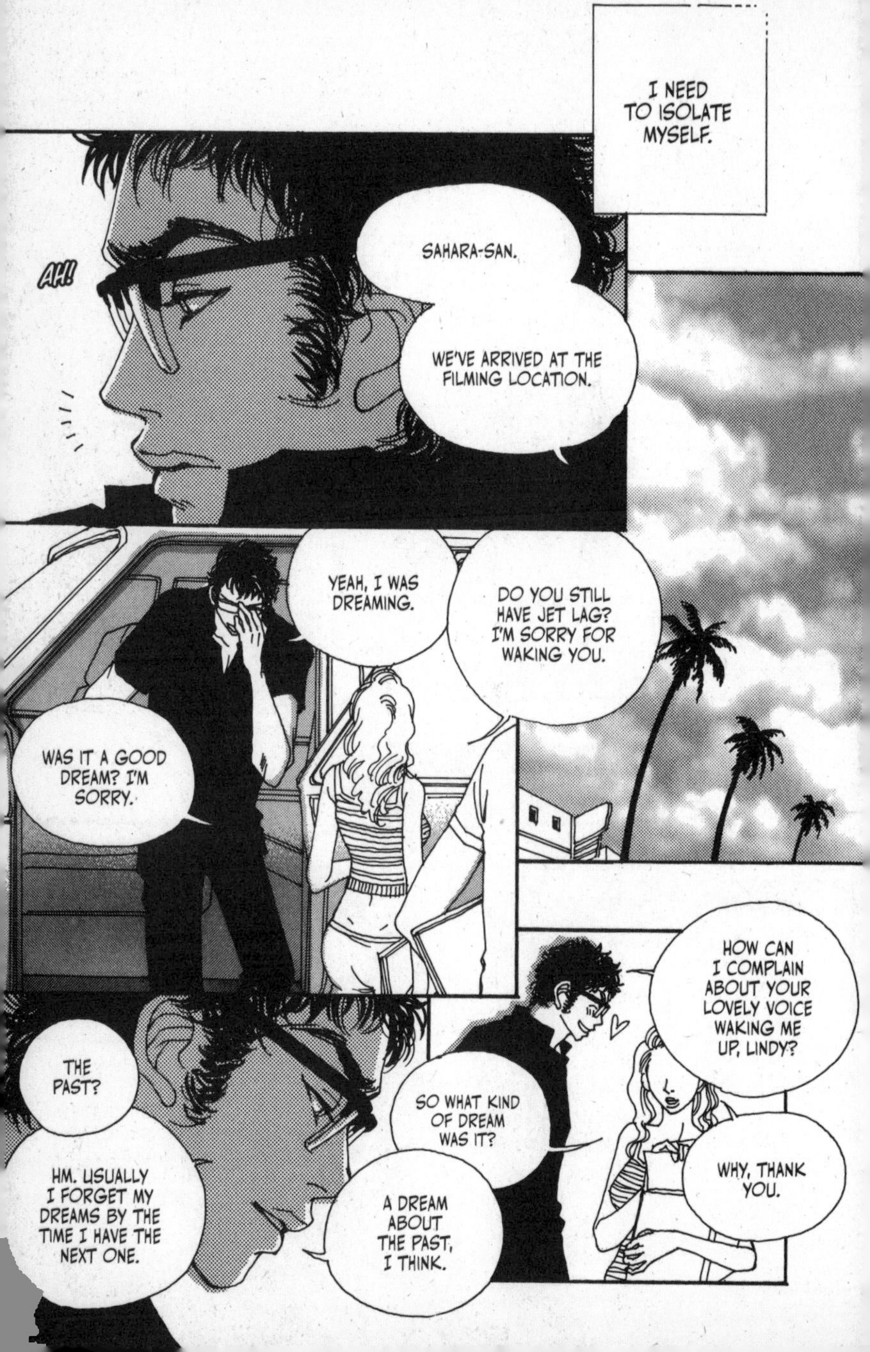
I NEED TO ISOLATE MYSELF.
SAHARA-SAN.
WE'VE ARRIVED AT THE FILMING LOCATION.
AH!
DO YOU STILL HAVE JET LAG? I'M SORRY FOR WAKING YOU.
YEAH, I WAS DREAMING.
WAS IT A GOOD DREAM? I'M SORRY.
HOW CAN I COMPLAIN ABOUT YOUR LOVELY VOICE WAKING ME UP, LINDY?
WHY, THANK YOU.
SO WHAT KIND OF DREAM WAS IT?
A DREAM ABOUT THE PAST, I THINK.
THE PAST?
HM. USUALLY I FORGET MY DREAMS BY THE TIME I HAVE THE NEXT ONE.

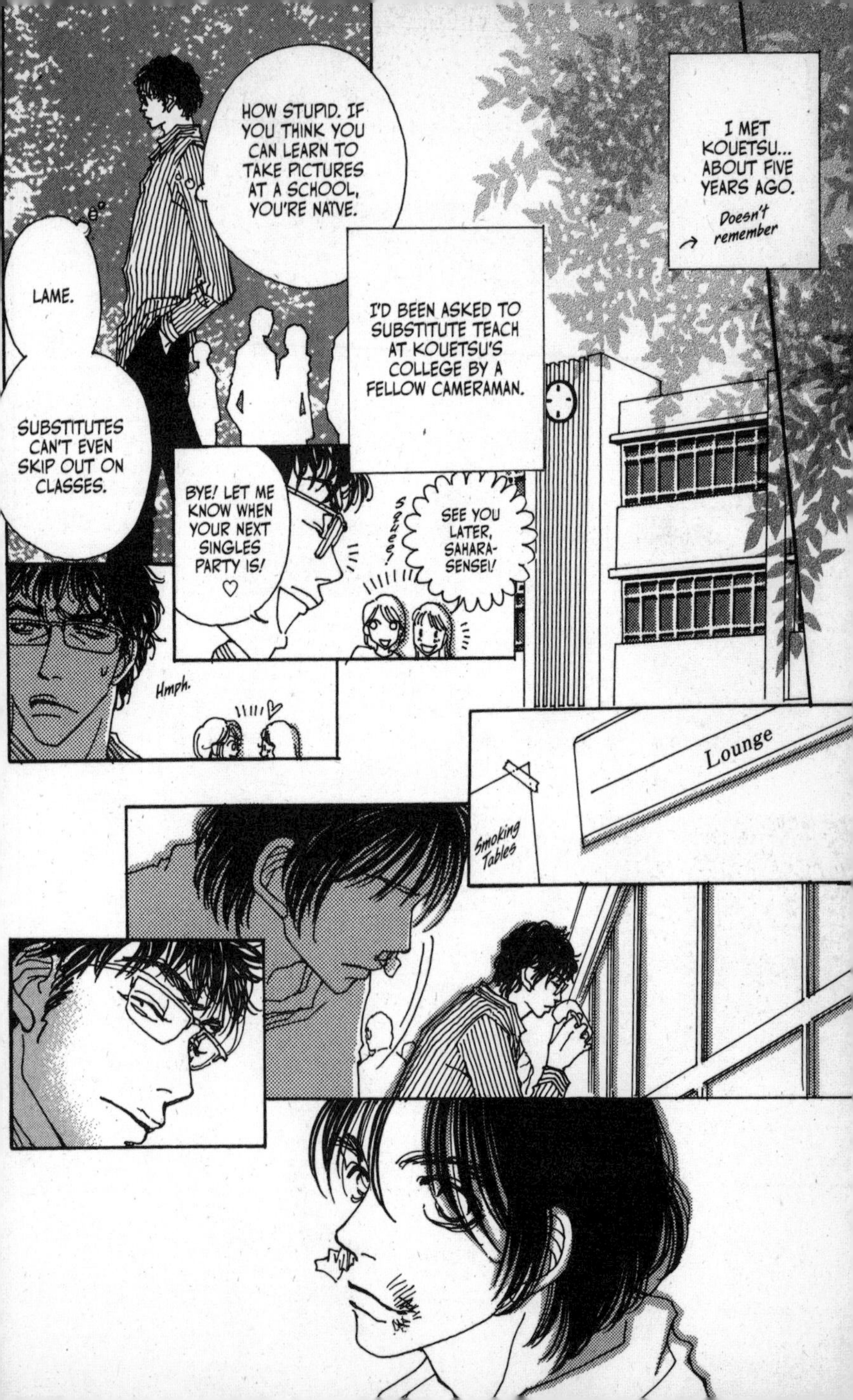
I MET KOUETSU... ABOUT FIVE YEARS AGO.
Doesn't remember
I'D BEEN ASKED TO SUBSTITUTE TEACH AT KOUETSU'S COLLEGE BY A FELLOW CAMERAMAN.
HOW STUPID. IF YOU THINK YOU CAN LEARN TO TAKE PICTURES AT A SCHOOL, YOU'RE NAÏVE.
LAME.
SUBSTITUTES CAN'T EVEN SKIP OUT ON CLASSES.
SEE YOU LATER, SAHARA-SENSEI!
Squee!
BYE! LET ME KNOW WHEN YOUR NEXT SINGLES PARTY IS! ♡
Hmph.
Lounge
Smoking Tables

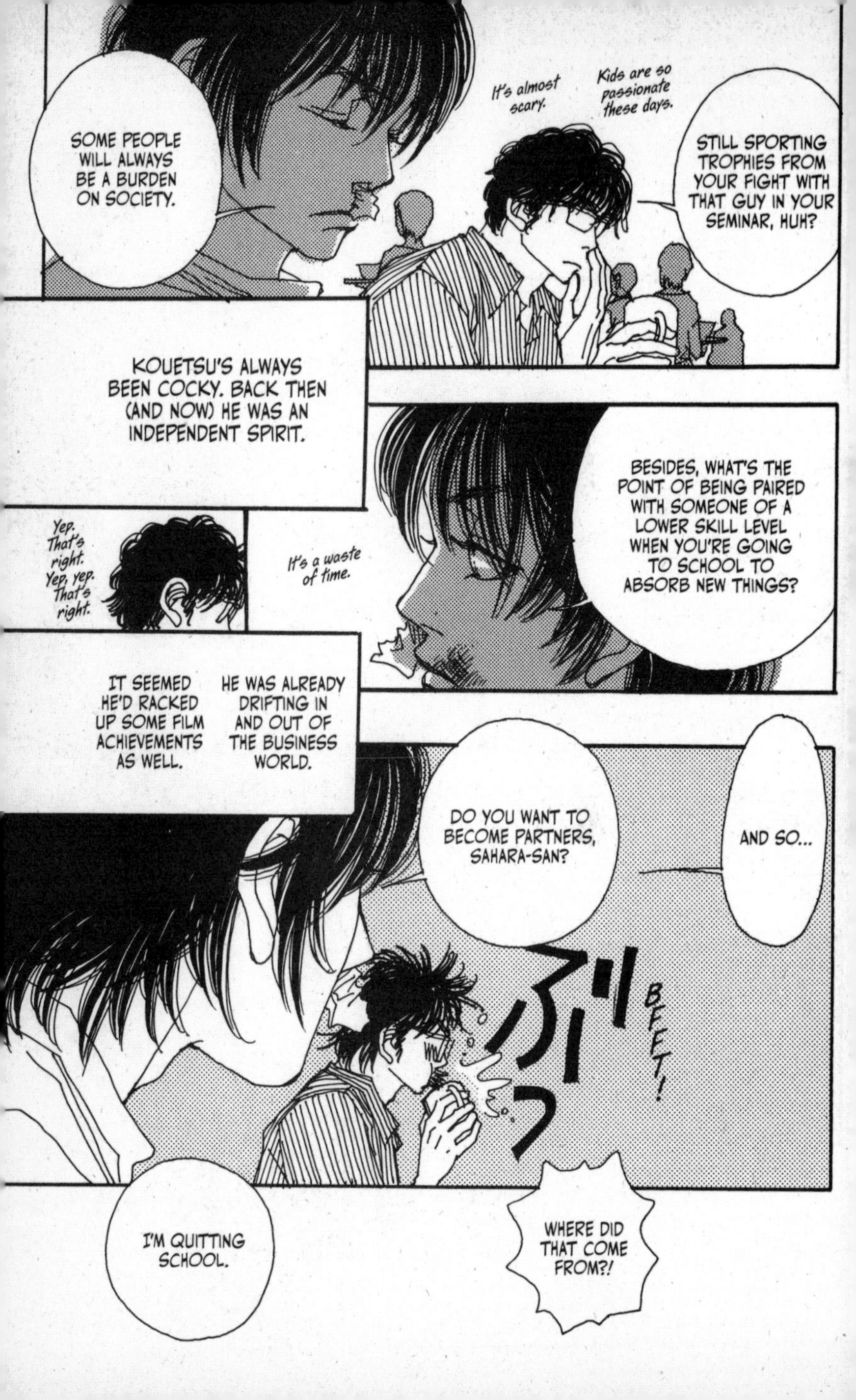
STILL SPORTING TROPHIES FROM YOUR FIGHT WITH THAT GUY IN YOUR SEMINAR, HUH?
Kids are so passionate these days.
It's almost scary.
SOME PEOPLE WILL ALWAYS BE A BURDEN ON SOCIETY.
BESIDES, WHAT'S THE POINT OF BEING PAIRED WITH SOMEONE OF A LOWER SKILL LEVEL WHEN YOU'RE GOING TO SCHOOL TO ABSORB NEW THINGS?
It's a waste of time.
KOUETSU'S ALWAYS BEEN COCKY. BACK THEN (AND NOW) HE WAS AN INDEPENDENT SPIRIT.
Yep. That's right. Yep, yep. That's right.
HE WAS ALREADY DRIFTING IN AND OUT OF THE BUSINESS WORLD.
IT SEEMED HE'D RACKED UP SOME FILM ACHIEVEMENTS AS WELL.
AND SO...
DO YOU WANT TO BECOME PARTNERS, SAHARA-SAN?
BFFFT!
WHERE DID THAT COME FROM?!
I'M QUITTING SCHOOL.

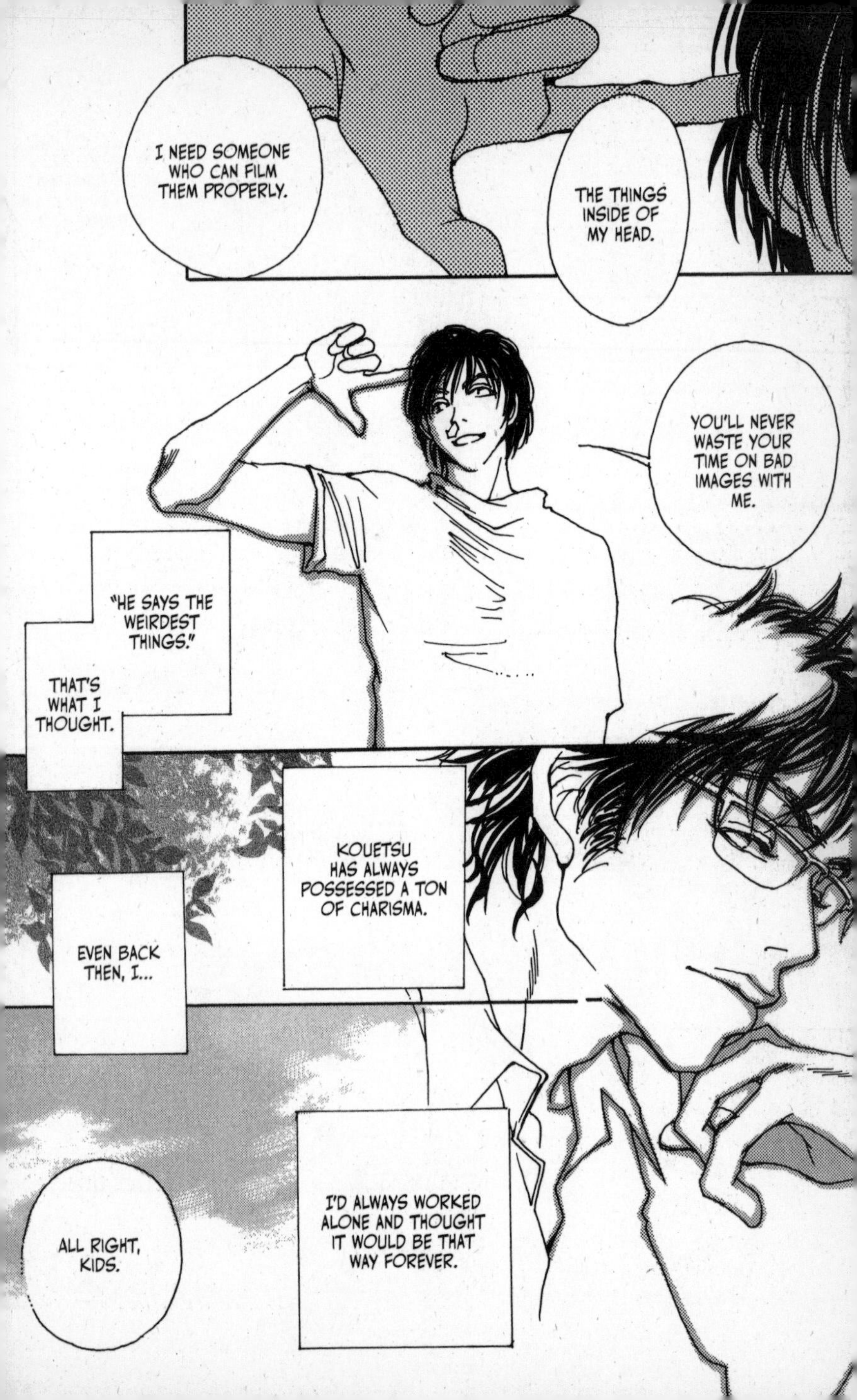
THE THINGS INSIDE OF MY HEAD.
I NEED SOMEONE WHO CAN FILM THEM PROPERLY.
YOU'LL NEVER WASTE YOUR TIME ON BAD IMAGES WITH ME.
"HE SAYS THE WEIRDEST THINGS."
THAT'S WHAT I THOUGHT.
KOUETSU HAS ALWAYS POSSESSED A TON OF CHARISMA.
EVEN BACK THEN, I...
I'D ALWAYS WORKED ALONE AND THOUGHT IT WOULD BE THAT WAY FOREVER.
ALL RIGHT, KIDS.

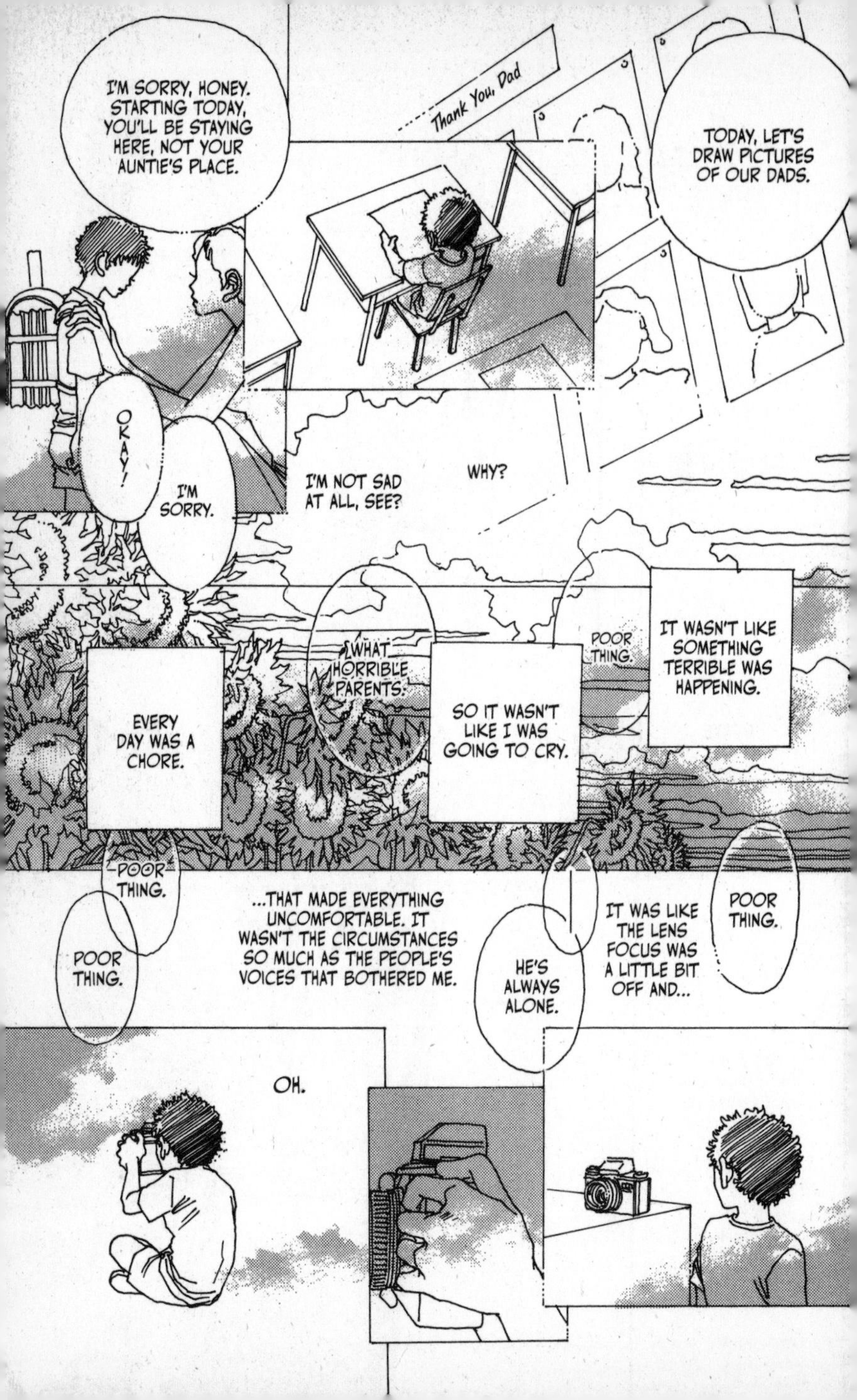
TODAY, LET'S DRAW PICTURES OF OUR DADS.
Thank You, Dad
I'M SORRY, HONEY. STARTING TODAY, YOU'LL BE STAYING HERE, NOT YOUR AUNTIE'S PLACE.
OKAY!
I'M SORRY.
WHY?
I'M NOT SAD AT ALL, SEE?
IT WASN'T LIKE SOMETHING TERRIBLE WAS HAPPENING.
POOR THING.
SO IT WASN'T LIKE I WAS GOING TO CRY.
WHAT HORRIBLE PARENTS.
EVERY DAY WAS A CHORE.
POOR THING.
IT WAS LIKE THE LENS FOCUS WAS A LITTLE BIT OFF AND...
HE'S ALWAYS ALONE.
...THAT MADE EVERYTHING UNCOMFORTABLE. IT WASN'T THE CIRCUMSTANCES SO MUCH AS THE PEOPLE'S VOICES THAT BOTHERED ME.
POOR THING.
POOR THING.
OH.

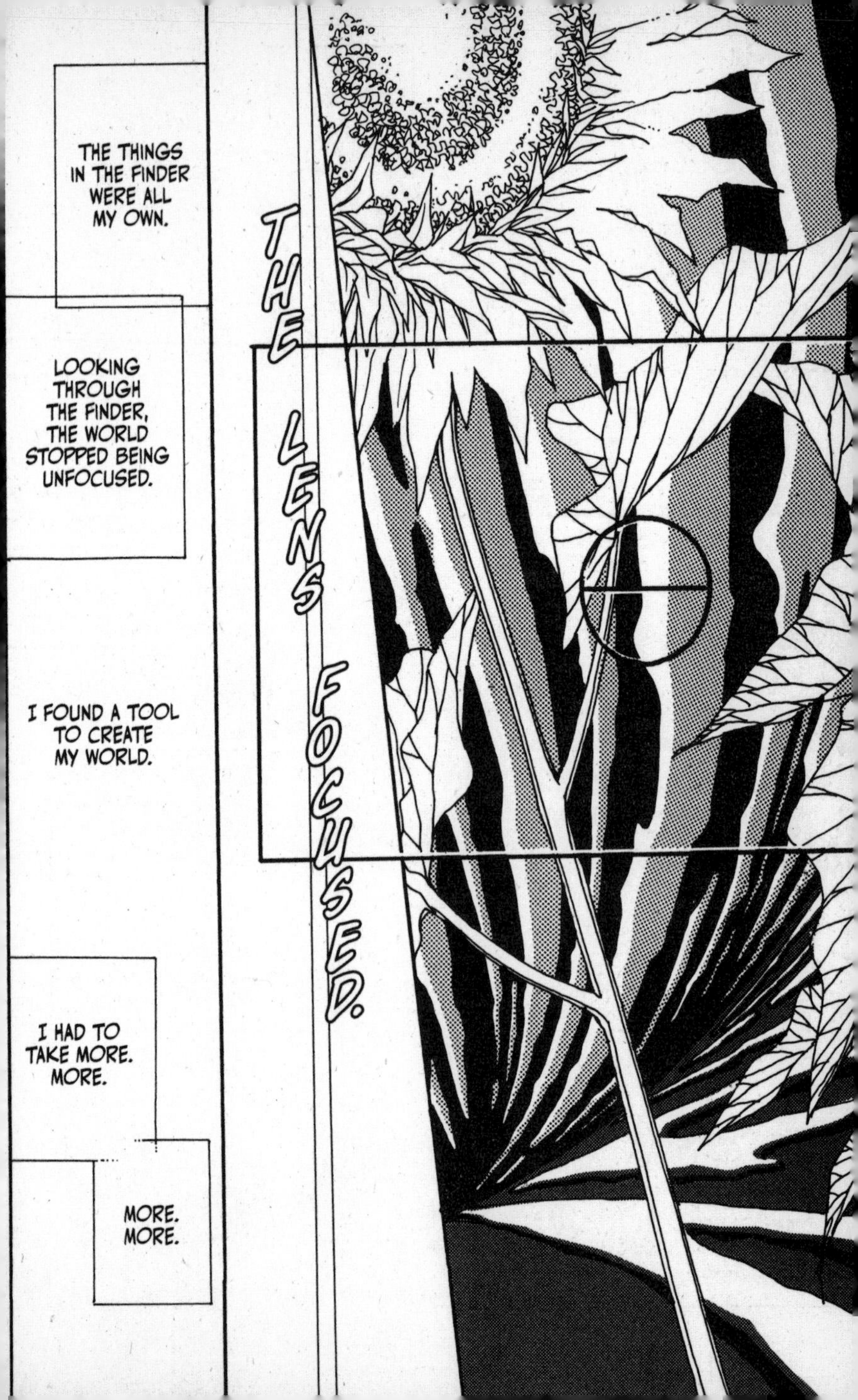
THE LENS FOCUSED.
THE THINGS IN THE FINDER WERE ALL MY OWN.
LOOKING THROUGH THE FINDER, THE WORLD STOPPED BEING UNFOCUSED.
I FOUND A TOOL TO CREATE MY WORLD.
I HAD TO TAKE MORE. MORE.
MORE. MORE.

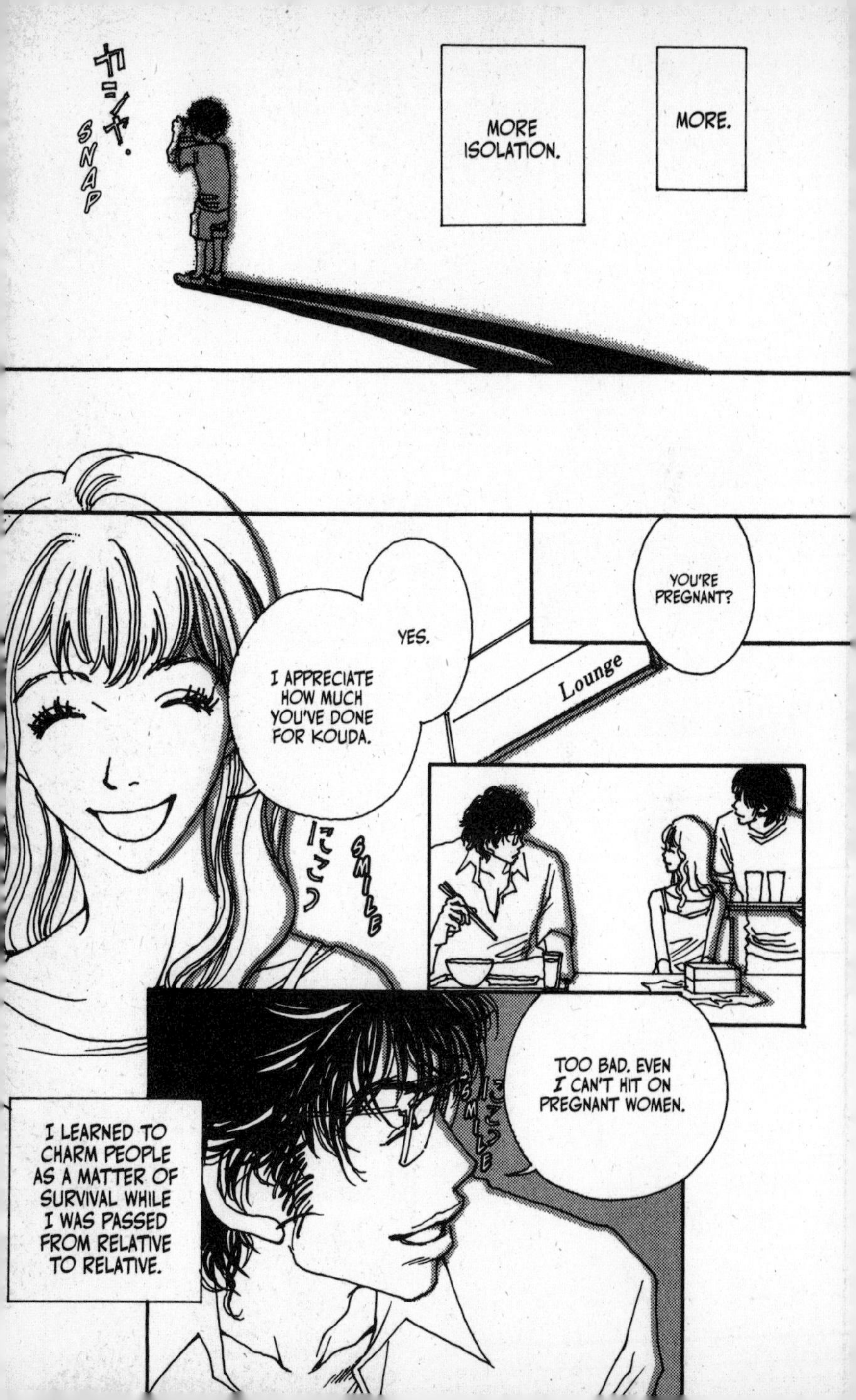
MORE.
MORE ISOLATION.
カシャ
SNAP
YOU'RE PREGNANT?
Lounge
YES.
I APPRECIATE HOW MUCH YOU'VE DONE FOR KOUDA.
にこっ
SMILE
TOO BAD. EVEN I CAN'T HIT ON PREGNANT WOMEN.
にこっ
SMILE
I LEARNED TO CHARM PEOPLE AS A MATTER OF SURVIVAL WHILE I WAS PASSED FROM RELATIVE TO RELATIVE.

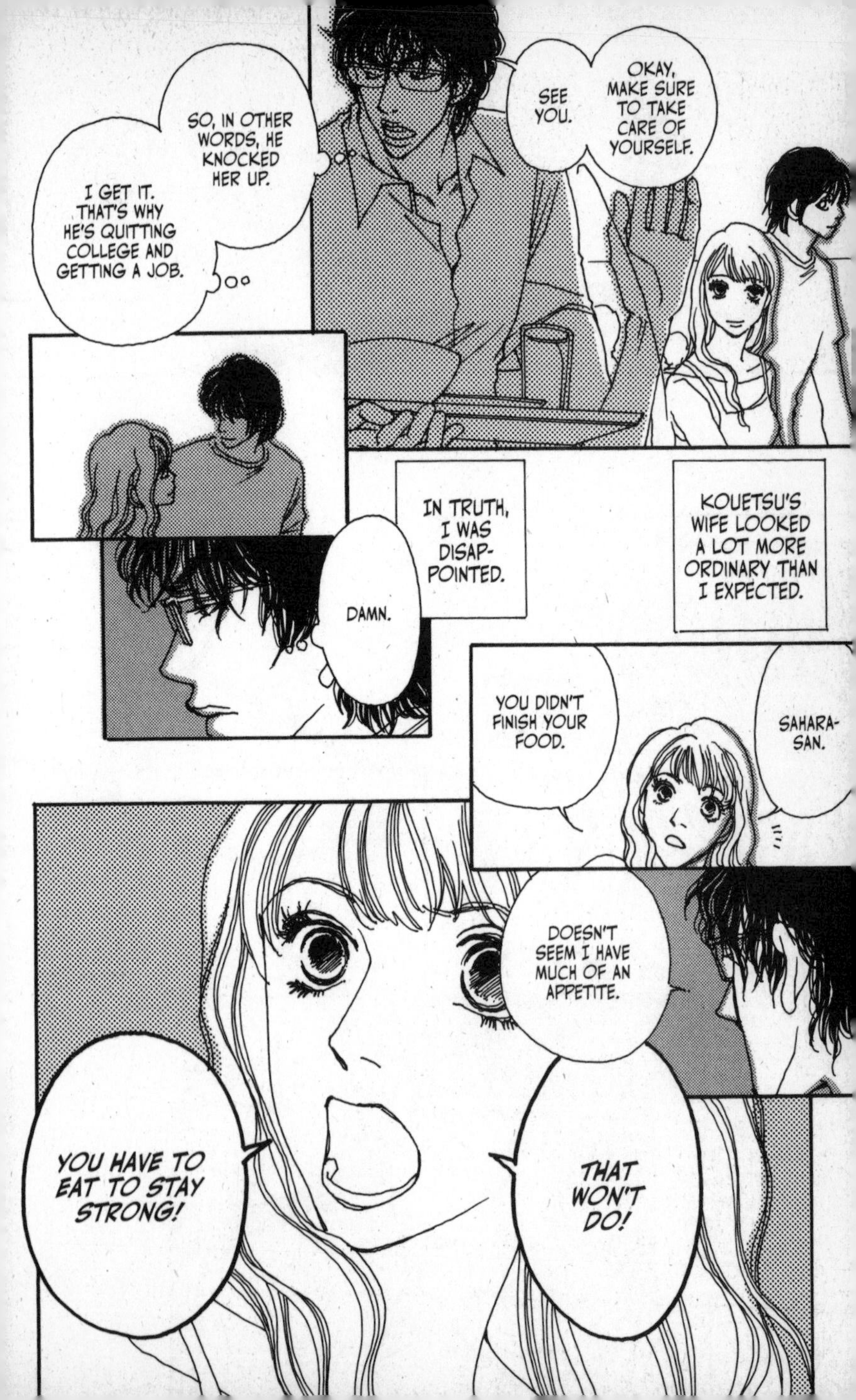
OKAY, MAKE SURE TO TAKE CARE OF YOURSELF.
SEE YOU.
SO, IN OTHER WORDS, HE KNOCKED HER UP.
I GET IT. THAT'S WHY HE'S QUITTING COLLEGE AND GETTING A JOB.
KOUETSU'S WIFE LOOKED A LOT MORE ORDINARY THAN I EXPECTED.
IN TRUTH, I WAS DISAP-POINTED.
DAMN.
SAHARA-SAN.
YOU DIDN'T FINISH YOUR FOOD.
DOESN'T SEEM I HAVE MUCH OF AN APPETITE.
THAT WON'T DO!
YOU HAVE TO EAT TO STAY STRONG!

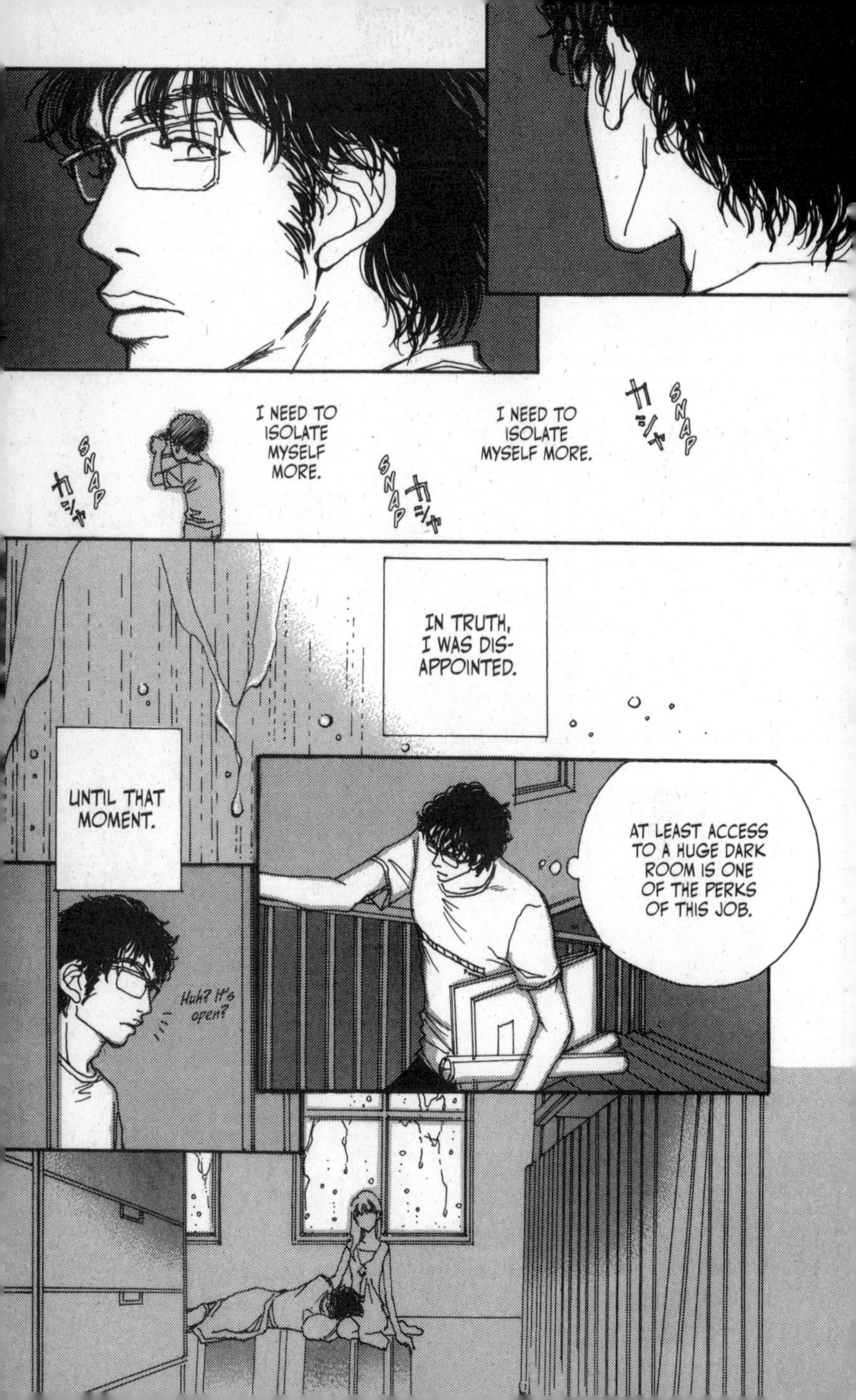
SNAP
カシャ
I NEED TO ISOLATE MYSELF MORE.
SNAP
カシャ
I NEED TO ISOLATE MYSELF MORE.
SNAP
カシャ
IN TRUTH, I WAS DIS- APPOINTED.
AT LEAST ACCESS TO A HUGE DARK ROOM IS ONE OF THE PERKS OF THIS JOB.
UNTIL THAT MOMENT.
Huh? It's open?

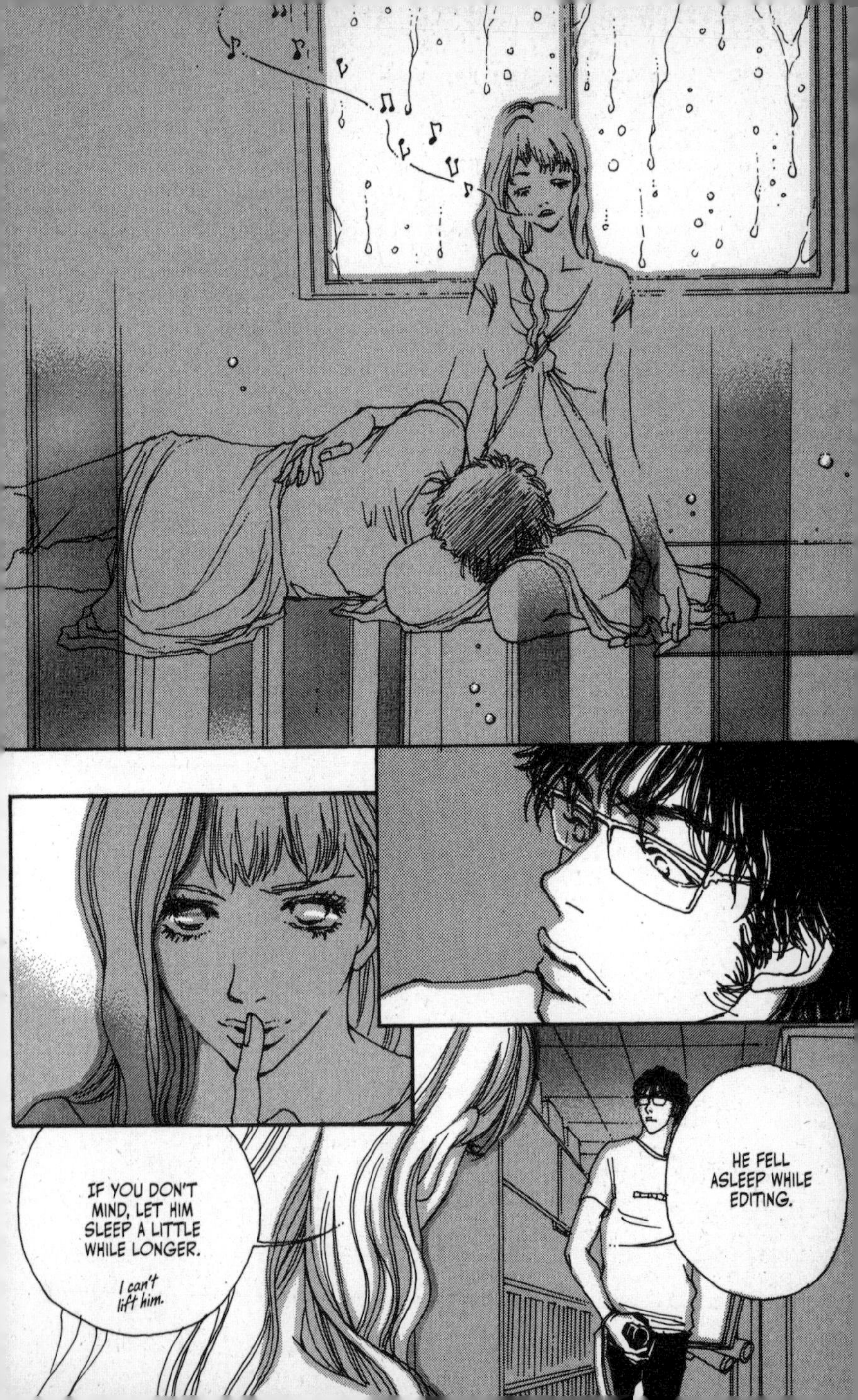
HE FELL ASLEEP WHILE EDITING.
IF YOU DON'T MIND, LET HIM SLEEP A LITTLE WHILE LONGER.
I can't lift him.

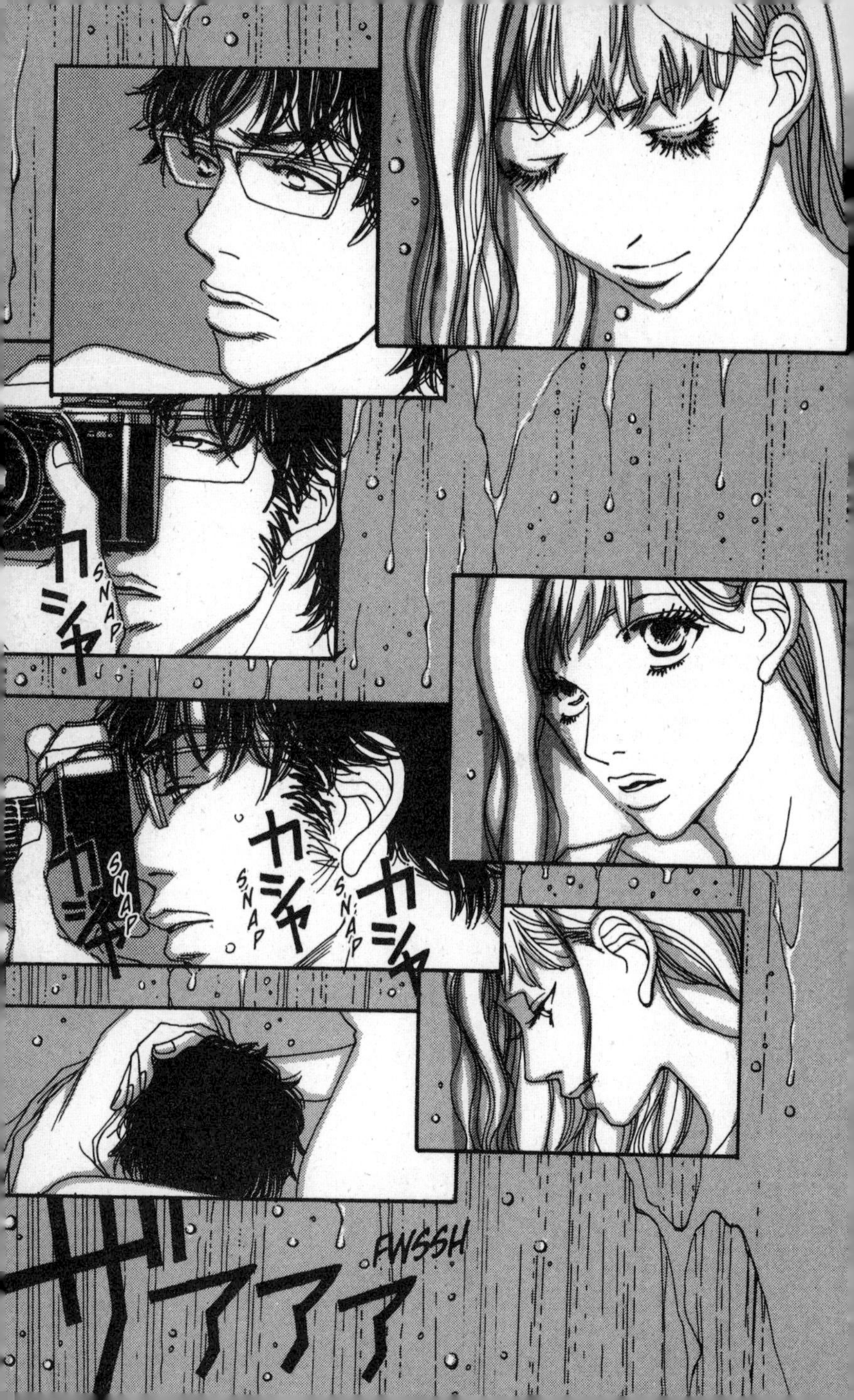

カシャ
SNAP
カシャ
SNAP
カシャ
SNAP
カシャ
SNAP
ザーアアア
FWSSH

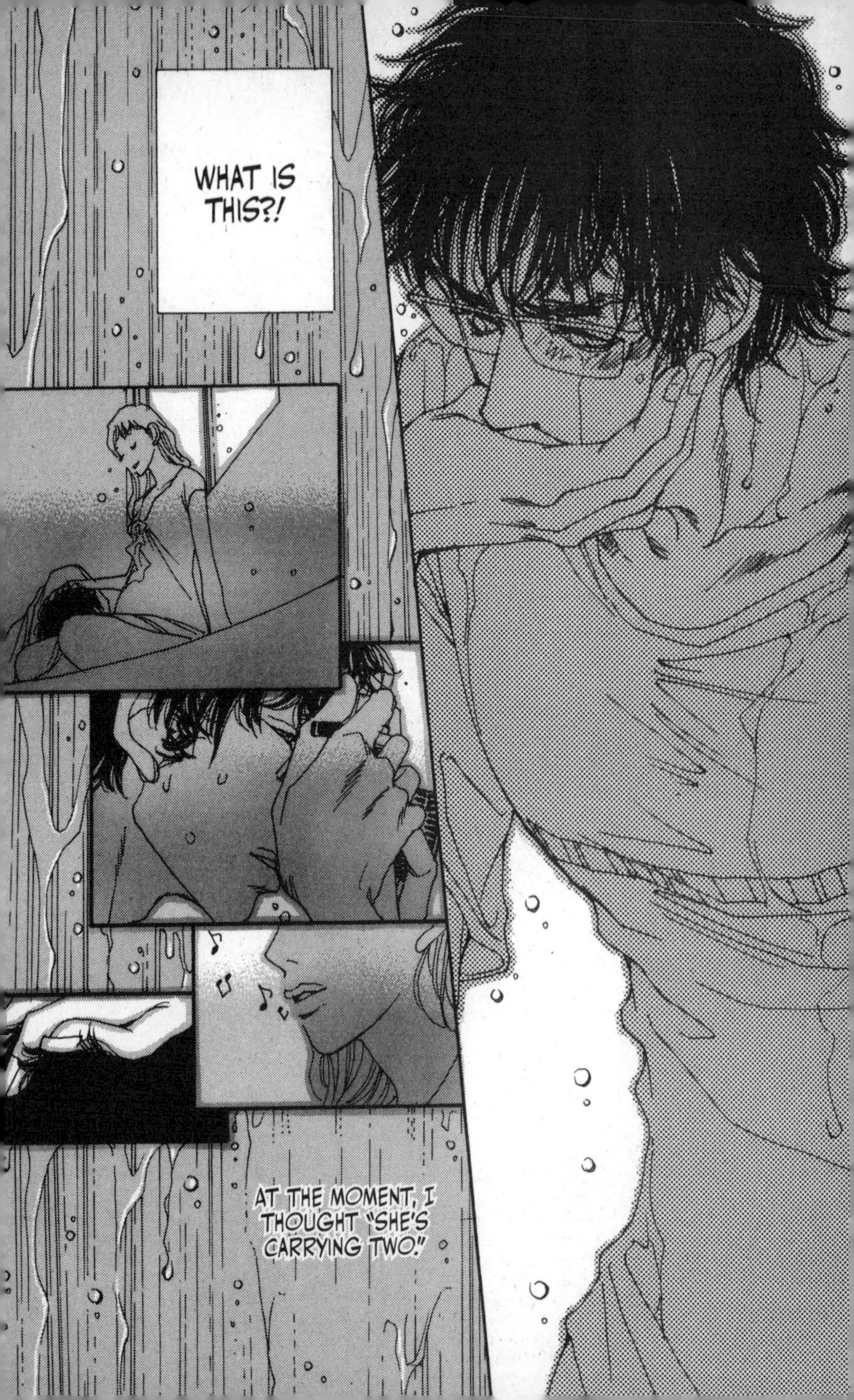
WHAT IS THIS?!
AT THE MOMENT, I THOUGHT "SHE'S CARRYING TWO."

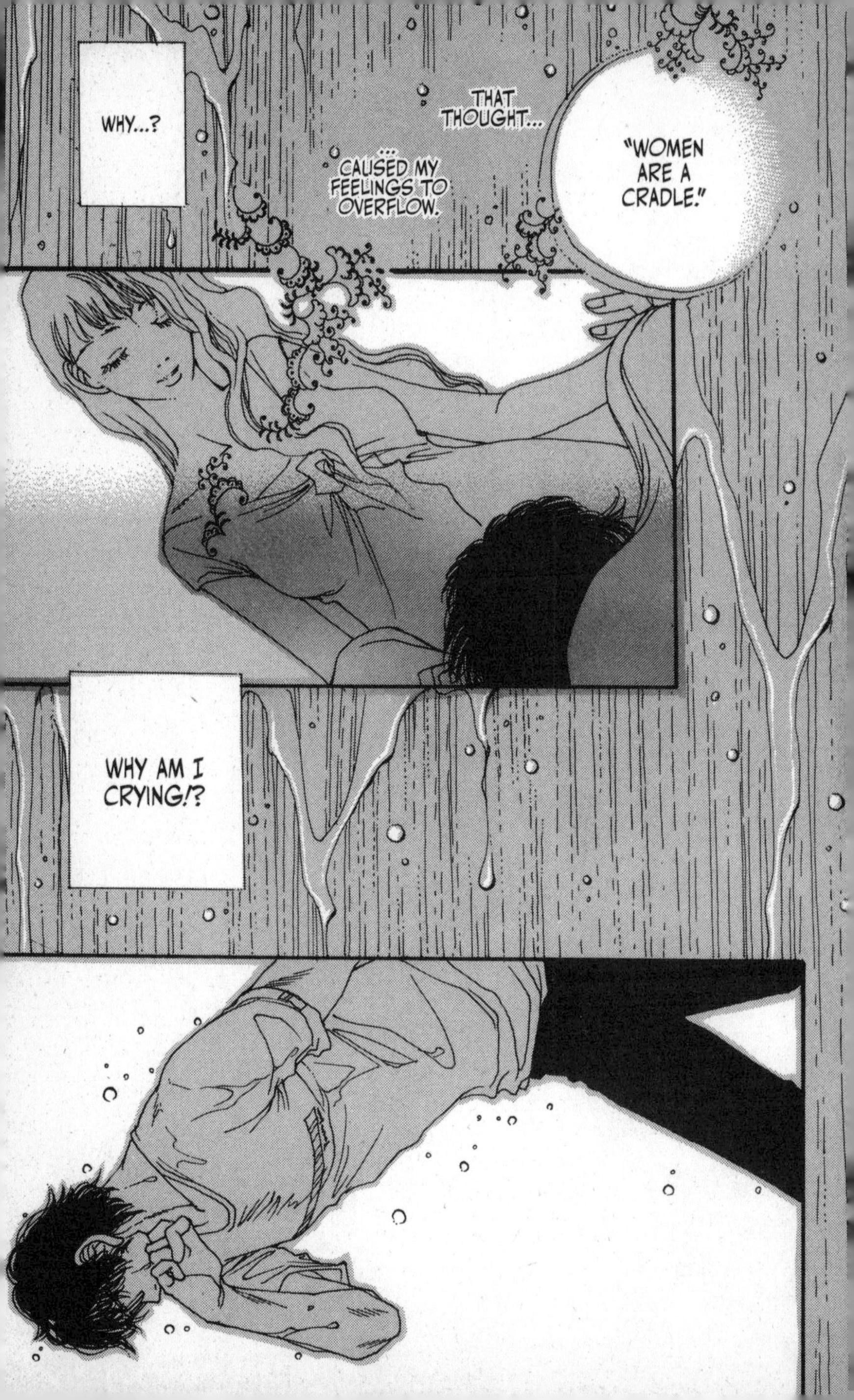
"WOMEN ARE A CRADLE."
THAT THOUGHT...
...CAUSED MY FEELINGS TO OVERFLOW.
WHY...?
WHY AM I CRYING!?

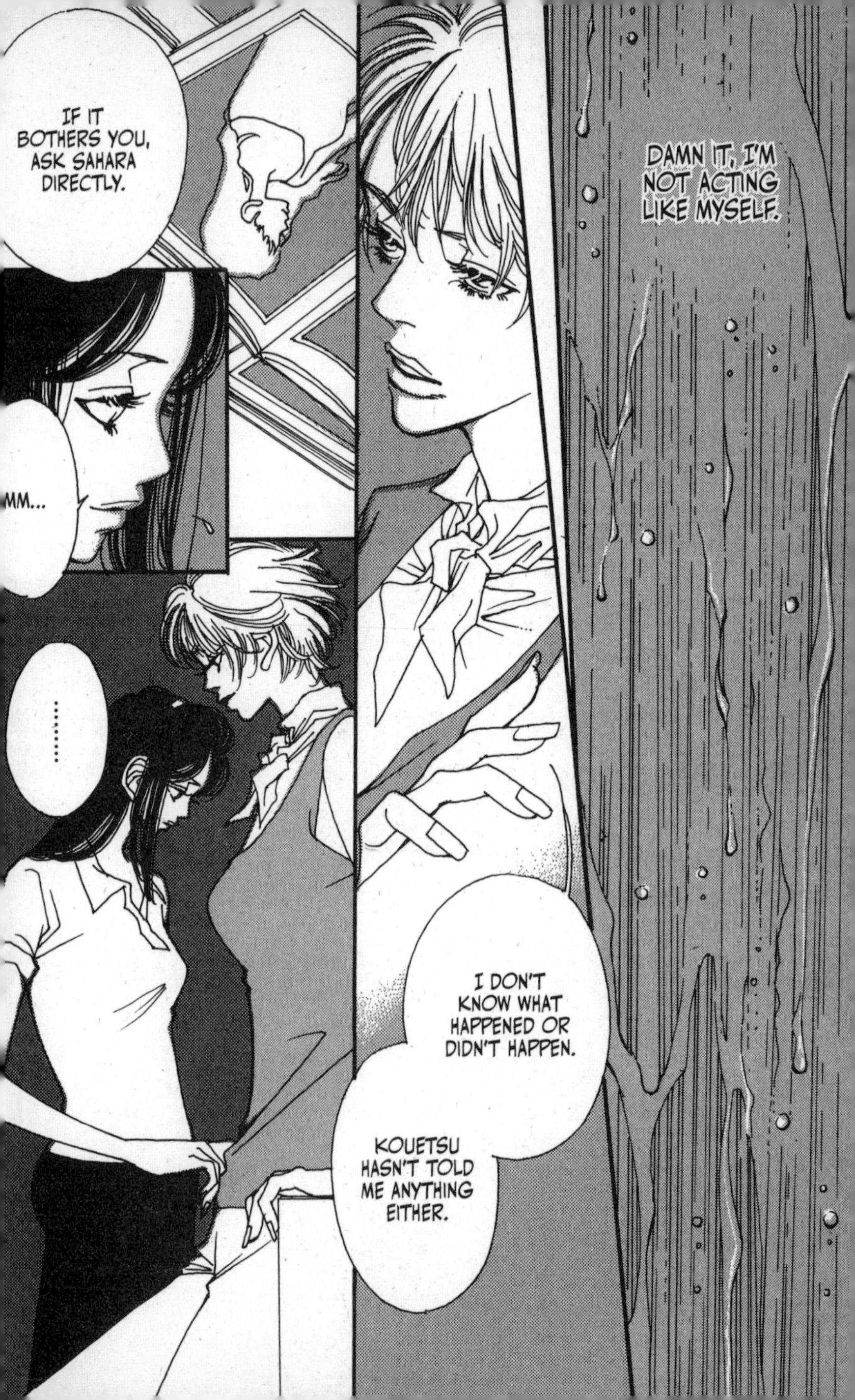
DAMN IT, I'M NOT ACTING LIKE MYSELF.
...
I DON'T KNOW WHAT HAPPENED OR DIDN'T HAPPEN.
KOUETSU HASN'T TOLD ME ANYTHING EITHER.
IF IT BOTHERS YOU, ASK SAHARA DIRECTLY.
MM...
....

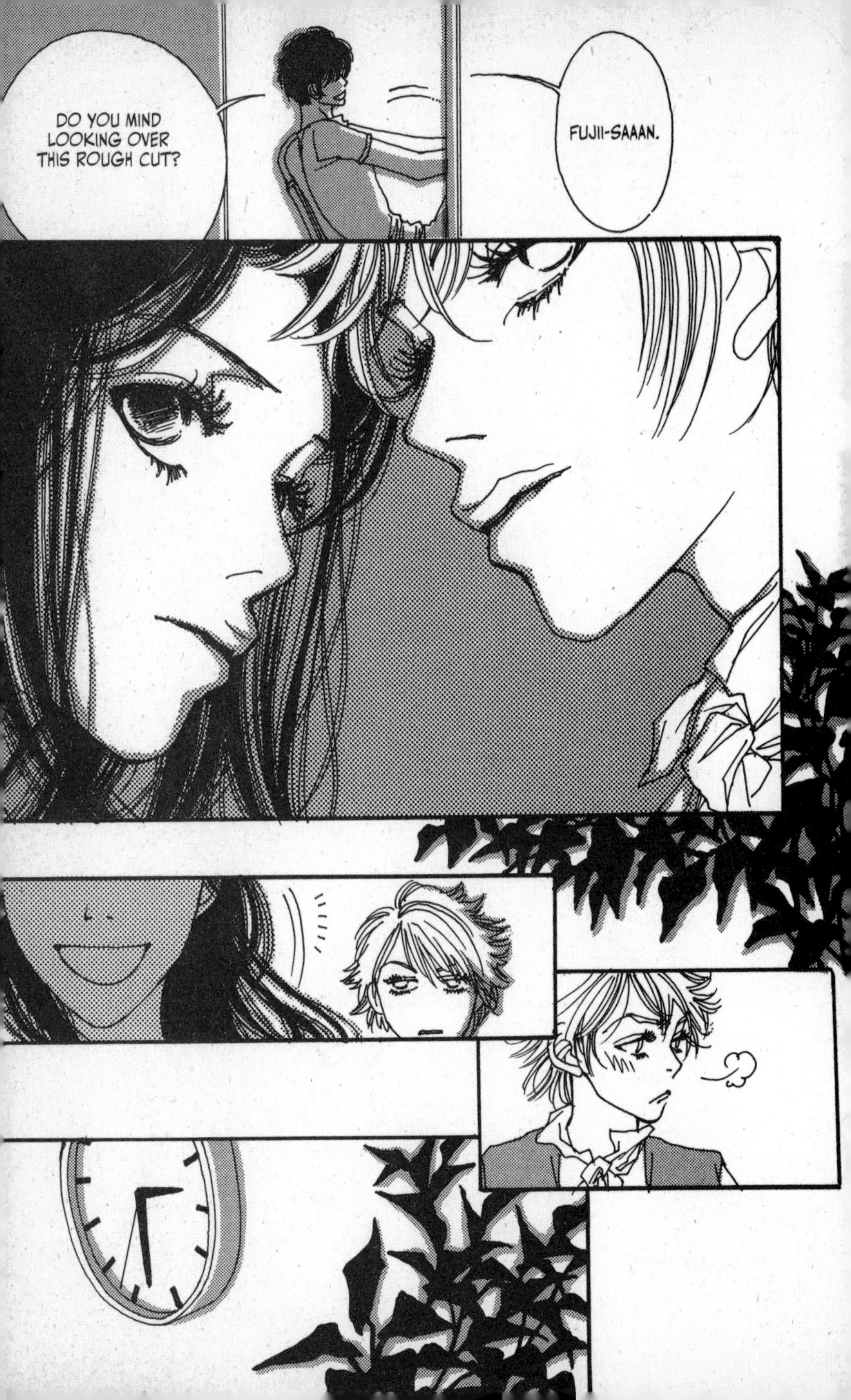
FUJII-SAAAN.
DO YOU MIND LOOKING OVER THIS ROUGH CUT?

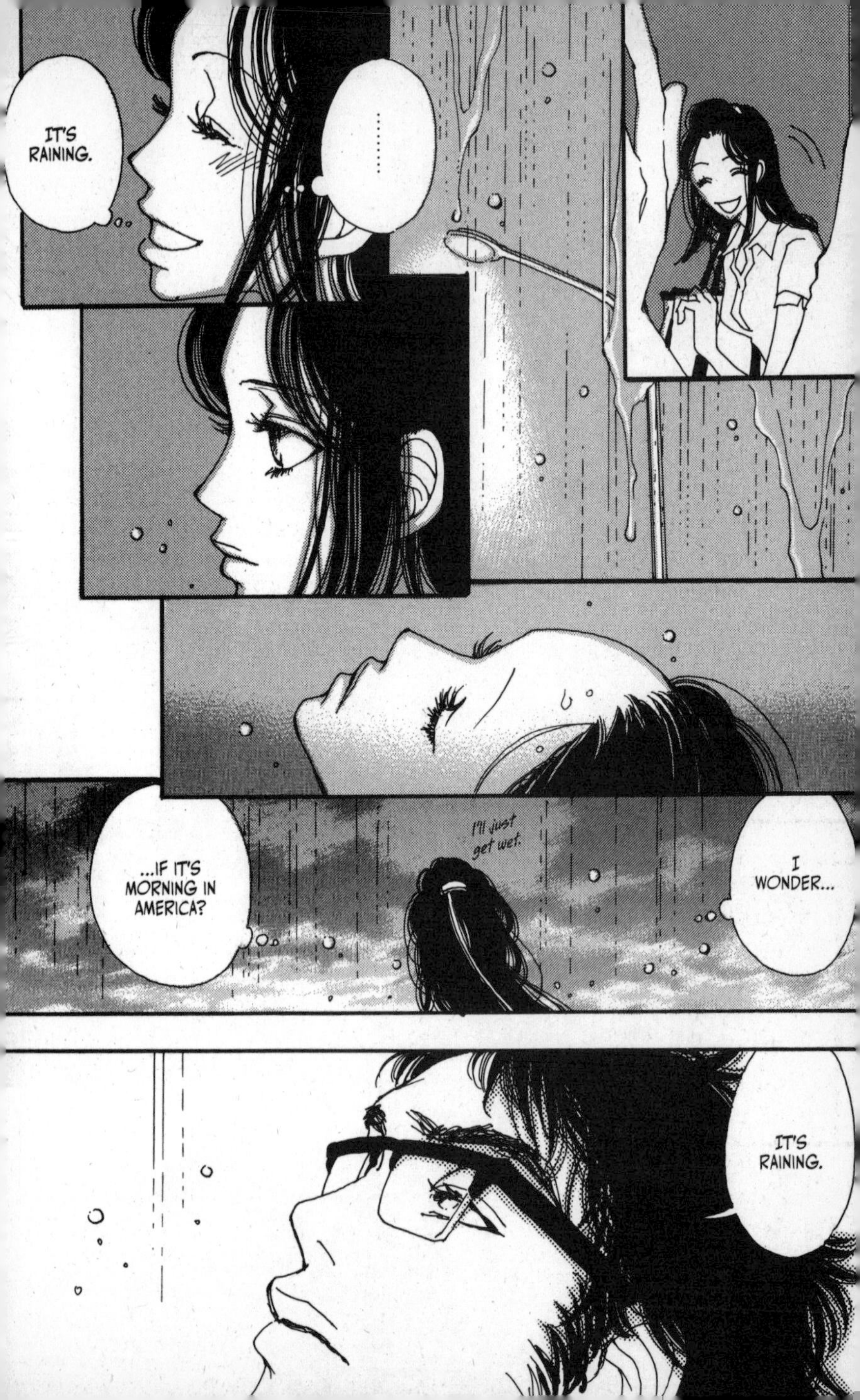
......
IT'S RAINING.
I WONDER...
I'll just get wet.
...IF IT'S MORNING IN AMERICA?
IT'S RAINING.

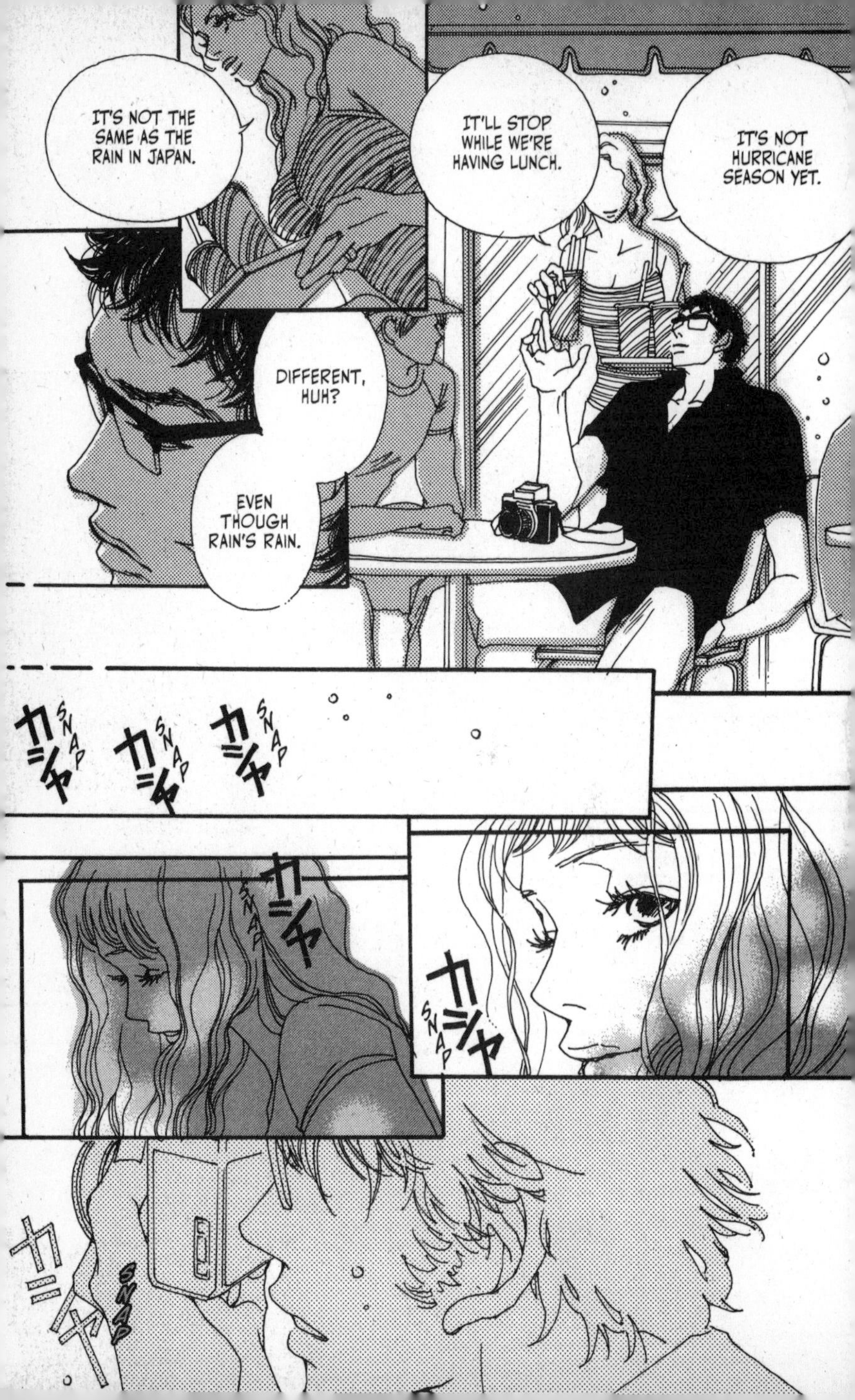
IT'S NOT HURRICANE SEASON YET.
IT'LL STOP WHILE WE'RE HAVING LUNCH.
IT'S NOT THE SAME AS THE RAIN IN JAPAN.
DIFFERENT, HUH?
EVEN THOUGH RAIN'S RAIN.
カシャ SNAP
カシャ SNAP
カシャ SNAP
カシャ SNAP
カシャ SNAP
カシャ SNAP

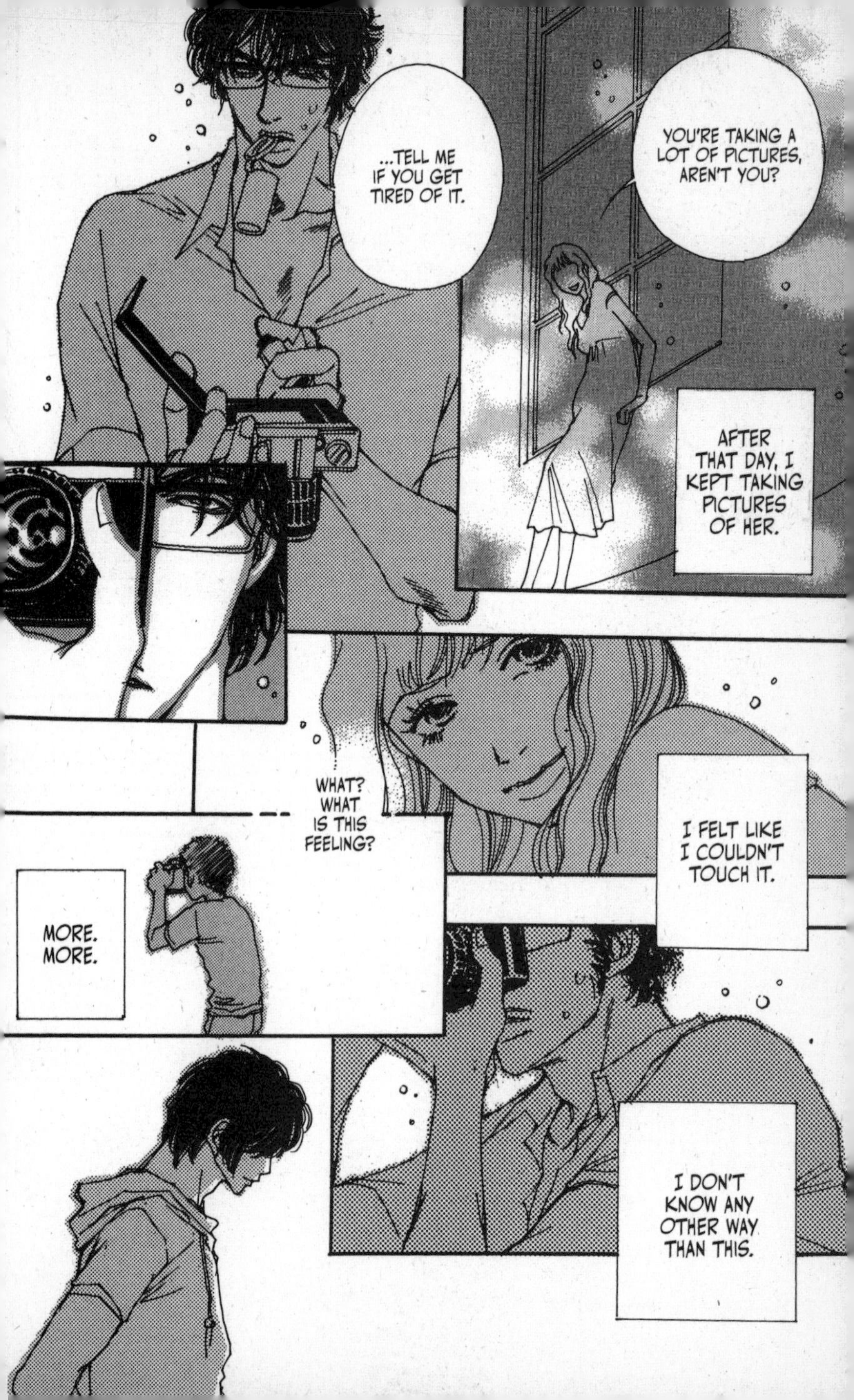
YOU'RE TAKING A LOT OF PICTURES, AREN'T YOU?
AFTER THAT DAY, I KEPT TAKING PICTURES OF HER.
...TELL ME IF YOU GET TIRED OF IT.
I FELT LIKE I COULDN'T TOUCH IT.
WHAT? WHAT IS THIS FEELING?
MORE. MORE.
I DON'T KNOW ANY OTHER WAY THAN THIS.

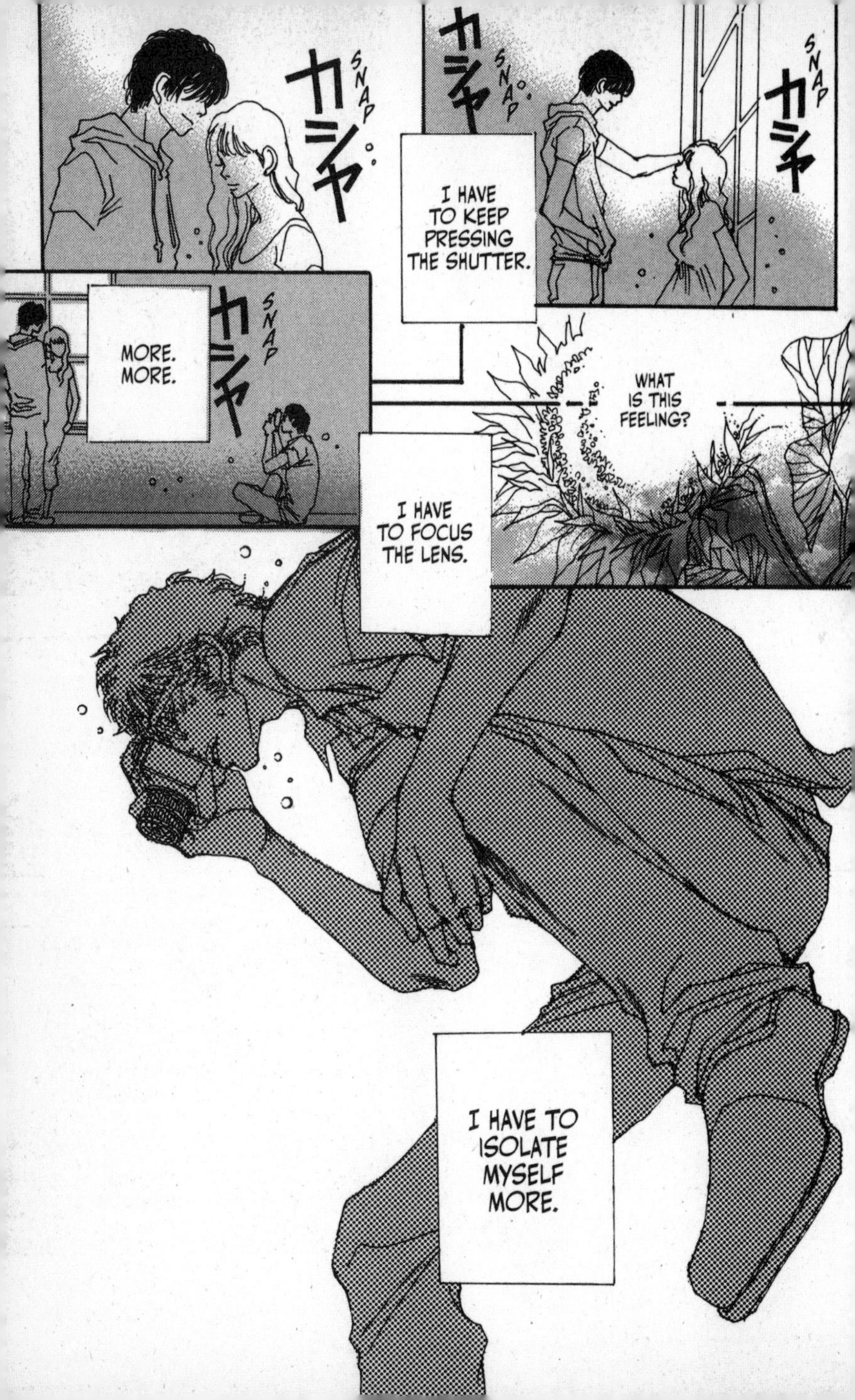
カシャ
SNAP
カシャ
SNAP
I HAVE TO KEEP PRESSING THE SHUTTER.
カシャ
SNAP
WHAT IS THIS FEELING?
MORE. MORE.
カシャ
SNAP
I HAVE TO FOCUS THE LENS.
I HAVE TO ISOLATE MYSELF MORE.

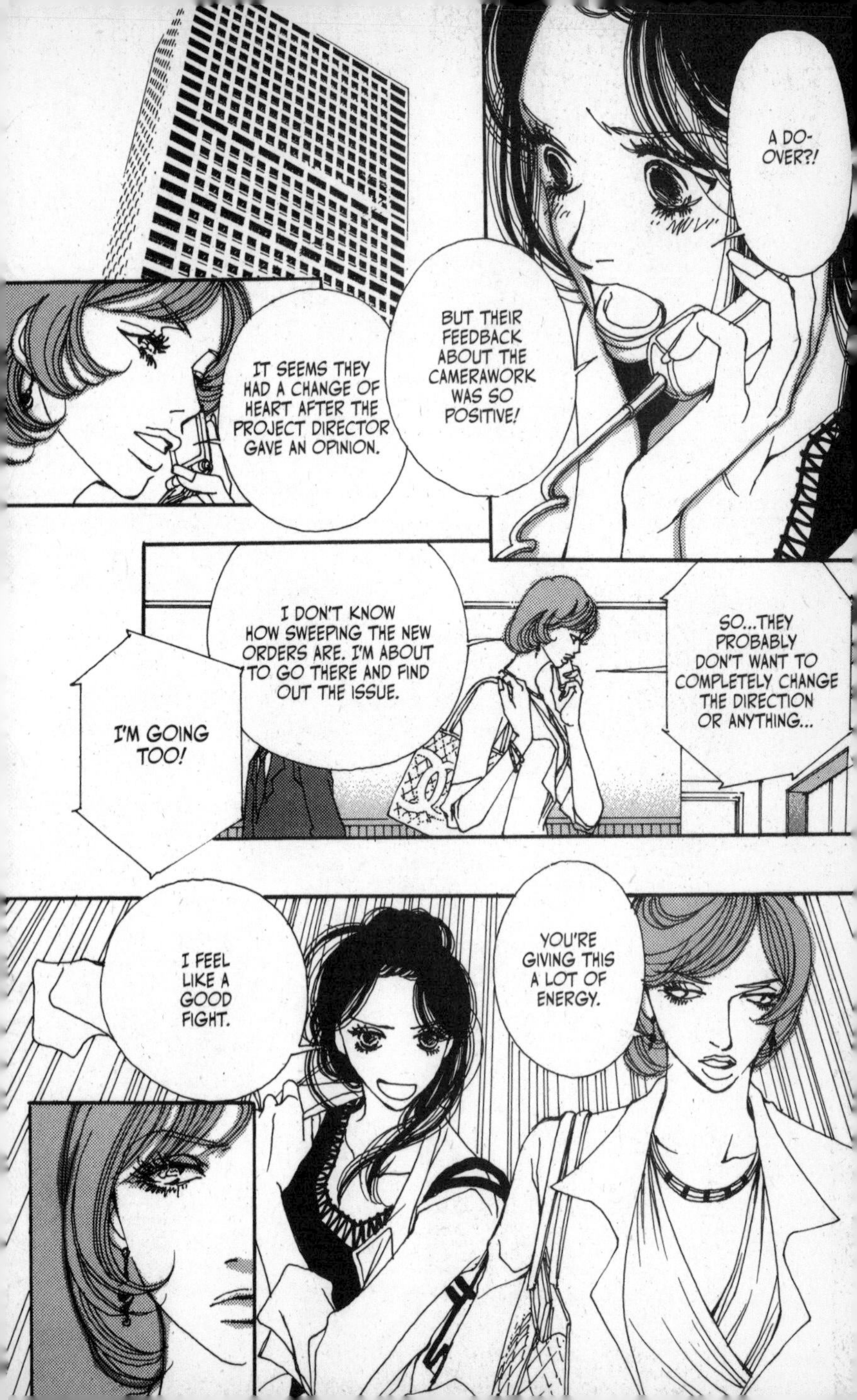
A DO-OVER?!
BUT THEIR FEEDBACK ABOUT THE CAMERAWORK WAS SO POSITIVE!
IT SEEMS THEY HAD A CHANGE OF HEART AFTER THE PROJECT DIRECTOR GAVE AN OPINION.
SO...THEY PROBABLY DON'T WANT TO COMPLETELY CHANGE THE DIRECTION OR ANYTHING...
I DON'T KNOW HOW SWEEPING THE NEW ORDERS ARE. I'M ABOUT TO GO THERE AND FIND OUT THE ISSUE.
I'M GOING TOO!
YOU'RE GIVING THIS A LOT OF ENERGY.
I FEEL LIKE A GOOD FIGHT.

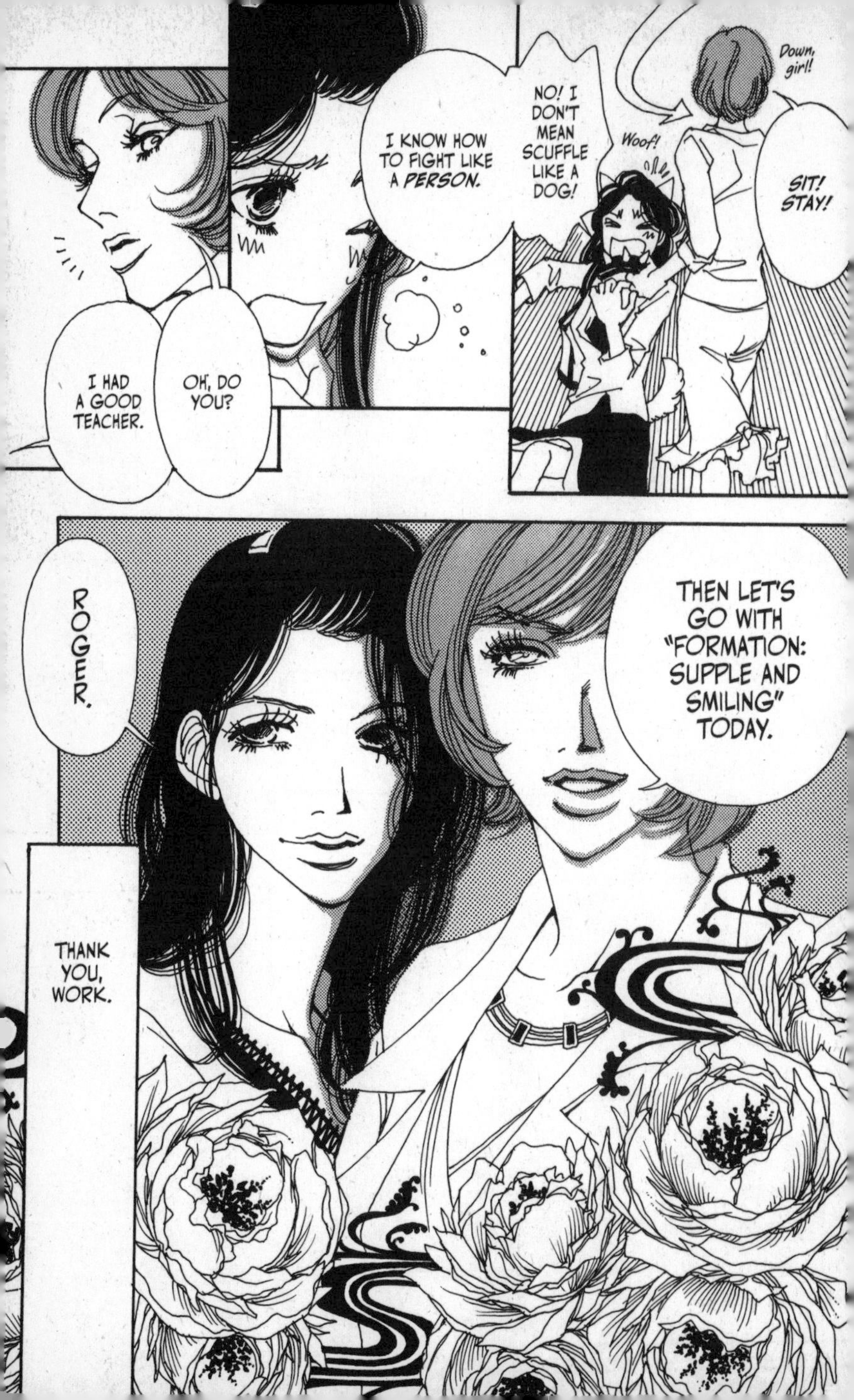
Down, girl!
NO! I DON'T MEAN SCUFFLE LIKE A DOG!
Woof!
SIT! STAY!
I KNOW HOW TO FIGHT LIKE A PERSON.
OH, DO YOU?
I HAD A GOOD TEACHER.
THEN LET'S GO WITH "FORMATION: SUPPLE AND SMILING" TODAY.
ROGER.
THANK YOU, WORK.

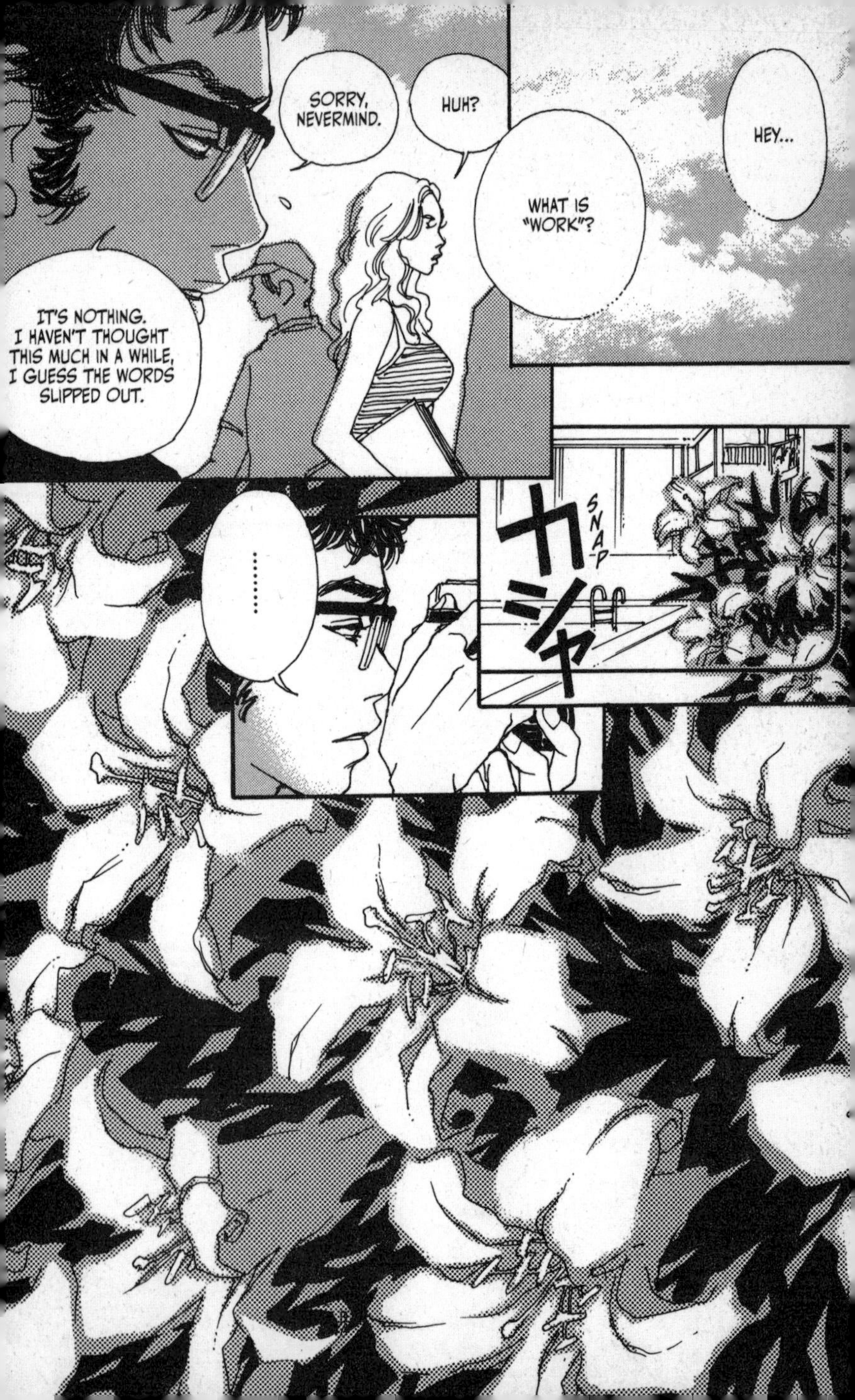
HEY...
WHAT IS "WORK"?
HUH?
SORRY, NEVERMIND.
IT'S NOTHING. I HAVEN'T THOUGHT THIS MUCH IN A WHILE, I GUESS THE WORDS SLIPPED OUT.
カシャ
SNAP
......

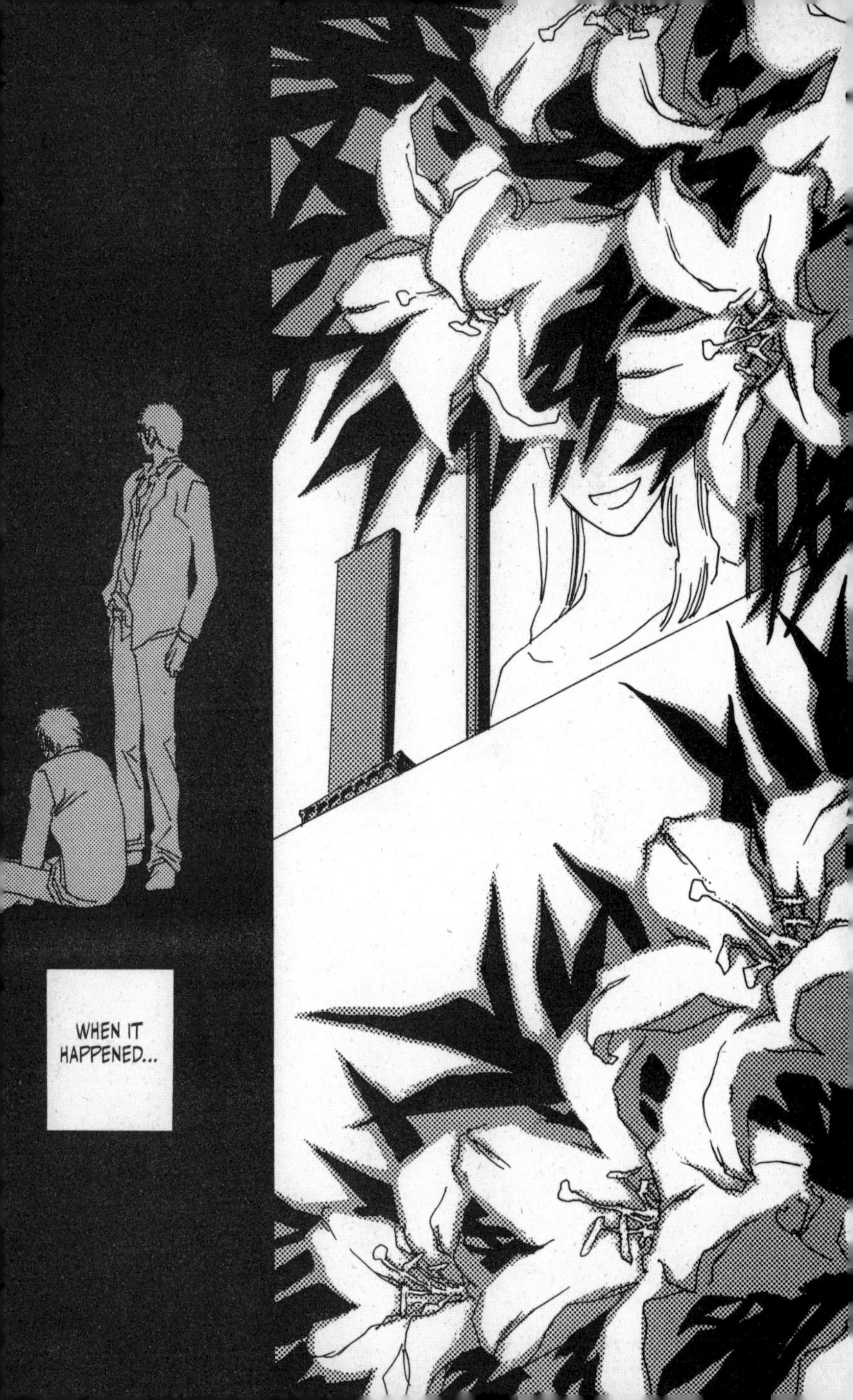
WHEN IT HAPPENED...

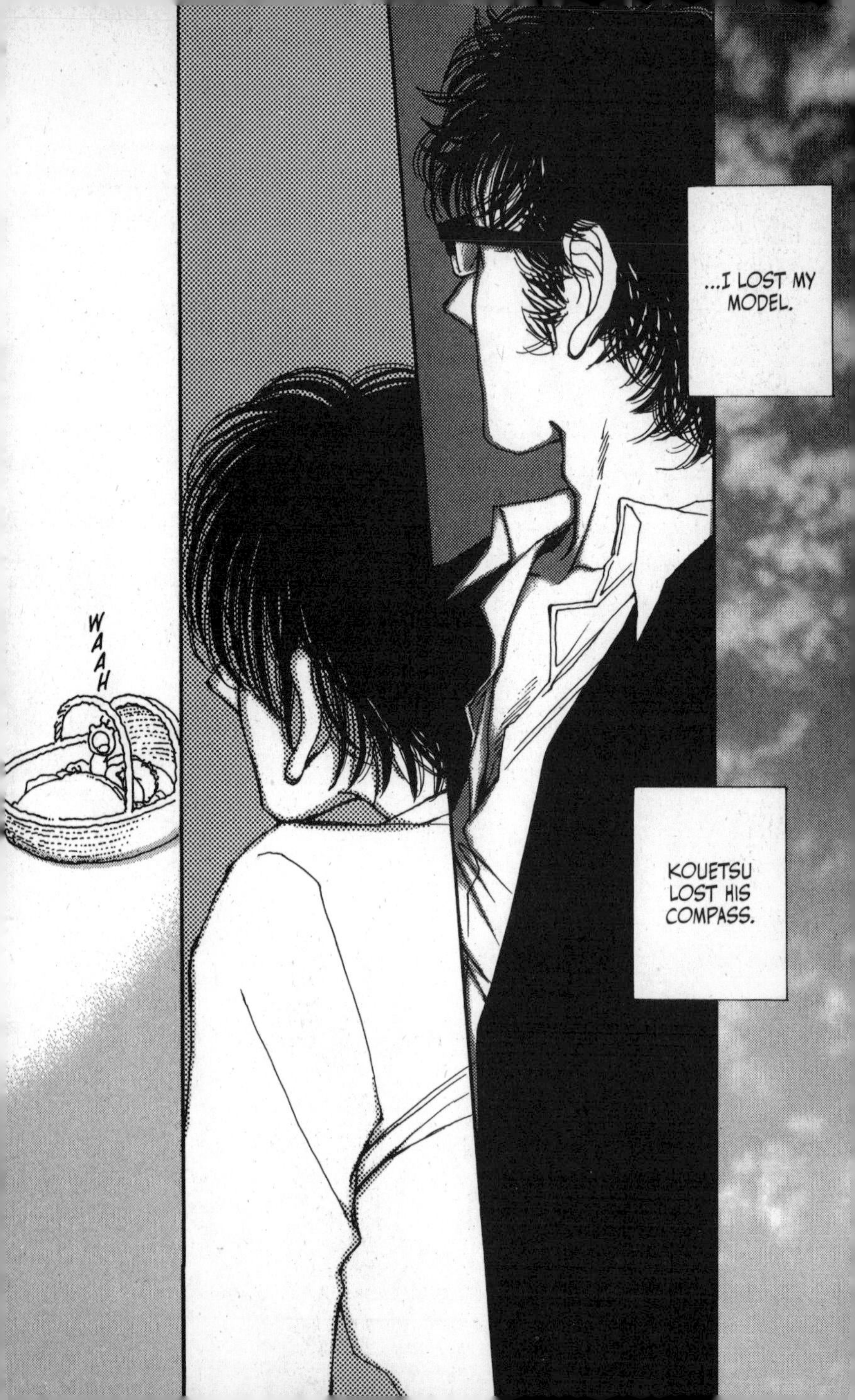
...I LOST MY MODEL.
KOUETSU LOST HIS COMPASS.
WAAH

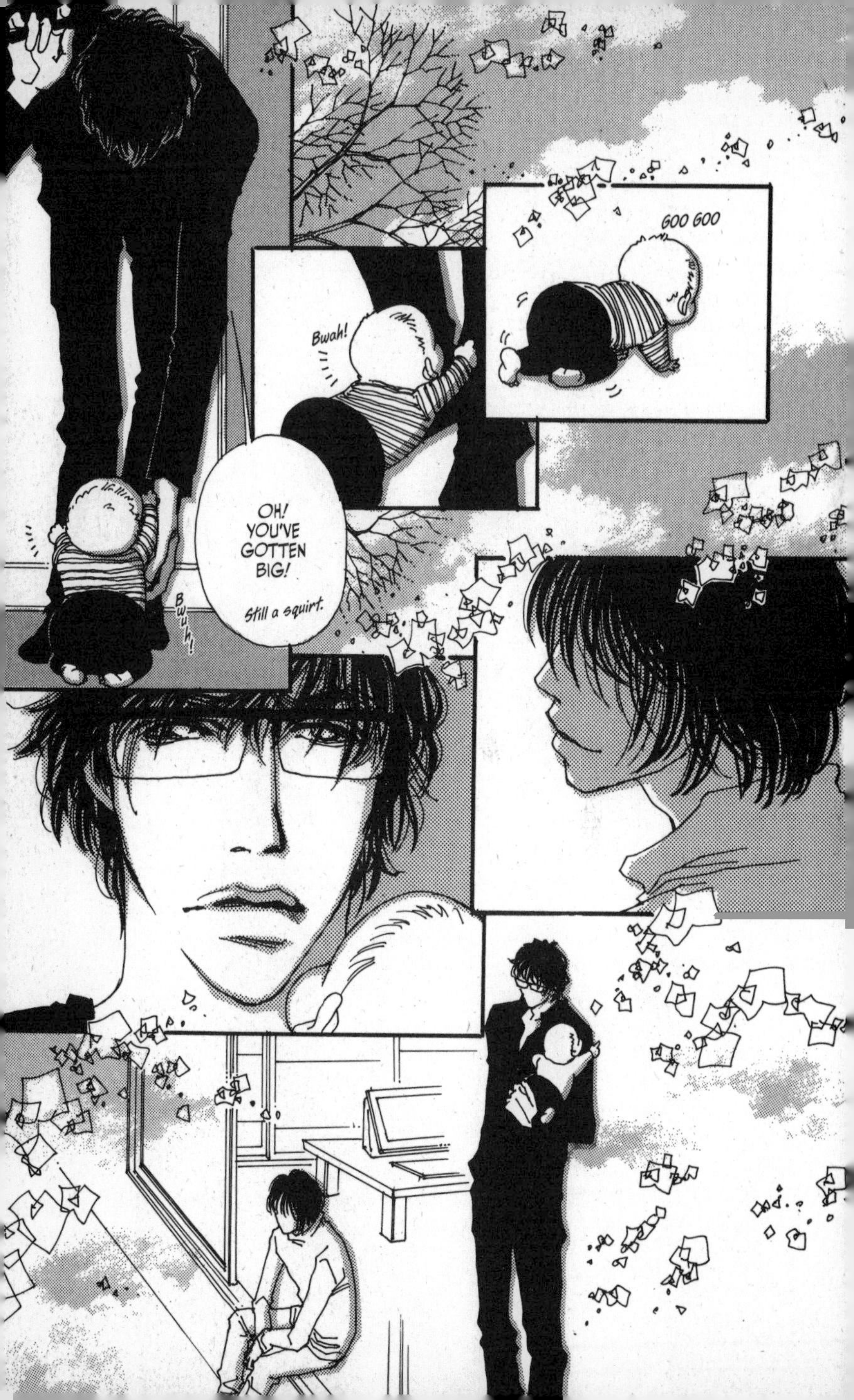
GOO GOO
Bwah!
OH! YOU'VE GOTTEN BIG!
Still a squirt.
Bwuh!

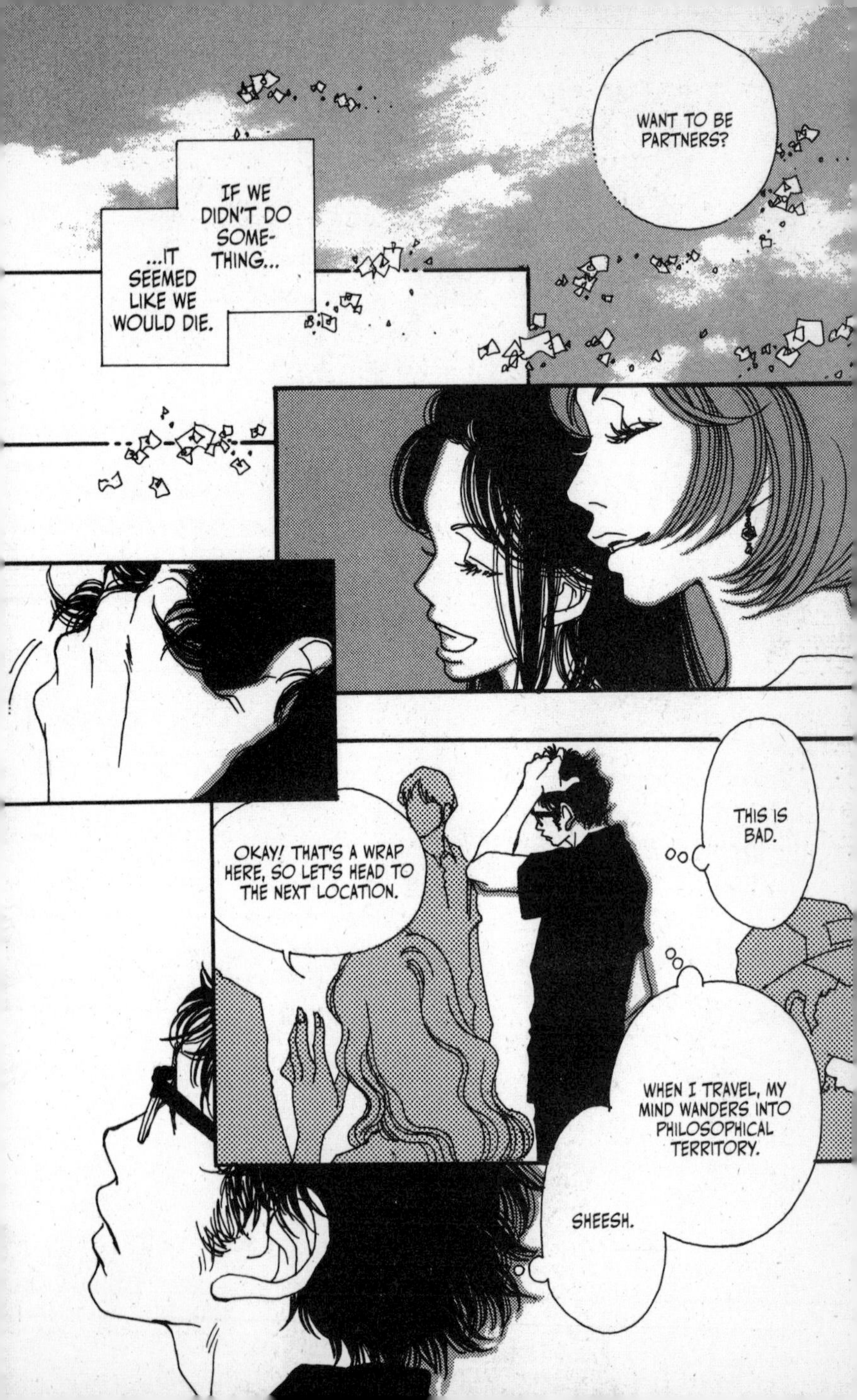
WANT TO BE PARTNERS?
IF WE DIDN'T DO SOME-THING...
...IT SEEMED LIKE WE WOULD DIE.
THIS IS BAD.
OKAY! THAT'S A WRAP HERE, SO LET'S HEAD TO THE NEXT LOCATION.
WHEN I TRAVEL, MY MIND WANDERS INTO PHILOSOPHICAL TERRITORY.
SHEESH.

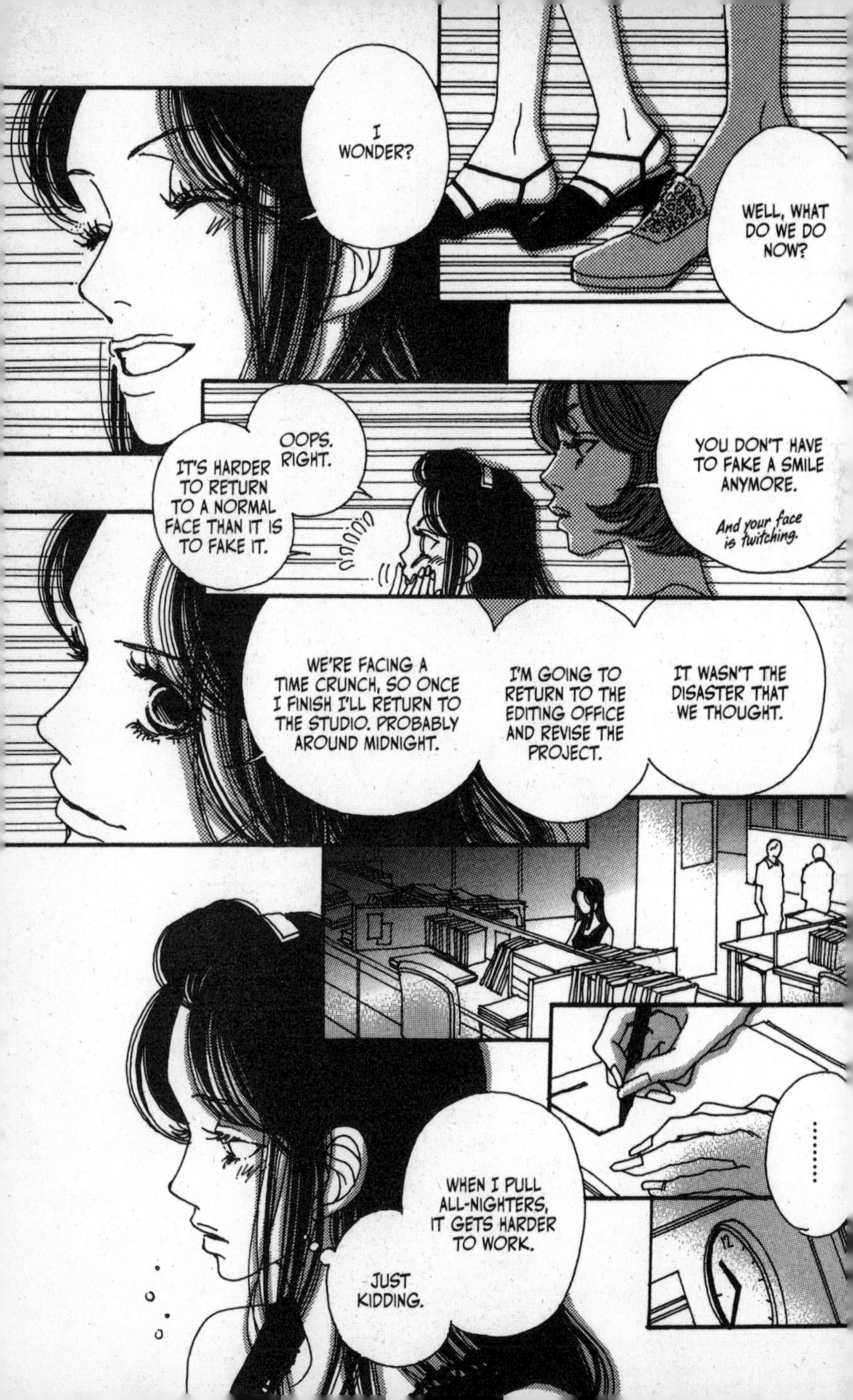
WELL, WHAT DO WE DO NOW?
I WONDER?
YOU DON'T HAVE TO FAKE A SMILE ANYMORE.
And your face is twitching.
OOPS. RIGHT.
IT'S HARDER TO RETURN TO A NORMAL FACE THAN IT IS TO FAKE IT.
IT WASN'T THE DISASTER THAT WE THOUGHT.
I'M GOING TO RETURN TO THE EDITING OFFICE AND REVISE THE PROJECT.
WE'RE FACING A TIME CRUNCH, SO ONCE I FINISH I'LL RETURN TO THE STUDIO. PROBABLY AROUND MIDNIGHT.
......
WHEN I PULL ALL-NIGHTERS, IT GETS HARDER TO WORK.
JUST KIDDING.

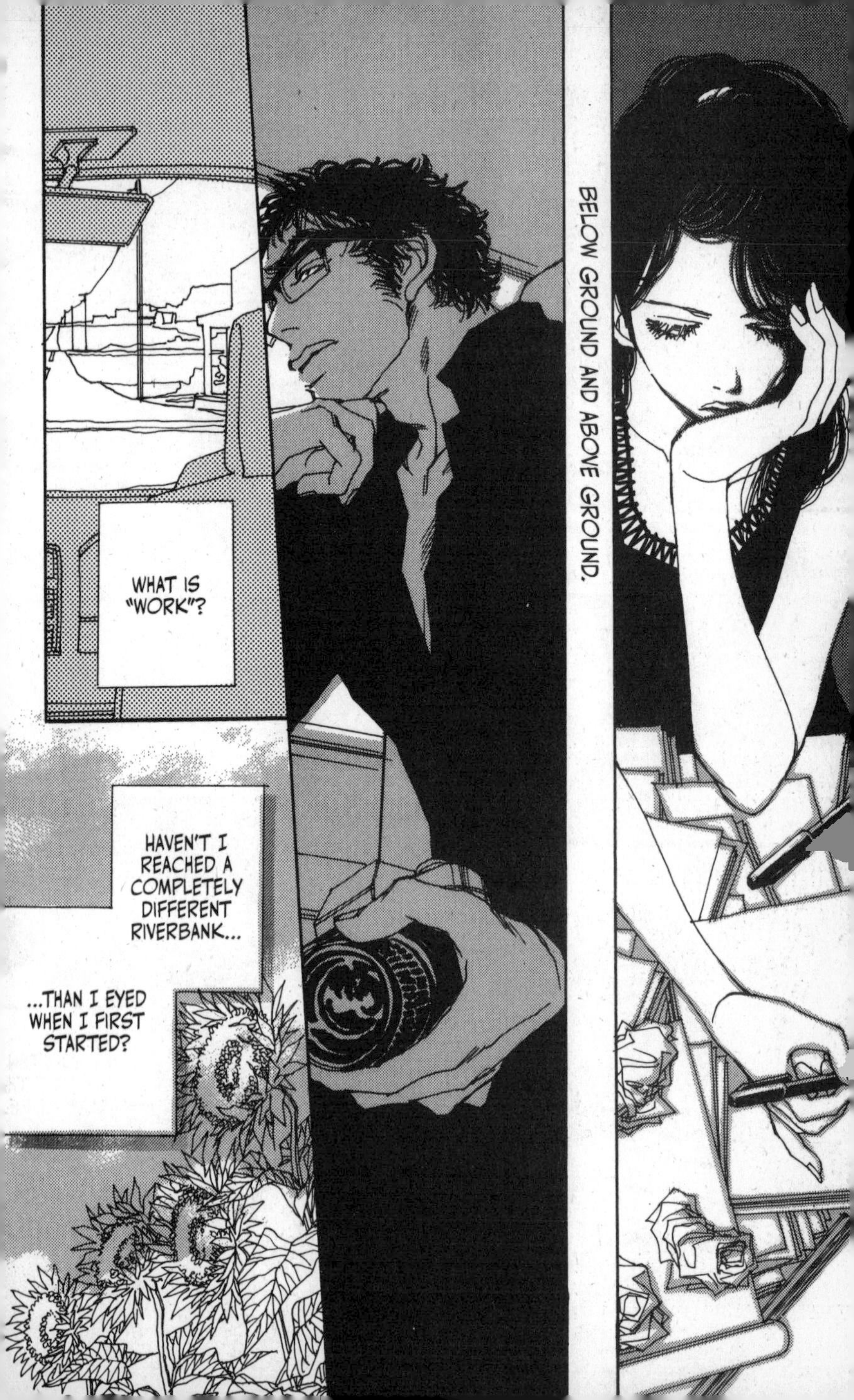
BELOW GROUND AND ABOVE GROUND.
WHAT IS "WORK"?
HAVEN'T I REACHED A COMPLETELY DIFFERENT RIVERBANK...
...THAN I EYED WHEN I FIRST STARTED?

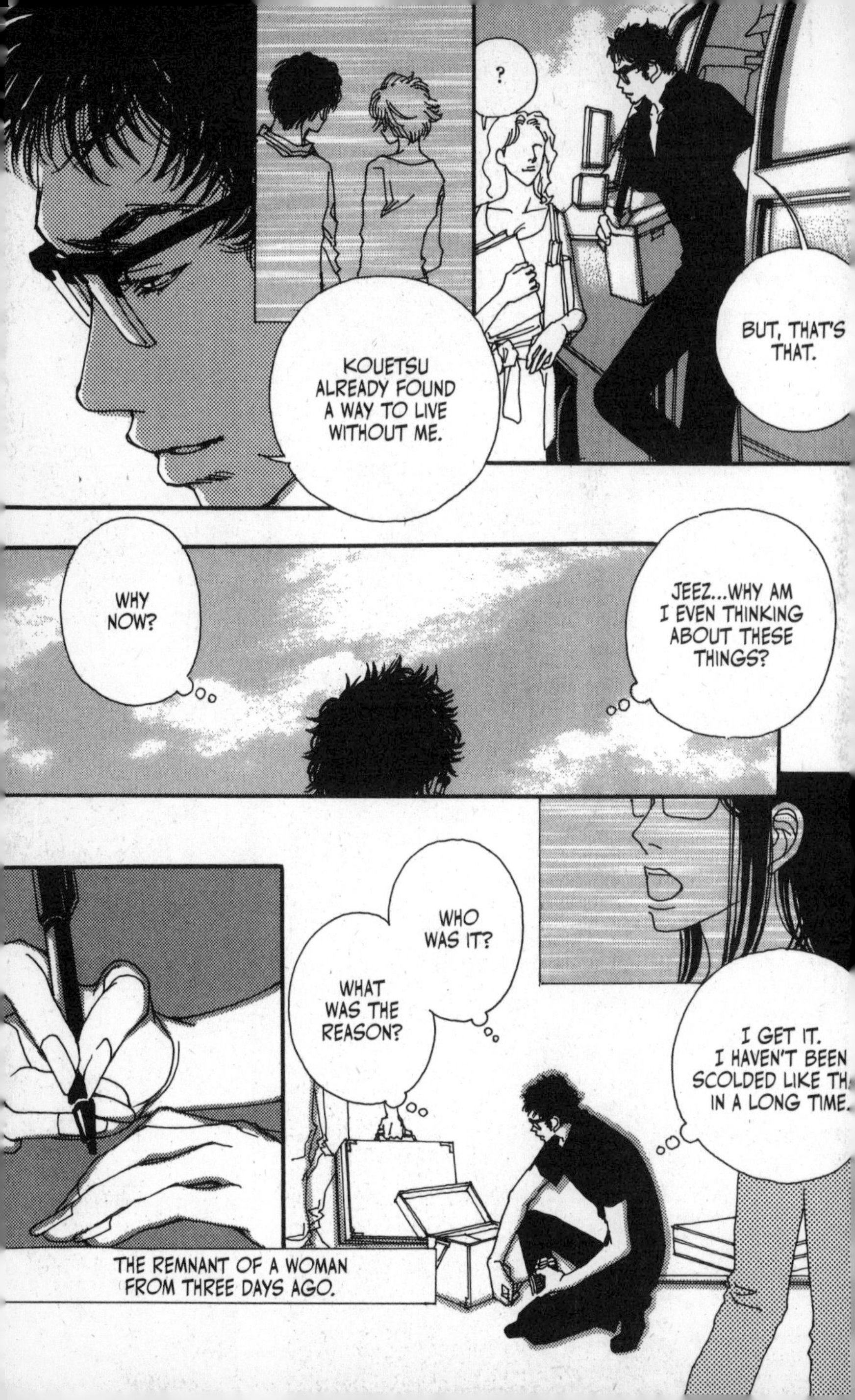
?
BUT, THAT'S THAT.
KOUETSU ALREADY FOUND A WAY TO LIVE WITHOUT ME.
JEEZ...WHY AM I EVEN THINKING ABOUT THESE THINGS?
WHY NOW?
I GET IT. I HAVEN'T BEEN SCOLDED LIKE TH IN A LONG TIME.
WHO WAS IT?
WHAT WAS THE REASON?
THE REMNANT OF A WOMAN FROM THREE DAYS AGO.

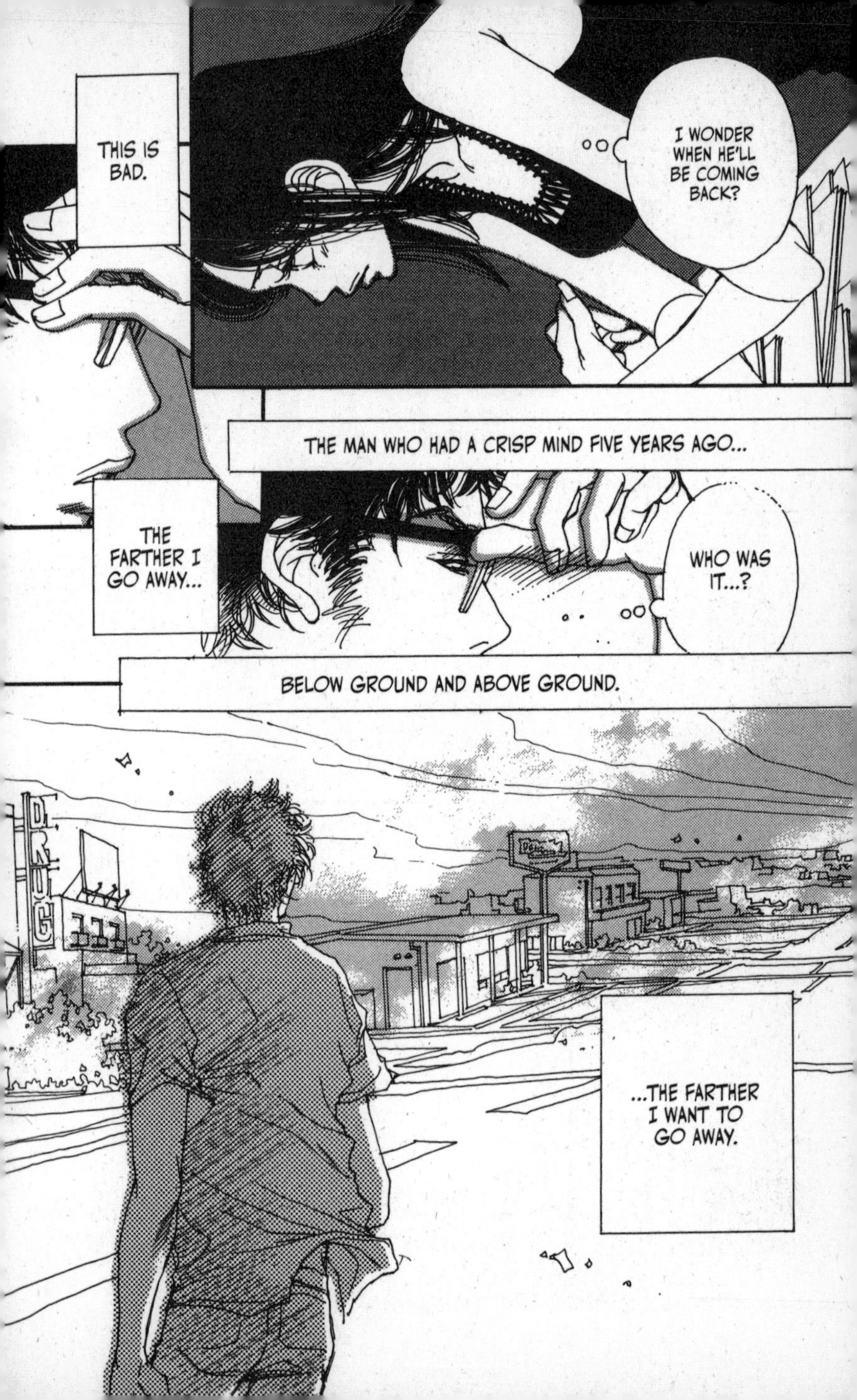
I WONDER WHEN HE'LL BE COMING BACK?
THE MAN WHO HAD A CRISP MIND FIVE YEARS AGO...
WHO WAS IT...?
THIS IS BAD.
THE FARTHER I GO AWAY...
BELOW GROUND AND ABOVE GROUND.
...THE FARTHER I WANT TO GO AWAY.

FILE. 29

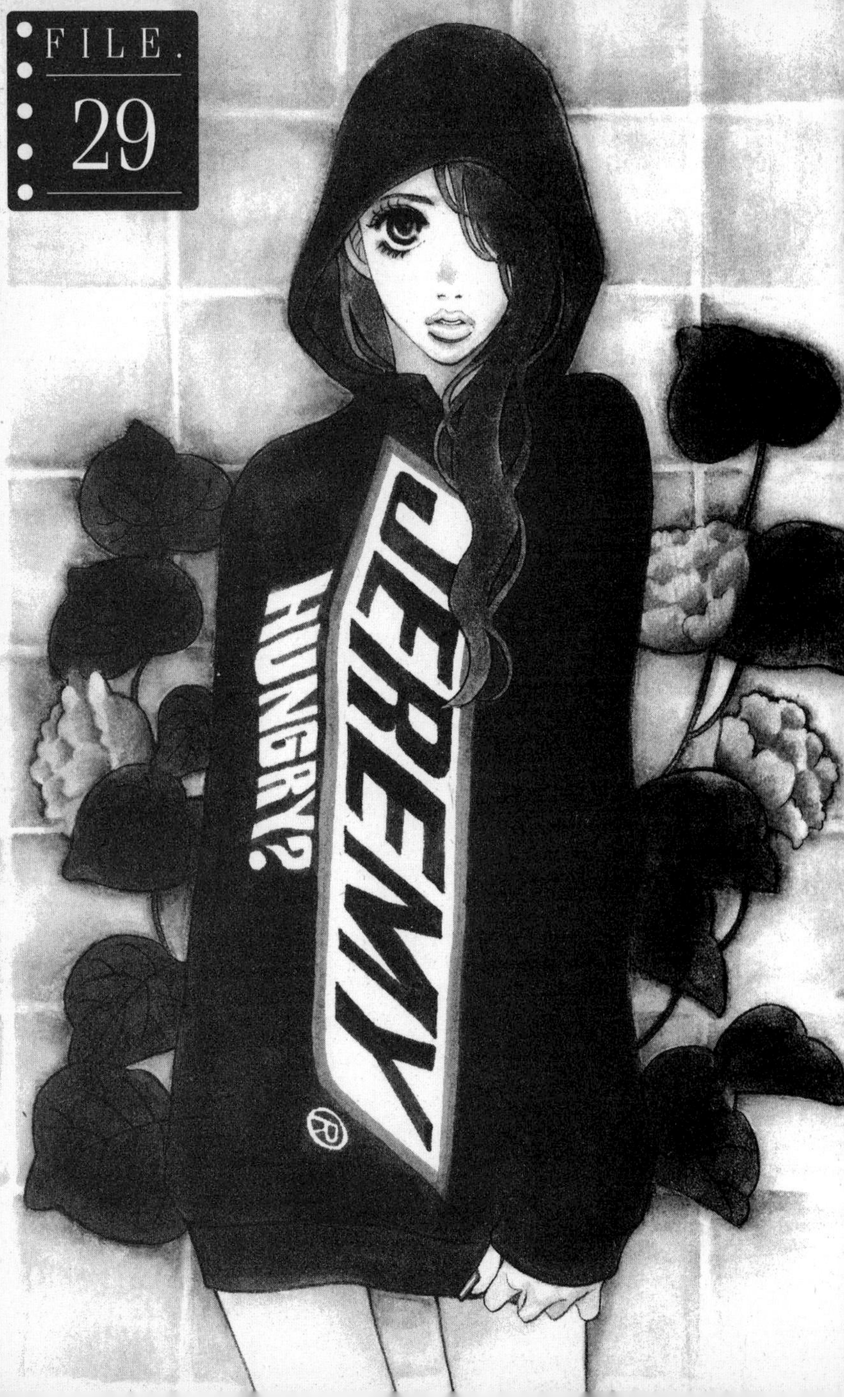
JEREMY
HUNGRY?

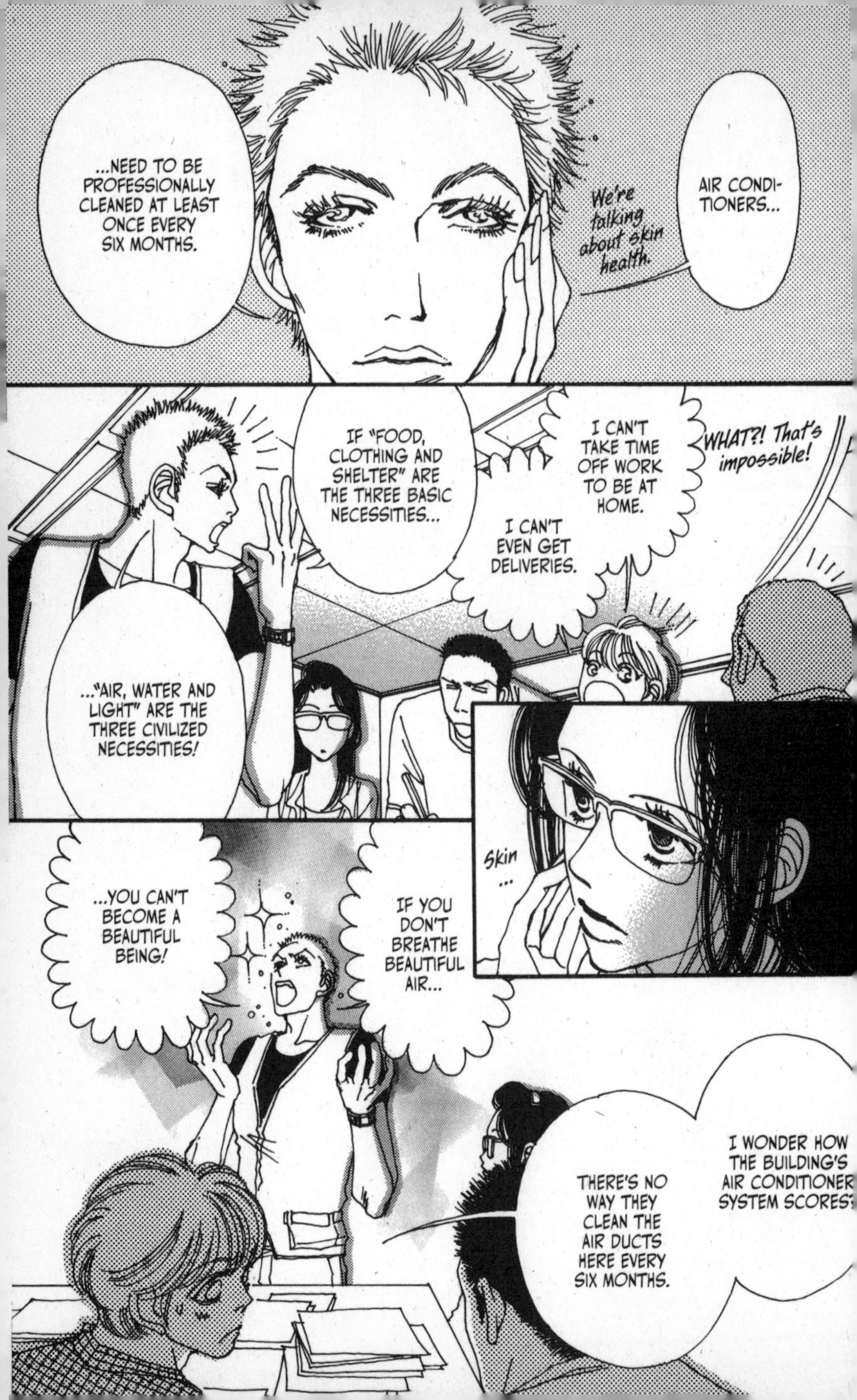
AIR CONDITIONERS...
We're talking about skin health.
...NEED TO BE PROFESSIONALLY CLEANED AT LEAST ONCE EVERY SIX MONTHS.
WHAT?! That's impossible!
I CAN'T TAKE TIME OFF WORK TO BE AT HOME.
I CAN'T EVEN GET DELIVERIES.
IF "FOOD, CLOTHING AND SHELTER" ARE THE THREE BASIC NECESSITIES...
..."AIR, WATER AND LIGHT" ARE THE THREE CIVILIZED NECESSITIES!
Skin ...
IF YOU DON'T BREATHE BEAUTIFUL AIR...
...YOU CAN'T BECOME A BEAUTIFUL BEING!
I WONDER HOW THE BUILDING'S AIR CONDITIONER SYSTEM SCORES
THERE'S NO WAY THEY CLEAN THE AIR DUCTS HERE EVERY SIX MONTHS.

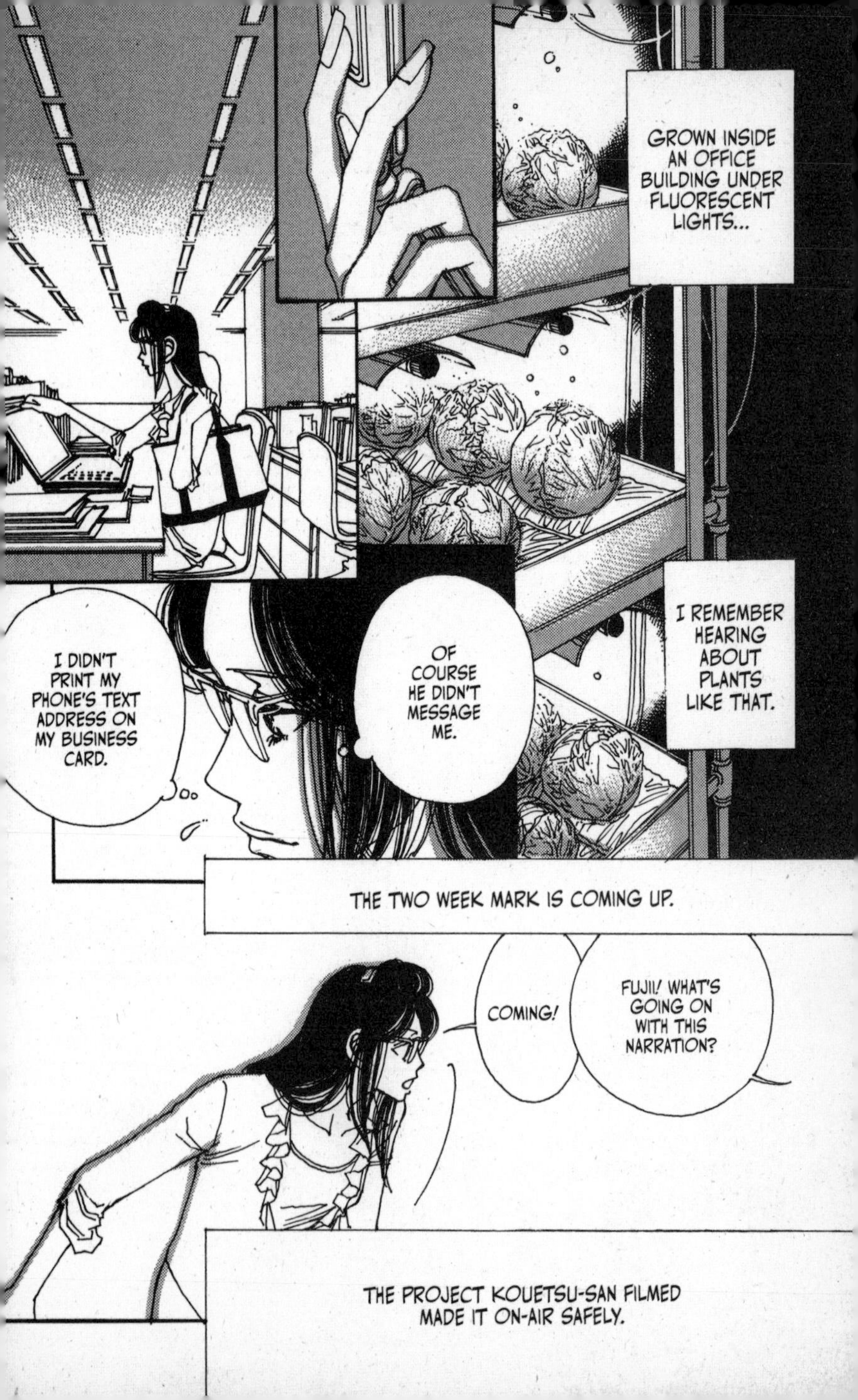
GROWN INSIDE AN OFFICE BUILDING UNDER FLUORESCENT LIGHTS...
I REMEMBER HEARING ABOUT PLANTS LIKE THAT.
OF COURSE HE DIDN'T MESSAGE ME.
I DIDN'T PRINT MY PHONE'S TEXT ADDRESS ON MY BUSINESS CARD.
THE TWO WEEK MARK IS COMING UP.
FUJII! WHAT'S GOING ON WITH THIS NARRATION?
COMING!
THE PROJECT KOUETSU-SAN FILMED MADE IT ON-AIR SAFELY.

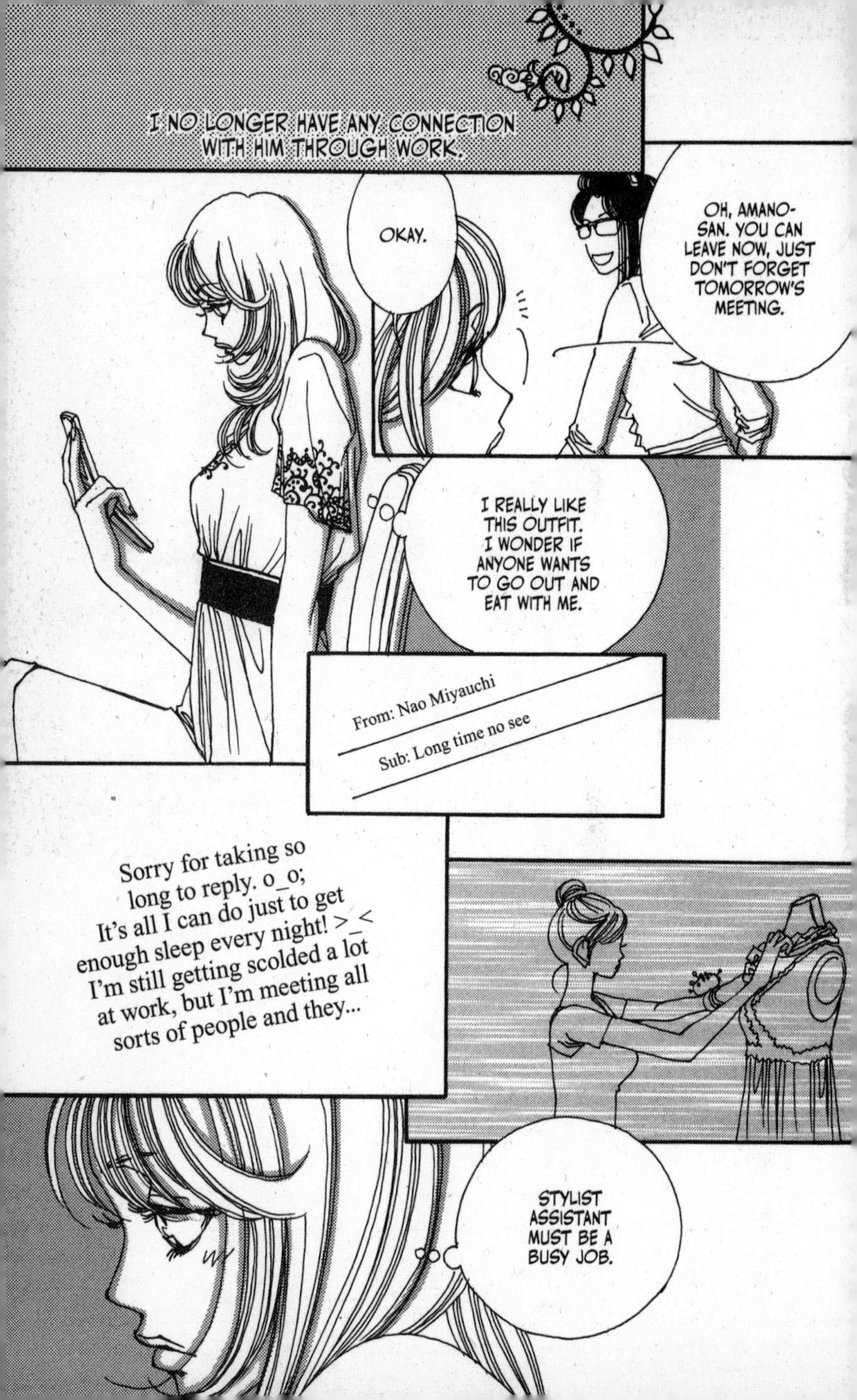
I NO LONGER HAVE ANY CONNECTION WITH HIM THROUGH WORK.
OH, AMANO-SAN. YOU CAN LEAVE NOW, JUST DON'T FORGET TOMORROW'S MEETING.
OKAY.
I REALLY LIKE THIS OUTFIT. I WONDER IF ANYONE WANTS TO GO OUT AND EAT WITH ME.
From: Nao Miyauchi
Sub: Long time no see
Sorry for taking so long to reply. o_o; It's all I can do just to get enough sleep every night! >_< I'm still getting scolded a lot at work, but I'm meeting all sorts of people and they...
STYLIST ASSISTANT MUST BE A BUSY JOB.

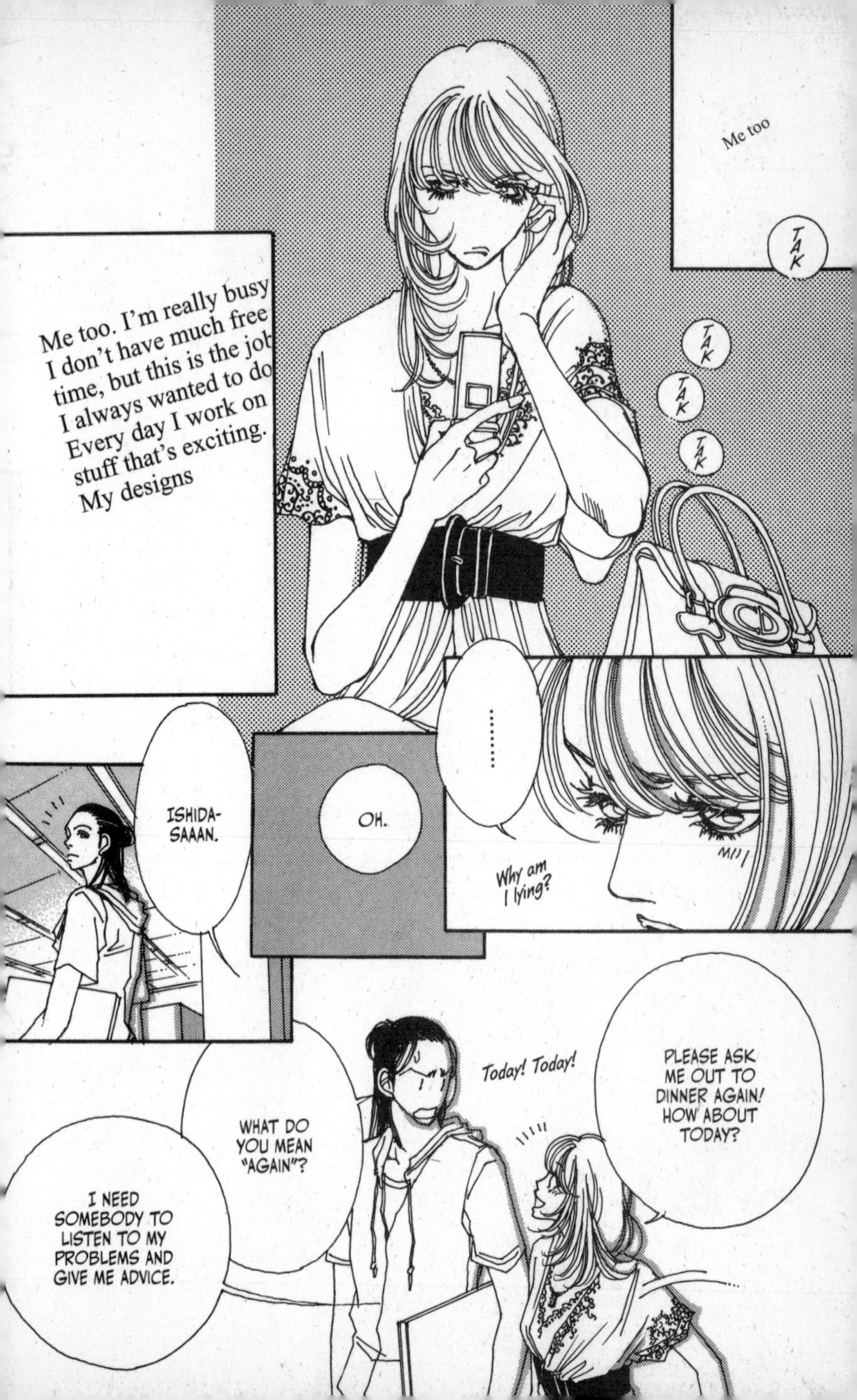

Me too
TAK
Me too. I'm really busy I don't have much free time, but this is the job I always wanted to do Every day I work on stuff that's exciting. My designs
TAK
TAK
TAK
......
Why am I lying?
OH.
ISHIDA-SAAAN.
PLEASE ASK ME OUT TO DINNER AGAIN! HOW ABOUT TODAY?
Today! Today!
WHAT DO YOU MEAN "AGAIN"?
I NEED SOMEBODY TO LISTEN TO MY PROBLEMS AND GIVE ME ADVICE.

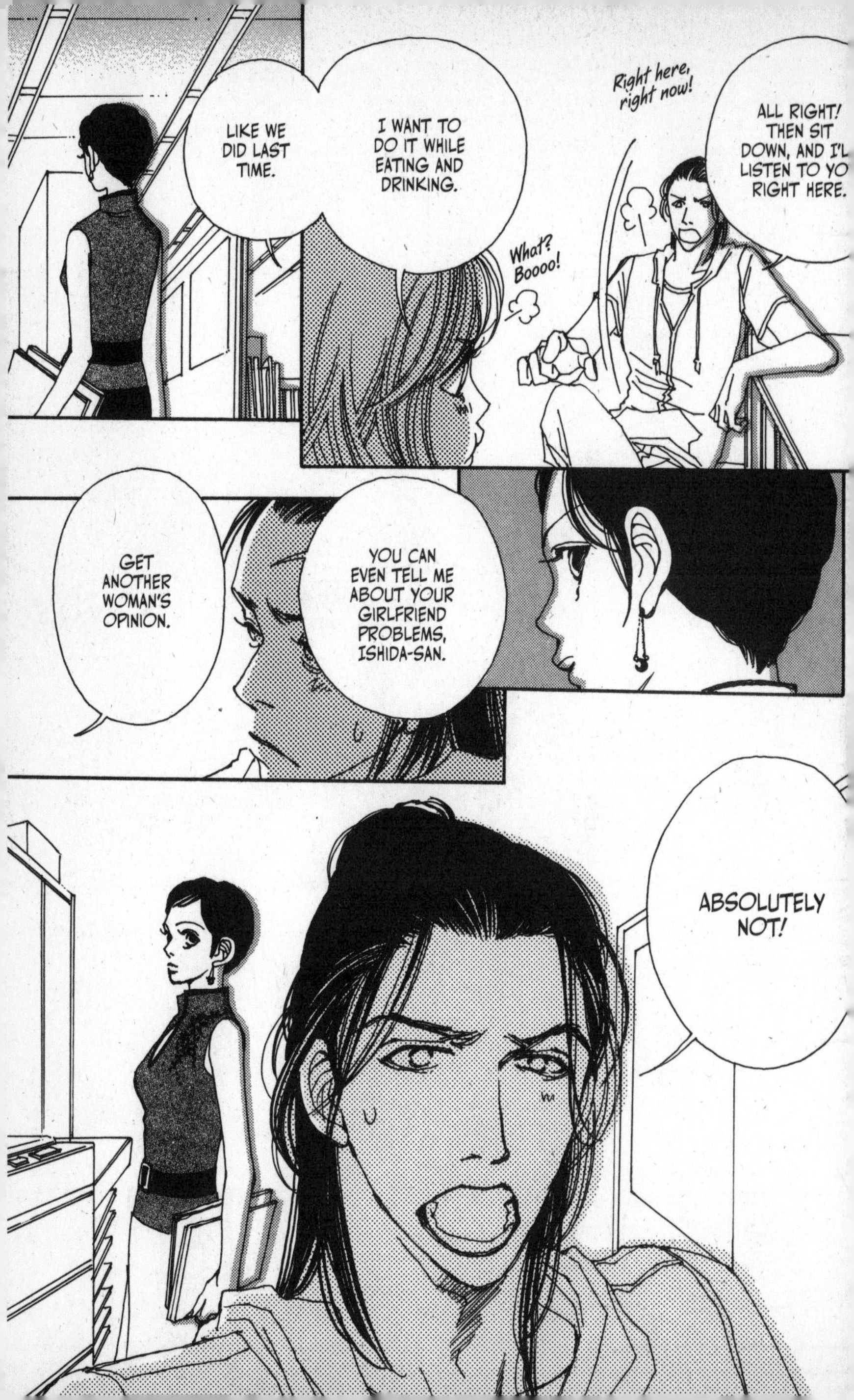
ALL RIGHT! THEN SIT DOWN, AND I'L LISTEN TO YO RIGHT HERE.
Right here, right now!
What? Boooo!
I WANT TO DO IT WHILE EATING AND DRINKING.
LIKE WE DID LAST TIME.
YOU CAN EVEN TELL ME ABOUT YOUR GIRLFRIEND PROBLEMS, ISHIDA-SAN.
GET ANOTHER WOMAN'S OPINION.
ABSOLUTELY NOT!

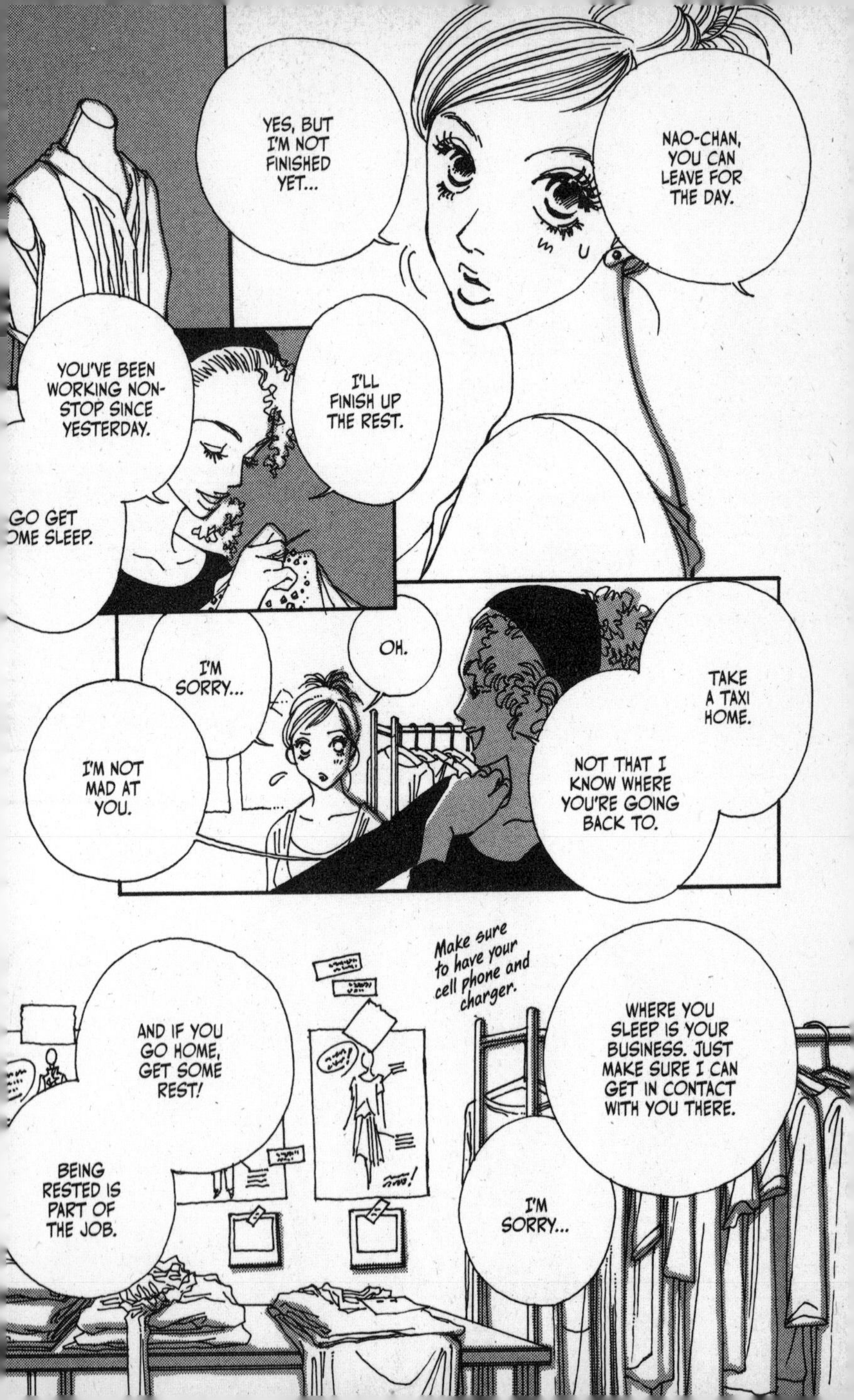
NAO-CHAN, YOU CAN LEAVE FOR THE DAY.
YES, BUT I'M NOT FINISHED YET...
I'LL FINISH UP THE REST.
YOU'VE BEEN WORKING NON-STOP SINCE YESTERDAY.
GO GET OME SLEEP.
TAKE A TAXI HOME.
OH.
NOT THAT I KNOW WHERE YOU'RE GOING BACK TO.
I'M SORRY...
I'M NOT MAD AT YOU.
WHERE YOU SLEEP IS YOUR BUSINESS. JUST MAKE SURE I CAN GET IN CONTACT WITH YOU THERE.
Make sure to have your cell phone and charger.
I'M SORRY...
AND IF YOU GO HOME, GET SOME REST!
BEING RESTED IS PART OF THE JOB.

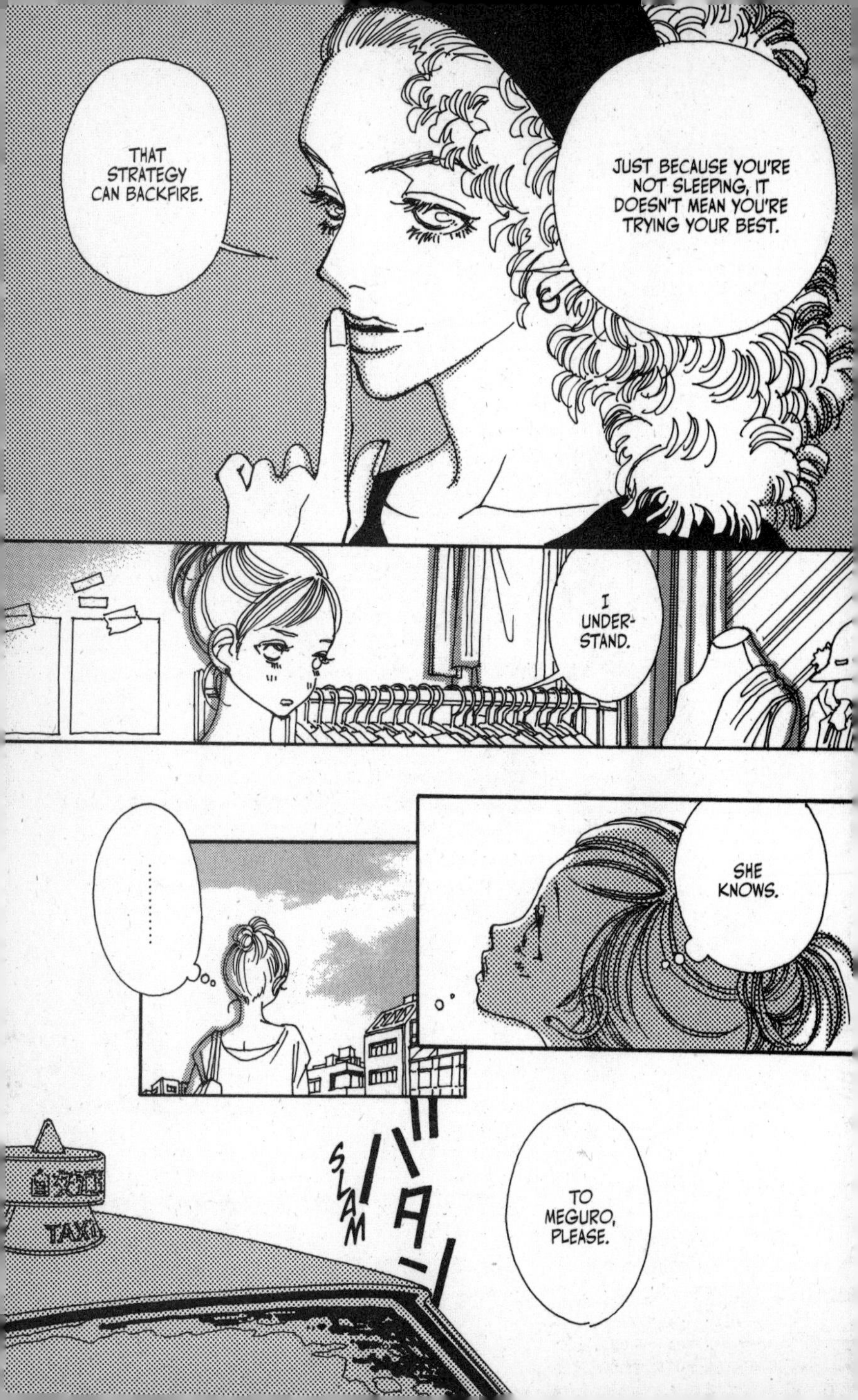
JUST BECAUSE YOU'RE NOT SLEEPING, IT DOESN'T MEAN YOU'RE TRYING YOUR BEST.
THAT STRATEGY CAN BACKFIRE.
I UNDER-STAND.
SHE KNOWS.
......
TO MEGURO, PLEASE.
SLAM
TAXI

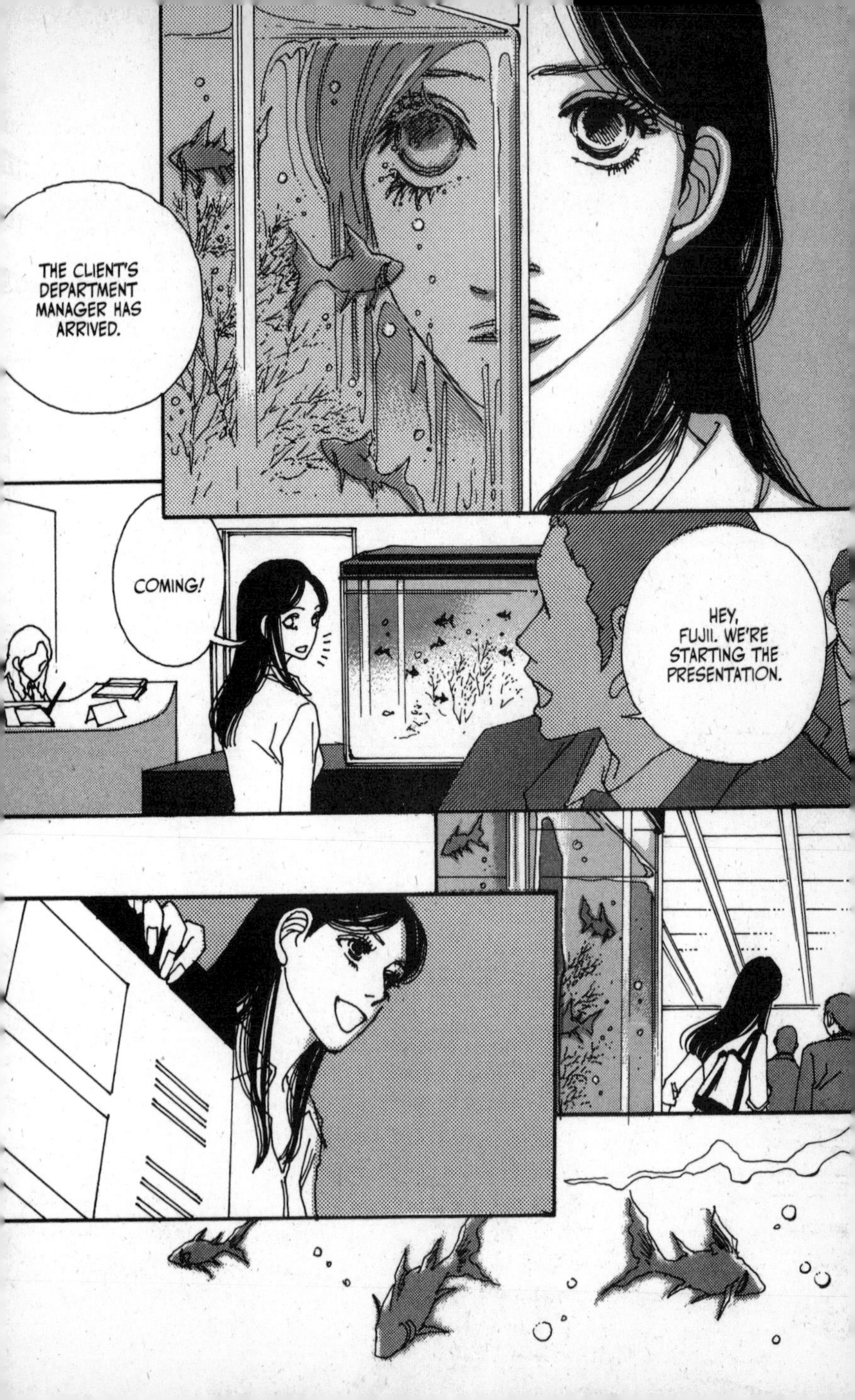
THE CLIENT'S DEPARTMENT MANAGER HAS ARRIVED.
HEY, FUJII. WE'RE STARTING THE PRESENTATION.
COMING!

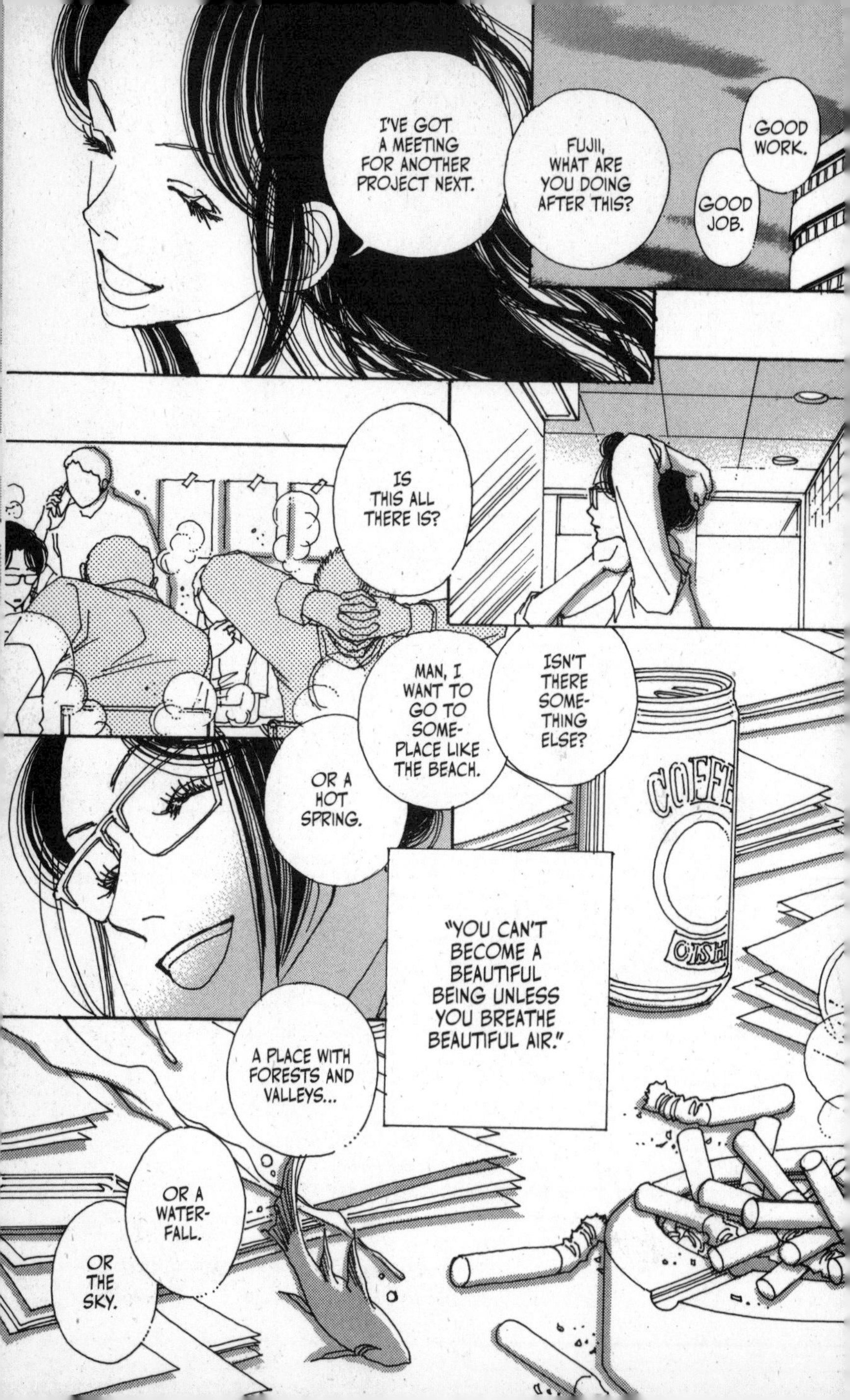
GOOD WORK.
GOOD JOB.
FUJII, WHAT ARE YOU DOING AFTER THIS?
I'VE GOT A MEETING FOR ANOTHER PROJECT NEXT.
IS THIS ALL THERE IS?
ISN'T THERE SOME-THING ELSE?
MAN, I WANT TO GO TO SOME-PLACE LIKE THE BEACH.
OR A HOT SPRING.
COFFE
OISH
"YOU CAN'T BECOME A BEAUTIFUL BEING UNLESS YOU BREATHE BEAUTIFUL AIR."
A PLACE WITH FORESTS AND VALLEYS...
OR A WATER-FALL.
OR THE SKY.

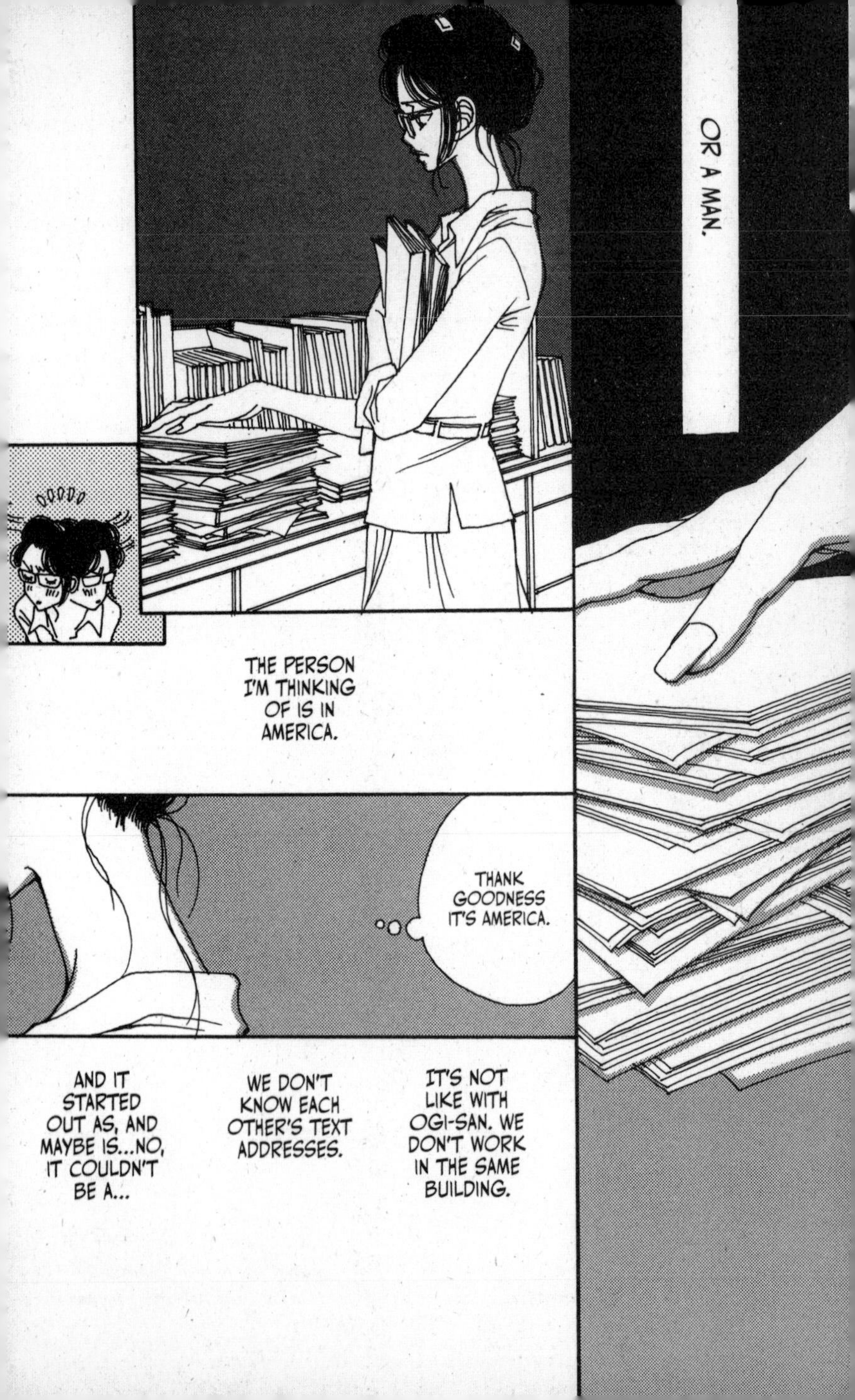
OR A MAN.
THE PERSON I'M THINKING OF IS IN AMERICA.
THANK GOODNESS IT'S AMERICA.
IT'S NOT LIKE WITH OGI-SAN. WE DON'T WORK IN THE SAME BUILDING.
WE DON'T KNOW EACH OTHER'S TEXT ADDRESSES.
AND IT STARTED OUT AS, AND MAYBE IS...NO, IT COULDN'T BE A...

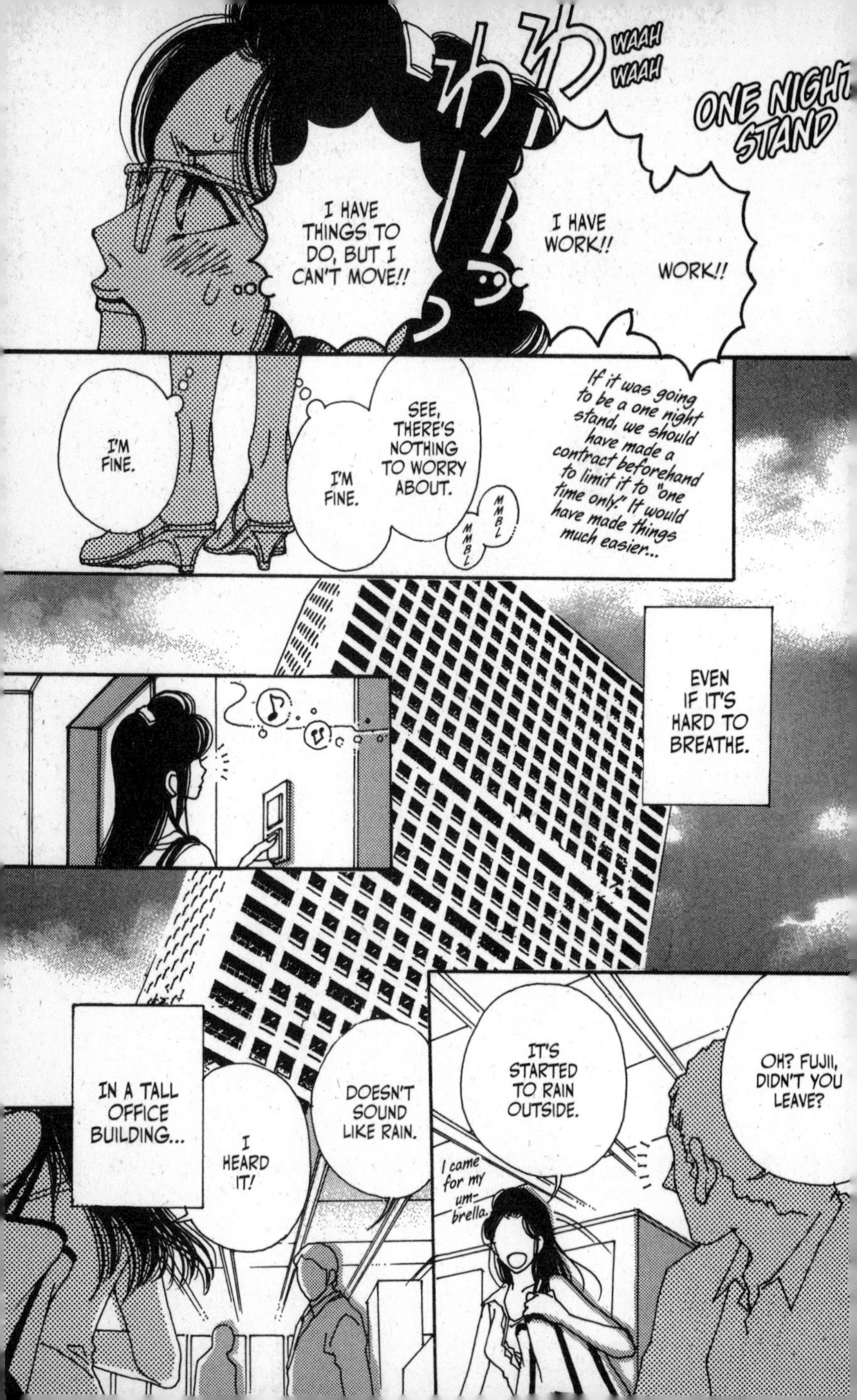

WAAH WAAH
ONE NIGHT STAND
WORK!!
I HAVE WORK!!
I HAVE THINGS TO DO, BUT I CAN'T MOVE!!
If it was going to be a one night stand, we should have made a contract beforehand to limit it to "one time only." It would have made things much easier...
MMBL MMBL
SEE, THERE'S NOTHING TO WORRY ABOUT.
I'M FINE.
I'M FINE.
EVEN IF IT'S HARD TO BREATHE.
OH? FUJII, DIDN'T YOU LEAVE?
IT'S STARTED TO RAIN OUTSIDE.
I came for my um-brella.
DOESN'T SOUND LIKE RAIN.
I HEARD IT!
IN A TALL OFFICE BUILDING...

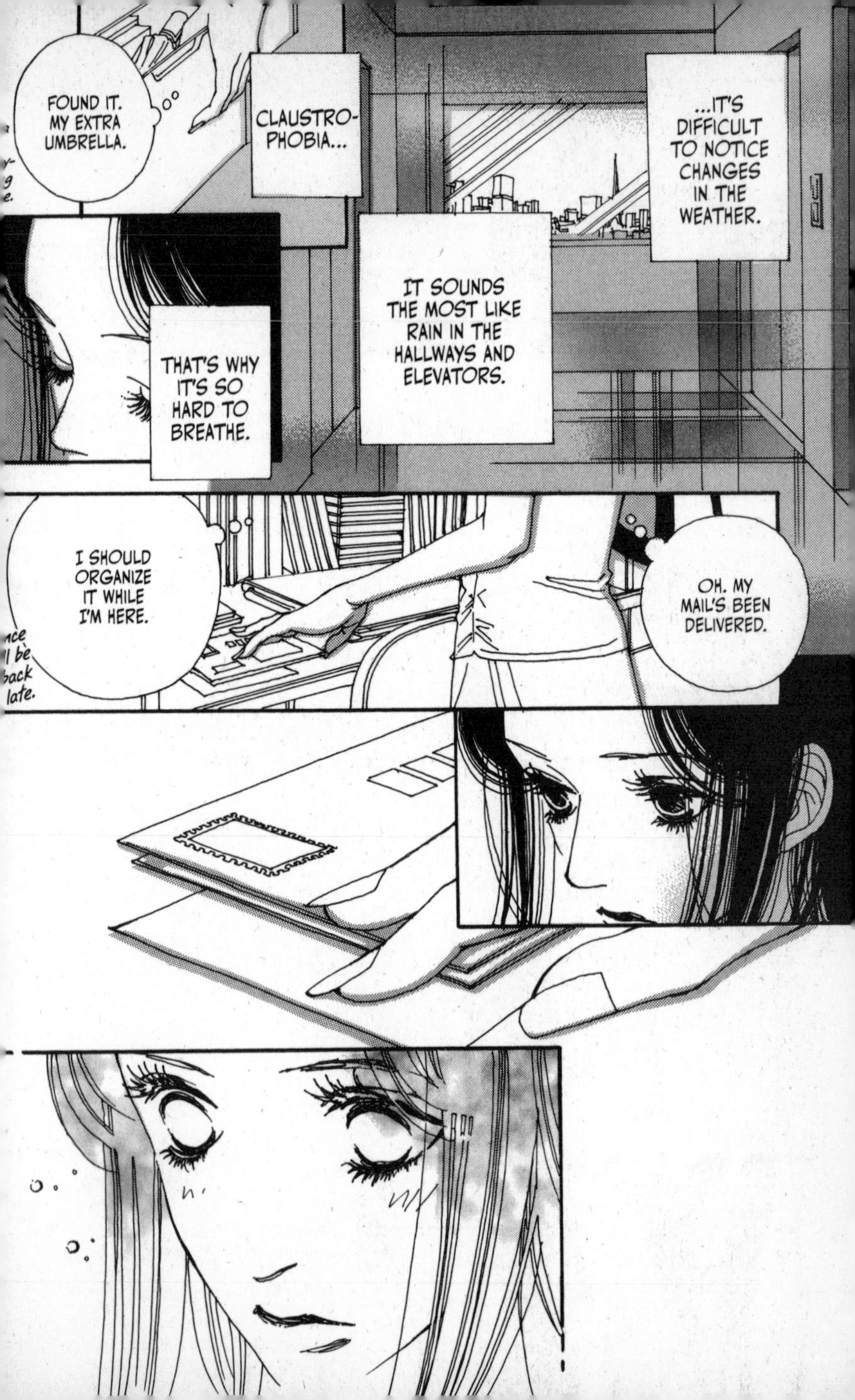
...IT'S DIFFICULT TO NOTICE CHANGES IN THE WEATHER.
IT SOUNDS THE MOST LIKE RAIN IN THE HALLWAYS AND ELEVATORS.
CLAUSTROPHOBIA...
FOUND IT. MY EXTRA UMBRELLA.
THAT'S WHY IT'S SO HARD TO BREATHE.
OH. MY MAIL'S BEEN DELIVERED.
I SHOULD ORGANIZE IT WHILE I'M HERE.

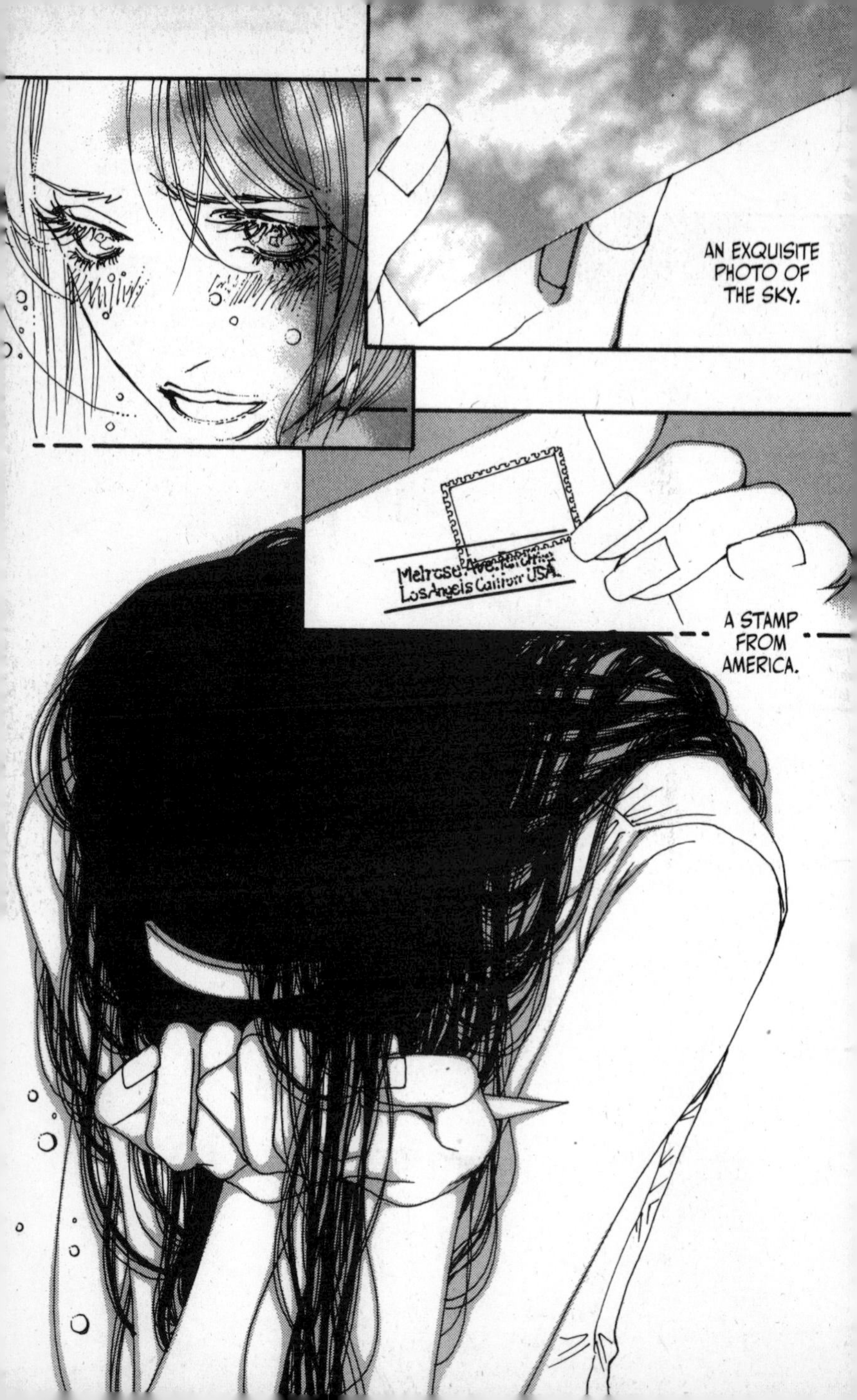
AN EXQUISITE PHOTO OF THE SKY.
A STAMP FROM AMERICA.

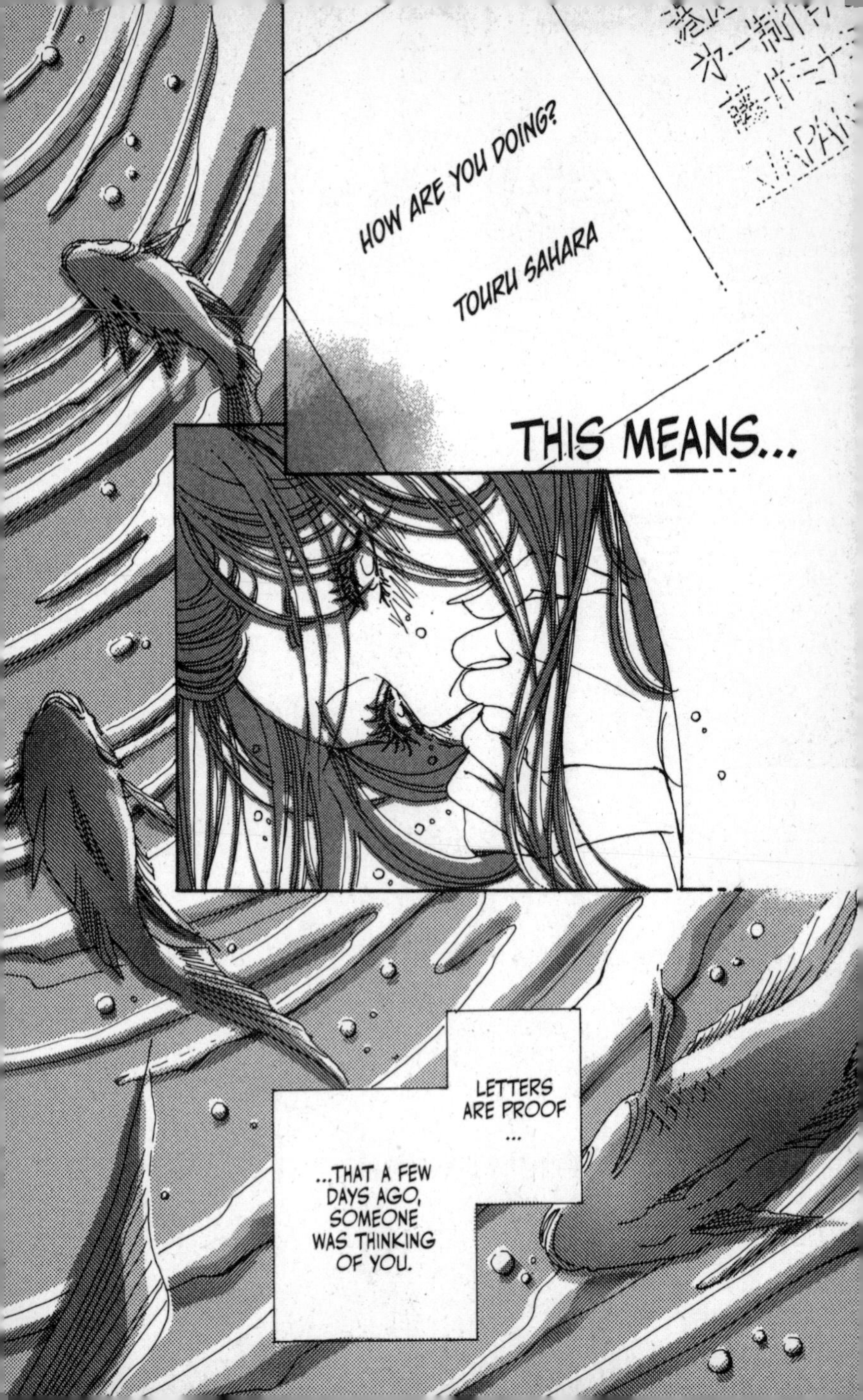
HOW ARE YOU DOING?
TOURU SAHARA
THIS MEANS...
LETTERS ARE PROOF ...
...THAT A FEW DAYS AGO, SOMEONE WAS THINKING OF YOU.

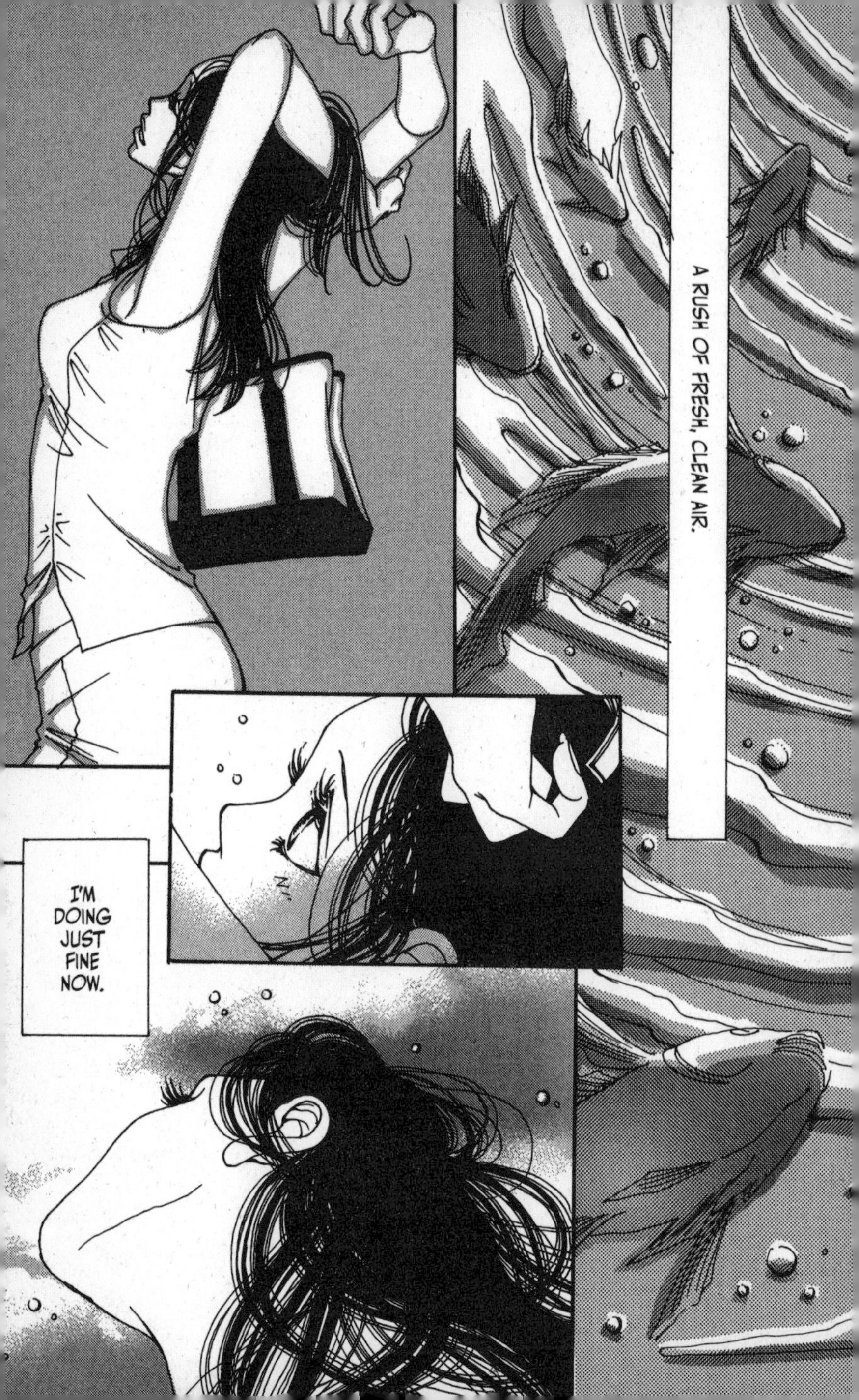
A RUSH OF FRESH, CLEAN AIR.
I'M DOING JUST FINE NOW.

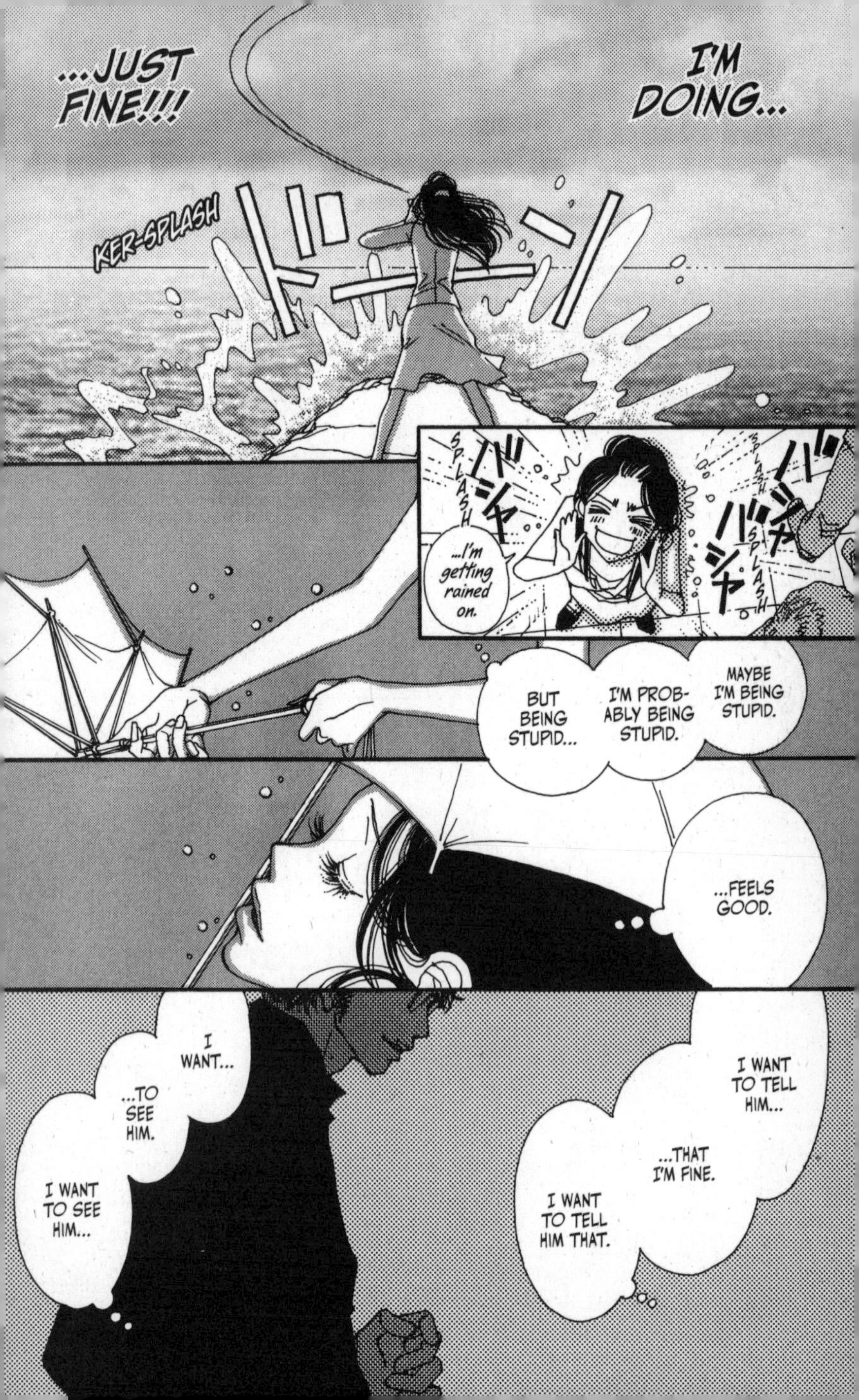
I'M DOING...
...JUST FINE!!!
ドーン
KER-SPLASH
バシャ
SPLASH
バシャ
バシャ
SPLASH
SPLASH
...I'm getting rained on.
MAYBE I'M BEING STUPID.
I'M PROBABLY BEING STUPID.
BUT BEING STUPID...
...FEELS GOOD.
I WANT TO TELL HIM...
...THAT I'M FINE.
I WANT TO TELL HIM THAT.
I WANT...
...TO SEE HIM.
I WANT TO SEE HIM...

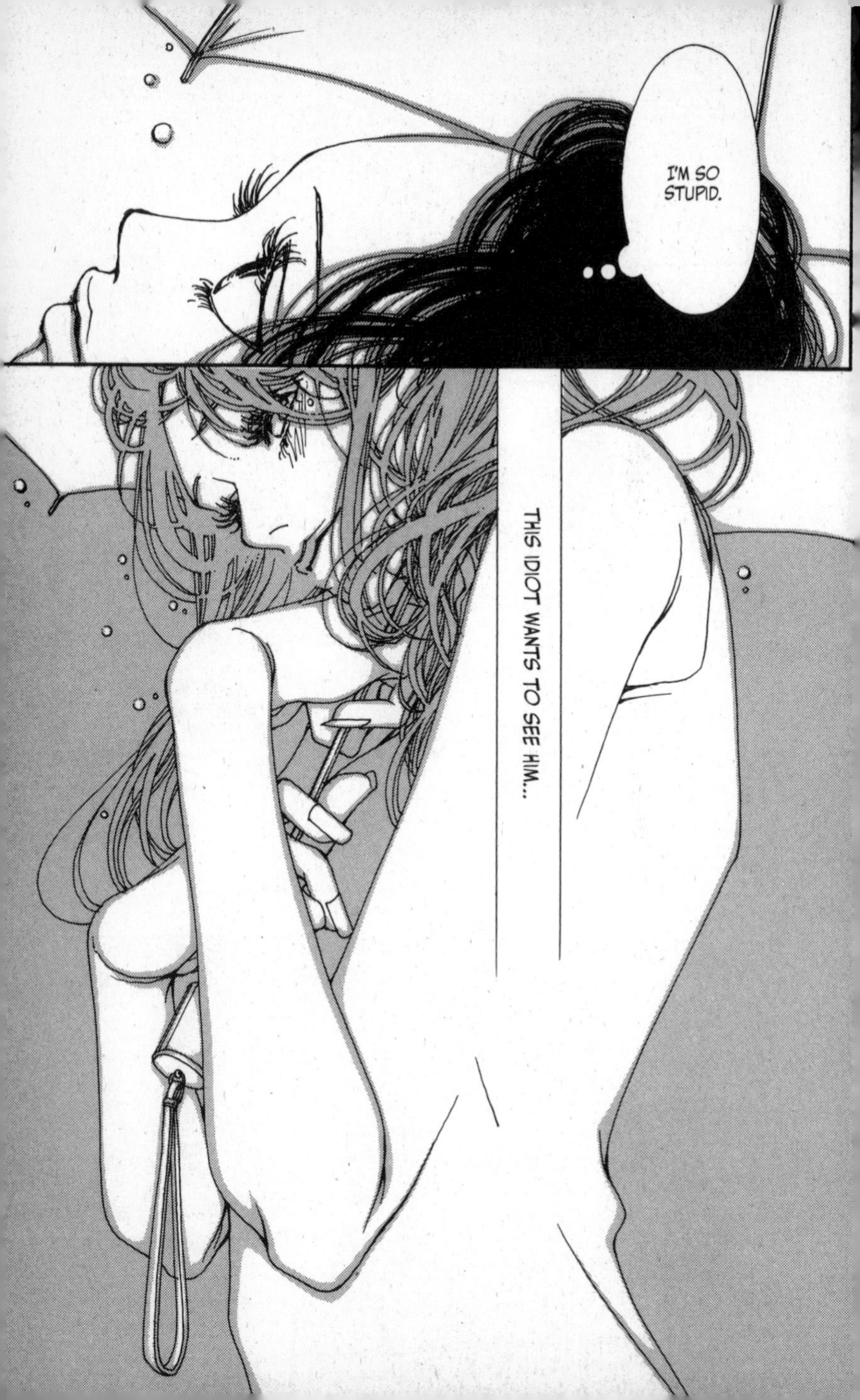
I'M SO STUPID.
THIS IDIOT WANTS TO SEE HIM...

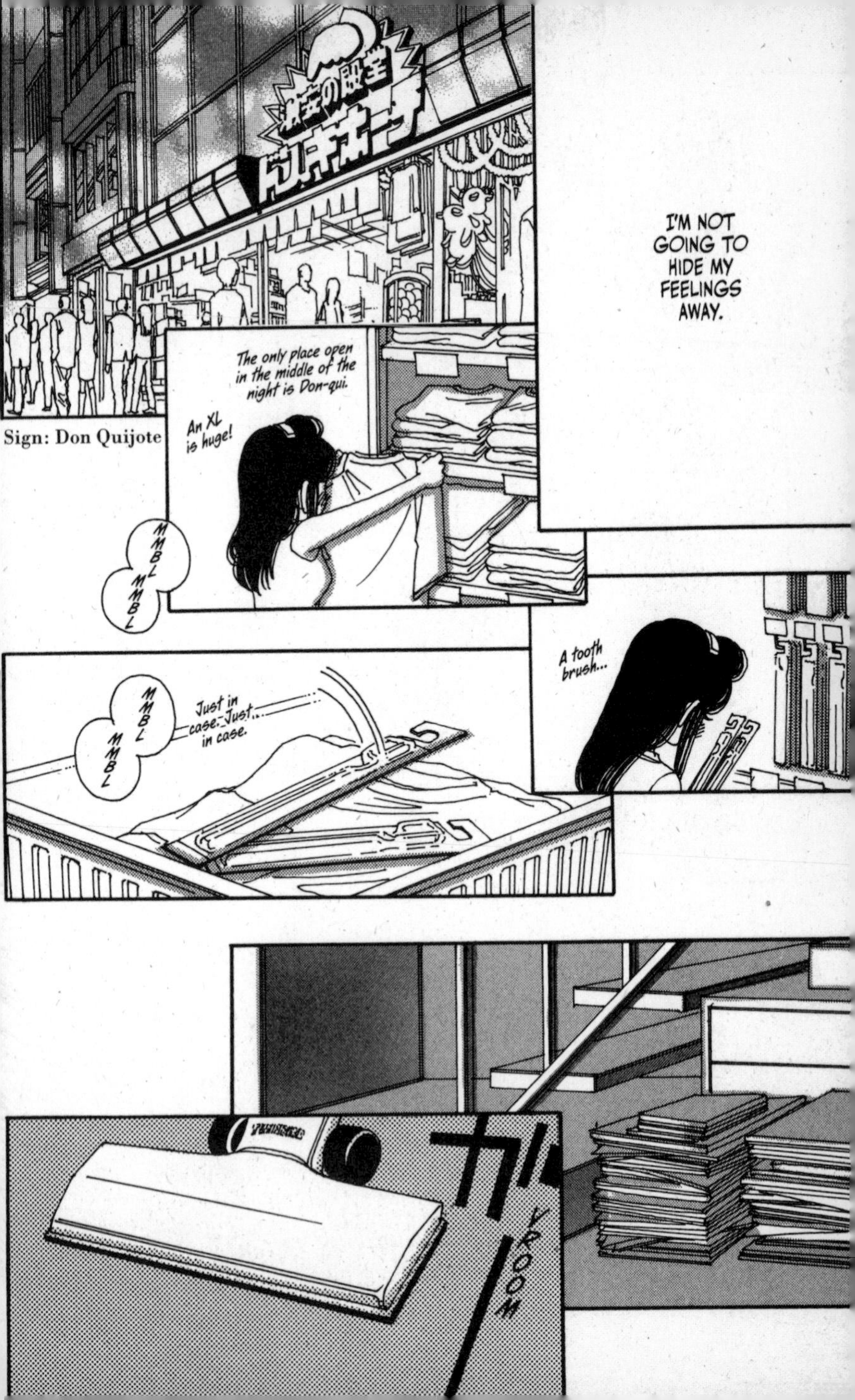
I'M NOT GOING TO HIDE MY FEELINGS AWAY.
The only place open in the middle of the night is Don-qui.
An XL is huge!
MMBL MMBL
A tooth brush...
MMBL MMBL
Just in case. Just in case.
VROOM
Sign: Don Quijote

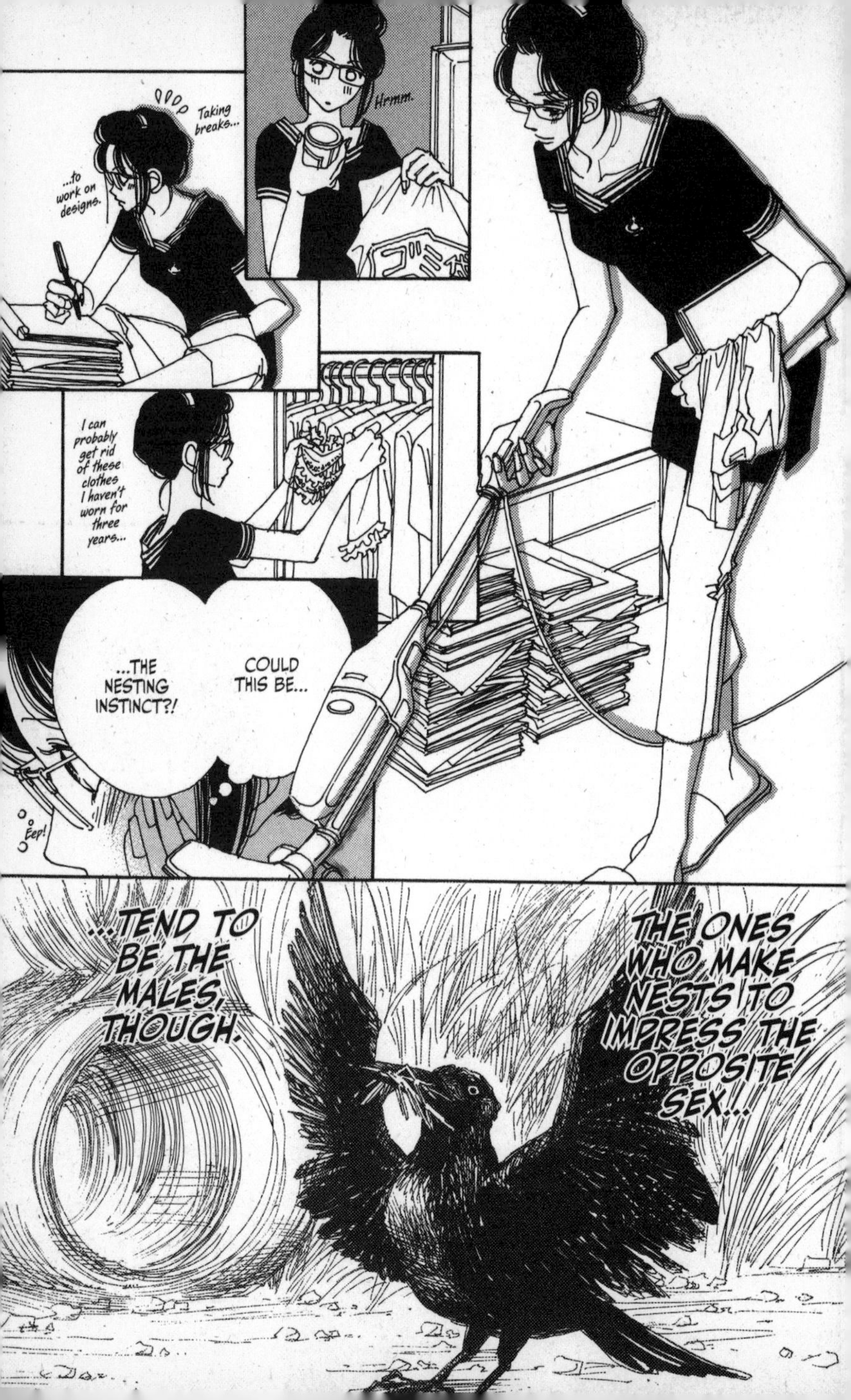
Hrmm.
Taking breaks...
...to work on designs.
I can probably get rid of these clothes I haven't worn for three years...
COULD THIS BE...
...THE NESTING INSTINCT?!
Eep!
THE ONES WHO MAKE NESTS TO IMPRESS THE OPPOSITE SEX...
...TEND TO BE THE MALES, THOUGH.

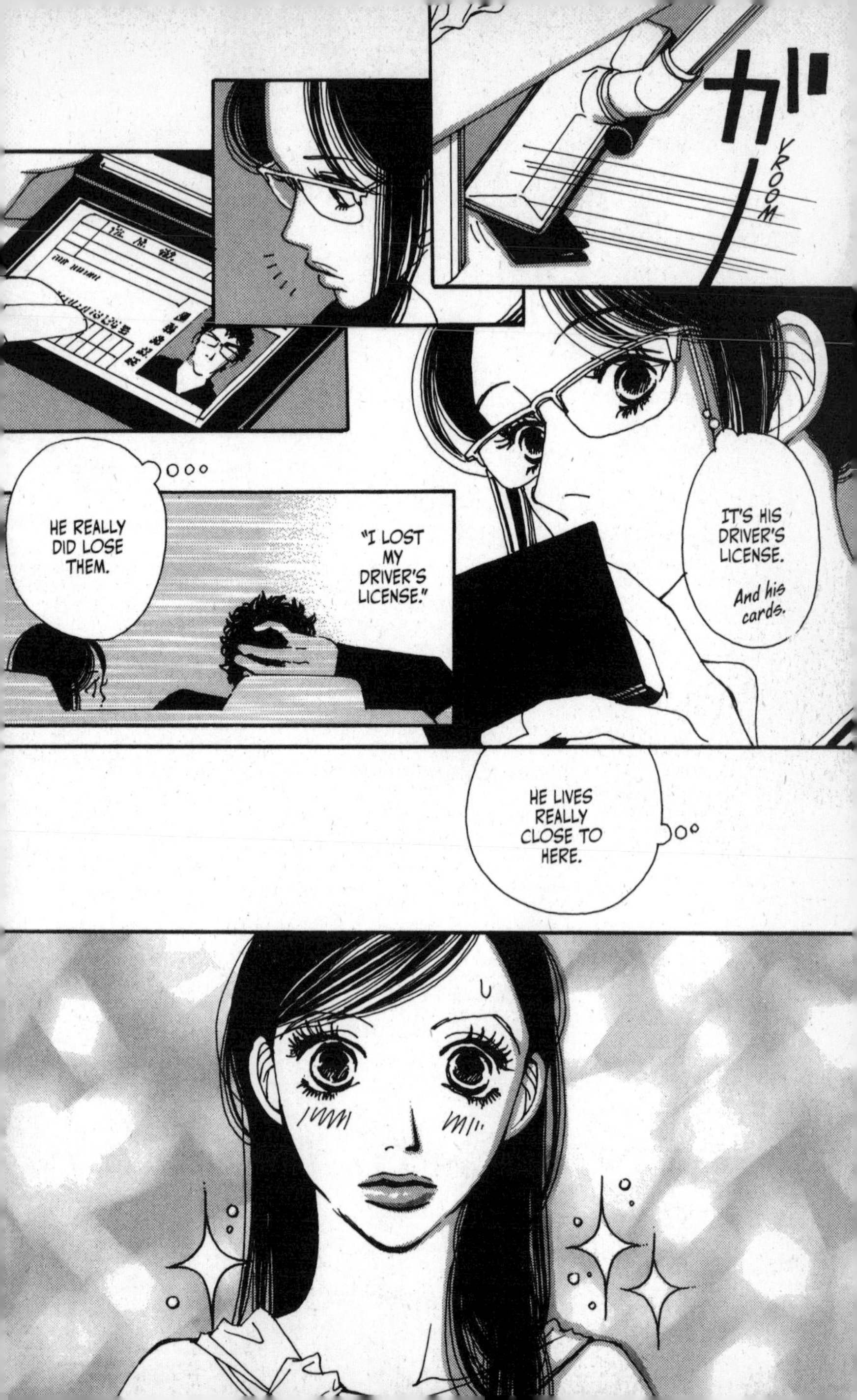
ガ
VROOM
IT'S HIS DRIVER'S LICENSE.
And his cards.
"I LOST MY DRIVER'S LICENSE."
HE REALLY DID LOSE THEM.
HE LIVES REALLY CLOSE TO HERE.

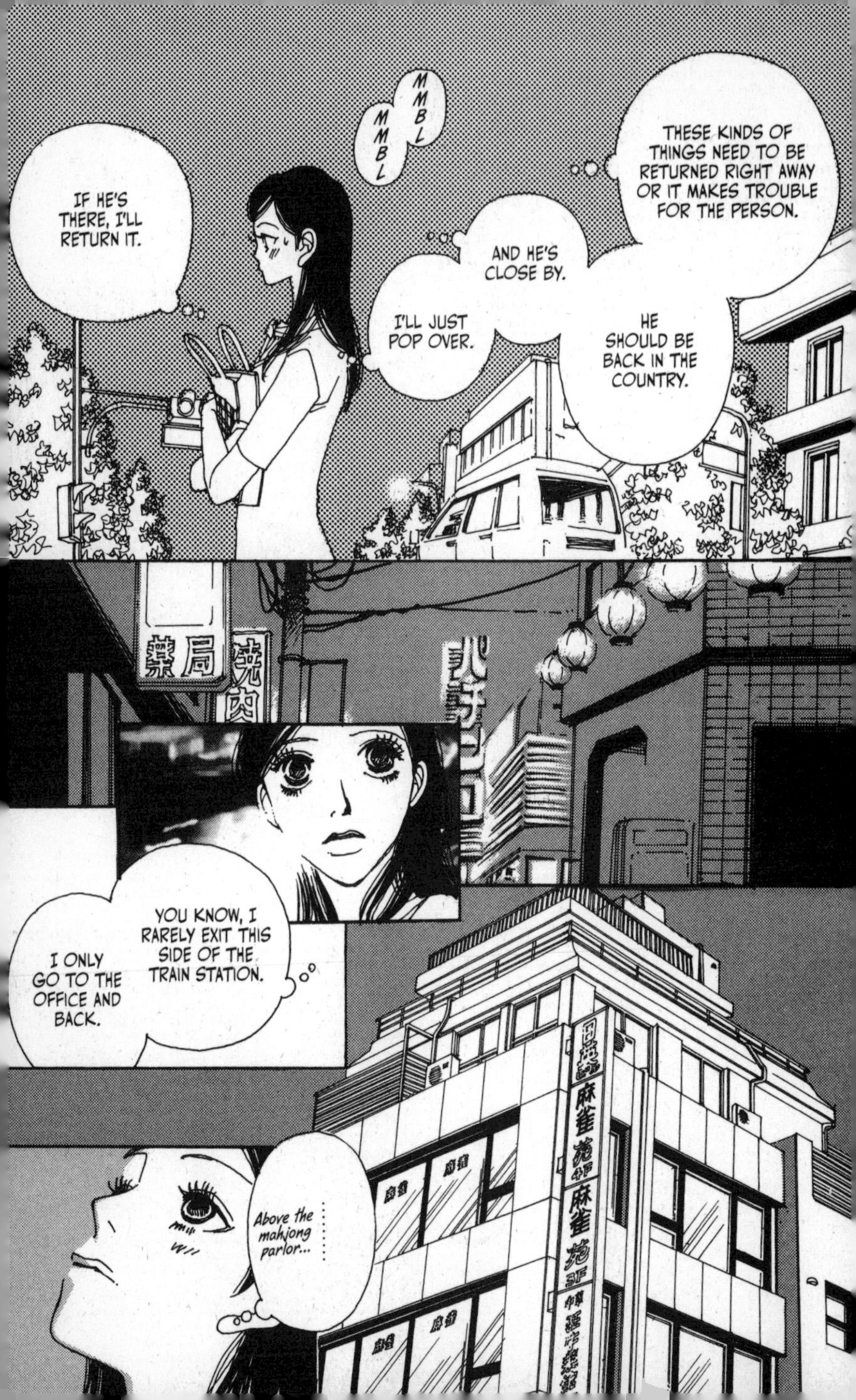
THESE KINDS OF THINGS NEED TO BE RETURNED RIGHT AWAY OR IT MAKES TROUBLE FOR THE PERSON.
HE SHOULD BE BACK IN THE COUNTRY.
AND HE'S CLOSE BY.
I'LL JUST POP OVER.
MMBL
MMBL
IF HE'S THERE, I'LL RETURN IT.
YOU KNOW, I RARELY EXIT THIS SIDE OF THE TRAIN STATION.
I ONLY GO TO THE OFFICE AND BACK.
Above the mahjong parlor...

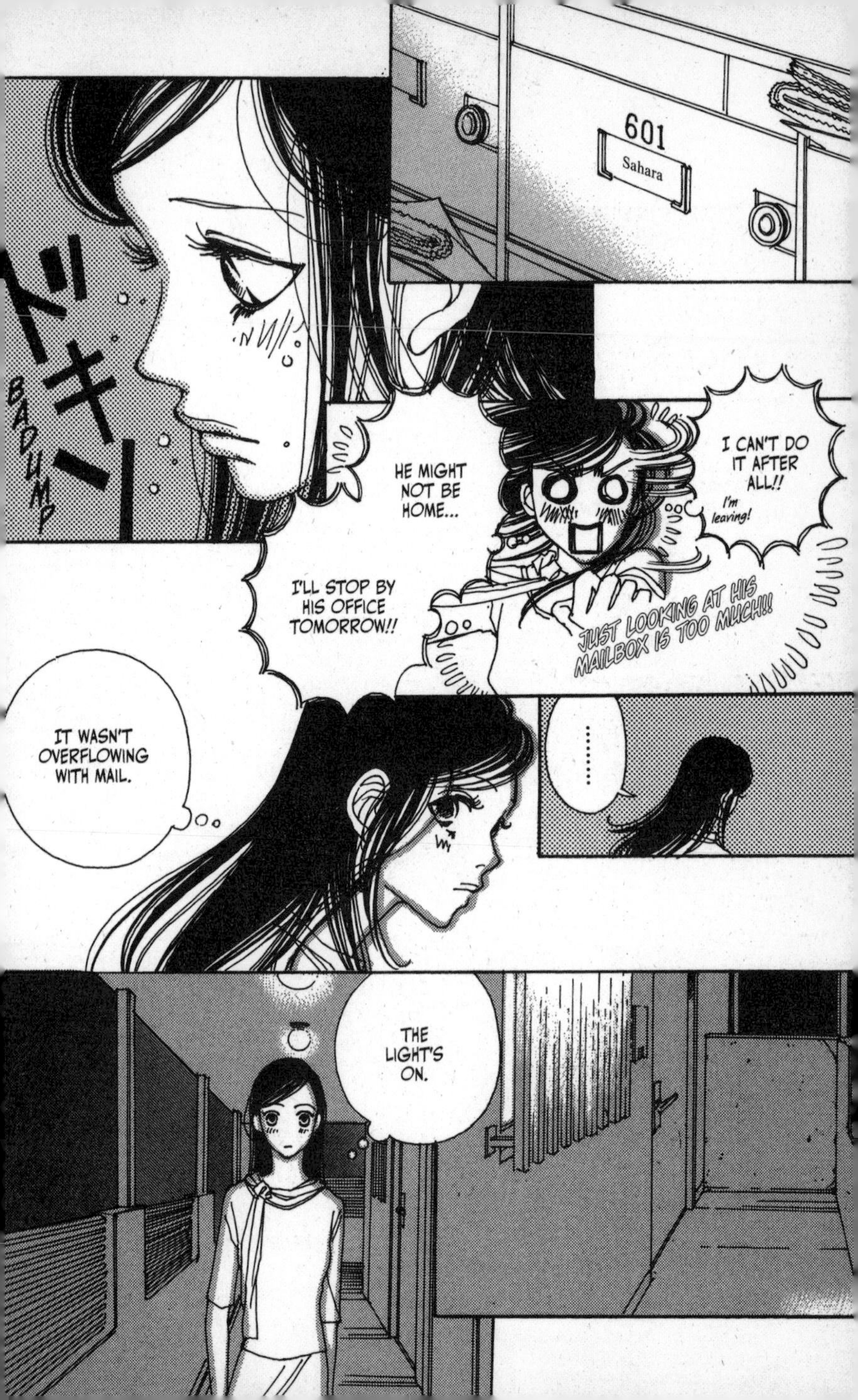
601
Sahara
ドキン
BADUMP
I CAN'T DO IT AFTER ALL!!
I'm leaving!
HE MIGHT NOT BE HOME...
I'LL STOP BY HIS OFFICE TOMORROW!!
JUST LOOKING AT HIS MAILBOX IS TOO MUCH!!
......
IT WASN'T OVERFLOWING WITH MAIL.
THE LIGHT'S ON.

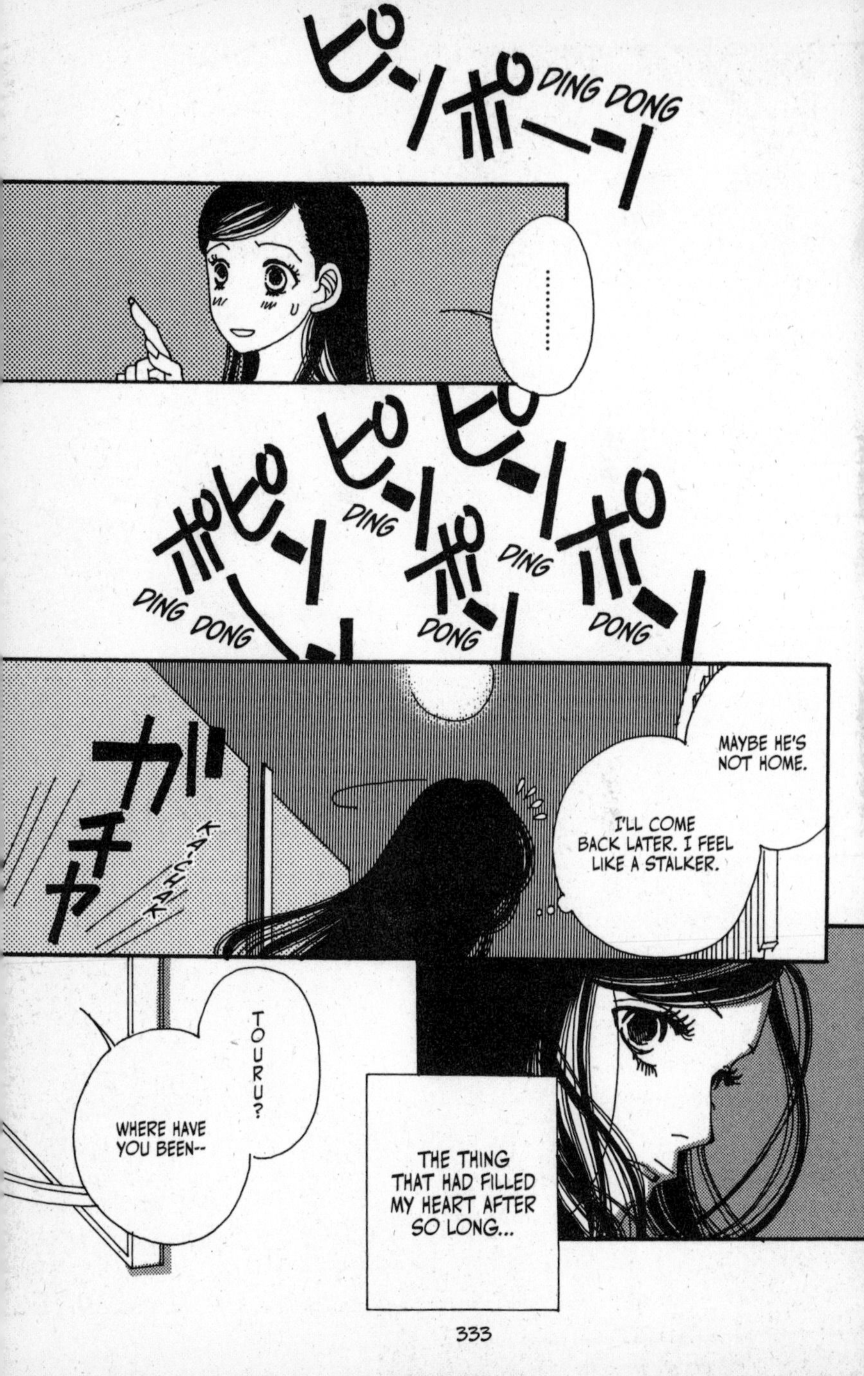
ピーンポーーン
DING DONG
......
ピーンポーン
DING
DONG
ピーンポーン
DING
DONG
ポピーン
DING DONG
MAYBE HE'S NOT HOME.
I'LL COME BACK LATER. I FEEL LIKE A STALKER.
ガチャ
KA-CHAK
THE THING THAT HAD FILLED MY HEART AFTER SO LONG...
TOURU?
WHERE HAVE YOU BEEN--

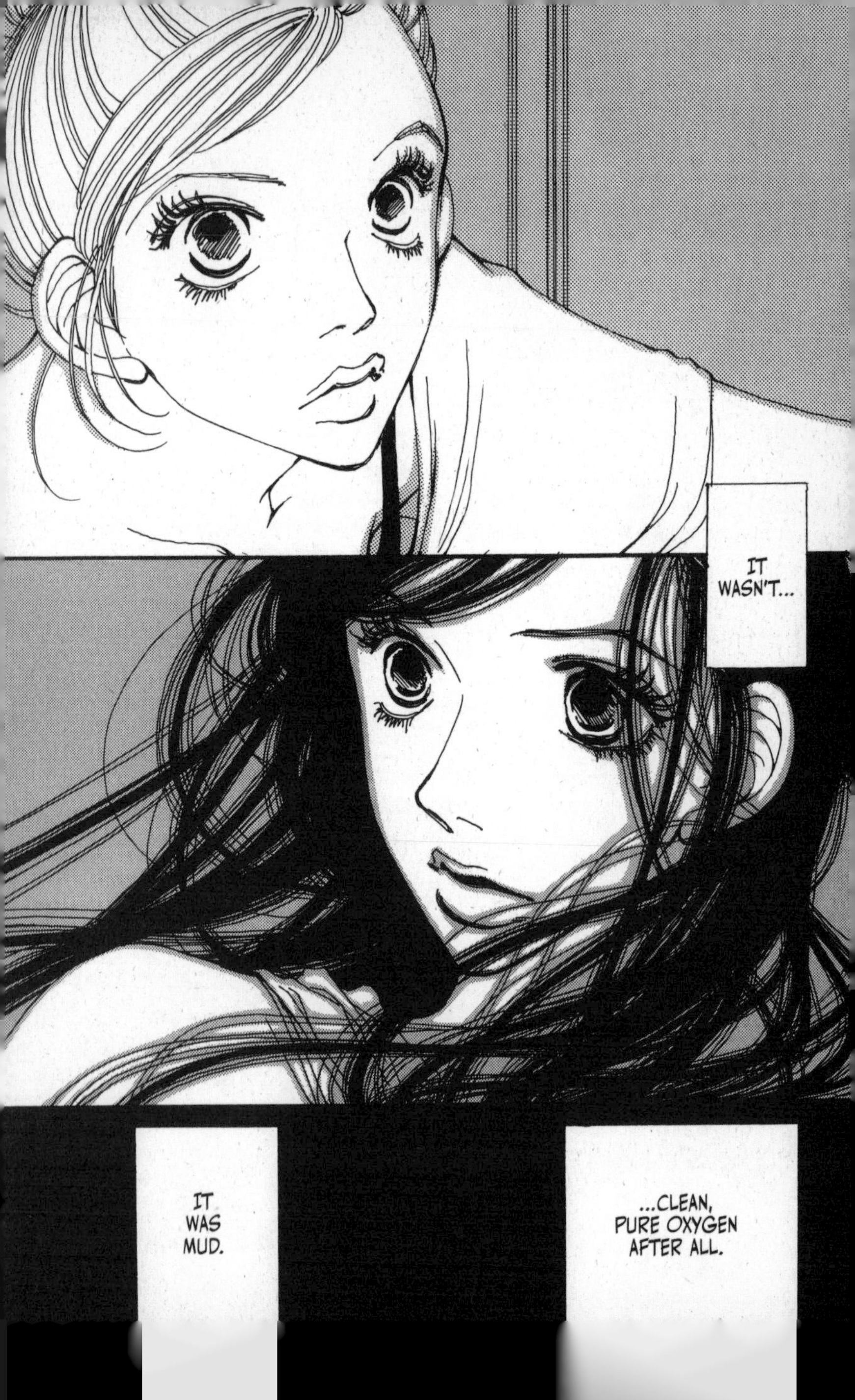
IT WASN'T...
...CLEAN, PURE OXYGEN AFTER ALL.
IT WAS MUD.

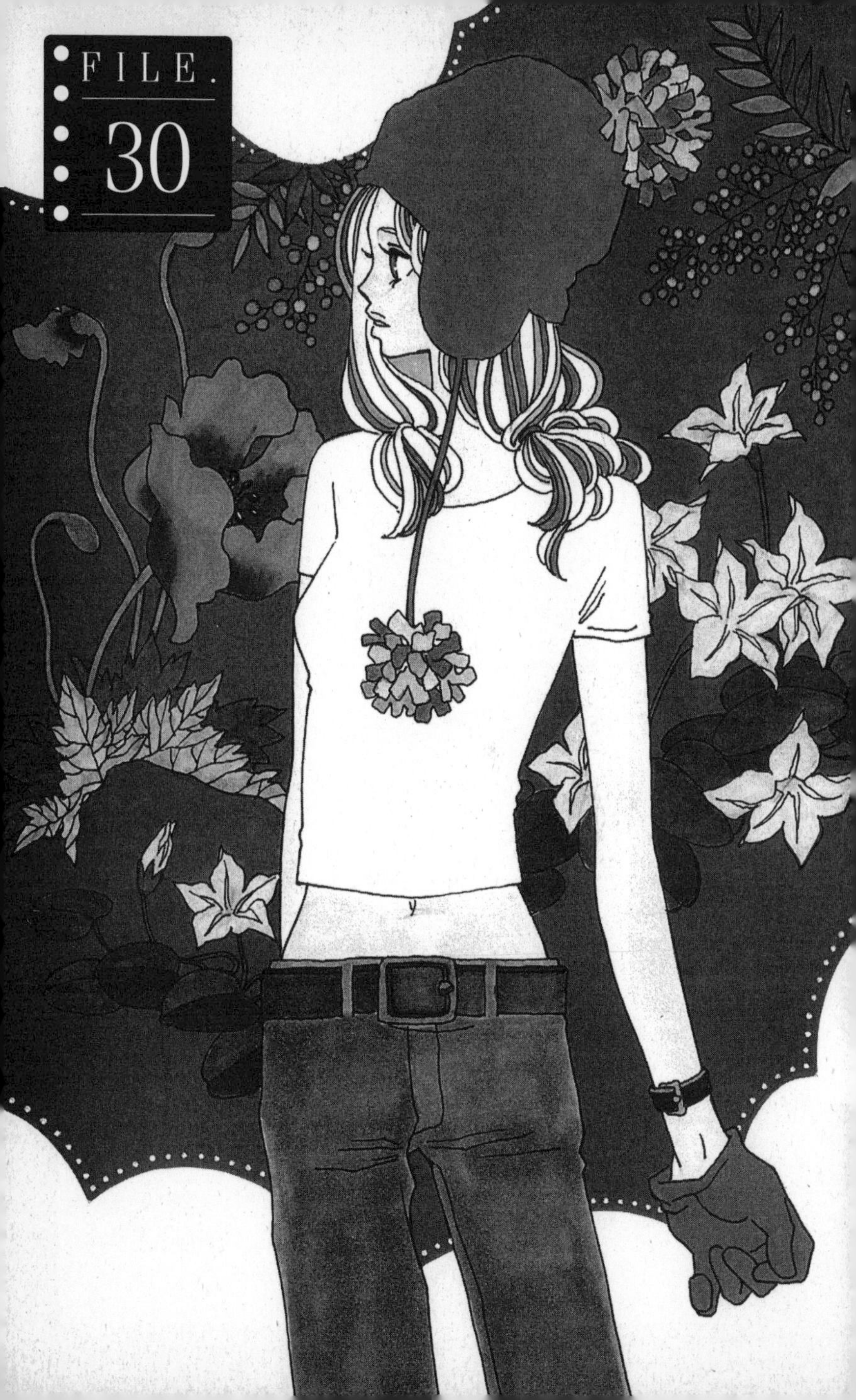
FILE.
30

OF COURSE, AT THIS AGE IT'S RARE TO FIND COMPLETELY CLEAN MEN.

THINGS CLING TO THEM WHEN YOU PULL.

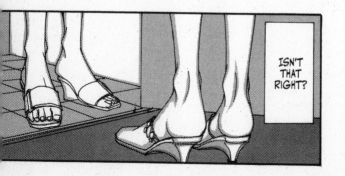

ISN'T THAT RIGHT?

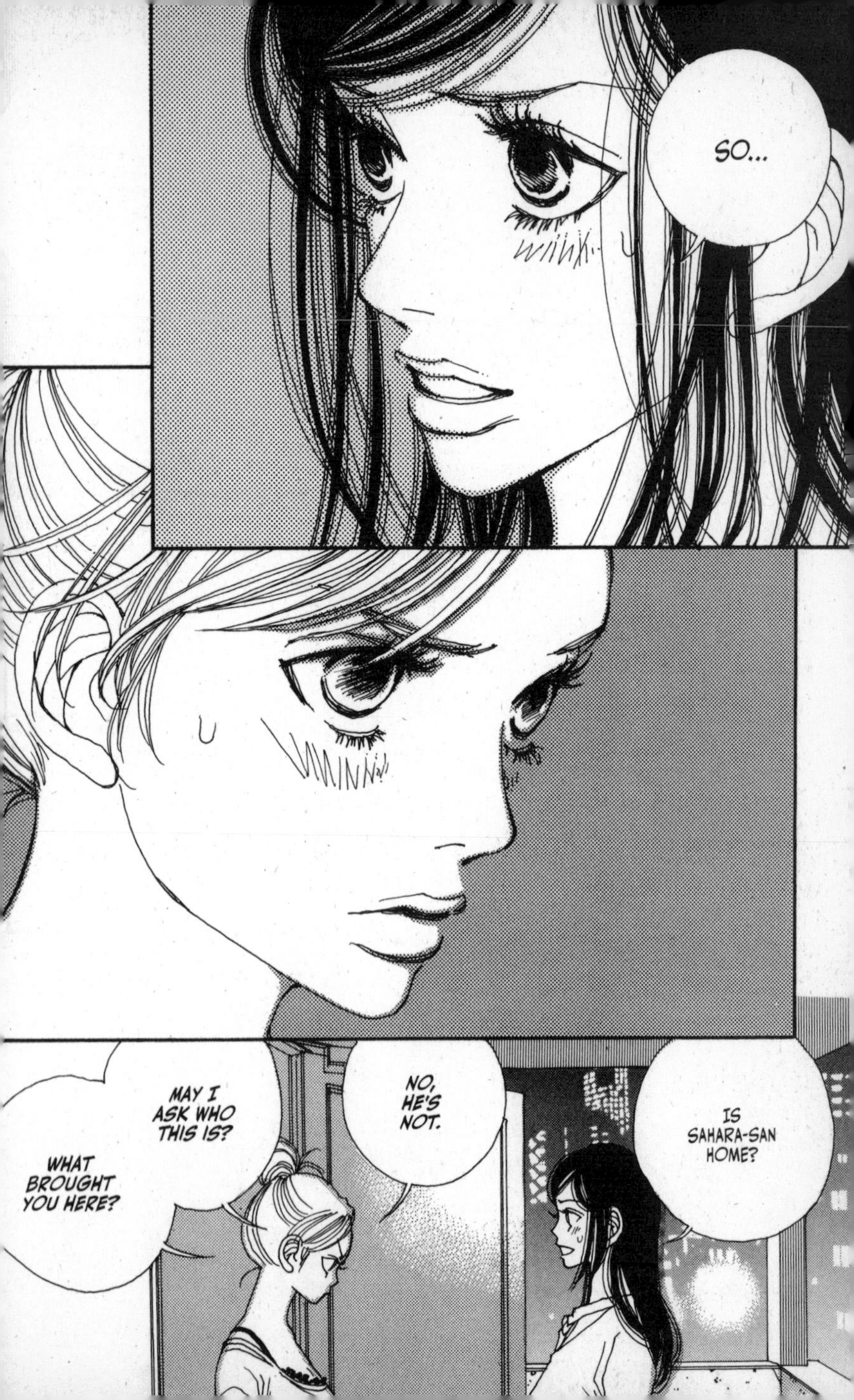
SO...
IS SAHARA-SAN HOME?
NO, HE'S NOT.
MAY I ASK WHO THIS IS?
WHAT BROUGHT YOU HERE?

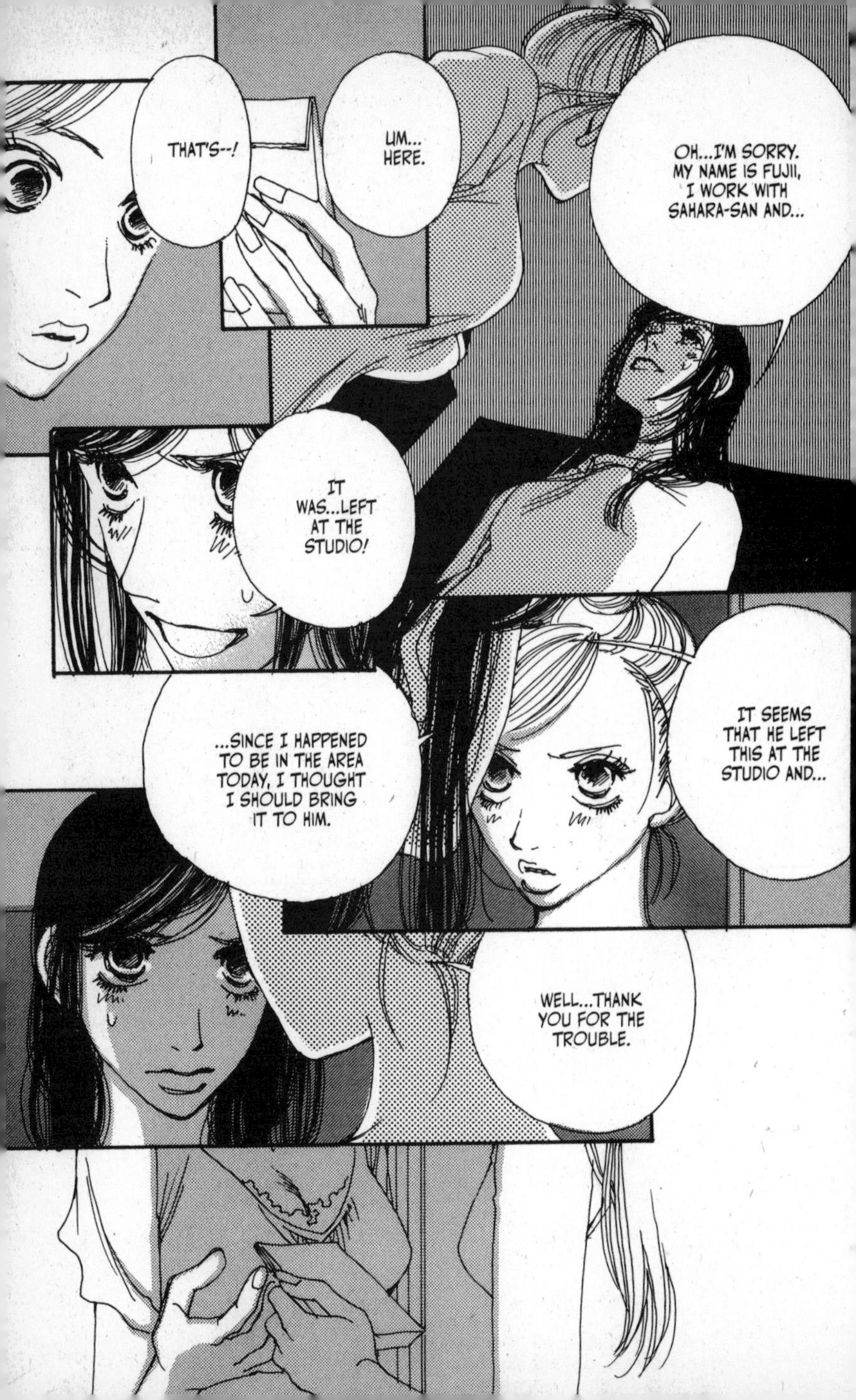
OH...I'M SORRY. MY NAME IS FUJII, I WORK WITH SAHARA-SAN AND...
UM... HERE.
THAT'S--!
IT WAS...LEFT AT THE STUDIO!
IT SEEMS THAT HE LEFT THIS AT THE STUDIO AND...
...SINCE I HAPPENED TO BE IN THE AREA TODAY, I THOUGHT I SHOULD BRING IT TO HIM.
WELL...THANK YOU FOR THE TROUBLE.

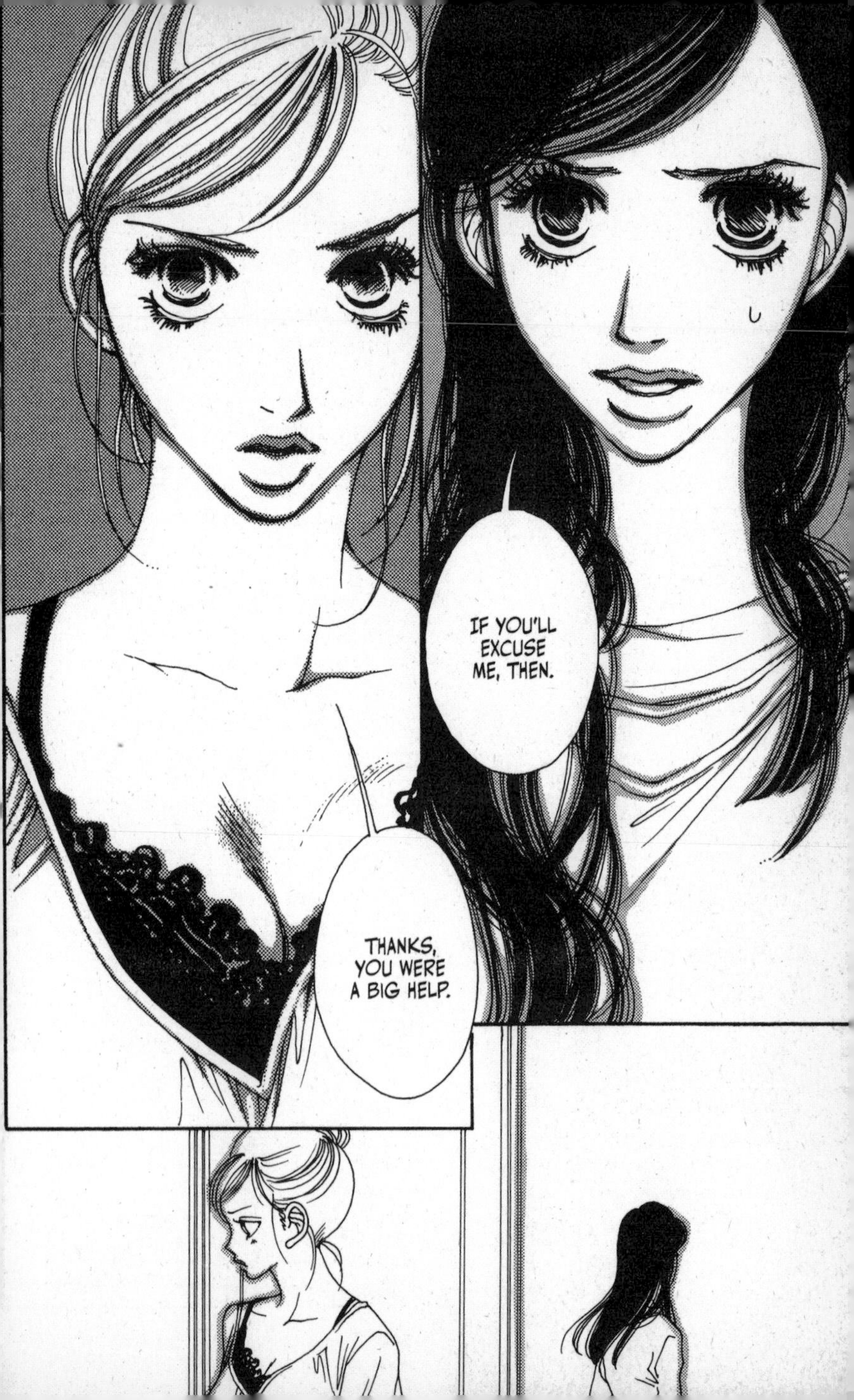
IF YOU'LL EXCUSE ME, THEN.
THANKS, YOU WERE A BIG HELP.

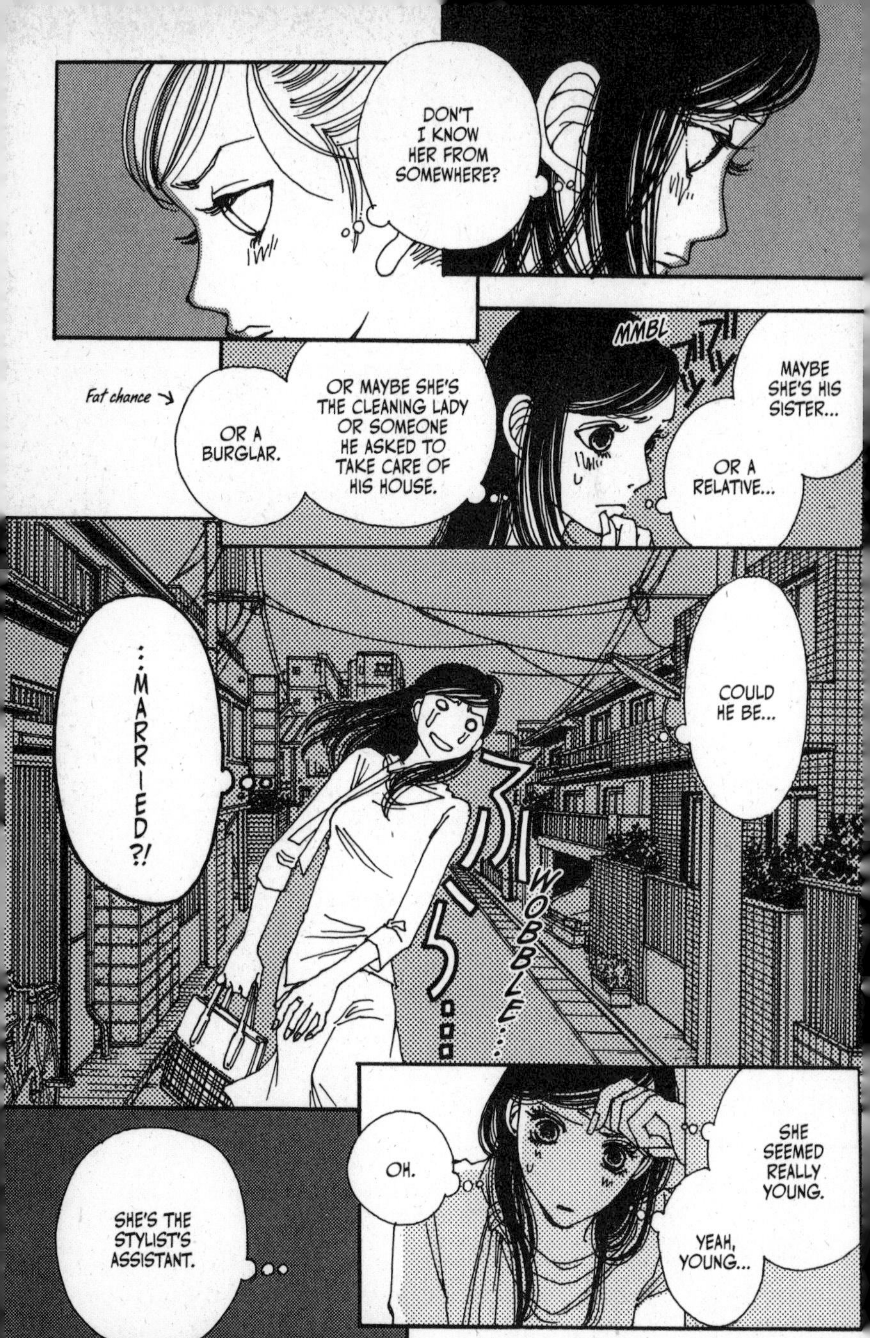
DON'T I KNOW HER FROM SOMEWHERE?
MMBL
MAYBE SHE'S HIS SISTER...
OR A RELATIVE...
OR MAYBE SHE'S THE CLEANING LADY OR SOMEONE HE ASKED TO TAKE CARE OF HIS HOUSE.
OR A BURGLAR.
Fat chance
COULD HE BE...
...MARRIED?!
WOBBLE...
SHE SEEMED REALLY YOUNG.
YEAH, YOUNG...
OH.
SHE'S THE STYLIST'S ASSISTANT.

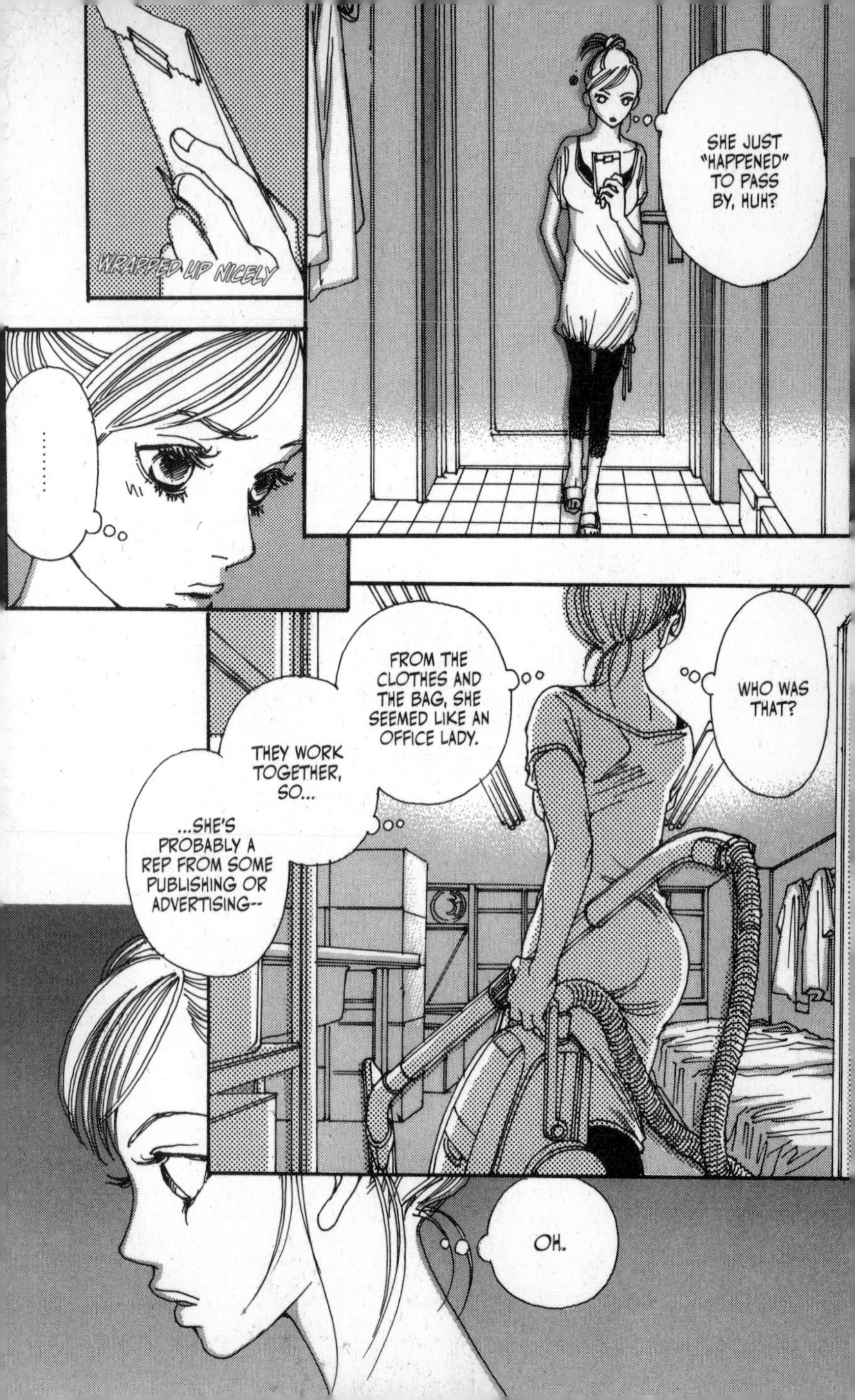
SHE JUST "HAPPENED" TO PASS BY, HUH?
WRAPPED UP NICELY
......
WHO WAS THAT?
FROM THE CLOTHES AND THE BAG, SHE SEEMED LIKE AN OFFICE LADY.
THEY WORK TOGETHER, SO...
...SHE'S PROBABLY A REP FROM SOME PUBLISHING OR ADVERTISING--
OH.

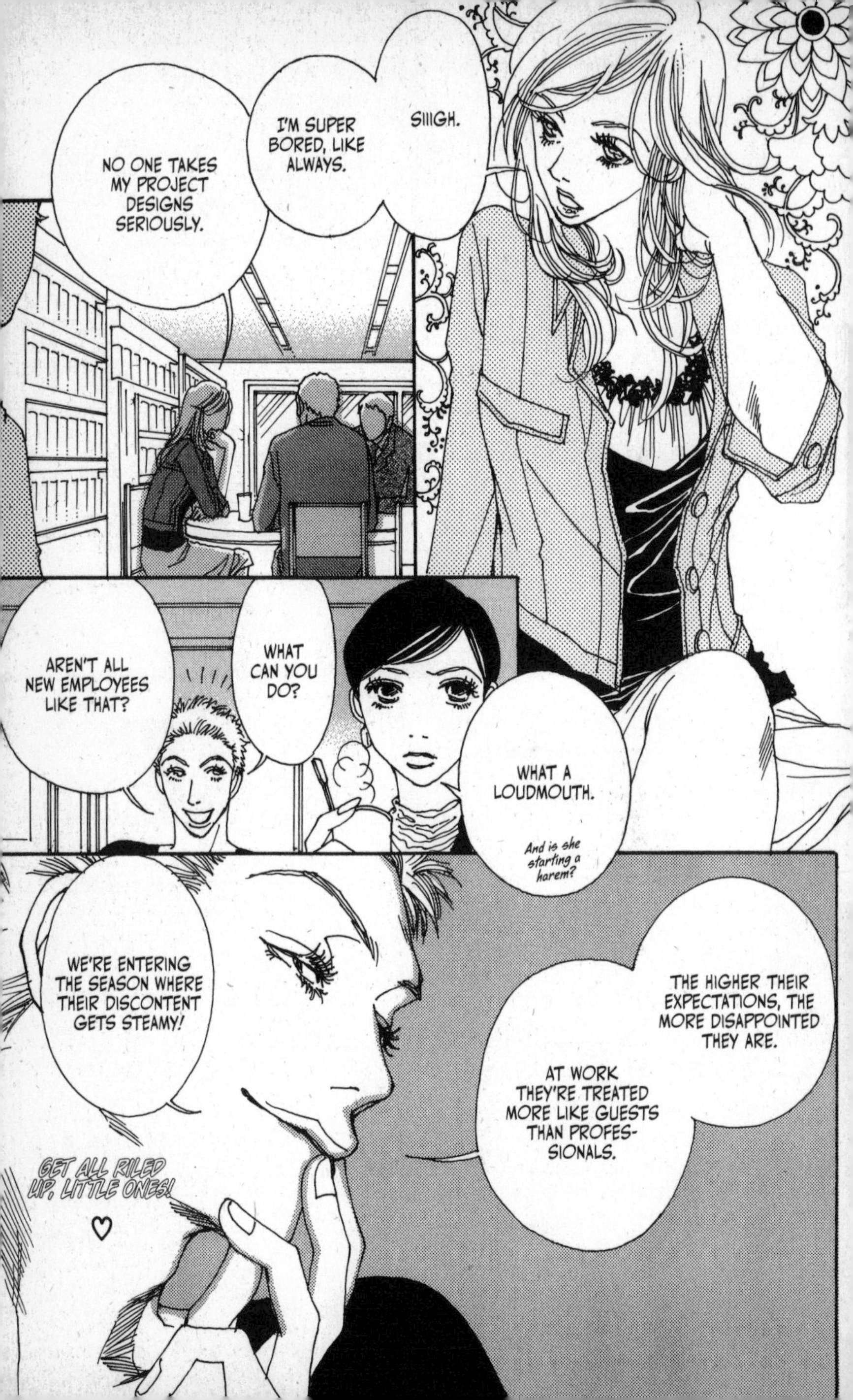
SIIIGH.
I'M SUPER BORED, LIKE ALWAYS.
NO ONE TAKES MY PROJECT DESIGNS SERIOUSLY.
WHAT A LOUDMOUTH.
And is she starting a harem?
WHAT CAN YOU DO?
AREN'T ALL NEW EMPLOYEES LIKE THAT?
THE HIGHER THEIR EXPECTATIONS, THE MORE DISAPPOINTED THEY ARE.
AT WORK THEY'RE TREATED MORE LIKE GUESTS THAN PROFES-SIONALS.
WE'RE ENTERING THE SEASON WHERE THEIR DISCONTENT GETS STEAMY!
GET ALL RILED UP, LITTLE ONES! ♡

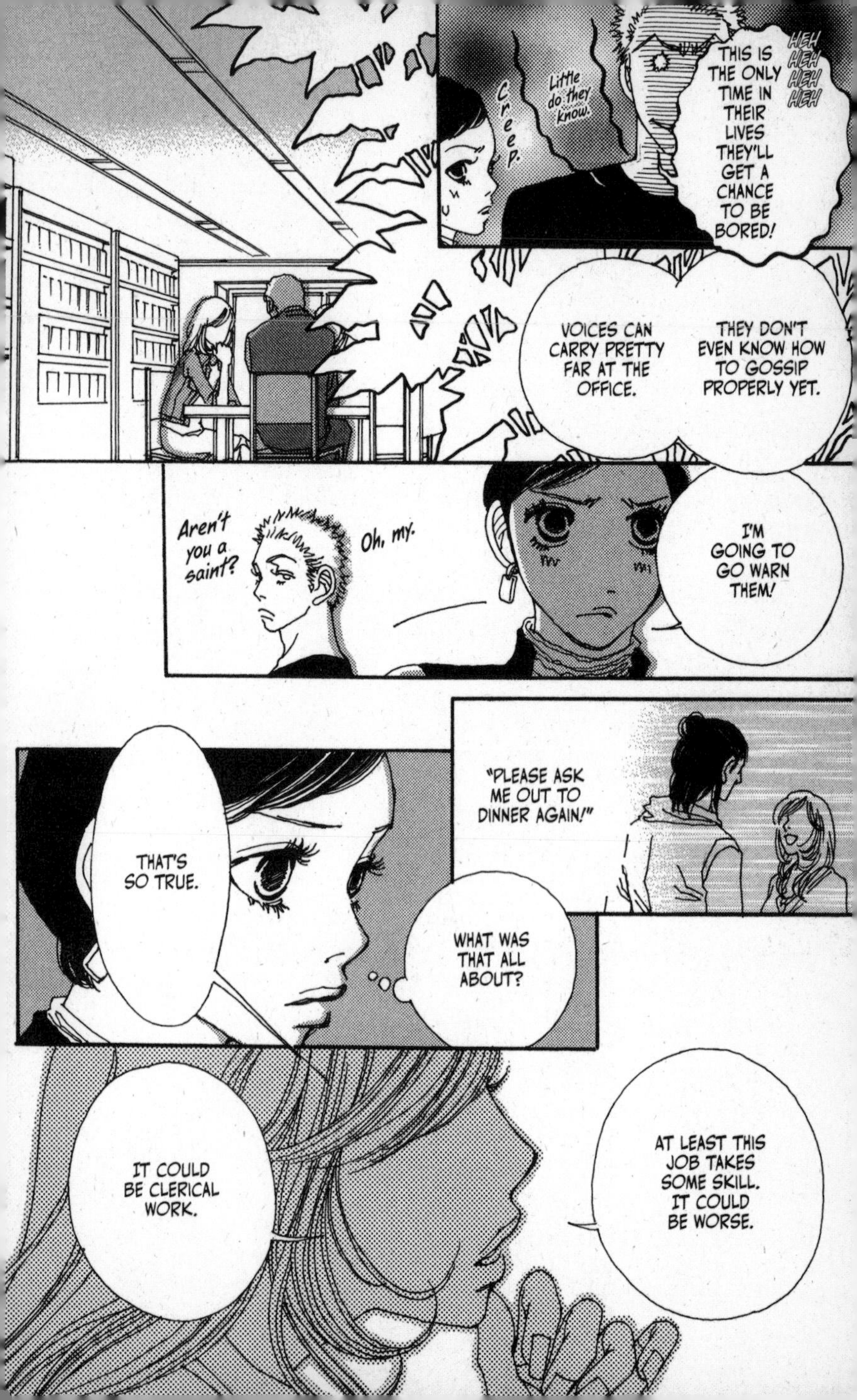
THIS IS THE ONLY TIME IN THEIR LIVES THEY'LL GET A CHANCE TO BE BORED!
HEH HEH HEH HEH
Little do they know.
Creep.
THEY DON'T EVEN KNOW HOW TO GOSSIP PROPERLY YET.
VOICES CAN CARRY PRETTY FAR AT THE OFFICE.
I'M GOING TO GO WARN THEM!
Oh, my.
Aren't you a saint?
"PLEASE ASK ME OUT TO DINNER AGAIN!"
WHAT WAS THAT ALL ABOUT?
THAT'S SO TRUE.
AT LEAST THIS JOB TAKES SOME SKILL. IT COULD BE WORSE.
IT COULD BE CLERICAL WORK.

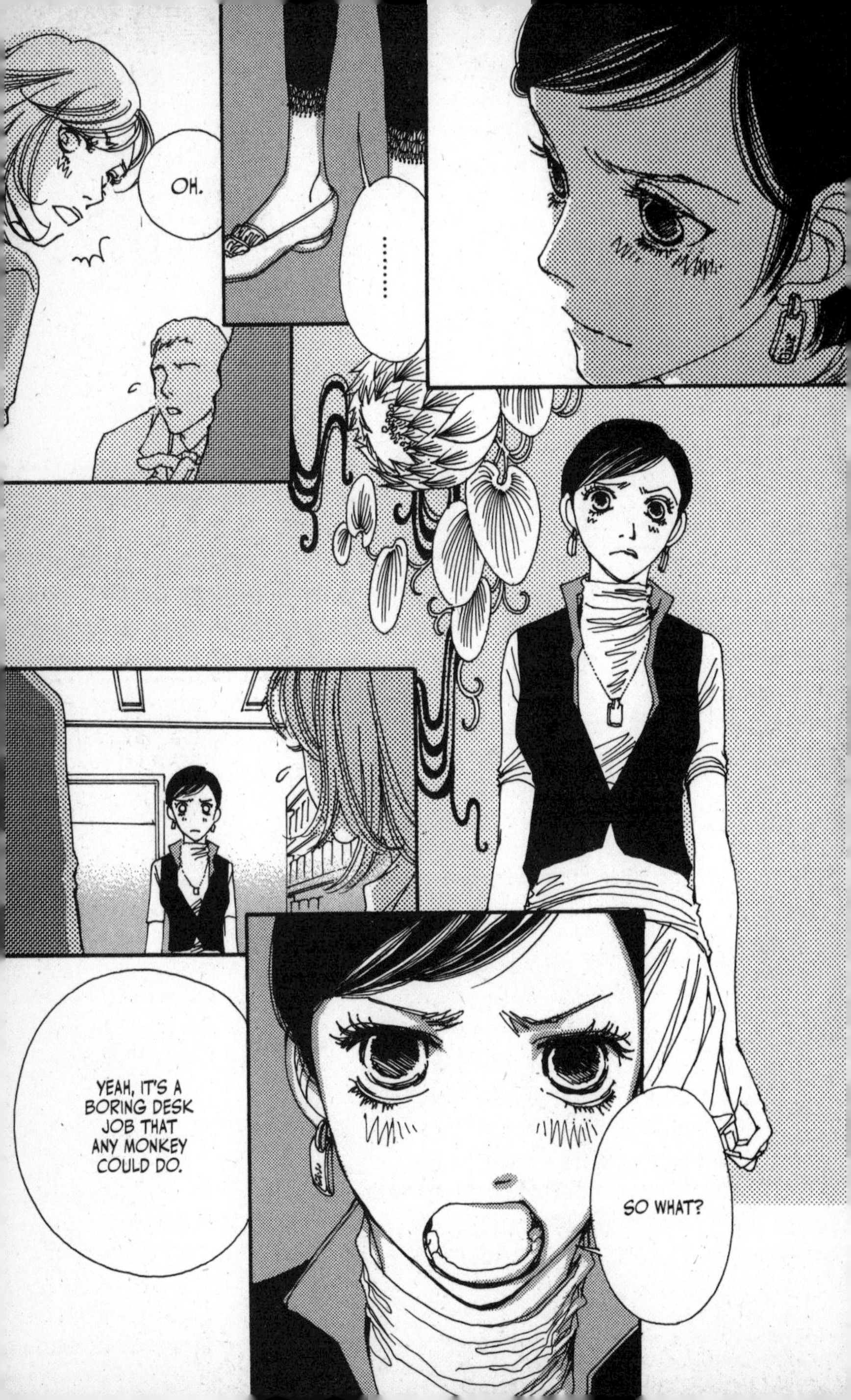
……
OH.
YEAH, IT'S A BORING DESK JOB THAT ANY MONKEY COULD DO.
SO WHAT?

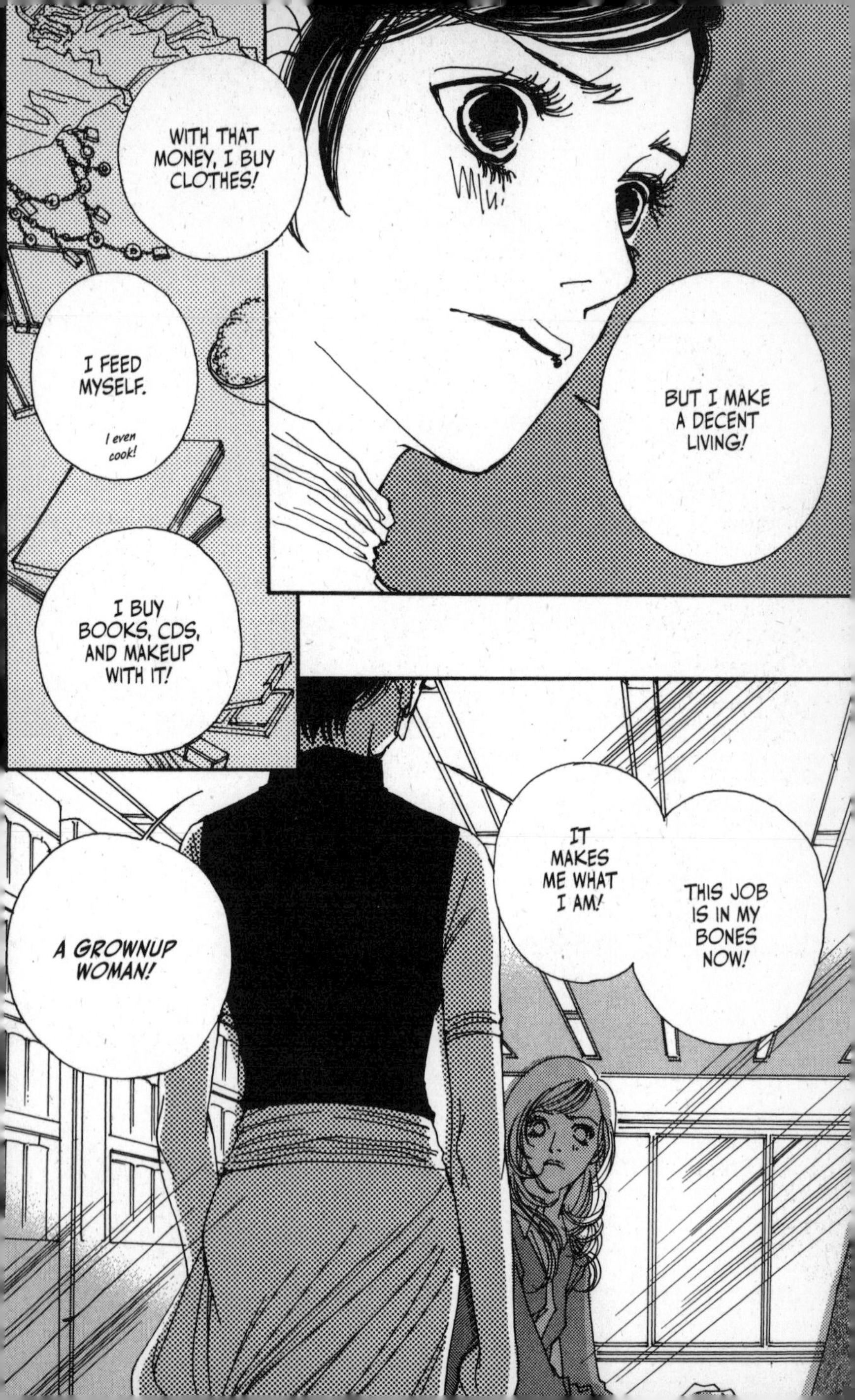
BUT I MAKE A DECENT LIVING!
WITH THAT MONEY, I BUY CLOTHES!
I FEED MYSELF.
I even cook!
I BUY BOOKS, CDS, AND MAKEUP WITH IT!
THIS JOB IS IN MY BONES NOW!
IT MAKES ME WHAT I AM!
A GROWNUP WOMAN!

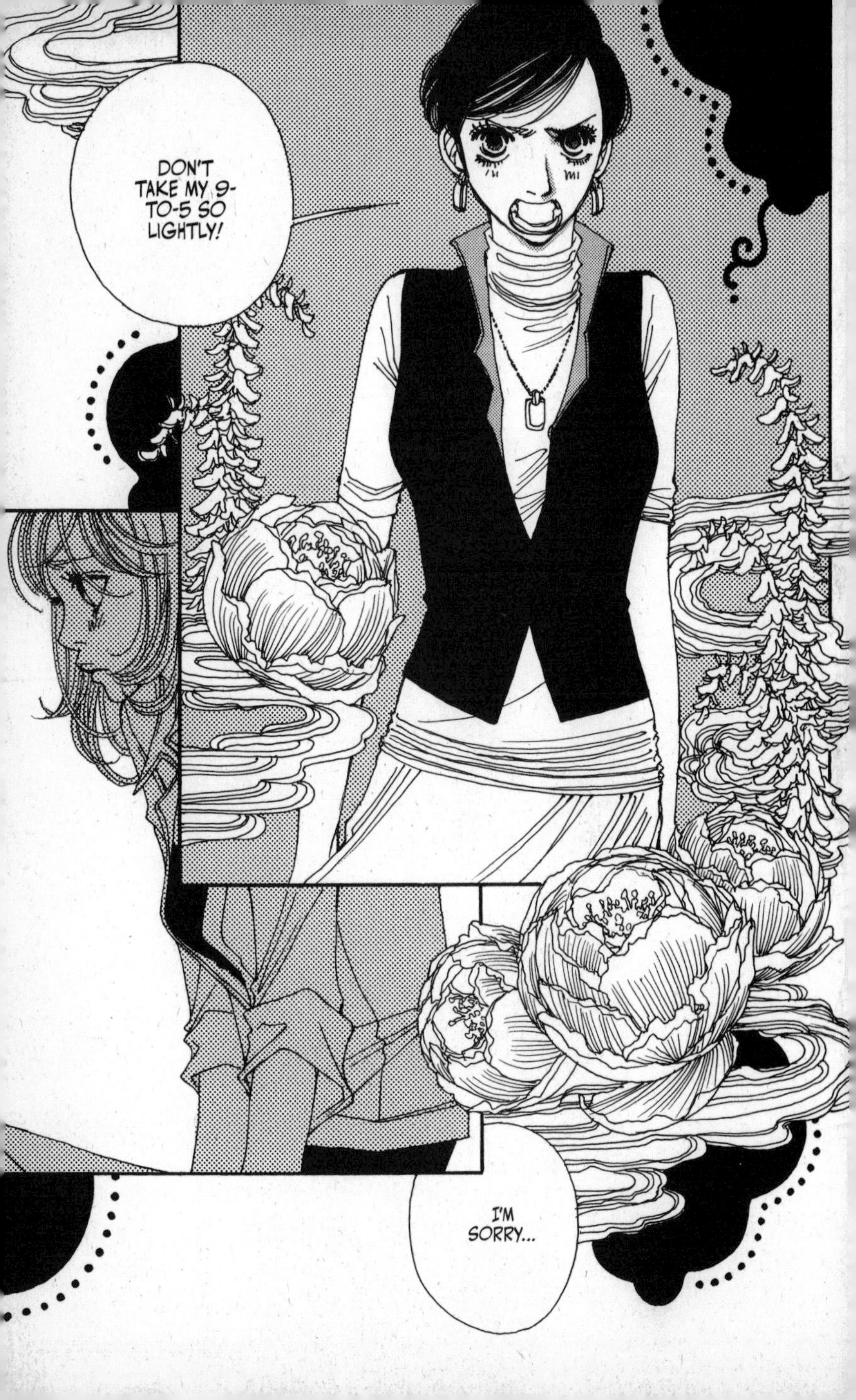
DON'T TAKE MY 9-TO-5 SO LIGHTLY!
I'M SORRY...

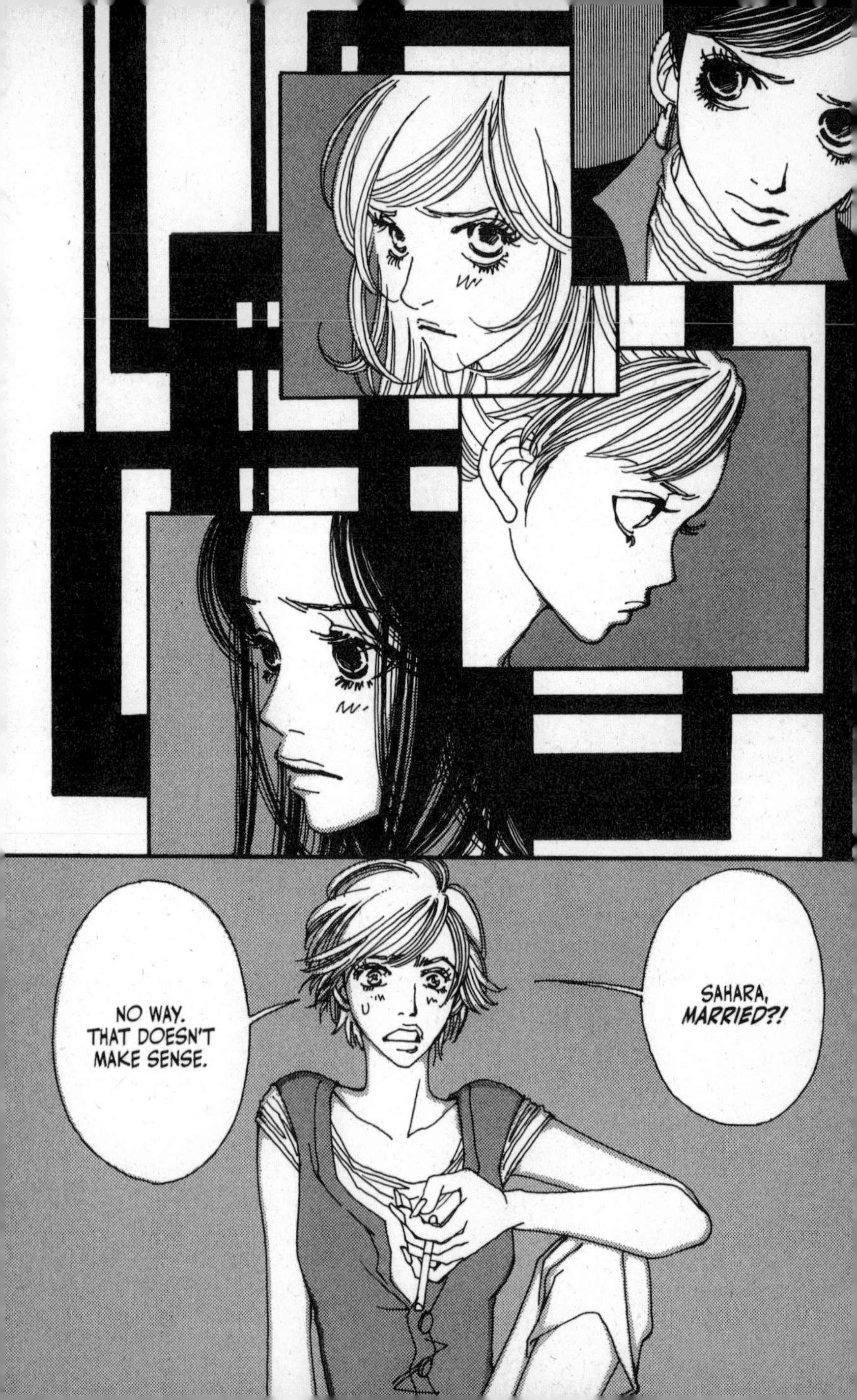
SAHARA, MARRIED?!
NO WAY. THAT DOESN'T MAKE SENSE.

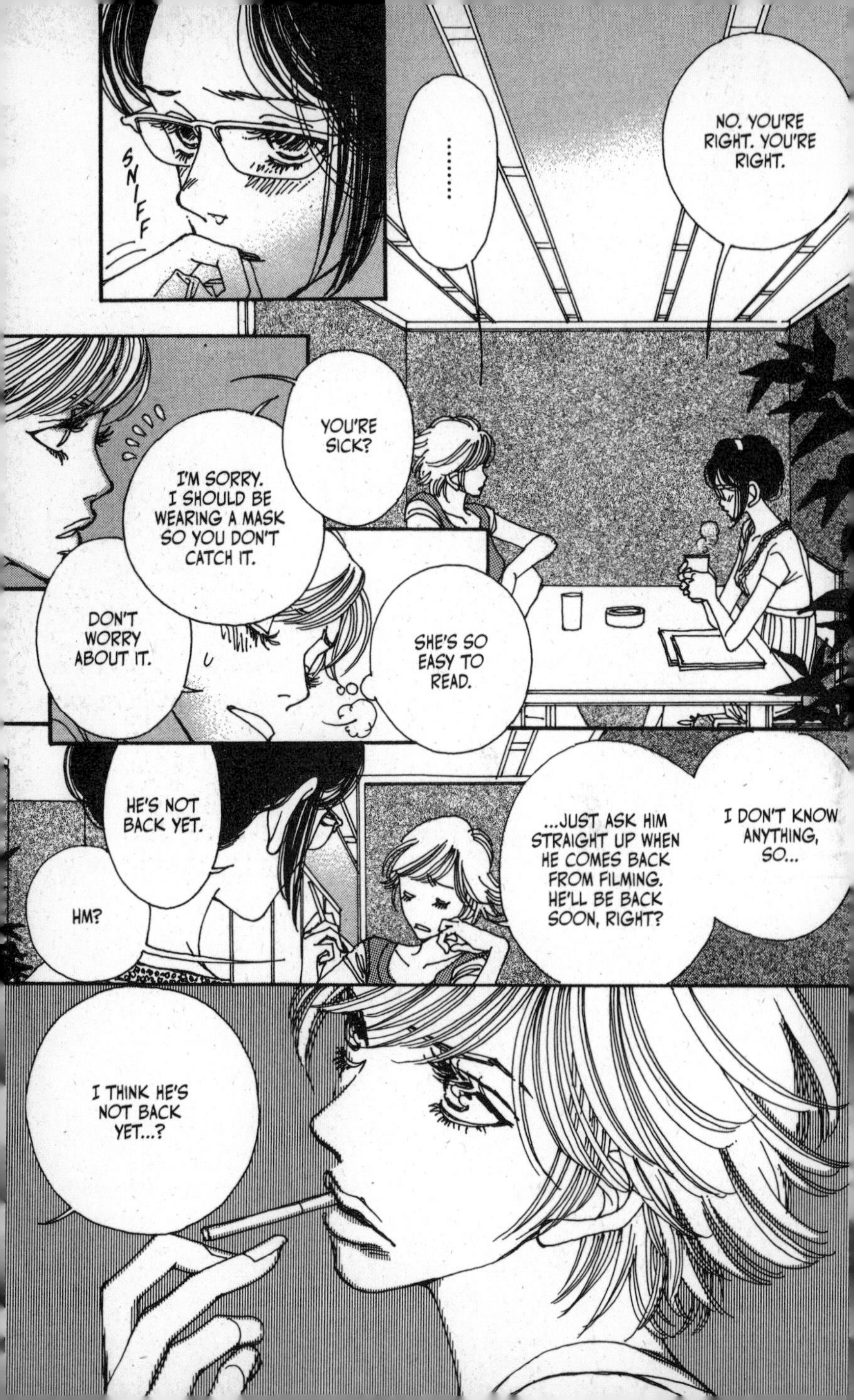
NO. YOU'RE RIGHT. YOU'RE RIGHT.
......
SNIFF
YOU'RE SICK?
I'M SORRY. I SHOULD BE WEARING A MASK SO YOU DON'T CATCH IT.
SHE'S SO EASY TO READ.
DON'T WORRY ABOUT IT.
I DON'T KNOW ANYTHING, SO...
...JUST ASK HIM STRAIGHT UP WHEN HE COMES BACK FROM FILMING. HE'LL BE BACK SOON, RIGHT?
HE'S NOT BACK YET.
HM?
I THINK HE'S NOT BACK YET...?

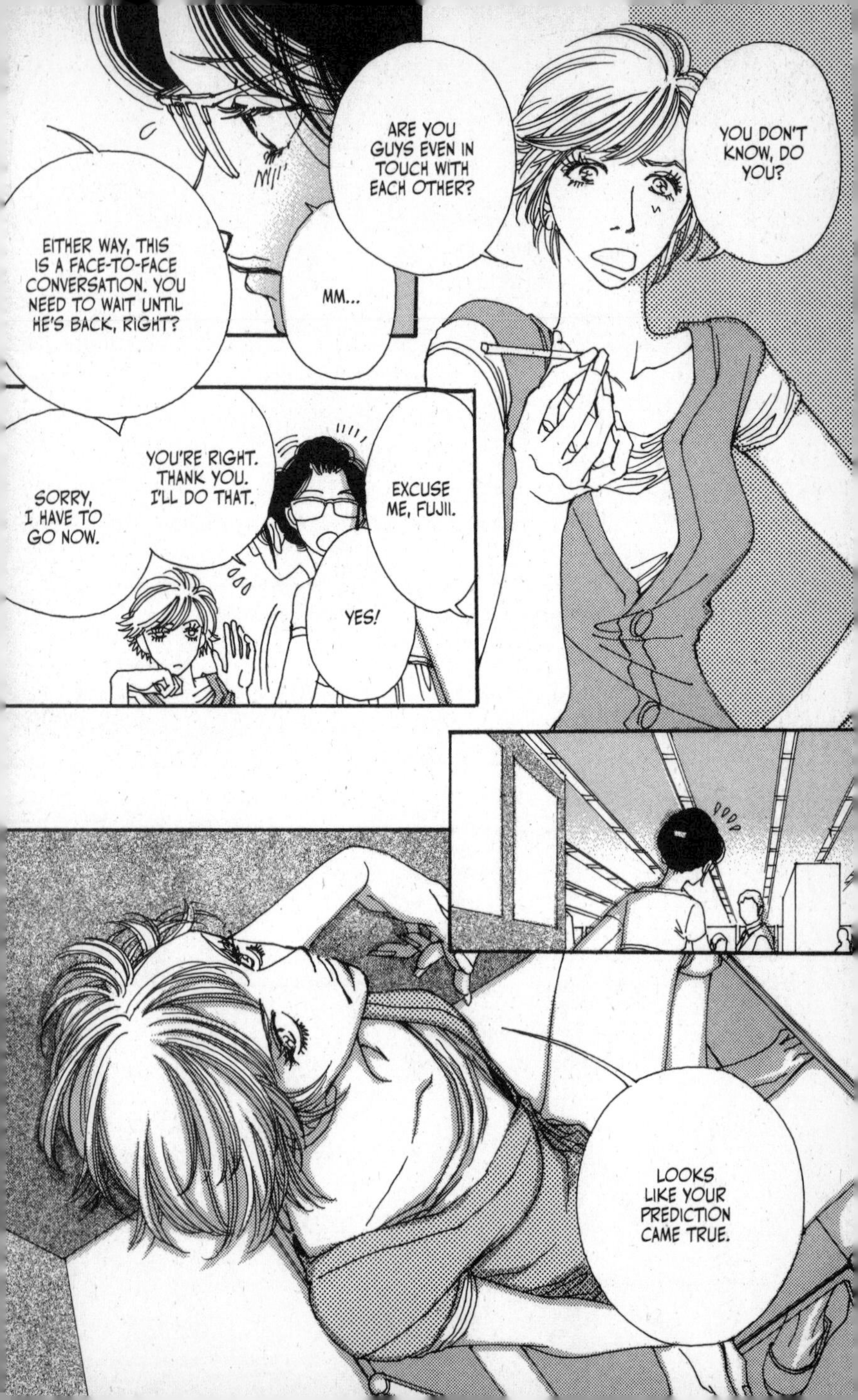
YOU DON'T KNOW, DO YOU?
ARE YOU GUYS EVEN IN TOUCH WITH EACH OTHER?
MM...
EITHER WAY, THIS IS A FACE-TO-FACE CONVERSATION. YOU NEED TO WAIT UNTIL HE'S BACK, RIGHT?
EXCUSE ME, FUJII.
YES!
YOU'RE RIGHT. THANK YOU. I'LL DO THAT.
SORRY, I HAVE TO GO NOW.
LOOKS LIKE YOUR PREDICTION CAME TRUE.

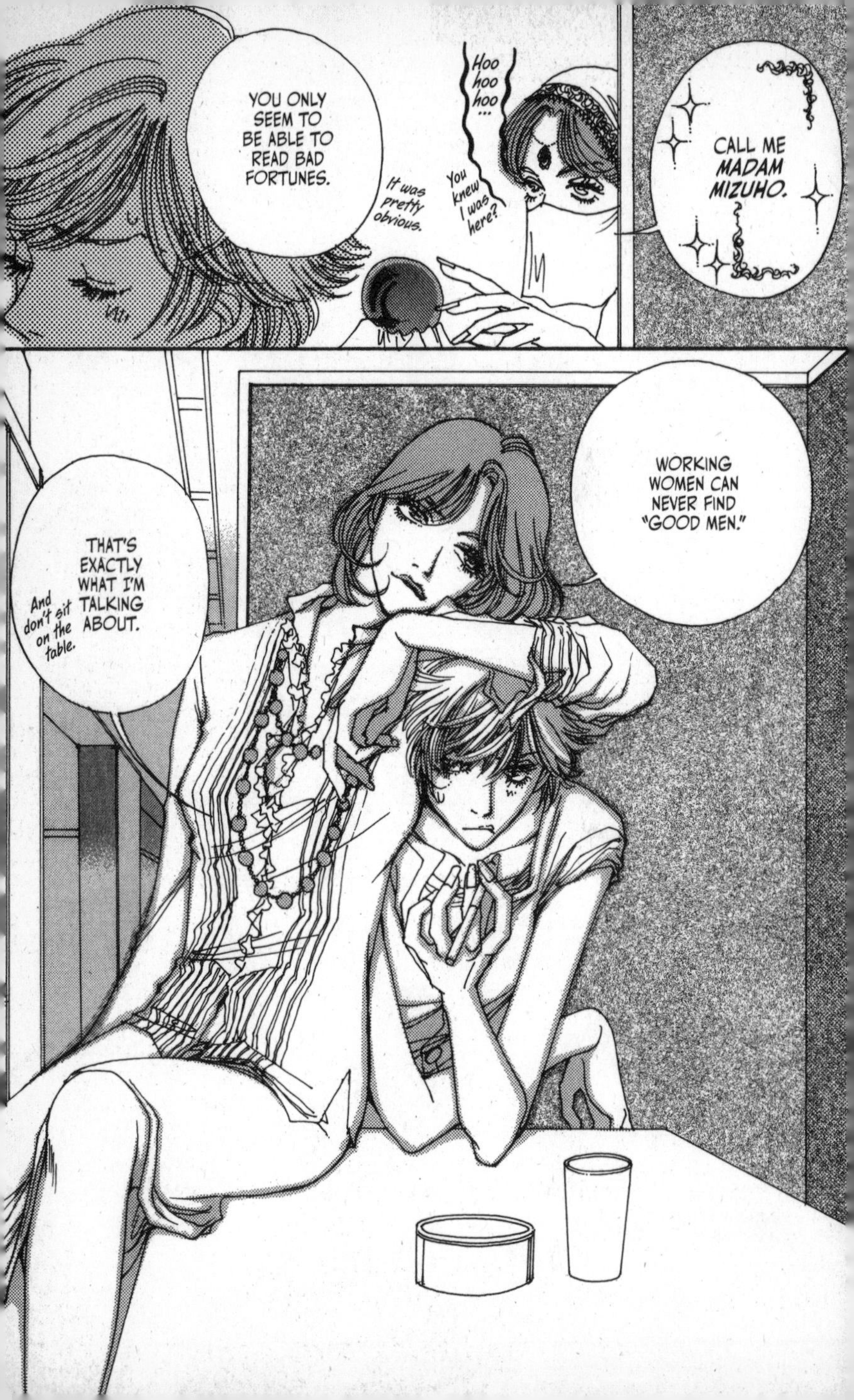

CALL ME MADAM MIZUHO.
Hoo hoo hoo...
You knew I was here?
It was pretty obvious.
YOU ONLY SEEM TO BE ABLE TO READ BAD FORTUNES.
WORKING WOMEN CAN NEVER FIND "GOOD MEN."
THAT'S EXACTLY WHAT I'M TALKING ABOUT.
And don't sit on the table.

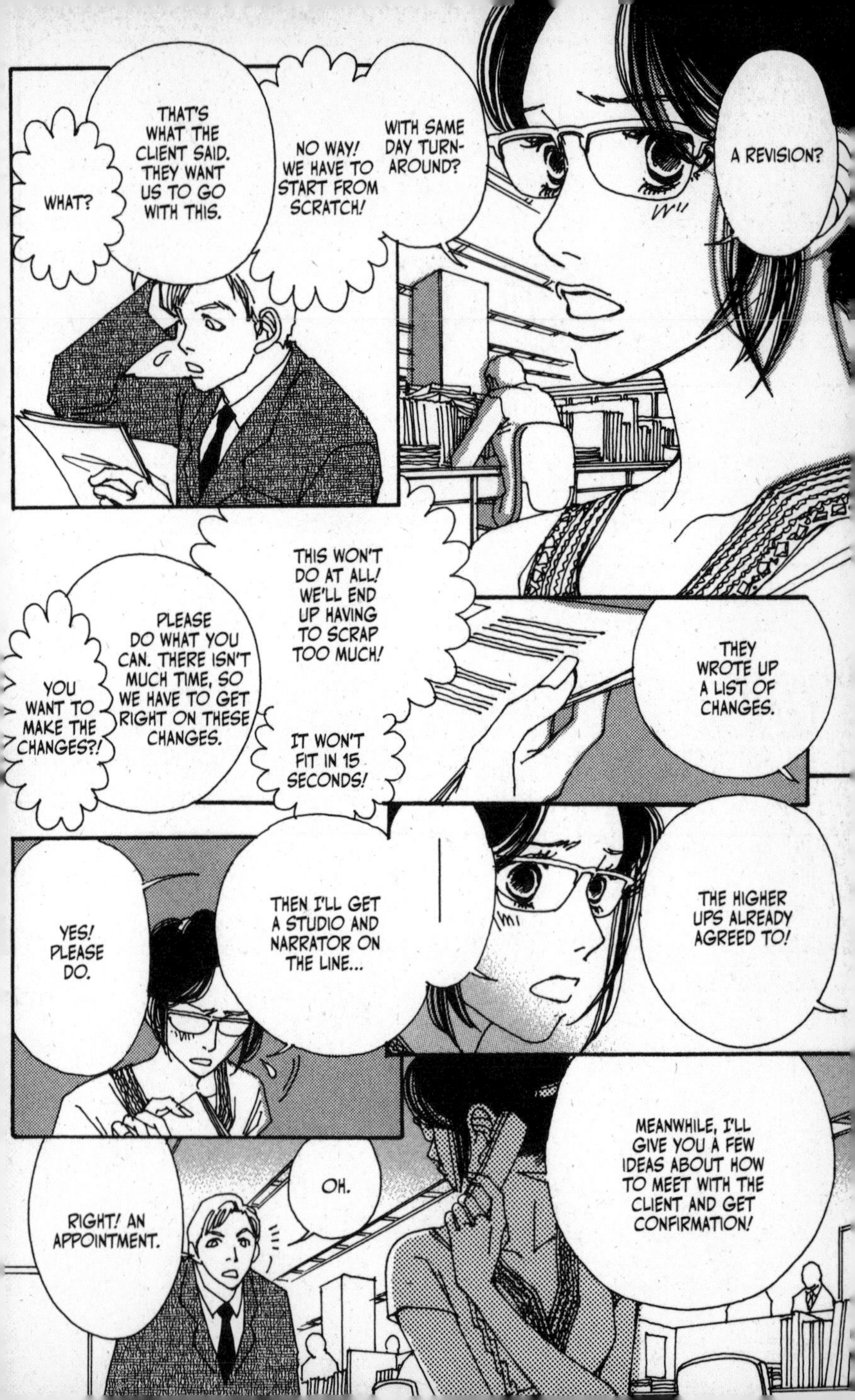
A REVISION?
WITH SAME DAY TURN-AROUND?
NO WAY! WE HAVE TO START FROM SCRATCH!
THAT'S WHAT THE CLIENT SAID. THEY WANT US TO GO WITH THIS.
WHAT?
THEY WROTE UP A LIST OF CHANGES.
THIS WON'T DO AT ALL! WE'LL END UP HAVING TO SCRAP TOO MUCH!
IT WON'T FIT IN 15 SECONDS!
PLEASE DO WHAT YOU CAN. THERE ISN'T MUCH TIME, SO WE HAVE TO GET RIGHT ON THESE CHANGES.
YOU WANT TO MAKE THE CHANGES?!
THE HIGHER UPS ALREADY AGREED TO!
THEN I'LL GET A STUDIO AND NARRATOR ON THE LINE...
YES! PLEASE DO.
MEANWHILE, I'LL GIVE YOU A FEW IDEAS ABOUT HOW TO MEET WITH THE CLIENT AND GET CONFIRMATION!
OH.
RIGHT! AN APPOINTMENT.

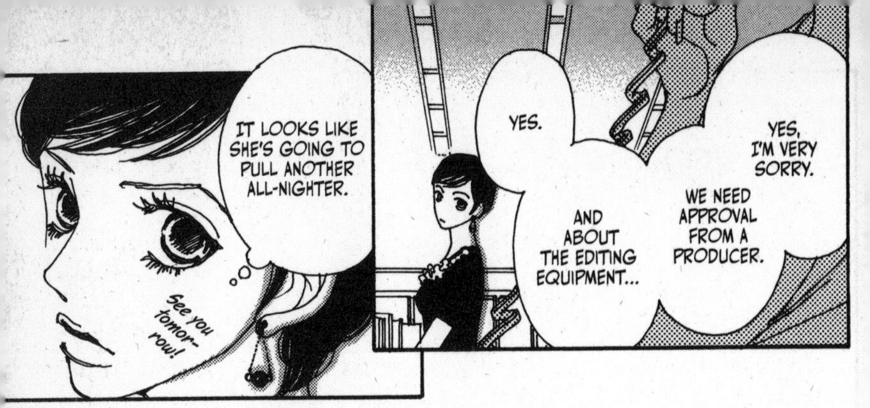
YES, I'M VERY SORRY.
WE NEED APPROVAL FROM A PRODUCER.
YES.
AND ABOUT THE EDITING EQUIPMENT...
IT LOOKS LIKE SHE'S GOING TO PULL ANOTHER ALL-NIGHTER.
See you tomorrow!

*Revision
To change a commercial that's already aired because of the product's sales or the client's circumstances, etc. Depending on the nature of the change, the commercial might need to be re-filmed. Other changes might include re-editing or altering the narration. Revisions are common, and a commercial can often be revised three or four times.

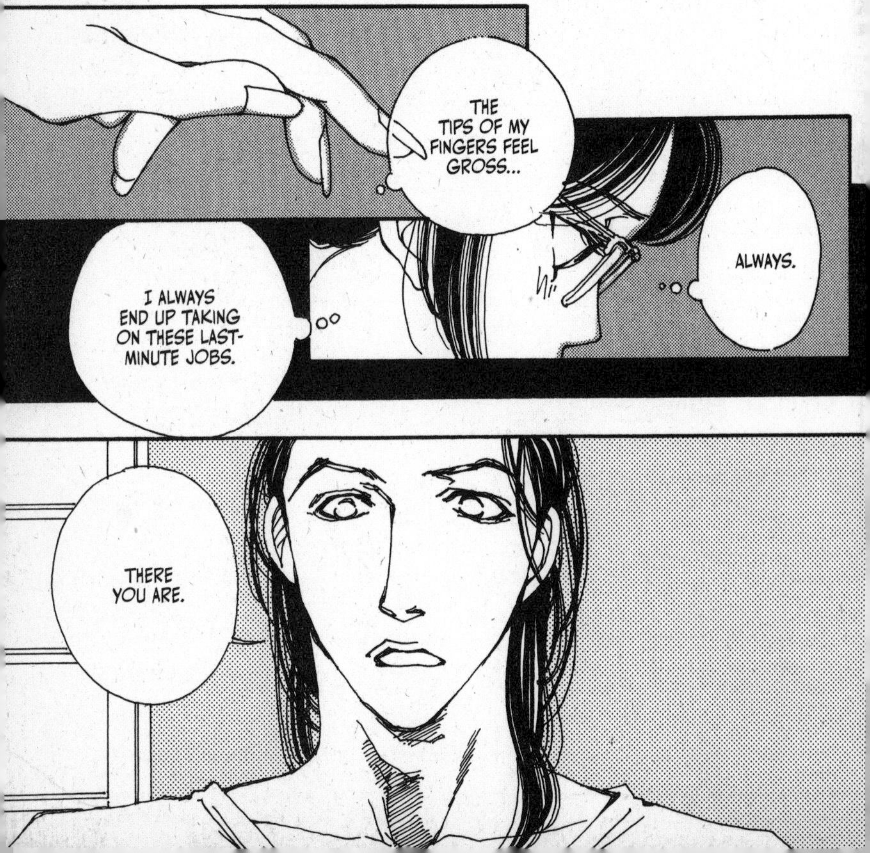
THE TIPS OF MY FINGERS FEEL GROSS...
ALWAYS.
I ALWAYS END UP TAKING ON THESE LAST-MINUTE JOBS.
THERE YOU ARE.

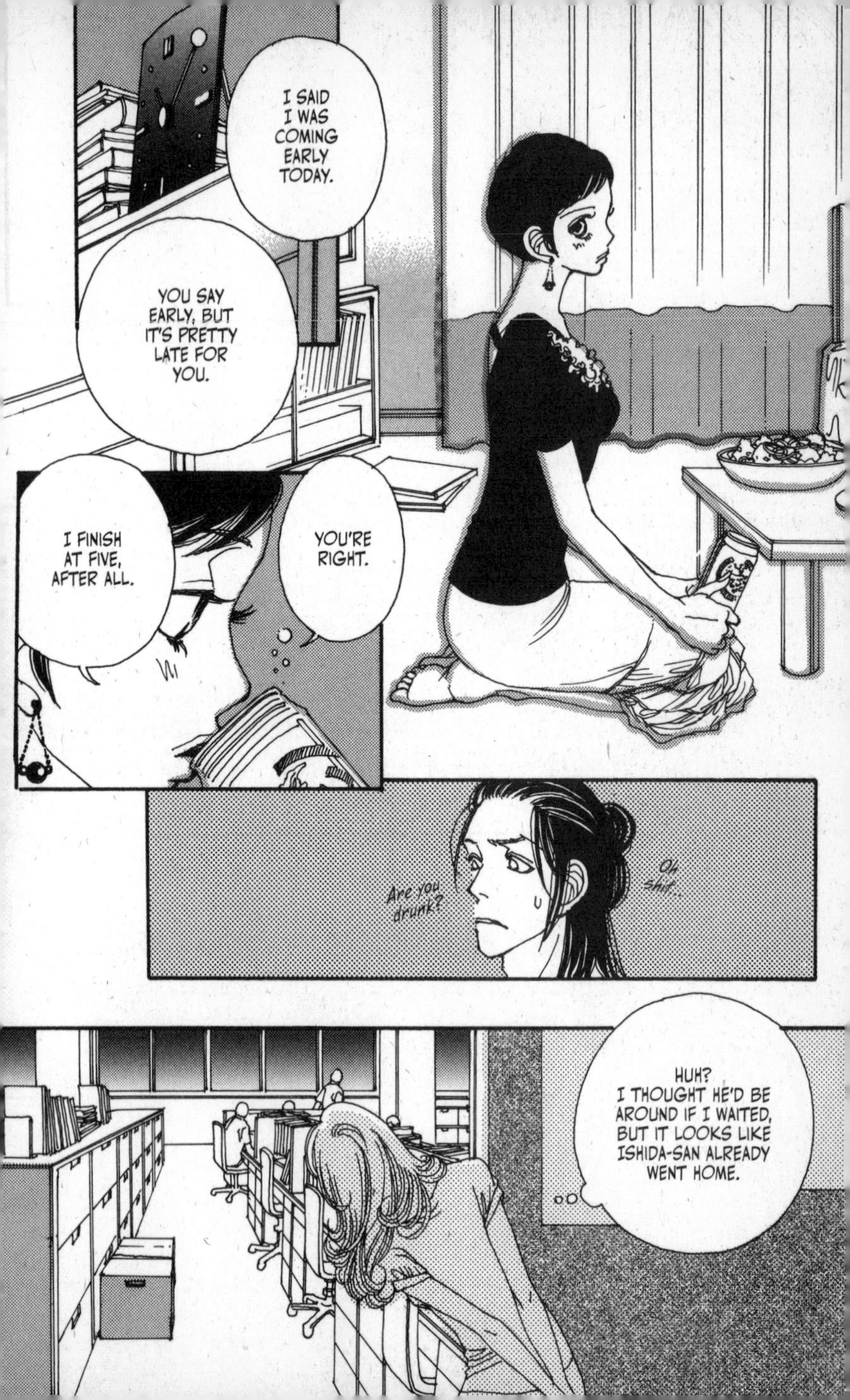
I SAID I WAS COMING EARLY TODAY.
YOU SAY EARLY, BUT IT'S PRETTY LATE FOR YOU.
YOU'RE RIGHT.
I FINISH AT FIVE, AFTER ALL.
Oh shit...
Are you drunk?
HUH? I THOUGHT HE'D BE AROUND IF I WAITED, BUT IT LOOKS LIKE ISHIDA-SAN ALREADY WENT HOME.

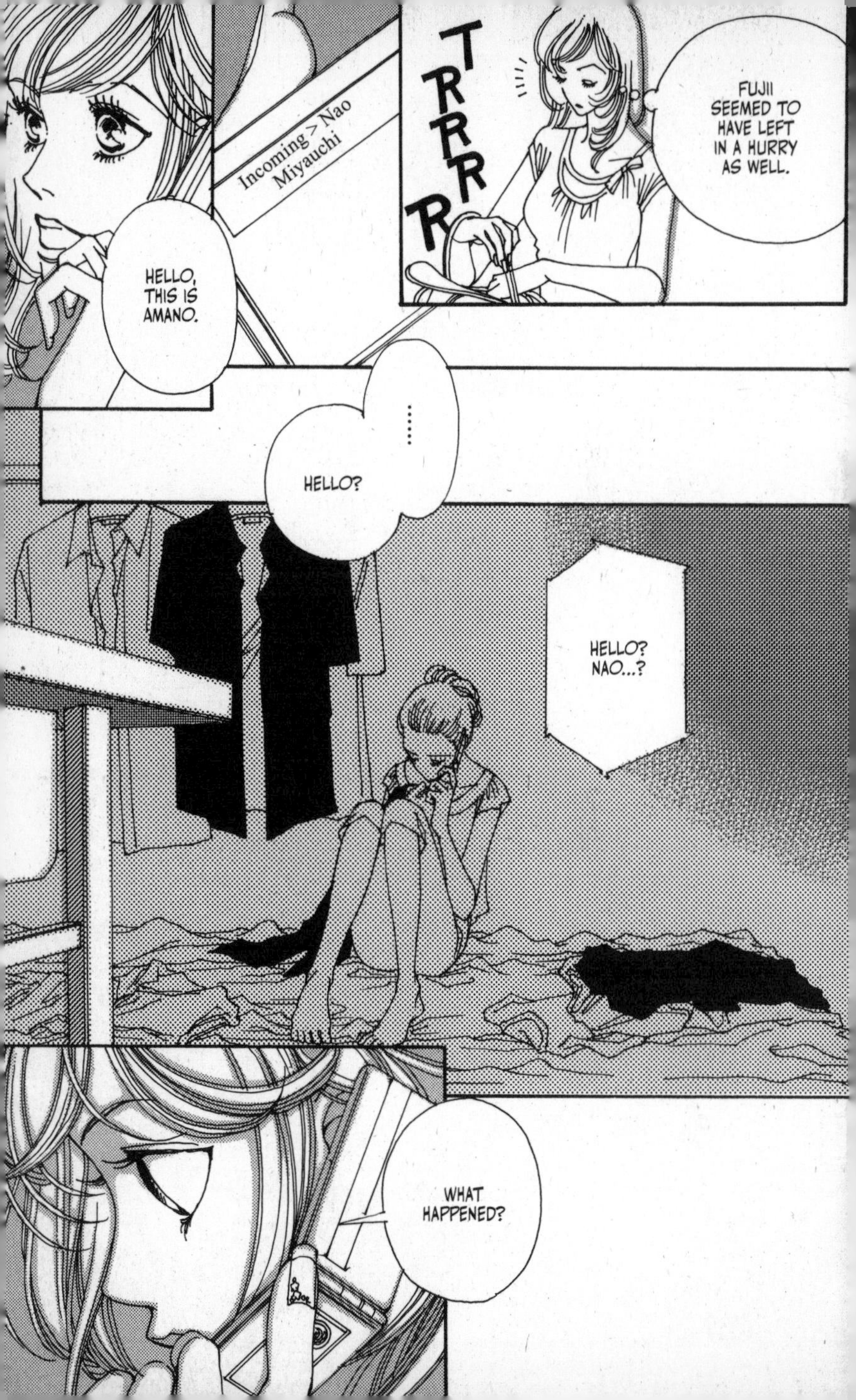
FUJII SEEMED TO HAVE LEFT IN A HURRY AS WELL.
TRRRR
Incoming > Nao Miyauchi
HELLO, THIS IS AMANO.
......
HELLO?
HELLO? NAO...?
WHAT HAPPENED?

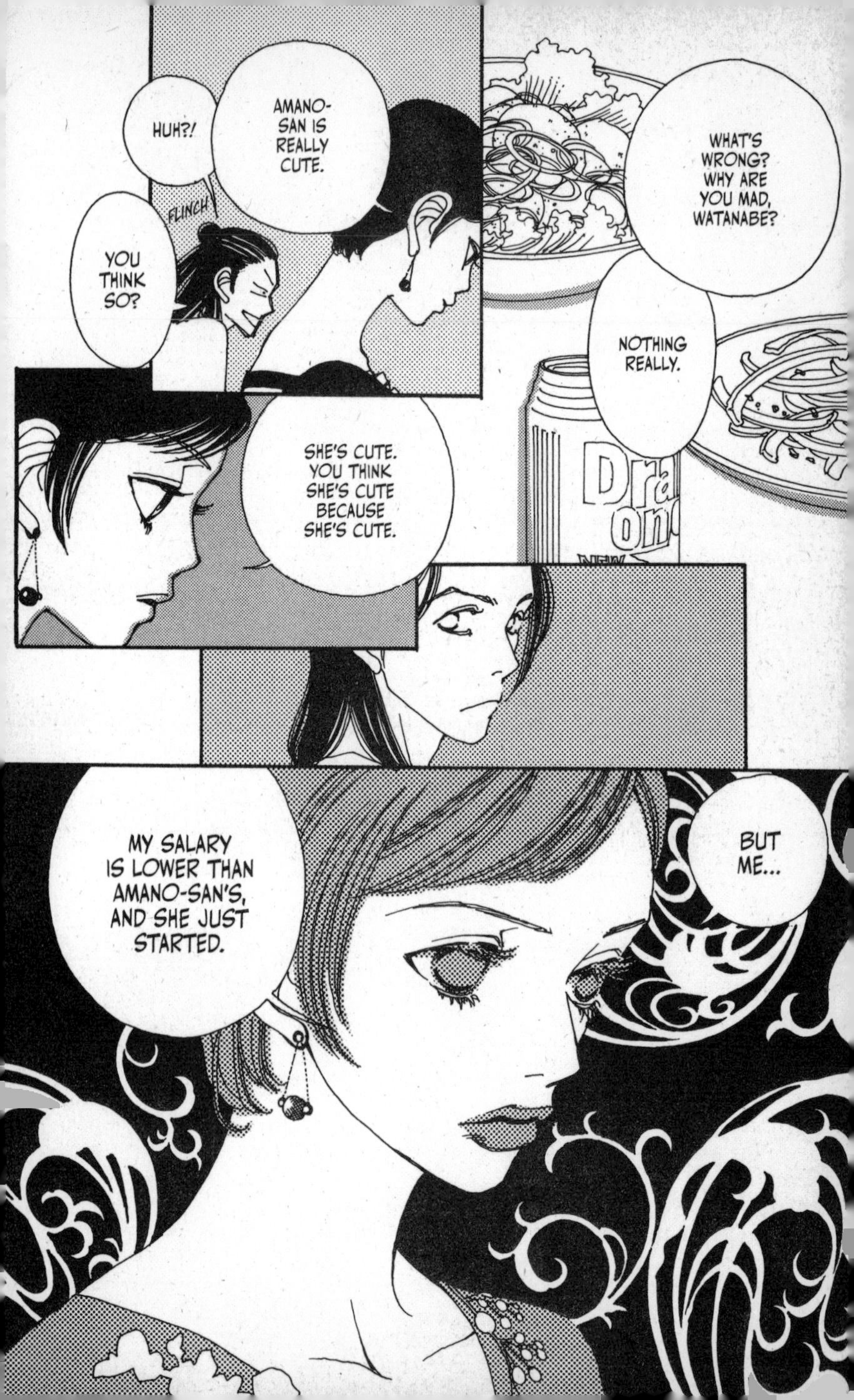
WHAT'S WRONG? WHY ARE YOU MAD, WATANABE?
NOTHING REALLY.
AMANO-SAN IS REALLY CUTE.
HUH?!
FLINCH
YOU THINK SO?
SHE'S CUTE. YOU THINK SHE'S CUTE BECAUSE SHE'S CUTE.
BUT ME...
MY SALARY IS LOWER THAN AMANO-SAN'S, AND SHE JUST STARTED.

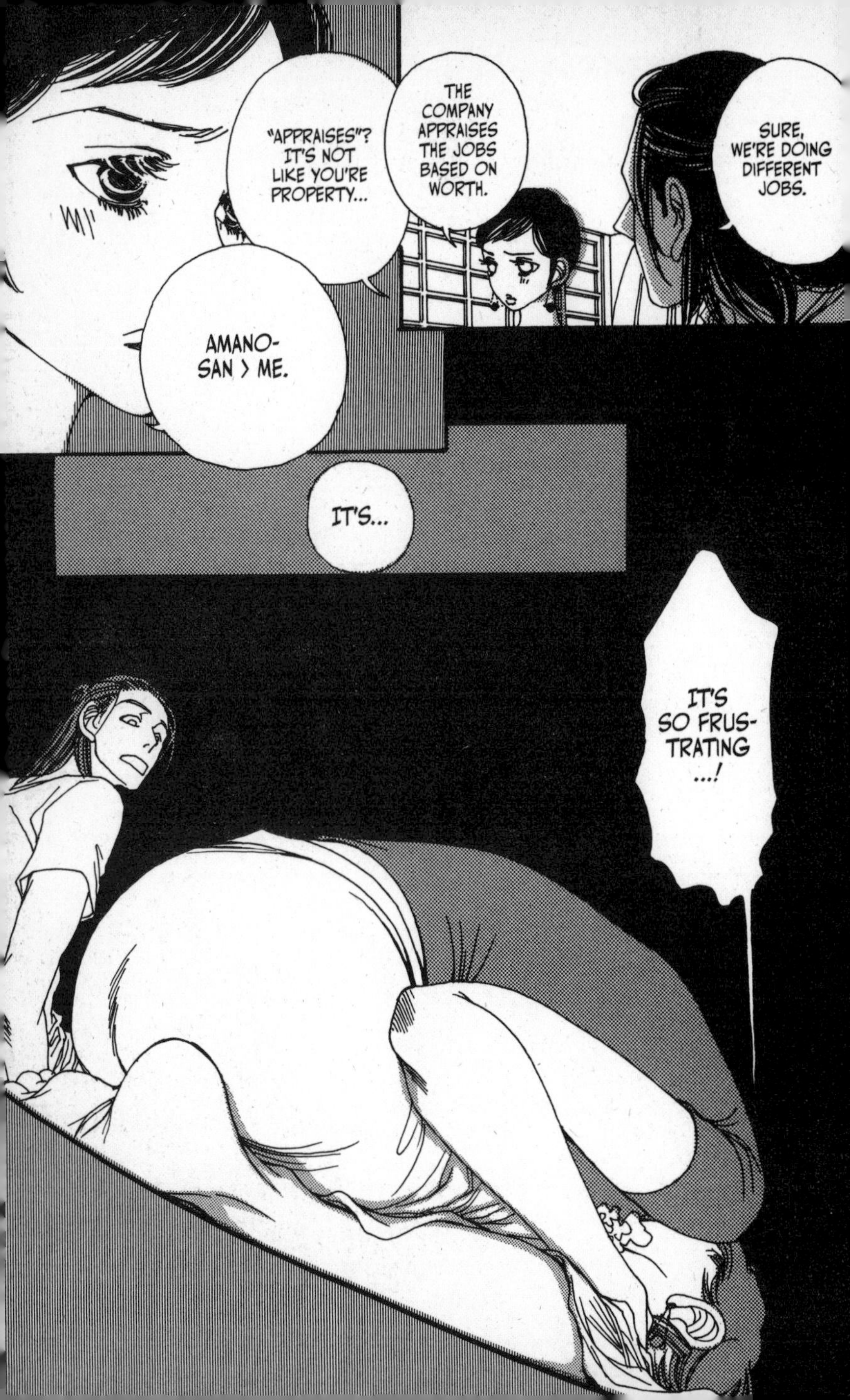
SURE, WE'RE DOING DIFFERENT JOBS.
THE COMPANY APPRAISES THE JOBS BASED ON WORTH.
"APPRAISES"? IT'S NOT LIKE YOU'RE PROPERTY...
AMANO-SAN > ME.
IT'S...
IT'S SO FRUS-TRATING ...!

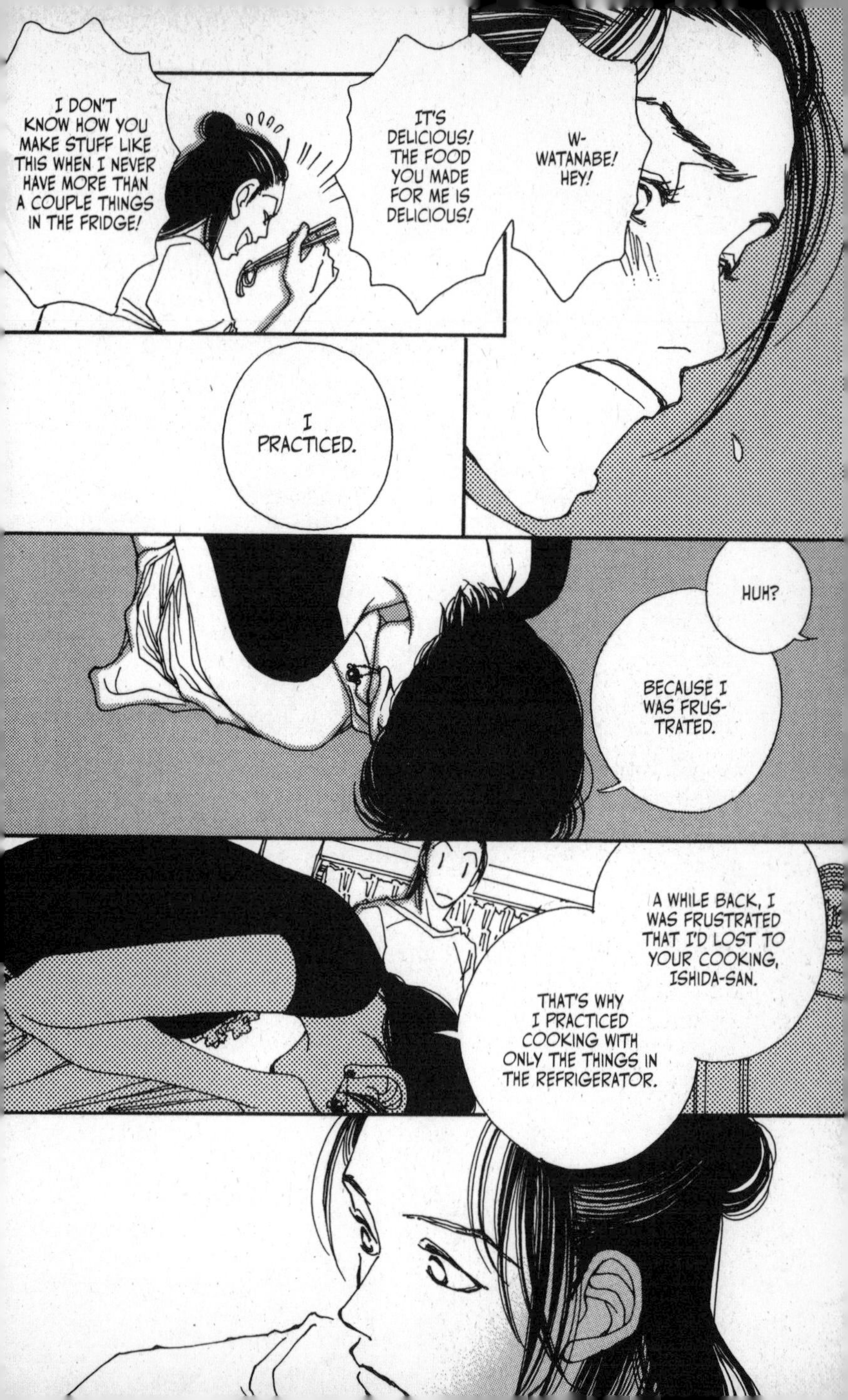
W- WATANABE! HEY!
IT'S DELICIOUS! THE FOOD YOU MADE FOR ME IS DELICIOUS!
I DON'T KNOW HOW YOU MAKE STUFF LIKE THIS WHEN I NEVER HAVE MORE THAN A COUPLE THINGS IN THE FRIDGE!
I PRACTICED.
HUH?
BECAUSE I WAS FRUS- TRATED.
A WHILE BACK, I WAS FRUSTRATED THAT I'D LOST TO YOUR COOKING, ISHIDA-SAN.
THAT'S WHY I PRACTICED COOKING WITH ONLY THE THINGS IN THE REFRIGERATOR.

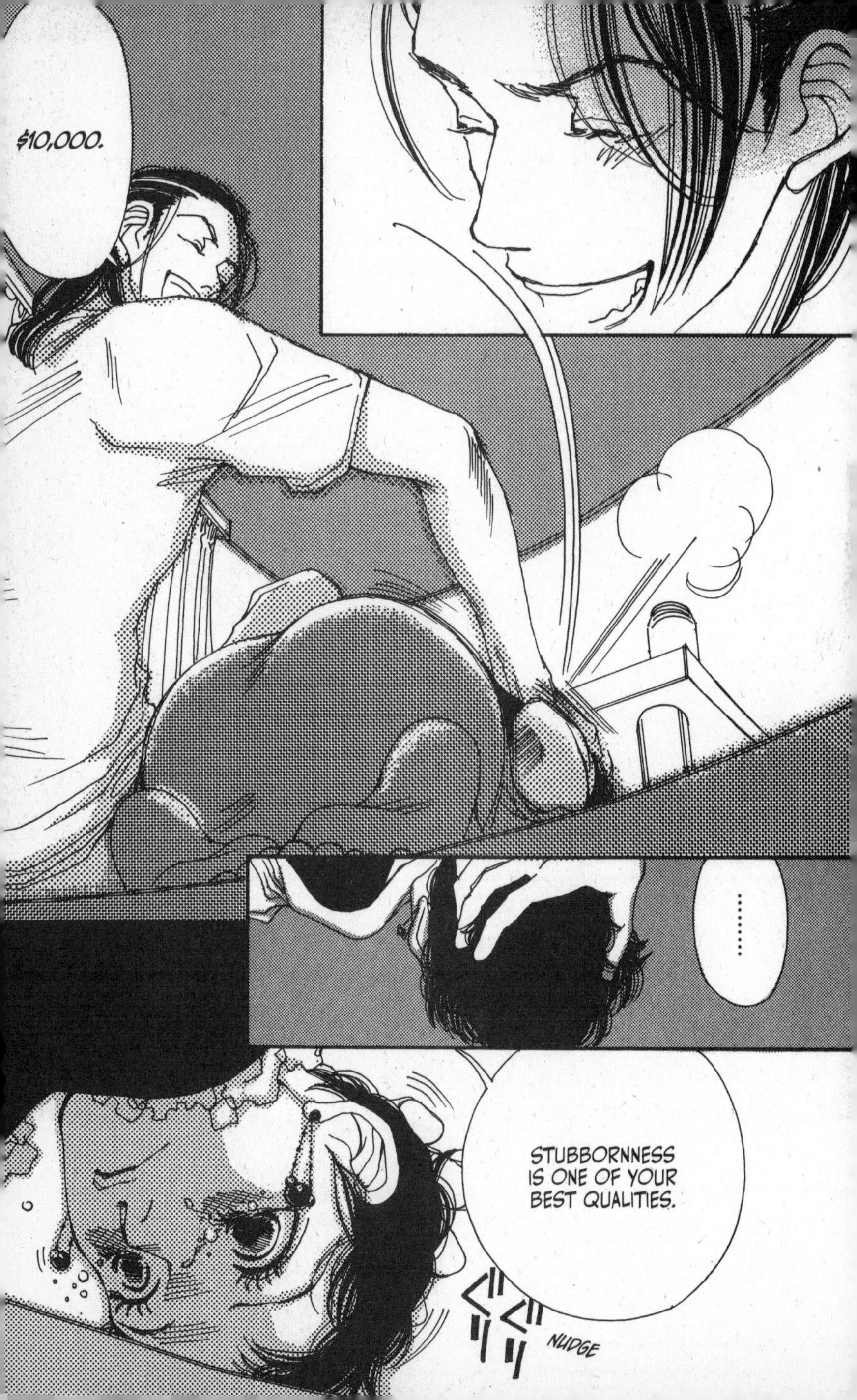
$10,000.
......
STUBBORNNESS IS ONE OF YOUR BEST QUALITIES.
NUDGE

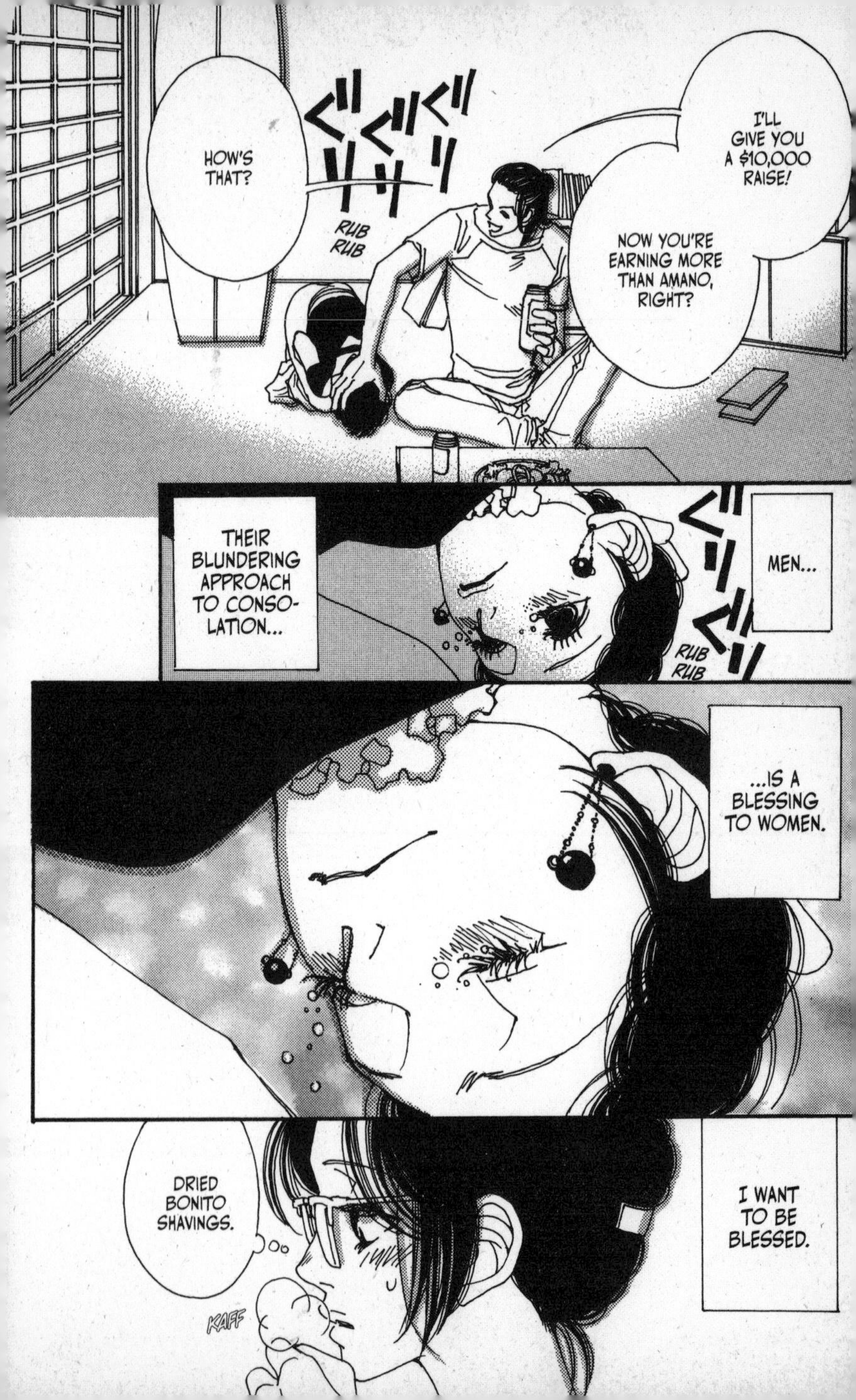

I'LL GIVE YOU A $10,000 RAISE!
NOW YOU'RE EARNING MORE THAN AMANO, RIGHT?
RUB RUB
HOW'S THAT?
MEN...
RUB RUB
THEIR BLUNDERING APPROACH TO CONSO-LATION...
...IS A BLESSING TO WOMEN.
I WANT TO BE BLESSED.
DRIED BONITO SHAVINGS.
KAFF

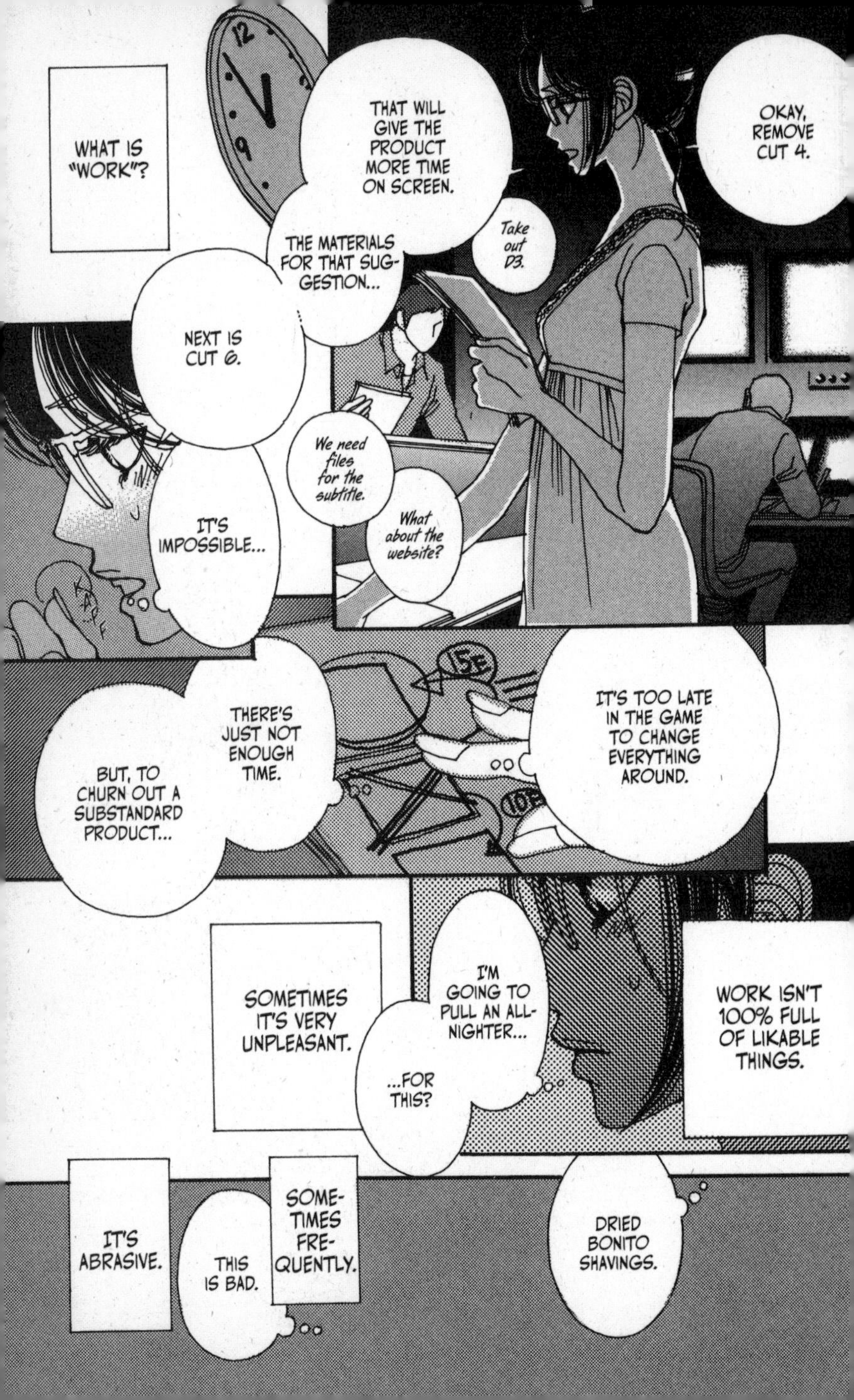
OKAY, REMOVE CUT 4.
THAT WILL GIVE THE PRODUCT MORE TIME ON SCREEN.
Take out D3.
THE MATERIALS FOR THAT SUGGESTION...
We need files for the subtitle.
What about the website?
WHAT IS "WORK"?
NEXT IS CUT 6.
IT'S IMPOSSIBLE...
IT'S TOO LATE IN THE GAME TO CHANGE EVERYTHING AROUND.
THERE'S JUST NOT ENOUGH TIME.
BUT, TO CHURN OUT A SUBSTANDARD PRODUCT...
WORK ISN'T 100% FULL OF LIKABLE THINGS.
I'M GOING TO PULL AN ALL-NIGHTER...
...FOR THIS?
SOMETIMES IT'S VERY UNPLEASANT.
DRIED BONITO SHAVINGS.
SOMETIMES FREQUENTLY.
THIS IS BAD.
IT'S ABRASIVE.

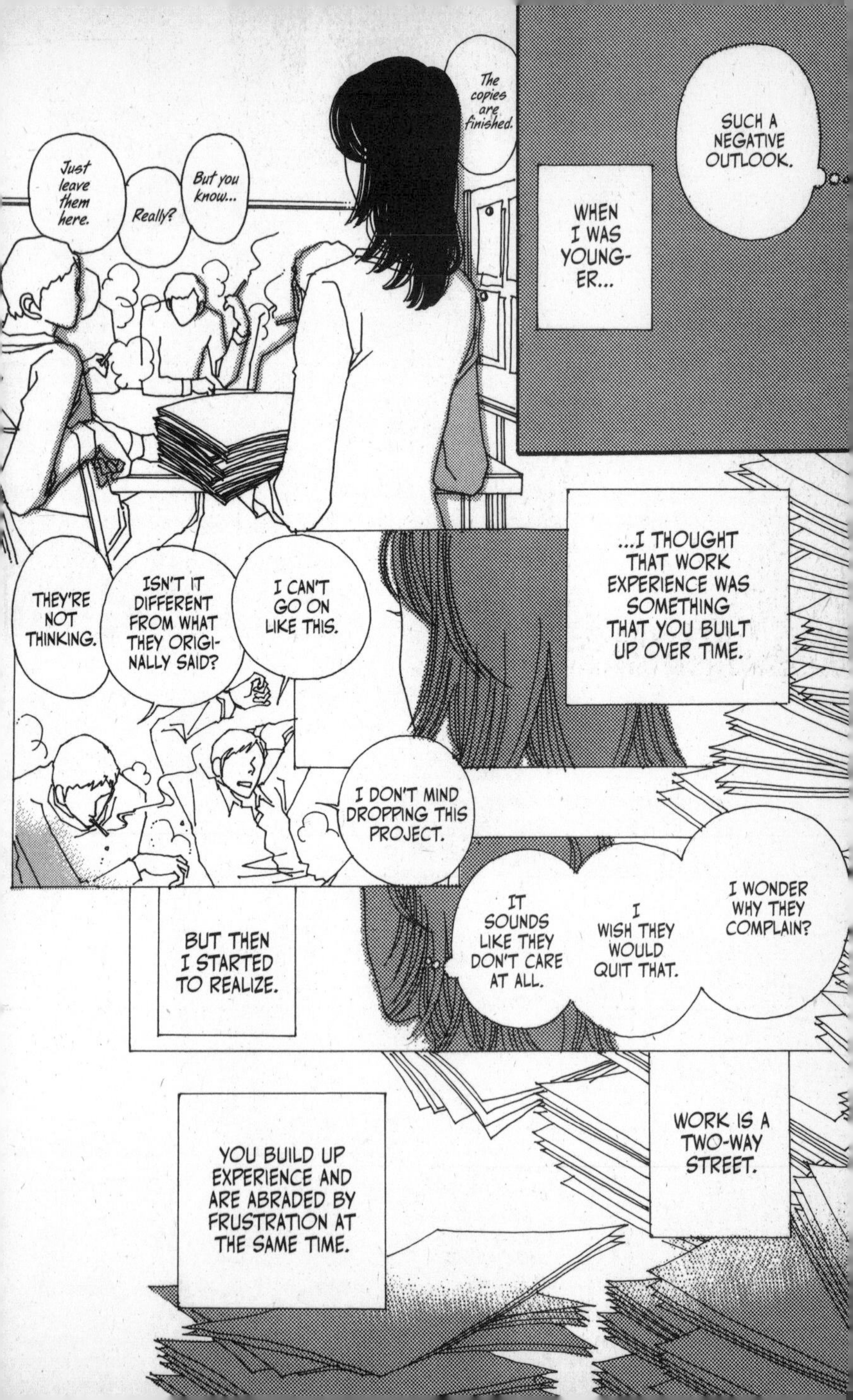
SUCH A NEGATIVE OUTLOOK.
WHEN I WAS YOUNG-ER...
The copies are finished.
But you know...
Really?
Just leave them here.
...I THOUGHT THAT WORK EXPERIENCE WAS SOMETHING THAT YOU BUILT UP OVER TIME.
I CAN'T GO ON LIKE THIS.
ISN'T IT DIFFERENT FROM WHAT THEY ORIGI-NALLY SAID?
THEY'RE NOT THINKING.
I DON'T MIND DROPPING THIS PROJECT.
I WONDER WHY THEY COMPLAIN?
I WISH THEY WOULD QUIT THAT.
IT SOUNDS LIKE THEY DON'T CARE AT ALL.
BUT THEN I STARTED TO REALIZE.
WORK IS A TWO-WAY STREET.
YOU BUILD UP EXPERIENCE AND ARE ABRADED BY FRUSTRATION AT THE SAME TIME.

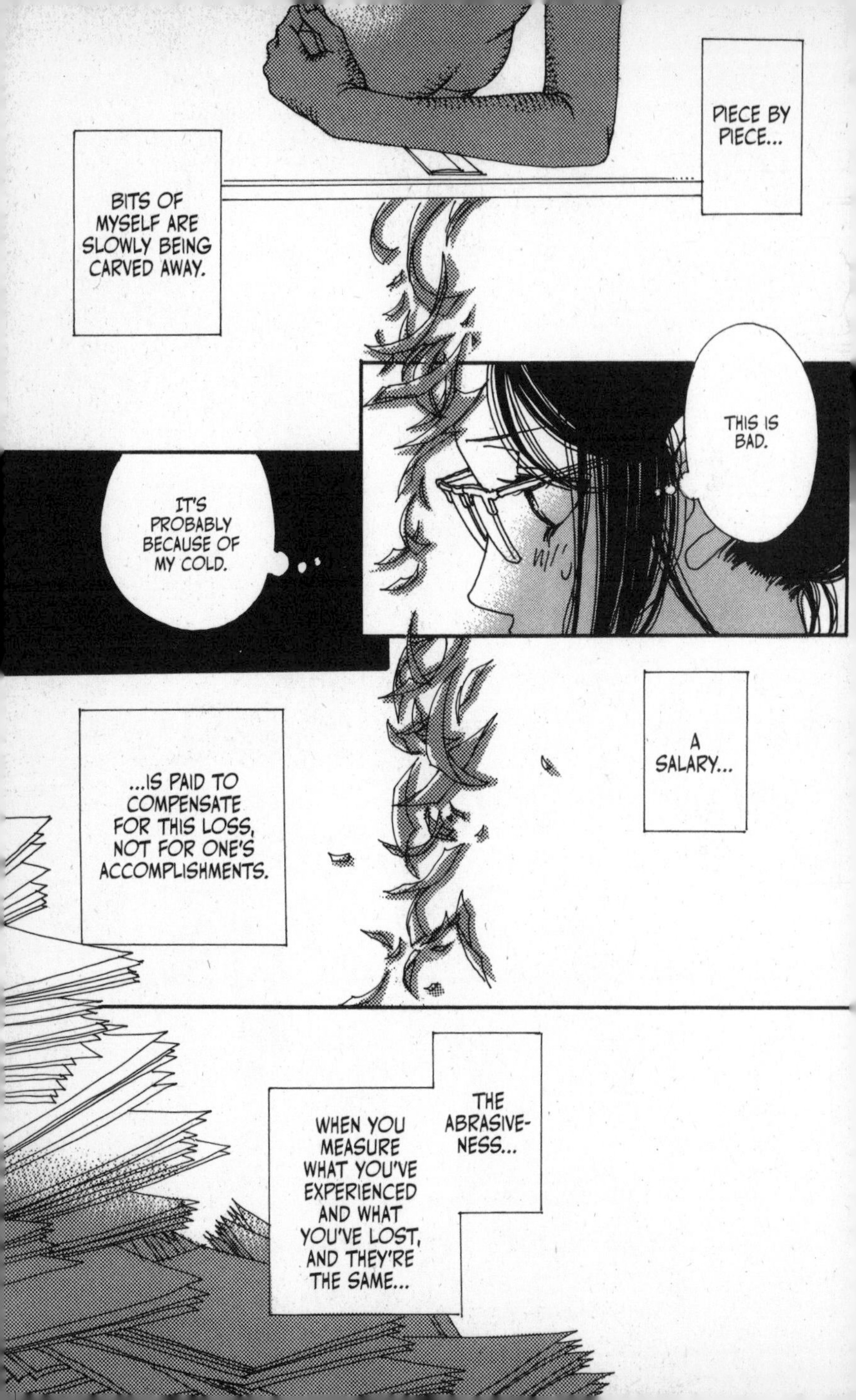
PIECE BY PIECE...
BITS OF MYSELF ARE SLOWLY BEING CARVED AWAY.
THIS IS BAD.
IT'S PROBABLY BECAUSE OF MY COLD.
A SALARY...
...IS PAID TO COMPENSATE FOR THIS LOSS, NOT FOR ONE'S ACCOMPLISHMENTS.
THE ABRASIVE-NESS...
WHEN YOU MEASURE WHAT YOU'VE EXPERIENCED AND WHAT YOU'VE LOST, AND THEY'RE THE SAME...

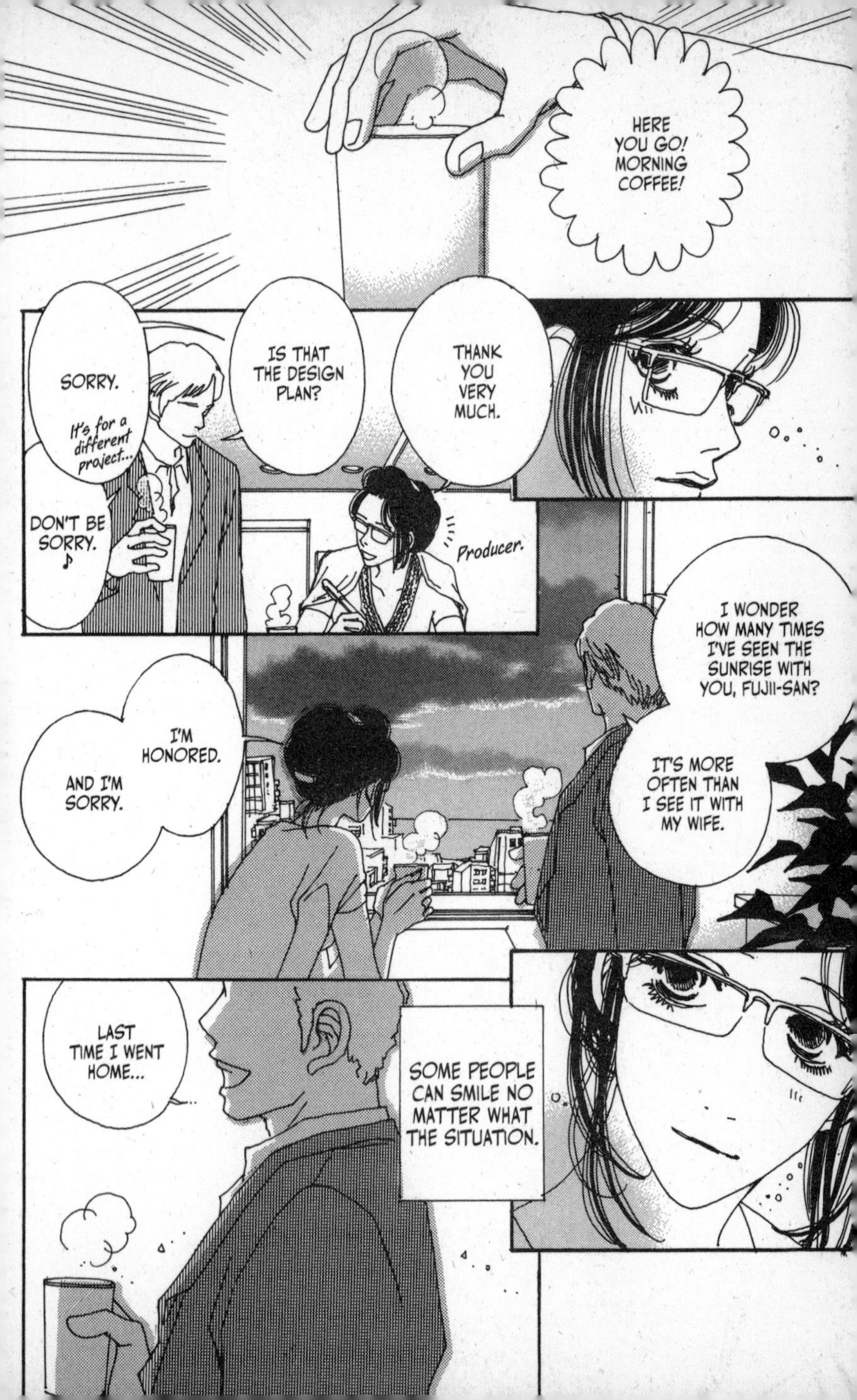
HERE YOU GO! MORNING COFFEE!
THANK YOU VERY MUCH.
Producer.
IS THAT THE DESIGN PLAN?
SORRY.
It's for a different project...
DON'T BE SORRY. ♪
I WONDER HOW MANY TIMES I'VE SEEN THE SUNRISE WITH YOU, FUJII-SAN?
IT'S MORE OFTEN THAN I SEE IT WITH MY WIFE.
I'M HONORED.
AND I'M SORRY.
SOME PEOPLE CAN SMILE NO MATTER WHAT THE SITUATION.
LAST TIME I WENT HOME...

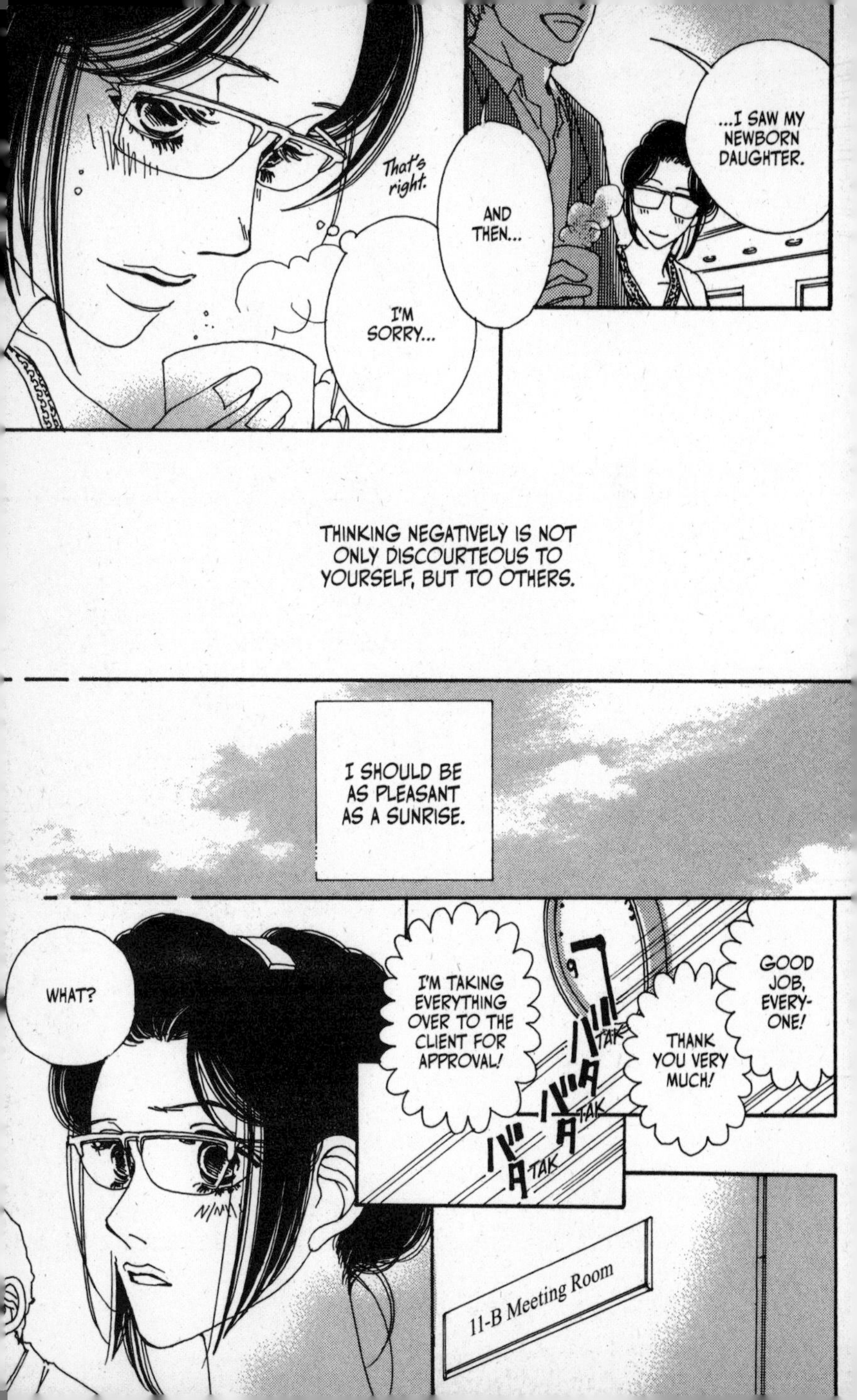
...I SAW MY NEWBORN DAUGHTER.
AND THEN...
That's right.
I'M SORRY...
THINKING NEGATIVELY IS NOT ONLY DISCOURTEOUS TO YOURSELF, BUT TO OTHERS.
I SHOULD BE AS PLEASANT AS A SUNRISE.
GOOD JOB, EVERY-ONE!
THANK YOU VERY MUCH!
I'M TAKING EVERYTHING OVER TO THE CLIENT FOR APPROVAL!
TAK
TAK
TAK
11-B Meeting Room
WHAT?

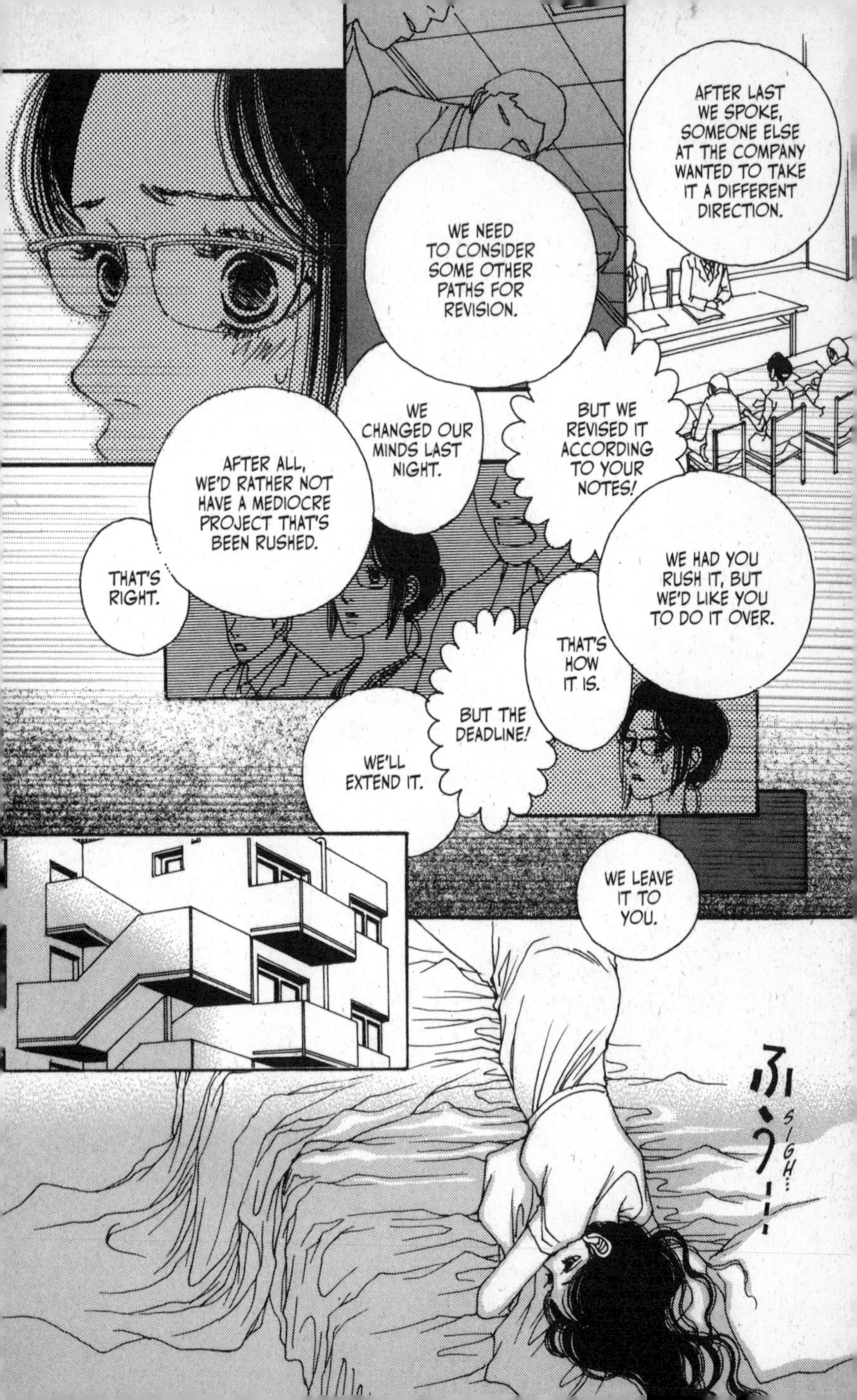
AFTER LAST WE SPOKE, SOMEONE ELSE AT THE COMPANY WANTED TO TAKE IT A DIFFERENT DIRECTION.
WE NEED TO CONSIDER SOME OTHER PATHS FOR REVISION.
BUT WE REVISED IT ACCORDING TO YOUR NOTES!
WE CHANGED OUR MINDS LAST NIGHT.
AFTER ALL, WE'D RATHER NOT HAVE A MEDIOCRE PROJECT THAT'S BEEN RUSHED.
THAT'S RIGHT.
WE HAD YOU RUSH IT, BUT WE'D LIKE YOU TO DO IT OVER.
THAT'S HOW IT IS.
BUT THE DEADLINE!
WE'LL EXTEND IT.
WE LEAVE IT TO YOU.
ふう
SIGH...

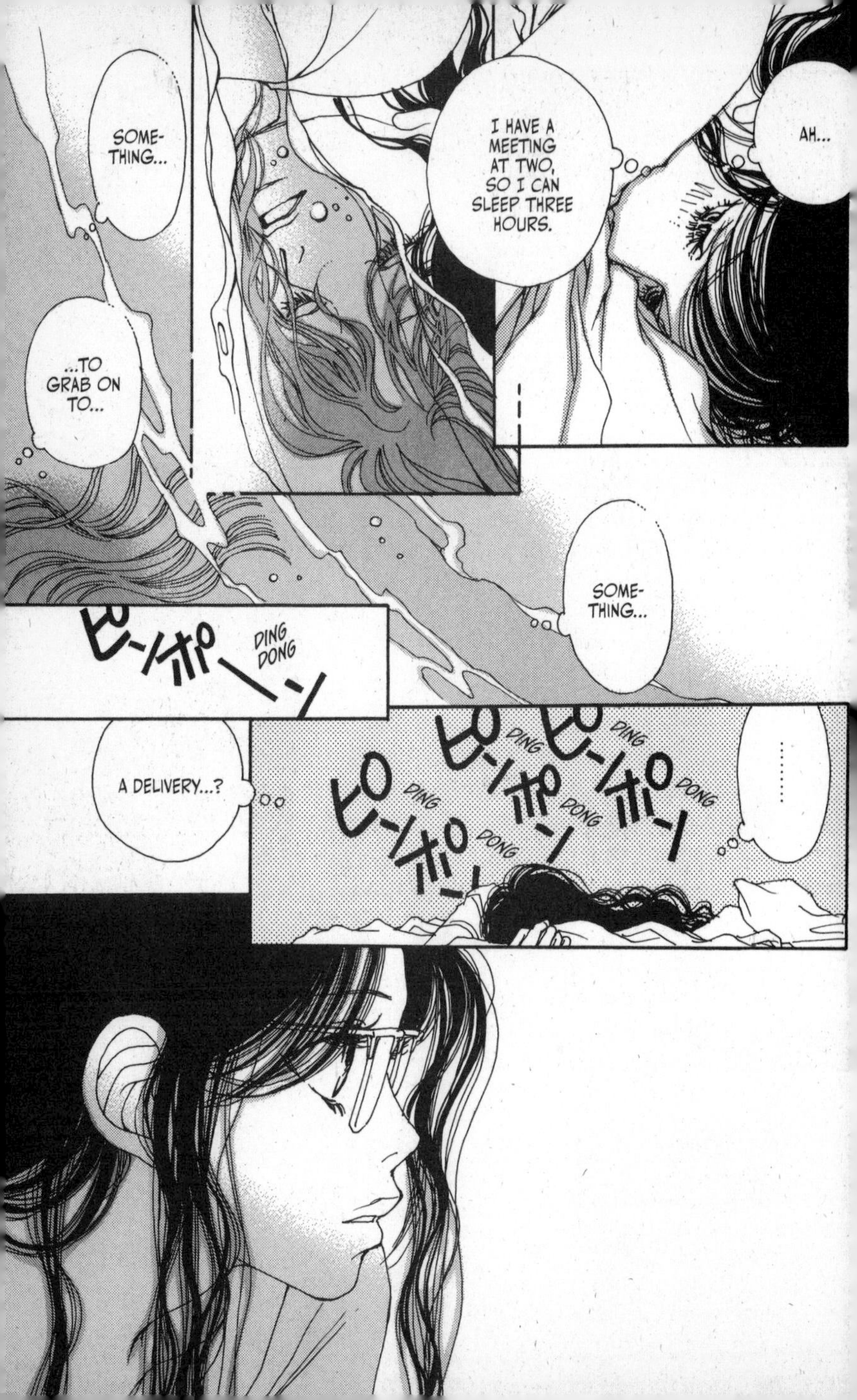
AH...
I HAVE A MEETING AT TWO, SO I CAN SLEEP THREE HOURS.
SOME-THING...
...TO GRAB ON TO...
SOME-THING...
ピーンポーン
DING DONG
......
ピーンポーン
DING DONG
ピーンポーン
DING DONG
ピーンポーン
DING DONG
A DELIVERY...?

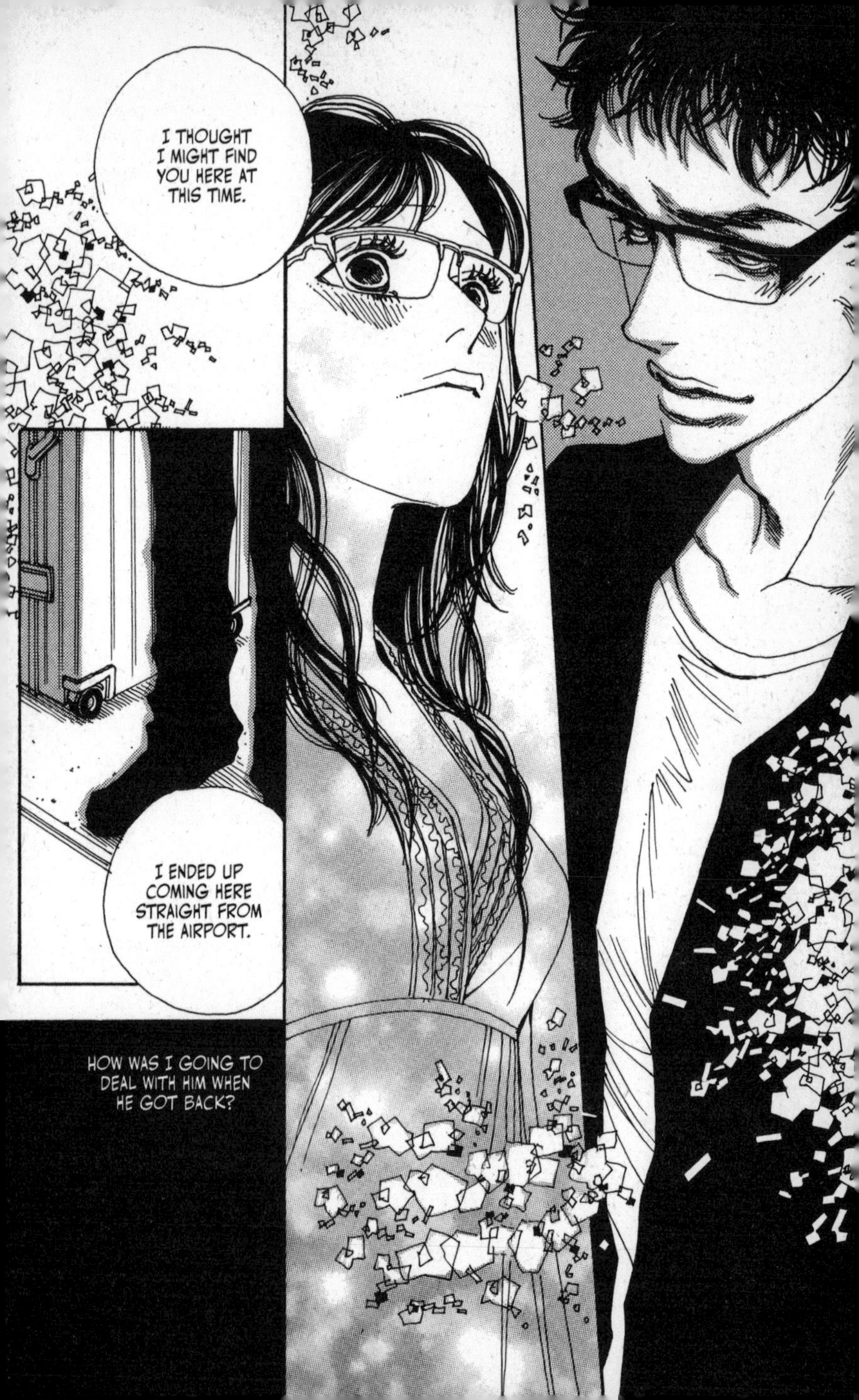
I THOUGHT I MIGHT FIND YOU HERE AT THIS TIME.
I ENDED UP COMING HERE STRAIGHT FROM THE AIRPORT.
HOW WAS I GOING TO DEAL WITH HIM WHEN HE GOT BACK?

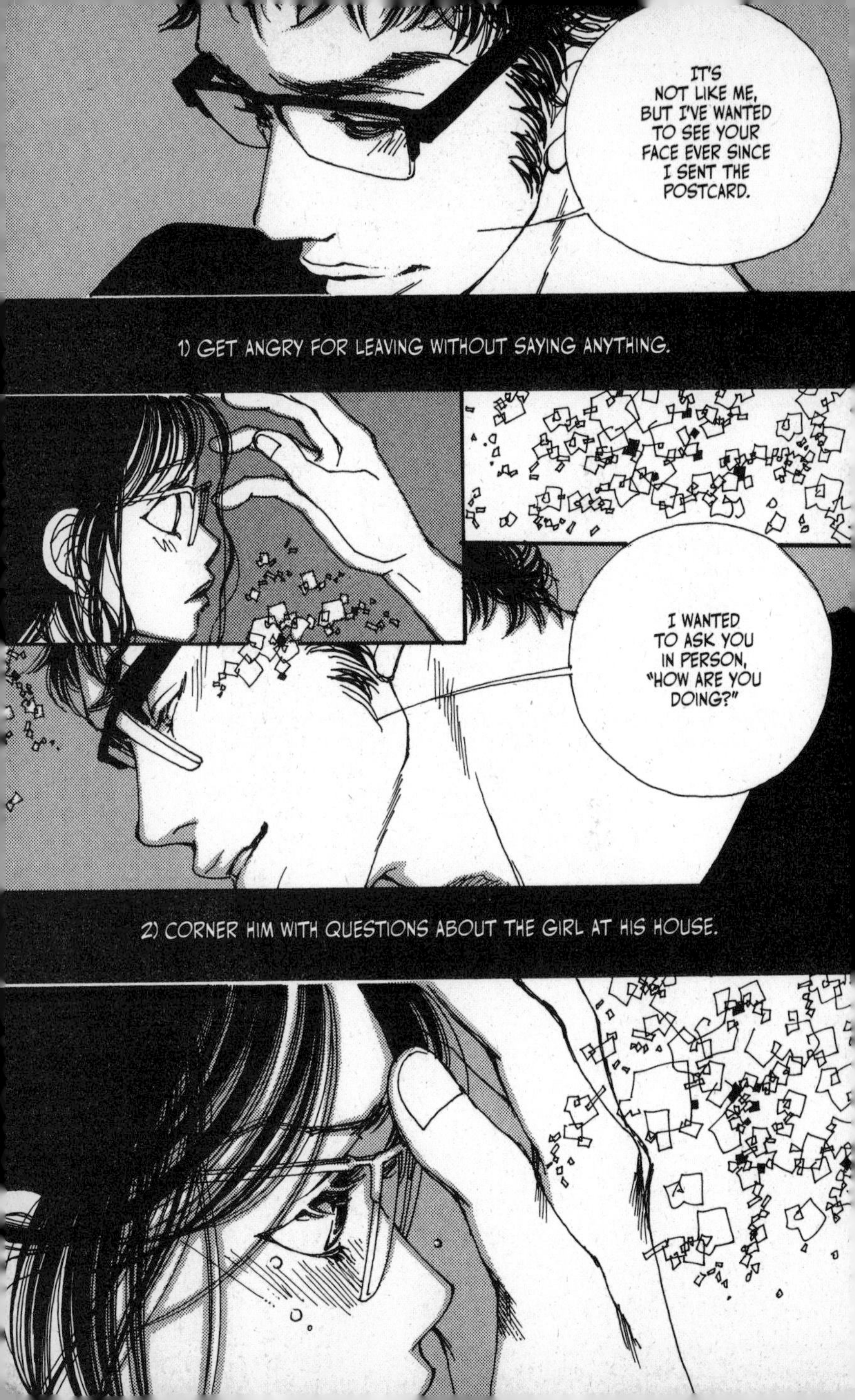
IT'S NOT LIKE ME, BUT I'VE WANTED TO SEE YOUR FACE EVER SINCE I SENT THE POSTCARD.
1) GET ANGRY FOR LEAVING WITHOUT SAYING ANYTHING.
I WANTED TO ASK YOU IN PERSON, "HOW ARE YOU DOING?"
2) CORNER HIM WITH QUESTIONS ABOUT THE GIRL AT HIS HOUSE.

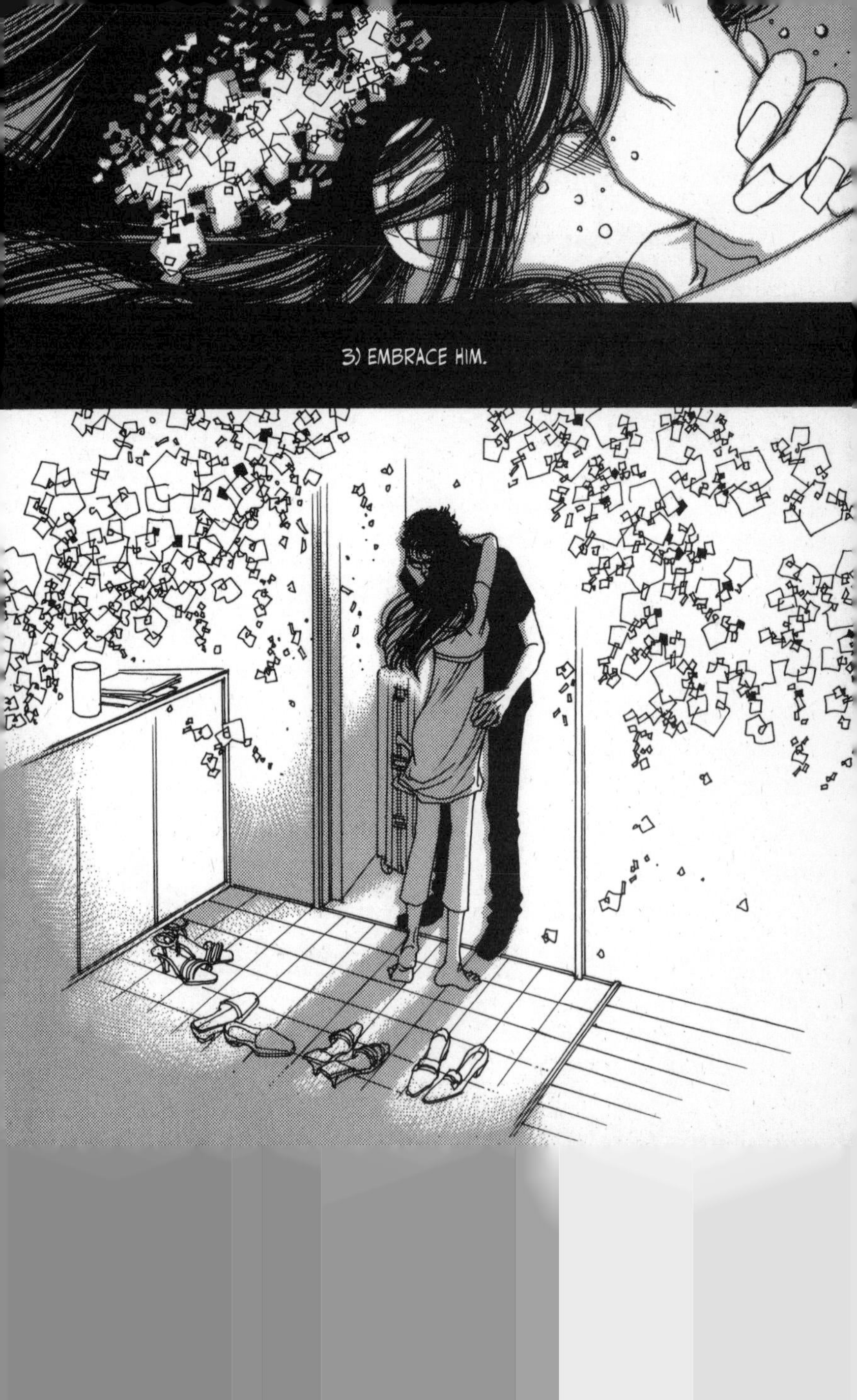
3) EMBRACE HIM.

✳ To Be Continued

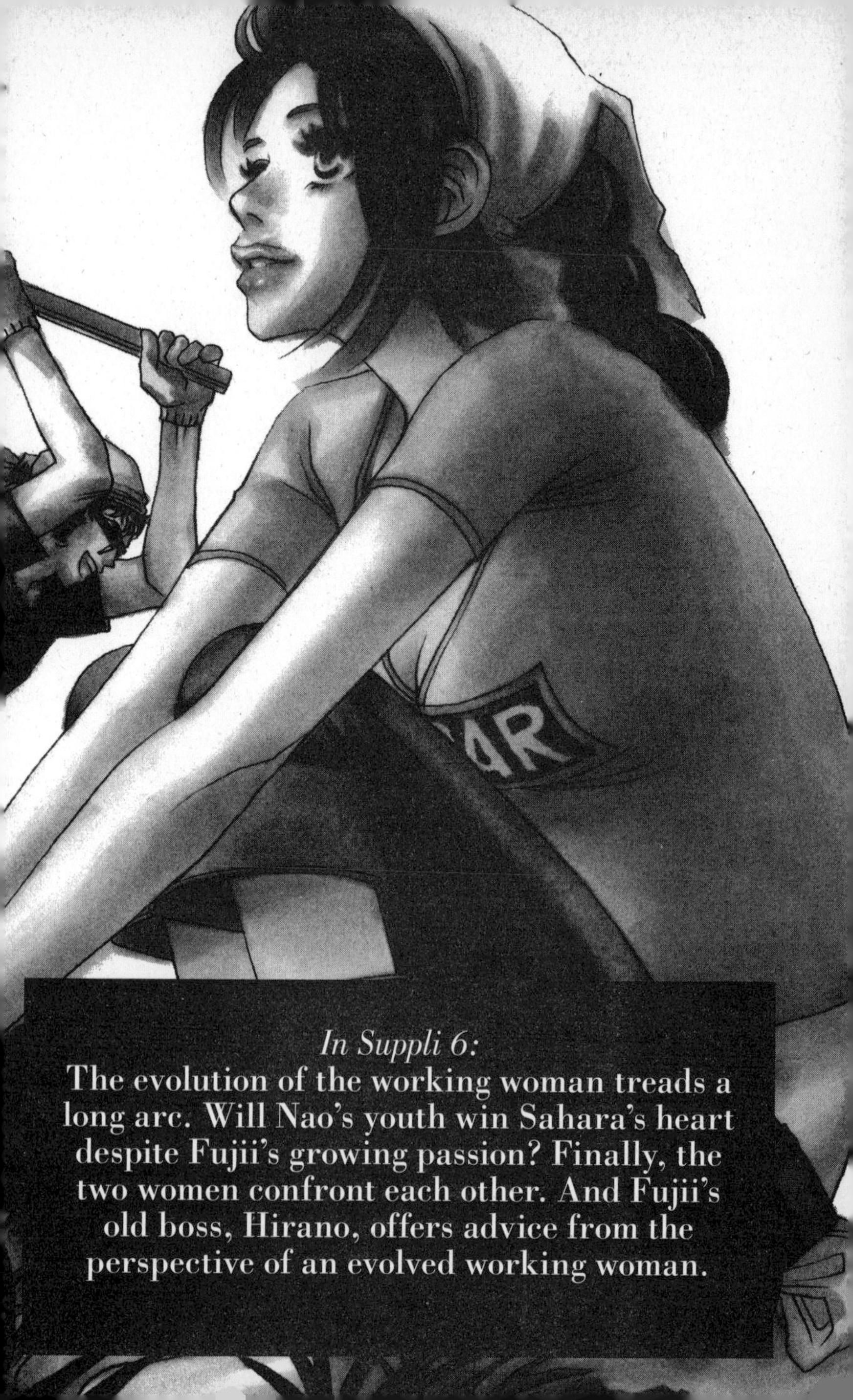

In Suppli 6:

The evolution of the working woman treads a long arc. Will Nao's youth win Sahara's heart despite Fujii's growing passion? Finally, the two women confront each other. And Fujii's old boss, Hirano, offers advice from the perspective of an evolved working woman.

Language and Cultural Notes on Suppli

Honorifics:

Suppli retains Japanese honorifics. Honorifics are suffixes used after names to denote respect, much like a "Mrs." or "Mr." a are commonly used in Japan. Unlike "Mrs." or "Mr." they are non-gender specific. They are generally placed after one's name.

-san. Equivalent to Mr. or Mrs. This is the most common suffix and the default level of respect. Minami Fujii is called "Fujii-sa by her co-workers.

-sama. Indicates a great level of respect or admiration and is used towards someone much older or of higher standing. Clos to "Lord" or "Lady" in English.

-kun. Indicates friendly familiarity, often used by older people addressing younger ones.

-chan. Indicates friendly familiarity.

-senpai. Used by younger students when speaking to or about their upperclassmen.

-sensei. Teacher.

Cultural Notes:

Fujii-san's office life includes a lot of references to Japanese culture. Here are notes on a few objects and practices.

File 22:

Sadako refers to **Sadako Yamamura**, the antagonist in *The Ring*. Her trademark limpid crawl is mimicked Tanaka's drunken sprawl for the door.

Himonya Park is a famous area in the Meguro district of Tokyo. In the Edo period, the park served as a falconi ground for the shogun.

"Minami" in "Minami Fujii" is the same word in Japanese for "south." When Sahara asks Minami if her name "like the direction," he's asking her if the kanji, or Chinese characters, in her name are the same that spell "sout The book's author uses katakana (a phonetic spelling system), so the Japanese readers don't know the answer Sahara's question either.

File 24:

Sakura, or cherry blossom, viewing is a seasonal activity in Japan. In Tokyo, where Fujii lives, sakura viewing tak place for about one week in early April.

File 25:

Baku are Chinese mythological creatures similar to tapirs, said to devour bad dreams. Various depictions portr them as having the head of an elephant and body of a lion, or other chimerical combinations.

"Kyushu boy" would be a young man from Kyushu, the southernmost island of Japan. This island is subtropical, a also removed from the city centers of Tokyo, Kyoto and the rest of the mainland.

File 26:

The lyrics **"Down, down the river"** refer to the folk story Momotaro, or "Peach Boy." According to the story, futu ogre-slayer Momotaro is found by as a baby floating down a river in a giant peach.

Host clubs are nightclubs where cute young men attend to female patrons.

Kabuki is a type of traditional Japanese drama, traditionally performed by only male actors.

File 27:

Ayu are a type of small (and delicious!) fish also known as "sweetfish." Amano is guessing that it's the ayu spawni season, spring.

Matsukiyo is Matsumoto Kiyoshi Drugstore, a popular drugstore chain in Japan.

Don-qui is an abbreviation of **Don Quijote**, a popular discount store in Japan and Hawaii.

Horizontal balloons in manga indicate that a speaker is using a language other than Japanese. In this ca English.

File 29:

Business cards in Japan are usually exchanged on the first meeting. It is normal for work associates like Fujii a Sahara to have each other's business cards.

Mahjong is a gambling game played with four players using tiles of different sets.

File 30:

Office lady, or OL, is the name for young female professionals looking to be "promoted" into marriage.

Masks resembling a doctor's are common attire for the sick in Japan. They prevent the spread of disease.

Dried bonito shavings are thin shavings of dried fish used in cooking.

NO ONE
IS SAFE ANYMORE

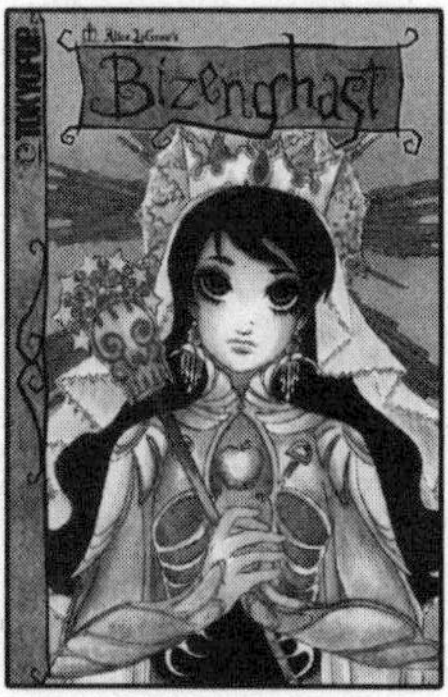
Bizenghast
TOKYOPOP

The final battle rages for the lives and souls of the inhabitants of Bizenghast, and no one is safe anymore. Shocking revelations of the town's dark history continue to emerge, and Dinah's struggle will go beyond the borders of the mausoleum...and into some of her worst nightmares...

VOLUME 7

PREVIEW AT www.TOKYOPOP.com/NoOneIsSafe

Bizenghast

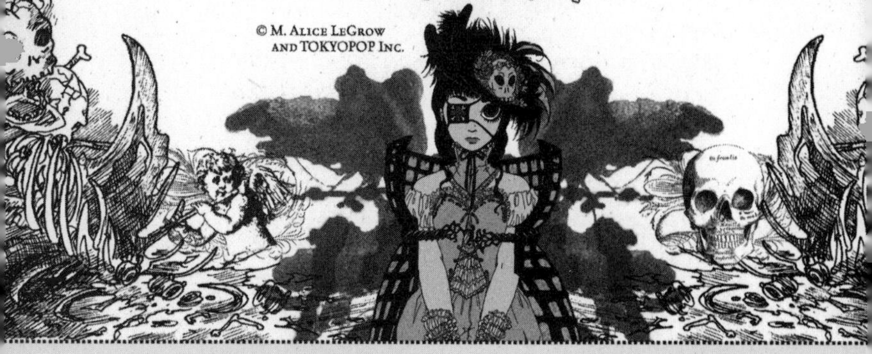

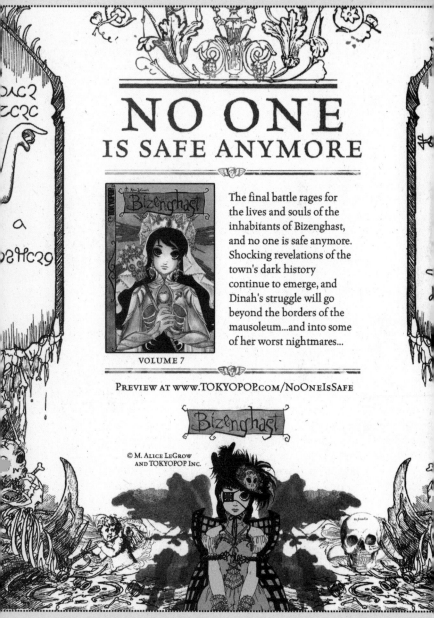

The second epic trilogy continues!

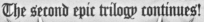

Ai fights to escape the clutches of her mysterious and malevolent captors, not knowing whether Kent, left behind on the Other Side, is even still alive. A frantic rescue mission commences, and in the end, even Ai's magical voice may not be enough to protect her from the trials of the Black Forest.

Dark secrets are revealed, and Ai must use all her strength and courage to face off against the new threat to Ai-Land. But will she ever see Kent again...?

"A very intriguing read that will satisfy old fans and create new fans, too."
— *Bookloons*

89/
11 Swg

STOP!

This is the back of the book.
You wouldn't want to spoil a great ending!

This book is printed "manga-style," in the authentic Japanese right-to-left format. Since none of the artwork has been flipped or altered, readers get to experience the story just as the creator intended. You've been asking for it, so TOKYOPOP® delivered: authentic, hot-off-the-press, and far more fun!

DIRECTIONS

If this is your first time reading manga-style, here's a quick guide to help you understand how it works.

It's easy... just start in the top right panel and follow the numbers. Have fun, and look for more 100% authentic manga from TOKYOPOP®!